Kingdoms in Peril

Volume 1

Kingdoms in Peril

Volume I

The Curse of the Bao Lords

Feng Menglong

Translated by Olivia Milburn

UNIVERSITY OF CALIFORNIA PRESS

University of California Press
Oakland, California

© 2023 by Olivia Milburn

Cataloging-in-Publication Data is on file at the Library
of Congress.

ISBN 978-0-520-38099-8 (cloth : alk. paper)
ISBN 978-0-520-38100-1 (pbk. : alk. paper)
ISBN 978-0-520-38101-8 (ebook)

Manufactured in the United States of America

32 31 30 29 28 27 26 25 24 23
10 9 8 7 6 5 4 3 2 1

Contents

Map: The Zhou Confederacy circa 500 B.C.E.   ix

List of Main Characters   x

Introduction   1

Chapter One   25

*King Xuan of Zhou hears a children's song and kills a woman
for no good reason.*

Grandee Du becomes formidable as he protests his innocence.

Chapter Two   39

*The people of Bao atone for their crimes by handing over a beautiful
woman.*

King You lights the beacon fires to tease the feudal lords.

Chapter Three   56

The chief of the Dog Rong invades the capital at Hao.

King Ping of Zhou moves east to Luoyang.

Chapter Four   72

Lord Wen of Qin sacrifices to Heaven in response to a prophetic dream.

Lord Zhuang of Zheng digs a pit in order to see his mother.

Chapter Five   86
After favoring the Duke of Guo, Zhou and Zheng exchange hostages.
To help Wey and defend against Lu, Song raises an army.

Chapter Six   102
Shi Que of Wey kills his only son in the cause of justice.
Lord Zhuang of Zheng fakes an edict and attacks Song.

Chapter Seven   117
Noble Grandson E, fighting from his chariot, shoots Ying Kaoshu.
The Honorable Hui comes up with a plot to usurp the title from Lord Yin.

Chapter Eight   132
To establish a new lord, Hua Du resorts to giving bribes.
Having defeated the Rong army, Zihu refuses a marriage alliance.

Chapter Nine   142
The Marquis of Qi gives Lady Wen Jiang in marriage to Lu.
Zhu Dan shoots King Huan of Zhou in the shoulder.

Chapter Ten   153
Xiong Tong of Chu oversteps his authority and declares himself king.
Zhai Zu of Zheng is blackmailed into establishing a concubine's
son as lord.

Chapter Eleven   168
Lord Zhuang of Song, being greedy for bribes, brings disaster
upon his army.
Zhai Zu of Zheng murders his son-in-law and forces his lord into exile.

Chapter Twelve   184
Lord Xuan of Wey builds a tower to steal another man's wife.
Gao Qumi takes advantage of the situation to change rulers.

Chapter Thirteen   198
Lord Huan of Lu and his wife travel to Qi.
The Honorable Wei of Zheng and his supporters are massacred.

Chapter Fourteen   210
Shuo, Marquis of Wey, returns to his state in defiance of the king.
Lord Xiang of Qi goes out hunting and meets a ghost.

Chapter Fifteen   226

Grandee Yong Lin plots the murder of Wuzhi.

Lord Zhuang of Lu fights a great battle at Ganshi.

Chapter Sixteen   238

After his release from imprisonment, Bao Shuya recommends Guan Zhong for office.

In the battle of Changshao, Cao Gui defeats Qi.

Chapter Seventeen   252

The state of Song takes bribes and executes Nangong Changwan.

The king of Chu raises his cup and steals Lady Gui of Xi.

Chapter Eighteen   268

Cao Mo menaces the Marquis of Qi with a sword in his hand.

Lord Huan invests Ning Qi with a noble title by firelight.

Chapter Nineteen   285

Having taken Fu Xia prisoner, Lord Li of Zheng returns to his country.

After murdering Prince Tui, King Hui of Zhou is restored to power.

Chapter Twenty   301

Lord Xian of Jin ignores a divination against establishing Lady Li Ji as his principal wife.

King Cheng of Chu puts down a rebellion and appoints Ziwen as Grand Vizier.

Chapter Twenty-one   320

Guan Yiwu cleverly explains the identity of the Yu'er.

Lord Huan of Qi's army brings peace to Guzhu.

Chapter Twenty-two   341

The Honorable You twice installs a ruler of Lu in power.

Master Huang of Qi is the only person to recognize the "Weishe."

Chapter Twenty-three   358

Lord Yi of Wey's love of cranes destroys his country.

Lord Huan of Qi raises an army to attack Chu.

Chapter Twenty-four   379

At the blood covenant at Shaoling, a Chu grandee is treated with ritual propriety.
At the meeting at Kuiqiu, the Zhou king is honored.

Chapter Twenty-five   401

Clever Xun Xi destroys Guo after borrowing a road.
Poor Baili Xi is appointed prime minister after feeding his oxen.

Chapter Twenty-six   420

A song about a bar to the door allows Baili Xi to recognize his wife.
After capturing the Treasure of Chen, Lord Mu discovers the truth of his dream.

Chapter Twenty-seven   435

Lady Li Ji plots the murder of Shensheng.
Lord Xian gives deathbed instructions to Xun Xi.

Chapter Twenty-eight   449

Li Ke murders two infant rulers in succession.
Lord Mu pacifies a civil war in Jin for the first time.

Chapter Twenty-nine   463

Lord Hui of Jin executes all his government ministers.
Guan Yiwu discusses the prime ministership on his deathbed.

Chapter Thirty   478

Qin and Jin fight a great battle at Mount Longmen.
Lady Mu Ji climbs a tower to demand a general pardon.

The Zhou Confederacy circa 500 B.C.E. Adapted from *Map of the Five Hegemons* by SY, CC-BY-SA 4.0

List of Main Characters

Volume One

The persons included in this list are characters who appear in multiple chapters of *Kingdoms in Peril*, and whose deeds would continue to be referenced long after they themselves were dead. Some of these historical individuals appear under various different names during the course of the book, as they inherited titles or achieved honors. In each section, rulers are listed first, followed by other important personages.

CHU (Xiong clan; king)

The kingdom of Chu, based along the middle reaches of the Yangtze River, became an increasingly powerful state during the early Eastern Zhou dynasty, and its monarchs declared themselves kings, indicating that they no longer recognized themselves as being under the authority of the Zhou king. The clever and competent kings of Chu often appear in *Kingdoms in Peril* as the main enemy of the Zhou Central States.

King Wu (r. 740–690 B.C.E.), personal name Tong: a powerful ruler in southern China, he declared himself king in around 704 B.C.E.

King Wen (r. 689–677 B.C.E.), personal name Zi: he significantly expanded Chu's territory, but came into conflict with Lord Huan of Qi.

King Cheng (r. 671–626 B.C.E.), personal name Yun: coming to the throne after the death of his older brother, King Cheng had a long and successful reign, only to fall victim to the machinations of Crown Prince Shangchen.

Dou Bobi: served as a senior minister during the reign of Kings Wu and Wen of Chu, and played an important role in the expansion of the kingdom at this time.

Dou Ziwen, personal name Guwutu: an illegitimate son of Dou Bobi, nevertheless inherited his father's honors and served as a senior minister under King
Cheng of Chu.

JIN (Ji clan; marquis)

The ruling house of Jin was descended from a younger brother of King
Cheng of Zhou (r. 1042/35–1006 B.C.E.). This border state, at the edge
of the Chinese world, grew enormously during the early Eastern Zhou
dynasty through the conquest of nomadic peoples. The increasing
power of Jin was, however, consistently contested and held in check by
its neighbor to the west: Qin.

Lord Xian (r. 676–651 B.C.E.), personal name Guizhu: his many wives and concubines, and their numerous offspring, were caught up in constant conflict
with one another resulting in much political chaos.
Lord Hui (r. 650–637 B.C.E.), personal name Yiwu: forced into exile by Lord
Xian and Lady Xi Ji, when captured by Qin after the battle of Longmen, his
life was spared through the intercession of his half-sister, Lady Mu Ji.
Lord Huai (r. 637 B.C.E.), personal name Yu: son of Lord Hui; married to a
daughter of Lord Mu of Qin.
Lord Wen (r. 638–626 B.C.E.), personal name Chong'er: second hegemon following on Lord Huan of Qi; succeeded to the title after many decades in
exile, to become the most powerful aristocrat of the age.

Lady Li Ji (d. 651 B.C.E.): one of Lord Xian's junior wives, who murdered or
forced into exile his other children in the interests first of her own son, Xiqi
(d. 651 B.C.E.), and then of her nephew Zhuozi (d. 651 B.C.E.).
Lady Mu Ji (d. c. 637 B.C.E.): daughter of Lord Xian and wife of Lord Mu of
Qin, she played an important role in trying to stabilize a series of civil wars
in Jin.
Scion Shensheng (d. 655 B.C.E.): the son of Lord Xian from an incestuous relationship with his father's wife, he committed suicide during conflict with
Lady Li Ji.
Xun Xi: a senior minister under Lord Xian of Jin, orchestrated his successful
campaigns against the states of Guo and Yu.

LU (Ji clan; marquis)

Lu was founded by a son of the first Duke of Zhou, a younger brother
of King Wu of Zhou (r. 1049/45–1043 B.C.E.), who held enormous
power at the beginning of the dynasty as regent to the infant King
Cheng. With the state of Qi, Lu dominated the political scene on the
Shandong peninsula, and the two ruling houses frequently intermarried,
with disastrous results. However, the demand that peace be preserved in
the region outweighed all other considerations.

Lord Huan (r. 711–694 B.C.E.): personal name Gui: came to the title after assassinating his half-brother, Lord Yin (r. 722–712 B.C.E.). The husband of the notorious Lady Wen Jiang, he was murdered by her brother, Lord Xiang of Qi.

Lord Zhuang (r. 693–662 B.C.E.), personal name Tong: the son of Lord Huan and Lady Wen Jiang, his rule was dominated by the problems caused by his father's murder, including navigating his relationship with his wife, Lady Ai Jiang, the daughter of Lord Xiang of Qi.

Lord Min (r. 661–660 B.C.E.), personal name Qi: murdered in childhood by his stepmother Lady Ai Jiang and her lover, the Honorable Qingfu of Lu.

Lord Xi (r. 659–627 B.C.E.), personal name Shen: brought order to the extremely chaotic situation in Lu following the murders of Lord Min and other claimants to the marquisate.

QI (Jiang clan; marquis)

The Jiang ruling family of Qi were descended from Jiang Ziya (dates unknown), a key advisor to King Wu of Zhou during his conquest of the Shang dynasty. After a series of damaging rulers at the very beginning of the Eastern Zhou dynasty, Qi began a prolonged period of florescence and expansion. This would see Qi dominating not just the Shandong peninsula, but the whole of the Central States, a position that was ultimately recognized by the Zhou king with the creation of an extraordinary, nonhereditary title of Ba, or "hegemon."

Lord Xi (r. 730–698 BCE), personal name Lufu: the indulgent father of the notorious incestuous couple Lord Xiang and Lady Wen Jiang.

Lord Xiang (r. 697–686 B.C.E.), personal name Zhuer: ordered the murder of his brother-in-law, Lord Huan of Lu, only to fall victim himself to assassins working for the Honorable Wuzhi of Qi (d. 685 B.C.E.).

Lord Huan (r. 685–643 B.C.E.), personal name Xiaobai: first hegemon of the Eastern Zhou dynasty. Coming to the title following the assassination of Lord Xiang and attempts to seize power by his cousin the Honorable Wuzhi and his older brother the Honorable Jiu (d. 685 B.C.E.), Lord Huan went on to dominate the political scene for decades.

Bao Shuya (d. 644 B.C.E.): a friend and contemporary of Guan Zhong, and a long-serving minister in Lord Huan of Qi's administration.

Chen Wan: a member of the ruling house of Chen, he served in Lord Huan of Qi's administration. His descendants changed their surname to Tian and eventually usurped the Jiang ruling house, founding the kingdom of Qi.

Guan Zhong (d. 645 B.C.E.), personal name Yiwu: a key advisor of Lord Huan of Qi and an important early Chinese political thinker.

Lady Ai Jiang (d. 660 B.C.E.): daughter of Lord Xiang of Qi, wife of Lord Zhuang of Lu.

Lady Wen Jiang (d. 673 B.C.E.): daughter of Lord Xi of Qi, wife of Lord Huan of Lu, and involved in a long-term incestuous relationship with her brother,

Lord Xiang. Lady Wen Jiang dominated the early reign of her son, Lord Zhuang of Lu.

Yi Ya: Lord Huan of Qi's cook and a key player in the conflict at the end of his reign.

QIN (Ying clan; earl)

The origins of the Ying ruling family of Qin remain highly obscure and very controversial. However, from the beginning of the Eastern Zhou dynasty, they became increasingly involved in the affairs of the Central States. They continued to remain highly isolated from most of the political upheavals during these years, except for maintaining a strong connection with the state of Jin. This connection was strengthened by marriage alliances, which brought the two families into close (if not always harmonious) relations.

Lord Wen (r. 766–716 B.C.E.), personal name unknown: received a series of prophecies concerning the future greatness of his family and state.

Lord Mu (r. 659–621 B.C.E.), personal name Renhao: presided over a major expansion in the power and prestige of Qin. Through his wife, Lady Mu Ji, he played a significant role in the establishment of a succession of Jin rulers and was closely allied with Lord Wen of Jin.

Baili Xi: a senior minister under Lord Mu of Qin, was claimed by Qin as a slave in the dowry of Lady Mu Ji of Jin.

SONG (Zi clan; duke)

The dukes of Song were descended from the Shang dynasty royal family, and they received lands and honors in order to allow them to continue to perform ancestral sacrifices for the Shang kings. The sensitive position of the dukes of Song, particularly for those unwilling to accept the authority of the Zhou king, was very challenging to negotiate; although treated with the utmost respect in theory, in practice the Song ruling house was often viewed with suspicion by its peers.

Lord Shang (r. 750–710 B.C.E.), personal name Yuyi: a very bellicose man, he was eventually killed in an assassination planned by a senior government official in Song, Hua Du (d. 682 B.C.E.).

Lord Zhuang (r. 710–692 B.C.E.), personal name Ping: installed in power after years in exile in Zheng following the assassination of his predecessor by Hua Du.

Lord Min (r. 692–682 B.C.E.), personal name Jie: murdered by one of his senior military officials, Nangong Changwan, over a stupid joke.

Lord Huan (r. 682–651 B.C.E.), personal name Yushuo: succeeded to the dukedom following Lord Min's murder.

Kong Fujia (765–710 B.C.E.): a senior government official in the time of Lord Shang, murdered by Hua Du. A sixth-generation ancestor of Confucius.

WEY (Ji clan; marquis)

The Wey ruling family were descended from a younger brother of King Wu of Zhou. Although very important in the founding of the Eastern Zhou dynasty, a succession of decadent and incompetent rulers reduced Wey to a condition of near terminal collapse, and it struggled to survive as an independent state within the Zhou confederacy.

Lord Wu (r. 812–758 B.C.E.), personal name He: a loyal supporter of King Ping of Zhou who helped put an end to the warfare ravaging the capital, under whose rule the state of Wey reached an apogee of power.

Lord Xuan (r. 718–700 B.C.E.), personal name Jin: notorious for his disorderly personal life, which included stealing his son's wife, Lady Xuan Jiang. Lady Xuan Jiang was the daughter of Lord Xi of Qi.

Lord Hui (r. 700–696, 688–669 B.C.E.), personal name Shuo: son of Lord Xuan and Lady Xuan Jiang, he played a key role in inciting the murder of his siblings.

Lord Yi (r. 668–660 B.C.E.), personal name Chi: noted for his peculiar affection for one variety of bird, the crane.

Scion Jizi (d. 701 B.C.E.): the original spouse of Lady Xuan Jiang, murdered by his father along with his half-brother, the Honorable Shou.

ZHENG (Ji clan; earl)

The state of Zheng was founded when King Xuan of Zhou (r. 827/25–782 B.C.E.) granted these lands to his younger brother, Prince You. The first Earl of Zheng was killed defending his nephew, King You, at the time of the fall of the Western Zhou dynasty. The clever, ruthless early rulers of Zheng would prove to be, by turns, loyal supporters of the Zhou kings and a serious challenge to their authority.

Lord Huan (d. 771 B.C.E.), personal name You: a loyal supporter of King You of Zhou who died by his side during the civil war that brought an end to the Western Zhou dynasty.

Lord Wu (r. 771–744 B.C.E.), personal name Juetu: a loyal supporter of King Ping of Zhou who played a key role in his installation as the founding monarch of the Eastern Zhou dynasty.

Lord Zhuang (r. 744–701 B.C.E.), personal name Wusheng: an intelligent, domineering man, in constant conflict with his mother and younger brother Gongshu Duan, and with King Huan of Zhou; the most powerful aristocrat of the entire Central States at the beginning of the Eastern Zhou dynasty.

Lord Zhao (r. 701, 697–695 B.C.E.), personal name Zihu: an important figure in his father's administration, he was forced into exile by the machinations of Lord Zhuang of Song.

Lord Li (r. 701–697, 680–673 BCE), personal name Tu: initially installed in power by Zhai Zu and Lord Zhuang of Song; a key supporter of Kings Xi and Hui of Zhou.

Lord Wen (r. 673–628 BCE), personal name Jie: his treatment of Lord Wen of Jin when the latter was in exile ensured constant conflict between their two states.

Gao Qumi (d. 694 B.C.E.): a senior military official in the state of Zheng, responsible for the assassination of Lord Zhao.

Gongshu Duan (d. 722 B.C.E.): Lord Zhuang's younger brother, much favored by their mother, whose attempt to usurp the title launched Zheng into a civil war.

Zhai Zu (d. 682 B.C.E.): a senior official in the state of Zheng, who played a key role in political machinations following the death of Lord Zhuang.

ZHOU (Ji clan; king)

The Zhou dynasty was founded in 1046 B.C.E., when the future King Wu of Zhou and his ally Jiang Ziya (founder of the state of Qi) defeated the last monarch of the Shang dynasty at the Battle of Muye. The Zhou kings went on to create the Central States by rewarding family members and key supporters with significant grants of land, which they ruled with considerable day-to-day independence. The loyalties of these aristocrats were increasingly frayed during the reign of King You, culminating in the uprisings that led to the fall of the Western Zhou. The establishment of the Eastern Zhou dynasty under the auspices of King Ping saw a monarch restored to the throne, but the authority of the Zhou monarchs had been comprehensively destroyed.

King Xuan (r. 827/25–782 B.C.E.), personal name Jing: the penultimate monarch of the Western Zhou dynasty, involved in supernatural events that brought about his death.

King You (r. 781–771 B.C.E.), personal name Gongnie: the final monarch of the Western Zhou dynasty. The conflicts between his oldest son and his favorite concubine Bao Si brought about the collapse of the dynasty.

King Ping (r. 770–720 B.C.E.), personal name Yiwu: the first ruler of the Eastern Zhou dynasty. He came to the throne following a devastating civil war, which forced the capital to move to Luoyang.

King Huan (r. 719–697 B.C.E.), personal name Lin: succeeded his grandfather King Ping following the unexpected death of his father, Crown Prince Hu, while a hostage in Zheng. His reign was marked by great conflict with Lord Zhuang of Zheng.

King Zhuang (r. 696–682 B.C.E.), personal name Tuo: his favoritism towards his younger son, Prince Tui (d. 673 B.C.E.), caused his eldest son and heir great problems.

King Xi (r. 681–677 B.C.E.), personal name Huqi: was forced into exile by Prince Tui and his supporters, and relied on Lord Li of Zheng's help to be installed in power again.

King Hui (r. 677–652 B.C.E.), personal name Lang: like his father, was also forced into exile by Prince Tui, and reinstalled by Lord Li of Zheng. In his later years, his favoritism of his younger son Prince Dai again caused serious political problems.

King Xiang (r. 652–619 B.C.E.), personal name Zheng: his reign was overshadowed by constant conflict with Prince Dai, which resulted in long periods of exile.

Bao Si (d. 771 B.C.E.): a famously beautiful woman, King You of Zhou's favorite concubine, and the manifestation of an ancient curse.

Prince Dai (d. 635 B.C.E.), younger son of King Hui of Zhou, and a highly charismatic figure, whose attempts to seize power were forgiven by his long-suffering relatives until he was finally executed by Lord Wen of Jin.

Introduction

Kingdoms in Peril is an epic historical novel covering the five hundred and fifty years of the Eastern Zhou dynasty, from the civil wars and invasions that marked the birth of a new regime in 771 B.C.E. to the unification of China in 221 B.C.E. This period saw the numerous states that made up the Zhou confederacy riven by intense and intractable conflict as they lurched from one crisis to the next. Every concept of what constituted a civilized society was tested again and again through centuries of political instability, and any momentary peace was soon threatened by the relentless intriguing of ministers, eunuchs, and harem favorites. It was a time when political life was punctuated with poisonings, assassinations, and sinister conspiracies, and those who escaped other murderous attacks might still fall victim to warfare or the rioting populace. As old certainties crumbled and hierarchies collapsed, it was no longer possible to maintain traditional social norms, and new opportunities opened up for the intelligent and able. Men and women were quick to take advantage of this, testing the boundaries and seeking self-advancement in ways that would have been impossible in a more stable environment. As an international market opened up for talented individuals, clever men increasingly sought to build careers abroad, secure in the knowledge that their social and ethnic background would not be held against them in a foreign country. Women too resisted traditional assumptions that their sphere should be confined to childrearing at home, and found that they were now expected—at least at the elite levels—to be able to provide sagacious advice, arrange murders, defuse political conspiracies, and, in the event of a crisis, potentially even to take over the running of the country.

Kingdoms in Peril was written in the 1640s, at the very end of the Ming dynasty, by the great novelist Feng Menglong (1574–1646). An expert in the history of the Eastern Zhou dynasty, he was inspired to write this novel by reading an earlier work on the same subject: *Tales of the States* (*Lieguo zhi*) by Yu Shaoyu (fl. 1522–1573). Horrified by the many mistakes and anachronisms this book contained, Feng Menglong decided to produce a new and improved account of the same historical events, which would explore the careers and personalities of the many remarkable individuals who lived through and defined this crucial era of Chinese history. In the course of the one hundred and eight chapters of the complete novel, he documents the collapse of the Zhou confederacy during the Spring and Autumn period (771–475 B.C.E.) and the slow rebuilding of civil society during the Warring States era (475–221 B.C.E.), which culminated in the unification of China under the First Emperor of the Qin dynasty (r. 246–221 B.C.E. as king; r. 221–210 B.C.E. as emperor). Thus, overall, this novel describes a grand arc, from stability to chaos and back again. As a novel about politics, much of the narrative in *Kingdoms in Peril* concentrates on the exercise of power. During the Eastern Zhou dynasty, there were two words in use to cover different aspects of the concept of power. *Quan* was used for the power that comes from quantifiable resources: the size of the army, the financial reserves in the treasury, the extent of the tax base, stockpiles of weapons, armor, and so on. *Shi*, on the other hand, refers to power that comes from taking advantage of the opportunities provided by a developing situation. It is the interplay between *quan* and *shi* that provides many of the most dramatic incidents in the history of this period, and therefore of this novel. Power that comes from circumstantial advantage could be utilized in all sorts of different contexts: whether it is a silver-tongued diplomat persuading a king to accept a disadvantageous treaty; a cunning general tricking the enemy commander into an unfavorable situation by playing to his prejudices; or a rival convincing a neglected wife to spy on her husband to set him up for assassination— these chinks in the armor allowed for stunning reversals of fortune.

Whether they were making history or being crushed by it, the characters of *Kingdoms in Peril* are presented in a way that reminds us of their human qualities. There are no heroes and villains here, just flawed individuals trying their best to survive in often impossible circumstances, all too often discovering that the choices available to them ranged from bad to worse. One of the key features of this novel is the emphasis on the terrible conflicts many of its characters faced—raised in an ethical system that valued loyalty, justice, benevolence, and filial duty and yet placed in circumstances in which they were torn between their duty to the ruler or the country and their love for family and friends. Regardless of whether they were monarchs, aristocrats, hereditary ministers, or clan leaders, members of the Eastern Zhou ruling elite almost always had complicated private lives, surrounded as they were by wives, concubines, mistresses, cronies, bodyguards, hangers-on, and hordes of servants, male and female. The ties of affection created within these households did not necessarily run neatly according to rank and status, where sons of the main wife held priority in the inheritance, followed by the children of concubines, while illegitimate offspring were generally treated little better than slaves. Although this social hierarchy might appear rigid, it could always be overturned by the intelligent; while ruthless ambition and violence occasionally found themselves tempered by loving relationships strong enough to withstand the brutality of the age. *Kingdoms in Peril* has long been recognized as a masterpiece for its exploration of the personalities of individuals caught up in momentous historical events.

KINGDOMS IN PERIL: HISTORICAL BACKGROUND

Kingdoms in Peril opens with a brief account of the political problems at the end of the Western Zhou dynasty, which were allayed with the accession of the highly competent King Xuan of Zhou (r. 827–782 B.C.E.). However, though the reign of King Xuan offered a temporary respite, the dynasty would collapse in a civil war during the reign of his son, King You (r. 781–771 B.C.E.). The fall of the Western Zhou dynasty is today understood as the result of multiple factors: natural disasters created enormous social disruption and forced many people to become refugees; attacks by powerful northern nomadic peoples increased; and the ensuing humanitarian crisis was exacerbated by an incompetent government riven with internal dissension. However, this is not how ancient Chinese people regarded these events. For them, the key figure in the fall of the Western Zhou was an accursed woman, Bao Si, the favorite slave-girl of the last king. She was believed to be the living embodiment of an ancient malediction, imposed upon the people of Zhou by the Bao lords, and hence predestined to bring about the fall of the dynasty. As a result, Bao Si came to represent a counterpart and antithesis to Hou Ji, the mythical founder of the Zhou royal house. Just as Hou Ji was born after his mother stepped in the footprint of a giant, and survived thanks to the protection of various birds and animals when his mother attempted to abandon her baby, Bao Si was born after her mother stepped in the footprint of a magical turtle, and survived an attempt to drown her as a baby through the intervention of the local wildlife. To an ancient Chinese audience, Heaven created Hou Ji to bring civilization to the world as the ancestor of the Zhou ruling house, and Bao Si was sent down to destroy everything that they had worked so hard to create.

In the year 771 B.C.E., Crown Prince Yijiu of Zhou, furious at having been dispossessed by his father, launched a rebellion against him. In the ensuing carnage King You and Bao Si were killed, together with vast numbers of government officials. The ordinary inhabitants of the capital were massacred, women were raped, and the city was pillaged by the crown prince's self-declared supporters. Faced with a burned palace and a ruined city, the newly enthroned Yijiu, now King Ping of Zhou (r. 770–720 B.C.E.), decided to move the seat of government permanently to the secondary capital at Luoyang. The immediate consequences of this decision were not necessarily apparent; however, it would gradually become clear that these events had completely destroyed the authority of the Zhou kings. With the center crumbling, violence began to spiral out of control. Over the course of the next few centuries, the states of the Zhou confederacy suffered social collapse and political cataclysm, from which no one would emerge unscathed. The violence spread outwards from each epicenter like the ripples when a stone is dropped into water. An assassination in one state would lead to further revenge killings, sucking more and more people into the maelstrom. The resulting political vacuum would result in popular uprisings, innocent people were slain, and foreign enemies invaded. Occasionally, an individual ruler and his ministers would try to make a stand and preserve the peace, but all too soon, that regime would pass away and the fighting would break out again. At the same time, centrifugal forces ripped the Central States apart, as power increasingly came to be vested in regimes more and more remote from the old center: the Zhou Royal Domain. This was a function of the way in which territory had been allocated since the founding of the Western Zhou in 1045 B.C.E. The political center consisted mainly of city-states, with limited opportunities for expansion. Over time it proved to be the peripheral regimes—sometimes even foreign kingdoms—that showed they had the capacity to expand rapidly, conquering their neighbors and recruiting ever vaster armies. The precise number of states within the Zhou confederacy at the beginning of the Eastern Zhou dynasty is not known, since not all are mentioned in surviving historical records and some appear only in inscriptions on ceremonial bronze vessels that have been excavated in modern times. However, there are thought to have been at least twelve hundred states in 771 B.C.E., at the beginning of the dynasty. By the end of the Spring and Autumn period in 475 B.C.E., these had been consolidated into seven vast countries, whose rulers were powerful enough to declare themselves kings. During the Warring States era, it became increasingly obvious to everyone that unification was necessary in order to bring the violence to an end. In the process, the seven kings of the Warring States would fight each other until there was only one left—Qin—which proceeded to unify China. However, before bringing about the unification of China, the future First Emperor would have to face numerous coup attempts launched by his closest family members, as well as running the gamut of assassins sent by his enemies. In the process, he found himself becoming increasingly isolated and paranoid, setting in train fresh bouts of violence from which the world of the Qin empire would be born.

THE AUTHOR: FENG MENGLONG

Feng Menglong was born into a gentry family in Suzhou in 1574, as the second of three sons. As with other young men of this kind of privileged background, he was destined for a career in the civil service. However, in spite of numerous attempts to pass the necessary examinations, he consistently failed, as a result of which the stellar career in government that he and his family had hoped for never materialized. In 1630, at the age of fifty-six, his scholarly achievements were finally recognized with appointment as a tribute scholar (gongsheng), which opened the way for him to receive a minor official appointment in Dantu County, Jiangsu Province. Having successfully completed this tour of duty, he served for four years as the magistrate of Shouning County in Fujian Province, from 1634 to 1638. On completing this second term of office, he retired and returned to live in Suzhou. That his ambitions to serve as a government official misfired so badly would have one important connection to Feng Menglong's career as an author: each candidate for the civil service examinations was required to choose one classical Chinese text for intensive study. In his case, Feng Menglong chose to specialize in the *Spring and Autumn Annals* (*Chunqiu*), a historical text that covers the events of the early Eastern Zhou dynasty. The fact that he never succeeded in passing the examinations should not be seen as a reflection of any lack of diligence, intelligence, or expertise on the subject: he would go on to produce three textbooks that would be regarded as standard works in the field for centuries to come. This academic training and specialism would prove crucial when writing *Kingdoms in Peril*. The language of the primary sources on which he based his novel is extremely difficult and requires many years of study to be able to read. A rigorous scholarly background can also be discerned in the structuring of *Kingdoms in Peril*. Feng Menglong was determined to produce a novel that was as historically accurate as possible, paying close attention to chronology (an issue of particular importance at a time when many states were using their own calendars), nomenclature, precise geographical locations, and so on. This attention to detail does not add to the literary qualities of the novel per se, but certainly serves to give readers the confidence that they are in the hands of a highly competent author.

Feng Menglong's place of birth was to have a very strong influence on his life and career. During the course of the Ming dynasty, Suzhou had emerged as the commercial capital of China. This ancient city, founded in 514 B.C.E., was originally constructed as the capital of the kingdom of Wu by its penultimate monarch, King Helü. Throughout the imperial era, it continued to be an important regional administrative center, and its location—dominating trade routes along the Yangtze River, the Grand Canal, and through the Lake Tai region—would make it the preeminent commercial hub where goods from every province of the empire were bought and sold. One of the many industries based in Suzhou was that of publishing, with numerous printing presses in operation producing everything from the cheap single-sheet texts handed out as amusing novelty fast-food wrappers to deluxe illustrated editions of the classics printed on the finest paper and elegantly bound for discriminating and wealthy customers. For an educated gentleman needing to make a living, becoming involved in the publishing industry was an obvious step. The majority of Feng Menglong's writings seem to have appeared before he was appointed to a government post in 1630, with the remainder dating to after his retirement in 1638. The dates of first publication of a number of his works are not known, and so the precise chronology of his development as an author remains unclear. However, it is evident that Feng Menglong was an extraordinarily prolific writer who was far from confining himself to a single genre. His popularity was such that a number of works by inferior authors were published with his name on the title page; a great deal of research has been done by modern scholars to identify and remove these spurious works from his oeuvre, and hence they are not included in the list below. However, in addition to writings that were published in his own name, he also appears to have produced some anonymous or pseudonymous works, where an attribution to Feng Menglong remains highly controversial.

The reception of Feng Menglong's writings has varied enormously. While his short story collections have consistently been very much admired and widely read, other writings that he produced have much more patchy histories. In general, the fall of the Ming dynasty can be said to have brought a significantly more conservative regime to power, and during the Qing dynasty (1645–1911) the government would ban many of Feng Menglong's writings—and indeed a great deal of late Ming literature—as indecent. This would particularly affect the reception of his two collections of folk songs, many of which are sexually explicit and describe pre- or extramarital relationships in positive (and sometimes humorous) terms. These song collections were rendered even more unacceptable by the fact that many pieces were produced in the female voice, and in some cases have explicitly female authorship. Both the *Mountain Songs* and the *Hanging Branches* collections have been virtually unobtainable until very recently. The *Anatomy of Love* was also banned because of the supposedly pornographic nature of the contents—this collection too has suffered neglect until modern times, when reprints have appeared to at last allow people to read these tales of love and lust again. While these writings survive, the impact of bans on Feng Menglong's anonymous and pseudonymous works is much harder to gauge, since by their very nature, their attribution to his authorship is controversial and uncertain. During the early part of his career as a writer, Feng Menglong appears to have authored at least one (and most likely more) short erotic novel(s). This kind of text was subject to extremely strict legal prohibitions during the Qing dynasty and beyond, and hence their role within his development as a writer has not been properly appreciated. However, this part of his oeuvre is particularly important given that one text that has survived, the *Scandalous History of Zhulin*, forms the basis of the tale of Lady Xia Ji in *Kingdoms in Peril*.

During the course of the Qing dynasty, an abridged version of *Kingdoms in Peril* was produced by Cai Yuanfang, an otherwise completely obscure eighteenth-century writer. His revised text, titled *Tales of the States of the Eastern Zhou* (*Dongzhou lieguo zhi*), proved to be enormously popular, to the point where Feng Menglong's original novel ceased to be reprinted. The difficulty of laying hands on a copy of the original text has served to confuse many readers as to the nature and extent of the abridgement. Most of Cai Yuanfang's changes are extremely minor, cutting a sentence here and a poem there. The most significant changes lie in the removal of much of the more sexually explicit material, which would fit with the conservative agenda of the government of the time and with changing tastes among readers. The present translation is based upon the critical edition of the text produced by Hu Wanchuan for the Lianjing Publishing Company as part of the *New Printings of Classic Chinese Novels* (*Zhongguo gudian xiaoshuo xinkan*) series. This reproduces the only surviving copy of the first edition, produced by Ye Jingchi—who also published many of Feng Menglong's other writings—which is preserved in the Naikaku Bunko in Japan. The Naikaku Bunko collection of Chinese literature comprises many important Ming and Qing editions purchased for the library maintained by the Tokugawa shoguns, which have not survived elsewhere.

It is not known when exactly *Kingdoms in Peril* was written, and there is no date of publication given on the only surviving copy of the first edition. However, there is a reference in the writings of Qi Biaojia (1603–45) to reading a copy in 1644 on a boat journey back to his hometown. Some scholars have suggested that this novel was published as early as the 1620s, but this would seem to be extremely unlikely for several reasons. First, as a very popular author with a large and devoted readership, it is hard to imagine that a major novel by Feng Menglong could exist for twenty years without anyone mentioning it. The second reason is practical: between 1620 and 1630, Feng Menglong appears to have been fully occupied with other writing projects. He produced a vast body of work during this decade, and the dates of publication of these writings are known. It would seem unlikely that with such a packed schedule it would have been possible to make room for the production of an additional one hundred and eight–chapter novel, particularly one that required very extensive background research. Finally, throughout the novel, Feng Menglong refers to himself as "an old man" or "a bearded old man" (*ranweng* or *ranxian*). This term of self-address is also found in other writings dating to the end of his life, and it would seem reasonable that he adopted it in his seventies, rather than in his late forties to early fifties. However, it is certainly true that Feng Menglong was an extraordinarily productive author, and considerable work remains to be done to elucidate the full scope of his literary legacy.

The dating of *Kingdoms in Peril* is significant, because it suggests that at some level the writing of this novel should be understood in the context of contemporary political events. During the reigns of the last Ming emperors, the regime lurched from one crisis to another: the Great Jiajing earthquake of 1556 killed nearly a million people and reduced vast areas of the northwest to ruins; Wokou pirate attacks of 1522–66 made life along the southern coast of China miserable for one and all (including repeated attacks on Suzhou and the surrounding area); and the Imjin War of 1592–98 obliged the bankrupt Ming state to go to the aid of its allies in Korea when under attack by the Japanese, thus worsening the political and economic situation at home. These events all took place during an era of global cooling, which saw crop failures, widespread famine, increased banditry, and significant social upheaval as hordes of refugees moved from one place to another struggling to find a way to survive. It was against this background of ever-intensifying misery that a rebel commander in the northwest, Li Zicheng (1606–45), came to power. In 1641, he would capture Luoyang, once the capital of the kings of the Eastern Zhou dynasty, and execute Zhu Changxun, King of Fu (1601–41), the uncle of the last Ming emperor. In 1643, the last of the Ming kings of Qin would surrender the city of Xi'an, and Li Zicheng would crown himself emperor of the Shun dynasty there on New Year's Day, 1644. From these lands, formerly the site of the Western Zhou capital, Li Zicheng would march on the city of Beijing, to bring the Ming dynasty to an end. The Chongzhen emperor (r. 1627–44), trapped within the Forbidden City, realized his peril too late: the city was under siege. On April 24, 1644, having ordered his wife and concubines to commit suicide and after murdering several of his children personally, the last Ming emperor hanged himself.

At the time that Feng Menglong wrote *Kingdoms in Peril*, the dreadful end of the Ming dynasty had not yet played out. The imperial family died and Beijing fell to the forces of Li Zicheng only in late April, 1644. The power vacuum that this created allowed the Manchu people to invade China from the northeast—the first wave of troops crossed the border in May, and was followed by further massive incursions over the next few weeks and months. The Manchu conquest would take decades and cost many millions of lives; indeed, it was not until 1683 that the last remnants of Ming loyalist resistance were mopped up on the island of Taiwan. However, the imminent collapse of the Ming dynasty would have been much on everybody's minds in the early 1640s, and this experience must have affected Feng Menglong's personal understanding of the historical events described in *Kingdoms in Peril*. Although no explicit parallel is drawn at any stage, and the author never mentions any contemporary relevance, it is because he does not have to. *Kingdoms in Peril* is a political novel, and it describes the exercise of power and the rise and fall of dynasties. When Li Zicheng was crowned as emperor in 1644, it was not by accident that he chose the city of Xi'an for this ceremony: this site was the location of the Western Zhou dynasty capital, and subsequently served as the capital for first the kingdom and then the empire of Qin, not to mention the Han and Tang dynasties. The legitimation of power by calling on the vestiges of past glory was a process that everyone understood—just as the rulers described in *Kingdoms in Peril* laid claim to the legacy of the founders of the Zhou dynasty, Li Zicheng wanted to see himself walking in the footsteps of the First Emperor of Qin.

• • •

The narrative of *Kingdoms in Peril* consists of three elements. There is the main story, which forms the bulk of the text. When writing *Kingdoms in Peril*, Feng Menglong made use of every single surviving ancient Chinese text relevant to this period in Chinese history, and the narrative is constructed using two techniques: translation and amplification. On the principle that nothing he could invent for his characters to say could possibly be as striking and characteristic as what they thought of for themselves, Feng Menglong relies heavily upon conversations reported in ancient texts, which he has translated from the classical Chinese of two thousand years earlier into the vernacular language of the early seventeenth century. Sometimes, however, his sources do not provide enough material to work with, and there the author resorts to amplification. Thus, for example, in the earliest account of the confrontation between Lord Huan of Lu and his wife over her incestuous adultery with her brother, *Zuo's Tradition* (*Zuozhuan*) simply says, "The lord upbraided her." This is amplified in *Kingdoms in Peril* into a dramatic interrogation sequence in which the angry Lord of Lu presses his evermore humiliated wife with a series of searching questions. In addition to the main narrative, Feng Menglong periodically incorporates quotations of poetry and prose into his novel. The presence of these literary works serves a couple of different purposes. Sometimes they act as a kind of punctuation, marking the end of a particular story sequence or the final appearance of an important character. In other instances, these writings highlight some aspect of the narrative that the author wished to emphasize, or provide a contrasting reading of the events described. Alternatively, they are there to remind the reader of the ongoing cultural significance of these events in China: these people and their actions have a legacy in Chinese literature that should not be ignored, and they have inspired some of the most important writers and poets of the past two thousand years. Finally, there are Feng Menglong's own comments, which are indicated in this translation by italics. These are intended to clarify unusual terms that he expected to be unfamiliar to his readers, to explain things that occurred outside the time frame covered by his book, or to note the precise location at which a particular event took place. This geographical information was included to remind his Chinese readership that these dramatic and often horrifying events occurred right there where they were living in the late Ming dynasty.

Feng Menglong and Late Ming Literature

Feng Menglong was a major figure in the late Ming Romantic movement. This would have personal implications as well as giving a particular flavor to his literary works. As a young man, he is known to have engaged in a series of intensely passionate relationships with courtesans in Suzhou, most notably with a woman named Hou Huiqing. Their relationship ended abruptly when Hou Huiqing was purchased from the brothel in which she was indentured by a wealthy salt merchant. The sudden end to their love affair seems to have been a devastating shock to Feng Menglong, and one from which he took long to recover. Society in the Ming dynasty was heavily segregated, and respectable women did not appear in public, so their opportunities to meet and mingle with men who were not close relatives were very limited. This meant that men desiring female companionship had little choice but to seek the company of courtesans, who not only provided sexual services, but were also trained as entertainers—singing, dancing, and playing music for the enjoyment of their clients. However, these courtesans were slaves, often sold into brothels as children, with virtually no control over their own lives. No matter how beautiful, charming, highly educated, and talented, there was little chance for them of leaving slavery. Even if they were bought out, the stigma remained: their engagement in sex work made them part of a legally circumscribed underclass. It is for this reason that courtesans were the focus of much late Ming

Romantic sensibility, for these women embodied the tragic side of the commercialism and commodification of the age. Feng Menglong's writings are interesting not only for the great sympathy he expresses concerning the fate of these women, but also because he clearly spent time discussing their lives with them, and records their thoughts and opinions. The respect he accords these women by allowing them an opportunity to speak for themselves is unusual and admirable.

One key feature of the late Ming Romantic movement in China was the tolerance that was expressed towards more unconventional relationships. As love came to be seen as an adequate justification for pretty much any attachment, no matter how frowned upon in society as a whole, it became possible to present a wide range of unconventional lifestyles in a positive light. Chinese society was traditionally monogamous, but polygynous—in other words, a man might only marry one wife, but he could have numerous concubines and junior consorts. Some individuals would take the Romantic ideal to extremes, expressing contempt for any social restraints and adopting a completely hedonistic way of life. For example, Zhang Dai (1597–1684) would write in his "Epitaph to Myself" (*Ziwei muzhiming*) that he "loved extravagance, loved luxurious houses, loved beautiful maidservants, loved pretty boys, loved colorful clothes, loved fine foods, loved pedigree horses, loved bright lights, loved red-light districts, loved the theater, loved loud music, loved antiques, and loved flower and bird paintings." Here, the maidservants and pretty boys should be understood as the focus of his sexual attentions, in the same way as the female denizens of the red-light districts and the male actors whom he met at the theater. As can be seen from the portrayal of unusual sexual relationships in *Kingdoms in Peril*, the author felt confident enough in his readers' engagement with these Romantic ideas to be able to describe brother-sister incest as an expression of true love. However, in *Kingdoms in Peril*, Feng Menglong does not shy away from documenting the appalling consequences of unrestrained lust—sexual obsession can lead to exploitation and abuse for the unfortunate victim, but worse than that, when these emotions afflict members of the ruling elite, there can be serious political consequences. In this novel, all too often, "love" leads to assassination, rioting, civil war, invasions, and the deaths of many innocent individuals as the situation gets completely out of control. As a result, *Kingdoms in Peril* can sometimes seem like an extended paean to the virtue of self-control and thinking through the consequences of one's actions.

In Feng Menglong's writings, women characters play an unusually prominent part, and they are accorded a deeper and more complex characterization than is often seen in premodern Chinese literature. The role of women in the history of the Eastern Zhou dynasty is not well-recorded, but wherever a female character does appear, the author makes every attempt to include her in the narrative in a substantive way. Hence, rather than portraying women as purely the ciphers—the unhappy victims of male lust—they appear in this novel in much more complicated guises: ambitious and intelligent participants in the government of the country, masterminds of cunning stratagems to turn events to their advantage, and persons of high moral values determined to preserve these qualities in the teeth of the dubious activities of their male relatives, as well as bewildered personalities who have blundered into situations far more complicated and serious than they can even begin to grasp. Some women are shown being as unrestrained and promiscuous as their male counterparts, while others strongly resent or suffer through the degradation of unwanted sexual attentions. The intelligent and strong female characters in this novel are every bit a match for their male peers. At the same time, the stupid and ignorant women are as just as dull as the worst of the men, and prove equally incapable of extracting themselves from the dangerous situations in which they find themselves.

THE WORLD OF *KINGDOMS IN PERIL*
Places

The majority of the action in *Kingdoms in Peril* focuses around the states of the Zhou confederacy, also known as the Central States, a civilization based around the Yellow River valley. This was a highly urban culture, found within vast walled cities, connected together by great highways. The people of the Central States lived either safely tucked away inside an array of moats, earthworks, fortifications, and huge pounded earth walls, or immediately outside the walls in suburban areas. The inhabitants of walled cities were "the people of the country" or "the people of the capital" (*guoren*), who formed the background audience for every public appearance on the part of the ruling elite. Although there was no mechanism for consulting the people of the capital about political decisions, monarchs and ministers were very conscious of the importance of their approval and support. Although far from being wealthy or socially advantaged, living cheek by jowl with the lords and clan chiefs inside the great walls of the city, the people of the capital could play a major role in historical events, providing enthusiastic support—even rioting—to ensure that a favored candidate took power or that unpopular legislation should be repealed. They had to be constantly propitiated with favorable treatment, and in times of famine or unrest, they required further generous gifts, because if mobilized against the government they could easily overthrow it.

In addition to the city residents, there were also those who lived immediately outside the walls in suburbs. In return for paying less tax towards the maintenance of these defensive structures, suburban dwellers risked losing their property and their lives in the event of a sudden attack. Politically, these people were also significantly less relevant than the inhabitants of the city, and their historical role was accordingly more restricted. The suburbs were, however, the location of the official guesthouses in which much diplomatic activity was centered. Ambassadors or distinguished visitors from foreign countries tended to arrive with heavily armed guards, even military units, and were therefore not allowed to stay within the confines of the city walls in case they were intending to cause trouble. Quite apart from these city and suburban residents, there were other people who had not assumed an urban lifestyle. A significant proportion of the population would have been agricultural workers, whether based on small farms or on the great manorial estates owned by grand aristocratic houses. In addition, within the confines of each state, it was possible to find *yeren* or "people of the wilds," who wished to live free of any government control, as well as bandits who had retreated to the margins of society, and nomadic or aboriginal peoples of one kind or another—such persons, individually or collectively, could occasionally play a major role in historical events. At the beginning of the Spring and Autumn period, many of the states within the Zhou confederacy were city-states, but over time increasingly such regimes were subject to conquest by more aggressive, powerful neighbors, creating the enormous kingdoms of the Warring States era.

The vast majority of the characters in *Kingdoms in Peril* are members of the ruling elite, and therefore they are to be found living in palaces, emerging periodically in order to attend ceremonies at the ancestral temple, to visit their hunting parks, or to go on campaign against their enemies. Other travel involved attendance at international meetings or blood covenants, designed to keep the peace between warring factions. When travel took place outside the confines of one's own country, the most important associated architecture was the sacrificial altar, erected upon a pounded earth platform, where agreements could be made and oaths sworn. Building such structures was an opportunity to show off one's wealth and ability to mobilize the resources of the population not only of one's own country, but also of one's neighbors. Meanwhile, within each state, ruling families in the Eastern Zhou dynasty took particular pride in constructing towers, and a great many significant historical events took place in or around these structures. Since constructing high-rise buildings was beyond the capability of architects in this period, towers were multilevel structures constructed on top of massive, stepped pounded earth foundations. From the outside, the tower might appear to be as much as ten or twelve stories high, but in fact, each part of the structure was only a couple of stories, with the impression of height achieved by building up the core on which it was erected. These towers quickly became an essential feature of elite life for the aristocracy of the Central States and their neighbors: they were a form of conspicuous consumption, which could be used to impress both subjects and foreign visitors; they allowed the aristocracy the privilege of quite literally looking down on everyone else; and they provided a luxurious space for elite socialization in a slightly freer form than the highly ritualized formal events held in palace halls or ancestral temples.

The action of *Kingdoms in Peril* is not confined exclusively to the Central States. Three foreign regimes are treated in some detail in this novel, in accordance with their historical significance. All three were located along the Yangtze River: the kingdom of Chu was based inland, while Wu and Yue occupied the delta region. To the inhabitants of the states of the Zhou confederacy, Chu was an exotic kingdom of fabulous wealth and apparently limitless resources, whose lands stretched in a vast swath southwards from the Yangtze, ending somewhere in the jungles of Southeast Asia. Chu often appears in *Kingdoms in Peril* as a counterbalancing regime to the Central States; although the two regimes were frequently in conflict, both sides are accorded a more-or-less legitimate position in their disagreements. Meanwhile, the kingdoms of Wu and Yue are given particular prominence in this novel thanks to the fact that an exceptionally fine body of early literature survives about the rivalry between these two kingdoms, which would eventually coalesce during the early Eastern Han dynasty into a truly remarkable epic retelling of these events—*The Spring and Autumn Annals of Wu and Yue* (*Wu Yue chunqiu*), which is also the first historical novel to be written in the Chinese language. The dramatic incidents attendant on the rise and fall of the kingdom of Wu, culminating in the suicide of their last king, form a well-known and much-studied story cycle which remains popular right up to the present day. However, Feng Menglong was himself a native of the city of Suzhou, once the capital of the kings of Wu, and hence the setting of these famous events would have been familiar to him from his birth, so highlighting them in his novel was an expression of pride in his own hometown. Unlike some other accounts of the history of these ancient kingdoms, Feng Menglong accepts the foreign and alien characteristics of the Wu and Yue people: they are described here sailing about on boats around their riverine homeland, armed with the finest of swords, and dressed in magnificent feather regalia.

People

People in ancient China used a very extensive nomenclature. Each person was affiliated with a clan, and individual branches within a clan were distinguished by a separate surname. Surnames were often derived from job titles or geographical locations, which meant that two people might have the same surname but belong to different clans, thus indicating that they were unrelated. This was of considerable importance to marriage practice in ancient China, since any sexual relationship between persons of the same clan was regarded as incest. Within a family, brothers and sisters were also each allocated a one-character name to indicate birth order: *bo* for eldest son, *meng* for eldest daughter, and so on. For day-to-day use, individuals were designated by their style-names, which provided a respectful form of address for use by friends and strangers. Personal names tended to only be used by very close family members, and for anyone else to address one by one's personal name was considered extremely offensive. Because of this consideration, women's personal names never appear in historical texts (though many such names are documented in archaeologically excavated bronze vessel inscriptions), and in the case of men, even for some very famous individuals their personal names are simply not recorded. In addition to these names, persons might also be designated according to the job they performed or the title that they held. Furthermore, persons of aristocratic rank would normally receive a posthumous title, a one- or two-word summary of their career. These ranged from the highly positive and desirable Wen (cultured) and Wu (martial)—these were also the posthumous titles of the first two kings of Zhou—to pejorative terms such as Ling (numinous), which was normally reserved for rulers who had proved dangerously insane. These titles provide an immediate alert as to what to expect of the reigns of the kings and lords who bore them, and Chinese readers would have been strongly aware of these meanings, even if not familiar with the precise details of the careers of the individuals concerned.

For this translation of *Kingdoms in Peril*, in order to minimize confusion, men are commonly designated by only one name, and mostly I have chosen to use their personal name where this is known. In order to keep persons with identical or very similar names separate in readers' minds, I have sometimes used unusual readings of the Chinese characters. In the case of rulers, they are given two names in this translation: princes and aristocrats are called by their personal names prior to their accession, and afterwards, they are always designated by their posthumous titles. Women are generally named either according to their clan and posthumous title, or clan and birth-order designation. In the case of foreign individuals, particularly those living in nomadic or tribal groups, the nomenclature is very confusing for this early stage in Chinese history. Many of the names accorded to characters of this kind in *Kingdoms in Peril* seem to have been invented by Feng Menglong. So far as is known, these peoples did not have surnames, and hence their multicharacter names have been translated as a single word. The kingdom of Chu, which originally seems to have been culturally indistinguishable from the states of the Zhou confederacy during the Western Zhou dynasty, increasingly absorbed foreign influences as it expanded through the conquest of numerous aboriginal peoples, achieving independence during the early Eastern Zhou. As a result, their language took on new vocabulary from the different peoples absorbed into this polity, and they came to develop a unique nomenclature for their government officials that would have appeared profoundly alien and exotic to the people of the Central States. In order to preserve this linguistic feature, Chu titles have been translated using comparable Persian terms, which for an English-language readership carry many of the same connotations.

It is one of the striking features of *Kingdoms in Peril* that there are virtually no descriptions of what any of the hundreds of characters looked like. Instead, their individual personalities are rendered distinct through their words and deeds, and there is virtually no mention of their physical features or manner of dress. In part, this reflects the fact that early Chinese literature contains very few descriptions of what even the most important historical individuals looked like (except perhaps in the event of one person possessing an obvious physical peculiarity or disability), and there are merely a handful of known portrait sculptures that date from the classical era. Most early artistic representations of human beings in the Chinese tradition are generic types: servants, warriors, captives, entertainers, and so on, rather than being portraits of individuals. There seems to have been no widespread tradition of representing famous historical figures in art until the Eastern Han dynasty (25–220 C.E.); when such depictions became popular, they appeared in a wide variety of mediums including stone sculpture, low relief bronzes, and wall paintings. However, these are entirely imaginary re-creations of the appearance of individuals who lived and died many hundreds of years earlier. Rather than attempt to ascribe particular physical features to the men and women of the Eastern Zhou dynasty, Feng Menglong leaves the reader free to imagine the beautiful women and battle-scarred men who people the pages of his epic novel.

Much of the action within *Kingdoms in Peril* is concerned with politics at a national or international level. However, in some instances, arguments arose within the family, as disputes emerged over the inheritance of titles and land. Status within each family was determined by a number of factors. Of primary importance was position within the clan, since the most senior branch had priority over all the others in issues of inheritance, and would decide the distribution of clan property. Seniority among siblings was also important, since an oldest child would have priority over younger brothers and sisters. However, among the aristocratic houses of the Central States, concubinage was standard, and some elite men established extensive harems. Therefore, a distinction was also supposed to be maintained between the offspring of the main wife—known as *dizi* or "legitimate" children—and the *shuzi* (commoner) children born to concubines. This gave rise to some perfectly predictable problems. First, affection did not follow legal prioritization, and many fathers much preferred the intelligent and charismatic offspring of a much-loved junior consort to the children of their main wife, who was furthermore likely to have been chosen for her lineage and wealth rather than personal compatibility. Secondly, although not the main wife, lesser consorts might nevertheless be women associated with powerful factions at court, or taken from other aristocratic houses to confirm an alliance—unlike later eras, Eastern Zhou dynasty concubines could be vastly wealthy and powerful in their own right. Such women were not necessarily prepared to see their own children's interests set aside in favor of the offspring of the main wife. Finally, it might be that an aristocrat did not have children at all by his main wife but produced a plethora of potential heirs by junior consorts, in which case balancing claims made on the basis of maternal seniority and child birth order would potentially make selecting an heir immensely contro-versial. Concubinage provided an important mechanism for tying the interests of other powerful families to those of the ruling house, bringing stability to the regime. However, if badly managed, it could equally create appalling internal crises, in which rival heirs fought endless bloody battles with one another over the right of succession.

Ideas

The states of the Zhou confederacy lacked any kind of organized religion, with a hierarchy and textual tradition, but both religious and ethical con-siderations were crucial for how their people understood the world around them. Ever since the founding of the Zhou dynasty, the kings had claimed to be the representatives on earth of the supreme deity Heaven (*Tian*), and hence assumed the title of Son of Heaven. In a related claim, the Zhou kings declared that they possessed the Mandate of Heaven (*Tianming*), which legitimated their right to rule. Even as the Zhou kings lapsed into political irrelevance, they retained a very important religious function, and performed a series of ceremonies throughout the year that were believed to be crucial for the ongoing functioning of the entire realm. In a more limited way, the lords of the Central States also had a religious function, performing annual sacrifices at the altars of soil and grain. Any failure to perform these agricultural ceremonies was regarded as an existential threat to the entire country; lords thought to be unable to carry out the sacrifices were routinely dispossessed, and a cessation of rituals at the altars was synonymous with the fall of the state itself.

The people of ancient China believed themselves to be surrounded by a vast array of spirits and ghosts, who could be supportive or malevolent. In an attempt to safely navigate these forces, individuals called upon a wide range of mantic skills, including oracle bone cracking, casting hexa-grams (milfoil divination), and the interpretation of dreams, as well as seeking the advice of shamans who could communicate with the spirits in a trance. It is one of the striking features of *Kingdoms in Peril* (and indeed its source texts) that these divinations are always correct, and the person-ages who receive them are in extreme danger if they decide to ignore a warning divination. Obtaining the benevolent intervention of a ghost or spirit could come about by pure chance, though there are a number of instances in *Kingdoms in Peril* where a living person is rewarded for some act of kindness in the past. At the same time, deceased ancestors were always believed to take a kindly interest in their descendants, and this concept undoubtedly served to strengthen bonds of clan and family solidarity. This would have been reinforced at regular ancestral sacrifices and gatherings, at which elders could become acquainted with and offer patronage and support to promising younger members, creating a strongly corporate identity within the clan. As a result, loyalty to the clan head would often trump any consideration of duty towards the king or lord, or to the country as a whole. It is therefore not surprising that the social reforms that made the Qin unification possible were aimed at strengthening the position of the central government and nuclear families at the expense of the power of individual aristocratic clans.

Numerous ancient texts stress the moral qualities that were supposed to underpin Eastern Zhou dynasty society: benevolence, justice, respect, loyalty, and so on. These attributes seem to have been hymned because they were in very short supply. However, the concept of ritual propriety (*li*) does seem to have formed an important tool for promoting social cohesion. In the Eastern Zhou dynasty, everyone seems to have been armed more or less constantly. Men were supposed to remove their weapons in the presence of the ruler but otherwise would always have a sword strapped to their belts, while women had at least a hairpin to hand with which they could stab anyone who offended them. In a society that was at one and the same time very hierarchical and very unstable, a situation in which one individual appeared to disrespect another could easily end in bloodshed. Throughout the Eastern Zhou dynasty, a mastery of ritual continued to be highly admired because this offered a mechanism for interacting with other people that minimized the chance of conflict. Ritual, here understood in a social and not a religious sense, was a key part of the education of members of the ruling elite, since it continued to provide an essential technique for negotiating relationships with others in a highly formalized and nonconfrontational way.

FURTHER READING
Works by Feng Menglong

The following novels, short story collections, literary anthologies, essays, poems, and writings in other genres are of undisputed authenticity.

Historical Novels:

Quelling the Demons' Revolt (*Pingyao zhuan*), 1620.
Kingdoms in Peril (*Xin lieguo zhi*), c. 1643?

Short Story Collections:

The best-known of Feng Menglong's works today are collectively called the *Sanyan* or *Three Story Compilations*:

Stories to Instruct the World (Yushi mingyan), 1620 (also known as *Stories Old and New [Gujin xiaoshuo]*).
Stories to Caution the World (Jingshi tongyan), 1624.
Stories to Awaken the World (Xingshi hengyan), 1627.

Feng Menglong's other major collection of short stories is a compilation of eight hundred and fifty tales of romance, infatuation, and sexual obsession:

Anatomy of Love (Qingshi), 1628.

Anthologies of Fiction:

Feng Menglong produced an abridged version of an important collection of early Chinese fiction, compiled in 978.

Excerpts from the Extensive Records of the Taiping Reign-Era, 976–984 (Taiping guangji chao), 1626.

In addition, he edited a compilation of three short religious novels, where he was also the author of the first novel:

Random Gleanings from the Three Faiths (Sanjiao ounian), date unknown.

Textbooks:

Examples Drawn from the Unicorn Classic [Spring and Autumn Annals] (Linjing zhiyue), 1620.
New Light on the Central Ideas of the Spring and Autumn Annals (Chunqiu dingzhi canxin), ca. 1623.
Thesaurus to the Spring and Autumn Annals (Chunqiu hengku), 1625.

Folk Song Compilations:

Mountain Songs (Shan'ge), date unknown.
Hanging Branches (Guazhi'er), before 1619.

Song Compilations:

Celestial Airs Played Anew (Taixia xinzou), c. 1627.

Plays:

An Authoritative Edition of Chuanqi Dramas from the Studio of the Inky Simpleton (Mohan zhai dingben chuanqi), 1620s.

Joke Collections:

Treasury of Laughter (Xiaofu), after 1610.
The Book of Wit and Wisdom (Zhinang), 1625.
A History of Humor Old and New (Gujin xiaoshi), date unknown (also known as *A Survey of Stories Old and New [Gujin tan'gai]*).

History and Local History:

Expectant Gazetteer for Shouning County (Shouning daizhi), 1637.
An Account of Events of Shenjia Year [1644] (Shenjia jishi), 1645.
Grand Proposals for National Rejuvenation (Zhongxing weilüe), 1645.

Translations of Feng Menglong's Writings

The three volumes of the *Sanyan* compilation have been translated into English in their entirety:

Shuhui Yang and Yunqin Yang, *Stories Old and New: A Ming Dynasty Collection* (Seattle: University of Washington Press, 2000).
———, *Stories to Caution the World* (Seattle: University of Washington Press, 2005).
———, *Stories to Awaken the World* (Seattle: University of Washington Press, 2014).

There have been many translations of individual short stories by Feng Menglong, and these can often be found in anthologies of Chinese literature, including the following examples:

Cyril Birch, *Stories from a Ming Collection: The Art of the Chinese Storyteller* (Bloomington: Indiana University Press, 1958).
Yang Xianyi and Gladys Yang, *The Courtesan's Jewel Box: Chinese Stories of the Xth–XVIIth Centuries* (Beijing: Foreign Languages Press, 1981).
Ted Wang and Chen Chen, *The Oil Vendor and the Courtesan: Tales from the Ming Dynasty* (New York: Welcome Rain Publishers, 2007).
Shuhui Yang and Yunqin Yang, *Sanyan Stories: Favorites from a Ming Dynasty Collection* (Seattle: University of Washington Press, 2014).

In addition, there are three different English-language translations of Feng Menglong's other major novel:

Nathan Sturman, *The Sorcerer's Revolt* (Rockville: Silk Pagoda, 2008).
Lois Fusek, *The Three Sui Quash the Demons' Revolt: A Comic Novel Attributed to Luo Guanzhong* (Honolulu: University of Hawai'i Press, 2010).
Patrick Hanan, *Quelling the Demons' Revolt: A Novel from Ming China* (New York: Columbia University Press, 2017).

Other works of Feng Menglong translated into English include:

Hua-yuan Li Mowry, *Chinese Love Stories from "Ch'ing-shih"* (Hamden: Archon Books, 1983).
Ōki Yasushi and Paolo Santangelo, *Shan'ge, the 'Mountain Songs': Love Songs in Ming China* (Leiden: Brill, 2011).
Hsu, Pi-ching, *Feng Menglong's* Treasury of Laughs: *A Seventeenth-Century Anthology of Traditional Chinese Humour* (Leiden: Brill, 2015).

Translations of Key Source Texts

Kingdoms in Peril makes use of a very wide range of early Chinese texts, not all of which have been translated into English. Feng Menglong occasionally quotes the most important classical works, in particular the *Book of Songs* (*Shijing*):

Arthur Waley, *The Book of Songs* (London: George Allen and Unwin, 1937).
Bernhard Karlgren, *The Book of Odes* (Stockholm: Museum of Far Eastern Antiquities, 1950).

The historical texts used as a basis for this novel include *Spring and Autumn Annals* (a text on which Feng Menglong was a specialist), as well as *Zuo's Tradition, Stratagems of the Warring States* (*Zhanguo ce*), and compilations focusing on specific locales such as *Lost Histories of Yue* (*Yuejue shu*). *Kingdoms in Peril* also makes extensive use of the first of the official dynastic histories, *Records of the Grand Historian* (*Shiji*), which covers the history of China up until the reign of Emperor Wu of the Han dynasty (r. 141–87 B.C.E.):

William H. Nienhauser, ed., *The Grand Scribe's Records* (Bloomington: Indiana University Press, 1994–).
James Crump, *Chan-kuo Ts'e* (Ann Arbor: University of Michigan Center for Chinese Studies, 1996).

Olivia Milburn, *The Glory of Yue: An Annotated Translation of the Yuejue shu* (Leiden: Brill, 2010).

Stephen Durrant, Wai-yee Li, and David Schaberg, *Zuo Tradition/Zuozhuan: Commentary on the "Spring and Autumn Annals"* (Seattle: University of Washington Press, 2016).

A number of the source texts used by Feng Menglong are yet to be translated, or the translations were produced so long ago that they are unavailable outside specialized academic libraries. However, since the writings of Sun Bin were rediscovered in the 1970s, they have been translated a number of times:

Ralph Sawyer, *Sun Pin: Military Methods* (Boulder: Westview Press, 1995).

D. C. Lau and Roger Ames, *Sun Bin: The Art of Warfare: A Translation of the Classic Chinese Work of Philosophy and Strategy* (Albany: State University of New York Press, 2003).

There is also a full translation into English of the key work of state-craft to survive from the court of the First Emperor of Qin:

John Knoblock and Jeffrey Riegel, *The Annals of Lü Buwei* (Stanford: Stanford University Press, 2000).

Careful study of these source texts indicates just how faithful Feng Menglong was to the chronology they provide and attests to the accuracy with which he tried to convey the key events of this historical period. However, unlike the text that inspired the production of this novel, *Kingdoms in Peril* does not generally include later overtly fictional material, and so the myths, legends, prophetic dreams, encounters with ghosts, and so on that scatter the pages are in fact taken from the ancient sources.

Chapter One

*King Xuan of Zhou hears a children's song
and kills a woman for no good reason.*

*Grandee Du becomes formidable as he
protests his innocence.*

When Heaven and Earth emerged from primordial confusion,
The Three August Ones and the Five Gods held power in turn.
After this era of enlightened rule, yielding to the better man ceased,
After the Xia, the Shang and Zhou dynasties succeeded each other.
The Xia lasted for four hundred years, the Shang for six hundred,
But the Zhou kept on flourishing, longer than another.
When a worthless king moved to the east to escape the Dog Rong,
He destroyed the fabric of the state and placed the kingdom in peril.
Factions were formed in a fight for supremacy.
In Linzi, the first of the hegemons was shot to power.
Jin and Chu, Song and Qi each took it in turn to lock horns;
When storms blow through the forest, not a single branch is safe.
When the Five Hegemons failed, Wu and Yue took over,
As King Goujian rose to power by the shores of the Eastern Sea.
When the Six Ministers partitioned Jin, the Tian family usurped Qi;
The Seven Kingdoms divided into the Horizontal and Vertical Alliances.
Su Qin and Zhang Yi sent these Seven Kingdoms to their doom,
And twelve bronze statues were set up in Xianyang.
The Zhou capital at Luoyang was overgrown with weeds, its
    treasures lost,
The last remnants of its ruling house exposed to killing frosts.
Who could stop the killing? Who could restore peace?
Even the clearest streams ran turbid, as endless fighting boiled.
When will we see the golden age of King Cheng and Kang again?
These mountains and rivers hold fast to a legacy of greatness.

You will have heard how the Zhou dynasty held the position of the Son of Heaven after the attack of King Wu on the evil last king of the Shang dynasty, and how King Cheng and King Kang inherited the throne, both of them stamping their authority on the regime and building on the accomplishments of their predecessors. There were also the Duke of Zhou, the Duke of Shao, the Duke of Bi, the Grand Historian Yi, and so on—a group of wise ministers who supported the government and who were so skilled in the demands of civil administration that they had no need for the arts of war, whereby wealth was abundant and the people were at peace. After King Wu of Zhou the throne was handed down through eight generations until it reached King Yi, a man who was neither sober nor correct, and the feudal lords gradually became strong. In the ninth generation the throne passed to King Li, a violent and unrestrained man, who in the end was murdered by the people of the capital. This was the beginning of a great change, which would affect the people of China for a thousand years and more. Once again it was thanks to the sympathy and backing of the Duke of Zhou and the Duke of Shao that Crown Prince Jing was established as the monarch, taking the title of King Xuan. He was a true Son of Heaven, both enlightened and principled. He employed wise ministers such as Fang Shu, Shao Hu, Yi Jifu, Shen Bo, and Zhongshan Fu. They reinvigorated the righteous government that had existed under Kings Wen, Wu, Cheng and Kang, and the Zhou house flourished brightly.

There is a poem that attests to this:

As Kings Yi and Li succeeded each other, the kingdom lost direction;
Any plans to employ wise men and reform the government had to wait
  for King Xuan.
If the Gonghe regency had destroyed the rule of the flourishing Central
  States,
How could the Zhou dynasty have survived for eight hundred years?

Although it is said that under the rule of King Xuan righteous government prevailed, in fact he did not write out prohibitions in royal red ink, nor were the wise words of sage-kings written on the lintels and posts of every door as during the reign of King Wu. Although it is said that the Central States flourished, they did not reach the great heights achieved during the time of King Cheng and King Kang, when barbarian peoples from the far south presented pheasants as tribute to the Zhou king. In the thirty-ninth year of his reign, the Jiang and the Rong peoples rebelled against his rule. King Xuan rode on a chariot and personally led the campaign against them, only to be defeated in engagement after engagement at Qianmu, suffering a terrible loss of war chariots and soldiers. He planned to raise another army for a second campaign, but was alarmed to discover that the number of soldiers was insufficient, and so he personally conducted a census of the population at Taiyuan.

This Taiyuan is the place now called Guyuanzhou, and it bordered upon the territory of the Rong and the Di peoples. Taking a census means that the population registers of a particular place were checked to see how many people there actually were, and how many chariots and horses, how much grain and fodder, in order to make proper preparations before going on campaign.

The prime minister, Zhongshan Fu, came to court to remonstrate with him, but the king paid no attention. Later on, someone wrote a poem about this:

> Why were these dogs and pigs able to humiliate us with their sharp
>   blades?
> When you use a pearl to shoot a sparrow, both suffer severe injuries.
> The authority of the august one was flouted but he could not be
>   avenged;
> He decided to personally count his people, but it was all in vain.

When King Xuan returned from conducting his census of the population at Taiyuan, when he was not far from the capital at Hao, he hurried on by chariot, and thus by traveling day and night he soon reached the city. Suddenly he saw a couple of dozen little children in the marketplace, clapping their hands and singing, and they all harmonized. King Xuan then stopped his royal chariot and listened to them. Their song ran:

> The moon will rise,
> The sun will set.
> A rush quiver and a wild-mulberry bow
> Will bring destruction on the kingdom of Zhou.

King Xuan was appalled by these words, and so he ordered the charioteer to arrest and interrogate the children. At that time the children were terrified and ran away, so he was only able to grab hold of one very young and one slightly older child, who were made to kneel before the royal chariot. King Xuan asked them, "Who composed these words?"

The younger of the two children was too frightened to speak, so it was the older child who replied: "They were not composed by any of us. Three days ago, there was a child in a red dress who came to the marketplace and taught us to recite these four lines. I do not know why. Afterwards it spread, and all the children in the city came together to sing it, not just here."

"So where is the child in the red dress now?" King Xuan asked.

"I do not know where the child has gone since teaching us the song," he replied.

King Xuan was silent for a long time, and then he yelled at the two children to go away. Immediately he summoned the official in charge of the marketplace to promulgate the command: "From this point on, if a child sings this song, the parents and older siblings are also guilty of treason." That night he went back to his palace without a word.

The following day at the early morning court, the Three Dukes and the Six Ministers met below the main audience hall of the palace, where they bowed and made obeisance. King Xuan recited to the assembled ministers the children's song that he had heard the day before. "How do you explain these words?"

Shao Hu, the minister of rites, replied, "Wild mulberry is the name of a type of tree, a variety of mulberry that grows in the mountains. It can be used to make archery bows; that is why the song mentions a wild-mulberry bow. Rush is the name of a plant, and it can be woven to make quivers, therefore the song speaks of a rush quiver. In my humble opinion, I am afraid that the country is destined to suffer warfare."

The prime minister, Zhongshan Fu, then offered his opinion to the monarch. He said: "Bows and arrows are weapons used by the country in times of war. Your Majesty has recently been conducting a census in Taiyuan in the hope of taking revenge upon the Dog Rong. If you do not demobilize your troops, I am afraid that you will suffer the calamity of losing your crown."

Although King Xuan did not say anything, he nodded his head in agreement. Then he asked, "These words come from a child in a red dress. Who can this child be?"

The Grand Astrologer, Bo Yangfu, offered his advice to the monarch. "The baseless rumors generated on the streets and in the marketplace are what is known as gossip. Heaven has warned Your Majesty of the oncoming disaster by ordering Mars to take the form of a child and compose these words, teaching them to all the other little children and creating a children's song. At best this song reflects the fate of Your Majesty alone, at worst it is linked to the rise and fall of the dynasty. Mars is a fiery planet, and so it is colored red. Today we have gossip concerning the destiny of our kingdom; this is the way in which Heaven is warning Your Majesty of the danger you are in."

"If I now pardon the Jiang and Rong for their crimes," King Xuan asked, "and demobilize the troops in Taiyuan, as well as ordering that all the bows and arrows stored in the armories should be burned, and then command that no one should be allowed to make or sell them in the whole country, will disaster be averted?"

"I have observed the movements of the heavens, and the signs are already there," Bo Yangfu replied. "It seems as if the problem derives from Your Majesty's harem, for bows and arrows do not threaten you from the lands beyond the passes. It is certain that in a later generation there will be a queen who brings the calamity of civil war to this country. Besides which, the children's song said: 'The moon will rise, the sun will set.' The sun represents the king, while the moon is womankind. For the sun to set and the moon to rise, this means that *yin* will advance and *yang* will retreat, and thus it is clear that a woman will interfere in the government of the country."

King Xuan then asked: "I have placed my wife, Queen Jiang, in charge of the Six Palaces, and she has behaved with the utmost wisdom and circumspection. The concubines and junior wives that she presents to me have all passed through stringent selection procedures. So where will this dangerous woman come from?"

"The words of the song said 'will rise' and 'will set,' so nothing is going to happen for the foreseeable future," Bo Yangfu replied. "Furthermore, 'will' is a word that expresses future potential, rather than something that will definitely happen. If Your Majesty now averts disaster by instituting reform, this will naturally turn bad luck into good, in which case you will not need to go to the extreme of burning your bows and arrows."

King Xuan listened to his advice, but was not sure what to think. He then stopped the audience and drove back to the palace in a foul mood.

Queen Jiang welcomed him, brought him into her chambers, and seated him carefully. Afterwards, King Xuan told her what the ministers had said, reporting everything verbatim to his wife. Queen Jiang said, "Something very strange has happened in the harem; I was just about to report it to you."

"What strange thing?" the king asked.

"There is an old palace maid now in her mid-fifties, who served His Late Majesty," Queen Jiang replied. "Having been pregnant for more than forty years, last night she gave birth to a baby girl."

King Xuan was astounded and asked her for details: "Where is the baby?"

"I thought this was an evil omen," Queen Jiang said, "and so I ordered the servants to wrap the baby in a straw mat and throw her into the Qing River twenty *li* away from the city."

King Xuan immediately had the old palace maid summoned and asked her about the pregnancy. The old palace maid knelt and said: "I have heard that in the final years of King Jie of the Xia dynasty the guardian spirits of the city of Bao transformed themselves into two dragons that came to His Majesty's audience hall, their mouths dripping with drool and foam. Suddenly they spoke in the words of men and said to King Jie, 'We are the two lords of the city of Bao.' King Jie was terrified and wanted to kill the two dragons. He ordered the Grand Astrologer to perform a divination about it, but it was not auspicious. Then he wanted to expel them and ordered a second divination, but this too was not auspicious. The Grand Astrologer spoke. 'A guardian spirit has come to earth that is definitely a wonderful omen for Your Majesty. Why not ask their permission to collect their spit and store it? Spit is the pure essence of a dragon, and if you keep it safe it will bring good luck to you in the future.' King Jie ordered the Grand Astrologer to perform yet another divination, and this time it was extremely auspicious. Then he laid out silk cloths and presented a sacrifice in front of the dragons, collecting their drool in a golden basin, which he then placed inside a cinnabar casket. Suddenly a great storm blew up and the two dragons flew away. King Jie ordered that this casket should be stored in the treasury. From the time of the Shang-Yin dynasty to the present day has been six hundred and forty-four years, and the throne has passed to twenty-eight kings in succession.

"For the last three hundred years of our Zhou dynasty, no one ever opened the casket to look at it. In the last year of His Late Majesty's reign, the casket emitted a bright light, and the official in charge of the treasury reported this to your father. His Late Majesty asked, 'What is inside the casket?' The official in charge of the treasury took out the little docket that recorded the whole story of how the dragon's spit came to be collected and presented it to the king. Your father ordered him to bring it for inspection. A servant broke open the golden casket, and with his hands he lifted up the golden bowl to present it to the king. Your father stretched out his hand to take the bowl, but in a moment of clumsiness he dropped it on the floor, and the dragon's spit that it held spilled out across the audience chamber. Suddenly it metamorphosized into a tiny little turtle while the bowl went spinning across the floor of the hall. The servants chased the turtle, which headed straight to the harem, where in an instant it disappeared. At that time I was just twelve years old, and purely by chance I stepped on the turtle's footprint, which caused an unusual sensation within my body. After that my belly gradually swelled, as if I were pregnant. His Late Majesty thought it was most strange that I became pregnant without a man, and so he imprisoned me in the Cold Palace, where I have spent the last forty years. Last night my belly was painful, and then suddenly I gave birth to a baby girl. The palace guards did not dare to cover this up, and so they reported it to the queen. The queen said that this was an evil omen, which could not be kept within the confines of the palace. She ordered the servants to take the baby away and abandon her by the riverbank. My crime merits death!"

"This is a matter pertaining to a previous dynasty; it has nothing to do with you," King Xuan said. Then he told the old palace maid to withdraw. Afterwards, he ordered the palace servants to go to the Qing River to discover what had happened to the baby girl. Not long afterwards, the servants returned and reported, "She has already been carried away by the river waters." King Xuan saw nothing to be concerned about in this.

At court early the following morning, he summoned the Grand Astrologer, Bo Yangfu, and told him the story about the dragon's spit. Then he said, "The baby girl has already died in the river, so would you mind performing a divination about this, to see if the evil omens have dispersed or not?"

When Bo Yangfu had finished performing a milfoil divination, he presented the following oracle to His Majesty: "Where there are tears there is also laughter; where there is laughter there are also tears. A sheep is swallowed by a ghost; a horse is chased down by a dog. Beware! Beware! The wild-mulberry bow and the rush quiver."

King Xuan could not understand what this meant. Bo Yangfu explained his opinion to the king: "If we extrapolate from the twelve animals of the zodiac, Sheep is the zodiac sign Wei, and Horse is the zodiac sign Wu. Tears and laughter are indications of sadness and happiness, and they must refer to the events of the years Wu and Wei. According to my reading of events, although the evil omens have been expelled from the palace for now, they have not yet been eliminated completely."

King Xuan listened to his explanation and was obviously unhappy. Then he issued a command: "Search every house inside and outside the city for the baby girl and find her, dead or alive. Anyone who assists with her capture or who hands her over to the authorities will be rewarded with three hundred lengths each of cloth and silk. If someone has taken her in and looked after her without coming forward, and if one of the neighbors turns them in, that person will be rewarded accordingly, and the offender and his whole family will be executed."

He ordered Grandee Du Bo to take sole command of overseeing the implementation of this edict. Given that the words of the oracle had also mentioned the wild-mulberry bow and the rush quiver, he also commanded Junior Grandee Zuo Ru to keep an eye on the officials who toured the marketplace, to prevent anyone from either making or selling bows made from the wood of mountain mulberries or quivers woven from rushes. Anyone who disobeyed would be put to death. The head of the market officials did not dare to relax his vigilance, so he led a company of guards around to explain everything clearly and make sure everyone was obeying the regulations. At that time the people in the city respected the prohibition, but the people from the surrounding countryside were not yet aware of it.

When they made their rounds on the following day, they found a woman carrying several basket-work quivers, which she had woven out of rushes. There was a man with a dozen or more mountain mulberry-wood bows on his back, walking just behind her. This couple lived in a distant village, and they had hurried to get to the market by midday to trade, since they had to come to the city to sell their wares. Before they had even entered the gates to the city, they came face-to-face with the official in charge of the marketplace. He shouted, "Arrest them!" His subordinates first laid hands on the woman. The man saw that something was terribly wrong, so he threw his mulberry bows to the ground and ran away as fast as he could. The official put the woman in chains and, gathering up both the mulberry bows and the rush quivers, presented all of them to Grandee Zuo Ru.

Zuo Ru pondered the situation and said to himself, "The bows and quivers correspond exactly to the words of the children's song. Furthermore, according to the Grand Astrologer, the woman is the danger; so, having arrested her, I can go back and get further directions from His Majesty."

Keeping quiet about the man, he simply informed the king about the woman disobeying the prohibition on making or selling wild-mulberry bows and rush quivers, for which the punishment was death. King Xuan ordered the woman to be beheaded. The bows and quivers were burned in the marketplace, as a warning to anyone else thinking of either making or selling them. That was the end of this matter.

Later on, someone wrote a poem about this:

Without good government you cannot prevent dynastic change.
Who interpreted this children's song to justify the death of an innocent woman?
In going wrong, there are many opportunities to put right your mistakes,
But in such circumstances, what minister would dare to speak out?

• • •

Let us now turn to another part of the story. The man who had been selling mulberry-wood bows and who ran away as fast as he could at the first sign of trouble had absolutely no idea why the authorities would want to arrest him and his wife. He was desperate to discover what had happened to her, and so that night he stayed just ten *li* from the city walls. The following morning, someone told him: "Yesterday a woman was arrested by the North Gate for contravening the ban on the manufacture and sale of mulberry bows and rush quivers, and she was killed immediately after her arrest." This was how he found out that his wife was already dead.

Wandering through a desolate and uninhabited wasteland, he cried a few bitter tears. However, he was pleased to have escaped with his own life, and so he walked away as quickly as he could. Having traveled for about a further ten *li*, he arrived at the banks of the Qing River. Far in the distance he could see a flock of birds flapping around and cawing. As he got closer and looked more carefully, he could see that there was a bundle wrapped in a straw mat floating in the middle of the river. The birds were all pecking at it with their beaks, nudging it along and cawing, and it seemed as if they were moving it closer to the bank.

"How strange!" the man said to himself.

He waved away the flock of birds and waded out into the river to pick up the bundle. When he got to the grass-covered bank, he opened it up to have a look. The first thing that greeted him was a cry, for there was a baby girl inside. He thought to himself, "I have no idea who could have abandoned this baby, but given that a flock of birds were trying to get her out of the water, she must be a very important person.

If I take her home and raise her, there will certainly be something in it for me when she grows up." Then he took off his shirt and wrapped up the baby, holding her in his arms as he thought about where he could go to hide. He headed for the city of Bao, where he hoped he could find sanctuary with a friend.

An old man wrote a poem about the strangeness of this baby girl's birth:

A pregnancy delayed for forty years,
Plucked safely from the waters after three days immersion.
Born to be a scourge for the kingdom,
Royal laws have never overcome the will of Heaven!

After King Xuan had executed the woman selling mulberry bows and rush quivers, he thought that he had responded to the words of the children's song, and he felt entirely secure. As a result, he never spoke again about sending troops out from Taiyuan. No one even mentioned these events for many years. However, in the forty-third year of his reign, the time had come for a great sacrifice. King Xuan was spending the night in the Purification Palace, and after the second watch the sound of people's voices gradually faded into silence. Suddenly he saw a beautiful young girl walking slowly from the west, and she went straight into the main hall of the palace. King Xuan was worried that her presence would contravene the rituals of purification and fasting, and so he yelled loudly. He bellowed at his entourage to arrest her, but not a single person responded. The girl seemed completely unafraid. She walked into the main ancestral temple, where she laughed heartily three times and cried loudly three times. Then, without haste and without alarm, she tied up in a bundle the tablets dedicated to the seven main ancestral spirits commemorated in the shrine before walking away to the east. The king got up and was just about to go in pursuit himself, when suddenly he woke up with a start; the whole thing had been nothing but a dream! His heart was thumping erratically, but nevertheless he forced himself to go to the ancestral temple and perform the proper rituals. When the nine rounds of offerings had been presented, he went back to the Purification Palace and changed his clothes. He ordered his entourage to secretly summon the Grand Astrologer, Bo Yangfu, and informed him of what he had seen in his dream.

"Surely Your Majesty cannot have forgotten the words of the children's song three years ago?" Bo Yangfu asked the king. "I stick to my original opinion: the king will suffer because of a woman; the signs of evil have not been eradicated. There was a reference in the riddle to laughter and to tears, and now Your Majesty has had this dream, which corresponds exactly."

"We have already executed the woman," King Xuan said. "Is that not enough to extirpate the prophecy concerning the mulberry bow and rush quiver?"

"The Way of Heaven is mysterious indeed; it is only after the event that you realize the significance of what has gone before," Bo Yangfu said. "How can a peasant woman affect the destiny of nations?"

King Xuan sighed deeply and said nothing.

Suddenly he remembered that three years before he had ordered Grandee Du Bo to keep an eye on the situation in the marketplace and investigate the ill-omened girl, but nothing had been reported to the authorities. After the sacrificial meats had been distributed, King Xuan returned to court, and all his officials gave formal thanks for the gift of food that they had received.

"Why have you not reported all this time about the baby girl?" King Xuan asked Du Bo.

"When I searched, I found no trace of her," Du Bo informed His Majesty. "It was my belief that, since the woman we arrested had answered for her crimes, the children's song had already been fully borne out. I was deeply worried about the prospect that further investigations would merely result in a reign of terror for the people of the capital, and so I called a halt."

King Xuan was absolutely furious. "If this is indeed the case," he demanded, "then why did you not report it to me? Clearly you have been disregarding my orders, doing just what you feel like. I do not need disloyal ministers like you!" He then shouted at his guards: "Drag this man out of the Chao Gate and behead him as a warning to the populace!"

All the officials present were so terrified that their faces went chalkwhite. Suddenly, one of their number burst out from the midst of the serried ranks. Running forward, he grabbed hold of Du Bo, shouting: "No! No!"

King Xuan recognized him; it was Junior Grandee Zuo Ru, a good friend of Du Bo, who had come to serve at court with him. Zuo Ru kowtowed and said, "I have heard that under the sage-king Yao, the world suffered nine years of floods, but that this did not prevent him from becoming a god; in the reign of Tang, there were seven years of drought, which did not harm his rule as king. Given that the natural cycles of Heaven cannot be interrupted, how can you believe that human beings can be evil omens? If Your Majesty kills Du Bo, I am afraid that the whole country will be given over to rumors of witchcraft, and when foreigners hear about this, they are going to despise us. I beg that you will show him mercy."

"You have disobeyed my orders for the sake of your friend; this means that you value your friend more than your king!" King Xuan exclaimed.

"If my king is right and my friend is wrong, then it is proper that I should turn my back on my friend and obey my king," Zuo Ru proclaimed. "If my king is wrong and my friend is right, then it is correct that I offend against my king and agree with my friend. Du Bo has committed no crime that can possibly merit the death penalty, so if Your Majesty kills him, everyone will think that you are completely stupid. If I do not remonstrate and try and stop you, then everyone will believe that I am not loyal. If Your Majesty is determined to kill Du Bo, then I ask your permission to die with him!"

King Xuan's rage was unabated, and he said, "For me to kill Du Bo is a matter of as little moment as digging out a weed; do not waste your time and energy!" Then he gave his instructions: "Behead him now!" The guards dragged Du Bo out of the Chao Gate, and a short time later his head was displayed at the foot of the steps. Zuo Ru beat his breast and wept, but before King Xuan could order his execution, he drew his sword and committed suicide by cutting his throat.

A bearded old man wrote a lament:

Wise Zuo Ru!
In this direct remonstrance his argument was faultless.
At once he agreed with his friend,
And offended against his king.
He resigned his job for the sake of principle,
He cut his throat out of true friendship.
His name has been esteemed for a thousand years,
He has become a model for later generations.

Du Bo's son, Xianshu, fled to Jin. Later on, he was employed in Jin in the position of chief judge, and his sons and grandsons took the surname Shi. They were given a fief in Fan, as a result of which they changed their surname to Fan. Later generations were deeply moved by Du Bo's loyalty, and so they built a shrine to him at the site of his tomb. They called him by the honorific name of Master Du, and the place of worship was also known by the name of the Temple to the General of the Left. It has survived to the present day. However, this is something that happened much later on.

The following day, when King Xuan heard that Zuo Ru had cut his own throat, he began to regret his hastiness in having Du Bo killed. It was thus in a somber and depressed mood that he returned to the palace. That night, he could not sleep, and his mind was confused; subsequently, he had great difficulty in putting his words in the right order, and there were many things that he had forgotten, to the point where he was no longer capable of holding court. Queen Jiang realized that he was seriously sick, and so she never said a word of criticism again. In the autumn, in the seventh lunar month of the forty-sixth year of King Xuan's reign, he gradually recovered and felt sufficiently well that he wanted to go out of the city for some hunting to cheer himself up. His attendants promulgated his command: "The minister of works must prepare the chariots, the minister of war must arrange for a military escort, and the Grand Astrologer must conduct a divination to select an auspicious day."

When the time came, the king rode out on his fine chariot drawn by six stallions, with Yi Jifu on his right hand and Shao Hu on his left hand. The flags and standards fluttered and the arms and armor appeared in serried ranks, as all were gathered in the eastern suburbs before they set out. Near the eastern suburbs there was a flat plain, overgrown with wild plants, which had frequently been used for hunting before. It had been a long time since King Xuan had last set foot outside the palace, and so he felt in a very good mood. He issued commands to build a stockade and told the guards: "One, you are not allowed to trample the crops. Two, you are not allowed to burn the trees for firewood. Three, you are not allowed to disturb the people who live here. It does not matter whether you capture a great deal of game or very little, it should all be handed in and then everyone can have their fair share. Any selfish behavior will be investigated and punished."

Once these commands had been given, they all set out to do their best, each competing to be the finest hunter. Advancing and retreating, the men moved in a great circle. The charioteers exerted all their skill in driving left and right; in front and behind, the bowmen displayed their abilities. Eagles and dogs took advantage of every opportunity to bring down their prey, while the rabbits and foxes scuttled this way and that in terror. The bows resounded, and thus flesh and blood were torn apart; the arrows arched towards their targets, and fur and feathers flew into the air. The battue progressed, building pace. King Xuan was absolutely delighted. The sun had already begun to set in the west when he gave the order to call off the hunt. The officers and men picked up the animals and birds of every variety that they had captured and went home singing songs of triumph.

Before they had gone more than three or four *li*, King Xuan felt rather dizzy, perched high up on the royal chariot. Suddenly he caught sight of a little chariot far away in the distance, driving straight towards him. There were two people standing on the chariot, and they each held a vermilion bow in one hand and a scarlet arrow in the other. They shouted at King Xuan, "Your Majesty, it has been a long time since last we met!"

King Xuan stared at them fixedly: one was Senior Grandee Du Bo, and the other was Junior Grandee Zuo Ru. King Xuan was terribly alarmed, but when he rubbed his eyes, they and their chariot simply disappeared. He questioned the men standing to his right and left, but they both said that they had seen nothing. King Xuan was at once frightened and alarmed. Just at that moment Du Bo and Zuo Ru reappeared, driving the little chariot just in front of the king's horses. King Xuan was absolutely furious and shouted, "Insolent ghosts, how dare you come and interfere with my travels!"

He drew his precious sword Tai-e and brandished it into space. However, Du Bo and Zuo Ru both shouted back, "Deluded, unjust king! You have failed to institute good government and compounded your errors by executing innocent men! Today your time is up! We have come specially to avenge those you have unjustly put to death! Prepare to die!"

Before they had even finished speaking, they flexed their vermilion bows and drew back their scarlet arrows, sighting their shots straight at King Xuan's heart. King Xuan screamed and fainted on the royal chariot. Yi Jifu was so alarmed that his legs gave way beneath him, while Shao Hu's eyes were practically starting from their sockets. The king's attendants fussed around, making a ginger soup in the hope of bringing him around. Given that he never stopped crying with pain, they drove back as quickly as they could to the city, whereupon they carried King Xuan into the palace. The soldiers did not wait to receive their rewards but went home. Truly, this was a case of the rats leaving the sinking ship.

An old man wrote a poem, which reads:

Vermilion bows and scarlet arrows gave them the appearance of gods;
Amid a great army they galloped with spinning wheels.
Even a king who kills an innocent man should expect to be punished,
Not to mention an ordinary man in a village!

If you do not know what happened next in the life of King Xuan, READ ON.

Chapter Two

The people of Bao atone for their crimes by handing over a beautiful woman.

King You lights the beacon fires to tease the feudal lords.

When King Xuan went hunting in the eastern suburbs, he met the ghosts of Du Bo and Zuo Ru, who demanded his life. He consequently got sick, forcing his return to the palace. Every time he closed his eyes, all he could see was the pair of them. Knowing that he would not recover from this, he refused all medication. Three days later, his illness had become critical. By that time, the Duke of Zhou had long since retired from office on account of old age, and Zhongshan Fu was dead. Therefore, all King Xuan could do was to summon his old advisors Yi Jifu and Shao Hu to ask them to look after his son. The two ministers went straight in to stand in front of the king's bed, whereupon they bowed their heads and asked after his health. King Xuan ordered his attendants to help him up, and, leaning against the embroidered cushions, he spoke to his two advisors. "Thanks to the abilities of my ministers, I have ruled now for forty-six years. I have campaigned in the south and done battle in the north, and I have brought peace to the lands within the four seas. I never expected to be laid low by disease! Even though Crown Prince Gongnie is now no longer young, his character is still unformed. I hope that you, as my ministers, will do your utmost to support him; please do not allow the dynasty to decline!"

His two advisors bowed their heads and accepted his commands.

Just as they left the palace gates, they met the Grand Astrologer, Bo Yangfu. Shao Hu spoke privately to him. "After hearing the words of the children's song, I said that I was afraid that in the future there would be some disastrous change brought about by a bow and arrow. Now the king has met a powerful ghost that grabbed a vermilion bow and scarlet arrow and shot him. That is why his illness has become critical. The signs all correspond: His Majesty will die!"

"At night I observe the patterns of the heavens, and an evil planet is currently lying in ambush beyond the starry wall of the Purple Palace constellation," Bo Yangfu declared. "The state will suffer further disasters, for the king's death alone is not sufficient to warrant such portents."

"Heaven determines the lives of men, but men can also change what happens in the heavens," Yi Jifu remarked. "Lords just say that Heaven determines what happens and ignore the importance of men, but where does that leave us?"

When these words had been spoken, each went his own way. Not long afterwards, all the government officials gathered by the gates of the palace to ask after His Majesty's health. When they heard that the king was sinking, they did not dare to go home. That night, His Majesty died. Queen Jiang issued an edict summoning the old ministers Yi Jifu and Shao Hu to take control of officialdom, and they brought Crown Prince Gongnie into the palace to begin the funeral ceremonies; thus he was crowned King You in front of his father's coffin. The following year was declared the first year of his reign. He appointed his wife, the daughter of the Earl of Shen, as queen, and their son Yijiu became the crown prince. He granted his father-in-law, the Earl of Shen, the new title of Marquis of Shen.

A historian wrote a poem praising the revival in the fortunes of the Central States effected during the reign of King Xuan:

> Good King Xuan!
> His virtue encompassed the entire age.
> He struck awe into the inhabitants of the wilderness,
> He reformed the regime in response to an evil omen.
> With ministers like Zhongshan Fu outside and Queen Jiang inside the
>   palace,
> He instituted an era of prosperity and good government.
> He dealt with the poisonous relics of his father's regime,
> Thus the flourishing Central States set out their pennants.

Queen Jiang was overwhelmed with grief, and not long afterwards she too died.

King You was a violent and vicious man, and his temper was unstable. Although he was supposed to be in mourning, he carried on partying with his unsuitable friends; he drank wine and ate meat, seemingly lacking any feeling of sadness over the death of his father. After Queen Jiang passed away, he became even more shameless and lost himself in the pleasures of music and sex, never paying the least attention to the affairs of government. The Marquis of Shen remonstrated repeatedly, but he never listened, and so in the end he went back to his home. This is when the Western Zhou dynasty finally came to an end, as the last old ministers Yi Jifu and Shao Hu died one after the other. King You appointed the Duke of Guo and the Duke of Zhai in their stead, and Yi Jifu's son, Yi Qiu, took the final position as the third of the Three Dukes: the most senior officials serving in the government of the country. These men flattered the king while being greedy for titles and coveting ever-greater wealth. Everything that the king wanted, they would do without delay. At that time the only worthwhile senior member of the government was You, Earl of Zheng, who held the position of minister of education, but King You did not trust him.

One day King You did decide to hold court, and the prefect of Mount Qi reported: "The three rivers—the Jing, the Yellow River, and the Luo—have all suffered earthquakes on the same day."

King You laughed and said, "For mountains to crumble and lands to suffer earthquakes is all perfectly normal. Why bother to report it to me?" Then he dismissed the court and went back to the palace.

The Grand Astrologer, Bo Yangfu, took Grandee Zhao Shudai by the hand. He sighed and said, "Those three rivers all have their source at Mount Qi. How can they have suffered an earthquake? In the past, the Yi and the Luo Rivers ran dry and the Xia dynasty fell; later on, the Yellow River ran dry and the Shang dynasty collapsed. If these three rivers have all suffered an earthquake, then their source will be blocked. The pressure of these blocked waters will cause the mountain to crumble. Mount Qi is where the founder of the house of Zhou was born. If this mountain crumbles, can the destruction of Zhou be far behind?"

"If there is going to be a change of dynasty, when will it happen?" Zhao Shudai asked.

Bo Yangfu counted on his fingers and said, "Within the next ten years."

"How can you be so sure?" Shudai questioned him.

"Doing many good deeds creates good luck, accumulated evil causes disaster," Bo Yangfu said. "Besides which, ten is a 'full' number."

"The Son of Heaven is uninterested in government and he employs wicked men," Zhao Shudai said. "However, I have a job that allows me to speak to His Majesty, so I must do my very best to warn him of the dangers."

"I am afraid that there is no point," Bo Yangfu said.

The two men spoke in private for a long time, and someone immediately reported their conversation to Shifu, Duke of Guo. Shifu was afraid that Shudai would go into the palace and remonstrate, revealing all his evil deeds, so he went straight into the harem and related everything to King You concerning the secret discussions between Bo Yangfu and Zhao Shudai. He claimed that they were plotting to bring down the dynasty and misleading the populace with their wicked words.

"Silly men often speak wildly about the government," King You said. "This is just the same as a marsh releasing its vapors into the air. I really can't be bothered to listen to this!"

Zhao Shudai possessed a deep sense of loyalty and justice, and he repeatedly tried to get into the palace and remonstrate with the king, but he was never able to do so. A few days later, the prefect of Mount Qi again sent a letter to report to the king: "The three rivers have all run dry, Mount Qi has collapsed, and the homes of countless people have been buried by the landslides." King You was completely unconcerned. Instead, he ordered his attendants to find beautiful women with whom he could fill his harem.

Zhao Shudai then came forward and said, "A mountain has collapsed and rivers have run dry. This is a sign that something has gone very wrong deep within the system. The heights have collapsed into the valleys, which is an ill omen for the country. In addition to that, Mount Qi is where the Zhou dynasty began, and now this place has been destroyed overnight and become bare. Such a thing cannot have come about for a minor cause! Now is the time to improve the government, give succor to the people, and seek out wise men to assist in your administration, for there is still time to avert disaster. Surely it is not right that you pay no attention to gathering clever and talented men, but instead are seeking out beautiful women."

"The dynasty established its capitals at Feng and Hao many, many years ago," Shifu, Duke of Guo, said to the king. "Mount Qi is like a cast-off shoe; what has it to do with us? Shudai has long behaved with extreme arrogance, seizing every opportunity to slander and defame others. I hope that Your Majesty will investigate this situation with dispatch."

"Shifu is indeed correct," King You proclaimed. Then he ordered that Shudai be stripped of his offices and sent into exile in the wilds.

Zhao Shudai sighed and said, "You should not go into a city that is torn apart by violence; you should not try to live in a place suffering a civil war. I cannot bear to just sit and watch the Western Zhou dynasty go the way of the Shang."

In the end, he took his whole family to Jin, where he was the ancestor of the famous family of grandees, the Zhaos: Zhao Cui and Zhao Dun were both descended from him. Later on, the Zhao family and the Han family partitioned the state of Jin and took noble titles for themselves. This will all be described later on.

Someone wrote a poem bewailing this:

A loyal minister fleeing civil war set out for the north.
As generations passed, they were assimilated, gradually fixing their
    ambitions on the east.
Since antiquity old servants have been an important resource;
Once the trustworthy and wise have gone, the kingdom is bereft.

Grandee Bao Xiang, visiting from the city of Bao, heard that Zhao Shudai had been forced into exile, and he quickly rushed to court to remonstrate with the king. "Your Majesty does not seem to be worried about the coming disaster, but instead you devote your energies to alienating your wisest advisors. I fear that the country will be left at the mercy of others and the state altars are in danger."

King You was absolutely furious and ordered that Bao Xiang should be thrown into prison. From that point onwards, there was no way to remonstrate with the king, and his cleverest advisors left his service.

· · ·

It has already been described how the man who sold mulberry-wood bows and quivers of woven rushes picked up the ill-omened baby girl and took her to the lands of Bao, where he tried to raise her. She needed milk to drink, and by a fortunate coincidence he encountered the wife of Si Da, whose own baby girl had just died, so he gave her some cloth and begged her to take in the infant he had found. She grew up there and took the name Bao Si. The years passed until she was fourteen, at which point she was grown up, looking just like a girl of sixteen or seventeen who has reached the age of pinning up her hair. Her beautiful eyes were framed by elegantly arched eyebrows; her lips were carmine and her teeth were white, her hair like a raven cloud and her hands as pale as jade. She had a face as beautiful as flowers and as lovely as the moon; she was a woman for whom men would sack cities and overthrow kingdoms. Given that Si

Da lived in a poor and isolated hamlet and that Bao Si herself was still very young, even though she was so outstandingly good-looking, she had still not been betrothed.

Bao Xiang had a son named Hongde, who by chance was placed in charge of collecting taxes—a circumstance that took him to this humble village. Purely by coincidence, Bao Si left the house to draw water, and not even her rustic clothes and unkempt appearance could conceal the fact that she was incredibly beautiful. Amazed, Hongde wondered, "How can such a poor village produce such a lovely lady?" Then he made a secret plan: "My father is imprisoned in the fortress at Hao, and even though three years have passed he still has not been released. If I present this woman to the Son of Heaven, perhaps it will atone for my father's crime."

First he made inquiries of a neighbor about her name and surname; then, he went home to discuss the matter with his mother: "My father annoyed the king by his direct criticisms, but this is not a crime that cannot be pardoned. The Son of Heaven is a vicious and debauched man who has brought beautiful women from every corner of the realm in order to fill his harem. Si Da's daughter is exceptionally lovely, and if I buy her with silks and gold, we can request that Father be released from prison. This is the same plan as that used by San Yisheng to get King Wen out of prison."

"If this plan has a chance of working, I would not begrudge any amount of gold and silk," his mother said. "You must go as soon as you can!"

Hongde went in person to the Si house and struck a deal with Si Da to buy Bao Si for three hundred lengths of cloth, after which he took her home. Having bathed her in perfume, fed her the finest delicacies, clothed her in embroidered silks, and instructed her in proper behavior, Hongde took her to Hao. There he began by bribing the Duke of Guo with gold and silver, begging him to transmit the following message to the king: "Your humble servant, Bao Xiang, knows that his crime merits death ten thousand times. Xiang's son, Hongde, understanding that once his father is dead he can never return to life, has specially sought out a beautiful woman whose name is Bao Si, to be presented to Your Majesty in atonement for his father's crimes. I hope that Your Majesty will pardon him."

When King You heard this message, he ordered that Bao Si should be brought to the audience chamber. When she had made her obeisance, King You looked at her carefully. She was indeed of exceptional beauty, such as he had never seen before. She was so lovely that she was the cynosure of all eyes. The king was very pleased. Even though women had been presented from every corner of the kingdom, none could hold a candle to Bao Si. Without even letting Queen Shen know, he established Bao Si in her own separate palace and issued a royal edict pardoning Bao Xiang and releasing him from prison. He even restored his official position and titles. That night with great delight, King You slept with Bao Si for the very first time, an event that does not need to be described here. From that point on they were never apart; they drank from the same cup and ate from the same plate. For ten days in a row, the king did not hold court, leaving his ministers to wait at the gates of the palace, none of them even catching a glimpse of His Majesty. They all sighed and left. This happened in the fourth year of King You's reign.

There is a poem that attests to this:

He found a great beauty and made her famous throughout the realm;
From poverty and hardship overnight she was promoted to share the
    royal bed.
A playboy king overwhelmed with lust
Was unaware of the disaster long-concealed in the dragon's saliva.

From the moment that King You first laid hands on Bao Si, he was bewitched by her beauty. They lived together in the Agate Tower, and for three months at a stretch the king did not even enter Queen Shen's palace. Naturally, people were quick to tell Queen Shen exactly what was going on, and she could not restrain her anger. One morning she decided to take all the palace ladies in a delegation to the Agate Tower, where she found King You and Bao Si sitting curled up together. Neither of them even got up to acknowledge her arrival. Queen Shen could not keep quiet at this insult, and so she cursed Bao Si, saying, "Who is this diseased whore who dares to ignore palace regulations!"

King You, afraid that Queen Shen might actually physically attack the girl, shielded Bao Si with his own body, speaking up for her: "This is my new beauty, and I have not yet decided what rank to give her. That is the reason why you have not seen her before. You should not be so angry."

Queen Shen carried on cursing her for a while and then left, still in a towering rage.

"Who was that who just came in?" Bao Si asked.

"That was the queen," King You explained. "Tomorrow you should go and pay your respects to her."

Bao Si said nothing to this, but the following day she did not go to pay court to Her Majesty.

Meanwhile Queen Shen, living in her palace, became deeply depressed. Crown Prince Yijiu knelt before her and said, "Mother, you hold the rank of the head of the Six Palaces, so why are you so unhappy?"

"Your father favors Bao Si, completely disregarding the distinctions between wife and concubine," Queen Shen said. "If in the future that little whore gets her way, neither you nor I will know a moment's peace!"

Then she explained all the details to the crown prince of Bao Si's failure to come to pay court and her refusal to get up and welcome her. Without being aware of what she was doing, she began to cry. The crown prince said, "There is no problem. Tomorrow is the first day of the month, and so my father will have to hold court. You, Mother, can then take some of the palace servants to the Agate Tower to pick flowers, which will certainly lure that nasty little bitch out of the building so that she can look at you. I will then give her a real beating to teach her to know her place. If Father is upset about it, he can blame me; it has nothing to do with you."

"My son, do nothing precipitate," Queen Shen exclaimed. "Let this pass and we will discuss what to do another time."

The crown prince left the palace in a rage. Thus they passed a night.

The next morning, sure enough, King You held court, and all his ministers were present to congratulate him on the occasion of the first day of the month. The crown prince intentionally sent a couple of dozen palace servants to the Agate Tower, ordering them to go around picking any flower that they fancied and not to ask anyone for permission. Some servants came out of the Agate Tower to stop them, saying, "These flowers are grown for His Majesty, and Consort Bao enjoys them, so stop wrecking the place before you are severely punished."

"We have been ordered to do this by the crown prince, for he wants to present these flowers to Her Majesty the queen," the other palace servants said. "How dare you try to prevent us?"

At this point the two sides started shouting at each other, which alarmed Bao Si so much that she came out to discover for herself what on earth was going on. She was absolutely furious and wanted to show them who was in charge. Just at that moment, the crown prince suddenly emerged from hiding. Bao Si had no means to protect herself, so when the crown prince came upon his enemy, he glared at her. Then he took a step forward and grabbed her by the hair, shouting curses at her.

"Nasty little bitch, who the hell do you think you are? A nameless piece of scum flaunting yourself shamelessly and wanting to be a royal! Today I am going to teach you your proper place!"

He balled up his fist and started punching her. After he had hit her a few times, a number of the palace ladies started to get frightened, for they were worried that King You might blame them. They all knelt down and kowtowed, imploring: "Please forgive her, Your Highness! Please think of the effect that this will have on your father!"

The crown prince began to be afraid lest he had caused her life-threatening injuries, and so finally he stopped. Bao Si swallowed her humiliation and crept back to the Agate Tower in terrible pain. She was perfectly well aware of the fact that the crown prince was doing this for his mother's sake, and the tears coursed down her cheeks. Her attendants tried to cheer her up by saying, "Don't be so sad, my lady, His Majesty will deal with this himself."

Just as they were speaking, King You dismissed the court and went back to the Agate Tower. When he caught sight of Bao Si's disheveled hair and the tears sparkling in her eyes, he asked, "My darling, why have you not combed your hair today?"

Bao Si took hold of King You's sleeve and began to cry. She said, "The crown prince brought some palace servants to the tower to pick flowers. I did nothing to annoy him, but the moment the crown prince caught sight of me he started hitting and cursing me. If it were not for the intervention of some of the palace ladies, I really think he would have killed me. I hope that Your Majesty will see justice done!"

When she had finished speaking, she burst into tears and wept bitterly. King You now understood exactly what had happened. He told Bao Si, "You did not pay court to his mother; that is why things have been brought to this pass. This is an expression of Her Majesty's enmity; it is not the crown prince's own idea. Don't blame the wrong person."

"The crown prince is taking revenge for his mother and he wants me dead," Bao Si said. "Naturally it does not matter at all if I die, but having been favored by you, I find that I am now two months pregnant. This is not about me; it is about my baby's life! Please let me leave the palace, to save both my life and the baby's!"

"My darling, please look after yourself," King You said. "I know how to deal with this situation."

That very day, he issued a royal edict saying: "Crown Prince Yijiu is a brave but unprincipled man who has behaved with conspicuous lack of filial piety. I therefore exile him to the state of Shen, in the hope that his grandfather, the Marquis of Shen, can teach him to mind his manners! The crown prince's senior tutor, his junior tutor, and the other officials in his train have proved completely useless in instructing him, and so henceforth they are dismissed from their offices."

The crown prince wished to go to the palace to plead his innocence, but King You told the guards at the gates not to announce his arrival. Therefore, he could only get on his chariot and go to the state of Shen for good.

Queen Shen, wondering why she had not seen the crown prince come to the palace for such a long time, asked around among the palace servants. In the end, she discovered that he had already been exiled to Shen. Friendless and alone, she missed her son terribly and hated her husband, but she had no choice other than to pass her days concealing her tears.

. . .

After nine months of pregnancy, Bao Si gave birth to a baby boy that King You loved deeply. He gave him the name Bofu, meaning "Senior," to signal his intention of disinheriting his son by the queen in favor of this child by a woman of humble birth. However, without some adequate excuse it would be difficult to do so. Shifu, Duke of Guo, had guessed the king's wishes in this matter, and so he discussed the situation with Yi Qiu before secretly getting in touch with Bao Si.

"The crown prince has been exiled to his mother's people," he explained, "so the moment has come for Bofu to be proclaimed the heir to the throne. With Your Ladyship speaking to His Majesty across the pillow on the one hand and the two of us supporting your son's candidature on the other, there is no reason to worry that we might fail."

Delighted, Bao Si replied, "I rely on the support from the two of you. If Bofu is proclaimed crown prince and does indeed come to the throne, then he will share the kingdom with you."

From this point on, Bao Si secretly promoted her faction among the king's entourage and spoke day and night of the shortcomings of Queen Shen. She had her ears and eyes inside and outside the palace gates. If the wind so much as blew and the grasses moved, she knew all about it.

Queen Shen at this time lived alone and spent her waking hours in tears. There was, however, one old palace servant who knew her troubles. She knelt before the queen and said: "Since Your Majesty misses the crown prince so much, why do you not write a letter and send it secretly to the state of Shen asking him to apologize to the king for his mistakes? If he is reconciled with the lord of ten thousand years, then he will be summoned back to the East Palace, and you will be reunited with him. Would that not be wonderful?"

"It is a lovely idea," Queen Shen said, "but I have no one to take my letter."

"My mother, Old Woman Wen, knows a little about medicine," the palace servant said. "If Your Majesty were to pretend to be ill, then you could summon her to the palace to examine you and ask her to take your letter out. My older brother could then get it to Shen. This is a plan with no flaws."

Queen Shen agreed with this and wrote her letter. It read:

> The Son of Heaven is an unprincipled man and he trusts an evil bitch, with the result that we have been forced apart. Now the wicked slut has given birth to a son, so she is even more firmly in favor. You must send a letter to the king in which you pretend to be sorry for your mistakes: "I realize what I have done wrong and I have turned over a new leaf, so I hope that Father will forgive me." If Heaven ordains that you return to court, we will be reunited and can make other plans.

When she had finished writing her letter, she pretended that she was ill and took to her bed, summoning Old Woman Wen for a consultation. Naturally, someone immediately reported this to Bao Si. Bao Si said, "This must be about sending information out. Prevent Old Woman Wen from leaving the palace and conduct a body search. Then we will know the long and the short of it."

When Old Woman Wen came to the Queen's Palace, her daughter, the palace servant, had already told her exactly what was required. Queen Shen pretended to stretch her wrist out to allow her pulse to be taken, but in fact she was taking the letter out from her pillow. She told the old woman, "This must go to Shen under cover of darkness, for any mistake will be fatal."

She ordered one of the maids to give her a length of brocade and a length of silk gauze. Old Woman Wen put the letter in her bodice and picked up the silks; thus she left the palace with a flourish. The eunuchs guarding the palace gate stopped her to inquire, "Where did you get this silk?"

"I gave Her Majesty the queen a medical examination, and they are a present from her," the old woman explained.

One of the eunuchs demanded: "Are you taking anything else out?"

"No," she said.

She clearly wanted to leave, but one of the other eunuchs said, "If we don't search her, how will we know if she is smuggling something else out or not?"

He then grabbed the old woman by the hand and spun her around. The old woman did everything she could to get away and appeared in a complete panic. The eunuchs were suspicious, and became more and more determined to search her. They came forward together and ripped open the bodice of her dress. The corner of the letter was then revealed. The woman and the letter that the eunuchs had found were then taken to the Agate Tower and brought before Bao Si. Bao Si opened the letter and read it, which made her absolutely furious. She ordered that Old Woman Wen should be locked up in an empty chamber, so that no news of this could leak out. She then took the two lengths of silk and ripped them into shreds.

When King You came to the palace, the first thing he saw was the pieces of gauze and the remnants of the brocade, and he asked where they had come from. Bao Si choked back her tears and said: "Ever since I was so unfortunate as to be brought to your harem and receive your favor, the queen has hated and been jealous of me. Things are even worse now that I have given birth to your son, for her enmity is even greater. The queen has just sent a letter to the crown prince, and the last line says that they 'can make other plans'; this must mean some kind of plot against my life and that of my son. I hope that Your Majesty will see justice done for me!"

When she had finished speaking, she gave King You the letter to read. The king recognized the queen's handwriting and asked about the messenger.

"Old Woman Wen is here right now," Bao Si explained.

King You then ordered that she be brought before him. Without a word, he drew his sword and cut her down.

An old man wrote the following poem:

Before the letter had even left the palace harem,
The frosty blade was already spotted with the blood of an innocent
    victim.
In other circumstances, had he asked what was going on,
Old Woman Wen would have been recognized as a loyal subject.

That night Bao Si made a great play of her charms and affection for King You. Then she complained, "My fate and that of my son is in the hands of the crown prince."

"I am still in charge here, so what can the crown prince do?" King You asked.

"Sooner or later the crown prince will succeed to the throne," Bao Si pointed out. "The queen is holed up in her palace right now, eaten up with hatred and cursing me day and night, so if she and her son come to power, Bofu and I will die and our bodies will be left to rot without even a decent burial!" When she had finished speaking, she burst into tears.

"I would like to divorce the queen and demote the crown prince, sending you to live in the Queen's Palace and Bofu to live in the East Palace, but I am afraid that my ministers will not stand for it," King You said. "What can I do?"

"For a minister to listen to the king is a sign of his devotion, but for a king to listen to his ministers is just stupid," Bao Si pointed out. "Why don't you clearly express your intention to your most senior advisors and discuss the whole matter with the Three Dukes?"

"How right you are, my darling," the king said.

That very night Bao Si communicated her intentions to the Duke of Guo and Yi Qiu, so that they would be ready to say the right things at court.

The following day, when the ceremonies for the early morning court had been performed, King You summoned the Three Dukes and the senior ministers to the great hall of audience. He began by asking them, "Her Majesty the queen is jealous and eaten up with hatred, going so far as to curse me, which makes it inappropriate for her to keep the honor of being the wife of the Son of Heaven. Would it be legal for me to have her arrested and put to the question?"

Shifu, Duke of Guo, then advised the king: "The queen is the head of the Six Palaces. Even if she has committed a crime, you cannot have her arrested or interrogated in any way. If she really cannot maintain the dignity of the position that she holds, you ought to promulgate an edict of divorce and select another more suitable wife to fulfill the role of queen. This would indeed be a blessing for ten thousand generations!"

Yi Qiu also advised the king: "In my opinion, Bao Si would be a very suitable candidate. Given her virtue and purity, she would be able to take charge of the palace."

"The crown prince is in Shen," King You said. "If I divorce Queen Shen, how will the crown prince react?"

"I have heard it said that a mother derives her status from her son and her son likewise receives titles of nobility thanks to his mother," Shifu, Duke of Guo, explained to the king. "The Crown Prince has gone to live in Shen to avoid the consequences of his crimes, so the rituals that express the tender regard between a father and a son have long been discontinued. Besides which, if you divorce his mother, how can anyone expect you to keep him in place? We all support the investiture of Bofu as crown prince, and the whole country will rejoice at this resolution of the issue."

Delighted, King You immediately issued an edict sending Queen Shen to the Cold Palace and demoting Crown Prince Yijiu to the status of a commoner. He established Bao Si as queen and Bofu as crown prince. Anyone who tried to reason with the king was said to be part of Yijiu's faction and punished severely. This all happened in the ninth year of King You's reign. The civil and the military officials were all deeply disturbed by these events, but they knew that King You's mind was already made up and they would only get themselves killed to no purpose if they tried to do anything about it, so they simply kept their mouths shut.

The Grand Astrologer, Bo Yangfu, sighed and said, "Three warp threads have now been cut; the Zhou dynasty is doomed!" That very day he retired on the grounds of old age. There were many officials at this time who gave up their jobs and went home to till the fields. At court, only Yi Qiu, Duke Shifu of Guo, and Duke Yi of Zhai remained, together with a whole host of toadies and flatterers. King You spent day and night in the palace, enjoying himself with Bao Si.

Although Bao Si had been elevated to living in the Queen's Palace and monopolized the king sexually, she never ever laughed. King You wanted her to be happy, and so he summoned musicians to sound the bells and bang the drums, play the flutes, and pluck the strings, and the palace servants sang and danced as they came forward to present cups of wine. From start to finish, Bao Si maintained a countenance of stone. King You asked her, "If you don't enjoy music, my love, what do you like?"

"I don't like anything," Bao Si said. "However, I do remember that the other day when I ripped up the silk gauze and brocade, I found the sounds of rending very enjoyable."

"If you enjoy listening to the sound of silks being ripped to shreds, why on earth did you not mention it before?" King You responded. He ordered the official stores to send one hundred bolts of silk a day and ordered the strongest of the palace maids to rip them to pieces, just to entertain Bao Si. Strange to say, even though Bao Si clearly enjoyed the shredding of the silk gauze, she still never smiled.

"Why don't you laugh, darling?" King You asked.

"But I never laugh," Bao Si replied.

"I am determined to make you laugh, my love, even if only once," King You proclaimed. He then issued a command: "Anyone who can make Queen Bao laugh just once, regardless of whether they are part of the palace personnel or not, will be rewarded with one thousand pieces of gold."

Shifu, Duke of Guo, explained his plan: "Some years ago your father, His Late Majesty, was worried by the growing strength of the Dog Rong and became afraid that they would invade one day. Therefore, he had more than twenty beacon stations built below Mount Li. He also set up several dozen war drums. If there is ever an invasion by the barbarians, we should light the wolf beacons and send the smoke straight up into the sky; then the nearby lords will send their armies to come to our aid. If the great war drums are sounded at the same time, they will hurry to our side. The kingdom has been at peace now for many years, so the beacon fires have never been lit. If Your Majesty wants the queen to show her teeth in a smile, then you must take her to Mount Li. Light the beacons at night, and the relief armies of the feudal lords are sure to come. Seeing them rush to your assistance when there is no invasion will certainly make the queen laugh."

"That's a wonderful idea!" King You exclaimed.

He then traveled to Mount Li with Queen Bao. When it got dark, he had a banquet served at the Li Palace and issued a command for the beacons to be lit. It so happened that at that time You, Earl of Zheng, was at court, since as minister for education he was then the most senior official present. When he heard the command, he was very alarmed and rushed to the Li Palace to talk to the king.

"The beacons were built by His Late Majesty in preparation for some dire emergency—that is why the signal is trusted by the feudal lords," he said. "Now you want to light the fires for no good reason, to trick the feudal lords. If at some point in the future something goes wrong and you really need the beacons, the feudal lords will not trust in them again. How will you then call troops to your side in a crisis?"

"The kingdom is at peace, so why should we need troops by our side?" King You demanded angrily. "The queen and I have come here to the Li Palace for this very purpose, and I am not going to call it all off. I want to have a joke at the expense of the feudal lords, and if at some point in the future there is an emergency, any problems will be my fault and not yours!"

Therefore, he paid no attention to the Earl of Zheng's remonstrance but lit all the beacon fires and banged the great drums. The sound of the drums was like thunder, and the flames from the fires lit up the sky. The lords of the Royal Domain believed that the capital city of Hao was under attack, so they all appointed their generals and mobilized their troops, hastening that very night to Mount Li. When they got there, all they heard was the sound of flutes and pipes coming from the tower where King You and Bao Si were drinking wine and enjoying themselves. The pair sent someone out to apologize to the feudal lords, saying, "Thankfully we are not under attack; I hope you don't mind trekking all this way."

The lords just looked at each other, struck their flags, and went home. Bao Si was up in the tower. Leaning over the railing, she could see the feudal lords rushing forward and then hurrying back home, all for nothing. Without even realizing what she was doing, she clapped her hands and burst into peals of laughter.

"The smile of my beloved wife is the most beautiful thing in the world," King You remarked. "Shifu, Duke of Guo has done well." Then he rewarded him with one thousand pieces of gold.

The expression still in use today, "buying a laugh with one thousand pieces of gold," is derived from this story.

There is a poem by an old man that describes how the beacon fires were lit to play a joke on the feudal lords:

> One night at the Li Palace music was played on the flutes and the pipes.
> The blaze of countless beacons lit the skies.
> Pity the troops rushing through the darkness,
> Only to earn a laugh from Bao Si.

When the Marquis of Shen heard that King You had divorced his queen and put Bao Si in her place, he wrote a letter of complaint to the king:

> In former times King Jie favored Mo Xi and brought about the fall of the Xia dynasty, while King Zhou favored Da Ji, which caused the decline of the Shang dynasty. Your Majesty now favors and trusts Bao Si, which has led you to demote your legitimate heir and establish a lesser princeling in his place. This strikes at the heart of the relationship between a husband and wife and ruins the affection that should exist between a father and son. The horrors perpetrated under King Jie and King Zhou will be seen again in our own times; the kind of disaster that overtook the Xia dynasty and the Shang cannot be far away. I hope that Your Majesty will revoke this appalling edict, for perhaps that way the country will survive.

King You read this letter and then hit the table with his fist in a towering rage: "How dare this bastard speak such traitorous words!"

"The Marquis of Shen has seen the crown prince sent into exile, and he has been filled with resentment ever since," Shifu, Duke of Guo, said. "Now he has found out that the queen has been divorced and the crown prince has been demoted, so he is planning to rebel. That is the reason why he dares to criticize what you have done."

"In that case, what should I do?" King You asked.

"The Marquis of Shen actually never did anything for the crown; he received his title because his daughter was the queen," Shifu explained. "Now that she has been divorced and her son degraded from the position of crown prince, it would be entirely appropriate to strip the Marquis of Shen of his title, reducing him to his old rank of earl. You should also send troops to punish him for his crime, for that way you can avoid storing up trouble for yourself in the future."

King You followed his advice and issued an order stripping the Marquis of Shen of his title. He appointed Shifu as general with responsibility for gathering weapons and mustering chariots, for he wanted to raise an army to attack Shen.

If you want to know who won and who lost, READ ON.

Chapter Three

The chief of the Dog Rong invades the
capital at Hao.

King Ping of Zhou moves east to Luoyang.

After the Marquis of Shen sent his letter to the king, someone at the capital city of Hao was appointed to keep him informed of developments. This spy discovered that King You had invested the Duke of Guo as commander-in-chief and that he would be leading his troops to attack Shen any day now. He fled under cover of darkness to report to the Marquis of Shen. The Marquis of Shen was deeply alarmed, and said, "This is only a little country with a few soldiers; how can we possibly resist the might of the royal army?"

Grandee Lü Zhang came forward and said, "The Son of Heaven is an unprincipled man, and so he has divorced his wife and demoted his legitimate heir. Good and loyal ministers have lost their jobs, and everyone is furious about it. This is a situation in which His Majesty has become isolated. Now, the Dog Rong are a very powerful nomadic people, whose lands border with Shen. If you, my lord, were to send a letter to the chief of the Rong, asking to borrow troops to attack Hao, we could save the queen and force the Son of Heaven to pass his title to the former crown prince. This is the kind of thing that Yi Yin or the Duke of Zhou would have done. There is a saying that goes, 'The one who acts first controls the situation'; so this opportunity cannot be lost."

"What you say is absolutely correct!" the Marquis of Shen replied.

He then prepared a cart full of gold and silk and sent an ambassador to deliver them, together with his letter about borrowing troops from the Dog Rong. They agreed that on a certain day they would attack

Hao, promising that the Rong would be allowed to take all the gold in the royal treasuries and the silks in the storehouses.

The chief of the Rong declared, "The Zhou Son of Heaven has lost control of the government and his father-in-law, the Marquis of Shen, now summons me to kill this wicked man and support the establishment of the crown prince. This I am only too happy to do!" He then ordered the mobilization of fifteen thousand Rong soldiers, divided into three columns. A man named Bo Ding commanded the vanguard for the right-hand column, Man Yesu commanded the vanguard on the left-hand column, and the Rong chief himself commanded the central column. Their spears and sabers blocked the roads; their banners and pennons filled the sky. The Marquis of Shen mobilized his own army to assist. Like a great wave, they rolled towards Hao, killing everyone in their way. Before its inhabitants were even aware of the danger they were in, the royal city was under siege by three concentric circles of troops, and the water supply to the city had been cut.

When King You heard about this development, he cried out in great alarm: "Our plans are known and disaster has already overtaken us! The Rong army has moved before my troops have mobilized! What can I do?"

Shifu, Duke of Guo, presented his opinion to the king: "Your Majesty, you should send a man to Mount Li to light the beacons as soon as possible, for then troops from the lords are sure to come to your aid. If an attack is coordinated between those inside the city and those outside, we are sure to be victorious!"

King You did exactly what the duke suggested and sent a man to light the beacons. Not a single soldier came from any of the feudal lords' armies. The beacons having been lit once for fun, this time they assumed it was a joke as well, and so none of them mobilized their men. King You now realized that the relief troops were not coming. The Dog Rong attacked the city walls day and night.

"We do not yet know how strong these barbarians really are, so why don't you go and find out?" the king said to Shifu. "I ought to review our soldiers, and they can then follow in your wake."

The Duke of Guo was not a good general, but he had no choice but to follow orders. In command of a force of two hundred chariots, he opened the city gates and fought his way out. The Marquis of Shen had made camp on a hill, and when he looked out into the distance and saw Shifu coming out of the city, he pointed this out to the chief of the Rong, saying, "That bastard led the king astray and ruined the country; don't let him get away!"

The chief of the Rong heard this and shouted, "Who will capture him for me?"

"Let me go!" Bo Ding shouted.

He brandished his sword, whipped up his horse, and rode straight ahead to take on Shifu, Duke of Guo. Before they had even crossed swords ten times, Shifu was beheaded in front of his chariot by a single sweeping stroke of Bo Ding's weapon. The chief of the Rong and Man Yesu then advanced together, killing everyone in the way. With screaming and shouting, they fought their way into the city. If they came across a house, they set fire to it; if they came across a person, they raised their swords. Even the Marquis of Shen was not able to prevent them; he could only look on helplessly.

The city was in complete chaos. Before King You had even had time to carry out his inspection of troops, he saw that things were going really badly. He found a small chariot that would carry Bao Si and Bofu, and they left together by the Servants' Gate to the palace. You, Earl of Zheng, the minister of education, caught up with them and yelled, "Do not be afraid, Your Majesty, I will protect you!"

They departed the capital by the north gate and hurried in the direction of Mount Li. On the way, they came across Yi Qiu, who said, "The Dog Rong have set fire to the palace, and they are looting the treasury and storehouses. The Duke of Zhai has already been killed by the rebel army!"

King You was both heartbroken and desperate. You, Earl of Zheng, again ordered that the beacons be lit. The smoke from these fires pierced the heavens, but relief troops still did not come. The Dog Rong army pursued them to the foot of Mount Li, where they surrounded the Li palace, shouting, "Don't think you are getting out of this, you bastard!"

King You and Bao Si were so frightened they collapsed into a heap together, crying in each other's arms. You, Earl of Zheng, entered and said: "Things are in a desperate state! I will do my very best to protect you, Your Majesty, as we fight our way out of this encirclement, even if it costs me my life. We should go to my country first and then make plans to retake the capital."

"It is because I ignored your advice, my cousin, that things have come to this pass," King You said. "Today the lives of my family are in your hands."

The Earl of Zheng instructed some people to start a fire in front of the Li palace, in order to confuse the Rong soldiers. He himself led King You out of the back of the palace to try and break through the siege. The Earl of Zheng held a long spear with which he opened a route in front. Yi Qiu, who was responsible for protecting Bao Si and her son, pressed close behind King You. Shortly after they set out, they found their path blocked by Dog Rong soldiers led by the junior general, Gu Lichi. The Earl of Zheng gritted his teeth in rage, and they started to fight. After they had crossed swords a few times, with one spear-thrust the Earl of Zheng forced Gu Lichi off his horse. When the Rong soldiers saw how valiant the Earl of Zheng was, they all ran away.

When the royal party had gone on for about half a *li*, they again heard shouting behind them. The commander of the vanguard for the right-hand column, Bo Ding, was leading a great host in pursuit. The Earl of Zheng ordered Yi Qiu to protect them in front, while he himself guarded the rear. They fought on every step of the way, only to have to sustain a charge by the Dog Rong armored cavalry, which split them into two groups. The Earl of Zheng was isolated at the center of a phalanx of enemy troops, but he was completely unafraid. His spear flashed in and out, and none of the enemy frontline was able to resist. The chief of the Dog Rong ordered archers to shoot from every direction. The arrows fell like rain, making no distinction between friend and foe. How sad that such a fine aristocrat should die that day under a hail of arrows!

The commander of the vanguard of the left-hand column, Man Yesu, quickly brought King You's chariot to a halt. The chief of the Dog Rong spotted his royal robes and jade belt and realized that this was King You. He cut him down as he stood on his chariot with a single blow from his sword. In the same way, he killed Bofu. Bao Si was so beautiful that he could not bear to slay her, hence he ordered up a light chariot to take her back to his yurt, where he could enjoy her himself. Yi Qiu was hiding among the baggage on the chariot, from whence he was dragged out by the Rong soldiers and beheaded.

In all, King You was on the throne for eleven years. The man who sold mulberry-wood bows and rush quivers plucked a cursed baby out of the Qing River and fled with her to the state of Bao: that baby was Bao Si. She bewitched her ruler with her wicked wiles, causing him to bully and maltreat his true wife, and that is what brought about King You's death and his country's collapse. It was just as the children's song of earlier days had said:

The moon will rise,
The sun will set.
A rush quiver and a wild-mulberry bow
Will bring destruction on the kingdom of Zhou.

Everything corresponds to this prophecy. The plans of Heaven were already fixed in the time of King Xuan.

Master Dongping wrote a poem that speaks of this:

> Every means was used to extract a smile from the woman in the palace;
> The flickering light from the beacon fires is now red, now black.
> Having alienated himself from the lords, the king has no choice,
> But to allow the state altars to suffer at the hands of barbarians!

The Recluse from Longxi wrote a poem titled "An Evaluation of History":

> One laugh from Bao Si at Mount Li resulted in the battle cry of the Dog
>   Rong;
> The bows and arrows of the children's song have already proved to
>   be true.
> After eighteen years this karmic debt has been paid;
> Who can be said to be responsible for this?

There is also a poem that describes how neither Yi Qiu nor any of his cohort died a good death, which is a warning to treacherous ministers. The poem reads:

> Cunning words and slanderous speeches deluded your ruler;
> All you thought of was wealth and honors to last your lifetime.
> The whole court was butchered and killed together,
> Causing you to be cursed as a wicked minister for a thousand years.

There is also a poem praising the loyalty of You, Earl of Zheng. This poem runs:

> Shifu passed away and Yi Qiu died;
> The brave Earl of Zheng was killed the same day, protecting his king.
> Though all three can be said to have suffered for the Zhou royal house,
> Which one of them left an honorable reputation?

When the Marquis of Shen arrived inside the city walls, he saw that the palace had gone up in flames. He quickly led the troops from his own country into the palace, where everything in his path had been ruined and destroyed. First he went to release Queen Shen from the Cold Palace. Then he went to the Agate Tower, but there was no sign there of King You or Bao Si. Someone pointed and said, "They have already left by the north gate." He guessed that they were heading for Mount Li, so he quickly set off in pursuit. On the way, it just happened that he bumped into the chief of the Rong. As their chariots ran abreast, each asked after the other's labors that day. When the chief of the Rong said that the deluded monarch was already dead, the Marquis of Shen was deeply shocked; he said, "The only thing I ever wanted was to arouse His Majesty to a sense of his wrongdoing; I never thought that things would come to this pass! In later generations, those who are disloyal to their lords are sure to take me as a precedent!"

He immediately ordered his followers to collect the body and prepare to bury it with all proper ritual. The chief of the Rong laughed and said, "In spite of your high honors, you really are as silly as a woman!"

The Marquis of Shen then returned to the capital, where he prepared a banquet to be held in honor of the chief of the Rong. The treasures and jades in the treasuries had all been taken, but he still managed to gather together ten carts of silk and gold as a bribe, in the hope that this would satisfy the chief and he would go home. Who could have imagined that he thought that killing King You made him a matchless hero! His soldiers and horses occupied the capital and they ate and drank and made merry day and night, so it was clear that he had no intention of dismissing his troops and returning home to his own country. The populace all blamed the Marquis of Shen for this situation. There was nothing that the Marquis of Shen could do about it, so he secretly wrote three letters and sent his messengers to the three marchemont lords to arrange a meeting at which they would crown the new king.

The three marchemont lords were Ji Chou, the Marquis of Jin, to the north; Ji He, the Marquis of Wey to the east; and Ying Kai, the Lord of Qin, to the west.

He also sent someone to the state of Zheng to report the terrible death of the Earl of Zheng to his son, Scion Juetu, instructing him to raise an army to take revenge. Of this no more.

• • •

At that time, Scion Juetu was twenty-three years old, some six feet tall, and of exceptionally handsome appearance. When he heard that his father had been killed in battle, he was extremely upset and angry. He put on a mourning robe with a plain white silk sash, and, in command of an army of three hundred chariots, he sped overnight in the direction of the capital. Spies soon reported his movements to the chief of the Dog Rong, who made his preparations. When Juetu arrived, he wanted to advance his troops. The Honorable Cheng remonstrated: "Our troops have advanced by forced marches, so they are exhausted and have not yet had time to recover. We should build a fortified camp and wait for the troops from the other lords to arrive. After that we can join battle. This would be by far the best plan."

"Avenging my father is the most important thing," Juetu proclaimed. "Besides, the Dog Rong are arrogant and their ambitions have recently been satisfied, so we can attack them while they are off guard—thus we are sure to be victorious. If we have to wait until the forces of the other lords arrive, surely this will cool our own troops' ardor."

He commanded the chariots to drive straight towards the city walls. No banners showed on top of the walls, and the war drums were still; in fact, the place was completely silent. Juetu shouted loudly: "You barbarians are like dogs or sheep! Why don't you come out of the city and fight?"

There was no response from anyone on top of the walls. Juetu ordered the left and right columns to get ready to attack the city. Suddenly, they heard a loud noise from deep within the forest as the great gongs resounded and a military column came forward to attack. This was the chief of the Dog Rong's plan, for he had prepared an ambush outside the city. Terrified, Juetu rushed to pick up his spear to do battle. Then the sound of massive gongs also arose from the top of the city walls, and the gates were thrown open to allow a military column to attack from that side. In front of Juetu was the army commanded by Bo Ding, behind him was that of Man Yesu, and the two held him in a pincer movement. He could not withstand such an onslaught and ran away after suffering a terrible defeat. The Rong troops chased them for more than thirty *li*.

Juetu collected the scattered remnants of his army and told the Honorable Cheng, "I did not listen to your advice, and that has been extremely bad for us. Do you have any plan to offer now?"

"We are not far from Puyang now, and the Marquis of Wey is a trustworthy and competent man, so why not throw ourselves on his mercy?" the Honorable Cheng suggested. "If we can join forces with Zheng and Wei, then we can achieve our object."

Juetu did as he said and ordered everyone to march towards Puyang.

After traveling for two days, they saw a great cloud of dust, and in the distance they observed countless soldiers and chariots advancing in an unbroken wall. In their very midst was an aristocrat wearing a brocade robe and jade belt—due to his age his hair was white, but his movements were still graceful and refined. This lord was in fact Ji He, Lord Wu of Wey, and at that time he was already more than eighty years old.

Juetu stopped his chariot and called out loud: "I am Juetu, the Scion of Zheng. When the Dog Rong troops attacked the capital, my father was killed in battle. Now my army has also been defeated, so I have come specially to ask for your assistance."

Lord Wu made obeisance and replied, "Do not worry, we will do our very best to assist His Majesty. I have heard that the troops of Qin and Jin will soon arrive. There is no need to worry about those barbarians!"

Juetu yielded precedence to the Marquis of Wey, allowing him to go in front. Then he turned his chariot around and began the journey back to Hao.

When they were twenty *li* away from the city, they divided into two groups to make camp. He sent someone to find out news of the Qin and Jin armies, and the spy reported back: "To the west a bronze war drum is sounding loudly and the rumble of chariots can be heard, while high overhead there is an embroidered banner reading 'Qin.'"

"Although Qin is only an obscure minor state," Lord Wu remarked, "they are familiar with Rong customs and their soldiers are exceptionally fierce and good at fighting: the Dog Rong fear them greatly."

Before he had finished speaking, the spy who had gone north also reported back: "The Jin army has also arrived, and they have already made camp by the northern gate."

Lord Wu was very pleased, and said, "Now that troops have come from those two countries, everything is ready!"

Then he sent someone to greet the rulers of Qin and Jin. A short time later the two lords both arrived at Lord Wu's camp, and they asked after each other. The two lords saw that Juetu was wearing mourning clothes, and asked, "Who is this?"

"This is the Scion of Zheng," Lord Wu said. He then explained how the Earl of Zheng had died and King You had been killed. The two lords sighed without cease.

"I am old now," Lord Wu continued, "but I am still a loyal subject, and so I have not refused to do my duty. I have forced myself to come here at some cost. I am relying on your assistance to get rid of these stinking barbarians. What plan do you propose?"

"The only thing the Dog Rong care about is stealing silk and gold and raping women," Lord Xiang of Qin said. "Now, although they know we have arrived, they are sure not to have taken proper precautions. Tonight at midnight, we should attack in three directions at once—north, south, and east—but we will leave a gap at the West Gate, so they can escape that way. However, the Scion of Zheng will have his troops waiting in ambush there, so that when they run away he can attack them. That way our victory will be complete."

"What an excellent plan!" Lord Wu exclaimed.

. . .

Inside the city, the Marquis of Shen heard that the armies of four states had arrived, and he was very pleased. Then he and Xuan, one of the sons of the Duke of Zhou, secretly discussed the situation: "We will wait for them to attack the city, and then we will open the gates for them."

They further encouraged the chief of the Rong to send home some of his booty of treasure, gold, and silk. He ordered Bo Ding, the commander of the left-hand vanguard, to divide up his soldiers to escort the train; this served to reduce the Rong chief's military strength. They suggested that the commander of the right-hand vanguard, Man Yesu, should immediately take his troops out of the city walls to meet the enemy. The chief of the Dog Rong thought that this was sensible advice, and so he followed it to the letter. He told Man Yesu to make camp just outside the eastern gate to the city, opposite the fortifications of the Wey army. They agreed to do battle the following day, but unexpectedly in the middle of the night, the Wey army entered their camp. Man Yesu immediately drew his sword and leapt onto his horse, advancing to tackle the enemy. But what could he do with the Rong soldiers running around in confusion everywhere? Though he waved his arms, he could not stop the rout, and so he had to run away with his men. The three marchemont lords then gave their battle cries and launched their attack upon the city. Suddenly the city gates opened. The chariots and horses of the three lords advanced together, and no one offered the slightest resistance. This was the Marquis of Shen's plan.

The chief of the Rong woke in alarm from his dreams. Leaping onto a bareback horse, he made his way to the western part of the city, followed by just a few hundred of his men. There he came across the Scion of Zheng, Juetu, who barred his way, forcing him to do battle. Just as things were at this critical pass, it so happened that Man Yesu arrived with the remnants of his defeated army; in the chaos and confusion of the fighting, the chief of the Rong was able to escape unharmed. Juetu did not dare to pursue him, so he entered the city and met up with the other lords. By then it was broad daylight, which meant that Bao Si was not able to follow the Dog Rong chief, so she hanged herself.

Master Hu Zeng wrote a poem on this:

First in her brocade silk bower she was called the mother of the nation,
Then in a stinking yurt she became a traitorous slut.
In the end she could not escape the pain of the tightening noose;
Would it not have been better to accept being a mere concubine?

The Marquis of Shen arranged a great banquet to pay tribute to the marchemont lords. However, the guest of honor, Lord Wu of Wey, put down his chopsticks, got up from his seat, and addressed the company as follows: "Today our king is dead and his capital is in ruins, so surely this is not the moment for his subjects to be feasting."

The assembled multitudes all stood, and said, "Please tell us what we should do!"

"The country cannot be left without a monarch even for one day," Lord Wu proclaimed. "Now the former crown prince is in Shen, and we should crown him as king. What do you think, my lords?"

"Your words, Marquis, bring solace to the spirits of our former kings: Wen, Wu, Cheng, and Kang," Lord Xiang said.

"I have done nothing in this great enterprise, but escorting His Majesty to the capital is something that I am happy to undertake, in the knowledge that it would meet with the full approval of my father, the late minister of education," Scion Juetu announced.

Lord Wu was very pleased and lifted his beaker in a toast. Then, using straw from the mat on which he was sitting as an official tally, he went to prepare his chariots. Every state wanted its soldiers to assist.

"We are not going to launch a punitive expedition against the enemy, so why do I need so many soldiers?" Juetu pointed out. "My own forces are enough."

The Marquis of Shen said, "My state has three hundred chariots. I hope that you will allow them to lead the way."

The following day Juetu set off for the state of Shen, where he met Crown Prince Yijiu and told him that he had become king. Yijiu had stayed in Shen while all this was going on, and he had become deeply depressed, not knowing whether his grandfather had been successful or not in his mission. When suddenly he heard that the Scion of Zheng had been bestowed with a tally bearing the names of his grandfather, the Marquis of Shen, and the other lords, which commanded him to return to the capital, he was absolutely astounded. When he opened up the accompanying letter, he learned for the first time that King You had been killed by the Dog Rong. Since he still loved his father, he burst into loud sobs.

"As crown prince," Juetu said, "the security of the state altars should be your first concern. We hope that you will soon assume kingship and thus bring peace to your people."

"Everyone in the world now thinks that I am not a filial son!" Yijiu sobbed. "However, since the situation has come to this, I will just have to carry on alone."

Within a day, he arrived in the capital city of Hao. The Duke of Zhou was the first to enter the city walls, to clear out the palace. The king's grandfather, the Marquis of Shen, led the lords of Wey, Jin, and Qin, together with the Scion of Zheng, and the civil and military officials, to go thirty *li* beyond the city boundaries to meet the new king. A diviner determined an auspicious day for him to enter the city. When Yiqiu saw the palace reduced to ashes and cinders, he cried bitterly. He first gave audience to the Marquis of Shen, to whom he issued his commands; then he changed into formal royal robes and reported his accession at the ancestral shrines, thus assuming the position of monarch. Yijiu took the title of King Ping of Zhou: the Bringer of Peace.

King Ping ascended to the main audience hall, and the assembled lords and officials completed their ceremonial congratulations. King Ping summoned the Earl of Shen to come to the audience hall, where he said, "I was demoted and degraded: that I have been able to come to the throne is all thanks to the efforts of my grandfather. I therefore promote you to the rank of Duke of Shen."

The Earl of Shen declined, saying: "When rewards and punishments are not issued for good reasons, the government is not respected. That the city of Hao was destroyed and has been restored is thanks to the merit of all these lords in coming forward to help Your Majesty in a time of national crisis. I could not control the Dog Rong, and thus I have offended against our former kings, a crime that merits death! How could I dare to accept any reward?" He resolutely refused to accept the promotion three times. King Ping then ordered that he be restored to the rank of marquis.

Lord Wu of Wey reported to His Majesty: "Bao Si and her son received favors that exceeded all bounds, while Shifu, Duke of Guo, Yi Qiu, and the others led their ruler astray and brought disaster on the country. Even though they are dead, the nature of their crimes demands an exemplary punishment."

King Ping agreed with every point of this submission. Ji He, the Marquis of Wey, was promoted to become a duke. Ji Chou, the Marquis of Jin, was granted the lands of Henei as dependent territories. You, Earl

of Zheng, died in the king's service, so His Majesty bestowed upon him
the posthumous title of Huan: "The Brave." Scion Juetu succeeded to
the title and became an earl; in addition to that, he was granted one
thousand *qing* of land. The Lord of Qin originally just ruled a dependent territory, but now he was granted the title of Earl of Qin and numbered among the lords of the Zhou confederacy. Ji Xuan, the son of the
Duke of Zhou, was granted the office of prime minister. Queen Shen
was given the rank and honors of a queen dowager. Bao Si and her son
Bofu were both posthumously demoted to become commoners. As for
Shifu, Duke of Guo, Yi Qiu, and the Duke of Zhai, in remembrance of
the merits of their ancestors in earlier generations and given that they
had died in the king's service, though they were themselves stripped of
all titles and honors, His Majesty agreed that these could then be inherited by their sons and grandsons. Placards were erected encouraging
people to report crimes committed against them, and this consoled the
suffering inhabitants of the capital. A great banquet was held for all the
ministers and officials, at which everyone enjoyed themselves to the full,
and then they went home.

There is a poem that testifies to this:

On this day the officials met their generous master.
Now everyone is overjoyed at the prospect of peace.
From this time on the court will be meritorious, virtuous, and magnani-
    mous;
Our mountains and rivers can look forward to an era of florescence.

The following day the lords thanked the king for his munificence.
King Ping issued further appointments, whereby the Marquis of Wey
became minister of education and Earl Juetu of Zheng became minister
of personnel, and thus they stayed at court working in the government,
assisting Prime Minister Ji Xuan. Only the lords of Shen and Jin said
goodbye and left, on the grounds that their countries were too close to
the Rong and the Di peoples. The Marquis of Shen saw that Juetu was
of exceptionally fine appearance, and so he married his daughter to
him: she was Lady Wu Jiang. Of this no more.

. . .

After the Dog Rong caused all this trouble in the capital of Hao, they
came to know the routes into the Central States well. Even though they
were forced out of the city by the marchemont lords, their rapacity was
undaunted. They muttered among themselves about how hard they had

worked for so little gain, and they were deeply angry. Therefore the chief of the Rong again raised an army and invaded the borders of Zhou, taking control of half the lands of Qi and Feng. Gradually they pressed closer upon the capital at Hao, so that the beacon fires were lit month after month. After the conflagration at the palace, barely half of it remained standing. These smoke-stained walls and broken columns formed a very bleak and miserable vista. King Ping found his treasuries and storehouses empty, so he could not rebuild the palace. Furthermore, he was afraid that sooner or later the Dog Rong would be back, and thus he formulated a plan to move the capital to Luoyang in the east.

One day, when the early morning court was over, he spoke to his assembled ministers. "In the past, my ancestor King Cheng fixed the capital here at Hao, but he also built the city of Luoyang. Why was that?"

With one voice, his ministers replied: "Luoyang is the center of the world; when tribute is brought from the four directions, all roads lead there. That is the reason why King Cheng ordered the Duke of Shao to build houses there and the Duke of Zhou to raise fortifications: he gave it the title of the Eastern Capital. The architecture of that city is exactly the same as that of Hao. Every year that there is a great interstate meeting, the Son of Heaven must travel to the Eastern Capital to meet the lords there. This makes governing the people much easier."

"Now the Dog Rong are pressing ever closer upon the city of Hao, threatening us with a terrible disaster," King Ping said. "I want to move the capital to Luoyang, how would that be?"

Prime Minster Ji Xuan offered his opinion: "Now the palace and gatehouses have been destroyed, and it is not going to be easy to rebuild them. It will put the people to great trouble and waste our money, which the populace is sure to resent bitterly. If the Dog Rong barbarians take advantage of this anger to attack, how will we defend the city? Moving the capital to Luoyang is indeed the best idea."

Both the civil and the military officials were worried about the Dog Rong. They all said, "The prime minister is right in what he says!"

Only the minister of education, Lord Wu of Wey, lowered his head and sighed deeply.

"My dear old minister of education, why are you the only one to say nothing?" King Ping asked.

Lord Wu then made his opinion known to the king. "I am nearly ninety years of age now, and thanks to the fact that Your Majesty still appreciates me, I have been ranked among the six most senior ministers. If I do not speak out about what I know, then I am disloyal to my king.

If I go against the opinion of the majority in what I say, then I am not in harmony with my friends. However, though I can accept annoying my friends, I would never dare to be disloyal to my king. To one side of Hao are the lands of Xiao and Han, while to the other you have Long and Shu. It is enfolded by mountains and girdled by the river, with one thousand *li* of rich lands. Of all the auspicious sites in the world, none are better than this. Luoyang is indeed the center of the world, but it is sited on a flat plain with enemy territory on all four sides. The reason why our former rulers established two capitals was so that they could live in the Western Capital, where they could satisfy the demands of governing the country, going to stay in the Eastern Capital only when they need to prepare for royal progresses. If Your Majesty abandons Hao and moves to Luoyang, then I am afraid that this will fatally weaken the royal house."

"The Dog Rong have already seized control of Qi and Feng, and their power grows ever greater," King Ping pointed out. "My palace is in ruins; I have no means to make a majestic impression. The reason I propose a move to the east is because in fact I have no choice."

Lord Wu submitted his opinion: "The Dog Rong indeed have a wolf-ish nature; you cannot allow them into your home in any safety. When the Marquis of Shen borrowed troops from them, his plan failed, for in fact he was opening the door and inviting in robbers. He allowed them to burn the palace and murder the king. This is a crime that must be avenged. Your Majesty must now fix your ambition upon making the country strong, economizing on your own expenditure and demonstrating your love for your people, training your soldiers and developing their martial powers, for then you can invade to the north and campaign to the south just as our former kings did. You can then take the chief of the Rong prisoner and offer him in sacrifice at the shrines to your seven ancestors to wipe away our shame. If you decide to put up with this situation and swallow your anger, abandoning this place to the enemy, then they will take every foot of territory that we leave. I am afraid that they will gradually assert their authority, and their depredations will not stop at Qi and Feng. In the past, when these lands were ruled by the sage-kings Yao and Shun, they lived in thatched cottages with earthen floors. Likewise later, the sage-king Yu lived in a simple residence and did not believe himself to be humiliated thereby. Surely, for a majestic impression, the capital does not depend solely on the appearance of the royal palace, does it? I hope that Your Majesty will think this matter over carefully."

Prime Minister Ji Xuan then spoke again: "I think that what the old minister of education has said is correct in times of peace, but not in such a troubled age. Our former king neglected the government and destroyed the principles by which we have all lived, bringing wicked bandits down upon himself, but we are already in a position where we can draw a line under this matter and move on. Now Your Majesty has cleared away the ashes and debris of the invasion, and you have been formally invested as the monarch, but your storehouses and treasuries are empty, while your soldiers are weak and their morale is low. The populace is as terrified of the Dog Rong as they would be of wolves or tigers. If one day the Rong cavalry were to launch a lightning strike on us, the people's morale would simply collapse. Who here is willing to be responsible for that kind of national disaster?"

Lord Wu then spoke again. "The Marquis of Shen was able to summon the Rong, so he ought to be able to send them away again. Your Majesty should send someone to ask him, for he is sure to have a good plan."

While they were in the midst of this discussion, the king's grandfather, the Marquis of Shen, sent someone with an urgent message. King Ping opened the letter and looked at it. It read:

> The Dog Rong are making constant incursions and my country is on the verge of collapse. I beg Your Majesty to send troops to rescue us, for after all we are family.

"My grandfather cannot even take care of himself, so how can he help me?" King Ping exclaimed. "I have now made up my mind, we are moving east!"

He ordered the Grand Astrologer to select a day to move eastwards. Lord Wu of Wey said, "It is my job to act as minister of education, so I must point out that if you leave right away, the populace will simply panic. That would be an unforgivable dereliction of duty on my part."

Then they set a date for the move and issued placards that informed the people: "If you wish to follow His Majesty on the move to the east, make your preparations quickly and we will all leave together."

One of the court scribes prepared a text explaining all the reasons for the move, and His Majesty performed a sacrifice at the ancestral temple at which it was proclaimed. On the appointed day, the minister of rites carried the spirit tablets of the seven ancestral temples and rode in a chariot in advance of the rest. When Ying Kai, the Earl of Qin, heard that King Ping was moving east, he personally led his troops to protect the royal convoy. Too many ordinary people followed to be counted, helping the old along and carrying the babies.

Many years before, on the night when King Xuan was holding the great sacrifice, he dreamed that he saw a beautiful girl who laughed loudly three times and cried three times and then, without haste and without alarm, walked up to the spirit tablets of the seven ancestral shrines, gathered them up in a bundle, and walked away to the east. The three loud laughs represented Bao Si at Mount Li when she made fun of the lords rushing to the king's side in response to the beacons. The three cries were for the deaths of King You, Bao Si, and their son Bofu. The spirit tablets being gathered into a bundle and her walking east represented the move to the east that happened that day. Everything in the dream was borne out by subsequent events.

As the Grand Astrologer, Bo Yangfu, said: "Where there are tears there is also laughter; where there is laughter there are also tears. A sheep is swallowed by a ghost; a horse is chased by a dog. Beware! Beware! The wild-mulberry bow and the rush quiver!"

The sheep being swallowed by a ghost referred to the fact that, in the forty-sixth year of his reign, King Xuan died after meeting a ghost; this happened in the year of the Sheep. The horse being chased by a dog referred to the invasion by the Dog Rong, which happened in the year of the Horse, which was the eleventh year of the reign of King You. This marks the end of the Western Zhou. That the calculations of Heaven had been settled in advance can be seen from the miraculously accurate prognostications of Bo Yangfu!

If you want to know what happened after the capital moved to the east, READ ON.

Chapter Four

Lord Wen of Qin sacrifices to Heaven in
response to a prophetic dream.

Lord Zhuang of Zheng digs a pit in order to
see his mother.

It has been described how King Ping moved the capital to the east. When he arrived at Luoyang, he saw that the markets were bustling with people and the palaces were beautiful—no different, in fact, from the city of Hao of yore—and he was very pleased.

When the new capital was settled, the lords from every direction came to present their congratulations and to offer tribute of local products. It was only Chu who did not participate, and so King Ping discussed launching a campaign against them. His ministers remonstrated with him: "The barbarian Chu people have lived for a long time beyond our influence; King Xuan was the first to go to war and force them to submit to his authority. Every year they present tribute of just one cartload of sweet herbs, which is used to strain the libations offered in sacrifice. They are not tasked with anything else, and this tribute item represents their acceptance of our control. Now, the move of the capital has only just been completed and people have not yet settled in here, and yet Your Majesty wants to lead the army on a campaign in distant lands without even bothering to conduct a divination about whether this is auspicious or not! It would be better to treat them with leniency and bring them back under your control by making them appreciate your moral authority. If they stubbornly stick to their wicked ways, you should wait until you have sufficient military strength to make them understand their mistake. It will not be too late to punish them at that point." The discussions about a southern campaign were then shelved.

Lord Xiang of Qin reported his departure, returning to his own country.

"More than half of the lands of Qi and Feng have now been conquered by the Dog Rong," King Ping said. "If you are able to expel the Dog Rong, I will bestow all these lands upon you, as a small reward for your ongoing labors to support the royal house. Qin will then in perpetuity form the western bulwark of our nation; would that not be wonderful?"

Lord Xiang of Qin kowtowed and accepted the king's commands. Then he went home, whereupon he prepared his soldiers and horses with the intention of destroying the Rong people. Within three years, he had massacred the majority of the Dog Rong and killed both their great generals—Bo Ding and Man Yesu—in battle. After this, the chief of the Rong moved far away into the western wilderness, and so the lands of Qi and Feng came to belong to Qin in their entirety. Thus, they opened up one thousand *li* of territory and went on to become a great state.

A bearded old man wrote a poem about this:

> Once this was the hometown of Kings Wen and Wu.
> How could it be lightly abandoned to the Qin?
> If the Zhou dynasty had kept Qi and Feng as before,
> Would the ruler of Qin ever have become strong enough to declare
>   himself emperor?

The ruling house of Qin was descended from the sage-king Zhuanxu. Among his descendants was a man named Gaoyao, and in the time of the sage-king Yao he held the office of chief judge. Gaoyao's son, Boyi, assisted Yu the Great with the work of controlling the floods, burning the mountains, and firing the marshes to expel fierce animals. For the success of his labors, he was granted the surname Ying. During the time of the sage-king Shun, he had already served as a master herdsman.

Boyi had two sons: Ruomu and Dalian. Ruomu was enfeoffed with the lands of Xu, and during the Xia and the Shang dynasties his descendants were aristocrats from one generation to the next. In the time of King Zhou of the Shang dynasty, a descendant of Dalian named Feilian was such a good runner that he could race five hundred *li* in a day; his son Elai was so amazingly strong that he could skin tigers and leopards with his bare hands. Since this father and son were both exceptionally brave, they were much favored by the evil King Zhou of the Shang dynasty, and they encouraged him in his sadistic violence. When King Wen conquered the Shang, he executed both Feilian and Elai.

Feilian's youngest son was called Jisheng, and it was his great-grandson, Zaofu, who was favored by King Mu of Zhou on account of his excellent charioteering skills. Thus he was enfeoffed in Zhao and became the ancestor of the Zhao family of Jin. Among his descendants was a man named Feizi, who lived at Quanqiu and was a good horse-breeder employed by King Xiao of the Zhou dynasty. The king commanded him to raise horses in the region between the Qian and Wei rivers, whereby they multiplied greatly. King Xiao was very pleased and enfeoffed Feizi with the lands of Qin. His Majesty made him a minor border lord, ordering him to continue the sacrifices of the Ying family and granting him the title Ying-Qin. Six generations later, his descendant Lord Xiang was given the title Earl of Qin thanks to his efforts on behalf of the crown. Now he had also obtained the lands of Qi and Feng, and thus his power grew and his strength became greater, so he established his capital at Yong and for the first time began to conduct diplomatic relations with the other aristocrats. When Lord Xiang died, his son Lord Wen was established. This occurred in the fifteenth year of the reign of King Ping.

. . .

One day Lord Wen of Qin dreamed that in the wilds outside Fuyi, a yellow snake descended from heaven and rested on the mountain slope. Its head was as big as a cartwheel, and though its body was resting on the ground, its tail was high up in the sky. Then, in an instant, it changed into a little child, who spoke to Lord Wen as follows: "I am the son of God on High, and he appoints you as the White Emperor to take command of the western sacrifices." When he finished speaking, the child vanished.

The following day, Lord Wen summoned the Grand Astrologer Dun to perform a divination about this.

"White is the color that symbolizes the western regions," Dun proclaimed, "and Your Lordship has great possessions in the west. Thanks to the mandate that you have received from God on High, if you perform these sacrifices you will certainly receive great blessings."

Thereupon Lord Wen built a tall tower at Fuyi and established the Temple to the White Emperor there, a site also known as the Great Shrine. White oxen were used in the sacrifices held there.

On another occasion, a man from Chencang was out hunting and captured a beast that looked like a pig but had many spines. He injured but did not kill it and, not knowing its name, dragged it along with him intending to present it to Lord Wen. On the road he met two small children, who pointed at the animal and said, "The name of this animal is 'Wei,' and it usually lives underground, sucking out the brains of dead men. If you hit it on the head, it will die."

The Wei then spoke in the language of men and said, "These two children are in fact the finest of pheasants, and they are called the 'Treasures of Chen.' The man who captures the boy will become king, while he who captures the girl will become hegemon."

The two children, realizing that he had revealed their true identity, transformed themselves into wild birds and flew away. The girl stopped on the north slope of Mount Chencang, where she was changed into a stone bird. When the man looked around for the Wei, it too had disappeared. The hunter was amazed by these miraculous events and rushed to report them to Lord Wen. Lord Wen of Qin then established the Shrine to the Treasures of Chen at Mount Chencang.

On yet another occasion, there was a great catalpa tree at Mount Zhongnan that Lord Wen intended to have cut down to provide timber for the construction of his palace, but no saw could make an impression: when people tried to chop it down, their axes just bounced off. Suddenly there was a great storm, which stopped as abruptly as it had started. There was a man who spent the night at the foot of the mountain who overheard a group of ghosts congratulate the tree, to which the tree spirit replied politely.

One ghost inquired, "If Qin sent someone with their hair unbound to tie a crimson thread around your trunk, what could you do about it?"

The tree spirit was silent. The following day, the man reported to Lord Wen of Qin what the ghost had said. Lord Wen then did as he was told and again sent someone to chop down the tree. This time the tree was indeed felled, and a black buffalo came out of the trunk and leapt into the Yong River. After that, the people living by the riverside often saw a black buffalo emerge from the waters. Lord Wen heard about this and sent a cavalry officer to wait beside the river and attack it. The buffalo was so strong that it knocked the cavalry officer to the ground, whereupon his hair fell so that it covered his face. The buffalo was so scared by this that it did not dare to come out again. Accordingly, Lord Wen established the "Long-Haired Guard" in his army. He also built the Shrine to the Angry Buffalo, in which sacrifices were held to the spirit of the great catalpa tree.

. . .

At this time Lord Hui of Lu heard that the state of Qin was conducting sacrifices to God on High in defiance of all regulations. Therefore, he sent Chancellor Rang to Zhou to ask permission to conduct the suburban and ancestral sacrifices normally performed only by the Son of Heaven. King Ping would not permit this.

"My ancestor, the Duke of Zhou, performed acts of exceptional merit in supporting the royal house," Lord Hui said, "and the rituals and music for these occasions were created by him. If his descendants also make use of them, what is the problem? Furthermore, if the Son of Heaven cannot prevent Qin from doing this, then how can he stop us?"

Subsequently he too conducted the suburban and ancestral sacrifices in a manner comparable to the royal house, in defiance of the regulations. King Ping knew about this but did not dare to make an issue of it. From this time onwards, royal authority declined day by day and the aristocrats gained in power and authority, invading and attacking each other so that the world became ever more dangerous and unstable.

A historian wrote a poem that bewails this:

Since antiquity, kings and aristocrats have conducted different rituals;
Never before had a marquis performed the suburban sacrifices to
    Heaven!
Once Qin and Lu began to usurp these prerogatives,
Subordinate states gradually encroached upon royal authority.

It has been described how Juetu, the Scion of Zheng, succeeded to his father's title and became Lord Wu. Thanks to the civil war in Zhou, Lord Wu was able to obtain the lands of Dongguo and Kuai, and he moved his capital to Kuai, which was then renamed New Zheng. The city of Yingyang was renamed Jing, and he established a border pass at Zhi. From this time onwards, Zheng was increasingly powerful. Together with Lord Wu of Wei, Lord Wu of Zheng was the most important minister at the Zhou court. In the thirteenth year of the reign of King Ping, Lord Wu of Wei died and Lord Wu of Zheng was then in sole command of the government of Zhou. Since the Zheng capital was very close to Luoyang, he could spend some of the time at court and some of the time at home, coming and going at irregular intervals. There is no need to describe this further.

As mentioned above, Lord Wu of Zheng's wife was Lady Jiang, the daughter of the Marquis of Shen, and she gave birth to two children: Wusheng and Duan.

Why did she call her son Wusheng? When Lady Jiang was about to give birth, she did not realize that she was in childbed, and thus she had the baby while she was asleep. When she woke up, she realized what had happened and was deeply shocked; thus, she gave the baby a name that means "Born on Waking."

Her deep unhappiness made her unable to bond with her baby. Later on, she gave birth to her second son, Duan. Duan grew up to be an exceptionally brilliant young man, who was not only very handsome but also strong and good at archery; indeed, he excelled in all branches of the military arts. Lady Jiang loved and favored her second son: "If you usurped the title and became lord, would you not be ten times better than Wusheng?" Time and again she spoke to her husband, Lord Wu, about her second son's talents and how he should be appointed as heir.

"There is a fixed order among siblings that cannot be set aside," Lord Wu said. "Besides which, Wusheng has done nothing wrong, so how could I possibly set aside the elder and establish his younger brother?"

He appointed Wusheng as his heir and gave the tiny little city of Gong to Duan, so that he might enjoy some private revenue. Thus he took the title of Gongshu. Lady Jiang was extremely unhappy about this.

When Lord Wu died, Wusheng succeeded to the title and became Lord Zhuang of Zheng. He also replaced his father as the most senior official at the Zhou court. Lady Jiang saw that Gongshu was left power-less, and so she became very depressed. She spoke to Lord Zhuang about it: "You have inherited your father's position and enjoy several hundred *li* of land, while your own younger brother goes without. Do you really find this acceptable?"

"What would you like me to do, Mother?" Lord Zhuang asked.

"Why don't you enfeoff him with the city of Zhi?" Lady Jiang demanded.

"Zhi is utterly crucial for the defense of the realm," Lord Zhuang reminded her, "and our former lords left instructions that it should never be given away. In anything other than this I will follow your instructions."

"Well, the city of Jing would be the next best," Lady Jiang said.

Lord Zhuang fell silent. Lady Jiang got angry and snapped: "If that too is unacceptable, all that is left is for him to go into exile in another country and try and seek advancement there. That way he might at least be able to make a living!"

"That would not be right! That would not be right!" Lord Zhuang repeated. He then agreed to her demands and left.

The following day, he ascended to the hall of audience and summoned Gongshu Duan in order to enfeoff him with this land.

Grandee Zhai Zu remonstrated with him: "You cannot do this. Just as the sky cannot have two suns, our country cannot have two lords. The city of Jing has walls one hundred cubits long, its lands are broad and its people numerous; it is comparable in every way to the capital. Besides which, Gongshu is Her Ladyship's favorite child, and if you enfeoff him with a great city it will put him in the position of a second lord. Given that he has such support inside the palace, I am afraid that in the end he will cause us all serious trouble."

"But this is my mother's wish," Lord Zhuang said. "How could I dare to refuse?"

In the end, he enfeoffed Gongshu in Jing.

After Gongshu had thanked his brother for his generosity, he entered the palace to say goodbye to Lady Jiang. She sent away her servants and spoke privately to Duan. "Your older brother has never cared much for you in spite of your blood relationship; in fact, he has been consistently mean to you. I had to pester him just to get today's enfeoffment, and though I have forced him to accord with my wishes, I don't think in his heart of hearts that he is happy about it. When you get to Jing, you must recruit an army and prepare in secret. If there is a suitable opportunity, I will let you know. You can then mobilize your army and make a surprise attack on Zheng. I will help you from inside the palace, and thus we will conquer this country. If you could but take Wusheng's place, even if I die I will have no regrets!"

Gongshu accepted her instructions and moved to take up residence in Jing. After this, the people of Zheng took up calling him Taishu of Jing.

On the day that Taishu began his residence in Jing, the steward of the Western Ward and the steward of the Northern Ward both came to offer their congratulations. Taishu Duan said to them, "The lands that you administer now belong to me as part of my fief, so henceforward any tribute or tax revenue must be brought directly to me, and I want the army placed under my sole control. There must be no mistakes about this!"

The two stewards were well aware that Taishu was Her Ladyship's favorite child and that he hoped to succeed to the title himself. Today, seeing him looking so impressive, such an exceptionally brilliant man, they did not dare to disobey his orders; they simply agreed with him. On the pretext of going out hunting or shooting, day after day Taishu left the city to train his troops, and all the people of the two wards were

enlisted in the army rolls. Again, while pretending that he was out hunting, he made surprise attacks on Yan and Pinyan and captured both of
them. The stewards of these two towns escaped to Zheng and made a
detailed report to Lord Zhuang of how Taishu had led his forces to
capture these lands. Lord Zhuang just smiled silently.

One of his officials shouted out, "Execute Duan!"

Lord Zhuang raised his head to look at the speaker; it was his senior
minister, the Honorable Lü. "What esteemed opinion do you have to
offer, sir?" Lord Zhuang inquired.

"I have heard people say, 'A subject should never betray his ruler,
and if he does, he should be executed,'" the Honorable Lü stated.
"Now, Taishu Duan wants to take advantage of his mother's favoritism
and the impregnable defenses of the city of Jing to usurp your title; to
this end he trains his army day and night. Give me an army, my lord,
and I will march straight on Jing, arrest Duan, and bring him home;
that way disaster can be averted."

"Duan has not yet done anything wrong," Lord Zhuang pointed out,
"so how can I order his execution?"

"He has already taken over two wards and extended his control as
far as Pinyan. Surely you will not just stand by while the lands of our
former lords are partitioned?" the Honorable Lü retorted.

Lord Zhuang laughed. "He is Lady Jiang's favorite son and my own
beloved brother," he said. "I would much rather lose this land than
harm the relationship between us and upset my mother."

The Honorable Lü presented his opinion: "I do not care about losing
land; I am worried that you will lose the whole country. Your people are
already beginning to vacillate; they can see that Taishu is becoming
stronger, and they all harbor expectations. Any day now, the people of
the capital are going to start changing sides. You may treat Taishu leni-
ently now, but I am afraid that in the future he will not be so generous
to you! But by then it will be far too late!"

"Please do not speak so melodramatically," Lord Zhuang said. "Let
me think carefully about this."

The Honorable Lü went out and spoke to Grandee Zhai Zu. "His
Lordship is so concerned about family harmony that he is prepared to
put the whole country at risk. I am very worried about this!"

"His Lordship is a very clever man," Zhai Zu said. "He will certainly
not just sit still and wait for events to overtake him. There are too many
eyes and ears about the court; it would not be sensible to reveal his true
plans there. You are not just a minister but also a member of the ruling

house, so if you went to see him privately he would be sure to grant you an audience."

Thus the Honorable Lü went straight back to the palace and requested a second interview with Lord Zhuang.

"Why have you come back?" Lord Zhuang asked.

"Her Ladyship never wanted you to succeed to the title," the Honorable Lü said. "If she is plotting with your younger brother, they will have no difficulty in raising a rebellion in which case you, my lord, will not keep possession of the state of Zheng. I can neither eat nor sleep for worry, so I have come again to beg you to deal with this situation."

"This matter touches upon Her Ladyship," Lord Zhuang said.

"Surely Your Lordship must have heard of the way in which the Duke of Zhou executed his own younger brothers, the lords of Guan and Cai?" the Honorable Lü demanded. "If you don't deal with the things that must be dealt with, disaster will result. I hope that you will come up with a plan at the earliest possible moment."

"I made my calculations long ago," Lord Zhuang explained. "Although Duan has behaved badly, he is not yet in open rebellion against me. If I try and have him executed, Lady Jiang will certainly do her utmost to prevent it, and once everyone is gossiping about it, not only will they say that I am behaving badly to my younger brother, they will also accuse me of being unfilial. My current position is simply to accept whatever my younger brother does. He knows that my mother favors him, and as he sees his ambitions fulfilled he will become more reckless. I am waiting for him to commit treason, for then his criminal acts will be clear and no one in the country will dare to help him. Even Lady Jiang will be left with nothing to say!"

"Your Lordship has thought more deeply into this matter than I," the Honorable Lü said. "But I am afraid that the longer this goes on and the greater his strength grows, the more difficult it will be to get rid of him, just like trying to uproot bindweed. What will you do then? If you, my lord, are determined to wait until he attacks you, why not encourage him into open rebellion at the earliest possible moment?"

"What kind of plan did you have in mind?" Lord Zhuang asked.

"It is a long time since you last went to the royal court," the Honorable Lü pointed out, "thanks to the ongoing problems with Taishu. Now, if you put the word out that you are going to Zhou, Taishu will imagine that the capital is undefended, and so he will raise an army to attack Zheng. I will be ready with troops hidden in the vicinity of Jing. When he leaves the city, I will enter and capture it. You can then attack from the direction of Pinyan. With enemies in front and behind, even if Taishu Duan grows wings he will not be able to escape."

"What an excellent plan!" Lord Zhuang exclaimed. "Be careful that it is not discovered by anyone else!"

The Honorable Lü then said goodbye and left by the palace gates, at which point he sighed and said, "Zhai Zu was absolutely right!"

The following morning at court, Lord Zhuang gave orders that Grandee Zhai Zu would assume the regency while he himself went to the royal Zhou court to carry out his duties there. When Lady Jiang heard this news, she was absolutely delighted. "Duan will become lord!" she exclaimed. Then, she secretly wrote a letter and gave it to a trusted messenger to carry to Jing, in which she suggested the first week in the fifth month as a suitable date for him to make a surprise attack on Zheng. This all happened in the last week of the fourth month.

However, the Honorable Lü had already set ambushes on all the major roads, and when they captured the messenger, they killed him. The letter was then secretly conveyed to Lord Zhuang. Having broken the seal and read it, Lord Zhuang then resealed it and ordered someone to take the letter to Taishu, pretending to be Lady Jiang's messenger. The return letter fixed the date for the fifth of the fifth month. Lady Jiang was to raise a white flag above the barbican, so that he would know which gate she would open. When Lord Zhuang obtained this letter, he said cheerfully, "With this evidence in hand, can Lady Jiang carry on defending him?"

He then entered the palace and said goodbye to his mother, saying that he was on his way to Zhou. In fact, he traveled to Pinyan in slow and easy stages. Of course, the Honorable Lü had already led an army of two hundred chariots to lie in wait in the vicinity of Jing.

When Taishu Duan received the secret message from his mother, Lady Jiang, he discussed it with his son, Noble Grandson Hua, after which he sent Hua to Wey to request auxiliary troops, agreeing to pay a hefty price for them. He gathered all the people of the two wards and announced that an order had been received from the Earl of Zheng appointing him as regent. He performed a sacrifice to the flag and feasted his army, then left the city at the head of a magnificent procession. The Honorable Lü had earlier sent ten chariots into the city by stealth, with the soldiers disguised as merchants. They had orders to wait for Taishu to mobilize his troops, then they were to light bonfires at the gates. When the Honorable Lü saw the flames in the distance, he attacked. The people already inside the city opened the gates for him, and Jing fell without a fight. Afterwards, the Honorable Lü circulated announcements to pacify the populace, describing Lord Zhuang's filial conduct and how generous he had been to his younger brother, and how Taishu had forgotten his older brother's kindness and rebelled against him. Everyone in the city agreed that Taishu was in the wrong.

Taishu had set out with his army, but the following day he got the news that Jing had fallen. He was very frightened and immediately turned back, traveling under cover of darkness. He made camp outside the walls as he planned his attack on the city. However, his officers and men were deeply disaffected. Some of his troops had received word from their families in Jing: "Lord Zhuang is a very kind man; it is Taishu Duan who is neither good nor honest."

One man told ten, ten men told one hundred, and they all exclaimed: "How dreadful! We have supported the wrong side!" They started to disperse. When Taishu counted his troops, fewer than half were left. He knew that these people no longer supported him, so he fled to Yan, where he intended to muster more men. He did not realize that Lord Zhuang's army was already in place. Then he said, "Gong is my old fief." He went to Gong and shut the gates, intending to make his stand there.

Lord Zhuang led his army to attack him; given that Gong was just a little city, how could they resist the onslaught of a great army attacking on two fronts? It was like crushing an egg with Mount Tai—it was immediately overrun. When Taishu Duan heard that Lord Zhuang had arrived, he sighed and said, "Lady Jiang has ruined my life! How could I ever face my brother again?" Thus he committed suicide by cutting his own throat.

Master Hu Zeng wrote a poem reading:

A favorite brother, with many talents, in possession of a great fief,
In addition to which he had support from inside the palace.
Who would have imagined that wickedness would so easily be
    punished?
Though he lived at Jing, he died at Gong.

There is also a poem that speaks of how Lord Zhuang encouraged Duan's crimes, in order to prevent Lady Jiang from complaining about his treatment of his younger brother—a truly unscrupulous man. This poem runs:

The merits of your children depend entirely on how they have been
    brought up.

If you educate them badly, you will bring about disaster.
From the moment that he was separately enfeoffed in Jing,
Taishu's fate was in other people's hands!

Lord Zhuang lifted Duan's body and wept loudly, saying, "How could you be so stupid?" Then he searched his effects and found the letter sent by Lady Jiang among them. With Taishu's reply, he placed them together into one envelope and instructed someone to hurry back to Zheng and give these documents to Lady Jiang and Zhai Zu to read. He also commanded that Lady Jiang should be sent into exile in Ying. He swore: "Until we meet in the Underworld, I will not see you again!"

When Lady Jiang saw the two letters, she was terribly upset and ashamed; she also felt that she could not face meeting Lord Zhuang. Immediately she left the palace and went to live in Ying. When Lord Zhuang returned to the capital and found his mother gone, he began to miss her. He sighed and said, "I had no choice but to kill my brother, but I cannot endure being separated from my mother. I have committed a terrible crime against nature by even trying!"

The border officer at Ying was named Ying Kaoshu, a very upright and unselfish man who had a well-deserved reputation for being a good son and a good friend. When he saw that Lord Zhuang had sent his mother to live in exile in Ying, he remarked: "Even though a mother may not behave in a motherly way, a child must remain filial. Our ruler's actions are wrong!"

Accordingly, he obtained a couple of *hao* birds and sought an audience with Lord Zhuang, pretending that he was presenting him with an unusual wild delicacy.

"What are these birds?" Lord Zhuang asked.

"They are *hao* birds," Ying Kaoshu explained. "In the daytime they are too blind to see Mount Tai, but at night they are so sharp-sighted they can see the tip of an autumn hair. You could say that they know about the small but not about the large. When they are young their mother feeds them, but when they grow up they eat her. These are unfilial birds, and so we catch and eat them."

Lord Zhuang was silent. At that point the chef sent in a dish of steamed lamb, and Lord Zhuang ordered that a haunch be cut off and given to Ying Kaoshu to eat. Kaoshu removed the best meat, and he wrapped it up in paper and slipped it into his sleeve. Lord Zhuang was surprised and asked him what he was doing.

"My old mother is still alive," Ying Kaoshu explained, "but my family is very poor. Every day I go to pluck wild herbs to give her something nice to eat, but she has never had the opportunity to enjoy meat like this. Now you have given this to me, but my old mother hasn't been able to enjoy so much as a morsel—thinking about my poor old mother, how could I possibly swallow it? I am going to take it home and make it into a stew for Mother."

"You, sir, are a truly filial son!" Lord Zhuang exclaimed. When he had finished speaking, he could not stop himself from heaving a sad sigh.

"What is the matter, my lord?" Ying Kaoshu asked.

"You at least have a mother to look after so you can fulfill your duties as a son," Lord Zhuang said. "I may be a nobleman, but in this you are luckier than I."

Kaoshu pretended not to understand what he was talking about, and asked, "But Lady Jiang is alive and well, so how can you say you have no mother?"

Lord Zhuang then explained how Lady Jiang and Taishu Duan had plotted together to launch a surprise attack on Zheng and how he had then sent his mother into exile in Ying. "I have already sworn a deadly oath, and though I may regret this, it is too late."

"Taishu is dead now, so Lady Jiang has only one son left, and that is Your Lordship," Ying Kaoshu said. "If you don't look after her, then what is the difference between you and a *hao* bird? If you think that your oath to meet only in the Underworld is an insuperable obstacle to a reconciliation, then I have a plan that should resolve your problem."

"What plan can solve my problem?" Lord Zhuang inquired.

"Dig a tunnel," Ying Kaoshu replied, "and build an 'Underworld' at the bottom. I will go and fetch Lady Jiang, and tell her how much you have missed her. I am sure that Her Ladyship cares about you just as much as you do about her. If you meet her there, your oath never to see her except in the Underworld will not be broken."

Lord Zhuang was very pleased. He ordered Kaoshu to take five hundred workmen and dig a deep pit below Mount Niupi at Quwei. They dug down till they hit a bubbling spring, and then beside the spring they built a wooden chamber: the "Underworld." When everything was complete, they built a staircase down to it.

Ying Kaoshu then went to see Lady Wu Jiang, hinting that Lord Zhuang regretted what he had done and that he now wanted to be reconciled. Lady Wu Jiang was still upset, but also pleased by this news.

Kaoshu took Lady Wu Jiang to the chamber below Mount Niupi while Lord Zhuang rode there in his carriage. He went down the stairs, and when he got to the bottom, he prostrated himself and said, "I have been unfilial and for too long unaware of my faults; I hope you will forgive me, Mother!"

"You can blame me for everything," Lady Wu Jiang said. "It is not your fault!"

She lifted him to his feet, and they embraced and cried bitterly. Afterwards they climbed the stairway out of the pit. Lord Zhuang assisted Lady Wu Jiang into the carriage and took the reins himself to drive her home. When the people of the capital saw Lord Zhuang coming back with his mother, they all saluted him and acclaimed his filial piety. This all came about thanks to Ying Kaoshu's efforts.

Master Hu Zeng wrote a poem about this:

By swearing to meet his mother only in the Underworld, he broke a
    natural bond.
In general, he seems to have been quite different from normal people.
If Ying Kaoshu had not put aside his meat,
Would Lord Zhuang ever have been willing to see his mother again?

Lord Zhuang deeply appreciated the efforts Ying Kaoshu had made to restore the loving relationship between mother and son, so he gave him the title of grandee. He took charge of military matters together with Noble Grandson E. Of this no more.

. . .

It has been mentioned that Gongshu Duan's son, Noble Grandson Hua, went to obtain an army from Wey. However, before he even got halfway, he heard that his father had been killed, so he fled into exile in Wey. He complained that his uncle had killed his own younger brother and imprisoned his mother.

"The Earl of Zheng is an unprincipled man," Lord Huan of Wey proclaimed. "Let me punish him on your behalf!"

Accordingly, he raised an army to attack Zheng. If you don't know who won and who lost, READ ON.

Chapter Five

After favoring the Duke of Guo, Zhou and
Zheng exchange hostages.

To help Wey and defend against Lu, Song
raises an army.

When Lord Zhuang of Zheng heard that Noble Grandson Hua had raised an army and was coming to attack him, he asked his ministers to come up with a plan.

"If you cut down a weed but do not dig out the roots," the Honorable Lü remarked, "it will be back the following spring. Noble Grandson Hua is lucky to be alive, yet now he has been able to raise an army in Wey. I am sure that the Marquis of Wey does not know that Gongshu Duan was guilty of a surprise attack upon Zheng, and that is why he is prepared to raise an army to help Hua, on the pretext that they are rescuing his grandmother. In my humble opinion, it would be best to prepare a letter to be sent to the Marquis of Wey explaining clearly to him what is going on, for then he is sure to remove his troops and go back to his own country. Hua will then be isolated and we can capture him without having to fight."

"That is true," Lord Zhuang said. Subsequently, he sent an envoy with a letter to Wey. Lord Huan of Wey got the letter and read it:

Wusheng, bowing twice, respectfully presents this letter to the Marquis of Wey. A misfortune has overtaken my family in which blood relatives have hurt each other grievously; I am indeed ashamed to have to mention this to my neighbors. I enfeoffed my younger brother in Jing, which shows that I treated him well; that he took advantage of my generosity to cause trouble is indeed a failure of respect on Gongshu Duan's part. I believed it was most important to protect the patrimony that I had inherited from my ancestors, and that forced me into a position where I had to kill him. My mother, Lady Jiang, has always loved Gongshu Duan excessively, was deeply upset at this turn of events, and went to live in Ying, but now I have already welcomed her back and effected a reconciliation. Now the traitor Hua has concealed his father's crimes and fled to your country, as a result of which you, my lord, ignorant of the rights and wrongs of this matter, have sent your army to threaten my humble capital. I have done nothing wrong, and I hope that you will join me in executing the traitorous rebel. Do not destroy our long-standing close friendship! That would be the greatest boon to my country!

When Lord Huan of Wey finished reading this, he was very shocked. "Gongshu Duan offended against every moral principle, and thus he brought his death upon himself! By raising an army for Hua's sake, I have in fact been helping a traitor!" He ordered an envoy to go and bring the army back home.

Before the envoy had even arrived, Hua had already attacked and taken the undefended town of Pinyan. Lord Zhuang of Zheng was absolutely furious. He ordered Grandee Gao Qumi to take out two hundred chariots and recapture Pinyan. By that time, the Wey troops had already been demobilized and gone back home. Consequently, Noble Grandson Hua did not have the means to resist an attack, so he simply abandoned Pinyan and fled again to Wey. The Honorable Lü took advantage of this opportunity to set off in pursuit, and he kept going right up until he reached the suburbs of the Wey capital.

Lord Huan of Wey summoned all of his ministers and asked them to come up with a plan to defend the city.

The Honorable Zhouyu stepped forward and said, "We must stop their onslaught by sending our army out to do battle. What other choice do we have?"

"No! No!" Grandee Shi Que exclaimed. "Troops have come from Zheng because we helped Hua in his treasonous rebellion. The Earl of Zheng has already sent us a letter explaining this, and we should write back apologizing. That way Zheng's army will withdraw without us having to send our troops into battle."

"You are right," the Marquis of Wey said. He immediately ordered Shi Que to write a reply and take it to the Earl of Zheng. The letter read:

Wan, bowing twice, respectfully presents this letter to the Earl of Zheng. I made a terrible mistake in listening to the words of Noble Grandson Hua, who claimed that you had murdered your younger brother and imprisoned your mother, leaving your nephew with nowhere to go—hence I raised an army. Now having read your letter, I realize that it was Taishu of Jing who was in the wrong, and I regret my actions more than I can say. The very day that I read it I withdrew my troops from Pinyan. If that is not enough, I am prepared to arrest Hua and hand him over to you, that we may restore our old friendly relations. Let me know what you would like me to do.

Lord Zhuang of Zheng read the letter. Then he said: "Wey admits its mistake. What more can I ask for?"

Dowager Countess Lady Jiang, when she heard that Lord Zhuang had raised an army to attack Wey, was afraid that Noble Grandson Hua would be killed, leaving Taishu without any descendants. "Please remember that he too is a descendant of your late father, Lord Wu, and spare his life!" she tearfully begged Lord Zhuang.

Lord Zhuang spared him for Lady Jiang's sake; however, he also calculated that there was little that Noble Grandson Hua could do, given that he was isolated and friendless. He wrote a letter in reply to the Marquis of Wey, which read:

Having withdrawn your troops on receipt of my letter, the good relationship between our two countries is now fully restored. Even though Hua has com-mitted criminal acts, he is my wicked younger brother's only child, so I beg that you will allow him to stay in your country where he can continue the sacrifices to Taishu Duan's spirit.

At the same time, he ordered Gao Qumi's troops home. Noble Grand-son Hua grew old and died in Wey, but this happened much later on.

. . .

Since Lord Zhuang of Zheng was away from his office for such a long time, King Ping of Zhou summoned Jifu, Duke of Guo, to court. Their discussions went very well, and so the king complained to the Duke of Guo: "The lords of Zheng have been in sole control of the government for years and years, the son taking over from the father. Now the Earl of Zheng has not come to work for a long time, so I want you to take over the business of government. You must not refuse!"

The Duke of Guo kowtowed and said, "The reason that the Earl of Zheng is not present must be because he has been confronted with an emergency at home. If I were to replace him, the Earl of Zheng would not only hate me, he might well also be angry with Your Majesty! I do not dare to obey your order." He refused two or three times, and in the end withdrew and went home to his own country.

Originally, even when Lord Zhuang of Zheng was at home, he would leave someone in the royal capital to keep an eye on what was going on at court, and if there was any news they were to report to him directly. Now King Ping wanted him to share power with the Duke of Guo; how could he not know about it? That very day he rode in his chariot to Zhou, and when the morning court was over he presented his opinion: "Thanks to Your Majesty's sagacious generosity, my father and I have been in charge of the government in succession. Since I have but meager abilities, I am ashamed to hold high office. I would like to resign my job as senior minister and return to my remote fief, that I may preserve my integrity as a loyal subject."

"You have not come to work for a long time," King Ping said, "which has caused me great worry. Now today you are here, and I feel like a fish that has been put back into its water. Why would you want to suggest such a thing?"

Lord Zhuang again submitted his opinion: "My country was brought to the brink of disaster by my rebellious younger brother, so I have had to neglect my job here for a long time. Now my problems are pretty much resolved, and so I hurried to court, traveling overnight without sleep. However, it was rumored on the road that Your Majesty intends to entrust the government to the Duke of Guo. I know myself to be much less able than he is, so how would I dare to occupy this position when I cannot do the job properly? How could I cause Your Majesty such trouble?"

When King Ping heard Lord Zhuang mention the matter of the Duke of Guo, he was so embarrassed that he blushed scarlet. He forced himself to speak calmly. "With you being away for so long, I realized that you must have had a crisis at home. I wanted the Duke of Guo to take charge temporarily, until you were ready to return. The Duke of Guo refused my request, and I have heard that he is now back at home. What further concerns can you have about this matter?"

"The government is Your Majesty's government," Lord Zhuang said. "It is not something that belongs to my family alone. It is Your Majesty's decision whom to employ. The Duke of Guo is an exceptionally able man who will assist the government greatly. I ought to give up my job in his favor. Otherwise, your ministers will certainly say that I am greedy for power and privilege and that I have promoted and dismissed people purely on selfish grounds. I hope that Your Majesty will reconsider!"

"You and your father have given great service to the country," King Ping said, "and that is why you have both been charged, one after the other, with a senior government position, holding power for more than forty years. You and I have always gotten along so well together, but today you seem to be suspicious of me. How can I clear myself in your eyes? If you really do not trust me, then I will order Crown Prince Hu to go as a hostage to Zheng. How would that be?"

Lord Zhuang bowed twice and refused the king's offer, saying, "My participation in the government depends on whether I have a job as a minister or not, but since when has the Son of Heaven been required to send hostages to his own subjects? I am afraid that everyone will think that I have been bullying Your Majesty, a crime that merits ten thousand deaths!"

"You are quite wrong," King Ping said. "You administer your country well, and I want to send the crown prince to observe the way that things are done in Zheng. That will also resolve our current problem of miscommunication. If you insist on refusing, then you are going to annoy me!"

Lord Zhuang still did not dare to accept the royal command, and he refused again and again.

The officials present made the following recommendation: "In our opinion, if His Majesty does not send a hostage to Zheng, there is no way to resolve the Earl of Zheng's concerns. On the other hand, if a hostage is given unilaterally, then it will appear that the Earl of Zheng is taking advantage of his ruler. It would be better if king and minister exchange hostages, so that neither side has reason to doubt the other's sincerity; thus both parties will feel secure."

"That would be wonderful," King Ping agreed.

Lord Zhuang sent someone to go on ahead and collect Scion Zihu to serve as a hostage in Zhou; then he thanked the king for his magnanimity. Zhou Crown Prince Hu also went to Zheng as a hostage.

A historian wrote a poem criticizing the exchange of hostages between Zhou and Zheng, because from this time on all distinctions between ruler and subjects disappeared:

Your heart and stomach, your hands and feet cannot act independently;
For the parts of one body to turn against each other creates a deplorable
   situation.
This exchange of hostages was clearly a deal;
From this point on, royal prestige declined.

After the exchange of hostages was made, the Earl of Zheng stayed in Zhou to support the government and everything went well. King Ping reigned for fifty-one years and then passed away. During this time the

Earl of Zheng and Heijian, Duke of Zhou, together directed the affairs of the realm. They sent the scion Zihu home to Zheng, where he was instructed to collect the crown prince and bring him back to the capital to be crowned king. Crown Prince Hu was terribly upset about his father's death, to the point where he could not contain himself. His grief was so extreme that when he arrived in Zhou, he too died. His son Lin then came to the throne and took the title of King Huan. The aristocrats and lords all came to pay their respects at the funeral and pay court to the new Son of Heaven. Jifu, Duke of Guo, was the first to arrive, and he performed all the rituals in an exemplary fashion, impressing everyone who saw him.

King Huan was hurt that his father had died while still a hostage in Zheng, and when he saw how the Earl of Zheng had monopolized power in the government for so long, his heart was filled with anger and resentment. He discussed this matter with Heijian, Duke of Zhou, in private: "The Earl of Zheng held my father, the late crown prince, hostage in his country, so he cannot take me very seriously. I am afraid that he does not trust me, nor I him. The Duke of Guo is a very honorable man in all he does, and I would like him to take charge of the government. What do you think of this idea?"

Heijian, Duke of Zhou, presented his opinion: "The Earl of Zheng is a brutal and cruel man; as a subject, he is neither a loyal nor obedient. However, when we moved east to Luoyang, Jin and Zheng were our most significant supporters. If now at the very beginning of your reign you want to take the government away from Zheng and deliver it into other hands, this will make the Earl of Zheng very angry and may well push him into open defiance of your authority. You must think about this very carefully."

"I will not accept being under his control!" King Huan announced. "My mind is made up."

The following day King Huan held court in the morning, and he said to the Earl of Zheng: "You, sir, served our former ruler as a minister, so I would not dare to demote you to a lesser rank. Why don't you just resign?"

"For a long time I have wanted to wash my hands of government affairs," Lord Zhuang said, "so today I am happy to say goodbye."

He left the court in a towering rage. As he told his people, "The kid has turned his back on me, so I am not going to help him."

That very day he rode home on his chariot. Scion Zihu led all the officials out through the city walls to welcome his father and asked him why he had returned. Lord Zhuang quoted King Huan's words of dismissal, making everyone very uneasy about the situation. Grandee Gao Qumi came forward and said, "Our lords have worked for the central government for the last two generations and have achieved great things. Besides, when the late crown prince was a hostage in our country, we always treated him with the utmost respect. Now His Majesty gets rid of our lord and employs the Duke of Guo instead—this is really unjust! Why do we not raise an army and crush the Zhou capital, getting rid of the present king and installing a more sensible member of the dynasty? The other aristocrats all fear Zheng, hence we can act as hegemons!"

"You cannot do this!" Ying Kaoshu exclaimed. "The relationship between a ruler and a subject is like that between a mother and a child. Our lord does not bear grudges against his own mother, so how could he bear grudges against his ruler? Give it a few years before going back to Zhou to pay court, and the king is sure to have regretted it. You, my lord, should not destroy a relationship for which your ancestor laid down his life just because of a moment's anger."

"In my humble opinion, you could actually follow the advice of both these men," Grandee Zhai Zu said. "I will lead the army to the border with Zhou, and on the pretext that we have had a bad harvest, I will get food from Wen and Luoyang. If the Zhou king sends someone to force us to leave, then we have an excuse to attack. If, on the other hand, His Majesty says nothing, then you, my lord, can go to court in the knowledge that all is well."

Lord Zhuang agreed to this proposal and gave Zhai Zu command of a cavalry division, with orders to act as he saw fit given conditions on the ground.

When Zhai Zu arrived on the outskirts of Wen, he announced: "We have had a bad harvest and are running short of food, so we have come to beg one thousand bushels of millet from the Grandee of Wen."

The Grandee of Wen refused on the grounds that he had not yet received instructions from the king.

"The grain here is ripe and ready to eat," Zhai Zu proclaimed. "We don't need to ask politely, we can just take it!"

He sent out his officers and men, each armed with a sickle, and ordered them to fan out through the fields of wheat, harvesting as much they could. They came back with laden chariots. Zhai Zu was in command of a company of guards, and he came out to meet them. The Grandee of Wen knew the strength of the Zheng army and did not dare to fight them. Zhai Zu kept his forces there at the border for more than three months, making two incursions as far as Chengzhou. In the second week of the seventh month, he noticed that the early rice in the fields was ripe, so he told his troops to dress up as merchants; they each took a chariot and spread out to hide in the villages. At dawn, they all took out their swords and cut down the ears of rice, and by sunset they had gathered it in. Outside the suburbs of Chengzhou, not a single stalk was to be seen. By the time local officials were aware of the situation and ordered troops out of the city, the Zheng army was already long gone.

In both cases, reports were sent to the capital at Luoyang informing King Huan that the Zheng army had stolen wheat and rice. King Huan was furious and right away wanted to raise an army to punish them.

"While it is true that Zhai Zu of Zheng has stolen this wheat and rice," Heijian, Duke of Zhou, remarked, "this is just a minor matter, and the Earl of Zheng is not necessarily even aware of it. You cannot ignore your blood relationship with the Zheng ruling house just because you are cross with them. If the Earl of Zheng is unhappy about the situation, he will come in person to apologize to you and restore good feeling between you."

King Huan accepted this advice, but he ordered the border regions to pay more attention to defense and not under any circumstances to allow the army of any of the lords to cross into the Royal Domain. The matter of the stolen wheat and rice he decided not to pursue.

When the Earl of Zheng realized that the king of Zhou had no intention of punishing him, he found himself feeling increasingly guilty, so he decided he ought to go to court. Just as he was about to set off, a report suddenly came in: "An ambassador has arrived from the state of Qi."

When Lord Zhuang of Zheng met the ambassador, he said that he had received orders from Lord Xi of Qi to invite the Earl of Zheng to a meeting at Shimen. Lord Zhuang wanted to form an alliance with Qi, so he hastened to Shimen. When the two lords met there, they smeared their lips with blood to make a covenant and swore an oath of brotherhood, promising to support each other in all things.

"Is Scion Zihu married or not?" the Marquis of Qi asked.

"Not yet," the Earl of Zheng replied.

"I have a beloved daughter, Lady Wen Jiang, who has not reached the age of womanhood," Lord Xi explained, "but who is very clever. If you like, I will give her to your son to be his bride."

Lord Zhuang of Zheng agreed and thanked him. When he went back home, he told Scion Zihu about this.

"When your wife comes from an equivalent background, then it is a suitable match," Zihu said. "Now, the state of Zheng is small while Qi is huge, so there is no equality of status. I do not want to use my marriage as an occasion for social climbing!"

"This wedding was their idea, and if you become the son-in-law of the Marquis of Qi, you can rely on them for everything," Lord Zhuang pointed out. "Why do you want to refuse this match, my son?"

"It is my ambition to make my own place in the world," Zihu replied. "I do not want to have to rely on my in-laws!"

Lord Zhuang was pleased to see him so ambitious and did not want to force him to do something against his will. Later on when the Qi ambassador arrived in Zheng and heard that the Scion of Zheng was not willing to go through with the marriage, he went home to report the matter to Lord Xi. Lord Xi sighed and said, "The Scion of Zheng is a very honorable man. My daughter is still very young . . . We can discuss the matter some other time."

Later on, someone wrote a poem making fun of social climbing by wealthy families and admiring Zihu of Zheng's refusal of an advantageous match. The poem runs:

> When getting married, you ought to pick a girl of equivalent status;
> Whether aristocrat or peasant, you should first weigh up your own
>   position.
> How laughable to see vulgar social climbers
> Flaunt their wealth to buy an equally common girl!

Suddenly one day, just as Lord Zhuang of Zheng was discussing with his officials the topic of making an official visit to Zhou, news came of the death of Marquis Huan of Wey. Lord Zhuang questioned the envoy, and that was how he discovered that the Honorable Zhouyu of Wey had assassinated his lord. Lord Zhuang stamped his feet, sighed, and said, "We are going to be attacked!"

"How do you work that out, my lord?" his officials asked.

"Zhouyu is good with soldiers," Lord Zhuang said. "Now he has usurped the title, and he will use his fearsome reputation as a military commander to achieve his ambitions. We have had our disagreements with Wey, so when he wants to test his army out he is certain to pick us first. We must prepare."

. . .

Why did Zhouyu of Wey assassinate his lord? The principal wife of Lord Zhuang of Wey, Lady Zhuang Jiang, was the younger sister of Dongguo Dechen of Qi—although she was very beautiful, she never had any children. His most senior concubine was a woman from Chen, Lady Li Wei, but she too never had any children. Lady Li Wei's younger sister, Lady Dai Wei, followed her sibling as a junior wife to the Lord of Wey, and she gave birth to two sons named Wan and Jin. Lady Zhuang Jiang was not at all jealous by nature, and she brought Wan up as if he were her own son. She also presented one of her own palace maids to Lord Zhuang, and Lord Zhuang regularly had sexual relations with this woman, as a result of which she gave birth to a son: Zhouyu. The Honorable Zhouyu was a cruel and violent man, with a great love of military matters and no topic of conversation other than warfare. Lord Zhuang loved Zhouyu inordinately and let him get away with everything.

Grandee Shi Que often remonstrated with Lord Zhuang, saying: "I have heard that if you love your children, you teach them to do right and do not allow them to do wicked things. Excessive favor leads to arrogance, and arrogance leads to trouble. If you want your title to be inherited by Zhouyu, my lord, then you ought to make him your heir. Otherwise, you should gradually bring him under control so that with luck we can avoid disaster from his arrogance, greed, debauchery, and violence!"

Lord Zhuang did not pay the slightest attention.

Shi Que's son, Shi Hou, was a close friend of Zhouyu's and often went out hunting with him, riding on the same chariot, whereupon they would cause considerable trouble to the local people. Shi Que beat his son fifty strokes for this and locked him up in an empty room, not allowing him to go out. Hou got out anyway, climbing over the wall, and afterwards he lived with the Honorable Zhouyu in his mansion, spending all his time with him. He never went home, and there was nothing that Shi Que could do about it.

Later on Lord Zhuang died and the Honorable Wan succeeded to the title, becoming Lord Huan of Wey. Lord Huan was a gentle and weak man. Shi Que knew that there was nothing to be done about it, so he resigned his job on the grounds of old age and stayed at home, neither attending court nor participating in the government. Meanwhile the Honorable Zhouyu behaved increasingly recklessly, and day and night he discussed plans for usurping the title with Shi Hou. At that time, the news of King Ping's death had already arrived and Prince Lin had just been established as King Huan, so Lord Huan of Wey wanted to go to Zhou to mourn the late king and congratulate His Majesty on his accession.

"Your plans can now succeed!" Shi Hou told the Honorable Zhouyu. "Tomorrow, when His Lordship sets off to go to Zhou, you must arrange for a banquet to be held at the West Gate and set an ambush of five hundred soldiers just outside the gate. When the wine has been passed around several times, take a dagger out of your sleeve and stab him. Any of his followers who don't submit to your authority, you can then immediately order to be beheaded. That way, your position as marquis is assured!"

The Honorable Zhouyu was thrilled. He ordered Shi Hou to arrange the ambush of five hundred soldiers outside the West Gate. Zhouyu drove his chariot himself and greeted Lord Huan at the official guesthouse, where he had already arranged for a banquet to be laid out.

The Honorable Zhouyu bowed and presented wine to His Lordship, saying, "My lord, you are going on a long journey, so I have arranged for drinks and a few snacks."

"How terribly kind of you, brother," Lord Huan said. "I will be gone for more than a month on this journey, so I hope that you will accept a temporary regency over the court, exercising your usual care and judgment."

"Of course I will," the Honorable Zhouyu said.

After the wine had circulated a couple of times, Zhouyu got up and presented his gold cup, full to the brim, to Lord Huan. Lord Huan drained it in a single draft, then filled his own cup and handed it to Zhouyu. Zhouyu stretched out his two hands to take it, only to pretend to lose his grip and drop the cup on the ground. He rushed to pick it up and took it away to wash it up himself. Lord Huan did not know this was nothing but a trick, so he ordered a new cup to be brought and poured wine into it, which he then wanted to give to Zhouyu. The Honorable Zhouyu took advantage of this opportunity and, quick as a flash, stepped behind Lord Huan, whipped out a short sword, and plunged it into his back, stabbing him through the chest. Lord Huan died immediately from this terrible injury. This happened on Wushen day in the third month, in the spring of the first year of King Huan of Zhou's reign.

All the ministers present, who had come to see their lord off, were well aware of Zhouyu's exceptional martial prowess. When Shi Hou led five hundred armed men into the guesthouse they all surrendered, knowing that they were in no position to resist. They loaded the corpse onto a chariot and carted it off for burial, announcing that Lord Huan had died of a sudden illness. The Honorable Zhouyu then became marquis, and he appointed Shi Hou as a senior grandee. Lord Huan's younger brother, Jin, fled to the state of Xing.

A historian wrote a poem bewailing the fact that Lord Zhuang of Wey's favoritism resulted in Zhouyu's rebellion:

When bringing up your children, make them understand the principle of
    justice;
If you let them become arrogant, there will eventually be trouble.
Lord Zhuang may not have treated Duan very well,
But it was better than being butchered like Lord Huan.

Just three days after the Honorable Zhouyu had succeeded to the title, rumors began to swirl outside the palace, saying that he had assassinated his older brother. He summoned Senior Grandee Shi Hou to discuss the matter, and said, "I want to establish my authority among my neighbors, which will bring my own people under control. What country should I attack?"

"None of our neighbors have particularly annoyed us," Shi Hou said, "with the exception of Zheng, which attacked us a few years back at the time of Noble Grandson Hua's rebellion. Our former ruler, Lord Zhuang, had to admit he had made a mistake and beg to be let off. This was a disgrace for our country, and if you, my lord, want to go on campaign, Zheng should be the target."

"Qi and Zheng made a covenant as Shimen," Zhouyu said, "and now they have become allies. If we attack Zheng, Qi is sure to go to their rescue. We cannot possibly hold out against two enemy states!"

"At the moment," Shi Hou remarked, "of all the states governed by families of a different surname from the Zhou ruling house, Song is the largest, and as a ducal house, the most important. Of the states governed by families of the same surname as the Zhou ruling house, Lu is the most respected—the king even addresses the Lord of Lu as 'Uncle.' If you want to attack Zheng, you must send ambassadors to Song and Lu, asking for them to send troops to assist you. If you also call upon the armies of Chen and Cai, then with five states in the alliance, is there any trouble that you cannot overcome?"

"Chen and Cai are little countries, and they always do just what the Zhou king says," Zhouyu pointed out. "Now there has been a breach between Zheng and Zhou. Chen and Cai are sure to know all about this, so if we call upon them to attack Zheng, they are sure to want to join in. However, Song and Lu are great states. How can we get them to help us?"

"My lord, you know something about the situation, but you do not know everything," Shi Hou explained. "In the past, Lord Mu of Song succeeded to the title on the death of his older brother, Lord Xuan, and when Lord Mu himself was dying, he was worrying about how to repay his brother's generosity. As a result, he decided to set aside the claims of his own son, Ping, and pass the title back to his older brother's son, Yuyi. Ping was furious with his father and jealous of Yuyi, so he fled to Zheng. The Earl of Zheng took him in and has consistently expressed his intention of raising an army and attacking Song, thus taking back the title that Yuyi now has. A joint attack on Zheng would be exactly what Yuyi desires. As for the state of Lu, the Honorable Hui is now in sole control of the government. It is Hui who has power over the army, and he treats the Lord of Lu as if he does not exist. If you send lavish bribes to the Honorable Hui, he will mobilize the Lu army for you."

Zhouyu was very pleased. That very day he sent ambassadors to Lu, Chen, and Cai, but he had problems with picking someone suitable to go to Song until Shi Hou recommended a man named Ning Yi, who came from Zhongmou in Wey: "This man is a very able diplomat; you should send him."

Zhouyu followed his advice and ordered Ning Yi to go to Song to ask for military assistance.

"Why do you want to attack Zheng?" Lord Shang of Song asked.

"The Earl of Zheng is an unprincipled man," Ning Yi explained. "He executed his younger brother and imprisoned his mother. Noble Grandson Hua fled for his life to our country, but even then he would not let it rest and raised an army to attack us. Our former lord was afraid of their might and had to apologize and submit to their authority with what good grace he could muster. Now my lord wants to expunge the insult inflicted on his late father, so we request your assistance, knowing that you hate Zheng too."

"I have no quarrel with Zheng," Lord Shang said, "so when you say that I 'hate them too,' is that not a mistake?"

"Please send away your entourage and I will finish what I have to say," Ning Yi whispered.

Lord Shang had his attendants leave. Leaning towards Ning Yi from the adjacent mat, he asked him, "What do you have to say?"

"Who gave you your title?" Ning Yi asked.

"I received it from my uncle, Lord Mu," Lord Shang replied.

"It has been common practice since antiquity that a son inherits on his father's death," Ning Yi pointed out. "Even though Lord Mu's generosity was comparable to the sage-kings Yao and Shun, there is nothing he could do to assuage the Honorable Ping's anger at being passed over in the succession. Though he now lives in a neighboring country, he has never for a moment forgotten about Song. Zheng took in the Honorable Ping, and their relationship is now secure. Should they one day decide to install Ping by force, may I remind you that the people of your country still remember the goodness of Lord Mu and have not forgotten his son? With support for a change of government both inside and outside the state, your position will be dangerous indeed! Right now you can claim to be attacking Zheng, but in fact you will be getting rid of the disaster that threatens you. If you, my lord, were to take charge of this matter and join us in raising an army, we can fight with the allied forces of Lu, Chen, and Cai. Zheng's destruction will then be assured!"

Lord Shang of Song had always been worried about the Honorable Ping, and so this conversation was just what he wanted to hear, and he agreed to raise an army. Marshal Kong Fujia, a descendant of King Tang of the Shang dynasty, was a very upright and just man. He now heard that Lord Shang had mobilized his troops after listening to Wey and he remonstrated: "Ignore the Wey ambassador! If this is about the Earl of Zheng having executed his younger brother and imprisoned his mother, then Zhouyu has also assassinated his older brother and usurped the title! What is the difference? I hope that you will think carefully about this, my lord."

However, Lord Shang had already made his promise to Ning Yi, so he did not pay any attention to Kong Fujia's remonstrance, but immediately mobilized the army.

The Honorable Hui of Lu accepted the lavish bribes offered by the state of Wey, and without even asking permission from Lord Yin, he raised a massive army and came to meet the rest. Chen and Cai also arrived on time, as was expected. Since the Duke of Song held the highest office of anyone present, he was invited to preside over the covenant. Shi Hou of Wey was appointed to head the vanguard, and Zhouyu personally led his army to cut off any retreat for Zheng. They gathered a great quantity of fodder and provisions, which they used to hold a feast for the soldiers from the other four states. The armies of the five allied countries in total numbered thirteen hundred chariots, and they laid siege to the East Gate of Zheng so that no one could go in or out.

Lord Zhuang of Zheng asked his ministers for a plan. Some spoke in favor of fighting and some of making peace, but no one agreed with anyone else. Lord Zhuang laughed and said, "There is not one single plan that will work for all the lords. Zhouyu has recently usurped his title, and he knows that his people feel no loyalty to him, so he keeps talking about an old enmity and has borrowed armies from four other countries simply because he wants to stamp his authority on the situation and force everyone to toe the line. On the other hand, the Honorable Hui of Lu is greedy for bribes from Wey, so this matter has nothing to do with His Lordship. Chen and Cai are not our enemies, and they will both be hoping for some kind of amicable solution. The real problem is that Song is angry about the Honorable Ping's presence in Zheng, so they really do want to fight. Therefore, I will send the Honorable Ping to live in Changge and the Song army will definitely go after him. Then the Honorable Lü can lead five hundred infantry out of the East Gate and do battle with Wey alone. Our troops will pretend to be defeated and run away, so Zhouyu will be able to claim that he has won a battle. Having achieved his ambition and with serious problems waiting for him back home, he certainly cannot keep his army out here for any length of time. He will have to make a speedy return to his capital. I have heard that Grandee Shi Que of Wey is very loyal, and sooner rather than later he will bring the rightful heir to power there. Zhouyu will have no time for anything other than protecting his own position, so how can he harm us?"

After this, Lord Zhuang sent Grandee Xia Shuying to escort the Honorable Ping safely to Changge, with one division of the army. He also sent someone to Song to say: "The Honorable Ping fled to our humble country in fear of his life, and we could not bear to execute him ourselves. Now he is expiating his offenses at Changge: do as you see fit with him."

Just as Lord Zhuang had anticipated, Lord Shang of Song moved his army to lay siege to Changge. When the troops of Chen, Cai, and Lu saw the Song army leave, they all wanted to strike their flags. Suddenly the report came that the Honorable Lü had come out of the East Gate to fight with Wey. The lords of three countries climbed up on the ramparts of their camps to watch.

Shi Hou led his forces to join battle with the Honorable Lü, but before they had even begun to fight, the latter had dropped his painted spear and fled. Shi Hou pursued him to the East Gate, but he had already entered the city. Shi Hou cut down all the grain growing around the East Gate and gave it to his soldiers. Then he gave orders to stand down the army.

"We have not yet won a decisive victory; how can we go home?" Zhouyu asked.

Shi Hou dismissed his attendants and then explained why the army should stand down. Zhouyu was very pleased.

If you want to know what Shi Hou said, READ ON.

Chapter Six

*Shi Que of Wey kills his only son in the
cause of justice.*

*Lord Zhuang of Zheng fakes an edict and
attacks Song.*

Shi Hou had been victorious in one engagement with the Zheng army and
then announced his intention of standing down the army, which his generals did not understand at all. They all went to report to Zhouyu: "Our
troops are all fired up and ready, on top of which we could take advantage of this victory to advance our army, so why are we going home?"

Zhouyu also thought this was odd, so he summoned Shi Hou and
questioned him about it.

"I have something to say, so please send away your entourage," Hou
replied.

Zhouyu ordered them to withdraw. Afterwards Shi Hou spoke. "The
Zheng army is strong, and in addition to that, their lord is a senior minister at the royal court. Now I have defeated them, which is more than
enough to give our army a fearsome reputation. My lord, you have only
recently been established and your authority is not yet secure. If you
stay too long abroad, I am afraid there will be a rebellion at home."

"Thank you for your advice," Zhouyu said. "I had not thought of
that!"

A short time later, representatives of the three states of Lu, Chen, and
Cai came to congratulate him, and each asked permission to demobilize. They lifted the siege and went home. From start to finish, the siege
had lasted just five days.

Shi Hou was very proud of his success and ordered the three armies
to sing triumphal songs as they swept Zhouyu of Wey home in glory.

However, they also heard the people in the wilds singing the following song:

> One hero dies, another takes his place.
> Songs and dancing are disrupted by warfare.
> When will there be peace?
> Why does no one care about the king at Luoyang?

"The people are still not at peace," Zhouyu said. "What should I do?"

"In the past when my father, Que, served as a senior minister, everyone in the whole country respected and trusted him," Shi Hou said. "If you, my lord, were to bring him back into the court, taking his advice in matters of government, your position would be secure."

Zhouyu ordered that a pair of white jade bi-discs and five hundred bushels of white rice should be bestowed upon Shi Que. Afterwards, he summoned him to court to discuss matters of state. Shi Que claimed that he was ill and resolutely refused to go. Zhouyu asked Shi Hou, "Your father refuses to come to court, so how about if I went in person to ask for his advice?"

"Even if you go, my father may well refuse to see you," Shi Hou said. "I will make a formal visit to him on Your Lordship's behalf."

Accordingly, he went home to see his father and conveyed the new lord's respect and admiration.

"The new lord has summoned me, what does he want?" Shi Que asked.

"The people are still not at peace, and so I am afraid that the position of the new lord is not secure," Shi Hou explained. "I beg you, Father, to come up with a good plan."

"When any lord succeeds to the title, the most important thing is to have his accession ratified by the royal court," Shi Que stated. "If our new ruler were to make representations to Zhou and obtain the robes, official hat, chariot, and trappings of an aristocrat from the Zhou king and thus be formally invested as lord, what could the populace say against him?"

"You are absolutely right," his son exclaimed. "However, if he just turns up at court for no good reason, the Zhou king is certain to become suspicious. We must first find someone to communicate the situation to the king's people."

"The Marquis of Chen is well-known for his loyalty to the Zhou king," Shi Que said, "and he never misses an opportunity to pay court or send an embassy. His Majesty is very fond of him. We have always been on good terms with the state of Chen, and recently we have borrowed an army from them. If our new lord were to go personally to visit Chen and beg the Marquis of Chen to communicate the situation to the king's people, he can then go to the royal court himself. Where is the problem?"

Shi Hou reported what his father had said to Zhouyu. His Lordship was very pleased and immediately prepared ceremonial gifts of jade and silk. He ordered Grandee Shi Hou to provide an armed escort as he traveled to the state of Chen.

As it happened, Shi Que had long been on terms of close friendship with Grandee Zizhen of Chen. Now he pricked his finger and wrote a letter in blood, which was sent in secret to Zizhen by a trusted messenger, asking him to communicate the contents to Lord Huan of Chen. The letter read:

> Your humble servant, Shi Que, bows one hundred times and presents this letter to the most sagacious lord, the Marquis of Chen:

> The state of Wey is small and Heaven has sent down a terrible disaster upon us, for we have suffered the trauma of the assassination of our ruler. This was carried out by his evil younger brother, Zhouyu, with the assistance of my son, Hou, who covets high honors. If these two wicked men are not punished, then rebellious subjects and wicked sons throughout the world will simply follow in their footsteps! I am an old man and the situation is beyond my control, so I can only say that I have let down our late lord. Now these two evil creatures are traveling together by chariot to your country, which is all part of my plan. I hope that you will arrest and punish them, thereby reestablishing the correct relations between ruler and subject, parent and child. This would indeed be a blessing not just for our country, but for the whole world!

When Lord Huan of Chen had finished reading the letter, he asked Zizhen, "What should we do about this?"

"If bad things happen in Wey, it is the same as if they happen in Chen," Zizhen replied. "Since they have come to Chen, let them be executed here; we cannot let them get away with this."

"Good," Lord Huan said. Then they worked out a plan to arrest Zhouyu.

When Zhouyu and Shi Hou arrived in Chen, they were completely unaware of Shi Que's plan. The ruler and minister made a state entry together. The Marquis of Chen sent the Honorable Tuo to meet them outside the city walls, and they stayed in an official guesthouse. Then he invited them to an audience the following day at the great ancestral temple, as commanded by the Marquis of Chen. When Zhouyu realized that the Marquis of Chen was treating him in the most respectful way, he was absolutely delighted. The following day huge bonfires were lit at the great ancestral temple as Lord Huan of Chen took the seat of honor, with the master of ceremonies on his left and the prime minister on his right. Everything was arranged in the most formal and correct way. Shi Hou was the first to arrive, and he noticed that above the gate to the great ancestral temple there was a white tablet reading: "Disloyal subjects and unfilial sons may not enter the temple!"

Shi Hou was rather alarmed. He asked Grandee Zizhen, "What do you mean by putting up this placard?"

"This instruction was given by the late marquis," Zizhen explained, "and His Lordship does not dare to forget it."

As a result, Shi Hou was not at all suspicious. A short time later, Zhouyu arrived. Shi Hou assisted him to get down from his chariot and led him to the guest's seat. The master of ceremonies and the prime minister then requested that he enter the temple. Zhouyu, all dressed up with jade pendants hanging from his belt and a staff of office in his hand, was just about to begin the ceremonies with a bow when Zizhen, who was standing beside the Marquis of Chen, shouted out, "A command has been issued by the Zhou Son of Heaven to arrest Zhouyu and Shi Hou for the murder of their ruler! Everyone else will go free!"

Before he had even finished speaking, Zhouyu had already been taken prisoner. In a panic, Shi Hou tried to draw his sword, but in the heat of the moment he could not get it out of the scabbard. He had to fight off his attackers with his bare hands, knocking two of them down. Soldiers had been stationed in the eastern and western wings of the temple, and they now came pouring out and laid bonds upon Shi Hou. The troops that had come with them from Wey could only watch from outside the temple precincts. Zizhen came out and read Shi Que's letter aloud. Then they realized that the arrest of Zhouyu and Shi Hou was all part of Shi Que's plan and that Chen was simply following his orders. Since he had right on his side, they simply walked away.

A historian wrote a poem bewailing these events:

Once Zhouyu invited Lord Huan to a barmecide feast.
Today in paying court to Chen, he suffers the same fate.
You could count on your fingers the number of days that he was lord;
The laws of Heaven still govern this world.

The Marquis of Chen intended to execute Zhouyu and Shi Hou as punishment for their crimes, but his ministers all said, "Shi Hou is Shi Que's own son, and we don't yet know what his intentions are. It would be better to ask Wey to send people here to discuss an appropriate punishment and thus avoid any future recriminations."

"You are quite right," the Marquis of Chen said. Then he imprisoned the pair separately. Zhouyu was confined in Puyi and Shi Hou at the capital. This was done so that they could not communicate. He also sent someone to report back to Wey, traveling under cover of darkness, to let Shi Que know that everything depended on him.

After Shi Que resigned his post on the grounds of old age, he never left the house. When he heard that an ambassador had arrived from Chen under orders from the marquis, he commanded his charioteer to hitch up the chariot and went to meet him. He also invited all the other grandees to a formal audience at court. Everyone was most alarmed. Shi Que went to court and personally met with all the officials and showed them the letter that he had received from the Marquis of Chen announcing that Zhouyu and Shi Hou had been arrested and that they were only waiting for the arrival of a grandee from Wey to carry out the executions. The officials all said, "This is a matter of the utmost importance for our country, so you must take charge!"

"The crimes of these two wicked men cannot be pardoned, and they must suffer an exemplary punishment in order to console the spirit of our late murdered lord," Shi Que proclaimed. "Who is prepared to go and oversee this?"

The Councilor of the Right, Chou, said: "Rebellious subjects and bad sons deserve to be executed. Although I have no particular merits, I know enough to be angry about what has happened here. I will preside over Zhouyu's execution."

The grandees all said, "The Councilor of the Right is the proper person to do this. But once Zhouyu has been punished as the main criminal, Shi Hou can be treated with leniency since he was nothing more than an accomplice."

Shi Que, absolutely furious, shouted: "Zhouyu's crimes were all aided and abetted by my son! If I ask the Lord of Chen to show leniency towards him, will that not look to everybody as if I am selfishly protecting my own child? I am prepared to go in person and kill him myself. Otherwise, how will I ever be able to face His Late Lordship?"

The royal delegate, Nou Yangjian, then said, "There is no need for you, sir, to get so angry. I will go."

Shi Que then sent Chou, the Councilor of the Right, to Puyi to preside over the execution of Zhouyu, while Nou Yangjian went to Chen to preside over the execution of Shi Hou. He also prepared an official chariot and brought the Honorable Jin back from exile in Xing.

When Zuo Qiuming got to this juncture of the narrative in the Zuozhuan, he wrote of Shi Que: "For the sake of justice, he cut off his family line. He really was a great minister!"

A historian wrote a poem as follows:

It is impossible to be both a good minister and a good father.
He gladly killed his son to avenge his lord.
Favoritism and partiality cause many problems,
But otherwise, how could he have established such lasting fame?

The Recluse of Longxi also wrote a poem explaining that the reason Shi Que did not kill Hou earlier was so that he would be able to execute both his son and Zhouyu in one. This poem reads:

Given that he understood that evil has root causes,
Why did he not deal with his traitorous son before?
Naturally, this old minister had long-term plans,
So he kept his son alive in order to lead Zhouyu astray.

The Councilor of the Right, Chou, and Nou Yangjian traveled together to the capital of Chen. First they went to have audience with Lord Huan of Chen, to thank him for his kindness in dealing with these two traitors. After that, they went their separate ways to carry out their appointed tasks. Chou, the Councilor of the Right, arrived in Puyi just as Zhouyu was taken in chains to the marketplace for execution. When Zhouyu caught sight of Chou, he shouted, "You are my subject, how dare you do this to me!"

The Councilor of the Right said, "Wey has already had a subject assassinate his ruler—I am just following your example!"

Afterwards, Zhouyu stretched out his neck for the executioner's axe.

Nou Yangjian stayed at the Chen capital, where he presided over Shi Hou's execution.

"I am ready to die," Shi Hou declared. "But I want you to take me back in a prison cart and let me see my father one last time; then you can kill me."

"It is in accordance with your father's commands that I have come here to preside over your execution," Nou Yangjian informed him. "If

you want to see your father, I will take your head home to show him!"
Then he drew his sword and beheaded him.

When the Honorable Jin returned home to Wey from Xing, he
reported Zhouyu's execution to the ancestral temple, then reburied
Lord Huan with all the proper honors. Afterwards, he established himself as the new marquis and took the title of Lord Xuan of Wey. He
honored Shi Que with the title Elder of the State and ordered that his
family should rank as ministers in perpetuity. From this time on, relations between Chen and Wey became even friendlier.

. . .

When Lord Zhuang of Zheng saw that the armies of the five allied
nations had departed, his first action was to send someone to get news
of what was happening in Changge. Suddenly a report came through:
"The Honorable Ping has escaped from Changge and is waiting outside
the palace gates to have audience with you."

Lord Zhuang summoned him and asked him what had happened.

"Changge has been overrun by the Song army," the Honorable Ping
informed him. "Once they gained control of the walls, I fled for my life
back here. I am begging you! Please protect me!" When he finished
speaking, he wept bitterly. Lord Zhuang consoled him and ordered that
he be taken to the official guesthouse and treated with the utmost courtesy. That very same day, he heard that Zhouyu had been killed in Puyi
and that Wey had already established a new lord.

"What Zhouyu did has nothing to do with the new lord," Lord
Zhuang announced. "The real mastermind of the attack on Zheng was
Song. They are going to have to pay for that!"

He summoned all his officials and asked them for a plan to attack Song.
Zhai Zu came forward and said, "We have just had five countries launch
an allied attack upon Zheng. If we now invade Song, the other four countries will be alarmed and will join together to defend them. In those circumstances we cannot win. The best plan would be to send an ambassador to make a peace treaty with Chen and then offer bribes of some kind
to Lu. If Lu and Chen are on our side, then Song will be isolated."

Lord Zhuang followed this advice and sent an ambassador to Chen
to conclude a peace treaty. The Marquis of Chen did not want to agree
to this, whereupon the Honorable Tuo remonstrated: "Good relations
between members of the ruling house and friendship with your neighbors are great boons for the country. If Zheng is here to make peace, we
cannot refuse."

"The Earl of Zheng is a very devious man," the Marquis of Chen said. "We should not trust him so lightly! He is up to something, or else why would he not try and make peace with the great states of Song and Wey, but instead send an embassy to us? He must have some kind of plan to split up our alliance. Besides which, we have just joined forces with Song to attack Zheng, so if we now make peace with Zheng, it will annoy Song. Where is the benefit to us of irritating Song for the sake of Zheng?" Accordingly, he announced that he would not see the Zheng ambassador.

When Lord Zhuang realized that Chen was not going to make peace, he said angrily, "Chen relies for its security on Song and Wey. Wey has just been through a major internal upheaval, so they only have time to consider themselves; they are not likely to put themselves out for anyone else! If I can make an alliance with Lu, then I can attack Song with the combined forces of Lu and Qi, thus revenging myself upon them. Afterwards I can turn my attention to Chen. That way we can pick them off one at a time."

Zhai Zu submitted his opinion: "You cannot do this. Zheng is strong and Chen is weak, and the request for a peace treaty came from us. Chen must have suspected that we planned to break up their alliance, and that is why they refused. If we order our people along the border to take advantage of their lack of preparation to invade them, we will certainly make great gains. Then we can send in our diplomats to hand back the prisoners of war and make it clear that we do not intend to take unfair advantage of them. They will certainly accept this arrangement. After making peace with Chen, we can then consider an attack on Song."

"Good," said Lord Zhuang.

Then he ordered the stewards of two wards, in command of five thousand infantry troops, to encroach upon the borders of Chen while pretending that they were merely going out hunting. They took many men and women prisoner and obtained a great deal of food, enough to fill more than one hundred carts. The officials at the borders of Chen reported the situation to Lord Huan, who was deeply alarmed. He immediately called a meeting of all his ministers to discuss what to do. Just then there was a report delivered: "Ying Kaoshu of Zheng is at the palace gates. He has a letter from his lord to deliver, and he is prepared to hand back all the prisoners and the food."

Lord Huan of Chen asked the Honorable Tuo his opinion: "What is Zheng up to with this embassy?"

"They must be serious about wanting peace," the Honorable Tuo explained. "Do not refuse a second time."

Lord Huan then summoned Ying Kaoshu for an audience. Kaoshu bowed twice and presented his letter. Lord Huan opened it and read it. The letter said:

> Wusheng bows twice and presents this letter to the most sagacious lord, the Marquis of Chen. You, sir, have been designated as His Majesty's favorite, while I too have had the honor of serving as a royal minister, so it is only right and proper that the two of us should be friends, working together to protect the dynasty. Recently, my request for a peace treaty was turned down, as a result of which my border officials suspected that there was some breach between our two countries. They invaded you without my knowledge or approval. I have not been able to rest since I discovered this, and so today I return all the prisoners and everything that was stolen. I send my junior minister Ying Kaoshu to make a formal apology. I wish to swear an oath of brotherhood with you and hope that you will agree to this.

When the Marquis of Chen had finished reading, he understood that Zheng was indeed serious about making a peace treaty. Having treated Ying Kaoshu with the utmost ceremony, he sent the Honorable Tuo on a return embassy to Zheng. From this point on the two countries were at peace.

Lord Zhuang of Zheng then said to Zhai Zu, "We have now made peace with Chen, so what do we do about attacking Song?"

"Song has a most noble title and is a large state," Zhai Zu said, "as a result of which even the royal court has always treated it with the greatest respect. It will not be easy to attack them. Just when you were on your way to pay court, you had to go and meet the Marquis of Qi at Shimen and then Zhouyu arrived with his army, as a result of which your audience with the king has been put off until now. If you go to Zhou and pay court to His Majesty, then you can pretend to have received a royal edict authorizing an attack and summon the armies of Qi and Lu to join you on campaign against Song. If you attack on this pretext, you are sure to be victorious."

Lord Zheng was very pleased and said, "Your plan is perfect."

At this time King Huan of Zhou had been on the throne for three years. Lord Zhuang of Zheng appointed Scion Zihu regent of the country and set off for Zhou in the company of Zhai Zu, with the aim of paying court to the Zhou king.

It so happened that this was the first week of the eleventh month, in the winter, which was the time when all the aristocrats had to pay their respects to the king. Heijian, Duke of Zhou, urged the king to pay more respect to Zheng in order to encourage harmony among the states. King Huan really did not like Zheng, and when he thought about how they had stolen his wheat and rice, he got more and more furious. Therefore, he asked Lord Zhuang: "How has the harvest been this year in your country?"

"Thanks to Your Majesty's benevolent influences, we have had neither flood nor drought," Lord Zhuang replied.

"A good harvest, then," King Huan remarked. "This year I imagine that I can keep the wheat from Wen and the rice from Chengzhou to eat myself!"

Lord Zhuang realized the import of King Huan's words and shut his mouth, requesting permission to leave shortly afterwards. King Huan did not hold a banquet for him, nor did he give him any gifts, but he did send someone with ten cartloads of grain and the message: "I hope this is enough for you to prevent starvation from breaking out."

Lord Zhuang deeply regretted this visit and said to Zhai Zu, "You, sir, encouraged me to come to pay court to His Majesty. Just look at the Zhou king's attitude! Every time he opens his mouth, he spews out resentment, and now he uses this grain to insult us. I want to refuse this gift, but what excuse can I give?"

"The reason why the aristocracy respect Zheng is because you have been ministers for generations and companions to the king," Zhai Zu reminded him. "If you are given something by His Majesty, it does not matter if it is expensive or not; it is still termed a 'heavenly favor.' If you were to refuse this gift, my lord, then it would reveal the rift between you and the Zhou king. If Zheng loses the support of Zhou, how will you make the lords respect you?"

Just as they were discussing this matter, Heijian, Duke of Zhou, suddenly requested permission to see Lord Zhuang. He had brought with him a private gift of two cartloads of silk. The speeches on this occasion were lengthy and formal, and it was a long time before he said goodbye and left.

Lord Zhuang asked Zhai Zu, "Why would the Duke of Zhou come here?"

"The Zhou king has two sons," Zhai Zu explained. "The older is Prince Tuo and the second is Prince Ke. The king loves and favors his second son, who has been brought up under the aegis of the Duke of Zhou. In the future, he is sure to conspire against the current crown prince. Therefore, the Duke of Zhou will be hoping to make an alliance with our country now, in order that he may have outside support. If you, my lord, take his silks, it will be very useful."

"How can we possibly make use of them?" Lord Zhuang asked.

"All your neighboring countries know that you have come to pay court to the king," Zhai Zu explained. "Now, the silks that you have been given by the Duke of Zhou can be spread out to cover the ten carts, which will then appear from the outside to be full of fine brocades. When you leave the capital, you can announce that these are gifts from His Majesty. If you add in some red lacquer bows and some black arrows, you can then lie and tell everyone that since the Duke of Song has not sent in tribute to the court for some time, you have received a royal mandate to lead your troops on campaign against him. You can use that as a call to rally other aristocrats and demand that they supply auxiliary troops. Anyone who does not respond, you can condemn as disobeying a royal command. The more fuss you make, the more convinced the other aristocrats will be and they will support you. Even though Song is a large country, can they resist the might of an army holding a royal mandate?"

Lord Zhuang patted Zhai Zu on the shoulder and said, "You really are a clever man! I will do exactly as you have suggested."

The Recluse of Longxi wrote a poem titled "An Evaluation of History":

> Silk is not at all the same thing as grain;
> Without a mandate, how could you falsely implicate the king?
> Since his weasel words were able to convince others,
> Suiyang was turned into a battlefield.

As Lord Zhuang left the borders of the Royal Domain, he proclaimed the whole way along the road that he had received a mandate from the king. He spread the news far and wide that the Duke of Song was being punished for his disloyalty, and everyone who heard him believed this to be true. This news was transmitted straight to the state of Song. Lord Shang was alarmed and frightened, so he sent an envoy to report this matter secretly to Lord Xuan of Wey. Lord Xuan then got in touch with Lord Xi of Qi, with the intention of making every effort to encourage the two states of Song and Zheng to make peace. They decided on a date and agreed to meet at Wawu, where they would smear their lips with blood and make a covenant, each agreeing to set aside their old hostilities. Lord Shang of Song again sent an ambassador with lavish gifts to Wey, and they agreed to meet beforehand at Quanqiu, to discuss the problem of Zheng. Afterwards, both traveled together to Wawu.

Lord Xi of Qi arrived at the appointed time, but Lord Zhuang of Zheng did not come. The Marquis of Qi said, "If the Earl of Zheng is not here, then the whole peace plan has failed." He prepared to set off back to his own country. The Duke of Song insisted that he stay and make a blood covenant. The Marquis of Qi appeared to agree to this proposal, but in fact he was determined to preserve his neutrality. For Song and Wey, on the other hand, this was an opportunity to reaffirm a long-standing alliance, after which all the parties dispersed.

At this time, King Huan of Zhou still wanted to dismiss Lord Zhuang of Zheng from the government and replace him with Jifu, Duke of Guo. Heijian, Duke of Zhou, did his very best to advise His Majesty against this course of action, so instead he employed Jifu as Senior Minister of the Right and gave him a major role in national affairs. The Earl of Zheng was officially the Senior Minister of the Left, but this was just an empty honorific office. Lord Zhuang realized this and said with a laugh, "At least the Zhou king cannot take away my title!" Later on, he heard that Qi and Song had formed an alliance, so he discussed future plans with Zhai Zu.

"Qi and Song have never gotten along well together," Zhai Zu stated. "This alliance is all down to the efforts of the Marquis of Wey. Although they have now made a blood covenant, neither side is wholeheartedly in favor of it. You, my lord, should now proclaim your royal mandate to both Qi and Lu, and ask the Marquis of Lu to bring the Marquis of Qi into the alliance to punish Song. Lu and Qi are not only neighbors, they have been linked by marriage alliances for many generations. With the Marquis of Lu on your side, Qi cannot be against you. You should also circulate invitations to states such as Cai, Wei, Cheng, and Xu, summoning them to join you, making it clear that this campaign is widely supported. If anyone refuses to participate, you can attack them."

Lord Zhuang agreed to this plan and sent an ambassador to Lu to set a date for the invasion of Song. Any land that they captured would be given to the state of Lu. The Honorable Hui was a very greedy man, and so he was happy to agree to this. He informed the Lord of Lu of the situation and then sent word to the Marquis of Qi summoning his people to meet Zheng at Zhongqiu. The Marquis of Qi appointed his younger brother, Yi Zhongnian, as general and sent him out in command of a force of three hundred chariots. The Marquis of Lu appointed the Honorable Hui as general and sent him out with a force of two hundred chariots, and they hurried to the assistance of Zheng.

Lord Zhuang of Zheng, supported by his finest generals—the Honorable Lü, Gao Qumi, Ying Kaoshu, and Noble Grandson E—took personal command of the Central Army. He raised the great flag named Maohu. On it was written the words "Punishing the Guilty by Royal Command" in large characters, and it was carried on a battle chariot. A red lacquer bow and black arrows were hung up on the chariot, along with the message "Ministers and Officers Punish the Guilty." Yi Zhongnian commanded the Army of the Left, while the Honorable Hui commanded the Army of the Right. This terrible, awe-inspiring force marched towards the state of Song, killing anyone in the way.

The Honorable Hui and his troops were the first to arrive at Laotiao, where the general guarding the city led out his forces to intercept them. However, the Honorable Hui's vanguard fought bravely, and they butchered the Song troops until they cast aside their armor and dropped their weapons to run for their lives. However, there was nowhere they could go: more than two hundred and fifty men were taken prisoner. The Honorable Hui then sent an urgent dispatch to the Earl of Zheng, setting up camp at Laotiao in the meantime. When the two of them met, he handed over all his captives and booty. Lord Zhuang was very pleased and could not stop praising him. He ordered that the general should receive the greatest rewards for this campaign, and he killed an ox to feast his officers. They were allowed to rest for three days. Afterwards, Lord Zhuang reorganized his troops before they advanced for the next stage. He ordered Kao Yingshu and the Honorable Hui to lead their forces to attack the walled city of Gao, with the Honorable Lü in support; likewise, he ordered Noble Grandson E and Yi Zhongnian to lead their forces to attack the walled city of Fang, with Gao Qumi in support. Headquarters would be located at Laotiao, with responsibility for coordinating dispatches from the front.

When Lord Shang of Song heard that the armies of three countries had already crossed the border, he went as white as a sheet. He quickly summoned Marshal Kong Fujia and asked him for a plan to deal with this emergency.

Kong Fujia submitted his opinion: "I have already sent someone to the royal court to investigate this matter, and they say there has been no order given to attack Song. The mandate that Zheng claims to have is nothing but a lie—Qi and Lu have fallen into Lord Zhuang's trap! However, given that these three armies have united, their strength is such that we cannot fight them. There is only one plan that can deal with the crisis in which we now find ourselves, and that is to make Zheng leave without having to do battle."

"Zheng is in a very advantageous situation," Lord Shang pointed out. "Will they be willing to simply withdraw?"

"Zheng has forged a royal mandate and used it to summon other countries to their side," Kong Fujia said. "However, only the two states of Qi and Lu have obeyed. In the campaign at the Eastern Gate, Song, Cai, Chen, and Lu were all on the same side. Lu covets the bribes offered by Zheng, and Chen has made a peace treaty with Zheng, so they have both changed sides. Those remaining are Cai and Wey. The Lord of Zheng is in personal command of the army here, and he has brought a massive number of chariots and soldiers with him, leaving his country empty. If you, my lord, were to send an ambassador armed with generous gifts to report this emergency to Wey, you could suggest that they form an alliance with the state of Cai to make a surprise attack on Zheng with their fastest troops. When the Lord of Zheng hears that his own state has been invaded, he will have to strike his flags and go home to deal with the situation. If the Zheng army goes home, why would Qi and Lu stay behind?"

"Even though this is a good plan, if you do not go in person to see it carried out, I am afraid that the Wey army will not necessarily mobilize straightaway," Lord Shang said.

"Let me take one division to show Cai what they need to do," Kong Fujia said.

Lord Shang mustered two hundred chariots and appointed Kong Fujia as general, and armed with gold, white jade bi-discs, silks and brocades, and other items of a similar nature, he traveled to Wey under cover of darkness to beg the lord of that state to send his army to make a surprise attack on Zheng. Lord Xuan of Wey took the gifts, and then he sent the Councilor of the Right, Chou, to lead an army to support Kong Fujia and explain that the previous situation was not at all what he had wished for. They marched straight on Yingyang. Although Scion Zihu and Zhai Zu quickly took command of the defense of the city, by then the area outside the walls had already been ravaged by the armies of Song and Wey, taking countless prisoners and seizing much valuable property.

Chou, the Councilor of the Right, wanted to attack the city, but Kong Fujia warned him against the idea: "In a surprise attack, you take advantage of the fact that they are completely unprepared, and having done that you get away. If we make camp below the walls and try to lay siege to them, when the Earl of Zheng brings his army back to rescue the city, we will have the enemy both behind and in front, which will place us at a serious disadvantage. It would be much better to ask permission to take our army home through the state of Dai, getting away without losing a man. I reckon that just as we depart Zheng, the Lord of Zheng will be leaving Song."

The Councilor of the Right, Chou, did what he said and sent someone to ask permission to take the army through Dai. The people of Dai suspected that this was just a ruse to make a surprise attack upon them, so they shut the gates to the city and positioned their soldiers on the ramparts. Kong Fujia was absolutely furious, and when they were about ten *li* away from the city, he and Chou, the Councilor of the Right, split their forces into two camps, one in front and one behind, and prepared to attack the city. The people of Dai held firm and made many sorties out of the city walls to do battle, as a result of which both sides sustained terrible losses. Kong Fujia sent someone to the state of Cai to ask for military assistance. Of this no more.

By this time, Ying Kaoshu had already captured the city of Gao and Noble Grandson E had also captured the city of Fang. Both sent messengers to report the good news to the main camp where the Earl of Zheng was based. They arrived just at the same time as the letter from Scion Zihu reporting the crisis at home.

If you do not know how the Earl of Zheng dealt with this situation, READ ON.

Chapter Seven

*Noble Grandson E, fighting from his chariot,
shoots Ying Kaoshu.*

*The Honorable Hui comes up with a plot to
usurp the title from Lord Yin.*

When Lord Zhuang of Zheng got the letter from Scion Zihu reporting the emergency, he immediately gave orders to stand down the army. Yi Zhongnian, the Honorable Hui, and the others then came in person to the main camp to see the Earl of Zheng and complain: "We were all just about to take advantage of these victories to push forward, but suddenly we hear that you have given the order to demobilize the army. Why is this?"

Lord Zhuang was a wily and cunning man, so he kept it a secret that Song and Wey had made a surprise attack on Zheng. "I received a royal mandate to punish Song," he said. "Now they have seen the might of our armies and lost two cities; hence, they have effectively suffered the penalty of having their lands partitioned. The dukes of Song are members of the former royal house, and our kings have always treated them with great respect—do I dare to ask for more? As for the two cities that we have captured, Gao and Fang, let Qi and Lu take one each. I would not dream of seeking any personal advantage from this."

"We mobilized our army as quickly as we could because we wanted to support the royal mandate you had received," Yi Zhongnian said. "For such a minor effort a small gift would be entirely appropriate, but not a whole city!" He refused again and again to accept it.

"Since you are resolute in your refusal, sir," Lord Zhuang said, "then both cities will be presented to the Marquis of Lu as a reward for the Honorable Hui's signal success at Laotiao."

The Honorable Hui did not refuse and clasped his hands together in a gesture of thanks. He ordered a couple of other generals to take their troops to guard the cities of Gao and Fang, but no more of this now.

Lord Zhuang held a great feast for the three armies. Before his departure, he killed a beast and made a blood covenant with Yi Zhongnian and the Honorable Hui: "Our three countries agree to come to each other's aid in times of trouble, and if one of us is attacked, the others will send soldiers and chariots to help. If any of us go back on our word, may the Bright Spirits turn against us!"

Yi Zhongnian returned home and had an audience with Lord Xi of Qi, at which he told him all about the capture of Fang. "At the covenant at Shimen," Lord Xi remarked, "we agreed to a mutual assistance covenant, so now, even though we captured the city, in principle it ought to belong to Zheng."

"The Earl of Zheng wouldn't take it, so both of them now belong to the Marquis of Lu," Yi Zhongnian explained. Lord Xi thought that the Earl of Zheng was a highly principled man and praised him greatly.

. . .

The Earl of Zheng, having stood down his army, was on the way home when he received another letter from the capital. This read:

Song and Wey have already moved their troops in the direction of Dai.

Lord Zhuang laughed: "I was absolutely sure they wouldn't be able to do much. Besides which, Kong Fujia is completely incapable of organizing an army. What kind of person takes out his rage on an innocent bystander when he should be running for his life? I have a plan to deal with him." Then he gave orders to his four generals, dividing the army into four columns, each with its own separate orders. They were told to advance in absolute silence, all moving in the direction of the state of Dai.

Song and Wey were joined together in the attack on Dai, and once they had asked the state of Cai to bring their army to assist in the battle, they were looking forward to imminent victory. Suddenly they received a report: "The state of Zheng has sent its senior general, the Honorable Lü, to command his soldiers in the relief of Dai, and they have made camp fifty *li* away from the city."

The Councilor of the Right, Chou, said, "That is the general who was defeated by Shi Hou; he really doesn't know the first thing about doing battle, so what are we afraid of?"

A short time later there was a further report: "The Lord of Dai knows that the Zheng army has come to his rescue, so he has opened his gates and allowed them to enter the city."

"We can capture Dai with a wave of our hands," Kong Fujia said. "Even though we were not expecting the Zheng army to come to their assistance, it is still only a matter of time; what can they do?"

"Dai now has their assistance, and the two armies will certainly be fighting on the same side," Chou, the Councilor of the Right, pointed out. "We should climb the walls of our camp to see if there is any movement within the city walls, in order to be prepared for any eventuality."

When the two generals were standing on top of the fortifications, pointing various things out to each other, they suddenly heard the sound of a battery of siege engines, and the standard of the state of Zheng was hoisted above the city walls. The Honorable Lü appeared in full battle dress. Leaning against the railings of one of the towers above the wall, he shouted: "Thanks to your efforts, generals, my lord has now obtained the city of Dai. Many thanks!"

It was Lord Zhuang of Zheng's plan all along to pretend to send the Honorable Lü in command of troops to rescue Dai, but in fact His Lordship was present personally on one of the battle chariots. The minute they entered the city walls of Dai, they threw the ruler of Dai out, along with all his army. The city had endured many days of warfare and siege, and everyone had heard of the Earl of Zheng's dread reputation, so who would dare to resist? This great city, independent for many centuries, fell to the state of Zheng without a fight. The Lord of Dai fled to Western Qin together with his entire family.

When Kong Fujia realized that the Earl of Zheng had obtained possession of the city of Dai just like that, he was so furious that he threw his helmet on the ground and said, "Today, either he dies, or I do!"

"That old bastard is a great tactician and he is sure to have arranged more nasty surprises for us," the Councilor of the Right, Chou, said. "If we are attacked both in front and from behind, our position will be very dangerous!"

"Your words are those of a coward!" Kong Fujia bellowed.

Just as he said that, an urgent report came in: "Someone has come from the city with a declaration of war." Kong Fujia promptly agreed to do battle on the following day. He held a meeting with the two states of Wey and Cai, at which they decided to withdraw the armies and horses of all three parties by twenty *li*, to prevent any sudden attack. Kong

Fujia established the central camp and Cai and Wey, the left and right camps respectively, less than three *li* apart.

After the camps had been set up, but before anyone had time to relax, they suddenly heard the sound of siege engines behind them; the lights of the fires illuminated the heavens, and the rumble of chariots assaulted the ears. Their spies reported: "The Zheng army has arrived!" Kong Fujia was furious. He grabbed his painted Fangtian spear and climbed onto his chariot ready to engage the enemy. But all that happened was that the sound of chariots ceased and the fires were all extinguished. Just as he was about to go back to the camp, on the left-hand side, the sound of siege engines could be heard and fires leapt up. As Kong Fujia again came out of the camp to inspect the situation, the fires died down, only for the rumbling to be heard on the right, as the whole place turned into a sheet of flames on the far side of the forest.

"This is a plot by that old bastard to confuse us!" Kong Fujia shouted. He gave the order: "Anyone who moves without authorization will be beheaded."

A short time later the flames shot up again on the left-hand side, and the ground was shaken by the sound of battle cries; then an urgent message arrived: "The Cai army in the left camp is under attack!"

"I will go to their assistance myself!" Kong Fujia bellowed. As he left the gate of the camp, he saw that fires were burning again on the right-hand side and did not know in which direction he should turn. He shouted to his charioteer: "Your job is to drive this chariot to the left!"

The charioteer was so flummoxed that he turned the chariot in completely the wrong direction, heading right, whereupon they ran into a group of soldiers and chariots and started fighting. It was only after some time that they realized that these people were part of the Wey army. When they had explained exactly who they were to each other, they joined forces and went back to the central camp, but it had already been captured by Gao Qumi. As they retreated hurriedly towards the main gate, they found that two other columns had just arrived: Ying Kaoshu on the right and Noble Grandson E on the left. Noble Grandson E took on Chou, the Councilor of the Right, while Ying Kaoshu fought with Kong Fujia, as the two columns went into battle. As dawn began to brighten in the east, Kong Fujia realized that he could not carry on fighting, so he cut his way out and ran. He ran straight into Gao Qumi, which resulted in another skirmish. Kong Fujia abandoned his chariot and escaped on foot, accompanied by his remaining band of some twenty soldiers. Chou, the Councilor of the Right, was killed in battle. The soldiers and materiel of the three states were all captured by Zheng. In addition, they took possession of the baggage train containing the people and animals captured in the outlying regions of the state of Zheng. Such was Lord Zhuang's brilliant plan.

A historian wrote a poem that runs:

> Ruler and minister, master and servant are sometimes hard to
> distinguish.
> Lord Zhuang's wisdom really was amazing.
> When the snipe and the clam are fighting with each other,
> The benefit goes to him who closes the net.

Lord Zhuang of Zheng had gained possession of the city of Dai and annihilated the armies of three countries, so his forces were overjoyed by their victory and sang songs of triumph as they marched homewards. Thereupon Lord Zhuang held a great banquet, at which he feasted the generals who had served under him on this campaign. The generals took it in turn to raise their goblets and toast him. Lord Zhuang looked very pleased and, raising his own cup, he said: "Thanks to the numinous powers of Heaven and Earth and my illustrious ancestors and the work of my ministers, every time I go into battle I am victorious and I strike terror into more senior lords. Can even the marchemont lords of antiquity be compared to me?"

The assembled company all shouted: "One thousand years of long life to our lord!" but only Ying Kaoshu remained silent. Lord Zhuang glared at him, whereupon he presented his opinion: "Your Lordship's words are not quite correct. The marchemont lords received a royal mandate that made them the most senior aristocrats in a particular region; thus they obtained a prerogative over military campaigns. Everyone carried out their orders; everyone responded to their commands. Now Your Lordship has pretended to receive a royal mandate in order to take your revenge on Song, but in fact this had nothing to do with the Zhou Son of Heaven. Furthermore, while you were on campaign, Cai and Wey turned against you to assist Song to invade Zheng, and such little states as Cheng and Xu did not make any move. Was the might of a marchemont lord so easily flouted?"

Lord Zhuang laughed and said, "You are quite right, sir. Cai and Wey have had their entire army defeated, which counts as punishment enough. Now I want to punish Cheng and Xu, so which country should be first?"

"Cheng borders on Qi; Xu borders on Zheng," Ying Kaoshu said. "If Your Lordship is happy to add to your reputation for transgressing royal commands, then you can make a formal declaration of their crimes and send a general to assist Qi in attacking Cheng, and then invite the Qi army to come and help in the attack on Xu. When Cheng is captured, its lands will belong to Qi, and when Xu is captured, its lands will belong to Zheng. That will not harm the friendship prevailing between your two countries. When the matter is concluded, you can present the spoils of war to Zhou, which should serve to conceal the true nature of matters from the eyes and ears of other people."

"Good," said Lord Zhuang. "We will do it in the order that you suggest."

Then he sent an ambassador to suggest attacking Cheng and Xu to the Marquis of Qi. The Marquis of Qi was delighted to hear of this idea, and he sent Yi Zhongnian in command of an army to attack Cheng, while Zheng sent its senior general, the Honorable Lü, to lead an army to assist him. They marched straight into Cheng. The people of Cheng were terrified and asked for a peace treaty with Qi, and the Marquis of Qi accepted this. He then sent an ambassador to follow the Honorable Lü back to Zheng to make inquiries about the date set for the attack on Xu. Lord Zhuang agreed to meet the Marquis of Qi at the regional meeting in Shilai and requested that the Marquis of Qi persuade the Marquis of Lu to participate. This happened in the spring of the eighth year of King Huan of Zhou.

The Honorable Lü became sick on the journey back to his home country, and not long afterwards he died. Lord Zhuang was so upset that he cried and said, "His death makes me feel as if I have lost my right arm!" He treated his family with great generosity, appointing his younger brother, the Honorable Yuan, as a grandee.

A senior ministerial appointment was made vacant by his demise. Lord Zhuang wanted to promote Gao Qumi, but the Scion Zihu secretly warned him against it: "Qumi is greedy and violent. He is not the proper person to be given high office."

Lord Zhuang nodded his head and appointed Zhai Zu as a senior minister instead, taking over the Honorable Lü's position. Gao Qumi received an appointment of equal seniority to that of a minister, of which no more will be said.

In the summer of that year, the two marquises of Qi and Lu both arrived in Shilai and agreed a date for military action with the Earl of Zheng: the first day of the seventh month in the autumn. They would all join forces when they met at the lands of Xu. The two marquises accepted their orders and said goodbye.

Lord Zhuang of Zheng went home, where he held a great muster of chariots and soldiers. He selected a day to report these events to the main ancestral shrine. Then he gathered all his generals on the training ground, whereupon he again set up the great flag, Maohu, placing it in an iron holder. This great flag was made with silk brocade and measured twelve feet square; it was fringed with twenty-four golden bells, and on it were embroidered four massive characters that read "Punishing the Guilty by Royal Command." The flagpole was thirty-three feet high. Lord Zhuang issued his orders: "Anyone who can carry this great flag and walk as normal will be appointed to lead the vanguard and will be granted a battle chariot in reward."

Before he had even finished speaking, one of his generals had already stepped out of the ranks. He was wearing a silver helmet on his head and was dressed in a purple robe and golden armor, his complexion was dark and he wore a curly beard, his eyebrows were thick and his eyes large: this was the Grandee Xia Shuying. He came forward and said, "I can carry it." He then grasped the flagpole in his hand, holding it tight. He advanced three steps, walked backwards three steps, and then took his place on a chariot without even breathing deeply. All the army officers shouted out in amazement.

Xia Shuying shouted, "Where is the charioteer? Drive this chariot for me!"

Just as he was about to thank His Lordship for his appointment, another general stepped out from the ranks. On his head he wore the pheasant-feather cap of a military officer, a green brocade headband, and he was dressed in rhinoceros-hide armor over a red robe. He said, "Holding the flag as you walk forward is nothing special. I can make it dance."

All those present stared at him, for this was Grandee Ying Kaoshu. The charioteer saw that Kaoshu had made a bold claim, so he did not dare move forward, but just stood where he was and awaited developments. He watched as Kaoshu took off his outer robe and reached out to undo the iron holder with his right hand, letting the flag stream out across his back. Then he jumped forward, the flagpole already firmly in his grasp. He quickly moved it to his left hand, turning his body smoothly as he tossed it over to his right hand. He was passing this enormous flagpole from his left hand to his right as if it were just an ordinary long spear, and as he danced there was a sound of swooshing. The flag rolled up, then unfurled, then rolled up again, amazing all who saw it.

Lord Zhuang was thrilled and exclaimed, "What a remarkable man! He deserves to receive this chariot and lead the vanguard."

Before he had even finished speaking, yet another young general had stepped out from the ranks. This was an exceptionally handsome man, wearing a purple and gold official hat and a green robe woven with gold threads. He pointed at Ying Kaoshu and shouted in a loud voice: "You can make the flag dance, and although I cannot, nevertheless this chariot is staying here!" He advanced with great strides.

Kaoshu saw that he looked extremely aggressive, so keeping hold of the flagpole with one hand, he grasped the crossbar of the chariot with the other and ran like the wind. The young general didn't give up, but grabbed a spear from a rack of weaponry and chased him out of the training ground. When he arrived at the main road, Lord Zhuang sent the grandee, Noble Grandson Huo, to talk some sense into him. The young general, seeing that Kaoshu was already far away, turned back angrily. He said, "That man seriously underestimates us members of the Ji clan. I am going to kill him!"

Who was this young general? He was a grandee and a member of the ruling house. His name was Noble Grandson E, and his style-name was Zidu. He was the handsomest of men and a great favorite with Lord Zhuang of Zheng.

Mencius says, "Anyone who does not recognize the handsomeness of Zidu must have no eyes." That saying referred to this man.

The favoritism that he received every day had made him arrogant, and he was both strong and brave. Neither he nor Ying Kaoshu had any time for each other. When he came back to the training ground, he was in an absolutely foul temper. Lord Zhuang praised his bravery and said, "You two tigers shouldn't fight each other. I know exactly how to deal with this situation." He gave another chariot and team of horses to Noble Grandson E and the same to Xia Shuying. The two of them thanked him for his kindness and left.

An old man wrote a poem that reads:

Military law always values impartiality;
Who would dare touch a chariot or draw a sword without orders?
Even though the ruling house of Zheng produced many brave knights,
It is always dangerous to keep people who don't respect ritual propriety.

On the first day of the seventh month, Lord Zhuang left Zhai Zu and Scion Zihu in charge of the country, and he himself led a great army to attack the city of Xu. The marquises of Qi and Lu were waiting for him, camped some twenty *li* from the city. When the three lords met, they behaved with great politeness to each other, and, after much bowing and scraping, the Marquis of Qi took the place of honor, with the Marquis of Lu on his right and the Earl of Zheng on his left. That day, Lord Zhuang held a great banquet, to feast these guests from far away. The Marquis of Qi took from his sleeve a document enumerating the crimes of the Baron of Xu in failing to present tribute and proclaiming that today they were in receipt of a royal mandate to punish him. The two lords of Lu and Zheng both read it, and together they raised their hands in a gesture of respect and said, "We have to do this; we have a right to send out this army." They decided that the following day, Gengchen, they would launch a joint attack on the city, but that beforehand they would order someone to shoot the document, setting out the reasons for the attack, into the city.

The following morning, the sounds of siege engines and the muster of troops could be heard in each of the three camps. The lords of Xu had the rank of baron and ruled a small city state. The walls were not particularly high, nor was the moat very deep, and now they were surrounded by the armies of three countries, in such a tight state of siege that not even a drop of water could escape. Panic reigned within the city. However, Lord Zhuang of Xu was a good ruler, much loved by his people, and since he wanted to make a stand, resistance had not yet crumbled. The two lords of Qi and Lu were not the original planners of this campaign, and so they did not really use their full might. It was the Zheng army that was doing all the work, with every soldier fighting hard and doing his very best.

Ever since Ying Kaoshu had stolen the chariot out from under the nose of Noble Grandson E, he was even more determined to show off what he could do. On the third day of the attack, Renwu, Ying Kaoshu was standing on a high chariot, holding the great flag Maohu against his chest, when with a bound he launched himself up onto the walls of Xu. Noble Grandson E was both sharp-sighted and quick-witted. Seeing that he was the first to climb up onto the walls of Xu, he was jealous of his success. Just as the masses of soldiers had their attention fixed on Kaoshu, he let fly a single assassin's arrow, which struck Kaoshu in the heart, killing him instantly. Kaoshu dropped the flag and fell from the wall.

Xia Shuying thought that Ying Kaoshu had been injured by one of the soldiers defending the walls, so he was deeply enraged—as incandescent as if the sun were in collision with Mars. He picked the great flag up from the ground, then with a leap he scrambled onto the walls and ran around them shouting, "The Lord of Zheng has control of the city walls!" The massed armies could see the flag fluttering in the distance, and they thought that the Earl of Zheng really had captured the city walls, so their bravery increased one hundred times as they marched on the city together, breaking open the gates and allowing the forces of Qi and Lu to enter. Later on, the three lords also entered the city, at which point Lord Zhuang of Xu formally surrendered. Then he lost himself among the throngs of soldiers and ordinary people, making his escape into exile in Wey.

The Marquis of Qi issued placards to pacify the people. He decided that he wanted to give the lands of Xu to the Marquis of Lu, but Lord Yin of Lu declined to accept it. Lord Xi of Qi said, "The original mastermind of this campaign was the Zheng, so since the Lord of Lu will not accept them, these lands ought to go to Zheng."

Lord Zhuang of Zheng had always coveted the lands of Xu, but seeing that the two lords of Qi and Lu were giving way to each other so politely, he pretended that he didn't want them either. Just as they were discussing this matter, a report was made: "Grandee Bai Li of Xu has brought a small child to request an audience." The three lords with one voice called for him to be admitted. On entering, Grandee Bai Li collapsed onto the ground in tears and kowtowed to them as he begged, "Please preserve the last descendant of Taiyue to perform sacrifices to his memory."

"Who is this child?" the Marquis of Qi inquired.

"My lord has no sons," Grandee Bai Li explained. "This is his younger brother, Xinchen."

The lords of Qi and Lu obviously felt very sorry for him. Lord Zhuang of Zheng realized what was happening, so he launched his own counterattack to Grandee Bai Li's plan. Changing his tactics completely, he said: "I was forced into punishing your lord for his crimes by a royal mandate, but if I profited from your lands, then this would not be a virtuous action. Now, although the Lord of Xu has gone into hiding, his ancestral sacrifices must still be carried out. His younger brother is here; furthermore, he has a grandee of Xu to rely on for advice. Here are a ruler and ministers ready to our hand, and we ought to give Xu back to them."

"I accept that my lord is ruined and the state is lost," Grandee Bai Li said. "I am just hoping to protect this orphan. This land is already under your control. How could we dare to expect you to hand it back?"

"I am entirely sincere in my offer to restore the independence of Xu," Lord Zhuang of Zheng said, "but I am afraid that this little gentleman is too young and cannot possibly be expected to take control of the government of the state. I will send someone to assist you."

He then divided Xu into two; the eastern part would be controlled by Grandee Bai Li on Xinchen's behalf, while the western part would be under the control of a grandee of Zheng, Noble Grandson Huo. In name this was done to assist Xu, but in fact it was the occupation of one half of the country. The two marquises of Qi and Lu did not realize that this was part of the plot and thought that it was an excellent solution, praising the Earl of Zheng's generosity. Grandee Bai Li and Xinchen bowed their thanks to the three lords, after which they each returned to their own country.

An old man wrote a poem about Lord Zhuang of Zheng's cunning plan. This runs:

In times of disaster, no one cares about their family members;
Who was prepared to speak up for the state of Xu?
The state was partitioned as a protectorate,
But they still used empty words to cozen outsiders!

Lord Zhuang of Xu died of old age in Wey, and Xinchen remained living under Zheng's control in the eastern part of Xu. He had to wait until after Lord Zhuang of Zheng died, and Scion Zihu and the Honorable Tu fought each other for many years—first with Tu in power and the other in exile, then with Zihu in power and the other in exile—to be able to escape from Zheng's aegis. At that time the state of Zheng was in chaos, and Noble Grandson Huo got sick and died, at which point Xinchen and Grandee Bai Li came up with a plan to take advantage of this opportunity to make their way to the Xu capital, where they restored the ancestral temples. This is a later part of the story.

When Lord Zhuang of Zheng returned to his country, he rewarded Xia Shuying lavishly, but he missed Ying Kaoshu terribly. He was furious that someone unknown had shot Kaoshu, so he divided up the hosts that had followed him out on campaign; to each regiment of one hundred men he gave a pig, and to each division of twenty-five men he gave a chicken and a dog. Then he summoned a shaman to create a curse that would bewitch the man responsible for Ying Kaoshu's death. Noble Grandson E was secretly laughing at all of this, but then three days after the curse was sworn, Lord Zhuang of Zheng personally led his grandees out to inspect the army, and a man with wild hair and muddy face rushed straight towards the Earl of Zheng. He knelt down and cried, saying: "Did your loyal subject Kaoshu do anything to betray the state in being the first to climb the city walls of Xu? And yet your wicked subject, Noble Grandson E, shot me dead because I had taken the chariot from him. I have appealed to God on High, and he has agreed that a life should be paid for with a life. I appreciate Your Lordship's remembrance of me; even in the Underworld, I feel your generosity and virtue!"

When he finished speaking, he gripped his own throat with his hand so hard that blood gushed forth, and he immediately died. Lord Zhuang recognized that this man was Noble Grandson E and quickly ordered someone to save him, but he had already stopped breathing. Apparently Noble Grandson E had been possessed by the wandering soul of Ying Kaoshu, and thus he personally reported to the Earl of Zheng who it was that had shot him. Lord Zhuang of Zheng sighed and wept, and he felt deeply sorry for the soul of Kaoshu. Thus he ordered that a temple should be built at Yinggu, where sacrifices could be made in his memory.

Today Dengfeng County in Henan Province is the ancient territory of Yinggu, and the temple there to Grandee Ying is also known as the Chunxiao or "Pure Filial Piety" Temple. There is also another shrine dedicated to him at Weichuan.

The Recluse of Longxi wrote a poem criticizing Lord Zhuang:

You should stop people fighting over a chariot before anyone gets hurt;
They caused chaos in the state without a thought for their lord.
If your ministers understand and fear the laws of the land,
Why would you need to bribe the Bright Spirits with chickens and dogs?

Lord Zhuang sent two ambassadors laden with gifts to the states of Qi and Lu, to express his thanks. What happened in the state of Qi, we do not need to discuss. However, in the case of the state of Lu, the ambassador returned still laden with gifts and money and with his official credentials unopened.

Lord Zhuang asked the reason for this, and the ambassador reported: "When I got to the Lu border, I heard that the Marquis of Lu had just been assassinated by the Honorable Hui, who has already established a new lord. Since my diplomatic credentials were made out to the previous ruler, I did not dare to hand them over without further instructions."

"The Marquis of Lu was a very gentle and generous man, not to mention a wise ruler," Lord Zhuang exclaimed. "How can he have been assassinated?"

"I have heard something about the reasons behind it," the ambassador said. "The principal wife of the former Lord of Lu, Lord Hui, died young, so his favorite concubine, Lady Zhong Zi, was appointed as his second wife. She gave birth to a son named Gui and wanted to establish him as the heir. Yin was one of his sons by another concubine. When Lord Hui died, his ministers wanted to establish him on the grounds of his seniority, but he supported his father's wishes, and every time they put it to him, he said, 'The country must belong to Gui, but since he is so very young, I will temporarily act as regent for him.' The Honorable Hui requested to be made prime minister, but Yin said, 'Gui is the lord, so you must make your request to him.' The Honorable Hui suspected that Yin was jealous of Gui, so he secretly said to him, 'I have heard that once a valuable thing enters a person's hands, it cannot be lent to other people.' You, my lord, have been recognized as having every right to inherit the marquisate and become the ruler of this state; the people of the capital are pleased to submit to your authority, and when you pass away, you could hand this inheritance to your sons and grandsons. Why do you insist on claiming a regency, giving rise to endless speculation? Now Gui is grown up, and I am afraid that in the future he will behave in a fashion detrimental to you, so I ask permission to kill him to get rid of this lurking menace. What do you think?' Yin just covered his ears and said, 'Are you insane, that you speak in such a reckless way? I have already sent people to Tuqiu to build me a palace with a view to spending my declining years there. Any day now I will be handing over power to Gui.' The Honorable Hui then withdrew in silence, regretting that he had spoken so plainly. He was frightened in case Yin reported what he had said to Gui, because when he took power he would certainly want to punish him for it. Late that night, he went to see Gui and told him the complete opposite of the truth: 'Yin has seen you gradually growing up and he is afraid that you will fight him for power, so today he summoned me into the palace and secretly ordered me to kill you.' Gui was alarmed and asked how he should deal with the situation. The Honorable Hui said, 'Since he is so wicked, there is no need for us to treat him with justice. If you want to avoid all disaster, you must kill him!' Gui said, 'He has been regent for eleven years. My ministers and my people trust and obey him, so if we fail in our attempt to kill him, we are sure to be in serious trouble ourselves.' The Honorable Hui then said, 'I have already come up with a plan for dealing with this situation. Before Yin was appointed your regent, he did battle with the Lord of Zheng at Hurang and was taken prisoner, being held at the home of the Yi family, who are grandees of Zheng. The Yi family worship a deity called Zhongwu, and Yin also secretly joined in this. He was plotting his escape to Lu and performed a divination about it, obtaining an auspicious result. He told the Yi family the truth about what he was up to, and since the Yi family believed that they were not appreciated in the state of Zheng, they fled to Lu with him. They then established a shrine to Zhongwu outside the city walls, and every winter they go in person to perform a sacrifice there. This year, after he performs the sacrifice, he is sure to stay at the house of Grandee Wei. I will send some bravos to join his train and mix among his entourage. They will stab him while he is deeply asleep without him noticing a thing. It will only take a minute.' Gui said, 'Although this is a good plan, how can we avoid ruining our reputations?' The Honorable Hui said, 'I will tell my bravos to run away and put all the blame on the Grandee Wei. What is wrong with that?' Gui got down on his knees and said, 'If this assassination succeeds, I will appoint you as prime minister.' The Honorable Hui put his plan into action and murdered Yin. Now, Gui has already been established as lord, the Honorable Hui has become prime minister, and they have punished the Wei family for the killing, but everyone in the country knows who is actually guilty. However, they are afraid of the Honorable Hui, who is very powerful, so they do not dare to speak out."

Lord Zhuang asked his ministers, "Which would be more advantageous for us, to attack Lu or to make peace with Lu?"

"Lu and Zheng have been allies for many generations, so it would be best to make peace with them," Zhai Zu said. "I imagine that not many days from now, the state of Lu will send an ambassador to us."

Before he had even finished speaking, the Lu ambassador arrived at the official guesthouse. Lord Zhuang sent someone to find out his intentions, and he said, "Since we have established a new lord, I have come on a special mission to reaffirm the good relations between our two countries and set a date for you to make a blood covenant with His Lordship."

Lord Zhuang treated this ambassador with the utmost generosity and the most perfect propriety. He set a date in the summer, in the middle of the fourth month, when they would meet at Yuyue to smear their mouths with blood and swear an oath that they would be at peace forever and never betray each other. From this point on, Lu and Zheng were in constant communication and regularly sent embassies to each other's courts. This happened in the ninth year of King Huan of Zhou's reign.

An old man, having read the history books to this point, would say that when the Honorable Hui obtained power over the army and attacked Zheng and Song on his own authority without considering anyone else's opinion, it was already clear that he would come to a sticky end. When he asked permission to kill his younger half-brother Gui, Yin told him of his wickedness. If his crimes had been revealed then, his body would have been exposed in the marketplace. In order that his younger brother Gui would believe that he was virtuous, he installed him in power. In spite of all this violence and wickedness, surely virtue will triumph in the end and evil will be punished!

There is a poem that bewails these events:

> This bumptious general is accustomed to going his own way;
> Frequent frosts do not mean that the ice freezes solid.
> The mansion at Tuqiu stands empty, its master died young;
> Who will now see justice done for the Wei family?

There is also a poem that criticizes the worship of Zhongwu as being not at all helpful. This poem says:

> Running away from Hurang, you brought this temple with you.
> Year after year, you sacrificed here to a private deity.
> If the spirit of Zhongwu had been able to help you,
> Why did it not send down a thunderbolt to slay the Honorable Hui?

As has already been mentioned, the Honorable Ping, the son of Lord Mu of Song, had fled into exile in Zheng at the end of the reign of King Ping of Zhou and at this time he was still living in the state of Zheng. Suddenly one day, a message arrived: "An envoy from Song has arrived in Zheng to meet the Honorable Ping and take him back to his state, where they want to appoint him the new ruler."

"Can it be that the Lord of Song wants to trick Ping into going home so that they can kill him?" Lord Zhuang asked.

"You need to meet the envoy," Zhai Zu said, "because he will have official documentation from his state."

Do you know what the documents said? If not, READ ON.

Chapter Eight

To establish a new lord, Hua Du resorts to
giving bribes.

Having defeated the Rong army, Zihu refuses
a marriage alliance.

Lord Shang of Song, whose personal name was Yuyi, repeatedly resorted to military force after he came to the title: the state of Zheng he had now attacked three times. This came about purely because the Honorable Ping was living in Zheng; he was afraid, and so he was determined to kill him. The chancellor of Song, Hua Du, had always been friendly with the Honorable Ping, and when he saw that Lord Shang had sent troops against him, although he did not dare to open his mouth to remonstrate and prevent this, in his heart he was very unhappy. Kong Fujia was the official in charge of military matters, so how could Hua Du not blame him? Every time he thought about trying to put an end to this butchery, he remembered that Kong Fujia was one of Lord Shang's most trusted appointees and that he had control of the army, so he did not dare to act. In the attack on Dai the whole army was killed or captured, and yet Kong Fujia was able to escape and return home. Thus the people in the capital were deeply resentful: "The Lord of Song does not care about his people; he just wants to fight at whatever cost to our troops. He has filled the country with widows and orphans, and there is barely a family left intact." Hua Du then sent trusted men into the wards and alleys to spread further rumors: "These repeated campaigns are all Marshal Kong's idea." The people of the capital believed that this was true, and they all hated the marshal. Hua Du was very pleased with the way that the situation was developing.

Later, he heard that Kong Fujia had married a second wife from the Wei family and that she was exceptionally lovely, beautiful beyond compare. Hua Du was desperate to see her. It happened one day that Lady Wei went home, in order to go on a trip with her family to the suburbs to visit the ancestral graveyard. It was spring: the willows were shedding their floss like smoke, and the flowers bloomed like silk brocade. All the ladies and gentlemen were welcoming the spring, and Lady Wei could not bear to keep the curtains on her carriage drawn, but kept stealing glances at the landscape outside. Hua Du happened to be traveling outside the suburbs and came across her by chance. When he discovered that this was the wife of Marshal Kong, he said in amazement: "That the world could indeed contain such a magnificent creature—her reputation is well-deserved." Day and night he thought about her, his mind in turmoil. "If my harem contained such a beauty, I would be happy for the rest of my life! But I will have to kill her husband in order to be able to lay my hands on her." Thus his determination to kill Kong Fujia became increasingly firm.

It was the time of the Spring Muster in the tenth year of the reign of King Huan of Zhou, so Kong Fujia gathered together chariots and horses and issued many strict orders. Hua Du then sent his most trusted men into the midst of the army to spread lies: "The Marshal is raising an army to attack Zheng. This was already settled in a meeting with the chancellor yesterday, so today he is disciplining his troops."

The officers in the Song army were all frightened and did not know what to do for the best. They crowded around the Chancellor's Gate to complain and begged him to go and speak to the ruler and persuade him not to go to war. Hua Du intentionally kept his gate shut tight, but he sent the gatekeeper to stand by the crack in the middle to keep them calm with promises. The army officers became more desperate in their demands for audience; the number of people in the crowd grew and grew, and many of them were armed. Seeing that it was getting late and they had still not been able to see the chancellor, they started to shout. There is an ancient saying to the effect that it is easy to gather people but difficult to get them to go away. Hua Du realized that the mood within the army was becoming dangerous, so he put on armor, buckled on his sword, and came out. He ordered the gate to be opened, commanding the army officers to stand to attention and not to just keep on shouting. He himself took his place opposite the gate and began by making a speech full of false sympathy in order to calm them down:

"Marshal Kong has sole control over the army; it is he who is responsible for your terrible losses. Our ruler trusts him absolutely and pays no attention to my remonstrance; within the next three days he intends to raise another army to attack Zheng. What have the people of Song done to deserve such a terrible fate?"

This news made the army officers so desperate that they gritted their teeth, and shouts began to rise up here and there of "Kill him!"

Hua Du pretended that he wanted to resolve the situation amicably. "You must stop that," he said, "because if Marshal Kong hears about it he will report you to the ruler, and then you will most likely be executed!"

The army officers were all seething: "Our fathers, sons, and cousins have fought in battles year after year, and more than half our number are now dead. Now there is going to be a muster again, and then we will go out on campaign. The generals of Zheng are brave and their soldiers are strong—how can we defeat them? Death awaits us either way, so it would be better to kill this bastard and prevent further suffering for our people. Then we can die without regret!"

"When catching rats, you must beware of traps," Hua Du said. "Even though the marshal is a wicked man, he is still a favorite of our ruler, so you must not do this!"

"If we have your support, Chancellor, we are not afraid even of our deluded and useless ruler!" the officers proclaimed. As they spoke, they grabbed hold of Hua Du's clothing and would not let go. They were all shouting: "We will go with you to kill the bastard!"

The next moment, they were assisting the charioteers to bring forward a chariot. Hua Du was thrust on board by a group of officers, and he was followed there by some of his own trusted subordinates. Shouting the whole way, they marched towards the private residence of Marshal Kong and surrounded it. Hua Du said, "Keep silent and wait for me to knock on the door, then we can strike!"

By this time, it was already dark. Kong Fujia was in the inner chambers drinking wine when he heard the sound of urgent knocking on the front door. He sent someone to ask who it was. The servant reported: "Chancellor Hua has arrived at your gate in person. He says he has something top secret to discuss."

Kong Fujia hurriedly straightened his clothes, put on his official hat, and came out of the main hall to welcome him. Just as he opened the main gate, the roar of shouting could be heard outside, and the army officers rushed in like a swarm of hornets. Kong Fujia panicked and tried to turn back, but Hua Du had already climbed the steps to the main hall and shouted, "The bastard is right here! Why don't you get him?"

Kong Fujia didn't even have time to open his mouth—his head had already fallen to the ground. Hua Du then led his most trusted men straight into the harem, where he captured Lady Wei, forced her onto his chariot, and left. Lady Wei, trapped on the chariot, had no idea how to escape, but she was able to untie her bonds without being noticed and wind them tightly around her neck. By the time she had reached the gate to the Hua mansion, she had already stopped breathing. Hua Du was very upset about this, giving instructions that her body should be taken out and buried in a shallow grave outside the suburbs, strictly warning his followers not to mention this to anyone. Alas! He did not obtain even one night of pleasure, but created ten thousand enemies; is this not a cause for regret?

The army officers took advantage of this opportunity to get into Marshal Kong's private residence and rob it completely. Kong Fujia only had one son, whose name was Mu Jinfu. At the time of these events, he was still a baby. Faithful servants of the family stole the boy away and fled to Lu. Later on he took his father's style-name as his own surname, founding the Kong family.

The great sage Confucius was his grandson in the sixth generation.

When Lord Shang of Song heard that Marshal Kong had been murdered, he did not know what to do. When he discovered that Hua Du had been part of the conspiracy, he was absolutely furious, and sent someone to summon him in order to punish him for his crime. Hua Du claimed that he was too ill to leave the house. Lord Shang ordered his chariot to be brought because he wanted to attend Kong Fujia's funeral in person. When Hua Du heard this, he quickly summoned some military officials and said, "As you know, our ruler loved and favored Marshal Kong. Now that you have murdered him, can you escape punishment? Our former ruler, Lord Mu, set aside the claims of his own son to establish the present lord, but he has shown himself utterly ungrateful. He has allowed the marshal to attack Zheng time and again. Now the marshal has been killed and disaster has been averted! We should now ensure the survival of our state by establishing the son of our former ruler as lord, thereby turning disaster into good luck. Would that not be wonderful?"

"You, Chancellor, took the words right out of our mouths," the military officials said. Then they gave orders to summon the army officers to lie in ambush around the gate to the Kong mansion. When His Lordship came out, the drums sounded and his bodyguards fled in panic. Lord Shang died at the hands of an enraged army. When Hua Du heard the news, he arrived wearing mourning clothes and the other mourners followed him. He ordered the drums to be sounded to summon the other ministers, charged a couple of generals in the rebellious army with the murder of the ruler, and had them executed, in order to conceal the true nature of what had happened from the populace. Then he announced: "The son of our former ruler, the Honorable Ping, is living in Zheng. The people have never forgotten their affection for His Late Lordship, so it is appropriate that we establish his son."

The officials agreed and withdrew. Accordingly, Hua Du sent an ambassador to Zheng to report the death of the ruler and to escort the Honorable Ping home. He also took many valuable objects from the treasuries of the state of Song and presented them to other countries, in order to garner support for Ping.

Lord Zhuang of Zheng had an audience with the Song ambassador and read through his credentials, though he already understood exactly why he had come. Afterwards, he arranged for a state carriage in which the Honorable Ping would travel home to become the new ruler. Just as he was about to depart, he bowed to the ground and wept, saying: "You, my lord, saved my life. Now I am fortunate enough to be able to go back to my country and continue the sacrifices to my ancestors. For the rest of my life I will support you—there is no question that I could ever turn against you."

Lord Zhuang also burst into tears.

When Honorable Ping returned home to Song, Hua Du supported his appointment as the new ruler, and he became Lord Zhuang. Hua Du himself continued to serve as chancellor. Each of the countries to which he had sent bribes accepted them. The Marquis of Qi, the Marquis of Lu, and the Earl of Zheng met together at Ji, in order to confirm the new Duke of Song's position and ensure that Hua Du was promoted to become the prime minister.

A historian wrote a poem that reads:

> During the Spring and Autumn period, assassinations were common-
> place.
> The tumult in Song and Lu occurred within only a few years of each
> other.
> If the other states had refused the bribes on offer,
> Would rebellious ministers and disloyal sons have been able to sleep
> peacefully?

There is also a poem that says that it was only right and proper that Lord Shang of Song should end up being assassinated when he was so cruel and jealous of the Honorable Ping. This poem says:

It was right that Lord Mu should give the state to his brother's son;
Unfortunately, Lord Shang loathed the Honorable Ping.
On this day, Shang died and Ping was established;
Surely, in the Underworld, he will be ashamed to see his father and
    older brother?

As Lord Xi of Qi turned back from the meeting at Ji, in the middle of
his journey he received an alarming message: "The chief of the Northern Rong has sent his two senior commanders, Daliang and Xiaoliang,
across the borders of Qi with an army of ten thousand men. They have
already destroyed Zhua, and now they are attacking Lixia. The defenders cannot hold out much longer and are sending urgent dispatches all
the time, so we beg Your Lordship to come home as soon as possible."

"The Northern Rong have invaded us many times, but all they did
was to steal a few things," Lord Xi said. "This time they have launched
a major incursion, and if they obtain great wealth from this, in the
future our northern border will know no peace."

Thereupon he sent ambassadors to the three states of Lu, Wey, and
Zheng to borrow troops from them, while he himself hastened to Lixia
with the Honorable Yuan and Noble Grandson Daizhong and others to
lead the defense against the enemy.

When Lord Zhuang of Zheng heard that Qi had been invaded by the
Rong, he summoned Scion Zihu and told him, "Qi and Zheng have
made a blood covenant together: every time Zheng uses its troops, Qi
will definitely come to assist them. Now they have come to beg for an
army, so we must help them immediately."

He selected three hundred chariots, appointed Scion Zihu as the
commander-in-chief, ordered Gao Qumi to assist him and Zhu Dan to
lead the vanguard, and then they traveled day and night in the direction
of Qi. When they heard that Lord Xi of Qi was at Lixia, they hastened
there to meet him. At this time the armies from the states of Lu and Wey
had still not yet arrived. Lord Xi was terribly pleased to see them. He
personally came out of the city to feast the Zheng forces and discussed
with Scion Zihu a plan to make the Rong withdraw.

"The Rong army uses foot soldiers, who can easily be advanced but
are also easy to defeat," Scion Zihu said. "We use chariots, which are
difficult to maneuver but also hard to defeat. However, it is the nature
of the Rong people that they underestimate the enemy and are lax in
military regulations; they also show themselves to be utterly ruthless
when they see there is profit to be made. If they win a victory, they are
not happy to see anyone else benefiting from it, and if they are defeated,

they don't assist each other—that means we can set a trap for them. Besides which, if they are anticipating a victory, they will certainly advance recklessly. We can send out a few troops to meet the enemy, and they can pretend to have been defeated and run away. The Rong are sure to come in pursuit, but we will have soldiers waiting in ambush for them. When the pursuing soldiers get caught up in the ambush, they are sure to be panicked into flight, and if we then chase after them, we are sure to win a great victory."

"That is a wonderful plan!" Lord Xi exclaimed. "The Qi army can lie in ambush to the east, to meet them head-on. The Zheng army can lie in ambush in the north, to chase down any stragglers. Attacked simultaneously in front and behind, this plan cannot fail!"

Scion Zihu accepted his orders to take the northern road, where he divided his forces to set ambushes in two different places.

Afterwards Lord Xi summoned the Honorable Yuan and explained the plan to him: "You must take your troops to set an ambush by the East Gate. You are to wait until the Rong army comes in pursuit before you come out and kill them."

He ordered Noble Grandson Daizhong to lead his troops out as bait for the enemy: "In this engagement, you must lose! Whatever happens, you are not allowed to win. If you can draw them over to the East Gate to where our soldiers are waiting in ambush, you will have achieved success."

Once everyone knew what they were doing, Noble Grandson Daizhong opened the gates and provoked battle. The Rong commander, Xiaoliang, grabbed his sword, leaped onto his horse, and ordered three thousand Rong infantry out of the camp to engage the enemy. After the two sides had crossed swords about twenty times, Daizhong was exhausted, and he turned his chariot to flee. However, rather than heading back towards the North Gate, he circled the city to the east. Xiaoliang did not let him off so easily and set off in hot pursuit. When Daliang saw that the Rong troops were winning, he sent the whole army off after them. When they got close to the East Gate, they suddenly heard the sound of siege engines going off like thunder, and the booming of bronze drums resounded in the heavens. The troops hidden in ambush in the brush rose up like a swarm of angry bees.

Xiaoliang cried out in haste: "We have fallen into a trap!" He turned his horse's head to flee, but ran bang into the middle of Daliang's forces. These troops immediately collapsed into chaos, and the whole army started to run. Noble Grandson Daizhong and the Honorable Yuan then joined forces to pursue them. Daliang instructed Xiaoling to go ahead to clear the route, while he covered the retreat, fighting every step of the way. The stragglers who got left behind were captured by the Qi army and beheaded.

The Rong soldiers got as far as Mount Que, and when they looked back, they saw that the pursuing army had fallen behind, so they could rest. Just as they were setting the cooking pots on the ground and getting ready to make food, a great cry rose up from the mountain ridge, and a general came riding forth to announce: "I am the senior general of the state of Zheng, Gao Qumi."

Daliang and Xiaoliang rushed to their horses, but they had no stomach for further fighting and decided to make a run for it. Gao Qumi followed them, slaughtering as many of their men as he could. After they had traveled another couple of *li*, they heard more shouting up ahead. This time it was Scion Zihu who led his forces out to attack them. The Honorable Yuan came up behind, in command of the Qi army, and the Rong troops were massacred as they ran in all directions trying to get away. Xiaoliang was hit in the head by an arrow shot by Zhu Dan—he fell from his horse and died. Daliang's horse was able to break through the encirclement, but he ran into Scion Zihu on his battle chariot and was unprepared to defend himself. He too was beheaded by Scion Zihu. Three hundred armored soldiers were captured alive, and there were countless dead. Scion Zihu presented the heads of Daliang and Xiaoliang, together with their arms and armor, in front of the Marquis of Qi's chariot.

Lord Xi was absolutely delighted and said, "If it were not for the fact that we had a great hero like you here today, the Rong would not have withdrawn so easily! Now the peace and stability of the state altars is all thanks to you!"

"I really did very little," Scion Zihu said modestly. "There is no need to praise me so extravagantly."

Lord Xi then sent messengers to the Lu and Wey armies, telling them not to bother coming any further. He commanded that a great banquet be held in honor of Scion Zihu. As they took their seats, he returned to an earlier topic of conversation: "My daughter is just of marriageable age," but Scion Zihu repeatedly refused the alliance.

After the banquet was over, Lord Xi sent Yi Zhongnian to speak secretly to Gao Qumi: "His Lordship greatly admires the heroic character of the scion and would like to be joined with him in this marriage alliance. In the past he sent embassies on several occasions to request this, but with no success. Today His Lordship mentioned the matter personally to the scion, and he resolutely refused. Do you happen to know the reason for this? If you can bring this about, you will be rewarded with two pairs of white jade discs and one hundred gold ingots."

Gao Qumi accepted the mission and went to see Scion Zihu, to tell him about how much the Marquis of Qi admired him: "If this marriage alliance is concluded, in the future you will have the support of a great state. Would that not be wonderful?"

"Some time ago, before all this trouble, the Marquis of Qi was kind enough to suggest this marriage alliance to me and I refused, because I really do not want to be thought a social climber," Scion Zihu explained. "Today, I have received my father's orders to rescue Qi and have been lucky enough to be successful. However, if I were to get married before going home, people would certainly say that I had forced them into this alliance. How could I ever clear my name?" Gao Qumi kept trying to persuade him, but with no success.

The following day, Lord Xi of Qi sent Yi Zhongnian to discuss the marriage alliance yet again, but Scion Zihu refused, saying, "It would be wrong to get married without my father's permission." He said goodbye and immediately set off homewards.

Lord Xi of Qi was angry and said, "My daughter is very beautiful, so there is no danger of her being left on the shelf!"

. . .

When Scion Zihu of Zheng arrived back in his own country, he reported on how he had refused this marriage alliance to Lord Zhuang.

"If my son is so successful on his own account, there is no need to worry that he will not make a good match," Lord Zhuang remarked.

Zhai Zu then spoke privately to Gao Qumi: "Our lord has many favorites in his harem, and the Honorable Tu, Yi, and Wei all covet the succession. If the scion contracted a marriage alliance with a great state, he would be able to rely on their support. If Qi had not proposed this alliance, you should have asked for it. What is to be done about the fact that he seems determined to clip his own wings? You were there—why on earth didn't you remonstrate with him?"

"I spoke to him about it," Gao Qumi said, "but what can I do if he won't listen to me?"

Zhai Zu sighed and left.

An old man wrote a poem about how Scion Zihu refused this marriage alliance. The poem runs:

A gentleman in carrying out his duties relies on the carrot and the stick;
Refusing this marriage alliance should not have brought disaster on him.
If he tried singing the Qi songs "Galloping Horses" and "The Broken
    Trap,"
Might not Lord Huan of Lu have lived to a ripe old age?

Gao Qumi had always been friendly with the Honorable Wei, but now having heard Zhai Zu's words, he became even closer to him. Scion Zihu spoke to Lord Zhuang about this: "Gao Qumi and the Honorable Wei are in private communication and have lots of secret dealings together. Heaven alone knows what they are up to!"

Lord Zhuang upbraided Gao Qumi according to what Scion Zihu had told him. Gao Qumi lied and said that there was nothing at all in it, then turned around and reported all of this to the Honorable Wei.

"My father wanted to appoint you as a senior minister, but the scion prevented him," the Honorable Wei said. "Now he wants to put a stop to our friendship! At the moment my father is still alive, but after he dies, what if he takes it out on us?"

"The scion is a very kind and friendly person and is incapable of harming others," Gao Qumi said. "You have nothing to worry about!"

However, from this point onwards there was a noticeable coolness between Scion Zihu and the Honorable Wei and Gao Qumi. Later on, Gao Qumi assassinated Zihu in order to establish Wei, an event that has its roots in this division.

Zhai Zu came up with a plan for Scion Zihu, whereby he would seek a marriage alliance with Chen and a treaty of friendship with Wey. "With the two states of Chen and Wey on your side, together with Zheng, they will act as the feet of a tripod. Your position will be assured." Scion Zihu thought that this was good advice.

Zhai Zu spoke to Lord Zhuang about this, and he sent an ambassador to Chen to request a marriage alliance, to which the Marquis of Chen agreed. Scion Zihu then traveled to Chen, married a lady from the Gui ruling family, and went back home with her. The Marquis of Lu also sent an ambassador to Qi to request a marriage alliance. Many things happened because the Marquis of Qi agreed to marry his daughter, Lady Wen Jiang, to the Marquis of Lu.

If you want to know what occurred, READ ON.

Chapter Nine

The Marquis of Qi gives Lady Wen Jiang in marriage to Lu.

Zhu Dan shoots King Huan of Zhou in the shoulder.

Lord Xi of Qi had two daughters, both of whom were exceptionally beautiful. The older daughter, Lady Xuan Jiang, married into the ruling house of Wey, a story which will be told below. His second daughter was Lady Wen Jiang, who was born with a gentle character and an exceptionally beautiful face; she was as pretty as a flower with lovely pale fragrant skin—a remarkable, kingdom-toppling beauty. In addition to that, she was both well-informed about contemporary issues and learned in history, and whenever she spoke, she was very refined and polite: this earned her the epithet Wen, meaning "Cultured."

Scion Zhuer of Qi was an alcoholic lecher. Even though he was called Lady Wen Jiang's older brother, they were actually born to different mothers. Zhuer was only two years older than Lady Wen Jiang, and they grew up together in the palace, playing with each other. When Lady Wen Jiang gradually grew up and revealed her full beauty, Zhuer was already becoming caught up in his affairs with other women, but seeing how lovely and clever Lady Wen Jiang was and how close the two of them had always been, he started to flirt with her. Lady Wen Jiang was not only innately vicious but also completely unrestrained by any sense of decency, so she would talk and joke with him, not avoiding even the most disgusting and degenerate gossip of the day.

Zhuer was tall and strong, with a handsome face, a very good-looking young man. He and Lady Wen Jiang would have made a wonderful couple. Unfortunately, the two of them were born into the same family as brother and sister, so it was impossible for them to get married. However, whenever they found themselves together in the same place, they did not observe proper segregation between the sexes, but instead leaned against each other and held each other's hands: in fact, they touched each other all over. It was only because they were prevented by the presence of their entourage and the palace servants that they did not actually share the same bed.

The Marquis of Qi and his wife spoiled their children and did nothing to control them, as a result of which their sons and daughters behaved like animals. They created the situation that led eventually to the assassination of Zhuer and civil war in Qi.

When Scion Zihu of Zheng defeated the Rong army so comprehensively, Lord Xi of Qi praised him as a great hero in front of Lady Wen Jiang, and when it came to discussions about a marriage alliance, she was deeply pleased by the suggestion. Then she heard that Scion Zihu had resolutely refused the match. This caused her to become depressed to the point where she became ill, running a temperature in the evening and shivering in the morning. Her mind was confused, and she just lay there in a daze. She did not really either sleep or eat.

There is a poem that testifies to this:

A sixteen-year-old, hidden deep in the harem, overwhelmed by emotion,
A love affair carves lines in her brow.
Only phoenixes escape the silken snare of love;
Wild birds and domestic fowl feel its pain.

Scion Zhuer, on the pretext of asking after her health, would from time to time burst into her chambers in the harem and sit by the head of the bed. He massaged and rubbed all over her body, asking where it hurt. However, since there were other people present, he went no further.

One day, Lord Xi of Qi decided on the spur of the moment to go and see Lady Wen Jiang. When he saw that Zhuer was right there in her room, he upbraided him: "Even though you are brother and sister, the dictates of ritual propriety demand that you keep a proper distance from each other. In future you can send one of your palace servants to ask after her; you should not come yourself." Zhuer agreed and withdrew. From this time onwards, the pair only saw each other rarely.

Not long afterwards, Lord Xi married Zhuer off to a daughter of the ruling house of Song, with junior wives taken from the states of Lu and Ju. Zhuer fell deeply in love with his new wife, so he became even further separated from his younger sister. Lady Wen Jiang was profoundly bored, living in seclusion within the harem, and she missed Zhuer a great deal, so her illness worsened. In fact, it was her emotions that were troubled, but she would have been hard put to explain this. Really, this was a case of "a dumb man swallowing his medicine: only he knows how bitter it is."

There is a poem that testifies to this:

> Spring flowers are drenched in spring rain;
> Deep in the harem a woman sleeps alone.
> Resentment has aged her,
> Her thoughts burn her breast.
> Often on bright moonlit nights,
> In her dreams she flies to meet her lover.

When Lord Huan of Lu came to power, he was already grown up but still not yet married. Grandee Zangsun Da came forward and said, "Since ancient times the rulers of states have become fathers by the age of fifteen. Now the position of Your Lordship's principal wife is still vacant, so in the future, where will the heir to your title come from? This is not the proper way to show respect for the ancestral temples."

"I have heard that the Marquis of Qi has a favorite daughter named Lady Wen Jiang," the Honorable Hui said. "He wanted to marry her off to Scion Zihu of Zheng, but the match was broken off. Perhaps Your Lordship might like to ask for her hand in marriage?"

"I suppose so," Lord Huan said. That very day, he sent the Honorable Hui to propose a marriage alliance with Qi.

Lord Xi of Qi requested permission to delay setting a date on the grounds that Lady Wen Jiang was unwell. The palace maids informed Her Ladyship that the Marquis of Lu had requested her hand in marriage. Lady Wen Jiang's depression resulted from having too much time to fret, but when she heard this news she gradually cheered up and her illness disappeared. When Qi and Lu met at Ji over the problems with the Lord of Song, the Marquis of Lu requested the marriage alliance in person, and the Marquis of Qi then set a date to meet the following year. In the third year of the reign of Lord Huan of Lu, he went in person to the lands of Ying in order to meet the Marquis of Qi. Lord Xi of Qi was moved by his obvious sincerity and agreed to the alliance. The Marquis of Lu paid the bride-price while still in the lands of Ying, and the ceremony was performed with much greater pomp and circumstance than would usually have been the case. Delighted, Lord Xi agreed that the wedding would take place in the ninth month of autumn; he would personally escort Lady Wen Jiang to Lu for the occasion. The Marquis of Lu then sent the Honorable Hui to Qi to collect the bride.

When Scion Zhuer of Qi heard that Lady Wen Jiang was going to be married abroad, all his old feelings for her revived. He sent one of the palace servants ostensibly to take a bunch of flowers to his younger sister, but in fact to deliver a poem to her:

> The peach tree is covered in flowers, a beautiful red cloud.
> If the owner does not pluck them, the flowers float away to wither and die.
> Alas! How sad!

Lady Wen Jiang got the poem and understood what he meant by it. She replied with her own poem:

> The peach tree is covered in blooms, how lovely they are.
> If you do not pluck them now, how can it flower again next spring?
> Go ahead! Hurry up!

When Zhuer read her poem in response, he realized that Lady Wen Jiang reciprocated his love, and she was constantly in his thoughts.

A short time later the Lu ambassador, the Honorable Hui, arrived in Qi to collect Lady Wen Jiang. Since Lord Xi of Qi loved his daughter so much, he was going to escort her personally to her new home. When Zhuer heard this, he said to his father: "I have heard that my younger sister is going to be married to the Marquis of Lu. This is a good thing, given that Qi and Lu have been on friendly terms for many generations. Since the Marquis of Lu does not come in person to collect her, she must have a close relative to escort her. You, my father, have many matters of state to attend to, so it really is not easy for you to get away. Since I have nothing important to do, I am happy to represent you on this journey."

"I have already told him that I agree to escort the bride myself," Lord Xi replied. "How can I go back on my word?" Before he had even finished speaking, someone came in to report: "The Marquis of Lu had halted his cortege at the city of Xuan. He is waiting there specially to meet his bride."

"Lu is a state in which propriety and decorum reign, and they have come to the midpoint to meet the bride, so that I don't have to go to the trouble of leaving the country," Lord Xi said. "I really have to go." Zhuer withdrew in silence, and Lady Jiang was also disappointed.

At that time, it was already the first week of the ninth month of autumn and the date of the wedding was almost upon them. Lady Wen

Jiang went to say goodbye to the denizens of her father's six palaces, and then she went to the East Palace to bid farewell to her older brother. Zhuer poured wine and served her himself, and they looked deep into each other's eyes, unwilling to let each other go. Given that his principal wife was present at this banquet and that his father, Lord Xi, had sent some of his palace maids to attend them, they could not talk openly, but they sighed bitterly in secret. When the time came for them to part, Zhuer stood in front of the chariot and said, "Be careful, little sister, and do not forget your 'go ahead.'"

Lady Wen Jiang replied: "Look after yourself, brother. We are sure to meet again in the future."

Lord Xi of Qi ordered Zhuer to guard the capital while he personally escorted Lady Wen Jiang to Xuan to meet the Marquis of Lu. The Marquis of Lu performed all the proper ceremonies to greet his father-in-law, held a banquet for him, and gave lavish gifts to all the people in his train. Afterwards, Lord Xi said goodbye and returned home. Meanwhile, the Marquis of Lu took Lady Wen Jiang back to his capital, where the wedding ceremonies would be performed. There were two reasons for such extensive ceremonies: one was that the state of Qi was a great country, the other that Lady Wen Jiang was of such exceptional beauty that the Marquis of Lu had fallen deeply in love with her. On New Year's Day they held an audience at the ancestral temple, and the wives of the grandees of Lu all came to pay court to the lord's principal wife. Lord Xi sent his younger brother, Yi Zhongnian, on a formal embassy to Lu to ask after Lady Wen Jiang. From this point on, the relations between Qi and Lu became very close, of which no more.

An anonymous author wrote a poem that speaks of Lady Wen Jiang's marriage. This poem runs:

> People have always been suspicious of the relations between men and
> women.
> How can brothers and sisters not be kept apart?
> Before leaving she told him to look after himself,
> Just encouraging him to ruin her reputation later on.

. . .

Let us now turn to a different part of the story. When King Huan of Zhou heard that the Earl of Zheng had forged a royal mandate in order to attack Song, he was absolutely furious and ordered Linfu, Duke of Guo, to take sole control of the government, refusing to employ the Earl of Zheng ever again. When Lord Zhuang of Zheng learned this news, he was angry with King Huan and did not go to court for five years in a row.

"Wusheng of Zheng really is so rude!" King Huan announced. "If we do not punish him, people will think that they can just get away with that sort of thing. I will command the six armies personally and go and make clear his crimes."

Linfu, Duke of Guo, remonstrated: "Zheng has produced royal ministers for generation after generation. Now you have dismissed him from office, which is why he does not come to court. You might feel that it is appropriate to give orders for a campaign against him, but you must not go yourself. That is quite sufficient to make clear the might of Heaven."

King Huan went bright red with anger and shouted, "Wusheng has kicked me around more than once. Today, either he dies or I do!"

He summoned the three states of Cai, Wey, and Chen and ordered them each to raise an army to attack Zheng.

At this time Bao, the Marquis of Chen, had recently died, and his younger brother, the Honorable Tuo, style-name Wufu, had then murdered Scion Mian and usurped the title, granting Bao the posthumous title of Lord Huan. The people of the capital refused to submit to the Honorable Tuo's authority, and many of them had run away. On receiving a royal mandate to raise an army—even though the Honorable Tuo was only just established—he did not dare to disobey the king's command, so he gathered together some chariots and soldiers and appointed Grandee Bo Yuanzhu to lead the army; they advanced towards the state of Zheng. Cai and Wey also each sent troops to join the campaign. King Huan ordered Linfu, Duke of Guo, to take command of the Army of the Right, with the troops of Cai and Wey under his aegis. His Majesty appointed Heijian, Duke of Zhou, to take command of the Army of the Left, with the troops from Chen under his authority. The king himself commanded the royal army in the center, with the Left and Right responding to his orders.

When Lord Zhuang of Zheng heard that the king's army had arrived, he summoned all his grandees to discuss a plan of action. None of his ministers dared to be the first to speak. Then the senior minister Zhai Zu said: "The Son of Heaven has come in personal command of his army to punish us for the fact that we have not been to pay court to him. Since he is absolutely correct in all his accusations, it would be best for us to send an ambassador to apologize, for then we can turn this disaster into a blessing."

"The king has stripped me of my powers in the government, and now he has turned his army against me," Lord Zhuang said furiously. "Three generations of loyal service to the Zhou royal house have been wiped out. If we do not do something to blunt his ardor, the state will be in great danger!"

"Chen usually enjoys good relations with Zheng, so they will only have sent auxiliary troops because they had to," Gao Qumi said. "Cai and Wey are our inveterate enemies, so they will definitely render good service to the king. The Son of Heaven is so enraged that he has taken personal command of the army—therefore, we should not send our troops against his vanguard. It would be better to wait behind strong fortifications and test his attitude. We can then either fight or make peace as appropriate."

The Honorable Yuan, Grandee of Zheng, stepped forward and said, "For a subject to attack his lord is not in accordance with our principles, so if we are going to do it, it had better be sooner rather than later. Although I am not very clever, I would like to make a suggestion."

"What is your plan?" Lord Zhuang asked.

"The royal army is divided into three parts, and we ought to divide our army into three to respond to them," the Honorable Yuan explained. "Our Left and Right armies should then both go into square formation. Our Army of the Left will face their Army of the Right, our Army of the Right will correspond to their Army of the Left, and Your Lordship will have to command our Central Army against the king."

"Will doing that make us victorious?" Lord Zhuang asked curiously.

"Tuo of Chen assassinated his ruler in order to usurp the title, and the people of his state have not yet submitted to his authority," the Honorable Yuan reminded him. "He has forced them to follow him on campaign, but in their hearts they are sure to want to cut and run. If you order our Army of the Right to attack the Chen troops first, given that they don't want to fight in the first place, they will certainly be routed. Then you order the Army of the Left to put Cai and Wey to flight— when they hear that Chen has been defeated, their morale will collapse. Afterwards we bring all our troops together to attack the king's soldiers. That way we will certainly win."

"You understand the enemy as if you held them in the palm of your hand," Lord Zhuang said. "It is just as if the Honorable Lü were still with us!"

Just as they were discussing this, an official from the border came to report: "The king's army has already reached Ruge, and the three camps are in constant communication."

"It would be nice to destroy one of their camps, because that would really put the cat among the pigeons," Lord Zhuang mused. Then he ordered Grandee Man Bo to lead one army out to the right, the senior minister Zhai Zu to lead one army out to the left, while he himself marched out with the generals Gao Qumi, Yuan Fan, Xia Shuying, Zhu Dan, and others in his wake. He hoisted the great flag Maohu over the Central Army. Zhai Zu came forward and said: "Maohu was used in the victory over Song and Xu. The slogan 'Punishing the Guilty by Royal Command' is perfectly acceptable when you are attacking an aristocratic house, but you cannot use it when you are fighting the king."

"I didn't think of that," Lord Zhuang said. Then he ordered that the great flag be changed and commanded Xia Shuying to take charge of the new battle standard. Maohu was placed in the armory and was never used again.

"I see that the Zhou king knows something of tactics, so when we join battle today, we should use an unusual array," Gao Qumi suggested. "I therefore ask permission to set the battle formation 'Shoal.'"

"What is the 'Shoal' formation?" Lord Zhuang asked.

"Twenty-five armored chariots form a troop and five armored men form a unit," Gao Qumi explained. "Each chariot in the troop has twenty-five armed men—that is five units—following it, to prevent the enemy from getting close. If someone on a chariot is injured, he is replaced with one of the foot soldiers, thus these chariots just keep on rolling forward and never turn back. This battle formation is very strong and very dangerous; it is hard to defeat and will usually result in victory."

"Good," said Lord Zhuang.

The three armies arrived near Ruge and made camp.

When King Huan heard that the Earl of Zheng had led his army out to do battle, he was so angry that he could not speak. He wanted to go out and fight himself, but Linfu, Duke of Guo, remonstrated with him and prevented this. The following day, both sides drew up in battle formation, and Lord Zhuang issued his orders: "The armies of the Left and Right must not move until you see the battle standard raised in the Central Army, at which point we will advance our troops in unison."

King Huan had prepared a long speech blaming Zheng for the whole thing, and he was waiting specially for the Earl of Zheng to appear so that he could deliver it in front of the whole army and thus assuage his anger. However, although the Earl of Zheng had put his troops into formation, they remained stationary, not moving a muscle. King Huan sent someone to provoke battle, but no one responded. It was only after midday, by which time Lord Zhuang estimated that the king's soldiers would be thoroughly fed up and bored, that he told Xia Shuying to wave the great battle standard. The two armies to left and right then sounded their drums together, with a sound like thunder, and began advancing at speed.

First, Man Bo cut his way through the Army of the Left. The Chen army had no intention of fighting anyway and immediately scattered in panic, running headlong into the Zhou troops. Heijian, Duke of Zhou, could do nothing to prevent this and was defeated in an utter rout. As this was happening, Zhai Zu cut his way through the Army of the Right, aiming always for where the flags of Cai and Wey were fluttering. These two countries could not hold out, but fled—each heading off in a different direction. Linfu, Duke of Guo, drew his sword and marched in front of the chariots, warning his officers: "Anyone who moves without orders will be executed!" This ensured that Zhai Zu did not dare to come too close. Linfu retreated gradually, without the loss of a single man.

At the same time, King Huan was with the Central Army and could hear the sound of drums in the enemy camps shaking the heavens, so he knew that they had come out to do battle. As he prepared to engage them, all he could see were officers and men in complete confusion, as army ranks had already disintegrated into chaos. Since they had seen the fleeing soldiers and knew that their camps on the right and left had already suffered losses, even the Central Army had begun to panic. Now the Zheng army advanced like a wall, with Zhu Dan in front and Yuan Fan behind, while Man Bo and Zhai Zu led their victorious troops to join forces in a massive attack. In the following massacre chariots were overturned and horses butchered, generals were killed, and soldiers died. King Huan issued orders for an immediate retreat and he himself brought up the rearguard, fighting every step of the way. Zhu Dan caught sight of an embroidered baldachin in the distance and guessed that it covered the Zhou king; straining his eyesight to the utmost, he let fly a single arrow, which struck His Majesty in the left shoulder. Fortunately, the king was wearing hard and thick armor, so he was not very seriously wounded. Zhu Dan sped forward in his chariot, but just at the critical moment, Linfu, Duke of Guo, drove out to rescue the king and crossed swords with Zhu Dan. Yuan Fan and Man Bo both advanced together, desperate to become heroes, when suddenly they heard the urgent clanging of a bell coming from the Central Army. They each collected their troops and turned back.

King Huan led his army to retreat thirty *li* before making camp. When Heijian, Duke of Zhou, arrived, he reported: "The people of Chen were not willing to fight; that is why they were immediately defeated."

"It is my mistake for employing the wrong people," King Huan said shamefacedly.

Zhu Dan and the others rejoined the main body of the army. When he saw Lord Zhuang of Zheng, he said, "I had shot the king in the shoulder and he was absolutely petrified. I was right in the middle of chasing him down and would have captured him, so why did you sound the retreat?"

"This whole situation came about because the Son of Heaven is a stupid man and he hates me in spite of all that I have done for him," Lord Zhuang said. "That we met in battle today is because he forced me into it. Thanks to the efforts of my ministers, the state altars have been preserved unharmed, and that is all that I wanted. What more could I ask for? Supposing that, as you say, you could have captured the Son of Heaven and brought him back, how would we have resolved the situation? It is not right to shoot the king. If by some evil mischance he had been killed, I would have to bear the reputation of a regicide."

"You are quite right, my lord," Zhai Zu said. "Now the martial reputation of our troops has been established beyond any shadow of a doubt and the Zhou king is terrified of us. We ought to send an ambassador to ask after him, so that he gradually comes to accept our sincerity and understands that Your Lordship did not intend to have him shot."

"We will put Zhai Zu in charge of this," Lord Zhuang said. He ordered that twelve head of cattle, one hundred sheep, and enough grain and animal fodder to fill more than one hundred carts should be sent to the royal encampment, traveling day and night.

Zhai Zu kowtowed again and again, explaining: "Your vassal, Wusheng, has committed crimes deserving of death, but he could not bear to think that the altars of state should be endangered, so he gathered an army to defend himself. He had no idea that some of his soldiers would not listen to his orders and actually harm the royal person. Wusheng is absolutely terrified! He immediately sent me to apologize for his crimes at the gate to your camp, to respectfully ask after your health, and to hand over these meager rations to temporarily relieve the needs of your army. Please, will Your Majesty be so generous as to pardon him?"

King Huan was silent and seemed somewhat shamefaced. Linfu, Duke of Guo, who was standing beside him, then replied on his behalf: "Since Wusheng appreciates that he has committed a crime, we can forgive him. Let his ambassador come forward and thank His Majesty for his magnanimity."

Zhai Zu bowed twice, kowtowed, and left. He then traveled to the other camps, asking each one, "Is everything well?"

A historian wrote a poem bewailing these events:

> He praised himself for shooting an arrow into the king's shoulder,
> He did not understand that a ruler and vassal are as far apart as heaven
>   and earth.
> Even in front of the royal encampment Zheng did not give way,
> Performing empty rituals to mislead the king.

A bearded old man wrote a poem criticizing King Huan, who should not have attacked Zheng without considering the consequences for his own army, thus bringing humiliation upon himself. This poem says:

> You do not use a valuable pearl to shoot a worthless sparrow;
> Surely there was no need for the king to participate himself.
> If he had announced that he was stripping Lord Zhuang of his title,
> Would Zheng not have been overawed by the might of the royal house?

King Huan's battered army returned to Zhou. He could not swallow his rage and wanted to proclaim to one and all that Wusheng of Zheng had committed the crime of lèse-majesté. Linfu, Duke of Guo, remonstrated with the king: "Your Majesty acted hastily, and thus you achieved nothing. If you now send out announcements in all directions, this will simply publicize your defeat. Among the aristocracy, apart from the three states of Chen, Wey, and Cai, everybody sides with Zheng. If you cannot punish him militarily, you will simply be laughed at by Zheng. Since Zheng has already sent Zhai Zu to apologize for their crimes, you can make use of this occasion to appear magnanimous, and this will also allow you to open a new chapter in your relations with them."

King Huan was silent. From this time on, he never so much as mentioned Zheng again.

When the Marquis of Cai led his troops to attack Zheng under the leadership of the Zhou king, he discovered that the state of Chen was in chaos after the assassination of its ruler, since the people did not accept the usurpation of the title by the Honorable Tuo. Accordingly, he led his army to launch a surprise attack on Chen.

Do you know whether they won or lost? If not, READ ON.

Chapter Ten

*Xiong Tong of Chu oversteps his authority
and declares himself king.*

*Zhai Zu of Zheng is blackmailed into
establishing a concubine's son as lord.*

Lord Huan of Chen had a son born to a concubine whose name was Yue. His mother was Lady Ji of Cai, and he was the nephew of Fengren, Marquis of Cai. When the troops of Chen and Cai attacked Zheng together, the state of Chen put Grandee Bo Yuanzhu in command as general. Meanwhile, the state of Cai appointed as general the Marquis of Cai's younger brother, Cai Ji. Cai Ji privately asked Bo Yuanzhu about the state of things in Chen. Bo Yuanzhu said, "Even though our new lord, Tuo, has taken the title, he has not been able to gain the allegiance of the people. The only thing he seems to care about is hunting— he is always heading out in plain clothes in pursuit of animals beyond the suburbs. He does not pay any attention to matters of state, and we are going to end up with a civil war soon."

"Why don't you execute him for his crimes?" Cai Ji inquired.

"I would love to, but I don't have the military capability," Bo Yuanzhu explained.

When the army of the Zhou king was defeated, the troops of all three countries returned to their own states. Cai Ji reported what Bo Yuanzhu had said to the Marquis of Cai.

"Scion Mian is dead," the marquis proclaimed, "so my nephew ought to succeed to the title. Tuo is a criminal who assassinated his ruler and usurped the marquisate; are we going to leave him to enjoy wealth and power forever?"

Cai Ji then presented his opinion: "Tuo loves hunting. We should take advantage of his absence from the city to make a surprise attack and kill him."

The Marquis of Cai thought that this was a good idea, so he secretly sent Cai Ji with one hundred chariots to wait at Jiekou. When Tuo came out hunting, they were going to ambush him.

Cai Ji sent spies out to collect intelligence. and they reported back: "The Lord of Chen left the capital three days ago on a hunting expedition, and he has made camp at Jiekou."

"My plan will succeed!" Cai Ji exclaimed.

He then organized his chariots and horses into ten divisions, and they all dressed up as huntsmen and moved forward as if taking part in a battue, coming upon the Lord of Chen just as he was shooting a deer. Cai Ji urged his chariot on and stole the deer. The Lord of Chen was so angry he forgot his noble position in trying to arrest Cai Ji. The man turned his chariot back, whereupon the Lord of Chen ordered his chariot and outrunners forward. Then he heard the clear notes of a metal gong being struck, and the ten divisions of huntsmen surged forward, taking the Lord of Chen prisoner.

Cai Ji shouted loudly, "I am none other than the younger brother of the Marquis of Cai. My name is Cai Ji. After the murder of His Late Lordship, I received my brother's orders to come and punish you for your crimes. I am here to execute Tuo, not to inquire into the acts of anyone else."

All the other people present bowed down and then prostrated themselves. Cai Ji comforted them one by one, saying, "Yue, the son of your former lord, is the nephew of the Marquis of Cai. Why don't you make him the new lord?"

They replied as with one voice: "That would make everyone happy! We are willing to lead the way for you!"

Cai Ji immediately beheaded the traitor Tuo, hung his severed head from the chariot, and galloped towards Chen. The group of people who had followed the Lord of Chen out on his hunting expedition now cleared the road for him, in order to make it obvious to one and all that the Cai contingent were here to punish a criminal and establish a new lord. As a result, there was no panic in the markets or at the wells, and the ordinary people lined the streets shouting acclaim. When Cai Ji arrived in Chen, he ordered that Tuo's head be offered in sacrifice at the temple to Lord Huan of Chen. Then he established Yue as the new lord, and he became Lord Li. This all happened in the fourteenth year of the reign of King Huan of Zhou. The Honorable Tuo was able to hold the title illegally for just one year and six months. For the sake of this fleeting period of wealth and power, he was happy to endure ten thousand generations of odium. Is this not stupid?

There is a poem that testifies to this:

He assassinated his ruler in the hope of achieving lasting power,
But his love of hunting would one day get him killed.
If criminals did not suffer exemplary punishment,
There would be a great many more regicides and patricides.

After the Honorable Yue was established, Chen and Cai got along well for many years with no conflicts at all. Of this, no more.

. . .

The most important country in the south was named Chu. The ruling house had the surname Mi and the title of viscount. The founder of this family was Zhongli, the grandson of the sage-king Zhuanxu, who held the office of Regulator of Fire under the sage-king Gaoxin. He was able to bring light and warmth to the world, thus he was known by the epithet Invocator of Brightness. When Zhongli died, his younger brother inherited his title as Invocator of Brightness. He had a son named Luzhong, who married the daughter of the ruler of the state of Guifang, and she was pregnant for eleven years. Then a cesarean was performed on the left side of her abdomen, and she gave birth to three sons, after which a cesarean was performed on the right side of her abdomen and she gave birth to another three sons.

The oldest was named Fan and was the founder of the Qi clan. He was enfeoffed in the wastes of Wey and took the title of the Earl of Xia. When Tang attacked the evil king Jie and founded the Shang dynasty, this family was all killed. The second son was named Shenhu, and he was the ancestor of the Dong clan. He was enfeoffed in the wastes of Han. In the time of the Zhou dynasty this had become the state of Hu, though they were later on killed by Chu. The third son was named Pengzu and was the ancestor of the Peng clan. He too was enfeoffed in the wastes of Han and took the title of the Earl of Shang. At the end of the Shang dynasty, this state began to decline. The fourth son was named Huiren. He was the founder of the Yun clan and was enfeoffed in the wastes of Zheng. The fifth son was named An and was the ancestor of the Cao clan. He was enfeoffed in the wastes of Zhu. The sixth son was called Jilian, and he was the founder of the Mi clan.

Jilian's most famous descendant was the exceptionally well-educated Yu Xiong, who was tutor to both King Wen and King Wu of Zhou, hence his children took Xiong as their surname. In the time of King Cheng, he wished to honor the descendants of those who had worked diligently for Kings Wen and Wu, so he sought out Yu Xiong's great-grandson Xiong Yi and enfeoffed him in Jingman with the lands appropriate to a viscount or baron. He made his capital at the city of Danyang. His descendant in the fifth generation was Xiong Qu, who was able to unite the people living between the Yangtze and the Han Rivers and thus presumptuously assumed the title of king.

King Li of Zhou was a very violent and unrestrained man, and Xiong Qu was afraid that he might come under attack. Therefore, he stopped using his royal title and did not allow anyone to call him by it. His descendant in the eighth generation was Xiong Yí, also known by his Chu language name of Ruo'ao. In the next generation these lands passed to Xiong Shun, who was also known by his Chu language name of Fenmao. When Fenmao died, his younger brother, Xiong Tong, murdered Fenmao's son in order to establish himself.

Xiong Tong was a violent man who enjoyed doing battle, and it was his ambition to restore the title of king. However, he could see that all the other aristocrats supported the Zhou ruling house and continued to pay court and send embassies to them, so there was nothing he could do but wait. When King Huan of Zhou was defeated in Zheng, Xiong Tong no longer had any doubts—his decision to take the royal title was made. His prime minister, Dou Bobi, then came forward and said, "Chu has not used the royal title for a long time. If you were to resume it now, I am afraid that it would cause great ridicule. You must first overawe the other aristocrats and make them submit to your authority; then you can assume this honor."

"How do I do that?" Xiong Tong asked.

"Of all the states east of the Han River, only Sui is of any significance," Dou Bobi replied. "Your Lordship should send your troops to the border with Sui and at the same time send an embassy there asking for a peace treaty. If Sui submits, then all the states between the Han and the Huai Rivers will give their allegiance to you."

Xiong Tong followed his advice and personally led a great host to camp at Xia, while at the same time sending Grandee Wei Zhang to ask for a peace treaty with Sui. Sui possessed one wise minister, whose name was Ji Liang, and one toadying minister, whose name was Shao Shi. The Marquis of Sui loved being flattered but did not like sensible advice, so

Shao Shi was much in favor. When the Chu ambassador arrived in Sui, the marquis summoned the two ministers to ask their opinions.

Ji Liang presented his advice: "Chu is strong and Sui is weak, and yet now they have come to ask us for a peace treaty. This means that they are up to something. You should agree to this, but make internal preparations so that when the time comes you can defend against them."

"I ask permission to accept this peace treaty, so I can go and inspect the state of the Chu army," Shao Shi said.

The Marquis of Sui then sent Shao Shi to Xia, with orders to make a blood covenant with Chu.

Dou Bobi, hearing that Shao Shi was on his way, instructed Xiong Tong: "I have heard that Shao Shi is a stupid man who has obtained favor by flattery. Now he has come here to find out what is going on, so we should hide our strong and battle-hardened troops and show him only the weak and the feeble. That way they will underestimate us and become increasingly arrogant. If they become complacent, they will lower their guard, and then we can accomplish all that we wish for."

"Ji Liang is with them," Grandee Xiong Shuaibi said. "What part will he play?"

"Right now—none," Dou Bobi assured him. "My plan is for the long term." Xiong Tong agreed to his strategy.

When Shao Shi arrived in the Chu encampment and looked about him, he just saw rotten and worn-out weaponry, and old or enfeebled troops—certainly they were in no fit state to do battle. He then became more and more haughty, and said to Xiong Tong, "Our two countries keep strictly within their own borders, so what do you mean by asking for a peace treaty?"

Xiong Tong came out with a pack of lies in return: "My humble country has suffered poor harvests for several years in succession, and my people are exhausted and half-starved. We have become deeply worried at the prospect of a number of small states forming an alliance to attack us. That is why we wish to form a brotherly alliance with your great state, so that we may be as close as lips and teeth."

"All the little states along the east bank of the Han River obey our commands," Shao Shi informed him. "You have nothing to worry about."

Xiong Tong then made the blood covenant with Shao Shi. After his visitor left, Xiong Tong issued an order to stand down the army.

When Shao Shi returned, he had an audience with the Marquis of Sui, at which he reported the weak state of the Chu army: "When the blood covenant was concluded, they immediately dismissed the army, from which you can see that they are very frightened of us. I would like to take an army in pursuit to make a surprise attack on them. If I cannot capture the entire army and bring them home with me, I am sure that I can take at least half of them prisoner. From now on Chu will never dare look Sui straight in the eye again!"

The Marquis of Sui thought that this was an excellent idea. He wanted to raise an army, but when Ji Liang heard about this, he rushed to the palace to remonstrate: "You must not do this! You must not do this! Since the time of Ruo'ao and Fenmao the state of Chu has instituted serious governmental reforms, and for many years now they have invaded and skirmished around the Yangtze and the Han Rivers. Xiong Tong murdered his nephew in order to take the title, which demonstrates that he is a very violent and cruel man. Now for no reason he has come here to ask for a peace treaty, which means that he must have some wicked plan in mind. He showed us his oldest and weakest soldiers as bait. If you go in pursuit, you are simply falling into his trap!"

The Marquis of Sui then performed a divination about it and it was not auspicious, so he did not go in pursuit of the Chu army.

When Xiong Tong heard that Ji Liang's remonstrance had prevented them from sending troops after him, he summoned Dou Bobi again to discuss the next stage in their plans. Bobi recommended a stratagem: "I suggest that you invite the aristocrats to meet you at Shenlu. If Sui comes, that means that they submit to your authority. If they do not, then you can attack them for having failed in their treaty obligations."

Xiong Tong accordingly sent messengers to tell all the states east of the Han River that they should be present at Shenlu on the first day of the first month of summer.

On the appointed day, representatives of the states of Ba, Yong, Pu, Deng, You, Jiao, Luo, Yuan, Er, Zhen, Shen, and Jiang were all there; only Huang and Sui had not arrived. The Viscount of Chu sent Wei Zhang to request an explanation of Huang, and the Viscount of Huang responded with an apology, transmitted by his ambassador. Xiao Tong also sent Qu Xia to request an explanation of Sui, but the Marquis of Sui paid no attention. Therefore, he led his troops to attack Sui, stationing them between the Han and the Huai Rivers.

The Marquis of Sui summoned his ministers to discuss a plan to counter the threat posed by Chu. Ji Liang came forward and proclaimed: "Chu has taken the initiative by bringing together the aristocrats, and they have sent their soldiers to keep an eye on us. Their advance guard is formidable indeed and should not be underestimated. It would be better if we apologized humbly and asked for a peace treaty. If Chu is prepared to listen to us and restore the long-standing good relationship between our two countries, that is already more than we can expect. On the other hand, if they do not listen, that way the fault will lie with Chu. If we have humbled ourselves before Chu and yet they still think they can bully us, then their officers will be rendered complacent; if we see Chu refuse our diplomatic overtures, then our officers will be angry. If we are angry and they are complacent, even if we have to do battle, we may still be able to turn the situation to our advantage."

Shao Shi, from his position beside the marquis, shook his fist and said, "Are you really that cowardly? Chu has come from far away, and they are marching to their deaths. If we do not do battle with them soon, I am afraid that they will run away just like last time, which would be a shame."

The Marquis of Sui was entranced by his speech. He then appointed Shao Shi to stand at his right hand on the chariot and ordered Ji Liang to drive him, as he personally commanded his army into battle against Chu, drawing up in formation below Mount Qinglin. Ji Liang leaned out from the chariot in order to observe the Chu army. Then he said to the Marquis of Sui, "The Chu forces have been divided into a Left and a Right army. It is the custom in Chu to give priority to the Left, so their ruler is certainly over on that side. Their finest soldiers will be concentrated where the ruler is. I request your permission to launch an attack on the right-hand army, for if the Right is defeated, the morale of the Left will also be badly affected!"

"Hiding from the ruler of Chu and not attacking him—aren't you afraid that Chu is going to laugh at you?" Shao Shi sneered.

The Marquis of Sui then followed his advice and advanced to attack the Chu army of the Left first. Chu opened up its formations in order to allow the Sui army forward, and as the Marquis of Sui advanced, killing the soldiers in his path, the troops that Chu had placed in ambush on all four sides rose up—every single one of them fierce and cruel, each of them strong and brave. Shao Shi crossed swords with the Chu general, Dou Dan, but before they had even fought ten bouts, he had been beheaded by Dou Dan and his body fell below the wheels of the chariot. Ji Liang fought as hard as he could to protect the Marquis of Sui, but the Chu forces would not back down. The Marquis of Sui abandoned his battle chariot and took off all his insignia so that he could mix unnoticed with the ordinary soldiers. Ji Liang cut a bloody swath through the enemy forces, breaking through several encirclements. When he counted up the remaining officers and men, he realized that only three or four out of every ten had survived.

The Marquis of Sui said to Ji Liang, "It is because I did not listen to you that things have come to this pass!" Then he asked, "Where is Shao Shi?"

One of the soldiers had seen the way that he died and reported this to the Marquis of Sui. This saddened the Marquis of Sui very much.

"That man has brought the country to its knees," Ji Liang growled. "Why does Your Lordship regret his death? The best plan now is to ask for a peace treaty as soon as possible."

"For the sake of the country, I must listen to you," the Marquis of Sui agreed.

Ji Liang then went to the Chu army to beg for a peace treaty.

"Your lord broke the terms of the blood covenant between us and refused to attend a meeting of the states," Xiao Tong bellowed at him, "and what is more, he then led his army to attack us! Now that your army has been defeated, you ask for a peace treaty—this proves your insincerity!"

Ji Liang heard this unmoved. He came forward slowly and said: "In the past, a wicked minister, Shao Shi, took advantage of our ruler's partiality for him to force him to mobilize the army, since he was greedy for rewards—this was not in fact our lord's idea. Now Shao Shi is dead and our lord is fully aware of the crime that he has committed against you, so he has sent me to kowtow below your battle standard. If Your Lordship pardons him, then he will lead all the rulers and chiefs of the lands east of the Han River to pay court to you, which represents their submission to your authority for the rest of time. Only Your Lordship can make a decision in this matter."

"Heaven does not sanction the destruction of Sui," Dou Bobi said, "and that is why the flattering and fawning minister has been slain. Sui cannot yet be conquered. It would be better to make peace with them, let them lead the lords and chiefs of the lands east of the Han River to praise Chu's hard work and virtue to Zhou and ask permission for the title of king to be granted to you in order to impress the Man and Yi barbarian peoples. This would be most advantageous for Chu."

"Very well," Xiong Tong agreed.

Afterwards, he sent Wei Zhang to speak privately to Ji Liang as follows: "His Lordship possesses all the land around the Yangtze and the Han Rivers; he would like to assume the title of king in order to impress and control the Man and the Yi peoples. We would request your assistance to lead the Man peoples to ask permission for this from the Zhou royal house. If this request is so fortunate as to succeed, it will be because you have bestowed this glory upon His Lordship. His Lordship will rest his troops while awaiting your response."

Ji Liang went home and reported this to the Marquis of Sui. The Marquis of Sui did not dare to refuse. He went as a representative of all the aristocrats living east of the Han River to praise Chu's hard work and virtue and request that the royal house allow Chu to assume the title of king, to allow them to control the Man and Yi peoples. King Huan refused. When Xiong Tong heard this, he said angrily, "My ancestor, Yu Xiong, served the two founding kings of the Zhou dynasty with exemplary loyalty, for which he was enfeoffed in a tiny country at Jingshan, far away from the Royal Domain. Now our lands are broad and our people are numerous, all the Man and Yi peoples submit to our authority, and yet the Zhou king does not grant us a more senior title— that means rewards are not being properly apportioned! Someone from Zheng shot the king in the shoulder, and yet the king did not launch a campaign against them—that means punishments are not being properly meted out! If His Majesty can neither give rewards nor punish those who offend him, how can he be called a king? Besides which, my ancestor, Xiong Qu, declared himself king, and I am now simply restoring this old nomenclature. What has this got to do with the Zhou king?"

He promptly had himself crowned King Wu of Chu in the midst of the Central Army, made a blood covenant with the people of Sui, and went home. All the states east of the Han River sent ambassadors to congratulate him. Even though King Huan was furious with Chu, there was nothing that he could do about it. From this time onwards, the Zhou royal house became increasingly weak and the power of Chu grew.

When Xiong Tong died, the title passed to his son, Xiong Zi, who moved the capital to Ying, became ruler of all the Man peoples, and quickly built up the military capability to invade the Central States. Master Hu Zeng wrote a historical poem:

A million men were stationed between the Han and Jiang Rivers.
Just as the sky cannot have two suns, how can there be two kings?
The people of Sui were so frightened they let him get away with it,
And this turned the Central Plains into a battlefield.

. . .

Let us now turn to another part of the story. Lord Zhuang of Zheng was profoundly grateful for the Honorable Yuan's work in securing the victory over the royal army, so he sent him to guard the great city of Liyi. This was quite comparable to receiving an enfeoffment as a border lord. Each of the grandees received rewards, with only Zhu Dan being omitted. Zhu Dan spoke to Lord Zhuang about this, but all he said was, "If I reward you for shooting at the king, people will criticize me." Zhu Dan was very angry and upset, causing an abscess on his back to break open, from which he died. Lord Zhuang privately issued the reward to his family and ordered that he should be buried with all due ceremony.

In the summer of the nineteenth year of King Huan of Zhou, Lord Zhuang of Zheng became seriously ill. He summoned Zhai Zu to stand by the head of his bed and said to him: "I have eleven sons and, in addition to Scion Zihu, the Honorables Tu, Wei, and Yi are all remarkably brilliant. The Honorable Tu seems to be cleverer and luckier than the other three, but none of them have the look of those who will die in their beds. I would like to change the succession in favor of Tu. What do you think?"

"Lady Man of Deng is your principal wife, and that makes Scion Zihu your legitimate heir," Zhai Zu replied. "He has held this position for a long time, and what is more, he has repeatedly done great things for the country—the people trust him and have given their allegiance to him. I cannot accept your order to dismiss your rightful heir in favor of a concubine's son."

"Tu's ambitions will not be satisfied with a subordinate position," Lord Zhuang pointed out. "If Zihu is to be established, the only way to secure the succession is to send the Honorable Tu to live abroad with his mother's family."

"No one knows a son as well as his parents," Zhai Zu said. "You had better give orders to this effect."

"Zheng will suffer a great deal of trouble from my children!" Lord Zhuang proclaimed. Afterwards, he sent the Honorable Tu to live in Song. In the fifth month, Lord Zhuang died and Scion Zihu was established as Lord Zhao of Zheng. He sent his grandees on embassies to various other countries and Zhai Zu was sent to Song, with instructions to see if the Honorable Tu was up to mischief.

The Honorable Tu's mother was a daughter of the Yong family of Song: her name was Lady Yong Ji. The Yong clan was a noble family that had provided Song with numerous officials, and Lord Zhuang of Song was very fond of them and employed them to fill a number of important posts. When the Honorable Tu was sent to live in Song, he missed his mother, Lady Yong Ji, very much and discussed with the Yong family his plans for how to return to Zheng. The Yong family reported this to the Duke of Song, who agreed to help them. When Zhai Zu arrived in Song at his embassy, the Duke of Song said happily, "The only person who can make it possible for the Honorable Tu to go home is Zhai Zu."

He ordered Nangong Changwan to set an ambush in the palace and wait until Zhai Zu entered the court. Once the ceremonies were completed, the armed soldiers rushed out and arrested Zhai Zu.

"What have I done wrong?" Zhai Zu shouted.

"We will discuss that in the arsenal," the Duke of Song replied.

Zhai Zu was then imprisoned in the arsenal, surrounded by armed guards. He was held completely incommunicado and was terrified to the point where he could no longer sit still. That evening the prime minister, Hua Du, went in person to the arsenal, carrying a bottle of wine, which made Zhai Zu feel even more frightened.

"His Lordship sent me on an embassy to reaffirm the good relationship existing between our two countries," Zhai Zu said. "I have had no opportunity to offend you. What has happened to anger you so much? Was there some problem with the ceremonial gifts that my lord offered you? Or did I fail to carry out my duties properly?"

"None of these things," Hua Du replied. "As everyone knows, the Honorable Tu is a descendant of the Yong family. Now he is living as a miserable exile in Song, which has made our ruler extremely unhappy. Besides which, Scion Zihu is a weak and feeble man, unsuitable to hold the position of ruler. If you could depose him, then my lord is happy to offer a marriage alliance between your family and the Song ruling house. I hope you will consider this offer seriously!"

"His Lordship was established by his late father's command," Zhai Zu pointed out. "If I were now to depose him, would not the other aristocrats punish me for committing a serious crime?"

"Lady Ji of Yong was much favored by the late Lord of Zheng, and sons are often ennobled because of their mothers," Hua Du assured him. "What is wrong with that? Besides, what country has escaped from assassinations and usurpations? The only thing that matters is power. If you have that, who will punish you?" Then he leaned forward and whispered in Zhai Zu's ear: "My lord was installed as duke as a result of the previous ruler having being deposed. You have no choice but to do as he says. As long as my lord is in power, everything will be forgiven."

Zhai Zu frowned and did not reply. Hua Du then continued: "If you refuse to do as we say, His Lordship will command Nangong Changwan to lead a force of six hundred chariots to install the Honorable Tu in Zheng by force. The day that the army sets out, you will be beheaded in front of the troops. This is then the last time that I will ever see you!"

Zhai Zu was absolutely terrified and could only agree. Hua Du demanded that he swear a solemn oath.

"If I do not establish the Honorable Tu, may the Bright Spirits kill me!" Zhai Zu muttered.

A historian wrote a poem criticizing Zhai Zu:

A man should not be moved by either favoritism or humiliation.
How could a senior minister have been threatened like this?
If as a loyal subject he had been resolute in his refusal,
The people of Song would not necessarily have killed him.

That very night, Hua Du went back to report to the Lord of Song: "From now on, Zhai Zu will do as we say!"

The following day, the ruler of Song sent someone to summon the Honorable Tu to a secret chamber, where he told him: "I have agreed to the Yong family's request to help get you back home. Now the state of Zheng has announced that they have established a new ruler, and they have sent me a secret message to say, 'If you kill the Honorable Tu, we will give you three cities as a thanks offering.' I cannot bear to do this, and that is why I am telling you this in secret."

The Honorable Tu bowed and said, "I have been very unfortunate, and so I have come to your country in exile. It is up to you whether I live or die. If, thanks to your help, I am able to see the ancestral temples of our former lords again, I will do whatever you want! You will receive a much greater reward from me than just three cities!"

"It is for your sake that I have imprisoned Zhai Zu in the arsenal," the Duke of Song informed him. "This is such an important matter that we will have to have his help to accomplish it. I am going to make a blood covenant with him."

He then summoned Zhai Zu and brought him face-to-face with the Honorable Tu; he also summoned the Yong family and explained that they were going to depose Zihu and establish the Honorable Tu. The three men then smeared their mouths with blood as they made the covenant. The Duke of Song naturally acted as the master of the covenant, and Prime Minister Hua Du officiated over the ceremonies. His Lordship also made the Honorable Tu swear an agreement with him, whereby in thanks for his assistance he would give him not only the three cities, but also one hundred pairs of white jade bi-discs, ten thousand ingots of gold, and an annual levy of thirty thousand bushels of grain. Zhai Zu signed his name to this as a witness. The Honorable Tu was so desperate to become the ruler of Zheng that he would have agreed to anything. The Duke of Song demanded that the Honorable Tu turn the government of the state over to Zhai Zu, and he agreed to that also. Having heard that Zhai Zu had a daughter, he asked that she should be given in marriage to Yong Jiu, a son of the Yong family. Yong Jiu would therefore go with them to Zheng for the marriage ceremony, and he was to be appointed to the office of a grandee. Zhai Zu did not dare to refuse.

The Honorable Tu and Yong Jiu both put on plain clothes, dressing up as merchants. They rode on a chariot behind Zhai Zu, arriving in Zheng on the first day of the ninth month and hiding themselves in his house. Zhai Zu pretended that he was ill and hence was unable to go to court, and the grandees all came to his house to ask after his health. Zhai Zu concealed one hundred warriors behind the tapestries lining the walls of his house, and then he invited the grandees into the room to see him. When they saw that Zhai Zu looked perfectly healthy, his gown and official hat on straight, they said in amazement, "You are obviously perfectly well, so why don't you go to court?"

"It is not me that is ill—it is the country that is sick," Zhai Zu told them. "Our former ruler loved and favored the Honorable Tu, entrusting him to the care of the Duke of Song. Now Song is going to appoint Nangong Changwan as general to lead a force of six hundred chariots to attack Zheng in support of the Honorable Tu's pretentions. Zheng has not yet stabilized after the change of ruler, so how can we resist them?"

The grandees looked at each other in consternation, and none of them dared to respond. Zhai Zu continued: "If we want to make the Song army go away, we will have to depose our lord. The Honorable Tu is here, and the whole thing can be resolved by a single word from you: yes or no!"

Gao Qumi had never liked Scion Zihu after he discovered that it was thanks to his remonstrance that he had not been appointed to the office of a senior minister, so he now stepped forward. Brandishing his sword, he proclaimed, "Your words bring a blessing on the state altars. We are willing to follow a new lord!"

The others heard what Gao Qumi said and suspected that this was all prearranged with Zhai Zu. They had also realized that there were people hidden behind the tapestries, so, terrified and trembling, they all voiced their agreement. Zhai Zu then called to the Honorable Tu to come out and made him sit in the seat of honor. Zhai Zu and Gao Qumi were the first to come forward and bow to him. There was nothing that the grandees could do; they too had to prostrate themselves on the ground in front of him. Zhai Zu had already written out a document to which all their names were attached, and this was now forwarded to Lord Zhao of Zheng. It read:

> Song had installed the Honorable Tu by force, and we have no choice but to serve him.

To this missive he added another, secret letter, which said:

> Your appointment was not in fact our former ruler's intention, but I insisted that it be done. Now Song has imprisoned me, installed the Honorable Tu by force, and demanded that I make a blood covenant with them. I was afraid that if I died, it would not help you at all, so I pretended to agree to this. Now their troops have arrived in the suburbs and your ministers have been so thoroughly terrified by this display of force from Song that they have joined this conspiracy and will go and welcome them. My lord, you had better accept this situation and go into exile temporarily, allowing me to take advantage of developments in the situation to plot for a restoration.

At the bottom of this letter, Zhai Zu had appended an oath: "If I fail, may Heaven punish me!"

When Lord Zhao of Zheng received the document signed by his ministers and this secret letter enclosed with it, he realized that his position was impossible and that he had nowhere to turn, so he said a tearful farewell to his wife, Lady Gui, and fled to the state of Wey.

On Jihai day in the ninth month, Zhai Zu installed the Honorable Tu, who took the title of Lord Li of Zheng. All government matters, whether major or minor, were entrusted to Zhai Zu. He married his daughter to Yong Jiu, and she became Lady Ji of Yong. Lord Li then appointed Yong Jiu to the office of grandee. The Yong clan was Lord Li's maternal relatives; when Lord Li was living in Song he had become very close to them, as a result of which he trusted and favored Yong Jiu no less than Zhai Zu.

When Lord Li assumed the earldom, the people of the state all submitted to his authority, and there was no civil unrest. The only people who were unhappy about this development were the Honorables Wei and Yi, because they were afraid that Lord Li would murder them. Therefore, that month the Honorable Wei fled to Cai, while the Honorable Yi fled to Chen.

When the Duke of Song heard that the Honorable Tu had been established, he sent someone with a letter of congratulation. Eventually this resulted in the two countries going to war, so READ ON.

Chapter Eleven

Lord Zhuang of Song, being greedy for
bribes, brings disaster upon his army.

Zhai Zu of Zheng murders his son-in-law
and forces his lord into exile.

Lord Zhuang of Song sent someone to Zheng with a letter of congratulation and demanded the three cities, together with the white jade discs,
gold, annual tribute of grain and so on. Lord Li summoned Zhai Zu to
discuss the matter with him.

"Originally I was so desperate to obtain possession of the state that
I agreed to all his demands and did not dare to disobey his orders,"
Lord Li said. "Now, however, I have succeeded to the title, and he comes
to insist upon repayment of the debt. If I do what he says, the storehouses and treasuries will be empty. Besides which, I have only recently
taken the title, so if I were to lose three cities, would I not become a
laughingstock among my neighbors?"

"You could refuse," Zhai Zu suggested. "Tell him: 'The populace has
not yet been pacified, and I am afraid that partitioning my territory will
cause civil unrest. However, I am willing to give the tribute and tax
revenue from the three cities to Song in perpetuity.' Give him one third
of the white jade discs and the gold that you promised, and apologize as
nicely as you can. As for the annual tribute of grain, ask permission to
begin next year."

Lord Li followed his advice and wrote a letter to report that he had
collected thirty pairs of white jade bi-discs and three thousand ingots of
gold, which he would present immediately, while the tax revenue from
the three cities he proposed to hand over at the beginning of winter. When
the ambassador went back to report this development, Lord Zhuang of

Song was extremely angry. "Tu was dead and I gave him life!" he shouted. "Tu was poor and I made him rich and noble! Everything that he agreed to give me originally belonged to Zihu and had nothing to do with Tu at all! How dare he refuse to hand over these things!"

That very day he sent an envoy back to Zheng to repeat his demands that he be given the quantities originally specified. Furthermore, he insisted that ownership of the three cities be transferred immediately, since he would not accept merely the tax revenue. Lord Li and Zhai Zu discussed this, and then presented him with a further twenty thousand bushels of grain. The Song ambassador collected this, but when came back again, he was armed with the following message:

> If you do not hand over the full amount as agreed, then you must send Zhai Zu to explain the situation in person.

"Song received great assistance from your late father, which they have not done the slightest thing to repay," Zhai Zu told Lord Li. "Now they are taking advantage of the fact that they assisted you to succeed to the title to make outrageous demands, and what is more, they are not even pretending to be polite in their messages. Do not listen to them! I ask your permission to send ambassadors to Qi and Lu to request that they intercede on our behalf."

"Will Qi and Lu be willing to help Zheng?" Lord Li asked.

"In the past His Late Lordship attacked Xu and Song with the assistance of Qi and Lu," Zhai Zu explained. "Besides which, the Marquis of Lu owes his title to your father. Even if Qi is not prepared to help us, Lu cannot refuse."

"What is your strategy for a tactful intercession?" inquired Lord Li.

"When Hua Du assassinated his ruler and established the Honorable Ping, our lord received bribes together with Qi and Lu: treasure sealed the deal," Zhai Zu reminded him. "Lu received the great bronze tripod from Hao, while we got a Shang dynasty libation vessel. If we inform Qi and Lu about the situation and hand the Shang vessel back to Song, then the Duke of Song will remember what we have done for him and, feeling ashamed, he will stop of his own accord."

Lord Li was thrilled and said, "Listening to your words is like waking from a nightmare."

Immediately he sent an ambassador charged with gifts and money to go to each of the two states of Qi and Lu, where they were to announce the establishment of a new ruler in Zheng and to make known that Song had forgotten all the kindness that it had received and was behaving in a most unpleasant way, constantly extorting money. When the ambassador who went to Lu passed this message on, Lord Huan of Lu laughed and said, "In the past when the ruler of Song sent gifts to us, it was just a single bronze tripod. Now he has obtained so much from Zheng, when will he be satisfied? I accept the mission and I will personally go to Song straight away to get your ruler out of this difficulty." The ambassador thanked him and took his leave.

The ambassador who went to Qi to transmit this message discovered that Lord Xi of Qi had only the fondest memories of Scion Zihu thanks to his success in defeating the Rong. Because of this he had offered him the hand of his daughter, Lady Wen Jiang, in marriage. Even though Zihu had always firmly refused, at the bottom of the Marquis of Qi's heart he retained very friendly feelings towards him. Now the state of Zheng had set aside Zihu's claims in order to establish Tu, so the Marquis of Qi was naturally extremely unhappy. He said to the ambassador, "What crime did the Lord of Zheng commit that you deposed him? Ruling you people must be very difficult! I am going to lead the other feudal lords to punish you!" He would accept neither the gifts nor the money.

When the ambassador reported this to Lord Li, he was very alarmed and said to Zhai Zu, "If the Marquis of Qi blames us for what happened, this is sure to lead to open warfare. What can I do to prevent this?"

"I ask your permission to muster the army and gather our chariots in readiness," Zhai Zu said. "When the enemy arrives, we can deal with them. What is there to be frightened of?"

Lord Huan of Lu sent the Honorable Rou to Song, and he arrived for the meeting at the appointed time. Lord Zhuang of Song said, "The Lord of Lu wants to make an alliance with us, so I will go in person to the border with Lu. How could I put him to the trouble of coming all this way?"

The Honorable Rou returned to transmit this message. The Marquis of Lu then sent another envoy to set a date to meet in the lands of Zhuo, at a place named Fuzhong. This happened in the ninth month, in the autumn of the twentieth year of the reign of King Huan of Zhou.

. . .

Lord Zhuang of Song and the Marquis of Lu met at Fuzhong. The Marquis of Lu apologized on Zheng's behalf and asked for clemency. The Duke of Song said, "I have behaved with much generosity towards the Lord of Zheng! He was like an egg that I warmed in my nest. Now he has returned to his state and succeeded to the title, so immediately he tries to renege on his agreement. If not for this egregious insult, how could I set aside all that I owe to his father?"

"Surely Zheng cannot have forgotten what Your Lordship has done for them?" the Marquis of Lu said. "But His Lordship has not been long in office, and the storehouses and treasuries are empty. Although right at this moment it is impossible for him to fulfill his treaty obliga-tions, it is only a matter of time. He is certainly not going to go back on his word—that I can assure you!"

"If the storehouses and treasuries are indeed bare, then I can forget about the jade and the gold, but handing over the three cities can be done with a word," the Duke of Song said. "Why can't this be resolved immediately?"

"The Lord of Zheng is afraid that if he does not preserve the legacy of his ancestors intact, he will become a laughingstock among the feu-dal lords," the Marquis of Lu reminded him. "That is why he wants to give you the tax revenue instead. I have heard that he has already col-lected ten thousand bushels of grain!"

"He has already agreed to give me twenty thousand bushels of grain annually," the Duke of Song argued, "and that is a completely separate issue from the three cities. He has not even given me half of what he promised. If that is the situation now, what can I expect in the future, when the dust has settled? Your Lordship is the only person who can resolve this situation now."

The Marquis of Lu now realized that the Duke of Song was unwilling to make even the smallest concession, so he gave up unhappily.

Once the Marquis of Lu had returned to his country, he sent the Honorable Rou as an envoy to Zheng, to tell them that the Duke of Song was not willing to compromise. The Earl of Zheng then sent Gran-dee Yong Jiu to present the Shang libation vessel to the Marquis of Lu with the following words: "This is a treasure of the state of Song that I do not dare to keep any longer. Please return it to the Song treasuries instead of the three cities. I also present thirty pairs of white jade discs and two thousand ingots of gold. I beg Your Lordship to speak up for us and get us out of this situation!"

Lord Huan of Lu felt that he had no choice but to go in person to the state of Song. He agreed to meet the Duke of Song at Guqiu. When the two lords had completed the formal ceremony of greeting each other, the Marquis of Lu explained that the Earl of Zheng was very unhappy about the situation and presented the white jade discs and the gold.

"Your Lordship mentioned that you have not even received half of what Zheng promised to give you," the Marquis of Lu said. "I told Zheng that this was unacceptable, and they have now done their very best to meet your demands."

The Duke of Song did not even say thank you, but asked, "When will they hand over the three cities?"

"The Lord of Zheng is deeply aware of his duties towards his inheritance from his ancestors, and therefore he feels it unacceptable to change the present borders to repay a private debt of honor," the Marquis of Lu said. "Instead, he presents you with a gift of equal value."

He ordered his entourage to hold up high an object wrapped in a yellow brocade carrying cloth. Kneeling down, they presented it to the Duke of Song. When the Duke of Song heard the words "private debt of honor," his brow wrinkled in a frown and he appeared displeased. When he opened the bundle and looked at it, he realized that this was the Shang dynasty bronze vessel that had once been presented by the state of Song to Zheng, and he suddenly looked very uncomfortable. However, he pretended not to recognize the object, and asked, "What is all this?"

"This was once a national treasure of your great state," the Marquis of Lu reminded him. "When the late Lord Zhuang of Zheng rendered such signal service to you, your state rewarded him with this valuable object. It was preserved as a treasure for many years by the dukes of Song, and hence the present Lord of Zheng does not dare to keep it for himself, but returns it to you. He hopes that you will remember the good relationship that you enjoyed in the past and decide not to partition his state. The late ruler of Zheng was the person you wanted to reward, not his descendants!"

When the Duke of Song was reminded of this history, he blushed and said, "I had forgotten all about that. I will go home and ask the treasury about this matter."

Just as they were in the middle of their discussions, a report suddenly arrived: "The Earl of Yan wishes to pay court to Song, and he has already arrived at Guqiu."

The Duke of Song invited the Earl of Yan to meet the Marquis of Lu. When the Earl of Yan had an audience with the Duke of Song, he informed him: "My lands border on the state of Qi, which regularly invades my territory. I am hoping that Your Lordship will do your best to persuade Qi to accept a peace treaty that will preserve my state altars intact." The Duke of Song agreed to do this.

The Marquis of Lu said to the Duke of Song, "Qi and Ji have been at daggers-drawn for generations, and they are always launching surprise attacks on Ji. If Your Lordship is going to ask for a peace treaty on behalf of Yan, then I will speak up for Ji, so that both of them can be left in peace and we can avoid open warfare."

The three lords swore a blood covenant at Guqiu together. Lord Huan of Lu returned to his state, and for the whole of that autumn and winter he heard nothing from Song.

Meanwhile, the state of Zheng received a constant stream of envoys from Song demanding money, so yet again they sent an envoy to beg the Marquis of Lu for assistance. The only thing that the Marquis of Lu could do was to arrange to meet the Duke of Song between Xu and Gui, in the hope of finally sorting out Zheng's problems. The Duke of Song did not turn up, but instead sent a messenger to report to Lu: "My lord has an agreement with Zheng. There is no need for Your Lordship to interfere."

The Marquis of Lu was furious and swore: "It is not acceptable for an ordinary member of the public to be so greedy and unreliable, let alone the lord of a state!"

He then turned his chariot towards Zheng and met the Earl of Zheng at Wufu, where they agreed upon a plan for a joint attack upon Song. A bearded old man wrote a poem about this:

Wicked men forced Zihu of Zheng into exile and assassinated Yin of Lu.
Having been rescued from similar disasters, they sympathized with one
    another.
It is because Lord Zhuang of Song was so greedy and demanding,
He simply forced Lu and Zheng to go to war.

Lord Zhuang of Song heard that the Marquis of Lu was furious with him, and he calculated that they would not be able to stay at peace much longer. However, he also heard that the Marquis of Qi was unwilling to help Tu, so he sent the Honorable You to Qi to make a peace treaty, while informing him of how badly Tu had behaved: "I really regret the whole thing. I am happy to join you in an attack on Tu that will restore the former ruler, Zihu, to the title. At the same time, I request that you make a peace treaty with the Earl of Yan."

Before the messenger had returned, Song border officials reported: "The two states of Lu and Zheng have raised armies to attack us. Their vanguards are extremely strong, and they have already begun to approach Suiyang."

The Duke of Song was terribly alarmed by this development, and he summoned all his grandees to discuss how to deal with the enemy. The Honorable Yushuo remonstrated with him: "The strength of an army depends on whether they are in the right or not. We have been trying to extort wealth from Zheng and we have broken faith with Lu, so they have everything in their favor. It would be better to apologize for your mistakes and ask for a peace treaty, so that we do not have to fight. That is the very best plan!"

"Their troops are at our gates," Nangong Changwan said. "If we plead for mercy before even a single shot has been fired, it will show our weakness. How can we keep the country together under those circumstances?"

"Changwan is right!" Prime Minister Hua Du exclaimed.

The Duke of Song then paid no attention to what the Honorable Yushuo had said, but gave orders that Nangong Changwan should be invested as general. Changwan recommended that Meng Huo should take command of the vanguard, and he left the city at the head of a force of three hundred chariots, divided into two lines to make a show of strength. The Marquis of Lu and the Earl of Zheng were both present in person, and they halted their chariots in front of their battle formations. The pair of them were determined to provoke battle with the Duke of Song. The Duke of Song was feeling ashamed of himself and claimed that he was too ill to leave the city.

Nangong Changwan could see two embroidered baldachins in the distance, and he knew these covered the rulers of the two states. He then clapped Meng Huo on the shoulder and said, "If you don't win a great victory today, you never will!"

Meng Huo responded to this by grasping hold of his iron lance and signaling for a frontal assault. The lords of Lu and Zheng saw how fierce the attack was, and retreated their chariots a step or two. To left and right they each selected a senior general to respond. Lu sent out the Honorable Ni and Zheng sent out Yuan Fan, each riding on an armored chariot. First they asked his name, and he replied: "I am Meng Huo from the vanguard."

Yuan Fan laughed and said, "An anonymous little soldier is not worth soiling my sword with. Send out a real general so that I can kill him!"

Meng Huo was absolutely furious. Lifting his spear, he aimed it straight at Yuan Fan. Yuan Fan parried it with his sword. The Honorable Ni then led out the Lu army, and his armored soldiers stood in serried ranks. Meng Huo did battle with the two generals without any sign of being overawed. The Viscount of Qin and the Viscount of Liang, who were serving as generals in the Lu army, now joined in, along with the Earl of Tan, a general in the Zheng army. Meng Huo was severely outnumbered, and he was shot in the right shoulder by the Viscount of Liang. He could no longer hold his spear and was taken prisoner. The officers and chariots under his command were then all captured; only about fifty foot soldiers were able to escape.

When Nangong Changwan heard about this defeat, he ground his teeth with rage: "If I don't recapture Meng Huo, how can I ever go home?" Then he ordered his oldest son, Nangong Niu, to take thirty chariots out to provoke battle. "You must pretend to be defeated and trick the enemy armies into pursuing you towards the West Gate. I have a plan to deal with them." Nangong Niu agreed and left.

He shouted out above the crossed halberds: "Tu of Zheng is a bastard who betrays all his friends! You are just going to get yourself killed! Why don't you simply surrender?"

General Zhu Dan of Zheng, with a cohort of bowmen, emerged from the ranks in a single chariot. Completely underestimating Nangong Niu on the grounds of his youth, they attacked him willy-nilly. After crossing swords a couple of times, Nangong Niu turned his chariot and fled. Zhu Dan did not want to let him escape, so he set off in pursuit. When they arrived at the West Gate, there was a great sound of siege engines. Nangong Changwan held the rear while his son turned his chariot around, and the two of them attacked in unison. Zhu Dan shot off a few arrows in the direction of Nangong Niu, but they did not hit him. He then started to panic, so when Nangong Changwan jumped into his chariot, he held out his hands to allow them to be bound.

When the senior Zheng general, Yuan Fan, heard that Zhu Dan had gone off to meet the enemy alone, he became worried that something might have gone wrong, so he set off in a hurry with the Earl of Tan and his auxiliaries. They arrived just in time to see the gates of the Song capital opened wide, as Chancellor Hua Du personally led a great host out of the city to help. He was met by the Lu general, the Honorable Ni, along with the Viscount of Qin and the Viscount of Liang. Battle raged between the two sides with unspeakable savagery, and they carried on killing until cockcrow the next morning. The Song army suffered terrible casualties. Nangong Changwan presented his captive, Zhu Dan, and asked permission from the Duke of Song to go to the Zheng camp and exchange him for Meng Huo. His Lordship agreed to this.

When the Song ambassador arrived at the Zheng camp, he explained the idea of an exchange. The Earl of Zheng agreed, and then both generals were carried out in cages in front of their assembled armies and the exchange was made. Zhu Dan returned to the Zheng camp, and Meng Huo went home to Song. On this day, both sides rested and no more battles were joined.

Meanwhile, the Honorable You of Song traveled to Qi to present his credentials. Lord Xi of Qi was perfectly happy to assist: "The Honorable Tu of Zheng threw out his older brother to usurp the title, which I consider to be downright wicked. Right now, however, I have business in Ji and I do not have the leisure to attend to this. If Song is willing to send an army to assist me in the attack on Ji, how would I dare to refuse to help you in your attack on Zheng?"

The Honorable You said goodbye to the Marquis of Qi and went back to report to the Duke of Song.

Just as the Marquis of Lu and the Earl of Zheng were in camp, discussing their plan to attack Song, they suddenly got the report that someone had come from the state of Ji to announce an emergency. The Marquis of Lu summoned him, and he presented him with a letter that read:

> The Qi army has attacked Ji, and things have reached a most critical state; ruin stares us in the face. I beg that you remember the marriage alliance between us and the many generations of peace and come at once to save us from disaster!

Lord Huan of Lu was deeply shocked and told the Earl of Zheng: "The Lord of Ji reports an emergency, so I will have to go to his assistance. We cannot take this city any time soon, so I think it would be best if you stood down your army. I reckon that the Duke of Song will not dare to try and extort anything from you again!"

"Since you are going to take your troops to rescue Ji, I would like to lead my humble forces in support!" Lord Li of Zheng proclaimed.

The Marquis of Lu was very pleased. He immediately gave orders to dismantle the stockade, and they set out together in the direction of the state of Ji. The Marquis of Lu first advanced thirty li, while the Earl of Zheng moved his army into position to protect his rear.

Song first got the report from the Honorable You, and subsequently heard that the enemy was on the move, but they were afraid that this was some kind of bait to entice their army into a trap, so they did not dare to set out in pursuit but sent spies out to find out what was going on. These agents now reported: "The enemy has withdrawn completely beyond our borders. They are on their way to the state of Ji." It was at this point that they could relax.

Chancellor Hua Du presented his opinion: "Qi agreed to help us make an attack on Zheng, so we ought to assist them in their attack on Ji."

"I am happy to go," Nangong Changwan announced.

The Duke of Song sent him out in command of an army of two hundred chariots and ordered Meng Huo to lead the vanguard. They traveled day and night to the assistance of Qi.

Lord Xi of Qi had agreed to meet the Marquis of Wey, and they planned to launch a joint attack on Ji, with the forces of Yan. Wey was just about to mobilize its army when Lord Xuan suddenly became seriously ill and died. His son and heir, Shuo, then succeeded to the title as Lord Hui. Even though Lord Hui was in mourning, he did not dare to withdraw from the campaign, so he led a force of two hundred chariots in support. The Earl of Yan was afraid of being swallowed up by Qi, so he wanted to take advantage of this situation to make a peace treaty. He personally led his forces out to join the others. The Marquis of Ji saw how many troops these three states could command and did not dare come out to do battle, but prepared to sit out a siege behind his deep moats and high walls. Suddenly one day, he received a message: "The two lords of Zheng and Lu have arrived to rescue Ji." The Marquis of Ji climbed the city walls to have a look. He felt like a man who had just been reprieved from hanging.

The Marquis of Lu was the first to arrive, and he met the Marquis of Qi in front of the army.

"My humble state has contracted marriage alliances with Ji for many generations," he said, "so when I heard that they had annoyed you, I came in person to beg you to forgive them."

"My ancestor, Lord Ai, was slandered by Ji, and as a result he was boiled alive by the king of Zhou," the Marquis of Qi complained. "Although this happened eight generations ago, this crime has not been avenged. You can help your relatives, I can avenge myself on my enemies, but today must end in a battle!"

The Marquis of Lu was furious and ordered the Honorable Ni to come forward on his chariot. Qi then sent the Honorable Pengsheng to attack him. Pengsheng was a match for ten thousand men, so how could the Honorable Ni withstand his onslaught? The Viscount of Qin and the Viscount of Liang both came forward, but even so they were not able to defeat him. All they could do was fight one another to a standstill. The two lords of Wey and Yan saw that Qi and Lu had joined battle and advanced to attack. The rearguard—the great army of the Earl of Zheng—had by now arrived. Yuan Fan led the Earl of Tan and his troops in a direct assault on the Marquis of Qi's main camp. The Marquis of Ji sent his younger brother, Ying Ji, to lead the army out of the city walls in support, with a great battle cry that shook the heavens. The Honorable Pengsheng did not dare to fight any more, but turned his chariot back as quickly as he could. The armies of six states then butchered each other.

The Marquis of Lu happened across the Earl of Yan and said: "The three states of Song, Lu, and Yan swore a covenant at Guqiu. The blood is not yet dry on our mouths, and Song has already broken the covenant—that is why I have attacked them. You are well aware of what Song has done, but you only seem to care about keeping good relations with Qi. Surely this is not a long-term plan for ensuring the security of your state?"

The Earl of Yan knew that he had not kept faith, so he hung his head as he slunk off, with the excuse that his army had been defeated and was running away. Wey did not have a senior general in command, and so its army was the first to crumble. The army led by the Marquis of Qi was also defeated and massacred, so that bodies lay strewn across the field and blood flowed like a river. Pengsheng was struck by several arrows and almost died. Just at this critical juncture the troops sent by the state of Song arrived, so Lu and Zheng were able to collect their forces.

Master Hu Zeng wrote a historical poem about this:

> Bullying the weak for your own greedy purposes,
> Thinking that a single city would be easily overturned.
> Before a single other state was destroyed, you had already been
>   defeated,
> Causing a thousand generations to laugh at the Marquis of Qi!

The Song army had arrived but had no time to rest before Lu and Zheng launched a surprise assault. The Song troops were not even able to make camp—they suffered a terrible defeat and had to withdraw. Each state then collected the remains of its army and returned to its own country. The Marquis of Qi turned his head to look at the walls of Ji and swore an oath: "Either Ji goes or I do; the two of us cannot share the same sky!"

The Marquis of Ji welcomed the lords of Lu and Zheng into his city and held a great banquet for them, while also issuing generous rewards to all the army officers.

Ying Ji came forward and said, "The Qi forces have failed, but this will only deepen their hated of Ji. Today with Your Lordships present, I hope that you will agree to a plan to guarantee our security."

"At present I have no idea how to do so," the Marquis of Lu informed him. "I will have to think of something."

The following day, the Marquis of Ji escorted them thirty *li* outside the city and cried when he said goodbye to them.

After the Marquis of Lu returned home, Lord Li of Zheng again sent an envoy asking for a peace treaty, to reaffirm the blood covenant made at Wufu. From this time on, Lu and Zheng formed one faction, and Song and Qi another. Just at this time the Honorable Yuan, Grandee of Zheng, died at Yue. Zhai Zu presented his opinion to Lord Li that the Earl of Tan should take over his duties. This happened in the twenty-second year of the reign of King Huan of Zhou.

Lord Xi of Qi was so angry about the defeat of his troops at Ji that he became unwell. That winter he became critically ill and summoned his heir, Zhuer, to his bedside, where he instructed him: "Ji has been our enemy for many generations. If you destroy Ji, then you are a filial son. When you succeed to the title, this must be the first thing that you do. If you cannot avenge me, do not enter my shrine!" Zhuer kowtowed and accepted the mission.

Afterwards, Lord Xi summoned Yi Zhongnian's son, Noble Grandson Wuzhi, and ordered him to bow to Zhuer. He instructed the latter: "This is my younger brother's only child, and I hope that you will look after him. You should let him keep the rank and emoluments that I have given him."

When he finished speaking, his eyes closed in death. The grandees helped Scion Zhuer through the mourning ceremonies and then installed him as Lord Xiang.

. . .

The hatred Lord Zhuang of Song felt for Zheng was etched into his bones, so again he sent out ambassadors armed with the gold and jade that he had taken from Zheng and bribed the four states of Qi, Cai, Wey, and Chen, begging them for troops with which he could take his revenge. Qi, though engaged in national mourning, sent Grandee Yong Lin in command of one hundred and fifty chariots to assist in the campaign. Cai and Wey also sent generals to attack Zheng in concert with Song. Lord Li of Zheng wanted to do battle, but his senior minister Zhai Zu warned him: "No! No! Song is a great state and they have raised an army large enough to raze our country to the ground. They have come in the sure and certain knowledge that they can defeat us. If we do battle, we will be at a serious disadvantage and the state altars will be in danger. Even if by some miracle we win, we will have made them our enemies for many generations to come and in future we will know no peace. It would be better to let them do what they want."

Lord Li vacillated and could not make up his mind. Zhai Zu issued an order that the common people should prepare to defend the city walls: "Anyone who tries to start a fight will be executed!"

When the Duke of Song saw that the Zheng army had not appeared, he sacked the eastern suburbs. They attacked and set fire to the Qu Gate and destroyed it; then they proceeded along the main highway and captured the great ancestral shrine. They stole all the great beams and took them home, where they were used to build the Lu Gate to the Song capital. This was intended as a form of humiliation.

The Earl of Zheng became very depressed. He sighed and said, "I am completely under Zhai Zu's control, so where is the fun in being the lord?"

The following year, in the third month of spring, King Huan of Zhou became critically ill. He summoned Heijian, Duke of Zhou, to his bedside and said, "It is ritually correct to select the eldest son of your principal wife when establishing an heir. However, I have always been very fond of my second son, Prince Ke, and today I entrust him to your care. If in the future his older brother dies and he comes to the throne, you are the only person who can support him." When he finished saying this, he died.

The Duke of Zhou accepted his commands and enthroned Crown Prince Tuo. He took the title of King Zhuang.

When Lord Li of Zheng heard that national mourning had been declared in Zhou, he wanted to send an ambassador to express his condolences.

Zhai Zu remonstrated resolutely: "Your father was an enemy of Zhou, and Zhu Dan shot the king in the shoulder. If you send someone to express condolences, they will take it that you are trying to humiliate them."

Although Lord Li followed his advice, in his heart he was increasingly angry.

One day he was traveling around his outer hunting park, accompanied only by Grandee Yong Jiu. Lord Li caught sight of a bird soaring up into the sky and singing, and he sighed bitterly.

Yong Jiu came forward and said, "It is spring and the weather is becoming warm, so all the birds are happy. You, my lord, are ranked among the aristocrats, and yet you seem to be unhappy. Why is this?"

"Birds are free to fly about and sing," Lord Li said. "They are not under anyone's control. My situation is worse than that of a bird, and that is why I am unhappy."

"Is it the man who holds the reins of power that is worrying Your Lordship?" Yong Jiu inquired.

Lord Li was silent. Then Yong Jiu remarked: "I have heard people say, 'A ruler is like a father and a subject is like a son.' A son should not cause his father to worry, for that is unfilial. A subject should not cause his ruler trouble, for that is disloyal. If Your Lordship can trust to my humble abilities, I will do my best to deal with this situation for you."

Lord Li ordered his entourage to move away and asked Yong Jiu, "Aren't you Zhai Zu's much-loved son-in-law?"

"Son-in-law yes, much-loved no," Yong Jiu told him. "My marriage with Lady Zhai was forced upon him by the Lord of Song, and such was never his intention. He speaks every day about his old ruler, of whom he is clearly still very fond. It is only because he is terrified of Song that he does not dare to plot a rebellion."

"If you can kill him," Lord Li said, "I will make a ministerial appointment a hereditary emolument of your family. However, I do not know if you have any plan to suggest."

"The eastern suburbs have been ravaged by the Song troops, and people have not yet rebuilt their houses there," Yong Jiu remarked. "Tomorrow Your Lordship should order the minister of education to commence reconstruction and instruct Zhai Zu to go there with food and clothing to succor the local people. I will then hold a banquet in the eastern suburbs in his honor and poison his wine."

"My life is in your hands, so please be very careful!" Lord Li said.

Yong Jiu returned home and met his wife, Lady Zhai. Although he was not at all aware of the fact, he looked somewhat scared. Lady Zhai was suspicious and asked, "Did something happen at court today?"

"Nothing at all," Yong Jiu informed her.

"I don't care what you say," Lady Zhai said. "I am going by your appearance, so something must have happened at court this morning. You and I are one; you should tell me what is going on, regardless of whether it is important or not."

"His Lordship wants to send your father to the eastern suburbs to succor the people, and I am going to hold a banquet there in your father's honor," Yong Jiu announced. "Nothing else happened."

"If you want to hold a banquet, why does it have to be out in the suburbs?" Lady Zhai asked.

"That was His Lordship's order. Don't ask any more questions."

Lady Zhai was more and more certain that something was terribly wrong, so she got Jiu drunk. When he was in a stupor, she asked him a cunning question: "His Lordship ordered you to kill Zhai Zu, have you forgotten?"

Jiu, half-asleep, replied thickly: "How could I dare to forget something so important?"

When he got up the following morning, Lady Zhai said to him, "You are going to murder my father. I know all about it."

"Nothing of the kind," Jiu told her.

"Yesterday you got drunk and said so yourself. Don't try to deny it!" Lady Zhai retorted.

"Well, supposing that it were true, what are you going to do about it?" Jiu asked.

"Once you get married you have to obey your husband," she said. "What more can I say?"

Yong Jiu then reported his plan in every detail to his wife.

"I am not at all sure that my father will go with you," she said. "The day before I will go home and find out what he is up to."

"When this is all over and I have taken over his position, you will share in the glory," Yong Jiu told her.

As they had planned, the day before the banquet Lady Zhai went to her father's house. She asked her mother, "Which is the closer relative, a father or a husband?"

"They are both your closest relatives."

She asked again: "But which of the two is closer?"

"A father is closer than a husband," her mother said.

"Why?" Lady Zhai inquired.

"Before a woman gets married, her husband could be anyone, but she always has her father," her mother pointed out. "After she gets married, she can always marry a second or a third time, but she can never have another father. A husband is just a man, but a father is the person who has given you life. How can a husband compare?"

Although her mother did not mean anything in particular by these words, they awoke Lady Zhai to a sense of her responsibilities. With tears streaming down her face she said, "For my father's sake, I must betray my husband!"

She secretly informed her mother about Yong Jiu's plan. Her mother was deeply shocked, and in her turn she told all to Zhai Zu.

"You don't need to say anything more," he said. "When the time comes I will deal with this."

On the appointed day Zhai Zu ordered his trusted lieutenant, Qiang Chu, to follow him in his train with a dozen or so knights, all of whom had concealed weapons about their persons. He also ordered the Honorable E to take about a hundred of his own troops out to the suburbs to prevent trouble. When Zhai Zu set out, Yong Jiu came halfway to meet him, and he had prepared a lavish banquet for him.

"With the state in such a mess, though the duties of ritual propriety cannot be entirely dispensed with, there is really no need to put yourself to all this trouble," Zhai Zu told him.

"The spring scenery outside the suburbs is very pretty, so I have prepared a little drinking party," Yong Jiu replied. As he finished speaking, he poured wine into a large goblet and then, kneeling down in front of Zhai Zu, he smiled and toasted him.

Zhai Zu pretended to reach out, but then with his right hand he grabbed hold of Yong Jiu's arm while with his left he dashed the cup to the ground. The earth bubbled and split. Then he shouted: "How dare you treat me in this way!" He screamed to his attendants: "Get him!"

Qiang Chu and the other soldiers rushed in, took Yong Jiu prisoner, and beheaded him right then and there, throwing his body into the moat. Lord Li had hidden his own men out beyond the suburbs to help Yong Jiu carry out the assassination, but they were soon discovered by the Honorable E, who cut them to pieces. When Lord Li heard this, he was appalled. "Zhai Zu will not forgive me!"

Lord Li fled to the state of Cai. Later on, someone told him that Yong Jiu had given away the plot to his wife and that was how Zhai Zu was able to make his preparations in advance. Lord Li sighed and said, "He involved a woman in matters of state. He deserved to die!"

When Zhai Zu heard that Lord Li had gone into exile, he sent Gongfu Dingshu to the state of Wey to welcome Zihu and restore him to his title of Lord Zhao of Zheng. He said, "I have kept my promise to our old ruler!"

Do you want to know what happened next? READ ON.

Chapter Twelve

Lord Xuan of Wey builds a tower to steal another man's wife.

Gao Qumi takes advantage of the situation to change rulers.

Lord Xuan of Wey had the personal name Jin. He was a debauched and unprincipled man. Before he succeeded to the title, he had an affair with one of his father's concubines, Lady Yi Jiang, and she gave birth to a son who was sent away to be brought up among the people: he took the name Jizi. When Lord Xuan inherited the title, he did not favor his principal wife, Lady Xing, but cared only for Lady Yi Jiang, who was treated as if they were actually married to each other. He wanted to install Jizi as his legitimate son and heir, and entrusted him to the care of the Honorable Zhi.

When Jizi grew up and reached the age of sixteen, a diplomatic mission was sent to Lord Xi of Qi to ask for the hand in marriage of his oldest daughter. When the ambassador returned to his country and Lord Xuan heard that the lady from Qi was extremely beautiful, he became overwhelmed with lust, but found it very difficult to express his new desires. He ordered carpenters to build a high tower overlooking the Qi River, with vermilion pillars and painted beams, great halls and lavish chambers, as magnificent as could be. This was called the New Tower. On the pretext of sending an embassy to Song, he got rid of Jizi; then he sent the Honorable Xie to Qi, to welcome Lady Jiang and take her to the New Tower. There he took her for himself: this was Lady Xuan Jiang.

People at the time composed a song about the New Tower to criticize Lord Xuan's lust and debauchery:

The New Tower is beautiful; the waters of the river run deep.
This hideous man is not good enough to wed this lovely girl.
The nets were spread for fish, but a wild goose became caught in them.
This hunchback has obtained the hand of a beautiful lady.

The terms hideous and hunchbacked refer to an ugly appearance, and they are used to describe Lord Xuan. This song describes how someone as lovely and striking as Lady Jiang should not have been given to this horrible old man. When later generations read the history of this time, they speak about the two daughters of Lord Xi of Qi, where the older— Lady Xuan Jiang—committed adultery with her father-in-law, while the younger—Lady Wen Jiang—committed incest with her own brother. Every moral principle and standard was destroyed by women like these.

There is a poem that bewails this:

Of the wicked beauties of this time, the two Jiang sisters stand out.
Right up to the present day, Qi and Wey see much moral laxness.
Heaven created these exceptional women to bring disaster on ruler and
    state;
How can they compare with the ugly Wuyan who assisted her hegemon-
    king?

When Jizi returned home from Song, he was ordered to go to the New Tower, where Lord Xuan ordered him to perform the rituals due to a stepmother for Lady Jiang. However, Jizi did not mind in the slightest.

After Lord Xuan took the lady from Qi, he moved to the New Tower and gave himself up to a life of pleasure, abandoning Lady Yi Jiang completely. In the following three years, Lady Jiang of Qi gave birth to two sons; the older was named Shou and the younger was named Shuo. The saying "When the mother is favored the sons are ennobled" has been handed down from antiquity. In this case Lord Xuan adored Lady Jiang of Qi to the exclusion of all others, and the affection that he had lavished on Jizi in the past was now transferred to Shou and Shuo. He decided that after his death he wanted the rivers and mountains of the state of Wey to go to the brothers Shou and Shuo. He was deeply pleased by this idea, and this meant Jizi was totally superfluous.

It so happened that the Honorable Shou was very filial and kind, and he always loved Jizi as his own brother, so every time he visited his parents he would be sure to say nice things about him. Jizi was also a gentle and respectful young man, who never behaved badly, so Lord Xuan found it difficult to make his intentions known. However, he secretly entrusted the Honorable Shou to the guardianship of the Honorable Xie, so that in the future he would have his support when he succeeded to the title.

Although the Honorable Shuo was born of the same mother as Shou, they were completely different characters. The Honorable Shuo, even though at this time he was still very young, was a naturally devious and deceitful person. He took advantage of the favor shown to his mother to secretly assemble a small private army, for he was determined to take power one day. He not only resented and disliked Jizi; even his own older brother, the Honorable Shou, seemed to him a tiresome excrescence. However, some things are urgent and others are less so, hence he made it his priority to get rid of Jizi. He would often say things to needle his mother: "Although Father loves you now, Jizi was there first. He is the elder while we are the younger brothers. In the future, the succession will be determined by seniority in the family. Besides, you took Lady Yi Jiang's place and she hates you for that. If Jizi becomes ruler, then she will become the mother of the country. What will we do then?"

Lady Jiang of Qi had originally been intended to marry Jizi but now served Lord Xuan as a concubine instead. After having given birth to her sons, she had come to feel that Jizi was a stumbling-block in her way, so she plotted against him with the Honorable Shuo. They were always slandering Jizi to his father.

One day it was Jizi's birthday, and the Honorable Shou held a party to celebrate. Shuo was also in attendance. Jizi and the Honorable Shou started chatting in a very friendly fashion. Shuo couldn't get a word in edgewise, so he left early on the grounds that he wasn't feeling very well, and went straight to see his mother, Lady Xuan Jiang of Qi. With tears streaming down his face, he trotted out one lie after the other: "I went to Jizi's birthday party with my older brother out of sheer goodwill, but Jizi drank wine until he was half-tipsy and then as a joke he called me his son. I didn't feel comfortable about that, so I complained, and then he said: 'Your mother was originally supposed to be my wife, so it would only be right if you referred to me as your father.' I waited a bit before trying to reply, but he got more and more excited and wanted to fight me. Luckily my brother was there to calm him down, so I was able to get away. I hope, Mother, that you will tell Father how terribly I have been humiliated. Please stand up for me!"

Lady Jiang of Qi believed every word he said. She waited for Lord Xuan to enter the palace, and then sobbed and cried as she told him what had happened. She even made up a few extra lines: "He also insulted me by saying: 'My mother, Lady Yi Jiang, was originally my father's stepmother, and he still made her his concubine. Your mother was originally my wife, so Father is only borrowing her temporarily—in the end she will come back to me along with the state of Wey.'"

Lord Xuan summoned the Honorable Shou and asked him about it. "Nobody said anything of the kind," Shou told him.

Lord Xuan half-believed him, but he still sent a palace eunuch to transmit a message to Lady Yi Jiang to upbraid her for not bringing up her son properly. Lady Yi Jiang had to swallow her rage. She had no one to confide in, and in the end she hanged herself.

A bearded old man wrote a poem bewailing this:

How can a father's concubine commit incest with his son?
Even animals would find the goings-on in Wey disgusting.
Even though Lady Yi Jiang hanged herself, it was far too late;
Why didn't she decide to preserve her virtue from the very start?

Jizi was deeply upset by his mother's death, but he was afraid that his father would be angry with him, so he could only weep in secret. The Honorable Shuo and Lady Xuan Jiang kept on slandering Jizi, saying that because his mother was forced to commit suicide, he was very angry about it and that in the future he would want to take revenge. To begin with, Lord Xuan did not believe a word of it, but there was nothing that he could do to control his wicked concubine and nasty son, who nagged him day and night. They were determined to force Lord Xuan to kill Jizi, so that in the future he would not be able to cause trouble for them. They would not allow Lord Xuan to ignore them. After much hesitation, he finally agreed to an anonymous assassination, whereby they would hire the killers to murder him on the open road to hide the truth from the eyes and ears of the populace.

It happened that at this time Lord Xi of Qi called a meeting to discuss the attack on Ji, and levied troops from Wey. Lord Xuan discussed the matter with the Honorable Shuo, and they decided to send Jizi to Qi, on the pretext of setting a date for the muster of the army. He would be marked out by a white battle standard. Jizi would have to travel through the wilds of Shen, because that was the main road to Qi. When his boat arrived there, he would have to disembark to travel overland, so this would be the best place to catch him unawares. The Honorable Shuo brought out his private soldiers, for now they would be very useful. He instructed them to disguise themselves as bandits and set an ambush in the wilds of Shen.

When they saw a white battle standard go past, they should come out of hiding and slay the person holding it. The standard would function as proof that they had carried out their mission, for which they would receive rich rewards. After the Honorable Shuo had made his arrangements, he reported them to Lady Xuan Jiang. She was absolutely delighted.

When the Honorable Shou saw his father send away his entourage and summon his younger brother for solitary consultations, he became suspicious. He entered the palace to see his mother, to sound her out. Lady Xuan Jiang did not know that there was any need for secrecy, so she told him the truth. She instructed him: "This was your father's idea, because he hopes to remove an obstacle from our path. You must not reveal this secret to anyone else."

The Honorable Shou realized that the plan was already set, so there would therefore be no point in even trying to remonstrate. Instead, he went privately to see Jizi and explained his father's plan: "This is the road that you will have to take when leaving the wilds of Shen, and you have little chance of making it out alive. It would be best if you go into exile abroad and afterwards make plans for the future."

"As a son, it is by obeying your father's orders that you show your filial piety," Jizi said. "Someone who disobeys his father's orders is a bad son. Is there any place in the world that does not have fathers? Even if I wanted to run away, where could I go?"

He straightened his clothing and stepped down into the boat, boldly setting out on his journey.

The Honorable Shou, with tears in his eyes, urged him to run away, but he would not go. He thought to himself: "My brother really is a good man! He knows perfectly well that if he dies at the hands of bandits on this journey, then Father will appoint me as his heir. A son cannot be without his father; a younger brother cannot be without his older brother! If I get there ahead of him, then I will die in his place and my older brother will escape. When my father hears of my death, he may be moved to regret what he has done. In this way I will be both a good son and a good brother, and my name will be famous for a thousand ages!"

He had some wine put on board another boat and set off quickly downriver to invite Jizi to a farewell party. Jizi refused: "I am on a mission for His Lordship, so it is not appropriate for me to delay."

The Honorable Shou took a goblet over to him in the other boat, filled it to the brim, and insisted that he drink it. Before he had even opened his mouth to speak, a tear had trickled down into the cup, which Jizi then grabbed and drank.

"The wine was polluted!" the Honorable Shou said.

"I drank it to show that I know you love me," Jizi told him.

The Honorable Shou wiped away his tears and said, "The wine that we drink today is to say goodbye forever. If you really care about me, then you should drink another cup!"

"Of course," Jizi responded.

The pair looked at each other with tears in their eyes, as they toasted one another. The Honorable Shou was keeping control of himself, but Jizi drank whatever was put in front of him until he was dead drunk, at which point he rolled over on his seating mat and went to sleep, snoring.

The Honorable Shou spoke to his older brother's followers: "Having received an order from His Lordship, there must be no delay. I will go on my brother's behalf!"

He grabbed the white standard from Jizi's hand and deliberately placed it at the prow of the boat, ordering his own servants to follow him. He told Jizi's entourage to stay behind and look after him. Shou took a wooden tablet from his sleeve and gave it to them, saying, "Wait until he has woken up, then show him this." Immediately afterwards, he ordered the boat to set sail.

When he approached the wilds of Shen, it was time to transfer to a chariot to travel overland. When he climbed up the bank, the assassins lying in ambush shouted and fell on him like hornets. They had seen a flag fluttering in the breeze as the boat sailed downriver and realized it was the white standard they were looking for, so they were sure he was Jizi.

The Honorable Shou drew himself up and said, "I am the oldest son of the Marquis of Wey, the lord of this state, and I am on a mission to Qi. Who are you? How dare you attack me?"

The villains all shouted: "We have received a secret order from the Marquis of Wey to cut off your head!" They drew their swords and slashed away at him. His followers, seeing that things had turned violent and not knowing the truth of the matter, all panicked and scattered. Poor Shou could only stretch out his neck for the sword. The assassins took his head, placed it in a wooden box, and then all boarded the ship. They took down the battle standard and began the journey home.

Jizi had never had a great capacity for wine. After a while, he woke up and did not see the Honorable Shou anywhere. One of his followers gave him the sealed wooden tablet. He broke it open and read it. There was an eight-word message written on it: "I have taken your place, you must flee!"

Jizi started to cry. "My younger brother has gone into terrible danger on my behalf. I must quickly go after him, otherwise they will kill him by mistake!"

Fortunately his servants were all present, so having climbed aboard the Honorable Shou's boat, Jizi ordered the sailors to row at full speed. They moved like a flash of lightning, like a bird rising from the flock. That night the moon shone like silver and Jizi stood looking unblinkingly out over the prow, his heart filled with concern for his brother. In the distance he caught sight of the other boat and said happily, "Thank Heaven my younger brother is still alive."

His followers reported: "That boat is coming towards us—it is not moving away!"

Jizi became anxious and ordered them to pull up alongside the other boat. As the two vessels approached one another, the bridge and deck were all clearly visible, but all he could see were the villains on board—there was no sign of the Honorable Shou. Jizi was getting more and more worried. In an effort to trick them into telling the truth, he called out: "Have you carried out the thing that His Lordship ordered you to do?"

The assassins, hearing him mention their secret instructions, assumed that he was someone that the Honorable Shuo had sent to check up on them, so they handed over the box containing the head and said, "We have done it!"

Jizi took the box and opened it to look. He saw the Honorable Shou's head inside. Then he raised his face to the sky and wailed: "Heavens! What injustice!"

The assassins were surprised by this and asked, "When a father kills his son, he is quite within his rights. Why do you call it an injustice?"

"I am the real Jizi," he told them. "I have offended against my father and so he gave orders to kill me. What has my younger brother Shou done to deserve to die like this? Quickly cut off my head and go home to present it to my father, to atone for my crime in allowing my younger brother to be killed by mistake!"

Among the villains there was someone who was acquainted with both these young men. Looking carefully in the moonlight, he said, "We really did kill the wrong one!" So the assassins decapitated Jizi and put his head in the box with the other. His followers all fled in terror.

In the *Odes of Wey* there is a song called "Riding on a Boat," which commemorates the two brothers competing to be the one that died. This song runs:

Two young men got on a boat, their shadows floated away.
I think of them, my heart is wrenched.
Two young men got on a boat, which then floated away.
I think of them, did they not come to harm?

The person who wrote this song did not dare speak clearly, but thinking about the two young men on board is a way to imply a tragic meaning.

The criminals arrived back in the Wey capital under cover of darkness and went first to have audience with the Honorable Shuo, presenting him with the white battle standard. Afterwards they told him that the two young men had both been killed, even though they were afraid of being punished for having murdered the wrong person. None of them realized that he would think of this as killing two birds with one stone and that they had done exactly what the Honorable Shuo had secretly hoped they would. He brought out gold and silk, and rewarded the murderers lavishly. That done, he went into the palace to see his mother and report: "The Honorable Shou took the battle standard and went on ahead, so he got himself killed. Fortunately Jizi then turned up and told them his real name, so he paid for my brother's life with his own."

Lady Jiang of Qi was horrified about the fate of the Honorable Shou, but she was pleased to get rid of Jizi and thus pull a thorn from her own flesh. In this instance, happiness and sadness were about equally balanced. Mother and son discussed the situation, and decided to break the news to Lord Xuan slowly.

As has been mentioned above, originally the Honorable Xie was looking after Jizi and the Honorable Zhi was looking after Shou. Both of them were getting worried about their disappearance and sent people to investigate. Eventually, they reported back what had happened. To begin with, these men had been rivals in the service of different masters, but now they shared a common tragedy. They discussed together as to what they should do. They waited until Lord Xuan held an early-morning court, and then the two of them went straight into the main hall, bowed down to the ground, and burst into wailing cries.

Alarmed, Lord Xuan asked what the reason for this was. The Honorable Xie and Zhi then spoke in unison, explaining that both Jizi and Shou had been murdered: "Please permit us to collect their heads and bodies to allow for a proper burial, so that we can complete the task with which we were entrusted!" When they finished speaking, their wailing became even louder.

Even though Lord Xuan was angry with Jizi, he adored the Honorable Shou, and to hear all of a sudden that his two sons had been murdered at the same time caused the blood to drain from his face with horror. For a long time, he did not say a single word. After the first pain was over, he became terribly sad, and his tears fell like rain. He kept sighing and saying, "It is all her fault! She lied to me!" He immediately summoned the Honorable Shuo to ask him about it, but Shuo denied all knowledge. Lord Xuan was furious and ordered him to arrest the murderers. He agreed, but given his role in the plot, it was hardly likely that he would hand them over.

After Lord Xuan received this shocking news, he missed the Honorable Shou terribly and became ill. Whenever he shut his eyes, he seemed to see Lady Yi Jiang, Jizi, and Shou together, crying and calling out to him. Prayers did not work, and within a couple of weeks he was dead. The Honorable Shuo presided over the funeral and inherited the title as Lord Hui. At this time, he was fifteen years old. He immediately stripped the Honorable Xie and Zhi of their offices. He had an older half-brother, the Honorable Ying, also known by his style-name of Zhaobo, who would not give his allegiance to him, and so had to flee into exile in Qi. Xie and Zhi loathed Lord Hui and often thought of how to take revenge for Jizi and the Honorable Shou, but the opportunity did not present itself.

. . .

Let us turn now to another part of the story. When Shuo had just assumed the title of Marquis of Wey, he assisted Qi in the attack on Ji only to be defeated by Zheng. Just as his fury was at its height, he suddenly heard that an ambassador had arrived from Zheng. When he asked why, he was informed that Lord Li of Zheng had fled into exile and the ministers all supported the restoration of their old lord, Zihu, Lord Zhao of Zheng. He was very pleased and immediately ordered chariots and attendants to escort Lord Zhao back to Zheng. Zhai Zu bowed twice and apologized for his earlier failure to protect his lord. Even though Lord Zhao did not punish him, he was displeased and treated him with less respect than in days of yore. Zhai Zu also felt that he needed to tread carefully, so he kept claiming that he was too ill to go to court.

Gao Qumi had never been a favorite with Lord Zhao, and now that he had returned to the country, he was worried that he would be executed. He secretly collected a team of assassins with a view to murdering Zihu and putting the Honorable Wei in power. At this time, Lord Li of Zheng was in Cai, where he had good relations developed through lavish gifts to the people of Cai. He sent someone to take a message to the Earl of Tan to say that he wanted the loan of Yue as a base of operations. The Earl of Tan refused. Therefore, he sent some people from Cai, dressed up as merchants, to travel around Yue and make friends with the Yue people. They agreed to help him. He took advantage of this opportunity to murder the Earl of Tan, whereupon Lord Li then moved to Yue. He raised the city walls and deepened the moat, mustering a great army with the best of equipment, with the intention of attacking Zheng which he now thought of as an enemy state.

When Zhai Zu heard this news, he was deeply alarmed and reported it immediately to Lord Zhao, who ordered Grandee Fu Xia to station the army at Daling to halt Lord Li's advance. Lord Li discovered that Zheng was making preparations, so he sent someone to take a message to the Marquis of Lu, requesting that he apologize to Song on Lord Li's behalf and promise that after he returned to power, he would hand over all that he had previously failed to deliver. When the Lu ambassador arrived in Song, Lord Zhuang of Song's greed was awakened and he agreed to install Lord Li in power, in concert with Cai and Wey. At just this time Shuo, the Marquis of Wey, was angry with Lord Zhao of Zheng because he had worked so hard to enable his restoration, but Lord Zhao had neither behaved politely nor even thanked him. That is the reason why the Marquis of Wey joined in the plot with the Duke of Song. Since he had only recently succeeded to the marquisate, he had never met any other lords, so he decided to go in person to meet the duke.

The Honorable Xie said to the Honorable Zhi: "Our lord has left the country to travel far away. This is our opportunity!"

"If we want to act, we must first decide who will take the title, so that the people have a ruler and so that we can avoid a civil war," Zhi replied.

Just as they were deep in their secret discussions, the gatekeeper reported: "The Grandee Ning Gui would like to see you." The two men welcomed him in.

"Have you forgotten the way those innocent young men suffered?" Ning Gui asked them. "Now our opportunity has come! Let us make no mistakes!"

"We were just discussing who should take the title, but we had not fixed upon anyone yet," the Honorable Zhi said.

"I have observed all the young members of the ruling house and only Qianmou is a good man, worthy of our support," Ning Gui said. "In

addition to that, he is the son-in-law of the Zhou king. He can strike
awe into the hearts of the people."

The three men then smeared their mouths with blood to seal their
agreement and then secretly met with the former followers of Jizi and
the Honorable Shou. They circulated a false rumor: "The Marquis of
Wey has attacked Zheng. The army has been defeated and His Lordship
killed." Then they installed the Honorable Qianmou in power.

After the formal morning audience with all the officials had been
completed, they proclaimed Shuo's wicked role in the death of his two
brothers and how that had led to his father's demise. They ordered that
a proper funeral ceremony be held for Jizi and the Honorable Shou, at
which they were reburied in new coffins. Then they sent an ambassador
to the Zhou king to announce the accession of a new lord. Ning Gui
took the army out to camp beyond the suburbs, in order to prevent
Lord Hui from returning home. The Honorable Xie wanted to execute
Lady Xuan Jiang, but Zhi stopped him, saying, "Lady Jiang has committed terrible crimes, but she is the younger sister of the Marquis of Qi.
I am afraid that if you kill her, you will anger Qi. It would be better to
keep her alive and preserve friendly relations with them."

They made Lady Xuan Jiang move into a separate palace, but she
received the same monthly stipend as before.

. . .

The four states of Song, Lu, Cai, and Wey united their armies in an
attack on Zheng. Zhai Zu was in personal command of the army as it
approached Daling, and he joined forces with Fu Xia to resist the
enemy. They changed their approach as the situation developed, making sure that they never suffered heavy losses. The four states were not
able to defeat them, so in the end they had to go home. Shuo, Marquis
of Wey, had achieved no success in the attack on Zheng, and as he
traveled homeward he heard that the Honorable Xie and Zhi had
rebelled and that Qianmou was already installed in power. He then fled
into exile in the state of Qi.

"You are and always will be my nephew," Lord Xiang of Qi told him.
He housed and fed him with great generosity, and promised that he would
raise an army to restore him to his country. Shuo then made a treaty with
Lord Xiang that said: "On the day that I am restored to power, every item
in the treasury will go to pay you back." Lord Xiang was very pleased.

Suddenly a report came in: "An ambassador from the Marquis of
Lu has arrived." The Marquis of Qi had earlier requested a marriage

alliance with Zhou. The Zhou king had agreed to this, and he sent the Marquis of Lu to preside over the marriage, for he could not attend in person when a royal princess was marrying a mere aristocrat. The Marquis of Lu wanted to go to Qi in person to discuss the arrangements. Lord Xiang remembered his younger sister, Lady Wen Jiang, whom he had not seen for a long time, and he decided to invite her too. He sent an envoy to Lu to request that Lady Wen Jiang come in person.

The grandees asked what date had been set for the attack on Wey.

"Qianmou is the son-in-law of the Zhou king," Lord Xiang of Qi reminded them. "Now I am planning a marriage alliance with the Zhou ruling house myself, so this matter will have to be delayed."

He was afraid that the people of Wey would kill or torture Lady Xuan Jiang, so he sent Noble Grandson Wuzhi to return the Honorable Shi of Wey to his own country in an effort to protect her. He also secretly instructed Wuzhi to encourage the Honorable Shi to seduce Lady Xuan Jiang into an affair, because he thought this would help in the restoration of Shuo to power. Noble Grandson Wuzhi followed his orders and went back to Wey with the Honorable Shi, where they had audience with the new lord, Qianmou. At that time the Honorable Shi's wife was already dead, and Wuzhi—just as the Marquis of Qi had instructed him to—discussed the possibility of a marriage between Shi and Lady Xuan Jiang with the lord and ministers of Wey. She expressed her willingness to accept this. All the ministers in Wey were enraged by the fact that Lady Xuan Jiang still held the title of senior wife to the late lord, so they were happy to see her stripped of these honors now. It was only the Honorable Shi who remembered her seniority within the family and refused to agree.

Wuzhi spoke privately with the Honorable Zhi: "This is not working, so how can I carry out His Lordship's commands?"

The Honorable Zhi was afraid that they would lose the support of Qi, so he came up with a plan. He invited the Honorable Shi to a banquet at which women entertainers served wine, and they kept on drinking until he was dead drunk. Then he was carried into the separate palace, where he was put overnight in the same bed as Lady Xuan Jiang. Since he was drunk, he slept with her, and though when he woke up he regretted this deeply it was already too late. Lady Xuan Jiang and the Honorable Shi then became man and wife. Later on they had five children together; the oldest boy, Qizi, died young, so it was their second son, the Honorable Hui, who became Lord Wen of Wey. Of their two daughters, one married Lord Huan of Song, the other Lord Mu of Xu.

A historian wrote a poem bewailing this:

How can you steal a son's wife and make her your own?
How long can the punishment for incest be delayed?
Lady Yi Jiang's example was followed by Lady Xuan Jiang;
There is nothing to be surprised at in this family's behavior.

This poem speaks of how in the past Lord Xuan of Wey had an inces-
tuous relationship with his father's concubine, Lady Yi Jiang, and she
gave birth to Jizi; now his son, the Honorable Shi, had an incestuous
relationship with Lady Xuan Jiang, and they had five children together.
The standards of behavior of one generation were followed by the next,
so what happened at the New Tower was far from unique.

. . .

When Zhai Zu came back from Daling, he came up with a plan to deal
with his old lord, the Honorable Tu, who was then living in Yue, so as
to put an end to the danger threatening Zheng. He thought about the
fact that Qi and Lord Li had originally become enemies at the time of
the attack on Ji, and that now Qi was planning to install Lord Li by
force, but had not gotten around to it. He also considered the fact that
a new lord had taken power and was doing a wonderful job. He was
well aware of the fact that the Marquis of Lu's principal wife came from
Qi, and that these two countries had made peace as a result. Therefore,
he presented his opinion to Lord Zhao that he should go armed with
presents to the state of Qi to make an alliance with them and then conclude a peace treaty with Lu. With the assistance of these two states,
they would be able to deal with Song. There is an ancient saying: "A
wise man may come up with a thousand plans, but he is sure to fail
once." Zhai Zu understood that he had to defend the state against Lord
Li's machinations, but he did not know that Gao Qumi's wicked plan
had long been maturing. It was only because he was worried about Zhai
Zu's intelligence that he had not struck long before.

Now, seeing that Zhai Zu was embarking on a long journey, Gao
Qumi decided that there was nothing to worry about, so he secretly sent
someone to invite the Honorable Wei to his house. Then he took advantage of the fact that Lord Zhao had to go on a winter journey to perform sacrifices at the solstice to set assassins in ambush on the way.
They suddenly emerged to kill him, though afterwards the word was
given out that he had been murdered by bandits. Afterwards, Gao Qumi
installed the Honorable Wei as the new Lord of Zheng and sent a messenger in his name, summoning Zhai Zu back to the country and ordering him to share power. Poor Lord Zhao of Zheng was able to return to

his country, but less than three years later he was murdered by a wicked minister.

An old man, reading history up to this present point, noticed that Lord Zhao knew that Gao Qumi was a wicked man right from the time when he was the Scion of Zheng, and yet, though he was the lord of the country twice, he was still not able to get rid of him. This means that he brought disaster down upon himself. Is this not a tragedy that could have been avoided had he been less gentle?

There is a poem that bewails this:

If you see evil, you should root it out;
How can you live with a tiger or a snake?
If you do not control other people, they will control you;
What is the point of knowing what Gao Qumi is like if you don't get rid
   of him?

Do you want to know what happened to the Honorable Wei? READ ON.

Chapter Thirteen

Lord Huan of Lu and his wife travel to Qi.

The Honorable Wei of Zheng and his supporters are massacred.

When Lord Xiang of Qi heard that Zhai Zu had come on a diplomatic mission, he greeted him happily. Just as he was about to consider a return mission, he was suddenly informed that Gao Qumi had murdered Lord Zhao of Zheng and established the Honorable Wei in power. He was very angry about this and raised an army with the intention of punishing them. Just then the Marquis of Lu and his wife were about to arrive in the state of Qi, so he had to put the matter of Zheng to one side and go in person to meet the marquis at the Luo River.

When Lady Wen Jiang, the wife of the Lord of Lu, saw the Qi ambassador come to meet them, she remembered how much she missed her older brother and decided to make the journey to Qi with Lord Huan, on the pretext of visiting her natal family. Lord Huan was besotted with his wife and did not dare to refuse her request.

Grandee Shen Xu remonstrated: "It has been a rule since antiquity that men and women should live separately. The rituals cannot be confused, for if they become unclear there will be social disorder. When a woman has married, if her father and mother are still alive, she is allowed to go home once a year to visit them. However, Her Ladyship's parents are both dead; there is no reason for a younger sister to pay a visit to her older brother. Lu is a state founded on the proper ritual principles—surely you are not proposing to do something that flies in the face of all our norms?"

Lord Huan had already made his promise to Lady Wen Jiang, so he did not listen to Shen Xu's remonstrance. The husband and wife set off together, and when their carriage arrived at the Luo River, Lord Xiang of Qi was already there. They greeted each other respectfully and made polite inquiries, then rode on to Linzi. The Marquis of Lu, in accordance with the instructions he had received from the Zhou king, discussed the marriage alliance between their two houses. The Marquis of Qi was absolutely thrilled, and he immediately held a great banquet in honor of the Marquis of Lu and his wife. Later on, Lady Wen Jiang went to the palace saying that she wanted to meet her old friends in the harem. No one knew that Lord Xiang had already built a secret room in which he had set out another private banquet in order to show his love for Lady Wen Jiang. Over the wine cups their eyes met in love and lust, without any thought for the proper principles of behavior. Thus this terrible thing happened. The two were so deeply in love that they could not bear to be parted, so she stayed overnight in the palace, and even when the sun was high in the sky, they lay in each other's arms and did not get up.

There is an anonymous poem about this:

A modest lady should preserve her delicate reputation,
But having experienced these illicit pleasures, how could she be without
 them?
A moment of passion brought a thousand ages of shame,
All because a younger sister fell in love with her older brother.

The pair were deeply in love and forgot all other considerations, sparing no thought for Lord Huan of Lu, all on his own outside the palace.

The Marquis of Lu was deeply concerned and sent someone to the palace gate to make a detailed inquiry. The report came back: "The Marquis of Qi has not yet married a principal wife, but he has a junior wife, Lady Lian, who is the cousin of Grandee Lian Cheng. She has already lost favor and has nothing to do with the Marquis of Qi. The reason that Lady Wen Jiang went to the Qi palace was because she loves her older brother. She has not met with any of the other harem ladies."

The Marquis of Lu knew that his wife was up to no good, and he wished that he could leap into the Qi palace and see for himself what was actually going on. Just then, someone came to report: "Her Ladyship has left the palace and is on her way back."

With difficulty, the Marquis of Lu settled himself for the wait. When she arrived, as if it were quite an ordinary question, he asked Lady Jiang, "Who were you drinking with last night in the palace?"

"With Lady Lian," she told him.

"At what time did you get up from your seats?"

"We had a lot to talk about after such a long separation and chatted until the moon shone high over the palace walls, so it must have been about midnight."

"Was your older brother present when you were drinking?"

"My older brother did not join us."

The Marquis of Lu laughed mirthlessly and continued his questions: "Doesn't he care about you? Why didn't he come and drink with you?"

"While we were drinking he did come and have one cup, but then he went away again."

"Why didn't you leave the palace when the party broke up?" the Marquis of Lu demanded.

"It was too late at night."

"Where did you sleep?"

"What on earth is the matter, that you feel it necessary to question me like this?" Lady Wen Jiang asked. "The palace has many empty rooms, and certainly there is plenty of space to put down a bed. As a matter of fact, I spent the night in the Western Palace, in the rooms that I had when I was a little girl."

"Why did you get up so late today?"

"I had a hangover from last night, and so today when I got up and did my hair and makeup, it took much longer than usual."

"Who was present where you spent the night?"

"The palace maids."

"Where did your brother sleep?" the Marquis of Lu demanded.

Lady Jiang went quite pink, and said, "It really isn't the place of a younger sister to speculate on where her brother sleeps."

"But I am afraid that your brother is very interested in whereabouts you sleep!" the Marquis of Lu retorted.

"Why do you say that?"

"Since ancient times men and women have been segregated," her husband said. "I know that last night when you stayed in the palace you slept with your older brother. You can't fool me."

Lady Wen Jiang tried to excuse herself and then burst into tears, feeling deeply ashamed and humiliated. Lord Huan of Lu was at this time within the borders of Qi state, so there was nothing that he could do.

Even though he was filled with anger and resentment, he had no way to express it. This really was a situation where anger had to be bottled up for his own safety. He sent a messenger to say farewell to the Marquis of Qi and then set off home, where he would deal with what had happened.

Lord Xiang of Qi was well aware that what he had done was very wrong, so when Lady Wen Jiang left the palace, he was worried about her and secretly ordered one of his trusted bodyguards, Shi Zhi Fenru, to follow her and find out what the Marquis of Lu said when he met his wife. Shi Zhi Fenru came back and reported: "The Marquis of Lu and his wife have quarreled with each other."

Lord Xiang was quite taken aback. "I guessed that the Marquis of Lu would be sure to find out eventually, but I had no idea that it would happen so quickly!"

After a short time, he had the ambassador from Lu coming to say farewell, and he knew that this was because the truth had been discovered. He insisted that they all make a journey to Mount Niu together, where there would be a banquet to say goodbye. He sent someone several times to insist upon this point, and in the end the Marquis of Lu had to give orders to drive his chariot out to the suburbs. Lady Wen Jiang was left behind at the guesthouse, in a deep depression.

Lord Xiang of Qi was very upset to think that Lady Wen Jiang was going home, and he was also afraid that henceforth the Marquis of Lu would treat him as a personal enemy, so he was determined to deal with this situation. When the party broke up, he ordered the Honorable Pengsheng to escort the Marquis of Lu back to the guesthouse, and instructed him that while they were riding on the chariot he should put an end to the Marquis of Lu's life. Pengsheng, recalling that he had been shot by an arrow from Lu during the attack on Ji, was very happy to accept this command.

That day a lavish spread was served at the banquet at Mount Niu, with singing and dancing for their entertainment. Lord Xiang was extremely respectful, while the Marquis of Lu hung his head and said nothing. Lord Xiang told his grandees to keep the wine circulating, and he ordered the palace maids and serving women to present the cups to the guests on their knees. The Marquis of Lu was torn with anger and depression, so he decided to drown his sorrows in drink. He became so sodden with wine that when the time came to say goodbye, he could not perform even this simple ceremony, so Lord Xiang ordered the Honorable Pengsheng to lift him onto the chariot. Pengsheng then rode off with the Marquis of Lu. When they were about two *li* from the city gates, seeing that the Marquis of Lu was fast asleep, he grabbed hold of him and crushed his chest. Pengsheng was a strong man with arms like iron, and he used their full force on the Marquis of Lu until his ribs cracked. Lord Huan screamed once before he died, his blood pouring down the chariot. Pengsheng told the others present: "The Marquis of Lu has become dangerously ill from drinking too much. We must go at full speed back to the city to report this to His Lordship."

Even though they knew that they had just witnessed a murder, nobody dared to say anything.

A historian wrote a poem that reads:

> No ambiguous relationship should ever be allowed between a man and
> a woman;
> It was too dangerous to allow both a husband and wife to leave the
> borders.
> If he had originally listened to Shen Xu's remonstrance,
> Would Lord Huan's body have lain stretched out in the chariot?

When Lord Xiang of Qi heard that the Marquis of Lu had died suddenly, he pretended to be upset and cry, and gave orders that the body should be placed in the most expensive coffin. He also sent someone to report this sad news to Lu. However, when the Marquis of Lu's escort returned to that state, they told the truth about the assassination on the chariot.

"The country cannot be without a ruler for as much as a single day!" Grandee Shen Xu proclaimed. "We must support Scion Tong through the funeral ceremony. Once the chariot carrying His Lordship's body has arrived back, we can hold the ceremony of accession."

The Honorable Qingfu, whose style-name was Meng, was Lord Huan's oldest son by a concubine. He waved his hands and said: "The Marquis of Qi has contravened every standard of proper behavior, and now he has also murdered my lord and father. Please give me three hundred chariots that I may attack Qi and make his crimes known to the world."

Grandee Shen Xu was impressed by his words and privately went to ask one of his advisors, Shi Bo, "Can we feasibly attack Qi?"

"You must not let your neighbors know about this unfortunate incident," Shi Bo told him. "Lu is weak and Qi is strong, so if we attack them. not only are we unlikely to win, but this disgusting scandal will also become widely known. It would be better to endure the situation.

However, you must insist upon an investigation of what happened in the chariot, which will force the Marquis of Qi to execute the Honorable Pengsheng. That way we have an explanation to give the other states. At the very least, Qi will have to grant us that."

Shen Xu reported this to the Honorable Qingfu. Afterwards, he asked Shi Bo to draft an official letter on behalf of the government. Since Scion Tong was in mourning for his father, he could not be involved, so the grandees of Lu sent this document to Qi in their own names. When Lord Xiang of Qi opened the letter and read it, the text said:

> Grandee Shen Xu and his fellows bow respectfully to His Lordship, the Marquis of Qi. Our lord received an order from the Son of Heaven to discuss a marriage alliance with you, so he did not dare to delay. He has gone but has not come back, and everywhere we hear rumors that he has been murdered on his chariot. If this killing goes unpunished, we will be humiliated before all the other aristocrats. We therefore request permission to execute Pengsheng.

When Lord Xiang had finished reading this, he sent someone to summon Pengsheng to court. The Honorable Pengsheng thought that he had done a great deed, so he went off quite happily. Lord Xiang cursed him in front of the Lu ambassador: "I ordered you to help the Marquis of Lu into his chariot and see him home when he had too much to drink, but you did not attend to him carefully and so he died. You are guilty of an unpardonable crime!" He shouted at his entourage to tie him up and behead him in the marketplace.

"The affair with your younger sister and the murder of her husband are your wicked deeds, yet now you put the blame on me," Pengsheng screamed. "If the dead have consciousness, then I will become a vengeful ghost! I will come back to claim your life!"

Lord Xiang put his hands over his ears and his entourage all laughed. His Lordship then sent someone to go to the king of Zhou to thank him for the proposed marriage alliance and set a date for the wedding. He also sent someone to escort the Marquis of Lu's body back to his home country. Lady Wen Jiang, however, stayed in Qi and did not go home.

Grandee Shen Xu led the Scion Tong to meet the coffin when it arrived in the suburbs. Then, he performed a ceremony of mourning in front of the coffin and succeeded to the title as Lord Zhuang of Lu. The civil and military officials Shen Xu, Zhuan Sunsheng, the Honorable Ni, the Honorable Yan, and Cao Mo formed the backbone of his administration. His older half-brother, the Honorable Qingfu, his younger half-brother, the Honorable Ya, and his younger brother by the same mother,

Jiyou, all participated in the government of the country. Shen Xu recommended Shi Bo for his talents, and he was appointed a senior knight.
The following year was the first year of Lord Zhuang of Lu's reign, and
also the fourth year of the reign of King Zhuang of Zhou.

Lord Zhuang of Lu discussed his role in the proposed marriage alliance between Qi and the royal house with his ministers.

"Our country has been humiliated three times," Shi Bo informed
him. "Does Your Lordship know that?"

"What do you mean by three humiliations?" Lord Zhuang inquired.

"His Late Lordship died in such a horrible way: that is our first
humiliation," Shi Bo said. "Her Ladyship has stayed in Qi and refuses
to come home, giving rise to all sorts of gossip: that is our second humiliation. Qi is our enemy and Your Lordship is still in mourning, and
yet you are proposing to preside over Lord Xiang of Qi's wedding.
If you refuse, then you will be disobeying a royal command, but if
you do not refuse, then you will be a laughingstock. That is our third
humiliation!"

Lord Zhuang of Lu looked alarmed and said, "How can we avoid
these three humiliations?"

"If you want people to treat you well, you must first behave properly," Shi Bo said. "If you want people to put their faith in you, you
must first behave in a trustworthy manner. You have not yet received a
royal mandate allowing you to take over His Late Lordship's titles, so
you should take advantage of the opportunity offered by this royal wedding to request a grant from Zhou that gives your late father a glorious
name to take down to the Underworld. This is the way that the first
humiliation can be spared us! Her Ladyship is in Qi, and you should
bring her back with all due pomp and ceremony, thereby completing
your filial duty towards your father. That is how the second humiliation
may be avoided! As for having to preside over the wedding, that is
going to be very difficult to deal with to everyone's satisfaction, so we
will need to use some stratagem to get out of it."

"What did you have in mind?" Lord Zhuang asked.

"If you order the construction of a special guesthouse beyond the
suburbs for the reception of the princess, we can send a grandee to meet
her and escort her to her wedding," Shi Bo suggested. "However, Your
Lordship should decline to appear in person on the grounds that you
are in mourning. Then you will not contravene the commands that you
have received from His Majesty the king; likewise, you will not destroy
your relationship with the important state of Qi, and you will make it

clear that you are performing the mourning rituals for your father in full measure. In this way we can escape the third humiliation!"

"Shen Xu told me that you are amazingly clever," Lord Zhuang remarked. "Clearly he is right!"

He followed this plan step by step. Lu sent Grandee Zhuan Sunsheng to Zhou to escort the princess to her wedding. They also asked for an official robe and hat and a jade baton and jade disc, which would show respect to the soul of the late lord in the Underworld. King Zhuang of Zhou agreed to this, and he selected someone to go to Lu to bestow these items to assuage the soul of Lord Huan. Heijian, Duke of Zhou, wanted to go, but King Zhuang refused him permission and sent Grandee Ying Shu instead. King Zhuang's younger brother, Prince Ke, had been much favored by His Late Majesty. When he was on his deathbed, he had entrusted the prince to the care of Heijian, Duke of Zhou. Hence King Zhuang suspected him of disloyalty and was afraid that he would seek to establish private contacts with foreign powers and create a faction loyal to Prince Ke. That is why he would not employ him on this occasion. Heijian was well aware that King Zhuang did not trust him. That night he went to Prince Ke's mansion and discussed the possibility of taking advantage of the princess's marriage to create a riot during which King Zhuang could be assassinated, after which the prince could take power. Grandee Xin Bo was aware of this plot and reported it to King Zhuang, who then executed Heijian and sent Prince Ke into exile. The prince fled to Yan, and that was the end of that.

Zhuan Sunsheng arrived in Qi, having escorted the Zhou princess there. In accordance with the orders he had received from the Marquis of Lu, he went to collect Lady Wen Jiang. Lord Xiang of Qi was extremely unwilling to be parted from her, but he was constrained by public opinion and so he had to let her go back. As they were about to be parted, they clung to each other and kept repeating: "We will meet again!" They both said goodbye with tears in their eyes. Lady Jiang was deeply in love and did not want to leave the Marquis of Qi. Furthermore, she had done so many dreadful things that she was embarrassed to go home. Every step she took was reluctant. When her carriage arrived in Zhuo and she saw how neat and clean the guesthouse there was, she sighed and said, "This place is neither in Qi nor in Lu, so I will stay here!"

She instructed her entourage to this effect and ordered them to report to the Marquis of Lu: "Your father's widow needs her own space—she would not be happy returning to the palace. I will come back when I am dead!"

The Marquis of Lu realized that his mother had no intention of returning home, and so he built a residence for her at Zhuqiu and invited Lady
Wen Jiang to live there. She then traveled between these two places, and
the Marquis of Lu kept in regular contact, sending her frequent presents.

*When later historians discuss this matter, they point out that on the
one hand Lord Zhuang of Lu was Lady Wen Jiang's son, and on the
other hand, she murdered his father. If Lady Wen Jiang had returned to
Lu, it would have been very difficult to know how to deal with her, so
letting her move between these two places allowed the Marquis of Lu to
behave as a filial son.*

A bearded old man wrote a poem that reads:

> Having murdered her husband, she could not face going home.
> Living in Zhuo she placed herself between Qi and Lu.
> If she had steeled herself to return to her old home,
> How could the demands of love and punishment have been reconciled?

• • •

When Lord Xiang of Qi murdered Lord Huan of Lu, the state was in
complete uproar, and everyone said, "The Marquis of Qi is an evil man
and he has done a truly disgusting thing." Lord Xiang was secretly very
worried, and so he sent someone to bring the princess to Qi as soon as
possible for the wedding. The populace still did not calm down, so he
thought it would be a good idea to perform a couple of virtuous actions,
in order to sway public opinion to his side. He thought to himself:
"Zheng has assassinated their ruler and Wey has forced their lord into
exile—these are both major problems. However, the Honorable Qianmu
of Wey is the Zhou king's son-in-law, and I am just about to marry a
princess myself, so it would not be prudent to set myself up in opposition to him. It would be better to punish Zheng, for then the feudal
lords will fear and respect me!" However, he was afraid that if he raised
an army to attack Zheng, he might not win. Therefore, he secretly sent
someone to take a letter to the Honorable Wei inviting him to a meeting
at Shouzhi, where they would swear a blood covenant.

The Honorable Wei was thrilled, and said, "With the Marquis of Qi
on our side, our state is a safe as Mount Tai!"

He wanted Gao Qumi and Zhai Zu to go with him, but the latter
claimed to be too ill to travel.

Yuan Fan asked Zhai Zu in private: "Our new lord wants to make
an alliance with the Marquis of Qi. You ought to support that, so why
do you not go?"

"The Marquis of Qi is a vicious and cruel man," Zhai Zu explained. "Having inherited such a great state, he has developed a wild ambition to become hegemon. In addition to that, our former ruler, Lord Zhao, was much loved in Qi and is sure to be remembered there. It is hard to understand what they are up to, but when a large state goes to all this effort to make an alliance with a small state, they are certainly planning something nasty. Those who go on this journey might well find themselves killed!"

"If you are right, then who will take over in Zheng?" Yuan Fan asked.

"It can only be the Honorable Yi," Zhai Zu told him. "He has all the appearance of a ruler of men. The late Lord Zhuang once commented on this."

"Everyone speaks of your wisdom, so I will take a chance on your being right yet again," Yuan Fan said.

On the appointed day, Lord Xiang of Qi sent the two generals, Prince Chengfu and Guan Zhifu, each in command of more than one hundred daring knights, to circle around to left and right, while his loyal henchman Shi Zhi Fenru followed close behind them. Meanwhile, Gao Qumi conducted the Honorable Wei up to the altar at which the blood covenant would be sworn. When the formal ceremonies of greeting the Marquis of Qi had been completed, one of his favorite ministers, Meng Yang, picked up the basin full of blood, and kneeling down in front of him requested that he smear the liquid across his mouth. Lord Xiang glared at him, and Meng Yang quickly stood up. Lord Xiang then grabbed hold of the Honorable Wei's hand and asked, "How did your former ruler, Lord Zhao, die?"

The Honorable Wei went bright red and was so frightened that he could not get a word out, so Gao Qumi answered for him: "His Late Lordship died of illness. Why do you ask?"

"I heard that he met with bandits on his way to perform the sacrifices for the winter solstice. That has nothing to do with him being ill!" Lord Xiang retorted.

Gao Qumi could not continue to cover it up, and so he was forced to say, "He was not at all well in the first place, and then he suffered the shock of being attacked by bandits. That is why he died so suddenly."

"His Lordship would have been well guarded on his journey, so where did these bandits come from?" Lord Xiang demanded.

"It is a common occurrence for noble sons and the children of concubines to fight to succeed to the title. and each will have their own supporters," Gao Qumi said. "If they take advantage of this kind of opportunity, who is to prevent it?"

"Have you captured any of the bandits?" Lord Xiang inquired.

"The crime is still under investigation, but so far we have found no clues," Gao Qumi said.

Lord Xiang shouted furiously: "The guilty parties are right here! Why do you need to carry out an investigation? You have received titles and emoluments from the state and in return you assassinated your lord because of your personal dislike for him. You dare to come out with these lies to my very face! Today I will take revenge for your former lord!" He shouted to the guards: "Hurry up and seize him!"

Gao Qumi did not dare to resist as Shi Zhi Rufen tied him up. The Honorable Wei then kowtowed and begged for mercy: "This has nothing to do with me. It is all Gao Qumi's fault. Please spare me!"

"If this was all Gao Qumi's fault, why didn't you punish him?" Lord Xiang demanded. "You can go and explain yourself to your brother in the Underworld!"

At a wave of his hand Prince Chengfu and Guan Zhifu both came rushing in, followed by their soldiers, and cut the Honorable Wei down. He died on the spot. Although he had been followed by a vast entourage, who would have dared to fight back in the face of such a great show of strength by Qi? In an instant they all scattered.

Lord Xiang said to Gao Qumi, "Your lord is already dead. Do you still hope to survive?"

"I know that I have committed a terrible crime, so I beg to be allowed to commit suicide," Gao Qumi said.

"If I let you kill yourself with a sword, it would let you off too lightly," Lord Xiang informed him. He then took him back to the capital and ordered that he be torn apart by chariots at the South Gate.

Being torn apart by chariots means that the criminal has his head and four limbs tied to five chariots, each facing in a different direction. Each of the chariots is drawn by a single ox, and when the oxen are whipped, they set off and the chariots move, which rips the body into five pieces. What is commonly called "sectioning a corpse by five oxen" refers to this terrible form of punishment. Lord Xiang wanted his virtuous act to be known to the other feudal lords, and that is why he used such a dreadful kind of execution, to make the whole thing as widely known as possible.

When Gao Qumi was dead, Lord Xiang ordered that his head be suspended from the South Gate, and a placard there proclaimed: "Let wicked ministers look at this!" He also sent someone to collect the Honorable Wei's body and head, to be dumped in a shallow grave somewhere outside the city walls to the east. He sent a messenger to report the matter to Zheng and say: "There is a standard punishment in Zhou law for wicked ministers and rebellious sons. Gao Qumi was the chief conspirator in the assassination of your former lord, and he then installed a concubine's son in power. I was deeply pained to hear about the terrible fate suffered by the late ruler of Zheng, so I have punished him on your behalf. I hope that you will now establish a new ruler who will continue the long-standing good relationship between our two states."

When Yuan Fan heard about this, he sighed and said, "I will never be as clever as Zhai Zu!"

The ministers then discussed the establishment of a new lord.

"Our old lord is in Yue, so why don't we bring him back?" Shu Zhan asked.

"Having gotten rid of him, we cannot bring him back without causing more trouble for the country," Zhai Zu said. "It would be better to establish the Honorable Yi."

Yuan Fan also supported this idea, so they brought the Honorable Yi back from exile in Chen. He then succeeded to the earldom. Zhai Zu became a senior grandee, Shu Zhan became a middle grandee, and Yuan Fan became a junior grandee. When the Honorable Yi took the title, he entrusted the government of the state to Zhai Zu. He worried about his people and the defense of the realm, so he sent ambassadors to reopen diplomatic relations with the states of Qi and Chen. He also accepted the domination of Chu and agreed to pay tribute to them annually, being a protectorate of that kingdom in perpetuity. Lord Li had no opportunity to take advantage of the situation, and from this time on Zheng gradually stabilized and became peaceful again.

Do you know what happened next? If not then READ ON.

Chapter Fourteen

Shuo, Marquis of Wey, returns to his state in defiance of the king.

Lord Xiang of Qi goes out hunting and meets a ghost.

When the Zhou princess arrived in Qi, she got married to Lord Xiang. The princess was a very refined and quiet young woman, always careful of her words and actions. Lord Xiang, on the other hand, was an unrestrained and debauched man, so the two of them did not get along well together at all. After the princess had been several months in the palace, she discovered that Lord Xiang had committed incest with his younger sister. After being silent for some time, she sighed and said to herself, "What a disgusting thing to do! He is worse than an animal! What terrible bad luck for me to have to marry such a wicked man! But such has been my fate!"

Her depression resulted in her becoming sick, and before the year was out she was dead.

After the death of the princess, Lord Xiang became even more uncontrolled. He missed Lady Wen Jiang intensely, so he would go quite regularly to Zhuo, with the excuse that he was going hunting. He would then send someone to Zhuqiu to escort Lady Wen Jiang to Zhuo in secret, and then they would pursue their incestuous pleasures day and night. He was afraid that Lord Zhuang of Lu would object to this and he wanted to threaten him with the might of the forces under his command, so he personally led his army to make a surprise attack on Ji, capturing the three cities of Ping, Zi, and Wu. His troops then moved to the city of Xi, and he sent a messenger to tell the Marquis of Ji, "Write a letter of surrender now, before we destroy you!"

The Marquis of Ji sighed and said, "Qi has been opposed to us for many generations. I will not bend my knee at the court of my enemies and beg to be allowed to live!"

He asked his wife, Lady Bo Ji, to write a letter and sent someone to Lu to ask for assistance.

Lord Xiang of Qi issued orders: "I will attack anyone who comes to the aid of Ji!"

Lord Zhuang of Lu sent an envoy to Zheng suggesting that the two of them should band together to rescue Ji. The Honorable Yi had just been installed as the new Earl of Zheng and was worried that Lord Li would make a surprise attack on them from Yue, so he did not dare to send out his army. He therefore sent a messenger to refuse. The Marquis of Lu was thus left without any support. Having advanced as far as the lands of Hua, he became more and more frightened of the strength of the Qi army, so having spent three days there he set off home. When the Marquis of Ji heard that the Lu army was retreating, he realized that he would not be able to hold out. He entrusted the capital city, together with his wife and children, to the protection of his younger brother, Ying Ji, and having said farewell to his ancestral temples, he wept bitterly. That night he ordered that the gates to the city be opened to allow him to leave. He was never seen alive again.

Ying Ji discussed the situation with his senior ministers: "Which is more important, the survival of the state or the preservation of our family sacrifices?"

The ministers all said, "The preservation of your family sacrifices is the most important!"

"If I can preserve the ancestral temples of Ji, any humiliation that I myself may suffer is worth it!" Ying Ji proclaimed.

Accordingly, he wrote a letter of surrender, expressing his wish to become a vassal of Qi, on the condition that he could preserve the ancestral temples in the city of Xi. The Marquis of Qi agreed to this. Ying Ji then presented the records of the lands of Ji and the census of their population to Qi, kowtowed, and begged for mercy. Lord Xiang of Qi took these documents and declared that thirty households living around the ancestral shrine should be responsible for continuing the sacrifices to Ji, and he appointed Ying Ji as Master of the Temple. Lady Bo Ji had been so terribly shocked by these events that she had died, so Lord Xiang of Qi ordered that she be buried with all the ceremony due to the principal wife of a lord, in the hope that this would please Lu. Lady Bo Ji's younger sister, Lady Shu Ji, had come with her to Ji when she got married and joined her as a junior wife. Lord Xiang wanted to send her back to Lu.

"It is proper for a married woman to follow her husband," Lady Shu Ji said. "In this life I have been a wife of the Ying family; when I am dead I will become a Ying ghost! If I leave here, where could I go?"

Lord Xiang agreed to let her spend her widowhood in Xi. Lady Shu Ji died there a few years later.

A historian praised this:

> As time goes by standards of behavior decline,
> Under constant attack from immorality and wickedness.
> The Marquis of Qi committed incest with his younger sister;
> Lord Xuan of Lu built the New Tower to marry his own daughter-in-law.
> Thanks to their evil actions and wolfish hearts,
> Morals were ruined and norms destroyed.
> Yet this junior wife from a minor state
> Preserved her virtue from start to finish.
> She was happy to stay and guard her husband's ancestral shrines,
> Rather than return to her own home state.
> How wonderful was Lady Shu Ji!
> The equal of the widow hymned in the song: "Cypress-wood Boat"!

Lord Xiang of Qi destroyed Ji in the seventh year of the reign of King Zhuang of Zhou.

In the same year Xiong Tong, King Wu of Chu, raised an army and attacked Sui on the grounds that they would not pay court to him. However, before he had even begun his campaign properly, he died. The prime minister, Dou Qi, and Marshal Qu Chong kept his death a secret and sent their very best troops to advance to put pressure on Sui. This state was thus terrorized into making a peace treaty. Qu Chong pretended to have received a command from his king to enter the city and make a blood covenant with the Marquis of Sui. It was only when the army had forded back over the Han River that they announced the king's demise. His son, Prince Xiong Zi, was then established as King Wen of Chu. There is no need to say more about this.

. . .

When Lord Xiang of Qi returned in triumph from having destroyed Ji, Lady Wen Jiang met her brother on the way. They then traveled to Zhuqiu, where she had prepared a magnificent banquet for him. She greeted him with the same ceremonies as would be used when two lords met, and they toasted each other again and again, as she gave a feast for the entire Qi army. Afterwards they went to Zhuo together, where they spent many happy nights in each other's company. Lord Xiang had Lady Wen Jiang write a letter summoning Lord Zhuang of Lu to Zhuo for a meeting. Lord Zhuang was afraid of disobeying his mother's orders, so he traveled to Zhuo to have audience with Lady Wen Jiang. Her Ladyship forced Lord Zhuang to treat Lord Xiang of Qi with the ceremonies due to an uncle from his nephew, and he had to express thanks for the way in which he had buried Lady Bo Ji. Lord Zhuang was not able to refuse—he had to obey. Lord Xiang was very pleased and treated Lord Zhuang with the utmost ceremony.

At that time Lord Xiang had recently had a daughter born to him, so Lady Wen Jiang proposed a marriage alliance, since at that time Lord Zhuang still had not married a principal wife.

"She is just a baby," Lord Zhuang said. "She isn't a suitable wife for me!"

Lady Wen Jiang was annoyed: "Do you want to create a breach with your mother's family?"

Lord Xiang was also concerned about the difference in their ages, but Lady Wen Jiang said, "We will wait another twenty years and then they can be married. That is not too late."

Lord Xiang was afraid that he might alienate Lady Wen Jiang, Lord Zhuang did not dare to disobey his mother's orders, and so the pair of them could only agree. As uncle and nephew, they would now become father-in-law and son-in-law, making their relationship even closer.

The two lords went hunting together in the wilds of Zhuo, and Lord Zhuang turned out to be a very fine shot, hitting his target with every arrow. Lord Xiang could not praise him enough. The local people made fun of Lord Zhuang of Lu, saying, "That is our lord's 'son.'" Lord Zhuang was furious and ordered his entourage to hunt those people down and kill them. Lord Xiang did not make the slightest protest.

A historian wrote a poem criticizing Lord Zhuang, since his concern for his mother and disregard of his father's memory meant that he did not take revenge:

Having bottled up your anger over the murder of your father for so
  many years,
How could you be happy to share a sky with such an enemy?
How can you blame the people who called you his "son,"
When you agreed to a marriage alliance with his daughter?

After the lords of Qi and Lu had gone hunting together, Lady Wen Jiang behaved with less and less restraint, and she spent all her time with Lord Xiang of Qi. Sometimes they were in Fang, sometimes they were in Gu, and the rest of the time they were in the capital of Qi, where they would openly live together in the palace, just as if they were husband and wife. The people of the capital composed the song "Galloping Horses" to criticize Lady Wen Jiang. This song runs:

> The galloping horses move quickly;
> The chariot is canopied, and the door is hung with vermilion trappings.
> The road to Lu is clear,
> The lady from Qi set out in the evening.
> The waters from the Wen sweep on;
> The travelers are in crowds.
> The road to Lu is clear,
> The lady from Qi travels at her ease.

"Quickly" refers to the appearance of the horses galloping at speed. The canopy would cover the chariot, while the door is the entrance at the back of the chariot. The vermilion trappings would be the red-dyed leather that was used to ornament the chariot. The crowds mentioned means that she was attended by many servants and followers.

They also composed the song "The Broken Trap" to criticize Lord Zhuang. This song runs:

> The broken trap lies in the pond, its fish are the bream and the *guan*.
> The lady from Qi goes to her home, her retinue like clouds.
> The broken trap lies in the pond, its fish are the bream and the tench.
> The lady from Qi goes to her home, her retinue like water.

A trap is used for catching fish. This song describes how a broken trap or net cannot control these large fish, which is an allegory for Lord Zhuang of Lu being unable to restrain Lady Wen Jiang, as a result of which her servants came and went without let or hindrance.

When Lord Xiang of Qi returned to his state from Zhuo, Shuo, Marquis of Wey, congratulated him on his success in destroying Ji and asked for a date to be set for the attack on Wey that was to restore him to power in his country.

"Now that the princess is dead, there really is no obstacle," Lord Xiang told him. "However, unless other aristocrats are involved, this will not be a strong coalition, so Your Lordship will have to wait a little longer."

The Marquis of Wey thanked him for this.

A few days later Lord Xiang sent ambassadors to the lords of Song, Lu, Chen, and Cai, suggesting that they launch a joint attack on Wey and install Lord Hui in power. His message said:

Heaven sent down a disaster upon the state of Wey, which created the wicked ministers, the Honorable Xie and Zhi. They took it upon themselves to depose a legitimately established ruler, forcing the true lord of Wey to seek sanctuary abroad. This happened seven years ago. I have not been secure in my own authority and have had many problems along the borders, which is why I have not punished them for this. Now, fortunately, I have some free time and I have gathered some tax revenue, which I propose to devote to following in Your Lordships' wake and assisting the restoration of the true lord of Wey, while punishing the one who usurped his title.

This happened in the winter of the eighth year of the reign of King Zhuang of Zhou.

Lord Xiang of Qi sent out a force of five hundred chariots and they were the first to arrive at the borders of Wey, together with Shuo, Marquis of Wey. The lords of the four other states all arrived for the meeting with their armies. Who were these four lords? They were Jie, Lord Min of Song; Tong, Lord Zhuang of Lu; Wujiu, Lord Xuan of Chen; and Xianwu, Lord Ai of Cai. When the Marquis of Wey heard that the armies of five countries had arrived, he discussed the situation with the Honorable Xie and Zhi, while sending Grandee Ning Gui to report this emergency to the Zhou king.

King Zhuang said to his assembled ministers, "Who can rescue Wey for me?"

Jifu, Duke of Zhou, and Bo, Duke of Xiguo, both said, "After the king attacked Zheng and failed to defeat them, our orders have been ignored. Now Zhuer, Marquis of Qi, ignores the relationship that exists between us due to his marriage to a Zhou princess and summons four other states to his aid to install the ruler of Wey by force. He has every right to do so, and his army is so strong that we cannot oppose him."

The very last person in the left-hand row of ministers stood forward and said, "You are both wrong, sirs! The support of four other countries just makes him strong, but how can you speak of his right to do so?"

Everyone present looked at the speaker: it was the junior Knight, Zitu.

"If a lord loses his country and others put him back in power, why do they not have a right?" the Duke of Zhou asked.

"Qianmou's accession has already been confirmed by a royal mandate," Zitu reminded him. "For Qianmou's position to be secure, we must get rid of Shuo. You do not appear to regard His Majesty's commands as right but argue that Lord Xiang should install Shuo by force—I really do not understand this!"

"Wars are won by the strongest side," the Duke of Xiguo said. "It has been a long time since anyone feared the royal house. When we attacked Zheng, even though His Late Majesty was personally present amidst his army, he was still shot by Zhu Ran. That happened two reigns back, but we still have not been able to punish anyone for it. Furthermore, the combined forces of these four countries are ten times that of Zheng. For us to go to Wey's assistance alone would be like throwing eggs at a rock and will only result in ruining our prestige still further. What is the point of that?"

"In this world, when right defeats might the situation is stable; when might defeats right there are constant problems," Zitu proclaimed. "When a royal command has been given, then it is clear who is in the right. Might may result in a temporary victory over a weak opponent; a victory that endures for a thousand years requires right. If you spurn what is right you may well achieve your ambitions, providing that no one comes forward to question you, but in that case the principles of justice that have been handed down from antiquity will be overthrown and the world will have to do without the king! In that case, will you still have the gall to call yourselves royal ministers?"

The Duke of Xiguo was not able to reply to this, but the Duke of Zhou said, "If we raise an army to rescue Wey, can you lead it?"

"Military strategy is the province of the marshal," Zitu said. "I have never held high office and have little talent in this line, so I really cannot carry out this task. However, if no one else is willing to go, then how could I refuse? I am willing to take the marshal's place!"

"If you go to rescue Wey, are you sure that you will be victorious?" the Duke of Zhou asked.

"Today, when I lead the army out of the capital, I will have right on my side," Zitu said. "Just like Kings Wen, Wu, Xuan, and Ping, we will be fighting for justice and upholding our word, making these four countries regret the crimes that they have committed. Any victory will be due to the blessings of the royal house; otherwise, I certainly would not dare to speak categorically on the subject."

Grandee Fu Chen now spoke. "Zitu's words are very brave. If we send him on this campaign, then the world will know that the royal house can still attract the services of able men."

The king of Zhou followed his advice. He told Ning Gui to return home to Wey to report that the royal army would be following close behind him.

The two dukes of Zhou and Xiguo were afraid that Zitu would indeed be successful, so they only gave him a force of two hundred armored chariots. Even so, Zitu did not attempt to shirk his responsibilities, and having made a report to the royal ancestral temples, he set off. At that time the armies of the five states had already arrived below the walls of the Wey capital, and the attack was at a critical phase. The Honorable Xie and Zhi were on patrol day and night, hoping that the royal army would arrive to lift the siege. Who would have guessed that Zitu would come with such a small force? How could he possibly withstand the ferocity of the hosts from the five states? They did not even wait for Zitu to make camp; they simply cut his army to pieces. The two hundred chariots melted away like snow in the sun.

Zitu sighed and said, "I received a royal mandate to come here. If I now die in battle, at least I will be a loyal ghost!" He killed a couple of dozen enemy soldiers before committing suicide by cutting his own throat.

A bearded old man wrote a poem commemorating this:

Even though he did not win a great victory,
The king's commands were always in his thoughts.
It is bravery and a sense of justice that marks out a great man;
It is not victory in battle that creates our heroes.

The officers guarding the walls of the Wey capital ran away when they heard that the royal army had been defeated. Qi's soldiers were the first to climb the walls, followed by the forces of the four other states. They then hacked down the city gates and let Shuo, Marquis of Wey, into the city. The Honorables Xie and Zhi, with Ning Gui, collected up the scattered remnants of their army and escorted Qianmou out of the city. They ran slap-bang into the Lu army, which resulted in another battle being fought. Ning Gui was lucky enough to be able to escape, but the other three were all taken prisoner by the Lu soldiers. Ning Gui knew that he could not possibly rescue them, so with the greatest regrets he fled into exile in the state of Qin. The Marquis of Lu handed his three prisoners over to Wey, but Wey did not dare to make a decision about them, so he presented them in turn to Qi. Lord Xiang of Qi called for the executioners, and the Honorables Xie and Zhi were beheaded on the spot. Qianmou was the son-in-law of the Zhou king, as indeed was the Marquis of Qi himself, so he pardoned him and sent him back to Zhou.

Shuo, Marquis of Wey, was then reinstalled in power to the chiming of bells and the banging of drums. He gave all the jade and other treasures in his storehouses to Lord Xiang of Qi. His Lordship said, "It was the Marquis of Lu who captured those three men alive. He too has done you a signal service." Then he gave half of what he had received to the Marquis of Lu. He got the Marquis of Wey to find some other rich items to give to the three states of Song, Chen, and Cai. This all happened in the ninth year of the reign of King Zhuang of Zhou.

After Lord Xiang of Qi defeated Zitu and released Qianmou, he was frightened that the Zhou king might punish him, so he appointed Grandee Lian Cheng as commander-in-chief and Guan Zhifu as his deputy and sent them to camp at Kuiqiu to guard the southeastern regions. As the two generals were about to set out, they asked Lord Xiang, "This kind of duty is very tough. We would not dare to disobey your orders, but when will our tour be completed?"

At that time Lord Xiang happened to be munching on a melon, and he said, "This is melon season, so next year when melon season comes around again, I will send people to take over from you."

The two generals then went to make camp at Kuiqiu. Their year-long tour of duty slipped by, and suddenly one day the soldiers in the camp were all eating fresh melons. The two generals thought of the terms of their agreement: "This is the time when we should be relieved. Why has His Lordship not sent anyone to replace us?"

They sent a trusted servant back to the capital to find out what was going on. He reported that the Marquis of Qi was enjoying himself at Gu with Lady Wen Jiang and would not be back for another month.

Lian Cheng, absolutely furious, said: "After the princess died, my younger sister should by rights have become Marchioness of Qi. Instead that bastard of a marquis pays no attention whatsoever to the proper standards of behavior, but spends all his time outside the state involved in this disgusting affair with his own sister, leaving us to rot in this hellhole. I am going to kill him . . . and you are going to help me do it!"

"His Lordship told us himself that he would send replacements in the melon season," Guan Zhifu said. "I am afraid that he has forgotten his promise, so we should remind him about it. If he still refuses to relieve us, then the army will be mutinous and we can make use of that."

"Good idea," Lian Cheng said. Then he sent someone to present a melon to Lord Xiang and beg to be relieved.

Lord Xiang was cross and said, "It is up to me whether replacements are sent out or not. How dare you come and ask for them? You will simply have to wait until the next melon season."

When the messenger came back and reported this, Lian Cheng was rendered speechless with rage. He said to Guan Zhifu, "Now is the time to strike! Do you have a plan to suggest?"

"To achieve this, we are going to need help in order to be successful," Guan Zhifu told him. "Noble Grandson Wuzhi is the son of the Honorable Yi Zhongnian. He was the younger brother of our deceased ruler, Lord Xi, by the same mother. The late Lord Xi was very fond of both Zhongnian and Wuzhi. From a very young age he was brought up in the palace, and his clothes and emoluments were no different from those of the Scion. After His Present Lordship was established, there was a time when Wuzhi went to the palace and His Lordship challenged him to a wrestling bout in which Wuzhi hooked Lord Xiang's feet out from under him and he fell to the ground. That displeased His Lordship very much. On another occasion Wuzhi was arguing with Grandee Yong Lin, and His Lordship was very angry that he would not give way, so he dismissed him from office and reduced his titles and honors by more than half. Wuzhi has been bottling up his resentment for a long time! He would be happy to rebel, but he needs help. If we get in contact with Wuzhi secretly, then he can support us from inside the capital and everything will go well."

"When will we attack?" Lian Cheng asked.

"His Lordship likes going to war and he also enjoys hunting," Guan Zhifu reminded him. "When a tiger leaves its lair, it is much easier to deal with. We will have to wait until we hear that he is leaving the capital, then we will have our opportunity."

"My younger sister is in the palace, and she deeply resents having lost His Lordship's favor," Lian Cheng said. "If we tell Wuzhi to get in touch with my sister secretly, she can keep an eye out for any opportunity and inform us immediately. That way there will be no mishaps."

He sent a letter to Noble Grandson Wuzhi by means of a trusted servant. It read:

You, sir, were loved by His Late Lordship as if you had been his own son, and now all of a sudden you have been stripped of all your privileges, which has caused much unease among the people. In addition to that, His Lordship behaves more unacceptably every day and the government is in chaos. We have been encamped at Kuiqiu for a long time, and yet even though melon season has come around again, he has not relieved us. The officers of all three armies are in mutinous mood. If there is any opportunity to do so, we plan to let slip the dogs of war and do our utmost to put you in power. My younger sister is immured in the palace, eaten up with resentment at having lost favor with His Lordship. She is willing to help you too by providing inside information. This opportunity should not be missed.

Noble Grandson Wuzhi was very pleased to get such a letter. He wrote back immediately:

Heaven abhors wicked men. Having received this expression of your innermost thoughts, I can only say that I honor your words. Please send further information as soon as possible.

Wuzhi then secretly sent a maidservant to take the original message to Lady Lian. He wrote an extra line of the top of Lian Cheng's letter: "The day that this matter is accomplished, I will make you my marchioness." Lady Lian agreed to help him.

In the tenth month of winter, in the eleventh year of the reign of King Zhuang of Zhou, Lord Xiang of Qi heard that in the wilds of Gufen there was a mountain called Beiqiu that was stuffed with game, so he wanted to go hunting there. He instructed Fei and other cronies to prepare chariots and muster an entourage, for the following month they would go there to hunt. Lady Lian sent one of her palace maids to take a message to this effect to Noble Grandson Wuzhi, and he immediately passed this information on to Kuiqiu. He set a date in the first week of the eleventh month for himself, General Lian, and General Guan to strike.

"When His Lordship leaves to go hunting, the capital will be empty," Lian Cheng said. "We can lead our soldiers straight in through the city gates and install Noble Grandson Wuzhi. How would that be?"

"His Lordship is on good terms with all his neighbors, so if he asks them to send their armies to punish us, how will we resist them?" Guan Zhifu reminded him. "It would be better to set an ambush at Gufen and assassinate that bastard, then have Noble Grandson Wuzhi succeed to the title formally. That is how this matter should be done."

At this time the soldiers stationed at Kuiqiu had been away from home for a long time, and they were all missing their families. When Lian Cheng issued secret orders that they were to prepare food and get ready to march on Beiqiu, both officers and men were happy to oblige. Of this no more.

. . .

On the first day of the eleventh month, Lord Xiang of Qi set out in his chariot, accompanied only by the knight Shi Zhi Fenru and his favorite servant, Meng Yang. They had hawks on their wrists and dogs on leashes, for they were getting ready to go hunting. Therefore, they did not want even one senior minister to accompany them. When they arrived at Gufen, a traveling palace had been built there to receive them, and they spent a day wandering around the neighborhood. The local people had presented wine and meat, so Lord Xiang held a party that lasted late into the night, and that evening he slept there. The following day he set out on his chariot for Beiqiu. The whole way, the road ran through a dense forest overhung with lush creepers. Lord Xiang halted his chariot on a high promontory and gave orders to burn the forest. Then he commanded his entourage to work a battue, and he let his hawks and dogs go. As the fire burned fiercely, foxes and rabbits ran around wildly. Suddenly an absolutely enormous wild boar leapt through the flames and charged straight for the high promontory, coming to a halt just in front of His Lordship's chariot. At that time everyone else was off shooting, and only Meng Yang stood by Lord Xiang's side.

Lord Xiang of Qi glanced at Meng Yang and said, "Shoot that boar for me."

Meng Yang stared at it wide-eyed and then cried out in alarm: "That is no wild boar! That is the Honorable Pengsheng!"

"How dare Pengsheng come and bother me!" Lord Xiang bellowed angrily. He grabbed hold of Meng Yang's bow and shot at the boar himself, but he did not hit it, even when he had shot three arrows in a row. The boar got up on its hind legs, its two front trotters placed together, and walked forward like a human being. It then uttered a chilling, painful scream, which scared Lord Xiang so badly that every hair stood on end. As he fell from his chariot, his left foot buckled under him and his embroidered silk shoe fell off. The boar picked this up in its mouth and walked away. Suddenly it disappeared.

A bearded old man wrote a poem about this:

Back then it was Lord Huan of Lu who died on top of a chariot,
Today it is you who meet a ghost while riding on your own vehicle.
By killing Pengsheng you made him yet more formidable;
There was no point in Zhuer bending the painted bow.

Fei and the other servants lifted up Lord Xiang and laid him flat on the bottom of the chariot, giving orders that the hunt should be called off and that everyone should go back to the traveling palace at Gufen for the night. Lord Xiang was still petrified, and his mind was exceedingly disturbed. The soldiers had already struck the second watch when Lord Xiang, tossing and turning and unable to sleep because of the pain in his left foot, said to Meng Yang, "Could you lift me up and help me to walk for a few steps?"

When he had fallen from his chariot earlier that day, he had been in such a state that he did not notice that he had lost a shoe, but now he discovered that one was missing, and he asked Fei to go and get it.

"Your shoe was carried off in the mouth of the wild boar," Fei informed him.

Lord Xiang felt curiously disgusted by this, and flying into a rage, he screamed: "It is your job to look after me! Surely you can keep an eye on my shoes! If it was carried off by the boar, why didn't you say so earlier?"

He grabbed hold of a leather whip and started belaboring Fei's back. He did not stop until blood had spattered all over the ground. After his whipping, Fei went out of the door holding back his tears, only to walk straight into Lian Cheng, who had come with a small group of soldiers to investigate what was going on. They immediately took Fei prisoner.

"Where is that bastard, our ruler?" they demanded.

"In his bedroom," Fei said.

"Is he asleep?"

"Not yet."

Lian Cheng raised his sword and was just about to behead him when Fei said, "Don't kill me! I will go on ahead and act as your eyes and ears." Lian Cheng did not believe him, but Fei continued: "I have just been severely beaten. I would be happy to kill that bastard myself!" He then stripped off his shirt to show them his back. When Lian Cheng saw how his back was raw and dripping with blood, he trusted every word he had said and released Fei from his bonds. He told him that he should keep an eye on the situation for them and then went back to summon Guan Zhifu and the bulk of his soldiers, who would actually carry out the attack on the traveling palace.

Fei went back, and when he ran across Shi Zhi Fenru, he told him that Lian Cheng was planning a revolt. Afterwards, he went to Lord Xiang's bedchamber and reported this to him. Lord Xiang was so appalled, he did not know what to do.

"It is too late to run away," Fei told him. "If someone dresses up as Your Lordship and lies down in your bed, you can hide behind the door. If we are lucky and the soldiers don't look too closely, you may yet escape!"

"Your Lordship has always been kinder to me than I deserve, so I am happy to act as your proxy," Meng Yang told him. "If I die, I will have no regrets!" He then lay down on the bed and kept his face turned towards the wall. Lord Xiang took off his brocade robe and covered him with it, then went to hide behind the door.

"What are you going to do?" he asked Fei.

"I will be helping Shi Zhi Fenru to hold off the rebels."

"Do you not mind the injuries that I inflicted upon you?"

"Even if you killed me, I would not mind. These injuries are nothing!"

Lord Xiang sighed and said, "You are indeed a loyal subject!"

Fei ordered Shi Zhi Fenru to take his men and defend the main gate, while he himself went the other way, holding a sword. He would pretend to welcome the rebels, but in fact he was hoping for an opportunity to kill Lian Cheng.

By this time the main force had already fought their way through the main gate: Lian Cheng, with a sword in his hand, was cutting a path through the defenders while Guan Zhifu and his troops were waiting outside the gate, to prevent anyone from escaping. When Fei saw the violence of Lian Cheng's attack, without a moment's hesitation he took a step forward and stabbed him. Who would have guessed that Lian Cheng was wearing double-thickness armor so the blade did not penetrate? The first sweep of Lian Cheng's sword cut off two of Fei's fingers; the second blow took off half of his head. Fei died in the middle of the gate. Shi Zhi Fenru then picked up a spear and came forward to fight, and they crossed swords a dozen times, Lian Cheng advancing all the way. Shi Zhi Fenru was retreating gradually when he lost his footing, stumbling over a stone step, and he too was beheaded by a single blow from Lian Cheng's sword.

When they entered His Lordship's bedchamber, his bodyguards had already fled in panic. There was only one person lying in bed amid the flowered curtains, and he was covered by a silk brocade gown. Lian Cheng raised his arm and let his sword fall. The head bounced down from the pillows. He lifted up a torch to light up the scene, but seeing that the head was that of a young and beardless man, Lian Cheng shouted, "That is not His Lordship!"

He ordered his followers to search the room, but there was no sign of anyone else. Lian Cheng was searching with a torch in his hand to light the way when suddenly he caught sight of one embroidered silk shoe sitting on the doorstep. He realized that someone was hiding behind the door. Who could that be if not Zhuer himself? When he pulled back the door to see, the wicked marquis collapsed in a heap from the pain in his foot; the other embroidered silk shoe was safe and sound on his right foot. The shoe that Lian Cheng had spotted was the one that had been carried off in the mouth of the wild boar. No one could imagine how it had come to be on the doorstep. It must have been the work of ghosts—how terrifying!

Lian Cheng recognized Zhuer, who was now as helpless as a baby bird, and with one arm he dragged him out from behind the door and hurled him to the ground. He cursed him: "You wicked bastard! You send your armies out year after year, getting your people killed for no reason other than that you enjoy fighting—that is not benevolent. You disobeyed your father's orders and dismissed Noble Grandson Wuzhi from office—that is not filial. You have had an incestuous relationship with your own younger sister and paid no attention to the proper standards of behavior—that is immoral. You have spared no thought for your soldiers stationed far away, and even when melon season came around again, you did not send replacements—that means that you have broken your word! If you fail in the four great virtues of benevolence, filial piety, morality, and trustworthiness, can you really be considered human? Today I will take revenge on behalf of Lord Huan of Lu!"

He hacked Lord Xiang to pieces and wrapped up the remains in the blanket on the bed. He and Meng Yang were buried together, their bodies covered by the door. In all, Lord Xiang of Qi ruled for only five years.

When historians discuss this matter, they point out that Lord Xiang paid no attention to his senior ministers but was very partial to some of his juniors. Shi Zhi Fenru, Meng Yang, Fei, and so on all benefited from his favoritism and encouraged him in his wickedness. Even though in the end they died for him, they cannot be considered in the same light as virtuous ministers who die out of loyalty. Lian Cheng and Guan Zhifu plotted this assassination because they had been on duty for a long time without relief; if Lord Xiang had kept his promises, they would not have done this. Before he was executed, Pengsheng shouted: "When I die I will become a vengeful ghost, then I will come back to claim your life!" The appearance of the wild boar was no coincidence.

A bearded old man wrote a poem commemorating the deaths of Fei and Shi Zhi Fenru. This poem reads:

To die for your ruler is a loyal and virtuous act,
But Fei and Shi Zhi Fenru are not remembered in this way.
If obeying a wicked ruler to the end earned you an honorable reputation,
Then would not Fei Lian and Chong Hu be of glorious memory?

There is also a poem bemoaning Lord Xiang of Qi's career:

Your evil actions caused the death of another lord,
And in turn your life was snuffed out by a wild boar.
Having done such wicked things, of course you had to die,
There is no doubt that this encourages people to do good!

Lian Cheng and Guan Zhifu collected their forces and set off at all speed for the Qi capital. Noble Grandson Wuzhi had recruited his own private army, and when he got the news that Lord Xiang was dead, he led his soldiers to open the city gates and allow Lian Cheng and Guan Zhifu into the city. The two generals issued a statement: "In accordance with the dying wishes of our late ruler, Lord Xi, we will install Noble Grandson Wuzhi as the new marquis."

Lady Lian was appointed as his marchioness, while Lian Cheng became a senior minister and received the honorific title "Leader of the Nation." Guan Zhifu became a middle-ranking minister. Although the other grandees were forced to take office, none of them obeyed willingly. It was only Yong Lin who kept kowtowing and apologizing for having argued with him in the past in a very demeaning manner. Wuzhi pardoned him, and he kept his post as a grandee. The Gao and Guo ministerial families announced that they were all far too ill to come to court, and Wuzhi did not dare to dismiss them from office. Guan Zhifu suggested to Wuzhi that he should issue placards, recruiting clever men to his service, in order to encourage people to look favorably on his rule. He also recommended a member of his own clan, Guan Yiwu, for his talents, and Wuzhi sent someone to summon him.

Do you know if Guan Yiwu was willing to respond to this summons? READ ON.

Chapter Fifteen

Grandee Yong Lin plots the murder
of Wuzhi.

Lord Zhuang of Lu fights a great battle
at Ganshi.

Guan Yiwu had the style-name Zhong. He was a very handsome man of great intelligence, who was learned in the classics and history. He was possessed of most remarkable talents, such as would define the age in which he lived. There was a time when he and Bao Shuya went into business together. When the time came to divide the profits, Guan Yiwu took twice as much for himself, which made Bao Shuya's followers unhappy. Bao Shuya told them, "Guan Zhong isn't greedy for this small sum of money. However, his family is poor and I am happy to let him have it!"

It also happened that several times he went out on campaign, and every time the army went into battle formation, he would immediately head for the rear, and when the time came for the army to go home, he was the first to leave. There were many people who laughed at him for being a coward. Bao Shuya said, "Guan Zhong has an old mother at home, and he has to stay alive to look after her. He certainly isn't afraid of fighting!"

There were also a number of occasions when Guan Yiwu was planning things with Bao Shuya, and the former's advice only made the whole situation worse. Bao Shuya's only response was to say, "Sometimes things go well and sometimes they go badly. When Guan Zhong meets with the right opportunity, he will not fail!"

When Guan Yiwu heard this, he sighed and said, "My parents gave me life, but it is Bao Shuya who really understands me!" From that point onwards they became the very best of friends.

Lord Xiang of Qi's oldest son was named Jiu, and he was the son of a woman from the state of Lu. His second son was called Xiaobai, and he was the son of a woman from the state of Ju. Since both were born to concubines, they had an equal right to succeed to the title, and both were looking to appoint advisors to support and instruct them. Guan Yiwu said to Bao Shuya, "His Lordship has two sons, and one of them will come to power—if not Jiu, then Xiaobai. You and I should each support one of them. That way when one of them succeeds to the title, we can recommend each other for office."

Bao Shuya thought his advice was very sensible. Guan Yiwu and another man, Shao Hu, acted as the Honorable Jiu's advisors, while Bao Shuya worked for the Honorable Xiaobai.

When Lord Xiang of Qi met Lady Wen Jiang at Zhuo, Bao Shuya said to the Honorable Xiaobai, "His Lordship's evil reputation has destroyed his credit among his own people, but if he were to keep within his current bounds, we would be able to cover the whole thing up. If, however, he keeps on coming and going between the capital and Zhuo, the gossip will be like water pounding against a dam, until it crumbles and overflows. You must remonstrate with him!"

Xiaobai did as he had been told and went to the palace to remonstrate with Lord Xiang: "Since the death of the Marquis of Lu, there has been enormous gossip. You must avoid any suggestion that you are involved in an illicit relationship!"

Lord Xiang was angry: "It is not appropriate for a child to talk about such things!" He threw his shoes at him, and Xiaobai ran away.

"I have heard it said that those who are especially wicked receive an exemplary punishment," Bao Shuya said. "We should go into exile abroad and await further developments!"

"In which country should we seek asylum?" Xiaobai asked.

"A great state would not be suitable: it would be best to go to Ju," Bao Shuya told him. "Ju is both small and close to Qi. Since it is only a little country, they will not dare to treat us badly, and it is so close that we can go home within a single day!"

"That's a good idea!" Xiaobai exclaimed.

Accordingly, they fled into exile in Ju. When Lord Xiang heard about this, he made no attempt to go after them.

After Noble Grandson Wuzhi usurped the title, he summoned Guan Yiwu.

"The executioner's sword is already at his throat, and he is still trying to drag other people down with him!" Guan Yiwu exclaimed. He and

Shao Hu then decided to flee into exile in Lu together with the Honorable Jiu, for Lu was his mother's state. Lord Zhuang of Lu let them live in Shengdou and gave them a monthly allowance.

In the second month of spring in the twelfth year of the reign of King Zhuang of Zhou, Noble Grandson Wuzhi of Qi began his reign and all his officials gathered at court to congratulate him. When they saw Lian Cheng and Guan Zhifu assume the positions of honor there, everyone was angry. Yong Lin knew that the others were unhappy with the situation, so he put a cunning question to them: "I have a client who has recently arrived from Lu, and he says that the Honorable Jiu is just about to attack Qi with the Lu army. Have you heard this news too?"

"We have not heard a word about it," the other grandees said.

Yong Lin said nothing more, but then, after the morning court was dismissed, the officials all got together and decided that they should go to his house and ask for more news about the Honorable Jiu's plan to attack Qi.

"What do you think about this, gentlemen?" Yong Lin inquired.

"His Late Lordship was a horrible man, but that is not his son's fault!" Dongguo Ya exclaimed. "We would all be happy to see him come back." Some of the grandees were in tears at this.

"Do you think I was happy to bend my knees to him?" Yong Lin demanded. "I accepted this humiliation in order to be able to survive, to plan for the future! If you are all happy to help, then we can get rid of this bunch of murderers and install the son of our late lord. Surely that would be a virtuous act!"

Dongguo Ya asked if he had a plan of campaign, and Yong Lin said: "Gao Jingzhong's ancestors have served as ministers in this country for many generations, and he is both admired and trusted by the people for his abilities. That pair of criminals, Lian Cheng and Guan Zhifu, would be delighted at even the smallest sign of regard from him, and they deeply resent the fact that he has not even noticed their existence. If we get Gao Jingzhong to give a banquet in their honor, they will be delighted to attend. I will pretend to have received news that the Honorable Jiu is raising an army, and I will report this to Noble Grandson Wuzhi. He is a stupid and cowardly man, who relies entirely on his advisors. If I then kill him, who will come to his rescue? We can use the lighting of beacons as the signal that Wuzhi is dead, and then we can capture and execute the two other criminals. It will be as easy as waving your hand!"

"Gao Jingzhong hates wicked men as if they were his own personal enemies," Dongguo Ya said. "He will be happy to do what he can for the sake of the country, whatever the cost to himself. I think we can do this."

He reported Yong Lin's plan to Gao Jingzhong, who agreed to play his part.

Gao Jingzhong ordered Dongguo Ya to take the invitations around to the houses of Lian Cheng and Guan Zhifu, and on the appointed day they both arrived. Gao Jingzhong raised his goblet and said, "Our late lord did many wicked things, and I expected him to bring the country to ruin. Now, thankfully, you two have helped a new ruler to power, and I have been able to preserve the ancestral temples of my own family. Thanks to my great age and poor health, I have not been able to attend court recently; however, in recent days there has been some improvement, and so I have arranged for a little banquet to thank you for all that you have done and to entrust my sons and grandsons to your care."

Lian Cheng and Guan Zhifu said all that was polite. Gao Jingzhong gave orders that the gates be shut and locked. "Today we are drinking and will not stop until we have enjoyed ourselves to the utmost." He warned the gatekeeper: "Do not let anyone come in! When you see the beacons lit inside the city walls, then come and report."

Meanwhile, Yong Lin concealed a dagger about his person and went to bang on the palace doors. When he was granted an audience with Wuzhi, he proclaimed, "The Honorable Jiu will arrive any moment at the head of the Lu army! Luckily we have time to plan for how to meet the enemy."

"Where is the Leader of the Nation?" Wuzhi asked.

"The Leader of the Nation has gone drinking somewhere in the suburbs with Grandee Guan," Yong Bin told him. "He has not yet returned. Your officials are all gathered at court, waiting for Your Lordship to come and discuss the situation with them."

Wuzhi believed him and went straight to the audience chamber. Before he had even sat down, the grandees rushed forward to grab hold of him, and Yong Lin stabbed him from behind. Blood poured out over his throne and he died right then and there. Wuzhi had held power for just over a month. How tragic!

When historians discuss these events, they say that Lord Xi's excessive affection for Yi Zhongnian and his son brought them to ruin.

There is a poem that bewails this:

His mother's love allowed Duan to raise an army;
His father's favoritism enabled Zhouyu to start a civil war.

If Lord Xi had observed proper distinctions between noble and commoner,
Both sides could have lived happily together and no one need have died.

When Lady Lian heard the news, she hanged herself in the palace.
A historian wrote a poem that says:

Because she was not favored, she participated in the attack on Lord
Xiang,
Who would have guessed that Wuzhi's love would also be so fleeting?
A month of being a marchioness finished at the end of a rope,
Would it not have been better living a lonely life in an empty palace?

Yong Lin ordered people to light the beacons outside the court, and
the smoke rose high up into the heavens. Gao Jingzhong was in the middle of entertaining his guests, when suddenly he received a message from
outside: "The beacons outside the palace have been lit." Gao Jingzhong
immediately got up and walked towards the inner apartments. Lian
Cheng and Guan Zhifu had no idea what he meant by this and were just
about to ask what was going on, when the soldiers lying in ambush in
the side rooms suddenly rushed out and cut the pair of them down.
Their followers were completely unarmed, and they were killed too.

Yong Lin and the other grandees gathered at the Gao mansion, where
they discussed their next move. They cut out Lian Cheng and Guan
Zhifu's heart and liver and sacrificed them to the shades of Lord Xiang.
Afterwards, they sent someone to the traveling palace at Gufen to find
Lord Xiang's body and rebury it in a proper coffin. They also sent someone to the state of Lu to collect the Honorable Jiu, for he would be their
new lord.

. . .

When Lord Zhuang of Lu heard what had happened, he was very
pleased and wanted to raise an army to help install the Honorable Jiu in
power. Shi Bo remonstrated: "Qi is strong and Lu is weak—it is to our
advantage that Qi does not have a ruler. I beg that you will do nothing,
just wait and see what happens."

Lord Zhuang could not make up his mind what to do for the best.
After Lord Xiang had been assassinated, Lady Wen Jiang returned to
the state of Lu from Zhuqiu. Day and night she urged her son to raise
an army to attack Qi to punish Wuzhi for his crimes and avenge her
older brother. Now she heard that Wuzhi had been killed and that an
ambassador had come from Qi to fetch the Honorable Jiu and make

him the new marquis, so her joy was unconfined. She was determined to see Jiu installed in power, and she encouraged Lord Zhuang to assist him. Lord Zhuang was unable to resist his mother's importunate urgings, so he ignored Shi Bo's advice. He took personal command of a force of three hundred chariots. Having appointed Cao Mo as the senior general, the Viscount of Qin and the Viscount of Liang to command the Left and Right armies, he escorted the Honorable Jiu to Qi.

Guan Yiwu advised the Marquis of Lu: "The Honorable Xiaobai is living in Ju, and Ju is a great deal closer to Qi than Lu is. If he gets there first, he will be the next marquis! I beg that you will give me a team of good horses, and I will go on ahead to stop him!"

"How many soldiers will you need?" the Marquis of Lu asked.

"Thirty chariots will be enough," Guan Yiwu assured him.

When the Honorable Xiaobai heard that the country was in chaos and without a ruler, he discussed the situation with Bao Shuya. Then he borrowed a force of one hundred chariots from the Viscount of Ju to escort him back to Qi. Meanwhile, Guan Yiwu and his troops traveled day and night. When they arrived at Jimo, they heard that the Ju forces had already passed through, and so they set off in pursuit. Having advanced another thirty *li*, they came across the Ju troops, who had halted their chariots in order to cook up a meal. Guan Yiwu caught sight of the Honorable Xiaobai sitting in one of the chariots, so he went up to him and bowed: "How are you, sir? Where are you going?"

"I am going to attend my father's funeral," Xiaobai said.

"The Honorable Jiu is your father's oldest son, so naturally he will be the chief mourner," Guan Yiwu insisted. "You should stay here. There is no need to put yourself to all this trouble."

"Please go away," Bao Shuya broke in. "We each serve our own master. There is nothing more to discuss!"

Guan Yiwu noticed that the Ju soldiers were looking angry and gearing up for a fight, and he was afraid that the small force under his command would be no match for them. Therefore, he pretended to accept the situation and leave. However, he quickly whipped out an arrow and fitted it to his bow. Taking aim at Xiaobai, he let it fly. Xiaobai screamed in pain, blood spurting from his mouth, as he collapsed on the chariot. Bao Shuya rushed to his aid, and everyone started shouting "Help!" They were all in tears. Guan Yiwu and his thirty chariots ran away as fast as they possibly could.

As he traveled back, Guan Yiwu sighed and said, "Luck is on the Honorable Jiu's side, so it is only right that he should become our ruler!"

He reported what had happened to the Marquis of Lu, who held a party for the Honorable Jiu to celebrate. His Lordship's mind was now completely at rest, so they proceeded slowly on their journey, having banquets all the way with important local officials. None of them had the slightest idea that the arrow had only struck the Honorable Xiaobai's belt buckle. Xiaobai knew that Guan Yiwu was a fine shot and was afraid that he might have better luck a second time, so in a flash of inspiration he bit down on his tongue so that the blood spurted from his mouth as he pretended to collapse. In the first instance, even Bao Shuya was completely taken in.

"Guan Yiwu has gone now, but he could easily come back again," Bao Shuya exclaimed. "We must not delay any longer!" He had Xiaobai put on some different clothes and made him ride in a closed carriage, as they hurried along the back roads to Qi.

When they approached Linzi, Bao Shuya entered the city ahead of the rest, riding alone in his chariot. He made the rounds of all the grandees praising the Honorable Xiaobai's qualities.

"The Honorable Jiu will arrive soon. How will you deal with him?" the grandees inquired.

"Qi has had two rulers assassinated one after the other, and a stupid man cannot deal with this situation," Bao Shuya said. "It is by Heaven's will that you summoned the Honorable Jiu and yet Xiaobai was the first to arrive. The Lord of Lu plans to install Jiu by force, and he is expecting to be generously rewarded for this. In the past, when Song established the Honorable Tu in power, they extorted endless amounts of money, which led to years of warfare. We have had so many troubles lately, how will we resist Lu's demands?"

"That being the case, how can we make the Marquis of Lu go away?" the grandees asked.

"When he finds out that we already have a lord, he will leave of his own accord!" Bao Shuya pointed out.

The grandees Xi Peng and Dongguo Ya both said, "You are right!" They welcomed Xiaobai into the city and installed him as the new ruler. He became Lord Huan of Qi.

An old man wrote a poem commemorating the shooting of the belt buckle. This poem reads:

> The Marquis of Lu triumphed as the people of Ju despaired.
> Who would have guessed the arrow hit only the belt buckle?
> From just this one incident during this conflict,
> We learn that only the wise can unite the feudal lords.

"Given that the Lu army has not yet arrived, we ought to make preparations to defend against them!" Bao Shuya announced. He sent Zhongsun Qiu to meet Lord Zhuang of Lu and inform him that Qi already had a new marquis.

When Lord Zhuang realized that Xiaobai was still alive, he was furious and said, "We have a system of primogeniture—how can a younger son become the new ruler? I cannot simply withdraw my three armies empty-handed!"

Zhongsun Qiu returned to report this message.

"If the Lu army refuses to retreat, what do we do?" Lord Huan of Qi asked.

"We use force to get rid of them!" Bao Shuya proclaimed. He then appointed Prince Chengfu to command the Army of the Right, with Ning Yue to assist him; and Dongguo Ya to command the Army of the Left, with Zhongsun Qiu to assist him. Bao Shuya helped Lord Huan of Qi to command the Central Army, and Yong Lin took charge of the vanguard. Each of these forces consisted of five hundred chariots. When the plan of campaign was set, Dongguo Ya said: "The Lord of Lu is sure to realize that we will be prepared to meet him, and so he will not dare to advance too quickly. Ganshi offers us advantageous terrain on which to camp our army. If we can place our troops in ambush before he arrives, we can catch him off guard. Victory will then be assured!"

"Good idea!" Bao Shuya exclaimed. He ordered Ning Yue and Zhongsun Qiu to take the troops under their command and set ambushes at two different sites; he also ordered Prince Chengfu and Dongguo Ya to take a circuitous route and come up behind the Lu army. Yong Lin went out to provoke battle and entice the enemy into an unfavorable position.

When Lord Zhuang of Lu and the Honorable Jiu arrived at Ganshi, Guan Yiwu came forward and said, "Xiaobai has just been established, but he has yet to gain the loyalty of his people. If we take advantage of this to act quickly, our coup will be successful."

"I thought you said that Xiaobai was already dead," Lord Zhuang sneered.

He issued orders to make camp at Ganshi. The Marquis of Lu was camped in front and the Honorable Jiu was camped behind him, separated by a distance of twenty *li*.

Early the following morning, spies reported: "The Qi army has arrived, and they have sent Yong Lin from the vanguard to provoke battle."

"Let us first defeat the Qi army, for then the people in the capital will naturally be scared witless!" Lord Zhuang declared. He ordered the Viscount of Qin and the Viscount of Liang to drive his battle chariot out in front of the army, whereupon he shouted for Yong Lin to come out in person: "You were the chief conspirator in the murder of your last ruler, and you asked us to help the Honorable Jiu. Now you seem to have changed your mind. Where is your sense of justice and good faith?"

He drew his bow and tried to shoot Yong Lin. Yong Lin pretended to be ashamed of himself and fled with his tail between his legs. Lord Zhuang ordered Cao Mo to pursue him. Yong Lin turned his chariot around to fight, but having crossed swords a few times, he fled again. Cao Mo did not want to let him get away—being a brave man, he grabbed his painted spear and set off in hot pursuit, only to find himself surrounded by Bao Shuya and a great host of soldiers. Cao Mo was completely encircled. He tried to break out first to the left and then to the right. He was finally able to escape, but he left with two arrows stuck fast in his flesh.

The two Lu generals, the Viscount of Qin and the Viscount of Liang, were worried that Cao Mo had gotten into trouble, and so they came forward to help him. Suddenly they heard the deep rumble of siege engines to both left and right, and the troops set in ambush by Ning Yue and Zhongsun Qiu rose up. Bao Shuya and the Central army advanced towards them like a wall. There was no way that the Lu army could resist the enemy advancing on them from three directions, so they scattered and fled. Bao Shuya issued the order: "The man who captures the Marquis of Lu will be rewarded with a city of ten thousand households." He ordered the Central Army to shout this message to their fellows.

The Viscount of Qin grabbed hold of the Marquis of Lu's embroidered yellow banner and threw it to the ground. The Viscount of Liang picked it up again and hung it above his own chariot. The Viscount of Qin asked him what he was doing. The Viscount of Liang explained: "I am going to use it to trick Qi." When Lord Zhuang of Lu realized how critical the situation had become, he jumped down from his battle chariot and got into a light chariot instead, where he changed into plain clothes and prepared to flee. The Viscount of Qin kept close by, cutting his way through the encircling enemy. Ning Yue caught sight of the embroidered flag in the distance traveling along the lower road and thought it was the Marquis of Lu. He directed his troops to encircle him. The Viscount of Liang took off his helmet to reveal his face and announced: "I am one of the Lu generals. My lord is already far away."

Bao Shuya knew that the Qi army had already won a signal victory, so he sounded the bell in order to recall his forces. Zhongsun Qiu presented him with the armored chariot captured from the Marquis of Lu, while Ning Yue presented the Viscount of Liang. The Marquis of Qi beheaded him in front of the army. Since Prince Chengfu and Dongguo Ya had gone off with their armies in different directions and there was still no word from them, the Marquis of Qi ordered Ning Yue and Zhongsun Qiu to make camp at Ganshi, while he himself returned to the capital in triumph with the Central Army.

Guan Yiwu and the others had been left in charge of the heavy baggage at the rear camp. When they heard that the army ahead of them had been defeated, he told Shao Hu and the Honorable Jiu to hold the fort while he himself gathered all the men and chariots at his disposal to go to their assistance. When he met up with Lord Zhuang of Lu, he joined forces with him. Cao Mo also gathered up the scattered remnants of his army and came to join them. When they counted up their troops, out of every ten, they had lost seven.

"The army has no stomach for a fight, so we cannot stay here," Guan Yiwu ordained. He ordered them to strike camp that very night and set off home.

Before they had traveled even two days, they suddenly saw soldiers and chariots blocking the road. This was Prince Chengfu and Dongguo Ya, who were cutting off the Lu army's retreat. Cao Mo grabbed his halberd and shouted, "Run, Your Lordship! I will die here!" He glanced towards the Viscount of Qin: "You must help me!" The Viscount of Qin fought with Prince Chengfu, while Cao Mo took on Dongguo Ya. Guan Yiwu protected Lord Zhuang of Lu, while Shao Hu guarded the Honorable Jiu as they cut their way out. There was a young officer in red who came in hot pursuit of the Marquis of Lu—Lord Zhuang shot him through the head with a single arrow. Later on there was another man in white who came close, and again Lord Zhuang of Lu shot him dead. The Qi soldiers gradually fell back, and Guan Yiwu ordered his remaining troops to abandon their heavy armor, weapons, and equipment along the road and let the Qi troops have these things, since that would allow them time to escape. Cao Mo's left arm had been slashed to the bone by sword; nevertheless, he killed countless Qi soldiers and broke out of the encirclement. The Viscount of Qin died in battle.

When historians talk about Lord Zhuang of Lu forgetting that the Marquis of Qi murdered his father, to the point where in life they campaigned together and in death he supported his heir, they say he brought his defeat at Ganshi upon himself.

There is a poem that bewails these events:

The Honorable Jiu was his enemy's son;
Why should he raise an army to install him?
If he had remembered that he should not share the same sky with this
    man,
He would have helped Wuzhi rather than Jiu!

Lord Zhuang of Lu and the others were able to wrench themselves out of the tiger's jaws; then, like fish slipping through a broken net, they fled as quickly as they could. Xi Peng and Dongguo Ya came in pursuit and chased them across the Wen River. They captured all the lands on the north side of the Wen River within the borders of Lu and established guard posts there. The main body of the army then departed. The people of Lu did not dare to fight them, and so the Qi army went home in triumph.

Xiaobai, Marquis of Qi, held court early the next morning, and his officials offered their congratulations. Bao Shuya came forward and said, "The Honorable Jiu is now resident in Lu, and he has Guan Yiwu and Shao Hu to assist him. Lu is also prepared to help. As long as this menace exists, there is nothing to congratulate you about."

"What is to be done about this?" the Marquis of Qi asked.

"After the battle of Ganshi, the ruler and ministers of Lu must be very frightened," Bao Shuya said. "I will take the three armies to camp on the border with Lu, demanding to be allowed to execute the Honorable Jiu. Lu will be so terrified that they will have to accede to our demands."

"I will mobilize the army as you suggest," the Marquis of Qi said.

Bao Shuya then mustered chariots and horses and led a great host straight to the north bank of the Wen River, where he marked out the new border. He sent Xi Peng to take a letter to the Marquis of Lu, which read:

The subject of a foreign ruler, Bao Shuya, bows one hundred times to His Lordship, the excellent Marquis of Lu. A family cannot have two heads, and a country cannot have two rulers. His Present Lordship has already been presented at the ancestral shrines, so if the Honorable Jiu were to contest this we would be in the position of having two rulers. His Lordship is aware of the fact that Jiu is his older brother and therefore cannot bear to execute him himself, so we are hoping that you will do so on our behalf. Guan Yiwu and Shao Hu are His Lordship's enemies, and we ask you to hand them over so we can sacrifice them at the ancestral temple.

When Xi Peng was about to set out, Bao Shuya instructed him: "Guan Yiwu is a remarkably talented man, and I have spoken to His Lordship about summoning him into our service. Whatever happens, you must prevent his death."

"What do I do if Lu decides to kill him?" Xi Peng asks.

"Just mention the fact that he shot His Lordship's buckle, and Lu is sure to believe you," Bao Shuya advised.

Xi Peng agreed and then set off on his journey. When the Marquis of Lu received this letter, he summoned Shi Bo.

Do you want to know the result of their discussions? READ ON.

Chapter Sixteen

After his release from imprisonment, Bao Shuya recommends Guan Zhong for office.

In the battle of Changshao, Cao Gui defeats Qi.

When Lord Zhuang of Lu received Bao Shuya's letter, he immediately summoned Shi Bo to discuss the matter. "I led my troops into a terrible defeat because I did not listen to your advice. Which would be preferable: to kill Jiu or to let him live?"

"Xiaobai has only just succeeded to the title, and yet he was able to command a vast army and defeat us as Ganshi," Shi Bo said. "The Honorable Jiu simply cannot compare. Now the Qi army is at our borders. It would be better to kill Jiu and make peace with them!"

At this time the Honorable Jiu was living at Shengdou together with Guan Yiwu and Shao Hu. Lord Zhuang of Lu sent the Honorable Yan in command of an army to make a surprise attack on them, and Jiu was killed. They captured Shao Hu and Guan Yiwu alive. As they prepared to haul them back to Lu in cages, Shao Hu looked up at the sky and said sadly, "A son can die to prove his filial piety, a subject can die to demonstrate his loyalty—that is their duty! I would rather follow the Honorable Jiu into the Underworld than suffer the humiliation of being placed in fetters and chains." He killed himself by breaking his head open on one of the bars.

"Every ruler since time immemorial has had subjects who die and subjects who live," Guan Yiwu said. "I am going to return alive to the state of Qi, that I may proclaim the Honorable Jiu's innocence of any wrongdoing!" He was then chained and placed inside the cage.

Shi Bo spoke privately to Lord Zhuang of Lu: "I have observed Master Guan closely, and he seems to be deriving inner strength from something, as if he is sure that he will not be killed. He is a very remarkable man—if he escapes execution, he is sure to achieve high office in Qi and make His Lordship hegemon. Lu will then be in serious trouble. Why don't you beg Qi to let him live, my lord? If Master Guan survives, he will be very grateful to us. In that case, he will accept office here and we will have nothing to worry about from Qi!"

"He is a personal enemy of the new Marquis of Qi," Lord Zhuang said. "Even though we have put the Honorable Jiu to death, their anger will not be assuaged if we keep him!"

"Well, if Your Lordship feels that we cannot employ him ourselves, then we should kill him and hand his body back to Qi!" Shi Bo said.

"That is a good idea," Lord Zhuang agreed.

Xi Peng heard that Lu was going to kill Guan Yiwu, so he rushed to court and demanded an audience with Lord Zhuang, at which he proclaimed: "Guan Yiwu shot His Lordship and hit his belt buckle, so my lord now hates him more than he can say. He wants to wield the executioner's knife himself, in order to assuage his feelings. If you just hand back the body, it will be no use."

Lord Zhuang believed every word that he said and ordered the arrest of Guan Yiwu. He had Shao Hu's head sealed into a box and handed over to Xi Peng. Xi Peng expressed his thanks and left.

When Guan Yiwu was put into his cage, he understood Bao Shuya's idea, but he was still frightened: "Shi Bo is a clever man. Even though they have released me now, he may well change his mind and come in pursuit. In that case I will die!"

He came up with a plan to counter this and composed a song titled "Brown Dove," which he taught his guards to sing. The words ran as follows:

Brown dove, brown dove: it folds its wings and rests its feet,
It does not fly, it does not sing, it just sits at the bottom of its cage.
How vast are the heavens? How great is the earth?
Having met with disaster and encountered peril,
It stretches its neck and sings, almost seeming to cry!
Brown dove, brown dove,
Heaven gave you wings that you should be able to fly,
Heaven gave you feet so that you could run away,
But, having been caught by this net, who will save you?
If one day you should be able to break free,

I do not know if you will be able to fly to the treetops or soar into the sky.
The huntsmen are too close around you . . .

When his guards had learned this song, they sang it as they walked. They were so pleased with it that they forgot how tired they were. The chariots sped along and the horses galloped. In the space of a single day, they covered a distance that would normally have taken them two days to cross, and they had left the borders of Lu far behind them. Just as Guan Yiwu anticipated, Lord Zhuang of Lu changed his mind and sent the Honorable Yan in pursuit, but he did not catch up with them in time. He had no choice but to return empty-handed. Guan Yiwu looked up at the sky and sighed: "Today it is as if I have been reborn!"

When the party arrived at Tangfu, they found Bao Shuya already in residence. Catching sight of Guan Yiwu, he behaved as if he had found a treasure; he conducted him into the guesthouse, saying, "It is wonderful that you have arrived safe and sound!"

He immediately gave orders that his chains be struck off, but Guan Yiwu objected: "Unless you have received a command from His Lordship to do so, you should not have them removed on your own authority."

"Since you have made it here in one piece, I will go and recommend you to His Lordship's service," Bao Shuya promised.

"Shao Hu and I both served the Honorable Jiu, and I was unable to elevate him to the position of our lord," Guan Yiwu said. "Likewise, I did not commit suicide when he got into trouble. I have already brought enough shame on myself. How could I now take office under his enemy? If the dead have awareness, Shao Hu from his place in the Underworld would be ashamed of me!"

"A man who does great things does not worry about petty humiliations; a man who achieves a signal success does not care about minor restrictions," Bao Shuya proclaimed. "With your abilities you could govern the whole country, it is just that you have not met with a propitious opportunity. His Lordship is an ambitious and clever man. With your assistance he will put the state of Qi in good order and quite possibly go on to become hegemon. Your achievements will then define this generation, and your name will be famous among the lords. Why should you do something so pointless as to refuse this opportunity, simply in order to preserve an honorable reputation that no one cares about?"

Guan Yiwu was silent. They loosened his bonds for the duration of his stay at Tangfu. Meanwhile, Bao Shuya went back to Linzi to have an audience with Lord Huan. First he condoled with him, and then he congratulated him.

"Why are you offering your condolences?" Lord Huan asked.

"The Honorable Jiu was your older brother," Bao Shuya explained. "You had no choice but to kill him for the sake of the country. How could I fail to offer my condolences?"

"If that is so, why do you congratulate me?" Lord Huan inquired.

"Master Guan is a man of amazing abilities, far outstripping Shao Hu," Bao Shuya said. "I have just brought him back here alive. Your Lordship has just obtained a wise minister, so naturally I congratulate you!"

"Guan Yiwu shot me and hit my belt buckle," Lord Huan exclaimed. "I still have the arrow. That memory is a source of constant terror, and I would be happy to take my revenge by eating his flesh. How could I possibly appoint him to high office?"

"We each served our own master," Bao Shuya reminded him, "and at the time when he shot you in the belt buckle, he was working for Jiu and not for you. If you employ him, he will shoot down the whole world for you. Why make so much fuss about a belt buckle!"

"I will accept your advice and pardon him," Lord Huan said.

Bao Shuya then brought Guan Yiwu to live in his own house, and they spoke together day and night.

When Lord Huan of Qi rewarded those who had helped him succeed to the title, the two hereditary ministerial houses of Guo and Gao were both given additional grants of land. He wanted to appoint Bao Shuya as a senior minister, with responsibility for the government of the state.

"You, my lord, have behaved with great generosity to me," he said. "It is thanks to you that I have suffered neither cold nor hunger. However, I cannot possibly govern the country for you."

"I know what you can do, and I will not allow you to refuse," Lord Huan told him.

"I have been called a wise minister, but in fact I am just cautious and careful," Bao Shuya said. "I follow the rules of ritual propriety and stick to the letter of the law, and that is all. This is something that any ordinary official can do—not the mark of the kind of abilities that you need to govern the country. Someone who can govern the country well brings peace to the people inside the borders and pacifies the barbarians abroad; he honors the royal house and respects the aristocratic families. Then the country will be as stable as the great Mount Tai and Your Lordship will enjoy endless blessings. Your merits will be recorded on metal and stone and your name handed down for a thousand ages. How can I possibly sustain a mission comparable to serving a sage-king or assisting a monarch?"

Lord Huan was delighted and came forward on his knees: "Where is the man whom you describe?"

"It is up to you whether you recruit him to your service or not," Bao Shuya said. "The man whom you need is Guan Yiwu. There are five areas in which he excels: he is more benevolent and generous to the people than I; he does not lose control of the reins of government; people are more loyal to him and trust him greatly; he is better at spreading justice and ritual propriety in all directions; and when he holds the drumsticks at the gate to the army camp, he can make ordinary people go out to fight without thought of retreat."

"Please bring him to see me," Lord Huan exclaimed. "I would like to understand what exactly it is that he can do."

"I have heard people say that someone of humble origins cannot be set to keep watch over the noble; somebody poor cannot gain the respect of the rich; and somebody without connections cannot control those who are close to the ruler," Bao Shuya proclaimed. "If you want to employ Guan Yiwu, you will have to appoint him as prime minister, give him a very generous salary, and treat him with the rituals due to a father or an older brother. A prime minister is just as important as the ruler. If he is to be the prime minister and you order him around, then you are disrespecting him. If the prime minister is disrespected, Your Lordship will also be despised. A remarkable man must be dealt with in an exceptional way. Your Lordship should perform a divination to select an auspicious day and then travel out to the suburbs to welcome him. When everyone hears that you respect the wise and honor knights to the point where you can ignore a private enmity, who will not want to come and work in Qi?"

"I will follow your advice," Lord Huan said.

He ordered the Grand Astrologer to select an auspicious day to meet Master Guan outside the city. Bao Shuya escorted Guan Yiwu to the state guesthouse in the suburbs. On the appointed day, Guan Yiwu purified himself three times and ritually anointed himself three times. Then he put on an official hat, gown, and coat and held a staff of office just like a senior grandee. Lord Huan went out to the suburbs in person to meet him, and they drove back to court in the same chariot. The crowds who watched this were all amazed at the sight.

A historian wrote a poem about this:

Fighting with another aristocrat resulted in obtaining a prime minister,
But who could have imagined he would pick a prisoner?
It was because he could set aside his personal animosity,
That all within the four seas praised him as a hegemon.

When Guan Yiwu entered the court, he kowtowed and apologized for his crime. Lord Huan helped him up with his own hands and ordered that he be allowed to sit down in his presence.

"I am a prisoner who has been lucky enough to escape with my life!" Guan Yiwu said. "Would I dare to disobey the rules of ritual propriety?"

"I have a question for you," Lord Huan told him. "You must sit down, for I will not ask it until you do." Yiwu bowed twice and sat down.

"Qi is a state of one thousand chariots, and my grandfather was admired and feared by all the other aristocrats to the point where they called him the Lesser Hegemon," Lord Huan explained. "However, our former ruler, Lord Xiang, was very bad at governing the country, and this brought about serious civil conflict. I have now become the master of the state altars, but the people do not yet give their allegiance to me, and my powers do not extend very far. It is my intention to bring the government of the state into good order again, establishing a clear set of laws and statutes. What is the first thing that I must do to bring this about?"

"The four most important forms of social control are ritual propriety, justice, honesty, and shame," Guan Yiwu replied. "If these four principles do not hold the fabric of society together, then the country will be destroyed. Now, Your Lordship wants to establish a clear set of laws and statutes, so you must use these four principles of social control to make your people into useful members of society. It is only when the laws and statutes have been clearly established that you can extend the power of your country."

"If that is so, then how do I make my people into useful members of society?" Lord Huan asked.

"If you want to make your populace into useful members of society, then you must first love your people," Guan Yiwu replied. "Afterwards you can make use of them."

"What do you mean by loving the people?"

"Your Lordship must set your own clan in order, and likewise other families must put themselves in order. If you bring them together and let them share the same prosperity, then the people will be on good terms with one another. If you pardon those who committed crimes far in the past, repair ancestral temples that have fallen into abeyance, and continue family lines that have been broken off, then the people will flourish. If you lighten punishments and reduce taxes, then the people will become rich. If your ministers select capable officials to instruct the country, then your people will behave with ritual propriety. If you issue orders and then do not change them, then the people will be corrected. This is the way in which you love your people."

"I understand the way to love my people," Lord Huan said, "but how should I employ them?"

"The people can be divided into four categories: knights, farmers, artisans, and merchants. If the sons of knights become knights, if the sons of farmers become farmers, if the sons of artisans and merchants become artisans and merchants, then everything is as it should be. If you do not change their professions, the people will be at peace."

"The people may be at peace, but if our arms and armor are insufficient, what should I do?" Lord Huan inquired.

"If you wish to ensure that you have enough arms and armor, you must set up a system whereby people atone for their crimes with fines. The fine for a serious crime would be one set of rhinoceros-hide armor and one halberd. The fine for a minor crime would be a weapons rack, one shield, and one halberd. Alternatively, a minor crime could result in a fine of metal. Those simply suspected of a crime should be pardoned. Those who insist on bringing civil court cases should have to turn in a quiver full of arrows and then agree to an amicable arrangement. Once metal has been collected, the best quality should be used to make swords and halberds, which should then be tested on horses and dogs. The worst-quality metal should be used to make axes and hatchets and tested on the earth."

"Even if we have enough weaponry, what can be done about the fact that our funding is insufficient?" Lord Huan asked.

"Melt down the ore in your mountains to make coins, boil the waters of the sea in order to make salt, and you will make a vast profit by trading with the rest of the world. You should buy cheap products from other countries in order to facilitate trade. I will set up three hundred brothels that will be just for the use of itinerant merchants. That will make them happy to come, and so they will concentrate their trade here. Then you can tax it and use that money to support your military ambitions. In that case you will certainly have enough money."

"Even if we have enough money, my army is not very large, nor is it feared by my enemies. What can I do to improve this situation?" Lord Huan questioned him.

"Soldiers are respected when they are good, not because you have a lot of them. Their strength comes from their morale, not from their physical force. If Your Lordship were to put the divisions and units of your army into good order and improve the quality of your weaponry, then the other aristocrats would do exactly the same, creating an arms race that it is not certain you would win. If, on the other hand, you want to strengthen your army, then the best thing would be to keep silent about this fact while working secretly to achieve your aims. My idea is to use your internal government as a cover for the military command structure."

"What do you mean by internal government?" Lord Huan asked.

"Your internal government should divide the state into twenty-one districts," Guan Yiwu said. "Six of these districts would be for merchants and artisans, the other fifteen for knights. Merchants and artisans produce wealth, but the knightly class produces soldiers."

"Would that mean I have enough soldiers?" Lord Huan inquired.

"Every five families would constitute a neighborhood with a headman in charge. Ten neighborhoods would form a village, and each village would have an officer in charge. Four villages would form a community with a chief in charge. Ten communities would form a district, and each district would be under the control of a governor. That is how your whole society would come under military jurisdiction. Since each group of five families forms a neighborhood, they would provide five men to form a military unit, and the headman would lead them. Since every ten neighborhoods form a village, the fifty men they muster would form a brigade and the officer would command them. Since every four villages form a community, they would then provide two hundred men to form a company and the chief would lead them. Since every ten communities form a district, each district would muster two thousand men who would be led by their governor. Five districts would together muster one army of ten thousand men, and they would be commanded by the general. Our fifteen districts would create three armies with a total of thirty thousand soldiers. Your Lordship can then command the Central Army, while the representatives of the Guo and Gao ministerial families would each command one of the others. In each of the four seasons, a hunt should be held. The spring hunt is called a *Sou,* and this is when animals that are not pregnant are hunted. The summer hunt is called a *Miao,* and it is held in order to prevent damage to the crops. The autumn hunt is called a *Xian,* when animals are killed to accord with the change in the season. The winter hunt is called a *Shou,* in which ability in battle is tested by battues. These four hunts are used to get people accustomed to using weapons. The administration of units and brigades can be determined at the village level, and the administration of regiments in the army should be determined in the field. When your internal government structure has been implemented, people cannot move without an order. All the members of the same unit will pray together for success, and if someone dies, each one of them will be sad. Individuals will get along well together; families will become close. Living together generation after generation, playing together from infancy, should they have to fight at night, the mere sound of each other's voices will be enough to prevent them from killing each other by accident. When they go into battle during the day, they will be surrounded by their friends, which will prevent anyone from running away. Their long-standing mutual friendships will lead them to die for each other. If they live they will be happy; if anyone dies they will be sad—thus they will be strong in defense and invincible in battle. With thirty thousand men like this, you can conquer the world!"

"Having strengthened my armies," Lord Huan inquired, "can I use them in campaigns against the other aristocrats?"

"Not yet," Guan Yiwu replied. "Neither the Zhou royal house nor your neighboring states will support you. If Your Lordship wants the other aristocrats to serve you, then you had better show your respect for the Zhou royal house and establish friendly relations with your neighbors."

"How do I do that?" Lord Huan asked.

"Conduct a review of your border territory and return any lands that you have occupied," Guan Yiwu said. "Send diplomatic missions to them, armed with lavish gifts, but do not take anything in return. Then the states on our borders will trust us. You should select eighty wandering knights, give them chariots and horses, fine clothing, and a lot of money, and send them to travel all around the world encouraging wise men into your service. You should also send ambassadors with furs, silks, and similar treasures out in all directions to discover where rulers and their subjects are in conflict. If you select those who are already in trouble as the focus of your attack, you can expand your territories; if you choose to punish the wicked and those who have assassinated their rulers, then your authority will be established. If you do this, all the other aristocrats will come to pay court to Qi. After that, you can encourage them to serve the Zhou king, taking office at court and offering tribute, which will demonstrate how much you respect the royal house. Then, even if you wished to refuse the office of hegemon, you would not be able to."

Lord Huan spoke with Guan Yiwu for three days and three nights, and the two men got along very well together—neither felt in the least tired. His Lordship was very pleased. After fasting for three days, he reported to the ancestral temples that he wanted to appoint Guan Yiwu as prime minister. Yiwu refused the appointment.

"You have given me a plan for becoming hegemon, which will fulfill all my ambitions; that is why I want to appoint you as prime minister," Lord Huan said. "Why do you refuse to accept this?"

"I have heard it said that building a palace requires more than one plank, while filling an ocean demands that more than a single river flowing into it. If Your Lordship is indeed determined to fulfill this great ambition, you will need to employ five men."

"Who are these five men?" Lord Huan asked.

"In the polite rituals of diplomatic relations," Guan Yiwu replied, "in recognizing the right moment to advance and hang back, in bowing and giving way, in being firm in argument or gentle in discussions, I am no match for Xi Peng, so I ask your permission to appoint him as foreign minister. In opening up grasslands and extending the area of land under cultivation, collecting grain and promoting high yields, in getting the very best advantage out of the lands at our disposal, I am not as good as Ning Yue, so I ask your permission to appoint him as director of the state farms. In making sure that our chariots do not get stuck in ruts on the vast plains and that our officers do not turn tail, in drumming on our forces so that morale among the three armies is at its very best, I cannot possibly be compared to Prince Chengfu, so I ask your permission to appoint him as marshal. In judging difficult cases, in preserving the lives of the innocent and preventing the reputations of the guiltless from being besmirched, I cannot match Bin Xuwu, so I ask your permission to appoint him to head the Court of Judicial Review. In paying no attention whatever to Your Lordship's moods and presenting remonstrance that is totally loyal, in having no fear of death and sparing neither the noble nor the wealthy in his criticisms, I cannot be compared to Dongguo Ya, so I ask your permission to appoint him as official in charge of remonstrance. If Your Lordship wishes the country to be governed well and your army to be strong, you need these five. If you want to become hegemon, even though I am lacking in talent, I will do my best to achieve this for you."

Accordingly, Lord Huan appointed Guan Yiwu as his prime minister and bestowed one year's tax revenue from the markets in the capital upon him. As for Xi Peng and the other four men, just as he had recommended, one by one they were given high office and each took charge of the matters under his jurisdiction. Guan Yiwu had placards hung from the gates of the capital, encouraging people to suggest ways in which the country might be made richer and stronger. These were then categorized and put into practice.

On another occasion Lord Huan happened to ask Guan Yiwu, "It is my misfortune to enjoy hunting and women. Will this prevent me from becoming hegemon?"

"No," Guan Yiwu replied.

"If that is so, then what kind of conduct would?" Lord Huan asked.

"Not recognizing intelligent men, recognizing them but not giving them office, giving them office but not trusting them with important tasks, entrusting them with important tasks but allowing petty-minded people to interfere—all these things would prevent you from becoming hegemon."

"I understand," His Lordship said.

After this conversation, he employed only Guan Yiwu in the most important offices and gave him the honorific title Elder Zhong. The ceremonies performed for him were far more than those for the Gao or the Guo ministerial families: "In great matters of state, inform Elder Zhong first and then tell me. If something needs to be done, then do exactly what Elder Zhong says."

He also changed the way that the people of his state spoke, for he banned them from using the words Yi and Wu from Guan Yiwu's name. People started calling him Zhong, without any regard for social status. *This is when people in ancient times began calling each other by their style-names as a mark of respect.*

A bearded old man wrote a song about this, praising Guan Zhong's talent for good government, Bao Shuya's excellence in recommending him, and Lord Huan's magnanimity in appointing him. They all worked well together, creating a model for the ages:

The Spring and Autumn period was marked by terrible warfare;
Arrogant rulers and vicious ministers fought endless battles.
Jealousy and envy were everywhere to be seen,
And good men stayed poor, though happy to be at peace.
Yiwu had the intelligence to help the entire world,
He had plans to make the country great.
In shooting the buckle, by mistake he hit his future lord;
The blood spilled at Shengdu was naught but pointless pain.

Even though Guan Zhong and Bao Shuya were the closest of friends,
In releasing a prisoner without authorization he might be thought
    suspicious.
If the two had been suspected of forming a friendly faction,
His recommendation at the Qi court would have availed little.
Yet great rulers are capable of fine judgements:
His Lordship knew Bao Shuya was impartial.
After three purifications and three anointings, he went to the ancestral
    shrine;
In the space of a morning, a prisoner became a senior minister.
Lord and vassal were united:
In their discussions they agreed,
Dealing with their problems one by one,
Each stumbling-block removed in turn.
First he settled the principles by which the people would be governed,
Then he planned to make the country rich and the army strong.
On the one hand he stabilized the royal house and respected the Son of
    Heaven,
On the other he pacified the barbarians and affirmed the borders of the
    realm.
The founder of the state of Qi was much respected by the first Zhou
    king,
Now "Elder Zhong" found himself equally admired.
But just as a great building requires much timber,
He needed five men to help him in his endeavors.
Bao Shuya was not included among these five—
Each official was appointed on the basis of merit.
Thus we know that Guan Zhong and Bao Shuya were true friends;
Nepotism and cronyism remain only too common, alas!
From one end of the country to the other blew the winds of change,
Lord Huan became hegemon, a towering achievement.
In all the world, who can match Bao Shuya's vision?
Who can see the heroes in ordinary men?

When Lord Zhuang of Lu heard that the state of Qi had appointed Guan Zhong as prime minister, he was absolutely furious, and said: "I really regret not listening to Shi Bo's advice, for now I am being bullied by that brat." He held a great muster of chariots, because he was planning to attack Qi to take revenge for his defeat at Ganshi.

Lord Huan of Qi heard about this and asked Guan Zhong, "I have only recently succeeded to the title, and I do not want us to be in a constant state of war. What do you think of the idea of making a preemptive strike on Lu?"

"Neither the army nor the government is entirely loyal to you," Guan Zhong advised. "You cannot trust them yet." Lord Huan paid no attention to him but invested Bao Shuya as general. He led his forces to march on Changshao.

Lord Zhuang of Lu asked Shi Bo about this: "Qi is trying us too high. What can we do to stop them?"

"I can recommend someone who can deal with Qi," Shi Bo said.

"Whom do you mean?" Lord Zhuang asked.

"I know a man named Cao Gui: a recluse living in a village in Dongping," Shi Bo replied. "He has never held office, but he really would make an excellent general or prime minister!"

Lord Zhuang ordered Shi Bo to summon him, but Cao Gui just laughed at him: "If you noble meat-eaters cannot come up with a plan, then how can you expect anything of us peasant bean-eaters?"

"If a bean-eater has a plan, in future he will be eating meat," Shi Bo said. They then both had audience with Lord Zhuang.

"How will you fight Qi?" Lord Zhuang asked.

"In military matters victory is determined by the situation on the ground," Cao Gui said, "so there is no point talking about it in advance. I hope that Your Lordship will lend me a chariot, for then I can formulate a plan of campaign on the way."

Lord Zhuang was delighted with his words, and they then set off at all speed in the direction of Changshao, riding in the same chariot.

. . .

When Bao Shuya heard that the Marquis of Lu was on the way with his army, he drew his troops up into strict formation and waited for them. Lord Zhuang advanced in a straight line. Rendered complacent by the victory at Ganshi, Bao Shuya underestimated the resolve of the Lu army, so he issued orders that the drums should be sounded to tell his troops to advance and that the first to crush their resistance would be generously rewarded.

When Lord Zhuang heard the drums thundering, he too wanted to sound his drums and engage the enemy. Cao Gui stopped him with the words: "The Qi army has sent out its finest troops. We should wait for them here." He issued an order to the army: "Anyone who dares to make a sound will be beheaded."

The Qi troops hurled themselves against Lu's battle formations, but they stood as fast as iron. Since they could not break through, they had to retreat. A short time later, yet again their drums sounded with a ground-shaking noise. The Lu army was just as quiet as if they had not heard anything, and soon the Qi troops had to retreat again.

"Lu is afraid of having to do battle. Sound the drums again, and this time we will force them into flight," Bao Shuya commanded.

Cao Gui heard the drums resound and told Lord Zhuang, "Now is the time to defeat Qi! Quickly order the drums to be beaten!"

This was the first time that the Lu drums sounded but the third time that the Qi drums were beaten. The Qi army had attacked Lu twice with no result and had concluded that they did not want to fight, so their own hearts were now not in it. Who would have guessed that this time the drums would suddenly roll and the hacking of swords and the whistling of arrows would assault their ears like thunderbolts? They cut the Qi army to pieces, and, having sustained a dreadful defeat, they fled.

Lord Zhuang wanted to go in pursuit, but Cao Gui said, "I am not sure that would be a good idea. Let me investigate."

He got down from his chariot and looked all around at where the Qi army had been drawn up in formation, then he climbed back into the chariot and leaned out over the bar, looking into the far distance. After a long time, he said: "You can pursue them."

Lord Zhuang spurred on his chariot and chased them for thirty *li* before returning home. They collected countless pieces of baggage, suits of armor, and weapons.

If you do not know what happened next, READ ON.

Chapter Seventeen

*The state of Song takes bribes and executes
Nangong Changwan.*

*The king of Chu raises his cup and steals
Lady Gui of Xi.*

After Lord Zhuang of Lu had defeated the army of Qi, he asked Cao Gui, "Please, could you explain how drumming once could defeat an army that had drummed three times?"

"When fighting a battle, morale is the most important thing," Cao Gui said. "If your morale is good, then you will win. If your morale is poor, you will be defeated. Drumming is a way of exciting morale. The first time you drum, morale is splendid; the second time, it is poor; the third time, it is exhausted. I did not have the drums sounded in order to conserve the morale of our three armies; when they had drummed three times and were already exhausted, then I could drum once in the knowledge that our morale was wonderful. If you send confident troops into battle against demoralized ones, how can they not win?"

"When the Qi army had been defeated, what was it that you saw to begin with that meant that you would not let us go in pursuit, and what changed your mind later on?" Lord Zhuang asked. "Please, can you explain your thinking?"

"The people of Qi are very tricky, and I was afraid that they might have set an ambush somewhere," Cao Gui explained. "There was no reason to believe that we had put them to flight. However, from the appearance of their wheel ruts, I knew that the army was in chaos, and when I looked into the distance, I saw that their flags and banners were all over the place, because they were running away as fast as they could. That is the reason that I told you to pursue them!"

"You really are a military genius!" Lord Zhuang exclaimed. He appointed him to the position of grandee and generously rewarded Shi Bo for recommending such an impressive talent.

A bearded old man wrote a poem about this:

> Powerful Qi invaded another country only to bring disaster on themselves.
> Who would have guessed that an ordinary man held the winning hand?
> No wonder that the court fell silent on hearing this news,
> For meat-eaters rarely come up with good plans.

This happened in the spring of the thirteenth year of the reign of King Zhuang of Zhou.

. . .

When the Qi army returned home after its defeat, Lord Huan was furious and said, "If my armies return empty-handed, how am I supposed to make the other lords fear me?"

"Qi and Lu are both states of one thousand chariots, and our forces are pretty much equivalent to one another," Bao Shuya told him. "In this case, strength and weakness were determined by who was invading and who was resisting. At the battle of Ganshi, we were fighting on our home turf, and that is why we conquered them; in this battle at Changshao, the Lu troops were fighting on their own ground, and that is why we were defeated by them. Please, command me to raise an army from Song, for if Qi and Song were to join forces, we could achieve your ambitions!"

Lord Huan agreed to this. He sent an ambassador to make representations to Song and ask permission to mobilize their army. Ever since the time of Lord Xiang of Qi, the two states had regularly fought on the same side. When Lord Min of Song heard that Xiaobai had been established, he wanted to please him. He therefore agreed on a date for the muster of the army and announced that they would meet at Langcheng in the first week of the sixth month of summer.

On the appointed day, Song sent Nangong Changwan as the general and Meng Huo assisted him, while Qi sent Bao Shuya as the general and Zhongsun Qiu in support. They each led a great host to meet at Langcheng. The Qi army arrived from the northeast, the Song army from the southeast.

"Bao Shuya is extremely angry with us," Lord Zhuang of Lu announced, "therefore he has come to attack us. To this end he has obtained the assistance of Song. Nangong Changwan is so strong that he can lift a bronze tripod by himself—there is no one in our whole country who is his match. These two armies joined together will form a truly formidable force. When we lock horns with them, how will we withstand them?"

The Honorable Yan, Grandee of Lu, stepped forward and said, "Let me go and have a look at their army!"

On his return, he reported: "Bao Shuya is ready for us. His army is well-prepared. Nangong Changwan, on the other hand, thinks too much of his own merits and believes that no one can defeat him, so his units are in complete disarray. If we sneak out of the Yu Gate, we can take advantage of the fact that they are completely unprepared. Song can certainly be defeated. Once the Song army has been defeated, Qi will not remain here on their own!"

"You can't possibly defeat Nangong Changwan!" Lord Zhuang exclaimed.

"I can certainly try!" the Honorable Yan said.

"Then I will help in the attack myself," His Lordship said.

The Honorable Yan led a force of about one hundred mounted knights out of the Yu Gate, taking advantage of the fact that the moon was hidden behind the clouds. Likewise, they carried no battle standards and did not sound their drums. They managed to creep up on the Song camp without any of the soldiers being any the wiser. The Honorable Yan then ordered torches to be lit, and the sound of drumming shook the heavens as they launched their sudden assault. By the light of the flames they could see that they were under attack by a ferocious force, which threw the Song camp into panic. They rushed around in terror trying to get away. Even though Nangong Changwan was a very brave man, given that his troops were already running away in terror, he could not possibly fight, so he was forced to withdraw as quickly as he could. Lord Zhuang of Lu then arrived with his reinforcements, joining forces with the Honorable Yan to pursue the Song army through the night.

When they arrived at Chengqiu, Nangong Changwan said to Meng Huo, "Today we will have to die in battle. There can be no escape!"

Meng Huo agreed and set out, whereupon he came across the Honorable Yan and the two of them fought viciously. Nangong Changwan grabbed hold of a long spear and headed for the Marquis of Lu's chariot, stabbing anyone who stood in his way. The Lu soldiers were so frightened of this daring assault that they did not dare to come close. Lord Zhuang told his bodyguard, Chuan Sunsheng: "You are famous

for your strength. Now let us see which of you is better, you or Nangong Changwan?"

Chuan Sunsheng seized a great spear and set off to fight with Changwan. Lord Zhuang leaned out over the railings of his chariot and
watched them. He soon realized that Chuan Sunsheng could not possibly defeat Nangong Changwan. He looked around at his entourage and
said, "Fetch me the Golden Barb!"

Golden Barb was an arrow kept in the Lu armory.

His servants presented it to him, and Lord Zhuang nocked it to the
bowstring and sighted on Nangong Changwan. He let the arrow fly,
and it embedded itself in Nangong Changwan's left thigh. He fell to the
ground. His first thought was immediate escape, but Chuan Sunsheng
jumped down from his chariot and held him in an arm-lock as the rest
of the soldiers came up and took him prisoner. When Meng Huo saw
that the senior general had been captured, he abandoned his chariot and
ran away. Lord Zhuang of Lu was thus left in possession of the field,
and he had the bells sounded to recall his army. Chuan Sunsheng then
presented his prisoner. However, Nangong Changwan, even though he
had been severely injured in both the arm and the shoulder, was still
able to stand upright and showed no sign of being in pain. Lord Zhuang
was deeply impressed by his bravery and treated him generously. When
Bao Shuya realized that the Song army had lost, he turned back with his
entire army.

. . .

In this year Lord Huan of Qi sent his minister of foreign affairs, Xi
Peng, to report his accession to the Zhou royal court and to ask for the
hand in marriage of a princess. The following year Zhou sent Lord
Zhuang of Lu to preside over the wedding, at which a princess was married to the Lord of Qi. The states of Xu, Cai, and Wey each provided a
daughter of the ruling house as a junior wife. Since Lu was responsible
for presiding over this wedding, Qi and Lu now resumed diplomatic
relations. Having each suffered the humiliation of defeat in battle, they
swore brotherhood again.

That autumn there were terrible floods in Song. Lord Zhuang of Lu
said, "We have already reestablished relations with Qi, so how can we
remain on bad terms with Song?"

He sent an ambassador to express his condolences. Song appreciated
the gesture of sympathy made by Lu at the disaster they had suffered, so
they too sent an ambassador to apologize and to ask for the return of

Nangong Changwan. Lord Zhuang of Lu released him from captivity and allowed him to return home. From this point onwards, these three countries were at peace and the previous rifts between them were ignored.

An old man wrote a poem about this:

One side won at Ganshi, the other at Changshao;
They both saw the Song army collapse at Chengqiu.
No one can ever win forever, sooner or later there comes a defeat;
Would it not be better to make peace, so neither side is harmed?

When Nangong Changwan returned home to Song, Lord Min of Song made fun of him: "I used to respect you, but now that you have been imprisoned in Lu, I don't respect you in the least!" Nangong Changwan felt deeply humiliated and withdrew from court.

Grandee Qiu Mu privately remonstrated with Lord Min: "You should treat your ministers with ritual propriety and not make fun of them! If you make fun of him, then he won't respect you. If he doesn't respect you, he won't take you seriously, and that is only one step away from him not treating you with proper propriety. That is how rebellions are born. You must be careful!"

"Nangong Changwan and I often play such jokes on each other, and it has never caused any problems," Lord Min said.

. . .

In the fifteenth year of the reign of King Zhuang of Zhou, His Majesty became ill and died. Crown Prince Huqi was established as King Xi. Zhou's national mourning was reported in Song. At this time Lord Min of Song was enjoying a trip around Mengze with his palace ladies, and he invited Nangong Changwan to give a display of martial arts with his spear. Changwan had a particularly magnificent move in which he tossed the spear high up into the sky and then caught it again in one hand—he never missed. The palace ladies wanted to see this trick, and that is why Lord Min had summoned the general to accompany them on this trip. When Nangong Changwan received this order, he gave his display and the palace ladies couldn't stop praising him.

Lord Min was feeling a bit jealous, so he ordered a eunuch to bring out a *liubo* board and challenged the general to a game with the loser to drink a large golden goblet of wine as a penalty. Lord Min was very good at playing *liubo*, so Nangong Changwan lost five games in a row. The penalty was that he had to drink five goblets of wine, as a result of which he became very drunk. However, he still would not give up and challenged Lord Min to yet another game.

"You always lose at everything," Lord Min said. "How dare you think that you can beat me?" Nangong Changwan was upset, but he did not say anything.

Suddenly, one of the palace servants reported: "An ambassador has arrived from the Zhou king."

Lord Min asked why he had come and discovered that it was to report the death of King Zhuang and the coronation of a new monarch.

"Since Zhou has already established a new king, we ought to send someone to condole and congratulate," His Lordship said.

Changwan presented his opinion: "I have never seen the glories of the capital, so please let me go."

Lord Min laughed and said, "Is Song so lacking in capable men that we have to send an ex-prisoner as an ambassador?"

All the palace ladies burst out laughing. Nangong Changwan's face went bright red, and his humiliation turned to rage. He was already very drunk, and in his anger he paid no attention to the fact that he was a subject talking to his ruler. He cursed him: "You bastard! Don't you know that ex-prisoners can still kill people?"

Lord Min was now also angry. "Wretch! How dare you speak that way to me?"

He tried to grab the general's spear, because he wanted to stab him with it. Nangong Changwan didn't have time to pull the spear free, so he grabbed the *liubo* board and hit Lord Min with it. Then he punched him over and over again. It was a dreadful thing to happen, but Lord Min was beaten to death by Nangong Changwan.

The palace ladies ran away in terror. The general was still in a complete rage when he picked up his spear and left. When he arrived at the palace gates, he happened to run into Grandee Qiu Mu, who asked: "Where is His Lordship?"

"The bastard was rude to me, so I killed him!" Nangong Changwan announced.

Qiu Mu laughed and said, "You are drunk, general."

"I am not drunk. It is quite true," he declared. He showed him his hands, which were covered in blood.

Qiu Mu was appalled. He shouted, "The law does not permit the assassin of a ruler to live!" He raised his staff of office to attack him, but how could he withstand Nangong Changwan, who was as strong as a tiger? The general threw his spear to the ground and fought him with his bare hands. With his left hand he grabbed hold of the staff and tossed it away, while with his right hand he grabbed hold of the man's head so hard that he cracked the skull. When he pulled his hand away, it was clear that he had hit a vital spot. He truly was amazingly strong! With Qiu Mu dead, Nangong Changwan picked up his painted spear again and walked with slow steps towards his chariot. There was nobody at all around.

Lord Min of Song had been in power for ten years when, thanks to an ill-timed joke, he was felled by one of his own ministers. However, in the chaotic years of the Spring and Autumn period, there was nothing to be surprised at in the murder of a ruler. How sad! How sad!

A historian wrote a "Poem in Praise of Qiu Mu," which reads:

In these years when virtue and propriety failed,
All proper standards trailed in the dust.
There was no difference preserved between the court and the pot-house;
Rulers and subjects made each other the subject of improper jokes.
The ruler made a jest, the subject responded with his spear.
Brave Qiu Mu tried to attack the murderer with his staff.
He felt no awe at the other's strength,
And so his loyal heart spilt its blood.
His death was as weighty as Mount Tai;
His reputation shines as bright as the sun and moon.

When the Chancellor Hua Du heard about the murder, he grabbed his sword and climbed into his chariot, with the intention of raising an army to punish the guilty. When he arrived west of the Eastern Palace, he ran into Nangong Changwan. The general did not say a word to him, but stabbed him with a single blow from his spear. Hua Du fell from his chariot and was then dispatched with a second blow. After this, Nangong Changwan appointed Lord Min of Song's cousin, the Honorable You, to succeed him and threw the descendants of Lords Dai, Wu, Xuan, Mu, and Zhuang of Song into exile. These noble families mostly fled to Xiao, but the Honorable Yushuo went into exile in Bo.

"Yushuo is a very clever man," Nangong Changwan said, "and what is more, he is the late lord's younger half-brother, born to a concubine mother. If he stays in Bo, he will rebel against us. If we can kill Yushuo, we don't need to worry about the other nobles."

He sent his son, Nangong Niu, to lead the army to encircle Bo, assisted by Meng Huo.

That winter, in the eleventh month, Xiaoshu Daxin led the forces attached to the five noble clans descended from Lords Dai, Wu, Xuan,

Mu, and Zhuang of Song to rescue Bo, together with the army of the state of Cao. The Honorable Yushuo had mobilized the whole population of Bo, and they opened up the city gates to allow a double-pronged attack. Assaulted on two sides, Nangong Niu suffered a great defeat and was killed in battle. The whole of the Song army surrendered to the Honorable Yushuo. Meng Huo did not dare to return to Song, and so he went to try his luck in the state of Wey.

Dai Shupi presented his plan to the Honorable Yushuo: "Why don't we make use of the flags and banners of the surrendered army, and pretend that Nangong Niu has captured Bo and is now returning home in triumph with you as his prisoner?"

He sent a number of people off in different directions to spread the news. Nangong Changwan believed every word of it, ensuring that he was taken completely unawares. When the army under the command of the five noble families arrived at the capital, they tricked them into opening the gates. Once everyone was inside, the shout went up: "We just want the assassin Nangong Changwan! No one else has any cause for alarm!"

Nangong Changwan panicked and had no plan for dealing with this situation, so he rushed to the palace, for he thought he and the Honorable You should flee together into exile. However, he found that the palace had already been overrun by the army, and when one of the eunuchs came out, he informed him: "The Honorable You has already been killed by the soldiers!" Nangong Changwan sighed deeply.

Thinking that of all their neighbors Chen was the only state that did not maintain diplomatic relations with Song, the general determined to go into exile there. However, he remembered that he had an elderly mother at home, over eighty years of age, and he said, "I cannot abandon her to her fate!" He turned around and went home, lifted his mother into a cart, and then, holding his spear tight in his left hand, he used the right to push the cart along. He fought his way through the gate as fast as he possibly could, and nobody dared to try and stop him. The state of Song was more than two hundred and sixty *li* from Chen, and yet Nangong Changwan covered this distance in a single day, pushing a cart in front of him. This kind of remarkable strength has rarely been seen in the history of the world.

Having killed the Honorable You, the five noble families installed the Honorable Yushuo in power. He took the title of Lord Huan of Song. He appointed Dai Shupi as a grandee and selected the cleverest men from the five noble families to be grandees of the ruling house, while

Xiaoshu Daxin was sent back home to guard Xiao. He sent one ambassador to Wey, to ask them to arrest Meng Huo, and another ambassador went to Chen to demand they arrest Nangong Changwan.

The five-year-old Honorable Muyi was sitting alongside Lord Huan of Song at this time. He laughed and said, "Changwan won't come!"

"What does a little boy know about these things?" the Duke of Song demanded.

"Everyone respects brave men," Muyi said. "If Song has lost him, Chen will take him in. If we turn up empty-handed, why should they pay any attention to us?"

The Duke of Song was amazed. Accordingly, he ordered that they should be bribed with valuable gifts.

. . .

When the Song ambassador arrived in Wey, Lord Hui of Wey asked his ministers: "Should we hand Meng Huo over or not?"

His ministers all said, "He has thrown his lot in with ours. How can we possibly abandon him to his fate?"

The Grandee Noble Grandson Er remonstrated: "Evil is the same the world over. Evil in Song is just like evil in Wey, so what is the benefit to us of keeping a wicked man? Besides which, Song and Wey have been allies for a long time, so if we do not hand over Meng Huo, will not Song be angry? If we protect one man at the cost of embroiling the whole country in war, can this possibly be a good idea?"

"You are right," the Marquis of Wey said. He ordered that Meng Huo be put in chains and handed over to Song.

Meanwhile, when the Song ambassador arrived in Chen, he presented various treasures to Lord Xuan of Chen. Lord Xuan coveted these bribes, so he agreed to hand over Nangong Changwan. However, he was also worried that the general was so strong that he would be difficult to arrest. He understood full well that they would have to deal with him strategically. Therefore, he sent the Honorable Jie to talk to Changwan: "His Lordship regards your presence in his state as being the equivalent of having captured ten cities. No matter how many embassies Song sends, we will not hand you over. However, His Lordship was concerned that you might be worried, so he sent me to explain the situation to you. If you decide that the state of Chen is too small for you and your position would be better in a larger country, please just say you will put up with things for a couple of months more while we organize a chariot escort to send you off in state!"

"You have given me sanctuary," Nangong Changwan said with tears in his eyes. "What more can I ask for?"

The Honorable Jie lifted his cup and they toasted each other, swearing brotherhood. The following day Nangong Changwan went in person to the Honorable Jie's house to express his thanks, and Jie hosted yet another banquet in his honor. As they were drinking, he ordered his maids and concubines to come out to entertain them. Changwan got very drunk and lay down to sleep on his seating mat. The Honorable Jie then ordered his soldiers to wrap him up in a rhinoceros hide and tie the bundle together with ox sinews. The same day, Nangong Changwan's mother was arrested and the pair of them were sent back to Song that very night.

Nangong Changwan awoke mid-route and tried to burst his bonds, but the leather was strong and the sinews held firm: whatever he did, he was not able to escape. When they arrived at the Song capital, it was discovered that he had managed to split the leather so that his hands and feet were poking out. His military escort then hit him with their truncheons, breaking the bones in his legs. Lord Huan of Song ordered that he and Meng Huo should be dragged to the marketplace, where they were both cut to mincemeat. He ordered his cooks to pickle this meat, and a portion was presented to each of his ministers with the words: "Any minister who feels unable to serve his ruler loyally should look at this pickled meat!" Nangong Changwan's eighty-year-old mother was executed at the same time.

A bearded old man wrote a poem bewailing these events:

How sad that such a brave man should use his strength to such ill-effect.
He cared about his mother, but not at all about his ruler.
Faced with execution, it is too late for regrets.
Let this be a warning to traitors in the future!

Lord Huan of Song elevated Xiao to the position of a subordinate territory, in recognition of Xiaoshu Daxin's achievements in rescuing him at Bo, and Daxin became the Lord of Xiao. In remembrance of Hua Du's terrible death, he appointed his son to the post of marshal. From this point onwards, the Hua family became hereditary grandees of Song.

. . .

After the defeat at Changshao, Lord Huan of Qi deeply regretted having mobilized his army. He handed over all matters of state to Guan Zhong and spent his days drinking with his wives. If someone came to report on government business, Lord Huan would say, "Why don't you tell Elder Zhong about it?"

At that time there was a certain Shu Diao, who was one of Lord Huan's favorite servants. It was his ambition to take charge of the harem. Since normal men were not allowed in and out, he castrated himself. Lord Huan felt sorry for him, and favored and trusted him even more, to the point where he was always about his person. In the city of Yong in Qi there was a man named Wu, whom everyone called Yong Wu or Yi Ya. He was a highly intelligent man, a fine craftsman, an excellent shot, a good charioteer, but above all he excelled as a cook. One day Lady Ji of Wey fell ill and Yi Ya presented a particularly delicious dish to her. When Lady Ji of Wey ate it, she was cured, and this made her very fond of him. Yi Ya used his cookery skills to ingratiate himself with Shu Diao, and he recommended him to Lord Huan's service.

Lord Huan summoned Yi Ya and asked him, "I have heard that you are good at cooking?"

"I am indeed," he replied.

Lord Huan then said as a joke, "I have eaten birds and animals, crustaceans and fish many times, but there is one thing that I still do not know: what does human flesh taste like?"

Yi Ya withdrew, and at the midday meal he presented a platter of steamed meat that was as delicate in texture as suckling lamb and yet much more delicious. Lord Huan ate every last morsel, and then he asked Yi Ya, "What is this wonderful meat?"

Yi Ya knelt down and said: "It is human flesh."

Lord Huan was shocked. "Where did you get that from?" he asked.

"My son is three years old," Yi Ya explained. "I have heard people say that loyalty to your ruler comes above all considerations for your family. Your Lordship had never tasted human flesh, so I killed my son so you could eat him."

"You may withdraw," His Lordship said.

Lord Huan believed that Yi Ya must love him, so he favored and trusted him too. Lady Ji of Wey also constantly praised him. From this point on Shu Diao and Yi Ya were entrusted with important tasks both inside and outside the palace, but secretly they envied Guan Zhong.

This being the case, both Shu Diao and Yi Ya presented the same advice to their lord: "We have heard that a lord gives orders and his subjects obey them. Now, every time that someone asks Your Lordship's opinion, you always refer them to Elder Zhong. We are concerned that no one in the state of Qi really considers you."

Lord Huan laughed and said, "Guan Zhong is like my arms and legs. Arms and legs are part of the body—Elder Zhong is part of me. How could petty people like you understand this?" They did not dare to say anything more.

Within three years of Guan Zhong taking control of the government, the state of Qi was in impressive good order.

An old man wrote a poem about this:

If you suspect a person, do not give them office; if you employ them,
   trust them.
That is how Elder Zhong was able to bring good government to Qi.
Given that Lord Huan trusted him completely,
What could Shu Diao and Yi Ya do about it?

At this time, Chu was a very powerful kingdom. It destroyed Deng, conquered Quan, forced Sui to submit to its authority, defeated Yuan in battle, made a blood covenant with Jiao, and ordered Xi to raise an army for its use. All the little states east of the Han River were subordinate to Chu and gave tribute to it. The only exception was Cai, which held out against Chu trusting to the marriage alliance that it had made with the Marquis of Qi and its covenants with the aristocrats of the Central Plains. Xiong Zi was the second generation in the Chu ruling house to take the title of king, and he was assisted by Dou Qi, Qu Chong, Dou Bobi, Wei Zhang, Dou Lian, and Zhou Quan. They were casting speculative eyes on the region north of the Han River, gradually developing their plans for an invasion of the Central Plains.

Xianwu, Lord Ai of Cai, and the Marquis of Xi had both married daughters of the ruling house of Chen as their principal wives. The Lord of Cai was the first to get married, and he was followed by the Lord of Xi. Lady Gui, the principal wife of the Marquis of Xi, was an exceptionally beautiful woman, and on one of her visits home to Chen her route took her through the state of Cai.

"Given that my sister-in-law is visiting, I really ought to meet her," Lord Ai of Cai announced.

He sent someone to bring her straight to the palace for a banquet, at which he kept cracking salacious jokes, making it clear that he had no respect at all for his visitor. Lady Gui of Xi left in a rage. When the time came for her to go back to Xi from Chen, she deliberately avoided the state of Cai. When the Marquis of Xi heard how rudely the Marquis of Cai had behaved towards his wife, he wanted to punish him, so he sent an ambassador to take tribute to Chu. In private, he spoke to King Wen of Chu as follows: "Cai trusts that the Central States will protect them, and that is why they are not willing to pay tribute to you. If the Chu army were to pretend to attack me, I would ask for assistance from Cai. The Lord of Cai is a brave man who consistently underestimates the opposition, and he is sure to come to my rescue in person. I will then join forces with Chu to attack him, and we can take Xianwu prisoner. With Xianwu as your prisoner, you need have no worries that Cai will not pay court to you and offer you tribute."

King Wen of Chu was very pleased. Accordingly, he raised an army to attack Xi. The Marquis of Xi requested aid from Cai, and just as he anticipated, Lord Ai of Cai raised a great army and came in person to rescue him. Before they had even made camp, Chu soldiers who had been waiting in ambush rose up on all sides. Lord Ai was not able to withstand the onslaught, and so he headed towards the Xi capital city at all speed. The Marquis of Xi shut the gates and would not allow him in. This resulted in the Cai forces being massacred. The Chu army pursued the stragglers into the wilds of Shen, where they captured Lord Ai alive. They took him home with him. The Marquis of Xi held a great feast for the Chu army and escorted King Wen of Chu right up to the border as a gesture of respect. When Lord Ai of Cai realized that he had fallen into the Marquis of Xi's trap, hatred etched its way into his very bones.

When King Wen of Chu returned home, his plan was to kill Lord Ai of Cai and cook his body to be served as a sacrifice at his ancestral shrine. Zhou Quan remonstrated: "Your Majesty is trying to win over the Central Plains. If you kill Xianwu, the aristocrats will all fear you. It would be better to send him home and make a peace treaty with Cai."

He kept on remonstrating, but whatever he said, King Wen of Chu did not pay any attention. In the end Zhou Quan became furious, and, grabbing hold of the king's sleeve with his left hand, he drew his sword with the right and pointed it at him.

"Let us both die here and now!" he declared. "I cannot bear to think of Your Majesty making such a terrible mistake!"

The king of Chu was terrified. He kept repeating over and over again, "I will do whatever you say!" He then released the Marquis of Cai.

"It is the kingdom of Chu's good fortune that Your Majesty was prepared to listen to my advice," Zhou Quan said. "However, for a subject to threaten his ruler is a crime deserving of the death penalty. Let me submit to the headman's axe!"

"Your loyalty to me is clear to one and all," the king of Chu said, "so you have committed no crime."

"Even though Your Majesty has pardoned me, I cannot forgive myself!" Zhou Quan said. Right then and there, he cut off his foot with his sword, shouting, "Let anyone who disrespects His Majesty look at this!"

The king of Chu commanded that the foot should be preserved in the royal storehouse: "Let this remind me to listen to remonstrance!" He ordered a doctor to take care of Zhou Quan's injury. Even though he recovered, he could never walk again. The king of Chu appointed him as senior gatekeeper with responsibility for the gates of the capital, and he was given the honorific title of Taibo.

. . .

When the king of Chu released the Marquis of Cai and allowed him to return home, he held a great banquet in his honor to see him well on his way. Women musicians spread out through the banqueting hall, and there was an exceptionally beautiful girl who played the *zheng*. The king of Chu pointed her out to the Marquis of Cai and said, "That girl is the loveliest of them all. I will get her to give you wine."

He ordered that this girl should present a great goblet of wine to the Marquis of Cai, which he drained in a single draft. He then poured more wine into this goblet and offered a toast to the king of Chu.

The king of Chu laughed and said, "You have much more experience in these matters than I do. Is she the most beautiful woman you have ever seen?"

The Marquis of Cai remembered how much he hated the Marquis of Xi for encouraging Chu to attack him, and so he said, "The most beautiful woman in the world is Lady Gui of Xi. She really is a goddess!"

"What does she look like?" the king of Chu asked.

"She has eyes like a lake in autumn and a face like a peach blossom," the Marquis of Cai told him. "She is perfectly formed and lovely in her movements . . . indeed, I have never seen her like."

"If I could but see the Marchioness of Xi once, I can die without regrets!" the king of Chu proclaimed.

"With the power at your disposal, Your Majesty, you could have any woman that you want, no matter how grand her family—let alone the wife of a minor aristocrat!" the Marquis of Cai said.

The king of Chu was very pleased, and that day they enjoyed themselves to the utmost before the party broke up. The Marquis of Cai then said goodbye and returned home to his own country.

The king of Chu could not stop thinking about what the Marquis of Cai had said, and he decided that he wanted to lay hands on this Lady

Gui, so he traveled to the state of Xi on the pretext of making a progress through his realm. The Marquis of Xi came out to welcome him and stood on the left-hand side of the road. He treated him with the utmost respect, personally escorting him to the guesthouse that had been prepared for his reception, and holding a great banquet in his honor at the palace. The Marquis of Xi then came forward holding a goblet in his hands and toasted the king of Chu.

The king of Chu took the goblet in his hand and then said with a smile, "I did my best to repay the insults suffered by the marchioness. Now that I am here in person, why does Her Ladyship not come forward to toast me herself?"

The Marquis of Xi was in terror of the forces at Chu's disposal and did not dare to refuse. He just said yes, again and again, and immediately sent a message into the palace. Shortly afterwards they heard the sound of jade pendants chiming together as the marchioness, Lady Gui, arrived in full court dress. A separate place was laid for her, and she bowed twice and expressed her thanks. The king of Chu responded politely. Lady Gui picked up a white jade cup, filled it with wine, and came forward, her hands as pale as the cup that she held. The king of Chu was amazed. She was indeed as lovely as he had been told—a beauty rarely seen in this world. He wanted to take the cup from her himself, but Lady Gui handed it carefully to one of the palace servants, who then passed it to the king of Chu. He drained it in a single gulp. Again Lady Gui bowed twice, then she said goodbye and returned to the palace. With Lady Gui of Xi gone, the king of Chu found he wasn't really enjoying himself. When he left the banquet and returned to the guesthouse, he could not sleep that whole night.

The following day, the king of Chu hosted a return banquet at the guesthouse on the pretext of wishing to thank the Marquis of Xi for his hospitality. He secretly set an ambush there. The Marquis of Xi took his place and drank until he was somewhat tipsy. However, the king of Chu was merely pretending to be drunk when he said to the Marquis of Xi, "I really did my very best to avenge the insult offered to your wife, which is why my three armies are now here. How can your wife refuse to do the least little thing to pay me back?"

The Marquis of Xi apologized and said, "My state is tiny and poor, to the point where we cannot even act as your allies. Nevertheless, in the future my wife and I will do our very best to try and repay you."

The king of Chu thumped the table, shouting, "You have acted shamefully, and now you dare to try and use weasel words in my presence! Guards, why don't you seize him?"

The Marquis of Xi was in the middle of trying to explain himself, when the concealed soldiers rushed out and the two generals, Wei Zhang and Dou Dan, pinned him to his seating mat. The king of Chu then led his soldiers to the palace to search for Lady Gui of Xi.

When Lady Gui heard what had happened, she sighed and said, "It is my fault that this tiger was invited into our home!"

She ran out into the garden, with the intention of drowning herself in the well there. She was stopped by Dou Dan, who grabbed hold of her skirts and said, "Do you want the Marquis of Xi to get killed? What is the point of both of you dying?" Lady Gui of Xi said nothing.

Dou Dan took her to see the king of Chu, who said whatever nice things he could think of to console her, promising that he would not kill the Marquis of Xi and that the sacrifices at his ancestral shrines should be allowed to continue. He had Lady Gui of Xi crowned as his queen in the middle of the army and took her away, riding in the chariot behind his.

Since her face was as lovely as a peach blossom, she became known as Lady Peach Flower. Even today outside the walls of the city of Hanyang, there is a Peach Flower Cave, and above it there is the Temple to Lady Peach Flower, dedicated to Lady Gui of Xi.

During the Tang dynasty, Du Mu wrote a poem about her:

A lovely lady appeared in the palace of the kings of Chu;
In silence she endured many a spring.
Once Xi had been destroyed, her destiny lay in other places.
Not everyone is as brave as Green Pearl, leaping to her death.

The king of Chu gave permission for the Marquis of Xi to live at the Ru River and granted him ten households, to maintain the sacrifices to the ancestors of the Xi ruling house. The Marquis of Xi was torn between anger and depression, as a result of which he died. Chu really did behave very badly in this matter.

If you do not know what happened next, READ ON.

Chapter Eighteen

Cao Mo menaces the Marquis of Qi with a sword in his hand.

Lord Huan invests Ning Qi with a noble title by firelight.

In the spring in the first month of the first year of the reign of King Li of Zhou, Lord Huan of Qi held court. When he had finished receiving the congratulations of his assembled ministers, he said to Guan Zhong: "Thanks to your teachings, I have been able to govern the country well. Now my soldiers are well-trained and food supplies are ample, the populace is well-instructed in ritual propriety and in a sense of justice, so I would like to convene a blood covenant and establish myself as hegemon. What do you think?"

"There are many states that are stronger than Qi," Guan Zhong replied. "In the south there is Chu, while in the west there are Qin and Jin. Naturally they are very proud of how powerful they are, but they do not realize that it is necessary to show respect to the Zhou king. That is why none of them have been able to become hegemon. Even though Zhou is weak and in decline, they are still the only monarchs accepted by the entire country. Since the capital was moved to the east, many aristocrats have refused to go to court, and they have not presented tribute. That was followed by the Earl of Zheng shooting the king in the shoulder and the five countries resisting the orders of King Zhuang. The states of the Zhou confederacy no longer acknowledge their ruler. Xiong Tong proclaimed himself king, Song and Zheng both assassinated their lords—this has become normal, and no one dares to punish them. Now His Majesty, King Zhuang, has recently died and a new king has been established; at the same time, Song has become embroiled in Nangong Changwan's rebellion, and even though the main criminal has been executed, no new lord has been established in Song. Your Lordship ought to send an ambassador to Zhou and request an edict from the king, allowing you to call a great meeting of all the aristocrats at which you will select a new Duke of Song. Once the Lord of Song has been established, you should then use the respect you have shown to His Majesty to create a mandate to control the aristocrats, supporting the royal house on the one hand while pacifying the barbarians on the other. That way the weak states among the Zhou confederacy will find themselves supported while the aggressive will be restrained—if there is anyone who persists in causing trouble, you can lead the other aristocrats to attack them. When the aristocrats realize that we are acting out of no selfish motives, they are sure to pay court to Qi. That way you can become hegemon without having to mobilize a single soldier or chariot!"

Lord Huan was very pleased. He then sent an ambassador to Luoyang to congratulate King Li on his accession and to request a mandate to be allowed to convene a meeting at which to select a new Duke of Song.

"I am much to be congratulated that the Marquis of Qi has not forgotten his duties towards the royal house," King Li said. "My uncle seems to be the only person to be able to control the lords ruling lands north of the Si River. How could I begrudge him the mandate that he requires?"

The ambassador returned to report this to Lord Huan. His Lordship then reported this royal command to the states of Song, Lu, Chen, Cai, Wey, Zheng, Cao, and Zhu; and they agreed that on the first day of the third month they would meet at Beixing.

"How many soldiers will we need for this meeting?" Lord Huan asked Guan Zhong.

"You have received a royal command to convene these aristocrats," Guan Zhong replied. "Why do we need an army? This is supposed to be a friendly meeting!"

"I understand," Lord Huan said.

He ordered his officers to construct a three-level platform, thirty feet high. There were bells suspended on the left-hand side, while drums were placed on the right-hand side. The Son of Heaven's seat of honor was left empty, and to each side places were set for the various aristocrats who would be attending, with jade, silk, and bronze vessels, all much more lavish than would normally be seen. Several guesthouses were also made ready for their reception, and they were all most generously appointed.

On the appointed day, Yushuo, now Lord Huan of Song, was the first to arrive. He had an audience with Lord Huan of Qi and thanked him for his efforts to secure his title. The following day, Wujiu, Lord Xuan of Chen, and Ke, Viscount of Zhu, arrived one after the other. Xianwu, Lord Ai of Cai, also joined the meeting, looking for support against Chu. When the representatives of these four states realized that Qi had no military presence, they looked at each other and said, "The Marquis of Qi is really exceptionally sincere in his efforts to keep the peace!" They all ordered their own armies to retreat twenty *li*.

By this time it was already the end of the second month. Lord Huan asked Guan Zhong, "A lot of aristocrats still have not come. Should we set another date and wait for them?"

"There is a saying that three is a quorum,'" Guan Zhong said, "and we have already managed to collect the representatives of four states, so that is more than enough. If you set a new date, then you are not keeping your word; if you wait for them and they don't come, then you are openly demonstrating the humiliating weakness of the royal house. If you fail to keep your word the very first time you bring the feudal lords together, and you bring shame on the royal house, how in the future can you possibly become hegemon?"

"But what about the blood covenant?" Lord Huan asked. "And the meeting?"

"Clearly many people's hearts are not in it, but some feudal lords are waiting here for the meeting to be held and they have not gone away, so we can make the blood covenant with them," Guan Zhong suggested.

"Good idea!" Lord Huan said.

On the first day of the third month, before it got light, the lords of the five countries met below the platform. When they had finished their ceremonial greetings, Lord Huan clasped his hands together respectfully and reported as follows: "The royal government collapsed a long time ago, and now we are in a time of chaos and rebellion. I have received a mandate from the Son of Heaven to bring you all together to support the royal house. However, one person must take charge of this, and he will have the power to give orders that you will have to obey. Thus good government can be restored to the world."

The feudal lords discussed this pronouncement among themselves, and they wanted to recommend Qi for the position, but the ruler of the state of Song had the title of duke while Qi was only a marquisate; such an appointment would violate the proper order of things. Then they thought about recommending Song, but the Duke of Song had only just succeeded to the title, and he had required the support of Qi to achieve even this, so he was in no position to undertake such an important mission.

Just as they realized how tricky the whole thing was going to be, Wujiu, Lord Xuan of Chen, stood up from his seat and said, "The Son of Heaven commanded the Marquis of Qi to bring us all together here; who would dare to try and replace him? The Marquis of Qi is the only person who can preside over this covenant and meeting."

The other lords chorused: "Only the Marquis of Qi can undertake this mission! The Marquis of Chen is absolutely correct."

Lord Huan refused three times, to be polite, but then in the end he climbed up onto the platform and presided over the proceedings, seconded by the Duke of Song, followed by the Marquis of Chen, the Marquis of Cai, and the Viscount of Zhu, in that order. Once they had decided the issue of precedence, the bells chimed and the drums were struck, as they bowed ceremoniously to the Son of Heaven's empty seat and then to each other, using the ceremonial forms appropriate to older and younger brothers. Zhongsun Qiu lifted up the text of their agreement written out on bamboo slips and then knelt down to read it aloud: "On such and such a day, in such and such a month, in such and such a year, Xiaobai of Qi, Yushuo of Song, Wujiu of Chen, Xianwu of Cai, and Ke of Zhu assembled at Beixing, having received a command to this effect from the Son of Heaven. We agree to support the Zhou royal house together, to succor the weak and save those in danger. Anyone who betrays this agreement will be attacked by the other states."

The feudal lords then clasped their hands and accepted the mandate.

According to the Analects of Confucius, "Lord Huan brought the feudal lords together for nine meetings." This was the first.

A bearded old man wrote a poem that reads:

Five lords met together here, resplendent in their official robes;
This meeting at Linzi offered a gorgeous new spectacle.
Among this multitude, who can take first place?
Only the most respected of those present!

When the aristocrats present had finished toasting each other, Guan Zhong came up the steps and said, "Lu, Wey, Zheng, and Cao are all in contravention of a royal command, for they did not attend this meeting. We will have to punish them."

Lord Huan of Qi waved his hand to the other four lords and said, "My army is simply not sufficient to undertake such a task. I hope that you will help me."

The three lords of Chen, Cai, and Zhu all said at once: "We would not dare to disobey. Of course we will assist you."

Only Lord Huan of Song was silent.

Than evening when the Duke of Song returned to the guesthouse, he said to Grandee Dai Shupi, "The Marquis of Qi is becoming more and more presumptuous. Not only did he preside over the meeting even though he is clearly not important enough, he also now wants to take over our armies. It is going to be very difficult for us in the future."

"Half of the aristocrats disobeyed his orders," Dai Shupi pointed out. "This is because Qi is not yet strong enough to force everyone to come. If he succeeds in punishing Lu and Zheng, then he will become hegemon. If Qi becomes hegemon, it will be a black day for Song. Of the four states that have come here, Song is the only one that is of any importance, so if we do not hand over our armies, the other three states will also refuse. Besides which, the only reason that we came to this meeting at all is because we wanted a royal mandate to confirm your possession of the title of duke. You have participated in the meeting, so what are we waiting here for? Let us go home!"

The Duke of Song followed his advice. Just before dawn, he got up into his chariot and departed.

When Lord Huan of Qi heard that the Duke of Song had run away, betraying the terms of their agreement, he was absolutely furious and wanted to send Zhongsun Qiu in pursuit.

"It would not be right for you to pursue him," Guan Zhong pointed out. "You should ask permission to mobilize the royal army to attack him, and that will make your reputation. However, there is something much more urgent that you need to attend to."

"What can be more urgent than this?" Lord Huan asked.

"Song is far away, and Lu is nearby," Guan Zhong said. "Besides which, their ruling house is an important branch of the Zhou royal family. If you don't make Lu submit to your authority first, how can you possibly expect Song to obey you?"

"How should I make my attack on Lu?" His Lordship asked.

"Northeast of the Ji River there is a little state called Sui, which is a subordinate territory to the state of Lu," Guan Zhong said. "It is tiny and weak: in fact, only four clans live there. If you take your army there, they will surrender immediately. Once Sui is gone, Lu is sure to be frightened. After that, you can send an ambassador to complain about the fact that they did not attend this meeting, and you can also send a messenger to take a letter to the Dowager Marchioness of Lu.

The dowager marchioness has always insisted on making her son behave well towards his maternal relatives, so she is sure to do her utmost to push him into a reconciliation. With the Marquis of Lu under pressure at home from his mother's commands and worried about the military might of Qi on his very borders, he will have to beg us for a blood covenant. We will wait until he makes the request and then agree to it. After pacifying Lu, we can turn our troops against Song, overawing them with your position as the king's greatest supporter. Breaking them will be as easy as snapping a twig."

"Excellent!" Lord Huan exclaimed.

He personally led his army right up to the city walls of Sui, and they surrendered the first time he sounded his drums. Afterwards, he stationed his army at the Ji River.

. . .

Lord Zhuang of Lu was just as terrified as Guan Zhong had anticipated, and he called all his ministers together to come up with a plan.

"Qi has already invaded us twice, and it is not at all clear that they can win this time," the Honorable Qingfu said. "I would like to take the army out to fight them."

One of the other ministers screamed: "No! No!"

Lord Zhuang looked at him; the speaker was Shi Bo. "Do you have a different plan to suggest?" Lord Zhuang inquired.

"I have always said that Master Guan is a truly remarkable man," Shi Bo reminded him. "He now has charge of the government of Qi, and the army is under his control: that is one reason why this would be a bad idea. When he called the meeting at Beixing, he had received a mandate from the king to do so, and now they are complaining that we disobeyed a royal command. We are in the wrong here: that is the second reason it would be a bad idea. Your Lordship did all that was required in executing the Honorable Jiu for them, and you presided over the Marquis of Qi's wedding with a Zhou princess. You should not forget about the merit that you have accumulated and make them into your enemies: that is the third reason why this would be a bad idea. The very best plan would be to reaffirm the long-standing good relationship between our two countries and ask for a blood covenant; then we can get out of this mess without having to resort to warfare."

"I absolutely agree," Cao Gui put in.

Just as they were discussing this, a message arrived: "A letter has come from the Marquis of Qi."

Lord Zhuang looked at it, and this is what he read:

Your Lordship and I have both served the Zhou royal house together—we have loved each other like brothers and have been joined together in a marriage alliance. You did not attend the meeting at Beixing, but did I dare to criticize you? If you are now disloyal to me, then that is my fate.

The Marquis of Qi also wrote a letter to Lady Wen Jiang. She summoned Lord Zhuang and told him, "The ruling houses of Qi and Lu have intermarried for many generations. Even if you hate us, sooner or later you will have to make peace. Why not do it now?"

Lord Zhuang agreed and asked Shi Bo to write a letter in response. It read:

I have behaved very badly, taking panic at nothing, and you are absolutely right to criticize me, for I know that I have been at fault. Even though it might appear a blood covenant forced on me by an enemy army camped below my very walls, in fact I am entirely sincere about it. If you would withdraw to within your own borders, I will show my appreciation by offering parting gifts of jade and silk.

When the Marquis of Qi got this letter, he was very pleased and ordered his army to withdraw to Ke.

When Lord Zhuang of Lu was just about to set out to meet the Marquis of Qi, he asked, "Who wants to come with me?"

General Cao Mo asked permission to go, but Lord Zhuang said, "You have been defeated in battle three times by Qi. Aren't you afraid that they are going to laugh at you?"

"It is because I have been humiliated by these three defeats that I want to go." Cao Mo said. "I will expunge this humiliation in one fell swoop."

"What did you have in mind?" His Lordship asked.

"You deal with His Lordship, and I will deal with his ministers," Cao Mo said.

"For me to have to leave my country and beg him for a blood covenant is like being defeated all over again," Lord Zhuang said. "If you can expunge this humiliation, I will do whatever is necessary."

He set off with Cao Mo and traveled to Ke, where the Marquis of Qi had built a platform of pounded earth to prepare for their reception. The Marquis of Lu sent someone on ahead to apologize and ask for a covenant, and Lord Huan sent a return messenger to set a date for this.

On the appointed day, the Marquis of Qi ordered his best soldiers to line up below the platform, with blue, red, black, or white flags, facing north, south, east, and west respectively. Each unit was allocated a specific color and lined up under the command of its officers. Zhongsun Qiu was responsible for all of this. There were seven steps leading up to the platform, and each was guarded by knights holding yellow pennants in their hands. There was a further huge yellow standard suspended high above the platform, which had been embroidered with the words "Regional Hegemon." To one side there was a huge drum. Prince Chengfu had taken charge of all these arrangements. An altar had been set up in the middle of the platform, on which vermilion lacquer bowls and jade cups had been laid out—this was the equipment for collecting the blood of the sacrificial victim and swearing the covenant. It was Xi Peng who was in charge of this. Two places had been set, one beside the other, with an array of gold goblets and jade cups, all arranged by Shu Diao. West of the platform there were two stone pillars, with a black ox tethered to one and a white horse tied to the other: the butchers were getting ready to kill them. Yi Ya was in charge here. Dongguo Ya was responsible for making sure that the guests knew what they were supposed to be doing, and he was standing at the bottom of the steps waiting to receive the visitors. The prime minister, Guan Zhong, appeared immensely serious as he viewed these arrangements.

The Marquis of Qi gave his orders: "When the Marquis of Lu arrives, only he and one of his entourage will be allowed up onto the platform. Everyone else will have to stay at the bottom."

Cao Mo, wearing armor and with his hand on the pommel of his sword, followed closely on the heels of Lord Zhuang of Lu. His Lordship advanced slowly, and Cao Mo followed him up the steps, with no sign of being overawed by the occasion. Dongguo Ya came forward and said, "This is supposed to be a friendly meeting between our two lords, with both sides behaving with all due respect and propriety. Why are you armed? Please put down your sword."

Cao Mo glared at him, and their eyes locked. Dongguo Ya took a couple of steps backwards. Lord Zhuang then advanced up the steps with his minister and the two lords met, both expressing the most amicable sentiments. When the third drum-roll was over, it was time for them to approach the altar for further ceremonies. Xi Peng came forward with a jade cup full of blood; kneeling down, he requested that the Marquis of Lu smear his mouth with it. Just at that moment, Cao Mo drew his sword with his right hand while grabbing hold of Lord Huan's sleeve with his left—he looked absolutely enraged.

Guan Zhong rushed to shield Lord Huan with his own body, demanding: "What on earth are you doing?"

"Lu has been invaded repeatedly, causing us enormous losses," Cao Mo said. "Your Lordship spoke of succoring the weak and saving those in danger at this recent meeting—is it only us that this doesn't apply to?"

"What do you want?" Guan Zhong asked.

"Qi uses its military might to bully weaker states, and you have occupied our lands on the north side of the Wen River," Cao Mo said. "Today you must hand them back, and then His Lordship will make the covenant!"

Guan Zhong looked at Lord Huan. "You must agree to this!"

"Please let me go," His Lordship said. "I will grant your request!"

Cao Mo then let go of his sword. Taking the cup from Xi Peng, he came forward. When the two lords had smeared their mouths with blood, Cao Mo said, "Guan Zhong is in charge of the government of the state of Qi, so I would like the two of us to make a blood covenant too."

"Why do you insist on involving Elder Zhong?" Lord Huan asked. "I will swear an oath with you myself." Then he pointed up at the sun in the sky. "May anyone who prevents the return of the lands north of the Wen River be punished by Heaven!"

Cao Mo smeared his mouth with blood, bowed twice, and expressed his thanks.

When this was over, Prince Chengfu and the other persons present were all furious, and they asked Lord Huan for permission to arrest the Marquis of Lu, to avenge the humiliation wrought upon them by Cao Mo. Lord Huan said, "I have already agreed to Cao Mo's demands. Even an ordinary man should not betray his own promises, let alone the ruler of a state!" They had no choice but to stop.

The following day Lord Huan arranged for a banquet at the guesthouse, at which he drank happily with Lord Zhuang and said goodbye to him. Right then and there he ordered that the towns along the southern border of Qi should all be returned to Lu, along with the fields that they had captured on the north side of the Wen River.

In the past, people said that a forced covenant did not have to be kept. However, even under such circumstances Lord Huan made no attempt to get out of this agreement. Even though Cao Mo threatened him, Lord Huan refused to punish him. This is the reason why he made all the feudal lords submit to his authority and became hegemon over the entire world!

There is a poem that reads:

This juggernaut had swallowed all of eastern Lu;
What use was a foot-long sword against such military might?
Since other lords would only submit if he proved just and true,
He could not keep even a foot of land north of the Wen River.

There is also a poem that discusses the way in which Lord Huan of Qi was held hostage by Cao Mo, and how this made him the first knight-errant. This poem reads:

Amid a sea of pikes and spears,
A single sword carries out a heroic act.
The humiliation of three defeats was expunged in a single morning;
The very first knight-errant was this Cao Mo.

When the other aristocrats heard about what had happened at Ke, they were all deeply impressed by Lord Huan's sincerity and sense of justice. The two states of Wey and Cao both sent someone to apologize for their earlier behavior and to request a blood covenant. Lord Huan agreed that after the attack on Song, he would set a date for a meeting with them. He again sent an ambassador to Zhou, to report that the Duke of Song had contravened a royal command, and refused to attend the interstate meeting. Therefore he asked permission to mobilize the royal army to punish him. King Li of Zhou sent Grandee Dan Mie in command of the army to join Qi in the attack on Song. Spies reported that the two states of Chen and Cao had also mobilized their armies for this campaign, and that they were willing to march on ahead.

Lord Huan sent Guan Zhong on ahead in command of a single army to meet the forces of Chen and Cao, while he advanced more slowly with the main force, together with Xi Peng, Prince Chengfu, Dongguo Ya, and others. They would meet at Shangqiu. This happened in the spring of the second year of King Li of Zhou's reign.

. . .

Guan Zhong had a beloved concubine named Jing, who was a native of Zhongli, a clever and well-read woman. Lord Huan was very fond of feminine company, and whenever he went out on a progress, he was always followed by a bevvy of ladies. Likewise, Guan Zhong would bring along Jing.

On the day that Guan Zhong and the army left by the southern gate, they agreed that the first stage would take them some thirty *li* to Mount Nao. There, he happened to meet a local man wearing short trousers and a single shirt, with a bamboo hat on his head and bare feet, who was herding cattle at the foot of the mountain. This man sang a song as he beat time on a cow horn. Guan Zhong, perched up on his chariot, could see that he was no ordinary peasant, so he ordered someone to give him wine and food.

When the yokel had finished eating, he said, "I would like to have an audience with the prime minister, Elder Zhong."

"The prime minister's chariot has already gone by," the servant explained.

"I have a message for the prime minister that I hope you will pass on to him: 'How vast are the waters!'" the peasant said.

The servant caught up with Guan Zhong's chariot and reported what he had said. Guan Zhong was confused and did not understand it at all, so he asked his concubine Jing about it.

"I have heard that there is an ancient song titled 'The Waters,'" Jing said, "which runs: 'How vast are the waters, how numerous the fish! A gentleman has come to summon me and I will live at peace with him.' This man must want to serve in the government."

Guan Zhong immediately ordered his chariot to halt and sent someone back to summon him. The yokel stabled his oxen in the village and followed the messenger to have an audience with Guan Zhong, at which he simply folded his hands together and did not bow. Guan Zhong asked him his name, and he said, "I am a peasant from the state of Wey, and my name is Ning Qi. I came here because I heard that His Lordship is a good man who appreciates the talents of others. However, without connections to recommend me at court, I have ended up working for these villagers, herding their oxen."

Guan Zhong inquired into what he had studied, and his answers were impressively fluent. He sighed and said, "How many great men are like jewels hidden in the mud? If a clear stream does not happen to wash them free, how can they ever reveal themselves? My lord is traveling behind us with the main army, but he will be here soon. I will write a letter for you, which you can present to His Lordship, and I am sure he will give you a suitably important job."

Guan Zhong wrote the letter then and there, and sealed it. Having handed it to Ning Qi, the two of them said goodbye. Ning Qi then went back to herding his oxen at the foot of Mount Nao.

Lord Huan of Qi arrived three days later with the main army. Ning Qi stood by the side of the road in his short trousers and single shirt, with a bamboo hat on his head and bare feet, not seeming overawed in the slightest. When Lord Huan of Qi approached in his chariot, Ning Qi kept time by striking his cow's horn and sang a song:

> White stones shine on the beautiful Southern Mountain;
> Here there is a carp many feet long!
> Never meeting a Yao or Shun, who abdicated for a better man,
> Short trousers and a single shirt cover my battered frame.
> From feeding my oxen at dusk until midnight,
> The night seems endless—whence comes the dawn?

Lord Huan heard this song and was amazed by it, so he ordered his entourage to stop the singer and ask his name and place of origin.

"My name is Ning Qi," he said.

"You are just a herdsman, so why do you criticize the government?" Lord Huan asked.

"I am just an ordinary person, so how could I dare to criticize anyone?" Ning Qi retorted.

"It is His Majesty, the Son of Heaven, who has commanded me to lead the armies of the lords to bring peace to his realm, so that the ordinary people may carry on their livelihoods in peace, and even the very plants and trees may enjoy the spring just as in the time of the sage-kings Yao and Shun," Lord Huan said. "Your song mentioned something about not meeting with Yao and Shun and about a long night with no dawn in sight. If you are not criticizing the government, then what are you trying to say?"

"I am just a peasant, and hence I know nothing about the government of our former kings," Ning Qi replied, "but I have heard that in the time of Yao and Shun the wind blew once every ten days and the rain came once every five days; the common people ploughed the fields and so had enough to eat, and they dug wells and so obtained water to drink. This is what is called obeying the orders of the sages without thinking about it. These days, every rule and principle has been contravened and proper teachings are no longer spread among the people, and yet you speak as if it were indeed just like the time of Yao and Shun. I really don't understand this. I have heard that the sage-kings brought order to their officials and the lords obeyed their orders, they expelled all evil and the world was at peace, they were trusted though they did not speak and feared even when they were not angry. Now Your Lordship has seen

Song ignore the very first meeting that you held, and you were held hostage by Lu at the following blood covenant. You have been constantly at war, your people are exhausted and your coffers empty, and yet you can still speak about how the ordinary people carry on their livelihoods in peace, and even the very plants and trees enjoy the spring. I really don't see how you can have the gall. I have heard that Yao set aside the claims to the throne of his son Danzhu in order to allow the world to pass to Shun; Shun then ran away to hide at the Nan River. It was the ordinary people who pursued him there and forced him to take the throne—he had no choice but to become king. Now, Your Lordship murdered your own older brother in order to take control of the country, and you take advantage of the Son of Heaven and use him to bully the other aristocrats, which is so far removed from the virtuous behavior of our dynastic founders that I really don't know what to say!"

Furious, Lord Huan shouted: "How dare you speak to me like that?"

He gave orders that he should be beheaded. His entourage immediately arrested Ning Qi and tied him up. They were marching him out to be executed, but Ning Qi was completely unafraid. He just looked up at the sky and said, "The wicked king Jie murdered Long Feng, and the evil king Zhou slaughtered Prince Bigan. Now today I can make a third!"

Xi Peng presented his opinion to the lord: "This man is not awestruck by the sight of power, nor is he terrorized by the sight of military might. He is no ordinary herdsman. Your Lordship ought to pardon him!"

Lord Huan turned his head, and he was clearly no longer angry. He gave orders to loosen Ning Qi's bonds, and explained, "I said what I did in order to test you. You really are an exceptional knight."

Ning Qi felt among his clothing and pulled out the letter from Guan Zhong. Lord Huan of Qi broke the seal and read it. This is what the letter said:

Having received a command from Your Lordship, I took the army out, and when I arrived at Mount Nao I found a man there named Ning Qi from the state of Wey. This man is no ordinary herdsman—he is just the kind of talent that you need to recruit into your service. Your Lordship ought to make him a cornerstone of your administration. If you let him go to work for another country, you will regret it!

"You already had a letter of introduction from Elder Zhong," His Lordship said. "Why didn't you just present it to me?"

"I have heard it said that a clever ruler picks the people who can help him, while a clever minister picks a master who deserves his aid," Ning

Qi returned. "If it had transpired that Your Lordship hated unpalatable advice and merely wanted to be flattered, taking out your rage on your officials, I would rather have died than bring out the prime minister's letter."

Lord Huan was very pleased and ordered that he should ride in the chariot behind him.

That evening, when they made camp, Lord Huan ordered that bonfires be lit and quickly hunted out a formal hat and gown.

"Is Your Lordship looking for a hat and gown in order to invest Ning Qi with an official title?" the eunuch Shu Diao inquired.

"Exactly," Lord Huan said.

"Wey is not far away from Qi, so why don't you send someone there to check up on his background?" Shu Diao asked. "If he is indeed as clever as you seem to think, it will not be too late to invest him afterwards."

"This man is truly remarkable," Lord Huan retorted, "and in such a situation there is no need to hold to petty conventions. I am afraid that he may well have committed some minor crime in Wey. If we investigate his past, then we could easily find ourselves in a situation where we cannot invest him with a noble title. And yet it would be a great shame if we lost his services!"

He invested Ning Qi as a grandee by the light of the fires that he had lit, and he ordered him to take charge of the government of the state with Guan Zhong. Ning Qi changed into an official hat and gown, thanked him for his kindness, and left.

A bearded old man wrote a poem that reads:

A poor herdsman in short trousers and a single shirt,
He may not have come across a sage-king, but at least he met Lord Huan.
From the moment that he sang his song, keeping time by beating an ox horn,
He had no need to announce his arrival by any other means.

When Lord Huan of Qi arrived at the borders of Song, he found that Wujiu, Lord Xuan of Chen, and Shegu, Lord Zhuang of Cao, were already present. Shortly afterwards, Grandee Dan Mie arrived in command of the Zhou army. When they had finished greeting each other, they discussed the plan of campaign for the attack on Song.

Ning Qi came forward and said, "Your Lordship has already received a mandate for this campaign from the Son of Heaven, and you have assembled the lords to create an allied army; however, it would be better to win this battle with diplomacy rather than with force. In my humble opinion, you do not need to advance your troops. Although I have no particular merits to speak of, I would nevertheless like to be allowed to try to persuade the Duke of Song to agree to a peace treaty."

Lord Huan was very pleased and gave orders for a camp to be built on the border, while commanding Ning Qi to go to Song. Ning Qi rode in a little chariot accompanied by just a couple of other men and went straight to Suiyang, where he asked for an audience with the Duke of Song.

The Duke of Song asked Dai Shupi about this: "Who is this Ning Qi?"

"According to my information, he used to be a village herdsman, and has only recently been appointed to his current eminence by the Marquis of Qi," Dai Shupi explained. "He must be very persuasive, so he will have been sent here to talk you into something."

"How should I treat him?" the Duke of Song asked.

"When Your Lordship summons him in, you should behave rudely to him and see what he does," Dai Shupi recommended. "The moment he shows the least sign of reacting, I will tug on my sash, and that will be a sign for our soldiers to come in and take him prisoner. That should put a stop to whatever it is that the Marquis of Qi is planning!"

The Duke of Song nodded his head and instructed his guards to pay close attention. When Ning Qi came in, looking magnificent in an official robe and wide sash, he folded his hands respectfully in the presence of the Duke of Song. His Lordship, sitting on his throne, made no response. Ning Qi looked up at the ceiling, sighed, and said, "The state of Song is in terrible danger!"

The Duke of Song was alarmed, and said, "I am the most senior duke in the Zhou confederacy, in addition to which I am the most important of the feudal lords. What danger could possibly threaten me?"

"Who do you think to be cleverer, you or the Duke of Zhou?" Ning Qi asked.

"The Duke of Zhou was a sage!" His Lordship exclaimed. "How could I possibly be compared with him?"

"The Duke of Zhou lived at a time when the dynasty was flourishing; the world was at peace, and the barbarians from all four quarters offered tribute and submitted to the authority of our kings. And yet he still worked himself to the bone trying to persuade knights into his service. You, my lord, are descended from the royal house of the Shang dynasty, a defeated kingdom, you live in an era when many men are competing for power, and you only succeeded to the title after your two predecessors had been assassinated. Even if you were to do your best to imitate the Duke of Zhou and humble yourself to attract knights to join you, I am afraid that they would not come. If you take pride in your own power and behave arrogantly towards your clients, even if they have loyal advice to offer, is it possible that they would open their mouths in your presence? You really are in terrible danger!"

The Duke of Song was dumbstruck! Getting up from his seat, he said, "I have only been in power for a few days and I have not enjoyed the benefit of your instructions. You, sir, have said nothing that could possibly offend me!"

Dai Shupi, who was standing next to him, realized that the Duke of Song had been moved by what Ning Qi was saying, so he repeatedly tugged at his sash. The Duke of Song paid no attention to him. Then he said to Ning Qi, "You, sir, have come here for a reason. What would you like to say to me?"

"The Son of Heaven has lost power, and so the lords have scattered. There is no proper gradation of rank between rulers and their subjects, and every day you hear of assassinations and usurpations. The Marquis of Qi cannot bear to see the world descending into anarchy, so he has decided to respectfully uphold the commands that he received from His Majesty the king and become Master of Covenants for the Zhou confederacy. You took part in the meeting at which all this was decided and at which you were confirmed in your title. If you turn your back on the first part, is that not the same as calling your right to the title into question? His Majesty is very angry and has sent his ministers to speed around the various lords and collect an army to punish Song. Your Lordship has already betrayed a royal command, and now you are trying to resist His Majesty's armies. You don't need to do battle—it is already quite clear to me who will win and who will lose."

"What do you think I should do?" His Lordship asked.

"In my humble opinion," Ning Qi said, "you should make a formal offering of jade and silk, and then ask for a blood covenant with Qi. That way, on the one hand, you fulfill your duties as a loyal subject of the Zhou royal house, and on the other you will cement your good relationship with the new Master of Covenants. Without even moving a single soldier, you have made the state of Song as safe as Mount Tai."

"Thanks to my own stupidity, I did not stay until the end of the meeting," the Duke of Song said. "Now Qi has turned its armies against me, so will they be willing to accept my gifts?"

"The Marquis of Qi is a generous and large-minded man who is disposed neither to keep account of other people's faults nor to rake up old quarrels," Ning Qi assured him. "Just look at the state of Lu, which does not attend the meetings that Lord Huan calls and where they forced him to swear a blood covenant at Ke under pain of death! And yet he gave back to them all the land that he had conquered. You have at the very least attended meetings with him, so why would he not take your gifts?"

"What should I give him?" His Lordship asked.

"The Marquis of Qi likes to preserve good relations with his neighbors, treating them generously even if they do not reciprocate," Ning Qi said. "You could give him a sausage and he would consider it a suitable ritual gift. He is certainly not expecting you to empty out your treasury and storehouses!"

The Duke of Song was very pleased by this and sent an ambassador to go back to the Qi army with Ning Qi and ask for a peace treaty. Dai Shupi withdrew, feeling ashamed of himself.

When the Song ambassador had an audience with the Marquis of Qi, he apologized for their bad behavior and requested a peace treaty. He presented ten white jade cups and one thousand ingots of gold.

"All of this has happened because I received a mandate from His Majesty, the king," Lord Huan of Qi said. "Otherwise, how would I dare to take this task upon myself? I am afraid that I must trouble His Majesty's representative to report all this to the king."

Lord Huan handed over the jade cups and the gold to Grandee Dan Mie and reported the Duke of Song's intention to make peace.

"If you, my lord, are determined to pardon them and help them in restoring relations with the Zhou royal house, how could I dare to disagree?" Dan Mie said.

Lord Huan encouraged the Duke of Song to pay court to the Zhou king and suggested that once he had returned from this, they would set a date for another meeting. Grandee Dan Mie said goodbye to the Marquis of Qi and left. The rulers of Qi, Chen, and Cao then each went back to their own countries.

If you want to know what happened next, READ ON.

Chapter Nineteen

Having taken Fu Xia prisoner, Lord Li of
Zheng returns to his country.

After murdering Prince Tui, King Hui of
Zhou is restored to power.

Lord Huan of Qi returned to his state, and Guan Zhong presented his opinion: "Since the Zhou king moved his capital to the east, no one has been as powerful as Zheng. Zheng destroyed the state of Dongguo and made its capital city there; they have Mount Song in front of them and the Yellow River behind them, the Luo River to the right and the Ji River to the left, and they are guarded by the fastnesses of Hulao. Lord Zhuang relied on these natural defenses to be able to attack Song, to bully Xu, and to resist the might of the royal army. Now they have become allies of the kingdom of Chu. The ruling house of Chu claims the title of king illegitimately, but they have vast territories and a strong army, and they have conquered all the states along the north side of the Han River, setting themselves up as a rival power to the Zhou. If Your Lordship wants to support His Majesty, the Zhou king, and become hegemon over the other feudal lords, then you will have to deal with Chu. But before dealing with Chu, you will have to get Zheng on your side."

"I know that Zheng is the lynchpin of the Central States, and I have naturally been wanting to bring this state under my control for a long time," Lord Huan assured him. "The problem is that I simply have no idea how to do so."

Ning Qi came forward and said, "The Honorable Tu of Zheng was their ruler for two years, then Zhai Zu threw him out of the country and established Scion Zihu instead. Gao Qumi then murdered Zihu and put the Honorable Wei in power, only to have His Late Lordship kill the

Honorable Wei. Afterwards Zhai Zu was able to install the Honorable Yi. Zhai Zu was a subject, and yet he threw his ruler out of the country; the Honorable Yi was a younger brother, and yet he usurped the title of his older brother, thereby overturning every principle of good order and offending every standard of behavior. They ought to be punished. The Honorable Tu now lives in Yue and spends his days plotting attacks on Zheng. Zhai Zu is now dead, so there is no one in the state of Zheng who can withstand us. If Your Lordship were to order one of your generals to go to Yue and escort the Honorable Tu to Zheng, he would feel deeply grateful for Your Lordship's kindness and pay court to Qi!"

Lord Huan thought this a very good idea. He then ordered Bin Xuwu to take an army of two hundred chariots and make camp twenty *li* from the city of Yue. Afterwards, Bin Xuwu sent someone to inform them of the Marquis of Qi's intentions.

When Marquis Li of Zheng, formerly the Honorable Tu, heard the news that Zhai Zu was dead, he had secretly sent one of his closest supporters to the state of Zheng to find out what was going on. Now suddenly he heard that the Marquis of Qi had sent an army to escort him back home. He was very pleased and came out of the city to welcome them and held a great banquet in their honor.

Just as the Honorable Tu was deep in his discussions with Bin Xuwu, the trusted confidant whom he had sent to Zheng returned and made his report: "Zhai Zu is indeed dead, and it is now Shu Zhan who is the senior grandee."

"Who is Shu Zhan?" Bin Xuwu asked.

Tu, the Earl of Zheng, said: "He is a good minister, but a very poor general!"

The confidant reported another piece of information: "Something very strange has happened in the Zheng capital. There was an eight-foot snake living inside the South Gate, with an azure head and a yellow tail, and another snake living just outside the gate, over an ell long, with a red head and a green tail. They fought inside the gate for three days and three nights, without being able to determine a victor. The people of the capital all came out to see this, but none of them dared to get close. After seventeen days, the outside snake bit the inside snake to death. The outside snake then entered the city, slithered all the way to the great ancestral temple, and suddenly disappeared."

Bin Xuwu bowed to the ground and congratulated the Earl of Zheng: "Your Lordship is sure to take back your position."

"How can you know that?" the Earl of Zheng inquired.

"The snake from outside the city represents Your Lordship," Bin Xuwu explained, "and it was more than one ell long, which reflects the fact that you are the senior member of the family. The snake inside the city gates stands for the Honorable Yi—it was only eight feet long because he is your younger brother. After fighting for seventeen days the inside snake got injured and the outside snake entered the city: this corresponds to the fact that Your Lordship was forced into exile in the summer of the year Jiashen, and this is the summer of the year Xinchou, so seventeen years have passed. That the inside snake was injured and died means that the Honorable Yi will lose power, while the outside snake going to the main ancestral temple means that Your Lordship will once again preside over the sacrifices there. My lord, the Marquis of Qi, wants justice to spread through the world; therefore he plans to install Your Lordship in your proper place. The fight between the two snakes means that this is the moment to act. It is the will of Heaven!"

"I really hope that you are correct, sir," the Earl of Zheng said. "I will never forget your kindness to the end of my life!"

Bin Xuwu then explained his plan to the Earl of Zheng, and that very night he launched a surprise attack on Daling.

Fu Xia led his troops out of the city, and the two sides fought a battle. What he was not expecting, however, was that Bin Xuwu would send some of his troops in a flanking movement that allowed them to come up behind him. This enabled them to break through the defenses of Daling and hoist the battle standards and flags of the state of Qi over the city walls. Fu Xia realized that he would not be able to withstand the enemy, so he got down from his chariot and surrendered. Tu, the Earl of Zheng, loathed Fu Xia because he had been instrumental in keeping him in exile for seventeen years, so with gritted teeth he instructed his entourage: "Come back and report to me when you have beheaded him!"

"Don't you want to get back to Zheng, my lord?" Fu Xia shouted. "Why do you want to kill me?"

The Earl of Zheng asked him what he was talking about, and Fu Xia explained: "If you pardon me, I will take the Honorable Yi's head for you."

"What is your plan for killing the Honorable Yi?" the Earl of Zheng asked. "You are not just trying to trick me with honeyed words so that you can escape back to Zheng, are you?"

"The government of the state of Zheng is now all in the hands of Shu Zhan, and we are close friends," Fu Xia informed him. "If you pardon me, I will travel back secretly to the Zheng capital and come up with a plan with Shu Zhan to kill the Honorable Yi and present his head to Your Lordship."

The Earl of Zheng cursed him: "You deceitful old bastard, how dare you lie to me! The minute I release you and you get back to the capital, you and Shu Zhan will be coming up with some plan to prevent me recovering my rightful position!"

"Fu Xia's wife, Lady Nu Gu, lives in Daling," Bin Xuwu said. "We can keep her in prison in Yue as a hostage."

Fu Xia kowtowed and said, "If I fail to keep my word, you can execute my wife." He swore an oath by Heaven, and the Earl of Zheng released him.

Fu Xia traveled back to the Zheng capital, and that very night he had an audience with Shu Zhan. When Zhan saw Fu Xia, he was absolutely amazed. "You are supposed to be guarding Daling; what on earth are you doing here?"

"The Marquis of Qi wants to restore our true ruler to power in Zheng, so he has sent General Bin Xuwu in command of a great host to escort the Honorable Tu back home," Fu Xia explained. "We have already lost Daling. I escaped with my life and traveled back here under cover of darkness. The Qi army will arrive any moment now, and the situation is critical. If you can kill the Honorable Yi and open the gates of the city to welcome them, you will be able to keep your wealth and your noble title, and your life will be spared. This is your last chance to turn the situation to your advantage. If you do not take it, you will regret it!"

Shu Zhan listened to him in silence. After a long pause, he said, "I did suggest before that we restore our former lord, but Zhai Zu prevented this. Zhai Zu is now dead, which means that Heaven is helping him. It would be disastrous to go against the will of Heaven. I do not know if you have any plan of action to suggest."

"We should send a letter to the conspirators in the city of Yue telling them to bring their army here as soon as possible," Fu Xia suggested. "You can leave the city and pretend to counter their attack, for then the Honorable Yi is sure to climb up onto the city walls to watch the battle. I will look for an opportunity to deal with him, and you can then bring our old lord back to the city. That will work just fine."

Shu Zhan agreed to this plan. Secretly he sent someone to take a letter to the Honorable Tu to explain their scheme. Meanwhile, Fu Xia sought audience with the Honorable Yi and informed him that the Qi army was now supporting the Honorable Tu's pretensions and that Daling had been captured by them. The Honorable Yi was deeply alarmed and said, "I must send lavish gifts to Chu to request their assistance. When the Chu army arrives, we can attack in concert and the Qi army will be forced to withdraw."

Shu Zhan deliberately delayed as much as possible, so that two days later he still had not authorized an ambassador to go to Chu. Then spies reported: "The Yue army is at the foot of the city walls."

"I will take an army out to do battle," Shu Zhan said. "Your Lordship and Fu Xia should climb the city walls to take command of the defense of the capital."

The Honorable Yi believed that this would be the sensible thing to do.

The Earl of Zheng was the first to arrive with his army, and Shu Zhan fought several engagements with him. Then Bin Xuwu led the Qi army in a massive assault, and Shu Zhan turned around and fled. Fu Xia was standing on top of the city wall, and he shouted: "The Zheng army has been defeated!" The Honorable Yi was not at all a brave man, so he now decided to run away. Fu Xia came up behind him and stabbed him to death right there on top of the walls. Afterwards, Shu Zhan gave orders to open the gates, and the Earl of Zheng entered the city accompanied by Bin Xuwu. Fu Xia had gone on ahead to clear out the palace—when he found the Honorable Yi's two sons, he killed them. The people of the capital had always been fond of Tu, Lord Li of Zheng, and now that he had been restored to power, they greeted his arrival with thunderous acclaim. Lord Li rewarded Bin Xuwu generously and agreed that, in the tenth month of winter, he would go in person to make a blood covenant at the Qi court. Bin Xuwu accordingly said goodbye and went home.

A few days after Lord Li had been restored to power, everyone had pretty much settled down to this new state of affairs. He told Fu Xia: "You guarded Daling for seventeen years and used all the forces at your disposal to prevent me from getting back to my country. This might be described as loyalty to your old lord. And yet now you have assassinated your old ruler in order to put me in power simply because you didn't want to die. I cannot trust you. I must take revenge for the Honorable Yi!"

Lord Li shouted for his guards to arrest him, and he was beheaded in the marketplace. His wife, Lady Nu Gu, was pardoned.

A bearded old man wrote a poem about this:

The Honorable Tu of Zheng was a nasty piece of work:
Having forced someone to assassinate his enemy, he executed him.
If Fu Xia had not wanted to live a little longer,
He would have been praised for years to come for his loyal service!

It was Yuan Fan who had put the Honorable Yi in power in the first place. He was afraid of being punished, so he announced his retirement. Still, Lord Li sent people after him, and Yuan Fan hanged himself.

Having returned to power, Lord Li was determined to punish those who had forced him into exile, so he killed the Honorable E. Qiang Chu went into hiding in Shu Zhan's house, and Shu Zhan spoke up on his behalf. Accordingly, he was not executed, but had a foot cut off instead. Gongfu Dingshu went into exile in the state of Wey. Three years later Lord Li summoned him back and restored his office, saying, "I cannot let you be the last of your line!" Zhai Zu was already dead, so there was no point in pursuing that further. Shu Zhan was appointed as the senior minister, with Du Shu and Shi Shubing as grandees: the people of Zheng called them the "Three Good Men."

. . .

Lord Huan of Qi made it known that he had restored the Earl of Zheng to power, so that winter the two states of Wey and Cao both requested a blood covenant. It was his intention to hold a great meeting of all the feudal lords, at which beasts would be sacrificed and an interstate alliance agreed.

"Your Lordship has only just begun undertaking the duties of a hegemon, so your rule should be as simple and easy as possible," Guan Zhong reminded him.

"What do you mean by simple and easy?" Lord Huan asked.

"The states of Chen, Cai, and Zhu have served Your Lordship's interests with impeccable loyalty ever since the meeting at Beixing. Even though the Earl of Cao has not participated in any of the meetings you have called, he did assist in the attack on Song. You must not put these four states to any more trouble, or you will force them into revolt. Song and Wey do not ordinarily attend your meetings: in fact, this may be considered the first. You should wait until the feudal lords have all accepted you and then hold a blood covenant."

Before he had even finished speaking, it was suddenly reported: "The Zhou king has sent Dan Mie on an embassy to Song, and he has already arrived at the state of Wey."

"Make peace with Song," Guan Zhong suggested. "The state of Wey sits on an important crossroads, and so you ought to go in person to hold a meeting in Wey, to demonstrate how much you care for the other lords."

Lord Huan agreed to meet with the three states of Song, Wey, and Zheng at the city of Zhen. With Grandee Dan Mie and the Marquis of Qi himself, there would be five participants. No mouths were smeared with blood on this occasion; they just greeted each other politely and then went their separate ways. The lords were very happy with this development. The Marquis of Qi was astute enough to realize that people were pleased with him, so afterwards he held a great meeting of the states of Song, Lu, Chen, Wey, Zheng, and Xu at the city of You, at which a blood covenant was sworn. That was the first time he was appointed as the Master of the Covenant. This happened in the winter of the third year of the reign of King Li of Zhou.

. . .

After Xiong Zi, King Wen of Chu, obtained Lady Gui of Xi and made her his queen, he loved and favored her more than any of his other women. Within the space of three years she had given birth to two sons, the older of whom was named Xiong Jian and the younger Xiong Hui. Although Lady Gui of Xi had now spent three years in the Chu palace, she never said a word to the king of Chu. His Majesty found this behavior bizarre, and one day he asked her why she never spoke. Lady Gui of Xi burst into tears but did not reply. The king of Chu insisted on an answer, and in the end she replied: "I have had two husbands. Since I have not been able to die and thereby preserve my purity as a widow, how could I dare to speak to anyone?" She wept bitterly the whole time that she was talking.

Master Hu Zeng wrote a poem, which reads:

After Xi was destroyed, she entered the king of Chu's household.
Looking around, the spring winds have caused all the flowers to bloom.
Remembering the past, she does not speak, she even hides her tears,
Hatred creating her glorious reputation.

The king of Chu said, "This is all the fault of Xianwu of Cai. I will take revenge on your behalf. There is nothing for you to be so sad about."

He then raised an army and attacked Cai, penetrating their outer defenses. Xianwu, the Marquis of Cai, stripped his clothes to the waist as a gesture of surrender and offered all the jade and other treasures in his storehouses as bribes to Chu. The Chu army did indeed withdraw. This happened right at the same moment when Tu, the Earl of Zheng, sent an ambassador to report his restoration to power to Chu.

"Tu was restored to power two years ago, and it is only now that he reports this to me," His Majesty grumbled. "He really does not respect me at all."

The king of Chu raised yet another army to attack Zheng. The state of Zheng apologized for its lapse and requested a peace treaty, which the king of Chu accepted. In the fourth year of the reign of King Li of Zhou, the Earl of Zheng decided that he did not dare to pay court to Qi, for fear of what Chu would do if he did. Lord Huan of Qi then sent someone to complain about this, and the Earl of Zheng in return sent his senior minister Shu Zhan to Qi. He informed Lord Huan: "Our humble country is under siege by the forces of Chu, and His Lordship is involved in the defense of the capital day and night with no time for rest; that is why he has not been able to serve you as he did in the past. If Your Lordship could induce the Chu army to leave, naturally His Lordship would pay court to Qi."

Lord Huan found himself deeply irritated by this excuse, so he imprisoned Shu Zhan in the armory. Shu Zhan took advantage of a lapse in security to escape and make his way back to Zheng. From this time onwards, Zheng was allied with Chu rather than with Qi. Of this no more.

. . .

King Li of Zhou was on the throne for five years. Then he died and his son, Prince Lang, was crowned as King Hui. In the second year of the reign of King Hui, King Wen of Chu behaved with even more violence than normal, though he had always loved warfare. The previous year, King Wen of Chu had attacked the state of Shen in concert with the Lord of Ba, during which time he had constantly caused trouble and interfered with the Ba army. The ruler of Ba was absolutely furious about this, so he launched a surprise attack on the city of Nuochu in Chu and succeeded in capturing it. The general responsible for the security of Nuochu, Yan Ao, happened to be traveling around the Yong River and thus managed to escape. However, the king of Chu executed Yan Ao, which enraged the Yan family. In revenge, they made a deal with the Ba people that if they attacked Chu, the Yan family would provide assistance from inside the capital. The Ba army did indeed attack Chu, so the king of Chu led his army out to meet them and they fought a great battle at Jin. What no one was expecting was that a couple of hundred members of the Yan family would dress up as Chu soldiers and mingle with the army, with the aim of picking off the Chu king. The Chu army was thrown into confusion and the Ba forces took advantage of this, inflicting a terrible defeat on Chu. The king of Chu was shot in the cheek by an arrow and fled, but the ruler of Ba did not dare chase after him, so he regrouped his army and took them home. The Yan family went with them, and from that time onwards they lived in Ba.

When the king of Chu arrived back at the capital, he ordered that the city gates be opened for him that night.

Zhou Quan questioned him from inside the gates: "Did Your Majesty win?"

"I lost!" the king of Chu said.

"From the reign of His Late Majesty to the present day, the Chu army has won every battle it has fought," Zhou Quan said. "Ba is a tiny country, and yet we have been defeated even though Your Majesty was in personal command of the troops! How people will laugh at us! Huang does not pay court to Chu right now, so if you attack them and win, you will be able to resolve the situation with some credit to yourself."

He shut the gates and refused to allow the king back into the city. The king of Chu addressed his army officers furiously: "If we are not victorious in this campaign, I will never come home again!"

He moved his army to attack Huang. The king personally drummed his forces forward, and his officers and men fought to the death. They defeated the Huang army at Queling. That night when he was sleeping in the camp, the king of Chu dreamed that the Marquis of Xi appeared to him and said angrily, "What crime had I committed that you killed me? You occupied my territories, you raped my wife—I will appeal to God on High for justice!" He patted the king of Chu on the cheek with one hand, and the king of Chu screamed in pain. When he woke up, he discovered that his arrow wound had burst open and blood was pouring out. He immediately gave orders that the army should turn back, but they got only as far as Qiu, where he died during the night.

Zhou Quan went out to meet the cortege and take the body home for burial, whereupon His Majesty's oldest son, Xiong Jian, succeeded to the throne.

"I offended the king twice," Zhou Quan said. "Even though His Majesty did not execute me, how could I dare to live in such circumstances?

I will go to serve my king in the Underworld!" He instructed his family, "When I am dead, you must bury me at the entrance to His Majesty's tomb, that my descendants may know that my job is to guard the gates." He then cut his throat.

Xiong Jian was deeply grieved by this and ordered that his sons and grandsons should hold the office of official gatekeeper as a hereditary post.

The Confucian scholar Master Zuo Qiuming called Zhou Quan a man who really loved his ruler.

A historian wrote a poem refuting this assessment, which reads:

> He should have remonstrated rather than using force!
> It is very disrespectful that he shut the gate and did not let his ruler in.
> If this kind of deed is described as loyal or an act of love,
> Then rebels and criminals are bound to use it as an excuse.

When Lord Li of Zheng heard the news that King Wen of Chu was dead, he was very pleased and said, "Now there is nothing for me to worry about."

Shu Zhan came forward and said, "I have heard it said that relying on other people is dangerous and serving other people is humiliating. Your state is located between Qi and Chu, which leaves you the choice of being in danger or being humiliated: this is not a long-term strategy. Our former rulers, Lords Huan, Wu, and Zhuang, were ministers at the royal court for three generations, admired by the other states and respected by the aristocracy. Now a new king has just ascended the throne, and I hear that the two states of Guo and Jin have already paid court to him. His Majesty held a great banquet for them and gave them five pairs of jades and three horses. Your Lordship ought to pay tribute to Zhou, and then perhaps His Majesty will be pleased and will give you the opportunity to become a minister at court just as your ancestors were. Then you will not have to be afraid of even the largest states."

"Good idea," Lord Li said.

He sent Grandee Shishu to Zhou to request permission to pay court. Grandee Shishu came back and reported: "The Zhou royal family is in complete chaos."

"What do you mean?" Lord Li demanded.

"In the past, King Zhuang of Zhou had a favorite concubine who was a daughter of the ruling house of Yao. Her name was Wang Yao. She gave birth to a son, Prince Tui, who was much loved by King Zhuang, and His Majesty appointed Grandee Wei Guo as his tutor.

Prince Tui has always been exceptionally fond of oxen; he keeps several hundred beasts that he feeds himself, giving them only the finest fodder, and they sleep under embroidered blankets. He calls them his 'Lovely Beasts.' Whenever he goes in or out of the palace, his servants ride on the back of these oxen, and they trample down anyone who gets in the way. He also seems to have some kind of secret dealings with the grandees Wei Guo, Bian Bo, Zi Qin, Zhu Gui, and Zhan Fu, and they are all as thick as thieves. When King Li was alive, he did not attempt to control him. Although a new king was established, Prince Tui still had considerable seniority within the royal family, so he became ever more arrogant and unmanageable. The new king absolutely hates him and is trying to get rid of his faction, so he has stripped Zi Qin, Zhu Gui, and Zhan Fu of their lands. The new king also had plans to construct a garden next to the royal palace. Wei Guo had lands there and Bian Bo's house was there, both very close to the royal palace. The king seized their property with a view to extending his own domains. His Majesty was also angry because the royal chef, Shi Su, did not present him with the very finest of foods, so he cut his salary. Shi Su hated the king because of this. These five grandees and Shi Su rebelled against the king and supported the candidature of Prince Tui, basically in order to be able to attack His Majesty. The king, on the other hand, relied on Jifu, Duke of Zhou, and Liao, Duke of Shao, and various other supporters to fight them. When Prince Tui's cronies realized that they would not be able to win, they fled to exile in Su.

"In the time of King Wu of Zhou, Su Fensheng achieved great success as His Majesty's minister of justice. He received the title of the Duke of Su and was given the lands of Nanyang as his fief. After Fensheng's death, his descendants came under the control of the Di nomadic peoples, and they betrayed the king by serving these barbarians. They did not even have the grace to hand back their fief to the crown. In the eighth year of the reign of King Huan, the then Duke of Su was terrified of our former ruler, Lord Zhuang, so he gave us that part of his lands that was located closest to the Zhou capital, which alienated the ruling house of Su yet further from the Zhou king. The Marquis of Wey is furious because the Zhou king supported the pretentions of the Honorable Qianmou, so he has this old bone to pick with the royal house. The Duke of Su has now encouraged Prince Tui to seek sanctuary in Wey, and he has led an army to attack the royal capital in concert with the Marquis of Wey. Jifu, Duke of Zhou, was defeated in battle and fled into exile in Yan along with the king, Liao, Duke of Shao, and the other ministers. Although there are five grandees who are determined that Prince Tui should be crowned king, the populace does not accept him. If Your Lordship were to raise an army to put His Majesty back on his throne, that would be a meritorious act earning you ten thousand years of acclaim!"

"You are right," Lord Li said. "Besides which, Prince Tui is a weakling, relying entirely upon the support that he receives from Wey and Yan. The five grandees are all totally useless. I will send someone to talk some sense into them. It would be best if they realize the error of their ways without our having to resort to force."

He sent someone to go to Yan and escort His Majesty to the city of Yue, where he would reside temporarily. Lord Li had lived in Yue for seventeen years, so the palace there was in excellent order. He also sent someone to take a letter to Prince Tui, which read as follows:

> I have heard that some senior officials in Zhou have turned against the king, which is disloyal. For a younger brother to usurp his older brother's position is despicable. If you behave in a disloyal and despicable way, then you must expect Heaven to punish you. You, my prince, have made the mistake of listening to the advice of wicked ministers, and thus you played your part in forcing His Majesty into exile. If you would but regret what you have done and welcome the Son of Heaven back to his rightful domain, apologizing for the crimes that you have committed, you will not lose one jot of your wealth and nobility. If you cannot do that, you should withdraw to some remote region and take up office as a border vassal, which would also be a perfectly acceptable option. I hope that Your Highness will come to a decision quickly!

When Prince Tui got this letter, he hesitated, unable to make up his mind.

"Once you start riding a tiger, it is impossible to get off," the five grandees told him. "Surely you are not prepared to give up on being a ruler in command of ten thousand chariots and return to your old subordinate position? The Earl of Zheng is just trying to deceive you; don't listen to him!"

Prince Tui threw the Zheng ambassador out of the Royal Domain. Lord Li of Zheng then paid court to His Majesty at Yue, after which he launched a surprise attack on the royal capital at Chengzhou. The treasures and bronzes he captured were all shipped back to Yue. This happened in the third year of the reign of King Hui of Zhou.

That winter, Lord Li of Zheng sent someone to arrange a meeting with the Duke of Xiguo, at which they discussed raising an army to accomplish the righteous task of reinstalling the king. The Duke of

Xiguo agreed to help. In the spring of the fourth year of the reign of King Hui, the two lords of Zheng and Xiguo brought their armies together at Mi. In the fourth month, they launched a joint attack on the royal capital. Lord Li of Zheng led his armies to attack the South Gate, while the Duke of Xiguo commanded his troops to attack the North Gate.

Wei Guo rushed to the palace and demanded to have an audience with Prince Tui. Prince Tui had not yet finished feeding his oxen, so he refused to admit him.

"This is an emergency!" Wei Guo screamed. He had no choice but to forge an order from Prince Tui commanding Bian Bo, Zi Qin, Zhu Gui, and Zhan Fu to climb the walls and take command of the defense of the city. The Zhou people had never been prepared to obey Prince Tui anyway, and now that they heard that His Majesty had returned, they all started cheering and opened the gates to let him into the city. Wei Guo then wrote a letter that he planned to send to Wey to ask for help. Before he had even finished writing, he heard the sound of bells and drums. Someone rushed in to report: "The old king has already entered the city and is holding court as we speak!"

Wei Guo promptly cut his own throat. Zhu Gui and Zi Qin were killed by the army. Bian Bo and Zhan Fu were taken prisoner by the Zhou people and presented to His Majesty. Prince Tui fled through the West Gate. He ordered Shi Su to drive the "Lovely Beasts" in front of him as a vanguard. The animals were too fat to move quickly, so they were all captured by the pursuing troops. Every one of these oxen was killed on the same day that Bian Bo and Zhan Fu were beheaded.

A bearded old man wrote a poem bemoaning Prince Tui's stupidity:

> You used the favor shown to you to act with reckless arrogance,
> You took advantage of rifts at court to advance your wicked plans.
> What did you accomplish in your year as king?
> You just closed your doors and fed your oxen.

There is another poem that mentions that at this time Lord Huan of Qi had already become the Master of Covenants, and so he should have created a coalition to reinstall the king, rather than leaving it to Wei and Xiguo. This poem reads:

> An exiled Son of Heaven brought shame on the ancestral shrines;
> His restoration was thanks to the loyal assistance of Zheng and Xiguo.
> Why did Elder Zhong not come up with a plan to deal with this?
> Was he not the greatest strategist of the age?

When King Hui was restored to the throne, he rewarded Zheng with the lands east of Hulao, together with a royal belt with a bronze mirror hanging from it. He rewarded the Duke of Xiguo with the city of Jiuquan and several fine bronze wine vessels. The two lords thanked His Majesty for his generosity and went home. Lord Li of Zheng became sick on the way home, dying shortly after he had returned to his capital. His ministers arranged for Scion Jie to inherit his title and he became Lord Wen.

. . .

In the fifth year of the reign of King Hui of Zhou, Lord Xuan of Chen became convinced that the Honorable Yukou was plotting a rebellion and killed him. The Honorable Wan, whose style-name was Jingzhong, the son of Lord Li of Zheng and an old friend of the Honorable Yukou, was frightened that he too would be executed, and so he fled into exile in Qi. Lord Huan of Qi appointed him to the office of palace steward. One day, when Lord Huan was drinking with the Honorable Wan, it began to get dark. He ordered that all the lamps should be lit, so that they could carry on their party. The Honorable Wan refused to accept such an extravagant gesture, saying, "I am happy to drink during the day, but not at night. I do not think it appropriate to carry on by candlelight."

"You are very right!" Lord Huan said. He then left, marveling at the other's excellent appreciation of the demands of proper conduct.

Lord Huan thought that the Honorable Wan was a very clever man, so he gave him a small fief in Tian.

He became the ancestor of the Tian family.

The same year, Lord Zhuang of Lu was planning his wedding, and so he met Grandee Gao Xi of Qi in the lands of Fang.

After the death of Lord Xiang, Lady Wen Jiang, the Dowager Marchioness of Lu, suffered agonies missing her older brother day and night. In the end she became tubercular, and her eunuchs summoned a doctor from Ju to examine her condition. Lady Wen Jiang had been lonely for a long time and found her desires hard to control, so she made the doctor from Ju stay behind and held a banquet for him, which was the start of their affair. Later on, the doctor returned to Ju, but Lady Wen Jiang remained in communication with him. On at least two occasions she went to Ju, when she stayed at the doctor's house. The doctor from Ju subsequently introduced her to other lovers, but Lady Wen Jiang had become ever more sexually voracious with age, and she was deeply frustrated because none were such accomplished lovers as Lord Xiang.

In the eighth month of the fourth year of the reign of King Hui of Zhou, Lady Wen Jiang's illness took a turn for the worse and she died in her residence in Lu. As she lay on her deathbed, she told Lord Zhuang: "The daughter of the Marquis of Qi is already eighteen years old. It is high time that you were married and she took her position as the head of the Six Palaces. Whatever you do, you must not delay the wedding on the grounds that you have not completed full mourning for me. That would make it impossible for me to rest in peace!" Then she added, "Qi has plans to become hegemon. You should serve them loyally—do not destroy an alliance that now goes back many generations!" When she had finished speaking, she died.

Lord Zhuang held the funeral with all customary pomp and ceremony, but respecting his mother's dying wishes, he decided to hold the wedding that year.

"Her Ladyship has only just been buried, and these ceremonies cannot be hurried up," Grandee Cao Gui said. "You ought to wait until the three years of mourning are finished and then get married."

"This is done by my mother's orders!" Lord Zhuang reminded him. "The proper ceremonies can be over in an instant or they can be dragged out forever. Something between these two extremes is all that is necessary."

He waited one year, after which he discussed the engagement with Gao Xi, suggesting that he should go in person to Qi and hand over the betrothal gifts. Lord Huan of Qi suggested a further delay, on the grounds that the Marquis of Lu was still in mourning. However, in the seventh year of the reign of King Hui of Zhou, all had been decided and an auspicious date in the autumn had been picked for the wedding.

At this time, Lord Zhuang of Lu had been ruling for twenty-four years, and he was some thirty-seven years of age. With the intention of pleasing the daughter of the marquis, all his gifts were lavish and expensive in the extreme. But remembering that his father, Lord Huan of Lu, had been killed in Qi and that he was just about to marry the murderer's daughter, he felt deeply uncomfortable. He was sufficiently concerned that he completely rebuilt the ancestral temple dedicated to Lord Huan, ornamenting it with red lacquer pillars and carved beams, in the hope of consoling the spirit of the deceased. Grandee Yu Sun remonstrated, but His Lordship paid no attention.

That summer Lord Zhuang went in person to Qi, and in the eighth month, he and his wife, Lady Ai Jiang, arrived back in Lu, where she was installed as the marchioness. The wives of the grandees and other members of the ruling house performed the rituals for greeting the new marchioness, and they all gave her lengths of silk.

Grandee Yu Sun sighed and said, "When men give presents, the highest grade would be jade or silk, while at a lesser level they might give birds or other game, the difference demonstrating their respective ranks. When women give presents, it should be hazelnuts, chestnuts, dates, or perhaps a piece of meat—that shows their respect. If men and women give the same presents, there is no difference between them. But the preservation of distinction between men and women is one of the cornerstones of our society. If the marchioness is allowed to confound this, where will it all end?"

After Lady Ai Jiang married the Marquis of Lu, the alliance between their two countries became much stronger. Lord Huan of Qi and Lord Zhuang of Lu attacked Xu and Rong together. Xu and Rong then both became client states of Qi.

When Lord Wen of Zheng saw Qi becoming ever more powerful, he was afraid that they would invade him, and he sent an ambassador requesting a blood covenant.

Do you not know what happened after that? READ ON.

Chapter Twenty

*Lord Xian of Jin ignores a divination against
establishing Lady Li Ji as his principal wife.*

*King Cheng of Chu puts down a rebellion
and appoints Ziwen as Grand Vizier.*

In the tenth year of the reign of King Hui of Zhou, the two states of Xu
and Rong both submitted to the authority of Qi. Lord Wen of Zheng
realized that Qi was becoming more and more powerful. He was afraid
that they would attack him, so he sent an ambassador to ask for a blood
covenant. Accordingly, another meeting was held between the lords of
the four states of Song, Lu, Chen, and Zheng at which Lord Huan of Qi
presided, and they then swore a blood covenant together at You. Everyone in the world gave their allegiance to Qi.

Lord Huan of Qi then returned to his state and held a great banquet
for his ministers. The wine circulated until everyone was half-drunk.
Bao Shuya raised a brimming cup before Lord Huan and toasted him.

"This is such fun!" Lord Huan exclaimed.

"I have heard that enlightened rulers and clever ministers remember
their worries no matter how happy they are," Bao Shuya remonstrated.
"I hope that Your Lordship will never forget your time in exile, Guan
Zhong will never forget that he was a prisoner, and Ning Qi will never
forget feeding his oxen."

Lord Huan quickly got up from his seat, bowed twice, and said,
"That we all of us remember those days would be a great blessing for
the state of Qi!"

That day they enjoyed themselves to the full before the party broke up.

Suddenly one day, the message arrived: "The Zhou king has sent
Shao Boliao here." Lord Huan welcomed him and escorted him to a

guesthouse. Shao Boliao then proclaimed the mandate that he had received from King Hui to invest the Marquis of Qi as a regional hegemon, together with His Majesty's pious wish that he might model himself on the founding ancestor of the ruling house of Qi and concentrate his energies upon attacking the king's enemies. He also said: "Shuo of Wey supported Prince Tui in his rebellion, thus assisting a rebel to depose the rightful heir to the throne. I have swallowed my rage about this for ten years, leaving him unpunished to the present day. I would like you to deal with him on my behalf, Uncle."

In the eleventh year of the reign of King Hui of Zhou, Lord Huan of Qi led his army to attack Wey. At that time Lord Hui of Wey, formerly the Honorable Shuo, had been dead for some three years, and his son Chi had been established in his place as Lord Yi. Lord Yi did not ask why they had come but simply launched his army into battle, suffering a terrible defeat that forced him back to his capital. When Lord Huan arrived at the foot of the city walls, he proclaimed the royal mandate and listed all the crimes that Lord Hui had committed.

"These are all my late father's mistakes," Lord Yi said. "It has nothing to do with me." However, he sent his oldest son, the Honorable Kaifang, to go to the Qi army with five carts loaded with gold and silk, and beg them for a peace treaty.

"The legal principle was established under our ancestors that punishment cannot be extended to the children and grandchildren of the original criminal," Lord Huan proclaimed. "If you obey His Majesty's commands, what more can I ask for?"

The Honorable Kaifang saw how powerful Qi was, and he wanted to take office there.

"You are the oldest son of the Marquis of Wey, which means that by right of seniority the state will one day be yours," Lord Huan said. "Why would you want to give up the chance to be a ruler in order to work for me?"

"You are the greatest lord in the world, and if I could serve as a member of your entourage, holding your whip, then that would already be a great honor," the Honorable Kaifang replied. "Surely that would be better than becoming a lord?"

Lord Huan was impressed that the Honorable Kaifang admired him so much, so he appointed him to the office of grandee and favored him just as much as Shu Diao and Yi Ya. The people of Qi called these men the Three Nobles.

The Honorable Kaifang spoke many times to Lord Huan of the beauty of the Marquis of Wey's younger daughter. Lord Hui of Wey had already married one of his daughters to the Marquis of Qi, and now Kaifang was praising her younger sister. Lord Huan sent an ambassador with betrothal gifts, asking for the younger woman as a concubine. Lord Yi of Wey did not dare to refuse, so he escorted Lady Ji of Wey to Qi, where the Marquis took her into his household. The two women were then known as the Senior Lady Ji of Wey and the Junior Lady Ji of Wey. Both sisters were much favored by Lord Huan.

A bearded old man wrote a poem about this:

The case against the Marquis of Wey was rock-solid:
How could you use a royal command as an occasion to extort bribes?
You might speak about respecting the king and proclaiming justice to be
   done,
But in fact you came with greed in your heart.

. . .

Let us now turn to another part of the story. The ruling family of the state of Jin were members of the Ji clan, and they held the title of marquis. King Cheng of Zhou invested his younger brother, Prince Tangshu, with these lands, using a paulownia leaf instead of a jade scepter. Nine generations later, we come to Lord Mu. Lord Mu had two sons: the older was named Chou, and the younger was named Chengshi. When Lord Mu died, his son Chou was established in his stead, and he became Lord Wen of Jin. When Lord Wen died, his son was established as Lord Zhao. He was so in awe of his uncle's authority that he enfeoffed him as the Earl of Quwo with a large grant of land, while the state of Jin itself changed its name to Yi. This partitioned the state of Jin into two. Lord Zhao was in power for seven years, and then he was assassinated by Grandee Pan Fu, who installed the Earl of Quwo by force. The people of Yi would not accept this, so they killed Pan Fu and established Lord Zhao's younger brother, the Honorable Ping, as Lord Xiao of Yi. In the eighth year of the reign of Lord Xiao, Chengshi died and his son Shan was established as Lord Zhuang of Quwo. In the fifteenth year of the reign of Lord Xiao, Lord Zhuang attacked Yi. Lord Xiao suffered a terrible defeat in this battle against the invaders and was killed by Lord Zhuang. The people of Yi then appointed his younger brother, the Honorable Xi, as Lord E.

In the second year of Lord E of Yi's rule, he led his forces to attack Quwo. He was defeated and fled into exile in the state of Sui. His son Guang succeeded to the title, and he became Lord Ai of Yi. In the second year of Lord Ai's reign, Lord Zhuang of Quwo died and was succeeded by his son, Chengdai, who became Lord Wu of Quwo. In the ninth year of the reign of Lord Ai, Lord Wu of Quwo attacked Yi with his generals Han Wan and Liang Hong, and Lord Ai was killed in battle. King Huan of Zhou ordered his minister, Linfu, Duke of Guo, to install his younger brother Min as the new marquis: he took the title of Lord Xiaozi. In the fourth year of the reign of Lord Xiaozi, Lord Wu of Quwo tricked him into an ambush and murdered him. The two countries of Quwo and Yi were then reunited under the old name of Jin, and the capital was established at the city of Jiang. Lord Wu took all the treasures kept in the storehouses of Jin and carried them to Zhou, where they were presented to King Li. King Li was a greedy man, and so he issued a royal mandate that Chengdai was now the Marquis of Jin, with a fief of twelve thousand five hundred households. Chengdai held this title for thirty-nine years. When he passed away, his son, the Honorable Guizhu, succeeded him as Lord Xian of Jin.

Lord Xian felt a particular loathing for the noble families that were descended from the previous lords of Quwo, and he was worried that they might cause trouble for him. Grandee Shi Wei suggested a plan that would break up these nascent factions, and he tricked them into situations in which they were all killed. Lord Xian was very pleased with his efforts, and he appointed Shi Wei to be minister of works. Then he built an impressively large wall around the city of Jiang, in every way comparable to that of the capital of a great state.

When Lord Xian was still just the scion, he married Lady Jia Ji as his principal wife, but they did not have any children together. His junior wives included a niece of the chief of the Dog Rong, Lady Hu Ji, who gave birth to a son named Chonger, and a daughter of the Yun clan of the Lesser Rong, who gave birth to a son named Yiwu. In the last years of the reign of Lord Wu, he had requested a marriage alliance with Qi, and thus Lord Huan of Qi sent him one of his own daughters: she was Lady Qi Jiang. At this time Lord Wu was already pretty elderly and was no longer able to control his womenfolk, while Lady Qi Jiang was young and very pretty. Lord Xian fell in love with her and they began an incestuous relationship, which resulted in the birth of a son. He was sent away to be brought up secretly in the Shen family, and therefore he was given the name Shensheng.

When Lord Xian succeeded to the title, Lady Jia Ji was already dead, and he wanted to establish Lady Qi Jiang as his marchioness. At that time Chonger was already twenty-one years of age, and Yiwu was also older than Shensheng, but because Shensheng was the son of the marchioness, he took precedence over them in seniority if not in age. Shensheng was thus appointed as the scion. Grandee Du Yuankuan was made his senior tutor, and Grandee Li Ke was his junior tutor, with the aim that both should support and guide the scion. Lady Qi Jiang died shortly afterwards, giving birth to a daughter. Afterwards Lord Xian appointed Lady Jia Ji's younger sister, Lady Jia Jun, as his marchioness. They had no children together, but Lady Jia Jun brought up Lady Qi Jiang's daughter.

In the fifteenth year of Lord Xian's reign, he raised an army and attacked the Li Rong people. The Li Rong requested a peace treaty and gave two women from their ruling house to Lord Xian: the older was called Lady Li Ji, and the younger was called Lady Shao Ji. Lady Li Ji was as lovely as Lady Gui of Xi had ever been and as wicked as the temptress Da Ji. She was also extremely intelligent, but this concealed a vicious cunning. Whenever Lord Xian was present, she made a play of her affection for him and her loyalty, all the while making sure that she looked as attractive as possible. As a result, he let her participate in the government, and she gave very good advice. Lord Xian came to love and favor her above all others. They ate and drank together and were never to be found apart.

The following year, Lady Li Ji gave birth to a son called Xiqi. The year after that, Lady Shao Ji gave birth to a son named Zhuozi. Lord Xian was bewitched by Lady Li Ji and he was thrilled about their baby, so he forgot all about his earlier love for Lady Qi Jiang. He wanted to appoint Lady Li Ji as his marchioness, so he ordered the Grand Astrologer Guo Yan to perform a divination about it using a turtle shell. Guo Yan inspected the cracks and reported: "The change made by inordinate devotion will steal away the lord's good qualities. One is fragrant, one is disgusting, and after ten years it will still stink."

"What does that mean?" Lord Xian demanded.

"Change refers to some sort of problem," Guo Yan explained. "This means that if you are overly devoted to something or other, it will have a detrimental effect on your mind. That is why it says, 'The change made by inordinate devotion.' Stealing away refers to something being lost, and your good qualities are at present admired by one and all. If something has a detrimental effect on your mind, then you can no longer distinguish properly between good and bad. That is why it says, 'will steal away the lord's good qualities.' Pleasantly scented herbs are said to be fragrant, while those that smell unpleasant are said to be disgusting. If the fragrant cannot overcome the disgusting, corruption will endure for a long time. That is why it says, 'after ten years it will still stink.'"

Lord Xian was besotted by Lady Li Ji and did not believe a word that Guo Yan said, so he ordered another diviner, Astrologer Su, to perform a milfoil divination about it, in which he obtained the hexagram "Observing" and the words "Observing briefly: favorable for an unmarried woman."

"For a woman to live in the harem and observe what is going on outside from that vantage point is very proper," Lord Xian said. "What could be more auspicious than that?"

"Ever since the dawn of time, omens came first and numerology came second," Diviner Guo Yan reminded him. "A divination performed with a turtle shell qualifies as an omen while one performed with milfoil is simply numerology. You should pay attention to the turtle-shell divination and not to that obtained from milfoil."

"According to the strict rules of ritual propriety, a feudal lord cannot marry for a second time," Astrologer Su said. "That is the point made by the 'Observation' hexagram. How can marrying a second wife be called proper? If it is not proper, then how could it be beneficial? The wording found in the *Book of Changes* should not necessarily be interpreted as auspicious."

"If divinations actually worked, everything would be decided by the ghosts and spirits," Lord Xian said crossly.

In the end he paid no attention to what either Astrologer Su or the Diviner Guo Yan had said. He selected an auspicious day to go to the ancestral temples, and then he established Lady Li Ji as his marchioness and Lady Shao Ji as his secondary wife.

Astrologer Su spoke in private to Grandee Li Ke: "What are you going to do when the state of Jin collapses?"

Li Ke was very shocked, and asked him, "Who will be responsible for the destruction of Jin?"

"Who other than Lady Li Ji!" Astrologer Su retorted. Li Ke did not understand what he meant, and so the astrologer explained: "In antiquity King Jie of the Xia dynasty attacked the state of Shi, and they gave him a woman named Mo Xi as wife; King Jie's favoritism brought about the destruction of the dynasty. King Zhou of the Shang dynasty attacked the state of Su, and they gave him a woman named Da Ji as wife; King

Zhou's favoritism brought about the destruction of the dynasty. King You of Zhou attacked Bao, and the people of that state gave him Bao Si as wife; King You's favoritism brought about the destruction of the Western Zhou dynasty. Now Jin has attacked the Li Rong people and captured one of their women, whom he favors above all others—how can this not cause disaster?"

Just at that moment, the Grand Astrologer Guo Yan arrived, and Li Ke told him what Astrologer Su had said. Guo Yan responded: "Jin will certainly have to endure a civil war, but it is not clear whether or not the state will be destroyed. When Prince Tangshu was enfeoffed with these lands, he performed a divination that said, 'Your descendants will govern the lords well and reestablish the royal house.' With such an important task yet to be accomplished, how can Jin be destroyed?"

"When will this civil war occur?" Li Ke asked.

"Whether you do good deeds or bad, you will be repaid within ten years, because ten is a full number," Guo Yan told him. Li Ke recorded his words on a bamboo scroll.

Lord Xian loved Lady Li Ji so much that he wanted to establish her son Xiqi as his heir. One day, he discussed this with Lady Li Ji. She was very willing, but Shensheng had already been appointed as the scion, and she was afraid that the ministers would not accept a change in the succession made for no good reason. She was sure they would remonstrate and try to prevent this. In addition to that, Chonger and Yiwu were both very close to Shensheng and loved him very much. The three of them would definitely stand together. In such a situation, her faction could only fail.

She knelt down before Lord Xian and said, "All the aristocrats know that you have already appointed an heir. He is a clever young man and has done nothing wrong. I would rather commit suicide than see Your Lordship depose the rightful heir for the sake of myself and our son."

Lord Xian thought that she was in earnest and did not say anything more about it.

. . .

His Lordship particularly favored two of the grandees working in his administration. One was named Liang Wu and the other Dongguan Wu. They kept an eye on things outside the palace for Lord Xian and took advantage of the favor he showed them to bully other people. The inhabitants of the Jin capital called them the "Two Wus." There was also a young and handsome actor named Shi, who was much favored by the Marquis of Jin for his sharp intelligence and witty speech, to the point where he was allowed in and out of the palace without any hindrance. Lady Li Ji was having an affair with Shi, and they became closer as their relationship deepened. She told him that her dearest wish was to remove her husband's three older children to facilitate her plan to seize the succession for her own son.

The actor came up with a stratagem to help her: "You must send His Lordship's three sons far away from the capital on the pretext that they are needed to guard the borders. Then you will be left at the heart of things to carry out the next stage of your plans. However, in order to bring this about, you will need the support of at least some of the senior ministers, who can present this suggestion to His Lordship as 'loyal advice.' Your Ladyship should buy the 'Two Wus' into your service with presents of gold and silk. When we all tell His Lordship the same thing, he will have to listen to us."

Accordingly, Lady Li Ji gave silk and gold to Shi and told him to give half to each of the "Two Wus."

The actor Shi went first to see Liang Wu and said, "Her Ladyship would like to become friends with you, so she has sent me to give you some humble gifts."

Amazed, Liang Wu said, "What does Her Ladyship expect me to do for her? She must have given you some instructions! If you do not tell me exactly what is going on, I cannot possibly accept your presents!"

The actor then told Liang Wu of Lady Li Ji's plans, to which he responded, "This is impossible without Grandee Dongguan's assistance."

"Her Ladyship has prepared further gifts for him, just like yours," Shi assured him. They went to visit Dongguan Wu together, and the three of them discussed what they would do.

The following day, Liang Wu presented advice to Lord Xian: "Quwo was your original fief, and it is the site of the ancestral temples of our former lords. The cities of Pu and Qu are located close to the barbarian Di and Rong peoples, and these border territories are vital for our security. We need someone responsible in charge in all three places. If the home of your ancestors is left unattended, the people will despise you. If crucial border territories are left undefended, then the Rong and the Di will take advantage of this. If you send the scion to Quwo and the Honorable Chonger and Yiwu to Pu and Qu, respectively, Your Lordship can keep control in the capital and everything will go well."

"Do you think it is a good idea to send the scion away from the capital?" Lord Xian asked.

"The scion is Your Lordship's deputy, and Quwo is your secondary capital," Dongguan Wu assured him. "Who could be more suitable than the scion to take charge there?"

"Quwo is perfectly comfortable," Lord Xian said. "But Pu and Qu are right out in the wilds. How will my sons endure it?"

"If the houses are not enclosed within a wall, then they are indeed right out in the wilds," Dongguan Wu replied. "Once there is a wall, they become a city."

The two men praised this plan with one voice: "If you gain two cities in a single day, they can protect your present borders and assist in opening up new territory. Jin will soon become a great state!"

Trusting their advice, Lord Xian sent Scion Shensheng to live at Quwo and take control of the government of the city where his ancestors had lived. He was assisted in this task by his tutor, Du Yuankuan. Lord Xian sent the Honorable Chonger to live in Pu and the Honorable Yiwu to live in Qu, with a view to keeping control of these border regions. Hu Mao followed the Honorable Chonger to Pu, while Lü Yisheng escorted Yiwu to Qu. Lord Xian ordered Zhao Xi to build a wall around the city of Quwo, which was much higher and wider than the old one, and henceforward this was known as the New City. He also ordered Shi Wei to supervise the walling of the two cities of Pu and Qu. Shi Wei collected a bit of brushwood and piled up some earth, completing the work in a very lackadaisical manner. Someone said to him, "I am afraid that these walls will not hold."

Shi Wei just laughed and said, "In a few years' time when these cities become enemy strongholds, we won't want them to hold."

He then composed a song:

> Fox-fur cloaks have become confused:
> In this one state there are three lords,
> Whom should I follow?

A fox-fur cloak was a garment worn only by members of the nobility. Confused refers to a chaotic situation. This song describes a situation where there are so many members of the nobility that distinctions between the children of noble mothers and the sons of concubines and the divisions between older and younger siblings have become blurred. Shi Wei was aware of Lady Li Ji's plan to get rid of her husband's heir. That is why he spoke as he did. When Shensheng and his two brothers were sent away to live on the borders of the state of Jin, Xiqi and Zhuozi were left by His Lordship's side. Lady Li Ji did her best to ingratiate

herself with her husband and monopolize his favors, in the hope of
bewitching Lord Xian.

A bearded old man wrote a poem about this:

> Women's beauty has always been a cause of trouble,
> Thus Lord Xian was seduced into favoring Lady Li Ji.
> It was pointless to build these walled cities on the distant borders,
> When real danger lurked within the palace gates.

At this time Lord Xian created two new armies, and he took personal
command of the Upper Army. He appointed Scion Shensheng to command the Lower Army, and Shensheng then directed Grandees Zhao Xi
and Bi Wan in attacks on the three states of Geng, Huo, and Wei, in which
they were destroyed. The lands of Geng were given to Zhao Xi, and the
lands of Wei were bestowed upon Bi Wan as his fief. The scion had played
a major role in these successful campaigns, but Lady Li Ji was jealous of
any achievements he might make, so her plans to get rid of him were even
more vicious. However, this story must be set aside for the time being.

• • •

Prince Xiong Jian and Prince Xiong Hui of Chu were brothers, but even
though they were both born to the queen, Xiong Hui was much cleverer
and more talented than his older brother. This ensured that his mother
adored him and the people of the kingdom admired him greatly.
Although Prince Xiong Jian succeeded to the throne, he was very jealous of his younger brother and wanted to find some pretext to get rid of
him before he could cause trouble. However, there were many courtiers
who spoke up for Prince Xiong Hui, so he could not decide what to do.
Prince Xiong Jian had no interest in governing the country, for the only
thing that he enjoyed was hunting, so during the first three years of his
reign he achieved absolutely nothing. Prince Xiong Hui realized that
this was something that he could take advantage of, so he secretly gathered together a band of assassins, and while his older brother was out
hunting they attacked and killed him. It was reported to the dowager
queen that her oldest son had suddenly become violently ill and died.
Although the dowager queen was suspicious, she did not want to know
the truth. She directed all the ministers to support Prince Xiong Hui's
accession, and he was crowned King Cheng. Since Xiong Jian had never
governed the country, they did not think he counted as their ruler, so he
simply received the posthumous title of Du'ao, and they did not bury
him with royal rituals.

King Cheng of Chu appointed his uncle, Prince Shan, styled Ziyuan, as his Grand Vizier. Ever since the death of his older brother, King Wen, Prince Shan had been turning the possibility of usurping the throne over in his mind. He also coveted his sister-in-law, Lady Gui of Xi, who was such a beautiful woman, and he was hoping to seduce her into an affair. Prince Xiong Jian and Prince Xiong Hui were both still quite young and very respectful of their uncle, so he did not consider either a threat to his position. The only person he was worried about was Grand Vizier Dou Bobi, who was not only a very honest and unselfish man, but also very clever. It was only for this reason that he did not dare to try anything. However, in the eleventh year of the reign of King Hui of Zhou, Dou Bobi became sick and died. Prince Shan did not wait any longer, but ordered the construction of a mansion right next to the royal palace, where he had music played every day, with the intention of attracting the dowager queen's attention.

She heard the noise and asked one of her servants, "Where does that music come from?"

"From the Grand Vizier's new mansion!" the servant replied.

"His Late Majesty would exercise with a spear in order to practice his skills in the martial arts, so that he could campaign against the other lords," the dowager queen mused. "They came to pay court to us and sent tribute in an endless stream. It has now been ten years since the armies of Chu last went out into the Central States. The Grand Vizier appears to have no intention of altering this humiliating situation, but instead spends his time playing music to a widow. Is this not bizarre behavior?"

The servants reported her words to Prince Shan, who said, "I may have forgotten our ambitions in the Central States, but she has not! Let me attack the state of Zheng!"

He led an army of six hundred chariots out on campaign, with himself in command of the main army. Dou Yujiang and Dou Wu held the great flag marking the vanguard, while Royal Grandson You and Royal Grandson Jia took charge of the rearguard. In a great wave, they launched their attack on the state of Zheng.

. . .

When Lord Wen of Zheng heard that the Chu army had arrived in force, he immediately summoned his officials to discuss the situation.

"The Chu army is massive and we cannot resist them," Du Shi advised him. "You had better ask for a peace treaty."

"We have recently made a blood covenant with Qi, so they will have to come and rescue us," Shi Su said. "We should just sit behind the city walls and wait for them."

The Scion of Zheng, the Honorable Hua, was only a boy, but he was tough, and he suggested fighting at the foot of the city walls.

"Having listened to all three of you, I think that Shi Shu is right," Shu Zhan said. "In my humble opinion the Chu army will soon be going home."

"The Grand Vizier is in personal command, so why would they withdraw?" Lord Wen of Zheng asked.

"Ever since the first time that Chu invaded us, they have never employed so many as six hundred chariots," Shu Zhan replied. "Prince Shan wants to be sure that he will win this battle, because he is trying to seduce the dowager queen. He needs to win, and that means that he is going to be worried about the possibility of losing. If the Chu army does indeed come our way, I have a plan to make them leave."

Just as they were in the middle of their discussions, a spy reported: "The Chu army has cut its way through the Jiedie Pass and broken through the outer city wall. Having passed through the Chun Gate, they are now at the Kui Market."

"The Chu army is getting close," Du Shu pointed out. "If you are not going to ask them for a peace treaty, then we should at least flee to Tongqiu and get away from them!"

"There is nothing to be afraid of!" Shu Zhan assured him. He ordered his soldiers to hide inside the city walls and had the gates flung open to reveal that the streets were full of people going about their business as normal and that no one looked in the least bit scared.

Dou Yujiang and the other people in the vanguard were the first to arrive. When they saw the state of affairs, they were deeply puzzled, for there seemed to be no panic inside the city at all. He said to Dou Wu, "For Zheng to be so relaxed means that they must be up to something— they are trying to trick us into entering the city. We should not advance just in case, but wait for the Grand Vizier to arrive so that we can discuss our next move." They made camp five *li* away from the city.

A short time later, Prince Shan arrived with the main army, and Dou Yujiang reported what he had seen inside the city. Prince Shan climbed up onto the top of a hill that would allow him to see inside the city walls. Suddenly he saw flags and battle standards unfurl in strict order and serried ranks of armored men moved into battle formation. After watching them for a moment, he sighed and said: "The 'Three Good

Men' of Zheng are inside the city, and they are all excellent strategists. If by some mischance I were to lose this battle, how would I ever be able to face the dowager queen? Let us make further investigations and find out exactly what is going on before we make any attack on this city!"

The following day, Noble Grandson You sent someone to report from the rearguard: "Our spies have reported back that the Marquis of Qi is on his way in command of an enormous host, accompanied by the lords of Song and Lu. They are coming here to rescue Zheng. I hope that General Dou will not advance any further. I am waiting for your commands and preparing to meet the enemy."

Deeply alarmed, Prince Shan said to his generals, "If these lords have indeed cut our retreat, we will have the enemy coming up behind us. In that case we are sure to be comprehensively defeated. We have already advanced as far as the Kui Market, which counts as a victory."

He secretly gave orders for everyone to keep quiet and take the bells off their horses, so that they could strike camp that night and disappear. They were afraid that the Zheng army would pursue them, so they did not take down their tents, and they left their battle standards in place in the hope of delaying them. The army crept past the border, and then they sounded their bells and banged their drums and went home singing triumphal songs.

The very first thing that Prince Shan did was to send a message to the dowager queen to say, "The Grand Vizier has returned in triumph!"

The queen dowager refused to pay any attention to him: "If the Grand Vizier has indeed routed the enemy and won a great victory, then this should be proclaimed to the people in order to make the consequences of disobeying our might clear, and announced at the ancestral temples to console the spirits of our former kings. It has nothing to do with me!"

Prince Shan felt very ashamed of himself. When King Cheng of Chu heard that His Highness had returned without even fighting a single battle, he was naturally deeply displeased.

. . .

Shu Zhan of Zheng was personally inspecting the soldiers patrolling the city walls, so he was up all night. When it got light, he looked out at the Chu tents. Pointing to them, he said, "The camp is empty. The Chu army has gone."

No one believed him, and they asked, "How do you know?"

"Those tents are where the generals would be staying, and they sound the bells there to act as warnings and to raise the army's morale,"

Shu Zhan explained. "Now you can see a whole flock of birds sitting on top of them and cawing, which means that the camp must be empty. I would guess that the lords have sent an army to rescue us and that Chu got to hear the news first—that is why they have left."

A short time later, spies reported: "The army that the lords sent to rescue us was on its way, but it had not yet crossed the border into Zheng when they heard that the Chu army had departed, so they have gone back to their own countries."

Everyone was deeply impressed by Shu Zhan's perspicacity. Zheng then sent an ambassador to thank the Marquis of Qi for his efforts to rescue them, and from this point onwards they felt great gratitude towards the state of Qi and did not dare behave disloyally to it.

. . .

Prince Shan of Chu was not at all happy about the unsuccessful result of his attack on Zheng, and he began to feel that usurping the throne was ever more pressing. However, he was in an even greater hurry to seduce the dowager queen into an affair. It so happened that she came down with some mild complaint, and so, on the pretext of asking after her health, Prince Shan went into the royal palace, taking all his furniture and bedding with him, and for three days he refused to leave. He had a bodyguard of several hundred armed men, and during this time they were on patrol outside the palace. When Grandee Dou Lian heard what was going on, he burst through one of the palace gates and went straight to the prince's bedroom, where he found His Highness arranging his hair in front of a mirror.

He upbraided him, saying, "Surely this is not the place where ministers perform their ritual ablutions? You should leave as soon as you can!"

"This palace belongs to my family," Prince Shan shouted. "It has nothing to do with you!"

"In royal and aristocratic houses, senior and junior members do not share the same roof," Dou Lian retorted. "Since you are a younger son, Grand Vizier, you are a subject of His Majesty. When you pass the royal gate, it is mandatory that you get down from your horse, and when you walk by the royal ancestral shrine, you are required to hurry respectfully. It would not be respectful for you to either cough or spit within the precincts of these two places, let alone spend the night there! The dowager queen is in residence here. Perhaps, Grand Vizier, you may have heard that men and women should observe the segregation of the sexes?"

Prince Shan was furious. "The government of the kingdom of Chu is in my hands. How dare you speak to me like that?"

He ordered his servants to put handcuffs on him and drag him off into the side chambers, since they could not throw him out of the palace.

The dowager queen sent one of her servants to report this crisis to Dou Bobi's son, Dou Guwutu, summoning him into the palace to deal with the problem. Dou Guwutu secretly sent a memorial to the king of Chu, informing him of the situation, and he arranged with Dou Wu, Dou Yujiang, and his son Dou Ban that at midnight they would surround the royal palace with their troops. When they did indeed attack Prince Shan's bodyguards, the bodyguards were terrified and ran away. Prince Shan was sleeping drunkenly with one of the palace maids in his arms, when he woke with a start from his dreams—grabbing a sword, he ran straight into Dou Ban.

"Is it you that is causing all this trouble, brat?" the prince shouted.

"I am not causing any trouble, but I am here to execute someone who is!" Dou Ban said. The two of them then started fighting in the middle of the palace. Before they had crossed swords more than a couple of times, Dou Yujiang and Dou Wu both arrived. Prince Shan calculated that he could not possibly defeat all of them. He tried to escape through one of the gates, but Dou Ban cut his head off with a single stroke of his sword. Dou Guwutu then released Dou Lian from his chains, and they all went and lined up outside the dowager queen's bedroom, whereupon they kowtowed and made sure that she was safe and well, after which they withdrew.

The following morning King Cheng of Chu held court, and when his officials had completed their ceremonial greetings, he ordered that Prince Shan's family should be killed to the last man and placards proclaiming his crimes should be erected along all thoroughfares.

A bearded old man wrote a poem about Prince Shan's attempt to seduce the dowager queen, which reads:

How sad that his infatuation resulted in his destruction!
He did not care about her noble position, and he did not care that she
　was kin.
There is no point blaming him for his wild and reckless behavior;
The dowager queen of Chu was the former marchioness of Xi.

• • •

Dou Guwutu's grandfather was named Dou Ruo'ao. He married the daughter of the Viscount of Yun, who gave birth to Dou Bobi. Ruo'ao died when Dou Bobi was still very young, and therefore he moved back with his mother to the state of Yun, where he spent his childhood popping in and out of the palace. The Viscountess of Yun loved him as if he were her own son. Her only daughter was, of course, Dou Bobi's first cousin, and they played together in the palace when they were little children. When they grew up, they did not restrain their affections and became lovers. This daughter of the Yun ruling house became pregnant, at which point her mother discovered what was going on and ordered that Dou Bobi should under no circumstances whatsoever be allowed into the palace. She forced her daughter to pretend that she was sick and shut her up in a single room. Eventually, her pregnancy came to term and she gave birth to a boy. The Viscountess of Yun ordered one of the palace servants to wrap the baby up in old clothes and smuggle it secretly out of the palace, to abandon it at the Meng Marshes. She wanted to keep all of this a secret from the Viscount of Yun, as she did not want her daughter's humiliation to be blazoned to all the world. Dou Bobi was ashamed of what he had done, and he returned to the kingdom of Chu with his mother.

It so happened that the Viscount of Yun went out hunting in the Meng Marshes and caught sight of a tiger squatting down. He ordered his entourage to shoot at it, but all the arrows fell to one side or the other. None of them hit the tiger, and the animal was completely unalarmed. The Viscount of Yun was surprised by this, so he sent someone into the marsh to take a closer look. He reported back: "The tiger is suckling a human baby. It is not at all scared of people."

"That must be some sort of supernatural beast," the Viscount of Yun commanded. "Do not alarm it!"

When the hunt was over, he went home and said to his wife, "I saw a strange thing in the Meng Marshes."

"What could it be?" she asked.

The Viscount of Yun then explained how the tiger had been suckling a human baby.

"There is something that you do not know, my lord," his wife said. "I abandoned the baby there."

The Viscount of Yun was startled by this news: "Where did the baby that you abandoned come from?"

"I hope that you will not blame me for what I have done," she said. "This baby was born to our daughter and our nephew, Dou Bobi, but I was afraid that giving birth to an illegitimate child would harm her reputation, so I ordered the servants to abandon it in the Meng Marshes. I know the legend that Lady Jiang Yuan gave birth to a baby after she stepped in the footprint left by a giant man, and that when she abandoned the baby on the ice, birds covered it with their wings. Lady Jiang Yuan decided that it must be a miracle, so she kept the baby and raised him to adulthood, giving him the name Qi, or 'Abandoned.' He became the Lord of Agriculture and was the ancestor of the Zhou royal house. If this baby has been suckled by a tiger, in the future he is sure to become a great man!"

The Viscount of Yun agreed with her and ordered someone to bring the baby back home. He commanded his daughter to look after her baby. The following year he escorted his daughter to Chu, where she was married to Dou Bobi.

In Chu dialect the word "suckled" is pronounced "gu," while the word "tiger" is pronounced "wutu." Since this baby had been suckled by a tiger, they called him Guwutu. His formal style-name was Ziwen. To this day in Yunmeng County there is a village called Wutu, and this is where Ziwen was born.

When Dou Guwutu grew up, it became clear that he would be able to bring peace to the people and govern the country. He was equally talented at interpreting the classical texts of antiquity as he was in the arts of war. His father, Dou Bobi, held office as a grandee of the kingdom of Chu. When Bobi died, Guwutu inherited his position. When Prince Shan died, the office of Grand Vizier became vacant and the king of Chu intended to appoint Dou Lian.

Dou Lian refused in the following terms: "Chu's greatest enemy is the state of Qi. It is because Qi employs Guan Zhong and Ning Qi that their country has become rich and the army powerful. I am not as clever as either of that pair. If you wish to reform the government, Your Majesty, and fight with the states of the Zhou confederacy, then you need Dou Guwutu."

The officials present all presented their opinion, and with one voice they said, "You need this man, so please give him this office."

The king of Chu agreed and appointed Dou Guwutu to the position of Grand Vizier.

"In Qi they have Guan Zhong, and everyone calls him by the honorific title of Elder Zhong," His Majesty said. "Now we need to make it clear that Dou Guwutu is equally respected in Chu, so he needs some kind of honorific style-name."

He decided to call him Ziwen and not to use his personal name again. Thus, in the thirteenth year of the reign of King Hui of Zhou, Ziwen became Grand Vizier of Chu.

He proclaimed: "Many disasters for our country have stemmed from the fact that His Majesty is weak and the aristocrats are strong. To counteract this, all holders of hereditary fiefs must hand back one half of their lands to the royal house."

Ziwen started the implementation of this policy by giving back half of the lands of the Dou family, and then the others did not dare to disobey. Having observed the well-protected situation of the city of Ying, with the Xiang River to the south and the Han River to the north, he moved the capital there from Danyang. He trained soldiers and instructed them in the arts of war, and he promoted clever men and employed the able in the government. He selected a man named Qu Wan from one of the aristocratic houses in the kingdom of Chu as being particularly intelligent and appointed him to the office of grandee. There was a man named Dou Zhang from his own family, who was exceptionally brilliant, so he sent him to take charge of the army along with the other members of his clan. He enfeoffed Dou Ban as Duke of Shen. The government of the kingdom of Chu was truly exemplary.

. . .

When Lord Huan of Qi heard that the king of Chu was giving office to a host of exceptionally clever men, and had instituted a serious program of government reform, he started to worry that this would put them in a position where they would be able to defeat the Central States. He wanted to raise a coalition army from the lords of the Central States to attack Chu, and he asked Guan Zhong for his opinion of this idea.

"The king of Chu governs a truly vast realm, his lands are extensive and his army is strong: hence not even the Zhou Son of Heaven can control him," Guan Zhong informed him. "In addition to that, he has now appointed Ziwen as the Grand Vizier, and he has brought peace to all four corners of his domain—you will not achieve your ambition of cowing Chu simply by using military might. Your Lordship has also only recently taken charge of the lords of the Zhou confederacy, and you have not yet been able to convince them that it is their job to protect each other. I am afraid that we cannot rely on the armies of the other aristocrats. You will have to enhance your reputation for virtue and for military prowess and then wait for a suitable moment to strike, for it is only under those circumstances that you will be successful."

"I have already destroyed the state of Ji to take revenge for a crime that they committed against my ancestor nine generations back, and I now possess all their territory," Lord Huan said. "The state of Zhang was originally a subinfeudated territory of Ji, and it has not yet submitted to my authority. I would like to destroy it too. How would that be?"

"Even though Zhang is only a tiny state, its ruling house is descended from the Great Lord, the founding ancestor of the state of Qi, and so they are members of the same clan as Your Lordship," Guan Zhong pointed out. "It would not be righteous to destroy another branch of your own clan. Your Lordship should send Prince Chengfu to take a great army out on patrol around the former state of Ji, making it look as if you might launch a further attack. Zhang will then be terrified into surrendering to you. Thus you will obtain their lands without the odium of having destroyed part of your own clan."

Lord Huan followed this plan, and the Lord of Zhang was indeed frightened into surrendering.

"Elder Zhong's plans always work!" Lord Huan exclaimed.

Just as he was discussing the government of the country with his ministers, suddenly he received a report: "The state of Yan has been invaded by the Mountain Rong, and they have sent someone here specially to ask for assistance."

"If Your Lordship wishes to attack Chu, you will have to deal with the Rong people first," Guan Zhong told him. "Once the Rong have ceased causing problems, you can turn all your attention to the south."

Was Lord Huan able to subjugate the Rong in the end? READ ON.

Chapter Twenty-one

*Guan Yiwu cleverly explains the identity
of the Yu'er.*

*Lord Huan of Qi's army brings peace
to Guzhu.*

The Mountain Rong people were one branch of the Northern Rong, and their kingdom was called Lingzhi or Lizhi. The state of Yan was located to the west, and Qi and Lu to the south and east. Although Lingzhi shared a border with these three states, taking advantage of the difficulty of the terrain and the strength of their armies, they neither paid court nor offered tribute, and they repeatedly invaded the Central States. On one occasion in the past when they invaded Qi, they were repulsed by Scion Zihu of Zheng. When they heard that Lord Huan of Qi was planning to make himself hegemon, they gathered together a great host of ten thousand horsemen and invaded the state of Yan, in the hope of breaking their communications with Qi. Lord Zhuang of Yan had no way to resist such a powerful enemy, so he sent someone by a circuitous route to report this emergency to Qi.

Lord Huan of Qi asked Guan Zhong what he should do, and he replied: "The greatest threats to our security today are Chu to the south, the Rong to the north, and the Di to the west. These are all serious problems facing the Central States, and it is your responsibility as the Master of Covenants to deal with them. Although the Rong cannot possibly defeat Yan, they still seem to want to attack them. Since Yan has been invaded, should we not save them?"

Lord Huan led his forces to rescue Yan. When the army crossed the Ji River, they found that Lord Zhuang of Lu had come out to the borders to meet them. Lord Huan informed him of his plans to attack the Rong.

"If Your Lordship can restrain these leopards and wolves and bring peace to the north, it is not just the people of Yan who will benefit—will I not also be among their number?" the Marquis of Lu declared. "I am happy to assist you by levying troops."

"The situation in the north is very dangerous," Lord Huan explained. "I would not dream of letting you participate. If my efforts are attended by success, then I will attribute it all to your support. If things go badly, I may yet need to borrow troops from you."

"I will be happy to oblige," the Marquis of Lu said.

Lord Huan said farewell to the Marquis of Lu and proceeded in a northwesterly direction.

• • •

The Viscount of Lingzhi was named Milu. He had already been ravaging the borders of the state of Yan for two months, during which time he had captured countless men and women. When he heard that the Qi army had arrived in force, he broke the siege and left. When Lord Huan's army arrived at the Ji Gate Pass, Lord Zhuang of Yan came in person to welcome them, and he apologized to the Marquis of Qi for putting him to all the trouble of going such a long way to rescue them.

"The Mountain Rong have gone," Guan Zhong said, "and for the moment their ambitions are satisfied. They have not yet experienced a genuine defeat. If our army were to withdraw, the Rong soldiers would simply come back. It will be best if we take advantage of the current situation to attack them, to prevent any further trouble."

"Good idea!" Lord Huan exclaimed.

Lord Zhuang of Yan requested permission that his whole army should form the vanguard, but Lord Huan said, "Your soldiers have already suffered so much! How can you bear to order that they form the vanguard of yet another attack? Your Lordship will lead the rearguard, providing me with reinforcements. That is quite enough."

"Eighty *li* east of here, there is a kingdom called Wuzhong," Lord Zhuang of Yan explained. "Even though these people are a branch of the Rong, they have nothing to do with the Mountain Rong. If we can get in touch with them, they may be willing to act as guides."

Lord Huan issued enormous quantities of gold and silk and ordered Xi Peng to make contact with them. The Viscount of Wuzhong sent his senior general Hu'erban in command of a cavalry force of two thousand men to help in the coming battle. Lord Huan again issued generous rewards to them and placed them at the head of his army.

When they had advanced two hundred *li*, Lord Huan noticed that the road ahead was getting ever more precipitous and dangerous, and he asked the Earl of Yan about it.

"This place is called Kuisi," the Earl of Yan explained, "and it is the most important route for the Mountain Rong to leave their country."

Lord Huan discussed the situation with Guan Zhong, and they decided that one half of their heavy baggage carts, loaded with grain, should be left in camp at Kuisi. They ordered the soldiers to cut down trees and pile up earth to create a fortress that would protect this road, and Bao Shuya would remain behind to guard it, with responsibility for keeping their forces supplied. The army was allowed to rest for three days, and then they weeded out any soldiers who were sick or exhausted, so that only the very best and strongest men were allowed to proceed.

. . .

When Milu, Viscount of Lingzhi, heard that the Qi army had come to attack him, he summoned his general, Sumai, to discuss the situation.

"They have come from a very long way away and must be exhausted," Sumai said. "If we make a sudden attack on them before they have had time to make camp, we will win a great victory." Milu accordingly gave him a force of three thousand horsemen.

Sumai issued orders that they should spread out and set ambushes in the mountain valleys, waiting for the Qi army to arrive before they struck. Hu'erban was the first to arrive at the head of the vanguard, and Sumai attacked him with only one hundred horsemen in support. Hu'erban, a brave and reckless man, grabbed hold of a long-handled mace with a heavy iron gourd-shaped head. Catching sight of Sumai in the distance, he tried to club him with it.

"One step at a time!" Sumai shouted. He drew a massive cutlass and prepared to fight back. When they had fought for a while, Sumai pretended to cut and run, drawing his enemy deep into the forest. When he called out, the soldiers lying in ambush throughout the mountain valleys all rose up and fell on Hu'erban's troops, forcing them to separate into two groups. Hu'erban was now caught in a desperate fight; his horse had been severely wounded, and he expected himself to be made prisoner at any moment. Fortunately, the main force of the Qi army had now arrived, and Prince Chengfu advanced his troops in an awe-inspiring show of force, killing Sumai's soldiers and rescuing Hu'erban from his predicament. Sumai left the field having suffered a terrible defeat. The majority of the Rong cavalry under Hu'erban's command had either been killed or injured in this battle, so when he had audience with Lord Huan, it was obvious that he felt deeply ashamed.

"Every general has battles that he wins and battles that he loses," Lord Huan told him. "You must not take it so much to heart." He presented him with a famous blood-horse, and Hu'erban was overcome with gratitude.

The main body of the army now advanced thirty *li* to the east, to a place called Mount Fulong. Lord Huan made camp alongside Lord Zhuang of Yan, right up at the peak of the mountain, while Prince Chenghu and Bin Xuwu established a secondary camp at the base of the mountain. Big chariots were lined up around the perimeter to form a kind of basic defensive wall, and a strict watch was kept. The following day Milu, Viscount of Lingzhi, came in person to provoke battle, accompanied by General Sumai, in command of ten thousand horsemen. They attacked several times, but the defensive wall of chariots held and they were not able to enter the encampments. By the afternoon, Guan Zhong, watching from the very top of the mountain, noticed that the number of Rong troops on the attack was getting less and less every time. The frustrated and tired soldiers were getting off their horses to lie on the ground, cursing.

Guan Zhong patted Hu'erban on the back and said, "If you want to expunge the humiliation they inflicted on you, now is the time."

Hu'erban accepted his command. He ordered that one part of the chariot wall should be opened and led out his remaining troops, killing everyone in their path.

"I am afraid that it is all a trap on the part of the Rong army," Xi Peng murmured.

"Of course it is," Guan Zhong said. Immediately, he gave commands that Prince Chengfu should take an army out of the left side of the camp and Bin Xuwu should take an army out of the right side of the camp, with a view to providing support by killing all the troops lying in ambush. The Mountain Rong were accustomed to setting ambushes, so when they realized that the fortifications the Qi army was using were going to hold, they sent some soldiers away to lie in ambush around the valley, while the remainder intentionally got off their horses and discussed their grievances to trick the Qi soldiers into leaving their camp. The minute Hu'erban reached these disgruntled soldiers, they all fled, leaving their horses behind them. Hu'erban was just about to set off in pursuit when he heard the sound of a bell proceeding from the main camp, so he immediately reined in his horse and went back. When Milu realized that Hu'erban was not coming after him, he gave a whistle to summon all the people hidden throughout the valley with the intention of attacking with all his might. Just at that moment, Prince Chengfu and Bin Xuwu's troops advanced in a pincer movement, cutting them to pieces. Having suffered a second terrible defeat, the Rong army withdrew, with many of their men and horses having been butchered.

Sumai now suggested a new plan: "If Qi wants to advance its armies, they will have to proceed through the valley of Mount Huangtai. If we cut down trees and pile up stones to block the road, as well as digging numerous defensive pits, we can set our troops to guard it. Even if they came with a million men, they would not be able to pass. There is also no water source within more than twenty *li* of Mount Fulong other than the Ru River. If we were to dam the Ru River, they will have no water to drink and their army would be thrown into chaos. Once that happens, morale will collapse. If we take advantage of that situation, we are sure to defeat them. However, you should also send an ambassador to ask for assistance from the kingdom of Guzhu and borrow troops from them to help in the attack. Then this plan is sure to succeed."

Milu was thrilled and followed every point in his plan.

After the Rong army withdrew, for three days in a row Guan Zhong saw no sign of them. He became more and more suspicious, sending out spies to investigate. They reported back: "The main road at Mount Huangtai has been cut."

Guan Zhong summoned Hu'erban and asked him, "Is there any other road that we can take?"

"We are only fifteen *li* away from Mount Huangtai," Hu'erban explained. "If we could go that way, we could march straight into their kingdom. If, on the other hand, we have to go by another route, then we will need to make a great detour to the southwest through the Zhimaling mountain range to the foot of Mount Qing. Skirting around to the east for several *li*, we can make our way into the lair of the Lingzhi. However, these mountains are very high and the roads are extremely dangerous; we cannot possibly take either horses or carts that way."

Just as they were in the middle of their discussions, General Lian Zhi reported: "The Rong chief has cut our water supplies. The army has nothing to drink. What are we going to do?"

"The route to Zhimaling takes us through the mountains the whole way, and it will be several days until we can get there," Hu'erban said. "If we don't have any water, we cannot possibly go."

Lord Huan issued orders that the soldiers should all dig for water amid the mountains, and the first person to find a spring would be heavily rewarded. Xi Peng stepped forward and said, "I have heard that ants live near water, so if we find an ant's nest, we can dig there."

The troops searched everywhere, but they could not find a single ant's nest anywhere, so they came back to report this and ask for further instructions.

"In the winter when ants need to keep warm, you will find them living on the south side of the mountains," Xi Peng told them. "In the summer when the ants need to keep cool, you will find them living on the north side of the mountains. Right now it is winter, so they are all going to be on the southern side. There is no point in digging around indiscriminately."

The officers did as he said, and sure enough they dug out a spring about halfway up the mountain, which provided very pure and clear waters.

"Xi Peng really is a sage!" Lord Huan remarked.

They named the water source the "Sage Spring," and Mount Fulong changed its name to Dragon Spring Mountain. Everyone congratulated each other on having found water.

When Milu heard that the Qi army was apparently not running out of water, he was very surprised and asked, "Are the Central States perhaps being assisted by the gods?"

"Even if the Qi army has water, as they advance further and further, they will find their food supplies running out," Sumai said. "We don't have to fight them—once their food is finished, they will have to withdraw." Milu agreed.

. . .

Guan Zhong ordered Bin Xuwu to pretend as if he were going back to Kuisi to collect more grain, but in fact he was to make his way through the mountains at Zhimaling, with Hu'erban leading the way. He had six days to accomplish this task. He instructed General Lian Zhi to go to Mount Huangtai and try and skirmish with the soldiers guarding it, thereby keeping Milu's troops busy and preventing them from suspecting anything. During these six days, the Rong army did not fight a single battle.

"According to my calculations," Guan Zhong said, "General Bin Xuwu must have arrived on their western flank by now. They don't seem to have attacked, but I cannot wait any longer."

He ordered all the soldiers to take a bag each and fill it with earth. Then he commanded that two hundred empty carts should be brought up, so that they could be sent on ahead. Every time they found a pit, they should fill it with bags of earth. The main body of the army advanced right up to the mouth of the valley, whereupon they gave a great battle cry and advanced, ripping apart the Rong barricades.

Milu believed himself to be completely safe, so he spent every day in drinking and making merry with Sumai. Suddenly he heard that the Qi army was launching a major assault and had broken through the first line of his defenses. He immediately leapt onto his horse and set off to meet the enemy. Before he had arrived at the front, a Rong soldier reported to him: "Another enemy army is advancing on us from the west."

When Sumai realized that their retreat had also been cut, he had no stomach for a fight, so he protected Milu as they escaped along a south-westerly route. Bin Xuwu pursued them for several *li*, but when he noticed that the road through the mountains was becoming ever more perilous and the Rong troops were riding their horses as fast as they possibly could, he turned back. The Rong army had abandoned count-less horses, weapons, cattle, sheep, and tents, and these were all now taken by the Qi army. They also recaptured vast numbers of the men and women who had been stolen from the state of Yan. The people of Lingzhi had never seen such a powerful force before, and they surren-dered immediately, offering their captors baskets of grain and beakers of water. Lord Huan of Qi did his best to soothe their fears and ordered that no one should kill any barbarians who surrendered. This greatly pleased the Rong people. Lord Huan of Qi summoned some of the sur-rendered Rong people and asked, "Where will your chief go? Which country will he throw his lot in with?"

"Our kingdom borders on that of Guzhu, and we have always main-tained good relations with them," they said. "Just recently His Lordship sent an ambassador to them to ask for an army, but it has not yet arrived. He will certainly have gone to Guzhu!"

Lord Huan inquired about Guzhu's military capabilities and how far away it was.

"Guzhu is comparable to any of the great states south and east of here," they explained. "As far back as the time of the Shang dynasty, they already had a walled capital. Just over one hundred *li* from here, you will find a river called the Bi'er, and once you have crossed it, you will have arrived at the borders of the kingdom of Guzhu. However, the route through the mountains is very steep and dangerous, and you will find it extremely difficult to get there."

"Guzhu has been party to the violent attacks the Mountain Rong has made upon others, and they are located near to where we are now," Lord Huan said. "We ought to punish them."

Just at that moment General Gao Hei arrived with fifty carts of dry provisions sent by Bao Shuya. Lord Huan had Gao Hei stay and form part of the vanguard. He also selected one thousand strong men from the surrendered Rong and placed them under Hu'erban's command, in order to make good the losses that he had suffered. Then he rested the army for three days, before setting off again. When Milu and his supporters arrived at Guzhu, they had an audience with the chief, whose name was Daliha, and in tears they prostrated themselves on the ground: "The Qi army is terribly strong, and they have invaded our country. Please give us some troops that we may take revenge on them."

"I wanted to raise an army to help you," Daliha told them, "but it was delayed for a few days by some minor problems. I was not expecting that in the interim you would suffer such a dreadful defeat. Here we are safe on the far side of the Bi'er River, which is so deep that it is impossible to plumb. I will have all the bamboo rafts detained in harbor—even if the Qi army grows wings, they will not be able to fly across. We will just have to wait until they decide to withdraw. Then we can go and attack them, winning back all your old territory. Isn't that much more convenient for us?"

The senior general, Commander-in-Chief Huanghua, said, "I am concerned that they might build rafts and use them to cross the river. You should send soldiers to guard the mouth of the river with orders to patrol day and night, to make sure that we are secure."

"If they start building rafts, surely we are going to notice," Daliha retorted. He paid no further attention to Huanghua's advice.

. . .

As has already been mentioned, the main body of Lord Huan of Qi's army set off, but before they had even advanced ten *li*, looking out into the distance they could see the road winding through a desolate mountain range, with strangely shaped rocks and steep precipices, all overgrown with trees and undergrowth and clumps of bamboo so dense as to make the road impassable.

There is a poem that testifies to this:

Twisting and turning to meet the pale clouds,
The road disappears among the rocks and cliffs.
Even the northern barbarians have to get off their horses here,
Afraid that the caves may conceal a mountain spirit.

Guan Zhong instructed the soldiers to take sulfur and saltpeter and some easily combustible material, scatter it among the trees and brushwood, and then set fire to it. Crackling and snapping, the whole mountain burst into flame. The trees simply vanished, and the foxes and hares that made their abode here disappeared. The flames leapt up into the sky, and the fires burned for five days and five nights. When this inferno was finally extinguished, he ordered them to level a road to take their chariots through the mountains.

The generals reported that the mountain was simply too high and too precipitous to make it possible to take chariots through.

"The Rong cavalry moves at great speed, so we need the chariots to have a chance of dealing with them," Guan Zhong informed them. He then composed two songs: "Going up the Mountain" and "Going down the Mountain," and he taught the soldiers how to sing them. "Going up the Mountain" ran as follows:

Amid majestic peaks the road winds in and out,
Magnificent trees cloak the rocky promontories.
The sun gleams coldly amidst the light clouds,
We push our chariots up the scree.
If the monarch of the winds could be hitched to our chariots,
If Yu'er could hold the whip,
We would move like birds borne on feathered wings.
Ascending this mountain would then be no problem.

"Going down the Mountain" ran as follows:

Climbing up the mountain is difficult, going down is easy;
The wheels spin and the horses' hooves clip.
As the chariots rumble along, we breathe more easily,
Another few turns and we will find ourselves on flat land.
We will fall on the Rong huts, putting out the flames of war,
For which we will be praised for the rest of time.

Everyone starting singing, harmonizing with one another, and the chariots moved at speed. Lord Huan climbed up to the top of Mount Bi'er, accompanied by Guan Zhong, Xi Peng, and the others, in order to observe the lay of the land. Lord Huan sighed and said, "It is only today that I realize how much stronger people are when they sing!"

"When they loaded the cage in which I was imprisoned onto the top of a cart, I was afraid that the people of Lu would come in pursuit, so I composed a song and taught it to the people guarding me," Guan Zhong explained. "They were so pleased that they forgot about feeling tired, and then they completed a journey that would normally take two days in a single day."

"How could that be?" Lord Huan inquired.

"When people are tired, their spirits sink, but if you can cheer them up, then they forget about their exhaustion!"

"You really understand the way that other people feel, Elder Zhong!" Lord Huan exclaimed. He urged on the chariots and infantry, and they all advanced together.

They traveled past several mountain ranges and climbed a ridge, only to see that all the carts and chariots in front, both large and small, seemed to have become stuck in a bottleneck. The officers reported: "The road here passes through a narrow cleft, with massive stone cliffs on both sides. Cavalry riding in single file can get through, but not the chariots."

Lord Huan looked alarmed and said to Guan Zhong, "If there is an ambush ahead, we are sure to be defeated!"

Just as he was hesitating, uncertain of what to do, suddenly he noticed something walking out of the cleft in the mountains. Lord Huan stared at it—it looked like a person, but it wasn't human; it looked like an animal, but it wasn't any beast that he recognized. It was about ten feet tall, wearing a red gown and a black hat, but both its feet were bare. It respectfully bowed a couple of times to Lord Huan as if it had come specially to meet him. Then it gathered up its gown in its right hand and ran quickly back into the narrow cleft in the rocks.

Lord Huan, amazed, asked Guan Zhong, "Did you see that?"

"See what?"

Lord Huan described its appearance, and Guan Zhong said: "That is the Yu'er that I mentioned in my song!"

"What is an Yu'er?" Lord Huan asked.

"I have heard that there is a god that lives in these northern mountains, and its name is Yu'er. It only appears to those who will become hegemons. It is only too appropriate that Your Lordship should see it! It came to meet you and bowed respectfully, because it hopes that Your

Lordship will go and attack your enemies; the fact that it gathered up its clothes means that there must be water up ahead; and that it used its right hand means that the water on the right-hand side is going to be deep, but on the left-hand side there will be a ford."

A bearded old man wrote a poem about Guan Zhong's disquisition on the Yu'er, which reads:

> Many things can be learned from the *Spring and Autumn Annals*,
> But where did Elder Zhong get to know about the Yu'er?
> Can it be that remarkable people transmit stories about strange things?
> Zhang Hua's *Records of Many Topics* must be full of lies.

Guan Zhong went on to say, "Although we may have problems with the river up ahead, fortunately this mountain cleft will be very easy to defend. Let the army make camp on top of the mountain while we send people out to investigate where to cross the river. Then we can advance our troops."

The people whom they sent to have a look at the waters were gone for a long time, but finally they reported back: "Less than five *li* from the foot of this mountain there is the Bi'er River. This is a very broad and very deep river, which does not freeze over even in the depths of winter. It ought to be possible to cross it on bamboo rafts, but they have all been sequestered by the chief of the Rong. If you turn right, the water is very deep indeed; we let down ten feet of rope and still had not reached the bottom. However, if you go left, the river broadens out and becomes shallow. If you cross it there, it does not even come up to the knee."

Lord Huan clapped his hands and said, "That corresponds exactly to the Yu'er's omen!"

"I have never heard that there was any part of the Bi'er River that was shallow enough to ford," Lord Zhang of Yan remarked. "This is a sign that the spirits must be helping Your Lordship to succeed!"

"How far are we now from Guzhu?" Lord Huan asked.

"Once you have crossed the Bi'er River, you proceed east past Mount Tuanzi, Mount Mabian, and Mount Shuangzi," Lord Zhuang of Yan said. "The journey past these three mountains is about thirty *li*. These are the sites of the tombs of three of the lords of Guzhu from the time of the Shang dynasty. Once you have gotten past these three mountains, you travel on for another twenty-five *li*, and then you reach the city of Wudi. That is the capital of the rulers of Guzhu."

Hu'erban asked permission to lead his troops on ahead to ford the river.

"The army should move in a single group," Guan Zhong told him. "Otherwise, if by some mischance you were to run into the enemy, it would be difficult for you to either advance or retreat. However, we ought to divide our troops into two columns."

He ordered his soldiers to cut down bamboo and tie the staves together with vines. In an instant, they had constructed several hundred rafts. They abandoned their remaining chariots on the far side of the mountain cleft and boarded the rafts. The soldiers led their horses down the mountain track, whereupon they were divided into two groups. Prince Chengfu and General Gao Hei commanded one army, which went right and crossed the river on the rafts. This was the main army. The Honorable Kaifang and Shu Diao followed Lord Huan in this group. Meanwhile Bin Xuwu and Hu'erban led the second army to ford the river to the left, and they would act as shock troops. Guan Zhong and General Lian Zhi followed Lord Zhuang of Yan in this group. The two forces would meet up at the foot of Mount Tuanzi.Daliha, from his base inside the city of Wudi, had no idea that the Qi army was on its way, but when he sent an officer to the river to investigate what was going on, he discovered that the river was covered with bamboo rafts as the army was being sailed across. He rushed back to the city to report this news. Daliha was deeply alarmed and ordered his commander-in-chief, Huanghua, to take an army of five thousand men to intercept the enemy.

"So far I have done nothing to help you," Milu said, "so let me send Sumai to act as your vanguard."

"It would be difficult for me to work with someone who has lost so many battles," Commander-in-Chief Huanghua said. He got on his horse and rode off.

Daliha now spoke to Milu. "Northwest of this city there is a mountain called Tuanzi, which overlooks the most important route to the east. If it would not be too much trouble, I would like you to hold it for me. Perhaps then you can assist in the coming battle, for I will be leading reinforcements out from this city."

Of course Milu agreed, but he was angry with Commander-in-Chief Huanghua for just dismissing him like that, and he was not at all happy about this situation.

Before Huanghua had even arrived at the mouth of the river, he ran into Gao Hei's vanguard, and the two sides started fighting. Gao Hei found it impossible to defeat Huanghua and was just about to retreat when Prince Chengfu arrived. Huanghua then abandoned Gao Hei and started fighting with Prince Chengfu. Even after they had crossed swords more than fifty times, it was still impossible to tell who would be the victor. Then the Marquis of Qi came up behind them with the main body of the army, with the Honorable Kaifang on the right and Shu Diao on the left. When they all joined in, Huanghua panicked and ran, abandoning his army to its fate. Of his five thousand horsemen, more than half were massacred by the Qi army, and the remainder simply surrendered.

Huanghua fled on horseback alone, but when he approached Mount Tuanzi, he saw that a vast army was already occupying the site. In the distance he could make out the flags of Qi and Yan, as well as the kingdom of Wuzhong. Bin Xuwu and his men had forded the river and taken control of Mount Tuanzi. Huanghua did not dare to approach, but abandoned his horse and rearranged his clothing so that he looked like a woodcutter. He was able to escape by following a little-known path through the mountains.

Having won a great victory, Lord Huan of Qi advanced his army to Mount Tuanzi, where they built a second camp next to the one constructed by the occupying army. Afterwards, they discussed the next phase of the campaign.

. . .

When Milu arrived at Mount Mabian with his army, his scouts reported: "Mount Tuanzi has already been captured by the Qi army." They made camp right where they were. Commander-in-Chief Huanghua's escape route took him past Mount Mabian, and he recognized some of the troops there as his own. He entered the camp and found Milu there.

"You have won so many battles, so what are you doing here on your own?" Milu taunted him.

Huanghua was so humiliated and angry that he could neither eat nor drink, but he accepted a pannier of roasted barley and got back on his horse, riding it as hard as he could. Huanghua was in a complete rage the whole way back to the city of Wudi. He then had an audience with Daliha and requested permission to take out an army to avenge himself.

"If I had listened to you earlier, things would not have come to this pass," Daliha said.

"It is Lingzhi whom the Marquis of Qi really hates," Huanghua reminded him. "The best plan now would be to cut off Milu's head and present it to the ruler of Qi together with a request for a peace treaty. That way he will withdraw without a battle."

"Milu came to me as a last resort!" Daliha said. "How could I betray him?"

At this point, Prime Minister Wulügu stepped forward and said, "I have a plan that could turn this defeat into a victory."

"What plan?" Daliha asked.

"North of our kingdom there is a region called the 'Dry Sea' or 'Mysterious Valley,' which is a desert with no trees or plants as far as the eye can see," Wulügu said. "It has always been the custom in our country to expose the bodies of the dead there, and their white bones can be seen on all sides. As a result, it is common to encounter ghosts there, even in broad daylight. Sometimes a cold wind rises up, and none of the people or animals who encounter that wind survive—when they are touched by it, they die. Sometimes there are sandstorms, and you cannot even see your hand in front of your face. If we can trick them into entering the Mysterious Valley, they will find the winding route through the sand dunes difficult to recognize, and by the time they realize that they are lost, they will be left prey to the poisonous snakes and vicious beasts that live there. If one of us pretends to surrender, he can then trick them into heading in that direction. Without fighting a single battle, we will be able to kill almost all of them! Then we can station our army where they can pick off any of the survivors who finally make their way out. Is this not a wonderful plan?"

Daliha was puzzled. "Will the Qi army be willing to set off there for no reason?"

"Your Lordship should temporarily vacate the city with your family and go and hide on the far side of the mountains," Wulügu told him. "You should also order the residents of the city to go and hide in the valleys to escape the Qi army: that will leave the whole place empty. Afterwards, our surrendered soldiers can inform the Marquis of Qi: 'Our ruler has gone out into the desert to collect reinforcements.' He is sure to set off in pursuit, thus falling into our trap."

Huanghua happily agreed to be the one to go and surrender. He set off with a cavalry force of one thousand men to execute this plan.

The whole way along the road, Huanghua was thinking to himself: "If I don't cut off Milu's head, will the Marquis of Qi believe me? As long as I am successful, surely my lord will not blame me!"

When he arrived at Mount Mabian, he asked to have audience with Milu. Milu was even then hesitating over whether or not he would be able to hold out against an onslaught by the Qi army and was delighted to discover that Huanghua had arrived with reinforcements. He came out to meet him wreathed in smiles. Huanghua took advantage of finding him completely off guard and immediately cut off his head. Sumai was furious, and, having grabbed a sword, he leapt onto his horse and started fighting him. The two armies then started fighting and killing one another, each in support of its own commanders. Sumai reckoned that he would not be able to win this battle, so he fled alone on horseback to Hu'erban's camp, where he surrendered. Hu'erban did not believe a word of his story and ordered his officers to arrest and behead him. The wretched ruler of Lingzhi and his ministers were all killed in the space of a single day, thanks purely to their incursions into the Central Plains. Is this not sad?

A historian wrote a poem that says:

Cradled between Mount Huangtai and the Ru River,
Lingzhi was located one hundred *li* from Zhou.
Where is the booty that you captured from the state of Yan now?
How sad that this kingdom should be destroyed and its people killed!

Huanghua gathered up the remnants of Milu's army and rushed to meet the Qi troops. He presented Milu's head, saying, "Our ruler has abandoned his capital to escape into the desert; he is planning to borrow troops from other countries to take his revenge on you. I tried to persuade him to surrender, but he would not listen to me. Having beheaded Milu, I now surrender to you, and I hope that you will at least let me serve you as a common soldier. If you like, I would be willing to lead your army in pursuit of our ruler, acting as your guide, in the hope that I may achieve some success in your service."

When Lord Huan saw Milu's head, he believed every word that Huanghua said, and ordered him to take his place in the vanguard. The army then advanced on Wudi. Sure enough, it was an empty city, and so he trusted his advice even more. He was afraid that Daliha would get away, so he instructed one division of Lord Zhuang of Yan's army to guard the city, while the remainder would set off after the Lord of Guzhu, in the hope of making a surprise attack on him under cover of darkness. Huanghua suggested that he should go on ahead to check out conditions along the road. Lord Huan ordered Gao Hei to go with him, while the rest of the army would bring up the rear.

When they arrived at the desert, Lord Huan ordered his army to advance as quickly as they could. After proceeding for some time, Huanghua suddenly disappeared. It was already getting late, and all they could see were lone and level sands stretching out in all directions, wreathed in dark mists, with banshees howling desolately and an icy wind cutting them to the bone. The cold was terrible, freezing them to the marrow, and cruel winds seemed to scrape the land bare. Both men and horses were terrified. A number of the animals simply collapsed.

At this time Lord Huan of Qi and Guan Zhong were riding along together. Guan Zhong said, "I have heard that in the north there is a very dangerous region called the 'Dry Sea,' and I am very much afraid that it is where we are now. You must not advance any further."

Lord Huan immediately gave orders to collect the army, but both the vanguard and the rearguard had already lost contact with them. They tried to light torches, but they were immediately blown out by the wind. Guan Zhong guarded Lord Huan as he turned his horse around and headed back. The army officers were ordered to strike their bells and bang their drums in the hope that it would counteract the melancholy effect of this place, and that the sound would enable all the troops to keep together. It was then that they realized that with the sky so overcast and the land so desolate, they had no idea in what direction they were proceeding. Having traveled blindly for a certain distance, by great good fortune the wind blew away all the clouds, so high in the sky they could see the sickle of the new moon. Then the generals of the vanguard and the rearguard, hearing the sound of the drums and the bells, caught up with the main body of the army, and they all made camp together. Lord Huan of Qi waited until dawn, but when he counted his army he discovered that Xi Peng was missing, together with a large part of the forces under his command. They were lucky that it was winter, and so many creatures were hibernating and the poisonous snakes did not leave their lairs, while the massive racket made by the army was enough to frighten away even the most vicious animal. Otherwise, there would have been many injured or killed.

Guan Zhong was fully aware of the perils of their situation. Realizing that there were no signs of human habitation anywhere, he made every effort to find a way out of the desert. However, it did not matter whether he went east or west, the sand dunes stretched out in every direction, rising and falling, with no sign of a road. Lord Huan was already extremely anxious. Guan Zhong then came forward and said, "I have heard that old horses are good at recognizing the routes by which they have traveled. The kingdom of Wuzhong borders on the lands of the Mountain Rong, and many of their horses will have come from the lands north of this desert. If Hu'erban could select some of the older horses in his possession, we can watch where they go and follow them. If we are lucky, they will find the way out."

Lord Huan followed his advice. Having selected a couple of old horses, they were turned loose and sent on ahead. They twisted and turned this way and that, but they did find a way out of the desert.

A bearded old man wrote a poem that says:

> Ants can sense the presence of water and horses can find the road;
> Creatures of other species can get you out of all sorts of problems.
> How stupid that so many useless men get good jobs;
> Who is prepared to set their dignity aside and listen to good advice?

When Commander-in-Chief Huanghua went on ahead with General Gao Hei, they proceeded along a road skirting around to the south side of the mountain, at which point Gao Hei realized that they had lost contact with the rest of the army. He told Huanghua to wait and allow the rest to catch up with them, but Huanghua insisted on pressing on as quickly as possible. Gao Hei became suspicious and reined in his horse, only to find himself taken prisoner by Huanghua. He was then dragged into the presence of the Chief of Guzhu, Daliha. Huanghua kept silent about the fact that he had murdered Milu, and simply said, "Milu died when his army was defeated at Mount Mabian. I then pretended to surrender in order to trick the main body of the Qi army into the 'Dry Sea.' I was able to take the Qi general, Gao Hei, prisoner, and I now await your further instructions."

"If you are willing to surrender to me, I will reward you," Dalihua told Gao Hei.

The latter glared at him and shouted, "My family has been treated most generously by the ruling house of Qi for many generations now—how could I be willing to act as your running-dog?" He also cursed Huanghua: "You tricked me here! I don't care if you kill me, but when His Lordship's army arrives, you will die and your country will be destroyed. It is just a matter of time! I am telling you now that it is too late for regrets!"

Huanghua was infuriated and drawing his sword, he cut off his head. *Gao Hei really was loyal to Qi!*

Daliha promptly reorganized his army and attacked the city of Wudi again. Lord Zhuang of Yan could not hold the city—his troops were too few and the residents had already fled—so he ordered people to light fires on all four sides and then rode out of the city on a chariot, killing all the enemy soldiers in his path. He managed to make his way to the camp at Mount Tuanzi.

. . .

When Lord Huan left the Mysterious Valley, before his army had even advanced ten *li*, they came across a small force. Sending someone out to investigate, they discovered that this was Xi Peng and his men. The army was then united, and they turned towards the city of Wudi. As they advanced, they could see a column of refugees walking back to the city, leading children by the hand and carrying the elderly.

Guan Zhong sent someone to make inquiries, and the answer came: "The Chief of Guzhu has already expelled the Yan army, and so we are going back to the city. We were hiding in the mountains, but now we can return to our homes."

"I have a plan!" Guan Zhong exclaimed. He asked Hu'erban to pick his most trusted officers and got them to dress up like the inhabitants of the city and mingle with the crowds, making their way into the city. At midnight they should light fires to help in the attack.

After Hu'erban had left with his men to carry out this part of the plan, Guan Zhong sent Shu Diao to attack the southern gate, while Lian Zhi attacked the western gate and the Honorable Kaifang attacked the eastern gate. He left the northern gate alone so that the people would have a way to escape the city. He ordered Prince Chengfu and Xi Peng to each take a circuitous route and wait in ambush outside the North Gate until such time as Daliha left the city, at which point they should kill him. Guan Zhong and Lord Huan of Qi made camp ten *li* from the city walls.

At this time Daliha was busy putting out the fires burning within the city and summoning its people back to set them to work. He made time to instruct Huanghua to put his forces in good order, so as to prepare for any further attacks. At dusk they suddenly heard the sound of siege engines on all sides, and reports came in: "The Qi army has arrived and they have surrounded the city."

Huanghua was not at all expecting an attack from the Qi army, so he was completely overwhelmed. He rushed with his soldiers and a host of city residents to the top of the city walls to see what was happening. At around midnight fires broke out in four or five places inside the city, so Huanghua gave orders to arrest the arsonists. As this was happening, Hu'erban led about a dozen men in an attack on the South Gate, which they then hacked open, allowing Shu Diao's army into the city. At this point, Huanghua realized that the situation was hopeless. He assisted Daliha onto his horse and started looking for a way to escape. When he heard that there were no enemy soldiers to the north, he ordered that the North Gate be opened. Before they had gone two *li*, they saw torches coming towards them from several different directions and the sound of drumming shook the ground. Prince Chengfu and Xi Peng's armies then attacked them from two directions. The Honorable Kaifang, Shu Diao, and Hu'erban, having captured the city walls, also joined in the attack. Commander-in-Chief Huanghua fought for as long as he could, but in the end his strength gave out and he was killed. Daliha was then taken prisoner by Prince Chengfu, while Wulügu was killed by his mutinous forces. At dawn Lord Huan of Qi entered the city, whereupon he ceremonially read out a list of Daliha's crimes and personally cut off his head, hanging it above the North Gate as a warning to other barbarians. He then issued instructions to calm the local people's fears. When the Rong people recounted Gao Hei's bravery right up until the moment of his death, Lord Huan was very upset. He ordered that his loyalty and honesty should be recorded in the official history of this campaign, though any further posthumous rewards would have to wait until they had been properly discussed following their return to Qi.

When Lord Zhuang of Yan heard that the Marquis of Qi's armies had entered the city in victory, he came as quickly as he could from the camp at the foot of Mount Tuanzi. When he had finished offering his congratulations, Lord Huan said, "When I received your message reporting the emergency that you had suffered, I came one thousand *li* to your assistance. Fortunately, this campaign has gone well and the two kingdoms of Lingzhi and Guzhu have been destroyed, opening up five hundred *li* of territory. I cannot possibly govern these lands, which are much too far away from my own, so I would like to give them to you."

"It is thanks to you that I have been able to preserve my own state intact," Lord Zhuang of Yan told him. "How could I possibly hope to gain more territory from this? You had better establish a new ruler here."

"These northern lands are remote and backward, so if I were to appoint a new ruler from one of the barbarian people who live here, sooner or later they would attack you again," Lord Huan said. "Your Lordship should not refuse this new grant of land. You are in constant communication with the other states of the Zhou confederacy; you have done your best to restore the good government that prevailed under your ancestor, the Duke of Shao; you present tribute to the Zhou court; and you have long formed a solid bulwark along the northern border. You and I, my lord, must do our best to emulate the glories of our ancestors." The Earl of Yan did not dare to refuse any longer.

Lord Huan generously rewarded the three armies that had participated in the attack on Wudi, and since the kingdom of Wuzhong had done so much to help them, he commanded that the lands below Mount

Xiaoquan should be given to them. Hu'erban bowed his thanks and left. Lord Huan allowed his troops to rest for five days, and then they set off, crossing back over the Bi'er River and making their way back to the stone cliffs where they had left their chariots. They then collected the troops that had been left on guard there and set off home. Observing the devastation as they approached Lingzhi, Lord Huan became upset and said to the Earl of Yan, "Although the chief of the Rong behaved very badly, seeing this damage is absolutely horrifying."

Bao Shuya came out from the camp at Kuisi to meet them.

"It is all thanks to your efforts that we never ran out of food," Lord Huan told him. He instructed the Earl of Yan to leave some soldiers guarding the fortress at Kuisi, and then turned his army homewards to Qi. The Earl of Yan personally escorted Lord Huan as far as the border. Since he was still unwilling to see him leave, he entered the borders of Qi with him. When they had gone some fifty *li* from the border with Yan, Lord Huan said, "It has been a rule since ancient times that when one feudal lord was escorting another, he would not set foot in the other's country. I am concerned that in the present circumstances it may appear that I have behaved ungenerously to you."

He commanded that all the territory that the Earl of Yan had passed through should be given to him, with the intention of apologizing for allowing him to make such a mistake. The Earl of Yan absolutely refused to accept this, but in the end he had to take the land and go home. Subsequently, he ordered the construction of a walled city called Yanliu, to commemorate how well the Marquis of Qi had treated them. At this point the state of Yan gained five hundred *li* of territory in the northwest and fifty *li* of territory in the east, which allowed it for the first time to become the dominant state in the north.

After Lord Huan rescued Yan and refused to take any land in return, the other aristocrats were all in awe of Qi's military might and the virtue of their behavior.

A historian wrote a poem, which says:

He took his troops a thousand *li* to tame these animals;
He was determined that they should pay tribute to the Zhou royal house.
In such matters it is never a good idea to rely purely on brute force;
To respect the king and pacify barbarians, you must know how to unite
the world.

When Lord Huan arrived back at the Ji River in Lu, Lord Zhuang of Lu yet again welcomed him there and held a banquet in his honor to congratulate him. Lord Huan deeply appreciated Lord Zhuang's thoughtfulness, so he presented one half of the booty that he had seized from the Rong to Lu. Lord Zhuang happened to know that Guan Zhong's fief was the city of Xiaogu, which lay close to the border with Lu, so he sent out a team of laborers to build a wall around it, with the intention of pleasing Guan Zhong. This all happened in the thirty-second year of Lord Zhuang of Lu's rule and the fifteenth year of the reign of King Hui of Zhou.

That year in the eighth month, Lord Zhuang of Lu died, and the state of Lu was thrown into turmoil. Do you want to know what happened in Lu? READ ON.

Chapter Twenty-two

*The Honorable You twice installs a ruler of
Lu in power.*

*Master Huang of Qi is the only person to
recognize the "Weishe."*

The Honorable Qingfu had the style-name Zhong, and he was the older
half-brother of Lord Zhuang of Lu, born to a concubine mother. He had
a full younger brother named Ya, who had the style-name Shu. This man
was therefore also one of Lord Zhuang of Lu's younger brothers. Lord
Zhuang had a further younger brother born to the same mother, whose
name was the Honorable You. This name was chosen for him because
when he was born, the character *You* appeared on the palm of his hand.
He had the style-name Ji. Although Lord Zhuang of Lu appointed all
three of his brothers to the office of grandees of the state, there remained
a distinction between those of noble birth and those whose mother was
a concubine. The Honorable You was also by far the cleverest, so he was
the one whom Lord Zhuang trusted and confided in.

In the third year of Lord Zhuang's rule, he happened to visit the Lang
Tower. From the top of the tower he spotted a young woman of
the Dang family named Mengren, who was exceptionally beautiful.
He ordered one of his servants to summon her, but Mengren refused to
respond to his advances.

"If you join my household, I will appoint you as my marchioness,"
Lord Zhuang said.

Mengren insisted that he make a blood covenant with her to this
effect, and Lord Zhuang agreed. Mengren then cut her arm, and they
swore a solemn oath in her blood. She moved into the tower to live with
Lord Zhuang; later on, she went home to the palace with him. After

little more than a year, she gave birth to a son, whose name was Ban. Lord Zhuang wanted to establish Mengren as his marchioness and requested permission from Lady Wen Jiang to do so, but she refused. She was determined to promote a marriage alliance between her son and her own natal family, so she selected Lord Xiang of Qi's newborn daughter to be her future daughter-in-law. At that time the girl was still only a baby, so they had to wait twelve years or so for her to grow up before she could get married. During this time, even though Mengren was not officially appointed as the Marchioness of Lu, for more than a decade she was in de facto charge of the Six Palaces. When Lady Ai Jiang finally arrived in Lu to become the marchioness, Mengren was already too ill to get out of bed. Shortly afterwards, she died and was buried with the ceremonies appropriate to a concubine.

Lady Ai Jiang did not have any children for a long time, but her younger sister, Lady Shu Jiang, had accompanied her in marriage, and she gave birth to a son named Qi. Among Lord Zhuang's other concubines there was Lady Feng, who was the daughter of the Viscount of Xugou. She gave birth to a son named Shen. Lady Feng wanted the Honorable You to undertake the guardianship of her son Shen, because she hoped that he would further his pretensions to becoming the heir to the title. The Honorable You simply said, "Ban is the oldest." That was the end of that.

Even though Lady Ai Jiang was the marchioness, Lord Zhuang could not forget that it was her father who had ordered his father's assassination; so although he was always scrupulously polite to her, he did not care for her very much. The Honorable Qingfu, on the other hand, was a very handsome and prepossessing man, and Lady Ai Jiang found him deeply attractive. She sent one of the palace eunuchs to take him a message in secret, and that was the beginning of their affair. As their love for one another developed, they became ever closer. They roped the Honorable Ya into their plans, agreeing that when Qingfu became the ruler of Lu, the Honorable Ya would become his prime minister.

A bearded old man wrote a poem:

Many dreadful things happened in Zheng and Wei,
But worse was to come in the state of Qi.
The state of Lu was humiliated by its determination to be allied to Qi,
As Lady Wen Jiang's example was followed by Lady Ai Jiang.

In the thirty-first year of Lord Zhuang's rule, there was no rain for the whole winter. Lord Zhuang decided to hold a rain-making sacrifice.

The day before the ceremony, a concert was held in the courtyard of Grandee Liang's residence. Grandee Liang's daughter was very beautiful, and the Honorable Ban was in love with her. They had been in secret communication for some time, and he had promised to make her his principal wife. This young girl put a ladder up against the wall, so that she could watch the concert. There she was spotted by one of the grooms, a man named Luo, who thought she was very lovely. From the foot of the wall he sang a song to her in the hope of seducing her, which ran:

> The lovely peach is most fragrant in the coldest winter.
> I long for you, but I cannot climb over this wall.
> I wish I had wings so that we might be together forever!

The Honorable Ban was also present at the Liang residence because he would be taking part in the rain-making ceremony the next day. When he heard the song, he went out to investigate; when he saw Luo, he was absolutely furious and whipped him three hundred times until blood had soaked into the ground. Luo kept begging for mercy, and in the end he released him. The Honorable Ban complained to Lord Zhuang, and Lord Zhuang said, "It was very rude of Luo, but you should have killed him rather than whipping him. Luo is a very brave and strong man whose like is not to be seen anywhere else in the world. Now that you have whipped him, he is sure to hate you."

This groom, Luo, was famous for his strength—he had once climbed the gatehouse at the Ji Gate and then jumped down. When he reached the ground, he had then jumped up again. Then, grabbing hold of one corner of the gatehouse, he had shaken it until the whole building shook!

Lord Zhuang suggested that the Honorable Ban kill Luo, because he was afraid of what such a strong man might do.

"He is just a groom," the Honorable Ban said. "Why should I worry about him?"

Luo did indeed hate the Honorable Ban, and thus he threw in his lot with Qingfu.

. . .

In the autumn of the following year, Lord Zhuang became critically ill. He found himself more and more worried about Qingfu. It was for this reason that he summoned the Honorable Ya and asked him who should be the next ruler of Lu. Just as he had expected, the Honorable Ya praised Qingfu's talents to the skies: "If he becomes the ruler of the state of Lu, then we will be at peace. Besides which, it has often been the custom in Lu for the title to be inherited by a brother rather than a son." Lord Zhuang did not respond.

When the Honorable Ya had left, Lord Zhuang summoned the Honorable You and asked him the same question. The Honorable You said, "Your Lordship made a blood covenant with Mengren. Even though she never became marchioness, is this any reason to demote her son?"

"Ya recommended that I appoint Qingfu as my heir," Lord Zhuang said. "What do you think of that?"

"Qingfu is a harsh and unpleasant man," the Honorable You replied. "He does not have any of the qualities of a good ruler. Ya is supporting his older brother's pretensions, but you must not listen to him. Even if it kills me, I will see Ban succeed you." Lord Zhuang nodded, for by that time he was already too sick to speak.

The Honorable You left the palace and immediately ordered a eunuch to take a message, purporting to be from Lord Zhuang, summoning the Honorable Ya to the residence of Grandee Zhen Ji, where he would receive a command from the Marquis of Lu. The Honorable Ya did indeed go straight to the residence of the Zhen family. The Honorable You had already prepared a bottle of poisoned wine and instructed Grandee Zhen Ji to poison the Honorable Ya. He handed a letter to him saying: "His Lordship commands that you should be ordered to commit suicide. If you drink this poisoned wine, then your descendants will inherit all your titles and emoluments. If you do not, then your whole family will be killed."

The Honorable Ya refused to obey this order, so Grandee Zhen Ji grabbed hold of his ear and poured in the poisoned wine. A short time later, blood poured from every orifice and he died.

A historian wrote a poem about the poisoning of the Honorable Ya, which reads:

> The Duke of Zhou executed his brother to keep peace in the Zhou royal
>   house,
> The Honorable You poisoned Ya to secure the state of Lu.
> To kill a relative for the sake of the country is an act of great merit;
> Was this kind of thing ever seen among later dynasties?

That evening, Lord Zhuang passed away. The Honorable You assisted Ban to preside over the obsequies, informing the country that the following year would be the first year of the rule of a new Marquis of Lu, and receiving messages of condolence from all the other states. This does not need to be described in any detail.

. . .

That winter in the eleventh month, when the Honorable Ban heard that his grandfather, Dang Chen, had become ill and died, he remembered how kind the Dang family had always been to him and decided that he would attend the funeral in person. Qingfu then secretly summoned the groom, Luo, and said to him, "Have you forgotten how much you hate Ban for whipping you? Even an ordinary man can control a dragon that is away from water, so why don't you take your revenge when he is visiting the Dang family? I will support you."

"If you, sir, are helping me, then I would not dare to disobey your commands!" Luo said.

He hid a sharp dagger in his clothing and rushed to the residence of Grandee Dang during the night. It was already past midnight when he arrived, so he climbed over the walls and hid outside the guest bedrooms. When it got light, one of the junior servants opened the door in order to go and get some water. Luo then burst into the bedroom. The Honorable Ban was already fully dressed and was in the act of putting on his shoes. In alarm he cried, "What are you doing here?"

"I have come to take revenge on you for the whipping I received last year!" Luo shouted.

The Honorable Ban groped for the sword that he had placed under his pillow to defend himself, and he did indeed succeed in cutting open Luo's forehead. Luo warded off his sword with his left hand, while stabbing the Honorable Ban with the dagger in his right hand. He succeeded in killing him by stabbing him in the ribs. The servants had rushed off to report this to the Dang family, and the menfolk all picked up weapons and attacked Luo, who was already so severely injured by the wound in his head that he could not fight any more. They hacked away at him until he was chopped to pieces.

When the Honorable You heard that the Honorable Ban had been murdered, he knew at once that Qingfu was responsible for this and was afraid that worse disasters would follow. He fled to the state of Chen and sought asylum there. Qingfu pretended that he knew nothing at all about what had happened, placing all the blame upon Luo, thus excusing himself in the eyes of the people of Lu. The dowager marchioness, Lady Ai Jiang, was in favor of Qingfu becoming the next Lord of Lu, but he said, "The two sons of His Late Lordship are still alive. I can't possibly kill both of them, nor can I take their place."

"What do you think of the idea of establishing Shen?" Lady Ai Jiang inquired.

"Shen is a grown man, which will make him difficult to control. It would be better to establish Qi."

He then held a funeral for the Honorable Ban. With the pretense of going in person to the state of Qi to report his death, he gave bribes to Shu Diao so that he would support the succession of the Honorable Qi to the title of Marquis of Lu. Qi was at that time only eight years old. Nevertheless, he became Lord Min of Lu.

Lord Min was the son of Lady Shu Jiang of Qi, and Shu Jiang was the younger sister of Lady Ai Jiang, the dowager marchioness. That made Lord Min the nephew of Lord Huan of Qi. Lord Min was terrified of Lady Ai Jiang and similarly frightened of the Honorable Qingfu, but he hoped that his mother's family would help him to deal with them. He therefore sent someone to make representations to Lord Huan of Qi and arrange a meeting at Luogu. At this meeting Lord Min tugged at Lord Huan of Qi's robes and, through his tears, told him what Qingfu had done.

"Among the grandees of the state of Lu, who is the cleverest?" Lord Huan asked.

"The Honorable You is the cleverest, but he has fled into exile in the state of Chen," Lord Min informed him.

"Why don't you invite him back?" Lord Huan asked.

"I am afraid that it will arouse Qingfu's suspicions," Lord Min said.

"But if it is done in my name, who would dare to try and stop it?" Lord Huan asked.

An ambassador went with an order signed by Lord Huan himself to summon the Honorable You back from Chen. Lord Min stayed at Lang, and met the Honorable You there, and then the two of them traveled back to the capital riding on the same chariot. He appointed the Honorable You to the position of prime minister, claiming that he had been ordered to do so by the Marquis of Qi and so he did not dare to refuse. This happened in the sixth year of the reign of King Hui of Zhou and the first year of Lord Min of Lu's rule.

. . .

That winter, the Marquis of Qi was still worrying about the situation in Lu, so he sent Grandee Zhongsun Qiu to investigate and find out if the

Honorable Qingfu was up to something. Lord Min had an audience with Zhongsun Qiu, at which he became completely hysterical, the tears pouring down his face. After that, Zhongsun Qiu went to have an audience with the Honorable Shen and discussed the state of affairs in Lu with him. It was clear that he was a very sensible and upright man.

"He would make a wonderful ruler," Zhongsun Qiu said to himself. He told the Honorable You to take good care of him and suggested that he should get rid of Qingfu at the earliest possible opportunity. The Honorable You answered him by stretching out his hand; Zhongsun Qiu immediately understood that he meant that it would be difficult to act without support.

"I will report all of this to His Lordship," he assured him. "If you have any problems, we will not just sit back and watch."

The Honorable Qingfu presented generous gifts to Zhongsun Qiu when he came to have an audience with him, but Qiu simply responded: "If you, sir, would but behave loyally to the country, we would all benefit thereby, not just me!" He refused to take any of his presents. Qingfu was alarmed by his words and left. Afterwards, Zhongsun Qiu said goodbye to Lord Min and went home.

"Until they get rid of Qingfu, Lu will not be stable!" Zhongsun Qiu exclaimed.

"Do you think I should raise an army to remove him?" Lord Huan asked.

"His evil deeds have not yet become known to all, so we have no excuse for punishing him," Zhongsun Qiu said. "I have observed him, and he is clearly a very ambitious man, who will never be content in a subordinate position. He will definitely plan a rebellion sooner or later, and when he does, then we can take advantage of this opportunity to execute him. That is the way that a true hegemon would proceed."

"Good!" Lord Huan said.

In the second year of the rule of Lord Min, the Honorable Qingfu's plans to usurp the title were nearing fruition, but he did not dare to proceed lightly, given that Lord Min was the Marquis of Qi's nephew and was supported loyally by the Honorable You. Suddenly one day, his gatekeeper reported: "Grandee Bu Yi is here to see you."

The Honorable Qingfu invited him to enter his library, at which point he noticed that Bu Yi was in a truly foul temper. He asked why he had come to see him, and Bu Yi replied, "My lands run alongside the estate owned by the Grand Tutor, Shen Buhai, and he has stolen them from me by force. I went to report the situation to His Lordship, but he not only made excuses for the Grand Tutor, he even suggested that I should let him have my lands! I will not accept this! I have come specially to see you in the hope that you will put in a word for me with His Lordship."

The Honorable Qingfu sent away his entourage, and then said to Bu Yi, "His Lordship is only a small child and knows nothing about anything, so even if I go to talk to him, he will not listen to me. If you help me, then I will kill Shen Buhai for you. How would that be?"

"As long as the Honorable You is here, I am afraid that there is nothing that you can do," Bu Yi said.

"His Lordship is just a silly little boy who often leaves the palace at night by one of the side gates to go and play in the marketplace. If you were to set an ambush by the side gate and stab him when he comes out, you could put the blame on robbers or some other kind of criminal, and who would be any the wiser? I will then become the new ruler of Lu, by order of Her Ladyship, the dowager marchioness, and Mother of the Country. Getting rid of the Honorable You will then be as easy as waving my hand."

Bu Yi agreed to this. He sought out an assassin and found someone by the name of Qiu Ya. Armed with a sharp dagger, he lay in wait at the side gate to the palace. Just as they had anticipated, Lord Min did leave that night, and Qiu Ya suddenly rose up from his hiding place and stabbed him to death. His entourage was screaming in alarm, but they nevertheless managed to arrest Qiu Ya. Bu Yi ordered his own personal guards to go and remove Qiu Ya from their custody. At the same time, Qingfu murdered Shen Buhai in his own home.

When the Honorable You heard of Lord Min's assassination, he rushed to the residence of the Honorable Shen under cover of darkness, shook him awake, and told him of what Qingfu had done. The two of them then fled into exile in the state of Zhu.

A bearded old man wrote a poem that reads:

First the Honorable Ban and then Lord Min was murdered,
Who was the real villain holding the knife?
This trouble in Lu all arose in the palace,
When getting married, why did it have to be a woman from Qi?

The people of the capital had always been very fond of the Honorable You, and when they heard that the Marquis of Lu had been murdered and that their prime minister had fled the country, they seemed to go berserk. Everyone hated Bu Yi and loathed the Honorable Qingfu, so that day all business ceased in the capital. A group of about one thousand people surrounded Bu Yi's house and eventually burst in to kill him. Next they went to attack Qingfu, the crowd growing ever bigger. Qingfu realized that he could not possibly stop this riot, so he began to make plans to run away. He thought to himself that the Marquis of Qi had come to power thanks to the assistance that he had received from Ju. Therefore, Lord Huan owed Ju something, and he might be able to get them to speak up on his behalf to Qi. Besides which, Lady Wen Jiang had earlier had an affair with a doctor from Ju, and Lady Ai Jiang, the present dowager marchioness, was her niece, so thanks to this connection he might be able to find sanctuary there. He dressed up in the garb of a merchant and fled to the state of Ju, riding on a cart piled high with the spoils of his time in power.

When Lady Ai Jiang heard that the Honorable Qingfu had fled to Ju, she began to worry about her own position, and she too thought about seeking asylum there. Her servants pointed out: "Your Ladyship has irritated the populace of the capital by your relationship with Qingfu, so if the two of you both go to the same state, would anyone find this acceptable? The Honorable You is currently living in Zhu, and he is the one whom everyone loves. If Your Ladyship were to go to Zhu, you could throw yourself on his mercy." She did indeed flee to Zhu and begged for an audience with the Honorable You. He, however, refused to see her.

When the Honorable You heard that Lady Ai Jiang and Qingfu had both left the capital, he made preparations to go back home with the Honorable Shen. He also sent someone to report the situation to Qi. Lord Huan of Qi said to Zhongsun Qiu, "The state of Lu has been left without a ruler. How about we go and annex it?"

"Lu is a state noted for upholding the proper ceremonies and rituals," Zhongsun Qiu reminded him. "Even though there has recently been a spate of assassinations there, that is just a temporary problem. The people there have never forgotten the lessons of the Duke of Zhou—this state cannot be annexed! Besides which, the Honorable Shen will make them an excellent and enlightened ruler, while the Honorable You will quickly put down any lingering murmurings of discontent. They will bring peace to the people of Lu, so it would be better to help them."

"If you say so," Lord Huan remarked. He then ordered the senior minister Gao Xi to take a force of three thousand armed men out of Nanyang. He instructed him to act as the situation on the ground demanded: "If the Honorable Shen does indeed make a good ruler, it is your job to support his installation as the new lord and to preserve the long-standing good relationship between our two countries. If, on the other hand, he does not, you are to conquer his lands."

Gao Xi accepted these commands and set off. Purely by coincidence, he arrived at the Lu capital at the same time as the Honorable Shen and You. When Gao Xi saw how impressive the Honorable Shen's appearance was and how sensible his comments in discussion were, he developed the greatest possible respect for him. Accordingly, he discussed the plan of campaign with the Honorable You. Between the two of them, they arranged the accession of the Honorable Shen to the marquisate of Lu, and he took the title of Lord Xi. He ordered his soldiers to assist the people of Lu in building a city wall around the Lu Gate, which would prevent any trouble from Zhu or Ju. The Honorable You ordered the Honorable Xisi to accompany Gao Xi back to Qi, to thank the Marquis of Qi for all that he had done to ensure the stability of their country. He also sent someone to Ju, with promises of lavish rewards if they would execute Qingfu.

. . .

When the Honorable Qingfu fled to Ju, he traveled in a carriage stuffed with state treasures of Lu. These he presented to the Viscount of Ju, using his doctor as an intermediary. The Viscount of Ju accepted this gift, but he coveted these further bribes from Lu, so he sent someone to tell Qingfu: "The state of Ju is only small, and I am afraid that we will be attacked simply because we have given you sanctuary. Please, could you go somewhere else?"

Before the Honorable Qingfu was able to set out, the Viscount of Ju had already given orders to arrest him. Qingfu remembered that he had earlier given bribes to Shu Diao, as a result of which they had become good friends, so he set off for Qi. Even though the Qi border officials were aware of the trouble that Qingfu had caused, they did not dare stop him without proper authorization, so they let him stay at the Wen River. By coincidence the Honorable Xisi arrived at the Wen River, having completed his embassy to Qi, and met Qingfu there. He wanted to take Qingfu back to Lu with him.

"The Honorable You has no intention of letting me survive, but if you would speak on my behalf and remind him of our common blood relationship with His Late Lordship, perhaps he might let me live," Qingfu said. "Even if he demotes me to the status of a commoner, I will remember his mercy until the day that I die!"

When the Honorable Xisi made his way back to Lu, he passed on Qingfu's message. Lord Xi wanted to agree to this, but the Honorable You said, "If you do not execute people who have murdered their own rulers, what kind of message does that send to later generations?" He then spoke privately with the Honorable Xisi and said, "If Qingfu would be prepared to commit suicide, we can let his son succeed to all his titles and emoluments, and sacrifices will be made to his memory."

According to his instructions, the Honorable Xisi went back to the Wen River. He was going to report this message to Qingfu, but found it hard to know how to put it into words. He just stood outside the gate and cried. Qingfu heard the noise that he was making and realized that it was Xisi. He sighed and said, "If he cries like that and does not come in to see me, it must mean that I cannot escape my fate." He undid his belt and hanged himself from the nearest tree. Afterwards, Xisi went in to collect his body for burial. He reported these events to Lord Xi, who was deeply depressed at the news.

Suddenly a report came in: "The Viscount of Ju sent his younger brother, the Honorable Yingna, to take his army to the border, but when he got there, he heard that Qingfu was already dead. He has now come specially to collect his reward."

"Ju did not arrest Qingfu, so why should they be rewarded?" the Honorable You demanded. He asked permission to take the army out to meet the enemy. Lord Xi undid the precious sword hanging at his side and bestowed it upon him. "This sword is named Menglao," he said, "and although the blade is less than a foot long, it is nevertheless of unparalleled sharpness. I hope that you will treasure it, Uncle."

The Honorable You hung this sword from his own waist, thanked His Lordship for his generosity, and left. He advanced his army to Li, where the Honorable Yingna of Ju was waiting for him with his troops drawn up in full battle formation.

"Lu has only just established a new lord, and the government of the state is still in chaos," the Honorable You mused. "If we fight and are not victorious, that will seriously disturb the morale of the people. Fortunately, the Honorable Yingna of Ju is both stupid and greedy, so I should be able to deal with him by stratagem rather than by force."

He walked out in front of the army and invited Yingna to a face-to-face discussion, at which he informed him: "The two of us may not get along, but that has nothing to do with our officers and men. I have heard that you, sir, are both strong and good at martial arts, so how about we each pick a weapon and fight a duel to determine the victor here?"

"That is a wonderful idea!" Yingna said.

The two both ordered their armies to draw back, and they faced each other on the battlefield, both of them brilliant warriors, making no mistakes even though they crossed swords more than fifty times. The Honorable You's son, Xingfu, who at that time was only eight years of age, was present amid the army, since he was much loved by his father. He was watching them fight, standing off to one side, and when he realized that his father could not possibly win, he shouted out, "Why don't you use Menglao?"

The Honorable You immediately realized what good advice this was, so he deliberately made a mistake, allowing Yingna to advance one pace. The Honorable You turned slightly to one side, to allow himself to draw Menglao from its scabbard, and then, with a single sweeping move of his hand, he cut the top of Yingna's head off. The blade of the sword showed not a single bloodstain—what a truly remarkable weapon! When the Ju army saw that their general had been cut down, they did not wait to fight but simply turned tail and fled. The Honorable You thus won a complete victory and returned to the court in triumph.

Lord Xi came out to meet him on his arrival in the suburbs, appointed him prime minister, and gave him a grant of land at Bi.

The Honorable You presented his opinion: "Qingfu, the Honorable Ya, and I were all grandsons of Lord Huan of Lu, yet I poisoned the Honorable Ya and ordered Qingfu to hang himself. This was for the sake of the state and I had no choice, but nevertheless my two brothers have been left with no one to carry on their family lines, while I have received a noble title and a rich grant of land. When I die, how can I face Lord Huan in the Underworld?"

"Your two brothers both committed wicked deeds," Lord Xi reminded him, "so how can they be rewarded?"

"They may have been planning to do wicked things, but they did not actually succeed," the Honorable You said, "nor did they die under the executioner's axe. It would be entirely appropriate to grant them posthumous titles to demonstrate that you understand how to treat your relatives well."

Lord Xi agreed to this proposal. Thus, he ordered Noble Grandson Ao to be adopted as Qingfu's heir, taking the surname Mengsun. Qingfu's style-name was Zhong, so his heirs ought to have had the surname Zhongsun, but in order to disassociate themselves from Qingfu's wicked acts, they changed the first character to Meng. The Mengsun family were given the city of Cheng as their fief. Noble Grandson Ci was adopted to become the Honorable Ya's heir, taking the surname Shusun, and they had their fief at Hou. The Honorable You then accepted the fief at Bi and was given further lands on the north side of the Wen River. His descendants had the surname Jisun. From this time onwards, the three families of Jisun, Mengsun, and Shusun were all pillars of the government of the state of Lu, and they became known as the Three Descendants of Lord Huan.

It was on this very day that the southern gate of Lu collapsed for no reason; people who knew about such things said that it was because it was too tall that it fell over all of a sudden. Later on, they realized that it was a portent of the future decline of the country and that omens were already manifesting themselves.

A historian wrote a poem that reads:

The strange sign on his hand was enough to proclaim his special nature.
How could the Honorable You accept this enfeoffment?
In a time of disorder Heaven helps the rebellious,
And all three families concerned were descended from Lord Huan.

When Lord Huan of Qi discovered that Lady Ai Jiang had taken up residence in Zhu, he said to Guan Zhong, "Neither Lord Huan of Lu nor Lord Min died a natural death—this is the fault of the Jiang family. If I do not punish her, the people of Lu are sure to be angry with me, which will destroy the good relationship so carefully built up over many years."

"Once a woman is married, she should obey her husband," Guan Zhong said. "If she commits a crime against her husband's family, it is not the place of her own relatives to punish her. If you are determined to do so, it should be done in secret."

"You are right," Lord Huan said.

He sent Shu Diao to Zhu, to escort Lady Ai Jiang home to Lu. When Lady Ai Jiang arrived at the city of Yi, they stayed there overnight. Shu Diao then informed Lady Ai Jiang: "Everyone is aware of your involvement in the assassination of two lords of Lu. When you get home, will you have the gall to present yourself at the ancestral temples? Why don't you kill yourself so that you can at least preserve some self-respect?"

When Lady Ai Jiang heard this, she ran to her room, bolting the door and breaking down in tears. At around midnight silence fell, and then Shu Diao broke open the door to find that she had hanged herself. Shu Diao reported her death to the official in charge of Yi. Having put him in charge of arranging the encoffining of the body, he sent a message to Lord Xi by carrier pigeon. Lord Xi met the cortege and went back to the capital with the coffin, where Her Ladyship was buried with all due ceremony. He said, "The loving relationship between a mother and her son never ends." She was given the posthumous title of Ai, and that is why she became known as Lady Ai Jiang. Some eight years later, realizing that Lord Zhuang had no officially recognized principal wife, Lord Xi arranged for Lady Ai Jiang to receive sacrifices with her husband in the main ancestral temple, which was more than generous of him.

. . .

After Lord Huan of Qi rescued Yan from its difficulties and pacified the situation in Lu, his awe-inspiring reputation became known far and wide and the other lords all submitted to his authority. Lord Huan also came to trust Guan Zhong even more than he had before. He was employed in the most senior positions in the government, while the Marquis of Qi himself spent all his time in hunting and drinking. One day when he was out hunting along the margins of a great marsh, with Shu Diao driving his chariot, his horses were moving swiftly and he was shooting well, when suddenly he stared straight ahead of him. For a long time, Lord Huan said nothing, and he seemed petrified. Shu Diao asked, "What are you staring at, my lord?"

"I think I have just seen a ghost," Lord Huan said. "It was certainly something very peculiar and frightening. After a while it just simply disappeared. I wonder, could it be a bad omen?"

"Ghosts belong to the realm of darkness. How could you possibly see one during the day?"

"My older brother went hunting at Gufen and saw that mysterious wild boar," Lord Huan reminded him. "That was during broad daylight too. Would you call Elder Zhong here to me as soon as possible?"

"Elder Zhong isn't a sage," Shu Diao said. "What would he know about the ghosts and spirits?"

"What do you mean, he isn't a sage?" Lord Huan demanded. "Elder Zhong was able to identify the Yu'er for me!"

"But in that instance, you described the appearance of the Yu'er to him first. Elder Zhong knows exactly what Your Lordship wants to hear, and he can dress things up to encourage Your Lordship to act in particular ways. However, today Your Lordship says that you have encountered a ghost, and you have not told anyone what it looks like.

If what Elder Zhong says about it and what you saw correspond, then he is indeed a sage!"

"Absolutely," Lord Huan agreed. He then drove his chariot home as fast as he could, but he still felt uncomfortable and frightened. That night he became really sick.

The following morning, Guan Zhong and the other grandees came to ask after his health. Lord Huan summoned him and told him about seeing the ghost: "I was so scared I cannot bear to speak about it. Please, could you describe its appearance to me?"

Guan Zhong was unable to do so. He said, "Please allow me to investigate this further."

Shu Diao was standing to one side and sniggering: "I knew that Elder Zhong would not be able to describe it!"

Lord Huan got more and more sick, and Guan Zhong was very worried about him. He hung a message on the gates of the city reading: "If there is anyone who can describe the ghost that His Lordship has seen, he will receive one third of my fief."

Afterwards, a man dressed in rags and wearing a straw hat arrived and asked to have audience with Guan Zhong. Guan Zhong folded his hands respectfully and came forward.

"Is His Lordship sick?" the man asked.

"He is."

"Has His Lordship become unwell as a result of seeing a ghost?"

"He has."

"Did His Lordship see a ghost in a great marsh?"

"Can you describe this ghost or not?" Guan Zhong asked. "If you can, you will share my fief!"

"Let me go and see His Lordship, and then I will describe his ghost," the man said.

Guan Zhong went into the palace to have an audience with Lord Huan in his bedchamber. Lord Huan was reclining exhausted among the pillows, with two women rubbing his back and another two women massaging his legs. Shu Diao presented him with some soup, which he helped him to drink.

"My lord, you are ill, but I have found the man who can describe what you saw, and I have brought him with me," Guan Zhong said. "Please give orders to summon him into your presence!"

Lord Huan had him brought in. When he saw this man dressed in rags and with a straw hat, he was very displeased. He asked, "The man whom Elder Zhong mentioned, the one who can analyze ghosts, is that you?"

"You have brought this injury upon yourself, my lord," he replied. "How could a ghost harm you?"

"So, is there indeed such a thing as ghosts?" Lord Huan demanded.

"There is," the man informed him. "In the water there are 'Wangxiang'; in the hills there are 'Shen'; in the mountains there are 'Kui'; in the wilds there are 'Fanghuang'; and in the marshes there are 'Weishe.'"

"Please tell me what a 'Weishe' looks like!" Lord Huan said.

"Ah, well, the 'Weishe' is as fat as a hubcap and as tall as a carriage pole, and it wears a purple gown and a red hat. That kind of creature really hates the sound of wheeled traffic, so when it hears such a thing, it stops still and holds its head in its hands. It is very rare indeed that a human gets to see one, and if you do see it, it means that you will become hegemon and rule over the entire world!"

Lord Huan of Qi burst out laughing, and without being at all aware of what he was doing, he sat up straight and said, "That must be what I saw!" His mood had improved enormously, and he was no longer feeling in the least bit unwell.

"What is your name?" Lord Huan inquired.

"My name is Master Huang, and I am a farmer from the western part of the state of Qi."

"I hope that you will stay and work for me!" Lord Huan of Qi said. He wanted to appoint him to the office of grandee. Master Huang resolutely refused, saying, "You, my lord, have shown your respect to the royal house, you have pacified the barbarians and brought stability to the Central States, succoring the common people, allowing them to experience the joy of living in an age of good government. All that I care about is being allowed to continue farming my land. I cannot take office!"

"You really are a great gentleman!" Lord Huan exclaimed. He rewarded him with a gift of grain and silk, and exempted his family from all taxes. He also rewarded Guan Zhong lavishly.

"Elder Zhong couldn't describe what it was that you saw, so why are you rewarding him?" Shu Diao asked.

"I have heard it said that someone who can only employ one person is stupid, while someone who can employ many different people is enlightened," Lord Huan said. "If it were not for Elder Zhong, would I have been able to hear Master Huang's explanation?" Shu Diao had to agree.

. . .

In the seventeenth year of the reign of King Hui of Zhou, the Di nomadic peoples invaded the state of Xing and then moved their armies to attack Wey. Lord Yi of Wey sent a messenger to Qi to report this emergency. The grandees all fought for permission to go and rescue them, but Lord Huan said, "The troops that we would send against the Di are exhausted and need to rest. We will have to wait until the spring; then we can unite the lords in a joint rescue!"

That winter, Grandee Ning Su of Wey arrived in Qi and reported: "The Di have already crushed Wey and killed Lord Yi. We hope that you will support the accession of the Honorable Hui."

The Marquis of Qi was deeply disturbed and said, "I committed an unforgiveable crime in not going to the assistance of Wey earlier!"

Do you know how the Di destroyed Wey? READ ON.

Chapter Twenty-three

Lord Yi of Wey's love of cranes destroys his country.

Lord Huan of Qi raises an army to attack Chu.

Lord Hui of Wey's son, Lord Yi, succeeded to the title in the ninth year of the reign of King Hui of Zhou. He was in power for nine years, during which time he showed himself to be pleasure-loving, lazy, and arrogant, and he demonstrably had no interest at all in governing the country. The thing that he loved most in all the world was one variety of bird, and that was the crane.

According to the *Classic of Appreciating Cranes* by Fuqiu Bo:

> Cranes are birds that represent *yang* and yet they can travel through *yin*. They represent the element Metal, and yet they rely upon the essence of Fire to survive. Metal corresponds to the number nine and Fire to the number seven, and so cranes undergo a minor transformation every seven years and a major transformation after every sixteen years. After one hundred and sixty years their transformations cease, and at one thousand and six hundred years old, their form becomes stable. Their bodies are pure, and that is why they are white. Their song can be heard in heaven, and that is why their heads are red. They eat water creatures, and that is why their beaks are long. They nest on land, and that is why their legs are tall. They can soar up into the clouds, so they are richly feathered but not fat. They regurgitate stones, cleansing their system that they may take in new sustenance; this means that they live incalculably long lives. When they move, they always come to rest on islands or sandbanks, but they never congregate in forests. They are the most important of birds, the steeds ridden by immortals. The very best of cranes can be described as follows: small neat nostrils means that they sleep little, long fine legs means that they are strong, a red pupil to the eye means that they have excellent vision, strong feathers means that they enjoy flying, a healthy body means that they

will produce good offspring, the lightness with which they step forward and the power when they step back indicate that they are good at dancing, and the extension in their hips means that they are good at walking.

There is a poem by Emperor Gao of the Qi dynasty in praise of cranes that testifies to this:

The eight winds allow you to dance, your wings outstretched,
Throughout the wilds your clear calls can be heard.
One morning you can no longer soar into the skies,
But are held captive in a garden at the lord's behest.

The cranes that Lord Yi of Wey kept as pets were all given the titles and emoluments of senior government officials; his favorite cranes enjoyed equivalent privileges to a grandee, while his lesser cranes were recognized as knights. If Lord Yi went on a journey, then his cranes went with him, divided into groups and riding in grand carriages. The one in the lead carriage was known as the "Crane General." The people who looked after His Lordship's cranes were also given government positions, and they ate much better than others, because they could make use of the cranes' grain allowance. Ordinary people might be starving or cold, but they would have no chance of receiving any alms.

Grandee Shi Qizi was a descendant of Grandee Shi Que and the son of Shi Daizhong, and he was a famously honest and upright man. Together with Ning Zhuangzi, he was one of the pillars of the government. The two of them repeatedly presented remonstrance, but they were totally ignored. The Honorable Hui—the future Lord Wen of Wey—was Lord Hui of Wey's brother, born from Lady Xuan Jiang's incestuous relationship with the Honorable Shi. The Honorable Hui realized that Wey was in serious trouble, so he found a reason to go to Qi, whereupon he married one of Lord Huan of Qi's daughters and stayed there. The people of Wey remained deeply conscious of the horrible way in which Scion Jizi had died, and when Lord Hui was restored to the title, they cursed him day and night: "If there is any justice, he will not long enjoy these luxuries!"

Jizi and the Honorable Shou had both died without children, and the Honorable Shi and Qianmou had also passed away, so the only wise and virtuous member of the Wey ruling house was the Honorable Hui. The people of that state secretly pledged their allegiance to him. When Lord Yi lost all control, the Honorable Hui fled the country, which caused everyone to feel considerable hatred and anger.

. . .

In the time of King Wen of Zhou's father, the Xunyu branch of the northern Di peoples was already very powerful, and they forced him to move his capital to Mount Qi. When King Wu of Zhou founded the dynasty, the Duke of Zhou went south on campaign against the kingdoms of Chu and Shu, while to the north he fought against the Rong and the Di—thus for many years the Central States were at peace. When King Ping moved his capital to the east, the southern Man barbarians and the northern Di peoples began to encroach again. The leader of the northern Di tribes was a man named Souman, who commanded an army of tens of thousands of archers. He began to make plans to invade the Central States. When he heard that Qi had attacked the Mountain Rong, Souman said angrily, "For the Qi army to come so far to attack us means that they consider us to be an easy target. I will have to teach them a lesson!" He ordered a cavalry force of twenty thousand men to attack Xing, and they promptly overran the whole state. When he heard that Qi was planning to come to the rescue of Xing, he moved his army in the direction of Wey.

It so happened that at that time Lord Yi of Wey was just about to set out on a journey with his cranes, when a spy reported: "The Di people have invaded." Lord Yi was very alarmed and immediately donned his armor and buckled on a sword, with the intention of going out to do battle to defend his realm. His people had all fled to the outlying villages or into the wilds and were not willing to join the army. Lord Yi then sent his minister of education to arrest them. A short time later he returned, having captured more than one hundred people. When he asked them why they had run away, they said, "You already have all that you need to resist the Di, why do you want us?"

"What is it that is all that I need?" Lord Yi asked.

The people answered: "The cranes."

"How can the cranes possibly resist the Di?" Lord Yi wondered.

"Well, if the cranes can't defend us against the Di, they really are useless. The reason why none of us obey you is because you have ruined us in order to raise these pointless birds as pets."

"I realize that I have done wrong," Lord Yi said. "I will set all my cranes free, and I hope that this will demonstrate my sincerity to the people!"

"You have to do this, my lord," Shi Qizi said, "but I am afraid that it is too late."

Lord Yi sent someone to release the cranes, but since they were used to being fed, they just wandered around their old aviaries and would not leave.

The two grandees, Shi Qizi and Ning Zhuangzi, personally walked up and down the main roads in the capital, proclaiming that Lord Yi had repented his mistakes, and the people were gradually persuaded to present themselves for military service. By that time the Di had already cut a swath through to the Rong Marshes—three reports to this effect arrived one after the other. Shi Qizi presented his opinion: "The Di army has a well-deserved reputation for bravery, and they will not be easy to fight. I therefore ask permission to go to Qi and request their help."

"In the past, having received a royal mandate, Qi attacked us," Lord Yi pointed out. "Though in the end they withdrew their armies, we never restored diplomatic relations with them. Why would they help us now? I think it would be better just to fight and decide the fate of the country once and for all!"

"I will take an army to fight the Di," Ning Zhuangzi said, "while Your Lordship stays here guarding the capital."

"If I do not go with you in person, I am afraid that no one will fight in my cause," Lord Yi pointed out. He gave Shi Qizi a semicircular jade *jue* and ordered him to assume a regency over the state. He said, "I hope that your decisions will be as firm as this jade!" Next, he presented an arrow to Ning Zhuangzi as he appointed him to take command of the defense of Wey, saying, "It is all down to the two of you. If I do not defeat the Di, I will never return."

The two grandees, Shi Qizi and Ning Zhuangzi, both broke down in tears.

Having given his final instructions, Lord Yi held a great muster of chariots and men. He appointed Grandee Ju Kong as his general with Yu Bo to assist him, while Huang Yi commanded the vanguard and Kong Yingqi took charge of the rearguard. The whole way along, the soldiers complained. Lord Yi went out at night to observe the morale of his army, and the soldiers were singing a song:

> Cranes eat government grain while people plough the fields,
> Cranes ride on carriages while people shoulder weapons.
> The vanguard of the Di army is too strong for us to deal with;
> When we fight, only few of us will survive.
> Where are the cranes now?
> As we set out on this journey in fear and trembling . . .

When Lord Yi heard this song, he became deeply depressed.

Grandee Ju Kong was far too strict in his application of military law, which alienated the people under his command. When they approached the Rong Marshes, he realized that the enemy army comprised just over one thousand men, all milling around in confusion. Ju Kong said, "People say that the Di are brave, but clearly this is just an empty reputation!" He commanded that the drums be sounded to signal the advance. The Di people pretended to be defeated, but this was merely to lure the Wey army into a trap. With a shout the barbarians rose up on all sides, and it was as if the sky had collapsed or the earth had split. As the Wey army found themselves surrounded on three sides, they had no time to think about the safety of anyone other than themselves. They had never wanted to fight in the first place, and now, seeing this ferocious enemy facing them, they abandoned their chariots and fled. Lord Yi found himself completely surrounded by the Di forces.

"There is no time to be lost!" Ju Kong shouted. "Take down your battle standard and get off this chariot, leaving all your insignia behind you! You might still be able to get away!"

Lord Yi sighed and said, "If I have any loyal troops left, they will see my flag and come and rescue me. Otherwise, what is the point of having a battle standard? If I have indeed been abandoned, let me die! At least that way I can apologize to my people for my errors."

A short time later, both the vanguard and the rearguard of the Wey army had been defeated. Huang Yi died in battle while Kong Yingqi cut his own throat. As the Di army closed in, Yu Bo fell from his chariot, having been shot by an arrow. Both Lord Yi and Grandee Ju Kong, one after the other, sustained serious injuries before the Di army cut them down. The whole army was then massacred.

A bearded old man wrote a poem about this:

The ancients instruct us to beware of becoming too fond of hunting,
But who would have imagined that cranes could destroy a country?
That day amid the smoke and flames of Rong Marshes,
Was anyone able to ride on the back of a crane to find the land of the
    immortals?

Among others, the Di army took prisoner Hua Longhua and Li Kong, the Grand Astrologers of Wey, and they were intending to kill them. Hua Longhua and Li Kong were both well aware that barbarians believe in ghosts, so they tricked them by saying, "We are Grand Astrologers, and it is our job to take charge of sacrifices and religious ceremonies in Wey. We will go in advance of your army to report your arrival to the spirits. If we do not do this, the ghosts and spirits will not help you, and you will not be able to capture this state."

The chief of the Di believed what they said, so he let them go and gave them a chariot to ride. Ning Zhuangzi was on patrol on the city walls with the guards when, looking out into the distance, he saw a single chariot approaching at high speed. He recognized the two men riding on it as the Grand Astrologers. He was most alarmed, and demanded, "Where is His Lordship?"

"The whole army has been massacred!" they screamed. "The Di forces are too strong, do not just wait there for them to come and kill you. Run away!"

Ning Zhuangzi wanted to open the gates to let them in, but Li Kong said, "We left with His Lordship but come back without him. How can we be described as good subjects? I am going to go and serve His Lordship in the Underworld!" He drew his sword and cut his throat.

Hua Longhua, on the other hand, said, "I cannot allow the records of the history of the state of Wey to be lost." Accordingly, he entered the city.

Ning Zhuangzi and Shi Qizi discussed the situation and arranged to take the surviving members of the ruling house of Wey, including the Honorable Shen, out of the city under cover of darkness, riding in little carriages. They headed off to the east. Hua Longhua went with them, carrying the historical records and other documents. When the people of the capital heard that the two grandees had already left, they fled for their lives, carrying their children in their arms. The sounds of sobbing and screaming could be heard on all sides. The Di army pressed on to take advantage of the victory that they had just won, and they marched straight on the capital of the state of Wey, killing anyone who had been left behind. Having captured the city, they divided up their army to go in pursuit of the survivors. Shi Qizi was leading the way while Ning Zhuangzi defended their backs, and they fought every step of the way. About half of the people in their train were killed by Di swords. When they arrived at the Yellow River, they were lucky enough to find that Lord Huan of Song had sent his army out to meet them. They got into boats there and crossed the river by the light of the stars. The Di troops withdrew, having stolen all the gold and grain to be found in the government storehouses and the people's homes in the state of Wey to fill their own chariots. They also razed the walls of the capital. Of this no more.

. . .

Grandee Hong Yan had been sent on an embassy to the state of Chen some time earlier. By the time that he had finished his duties and returned, Wey had been destroyed. When he heard that the Marquis of Wey had been killed at the Rong Marshes, he went there to look for his body. As he searched, he could see skeletons everywhere exposed to the elements, with lumps of flesh here and pools of blood there. He could not overcome his sense of horror. As he pressed on, he caught sight of the great battle standard flying to one side of the marsh. Hong Yan said to himself, "The flag is there, so the body cannot be far away." Having advanced just a couple of paces, he heard the sound of groaning. Looking around, he caught sight of a young eunuch lying on the ground, one arm reduced to a bloody stump.

"Do you know where His Lordship died?" Hong Yan asked.

The eunuch indicated a heap of flesh and said, "That is His Lordship's body. I saw them kill him with my own eyes. Thanks to the pain in my arm I could not move, so I just stayed here. I have been hoping that someone would come, so that I could tell them what happened."

Hong Yan looked at the body—the only part that had been left completely uninjured was his liver. Hong Yan bowed twice to it and wailed loudly; then he made a report on his diplomatic mission to the liver, performing the same rituals as if it were the full living human being. When this had been completed, Hong Yan said, "No one else has come to collect Your Lordship for burial, so I will use my own body as a coffin." He instructed his entourage: "When I am dead, you must bury me in these woods. You should wait for a new lord to be established, then you may tell him what I have done." He took the sword hanging by his side and used it to cut open his abdomen. Then he picked up Lord Yi's liver and inserted it into his stomach, dying a short time later. His servants buried him there, as he had wished. Afterwards, they lifted the eunuch onto the chariot and set off to ford the Yellow River, to find out if a new lord had been appointed.

. . .

Let us now go back to another part of the story. While Shi Qizi was assisting the Honorable Shen in boarding a boat, Ning Zhuangzi was collecting all the refugees he could find, and they followed after this last remnant of the Wey ruling house. When they arrived at Cao, they counted these men and women and discovered that they had only managed to save seven hundred and twenty people. Is it not a tragedy that the Di butchered so many innocent lives? The two grandees discussed the situation together, and they said, "We must have a new ruler! But what is to be done about the fact that so few have been able to escape?"

They went to the towns of Gong and Teng and removed one third of the population—more than four thousand people in total—and set them to building new houses in Cao. With the refugees this formed a populace of about five thousand. They established the Honorable Shen as the new Marquis of Wey, and he took the title of Lord Dai. Lord Huan of Song and Lord Huan of Xu both sent ambassadors to express their deepest sympathies about what had happened. However, Lord Dai had long been in very poor health, and he died just a few days after succeeding to the title.

Ning Zhuangzi then traveled to Qi, with a view to inviting the Honorable Hui to take the title.

"You should go home and look after your ancestral temples," Lord Huan of Qi told him. "If there is anything lacking, it is my fault."

He gave him a team of fine horses for his chariot, five sets of official robes, three hundred head of oxen, sheep, pigs, chickens, and dogs. In addition to that, he presented the future Marchioness of Wey with a chariot decorated in sharkskin, together with three hundred lengths of silk brocade. He commanded the Honorable Wukui of Qi to escort them to their new home with a train of three hundred chariots, together with a great deal of timber that they could use to build the main gate to the city. The Honorable Hui thus arrived at Cao. Hong Yan's entourage then arrived with the one-armed eunuch and reported on the fate of Lord Yi of Wey. The Honorable Hui ordered someone to prepare the necessary equipment and go to the Rong Marshes to encoffin the body; thus, a funeral was held for both Lord Yi and Lord Dai. He bestowed a title upon Hong Yan and determined to give his son an official position in order to proclaim his loyal service. The lords were much impressed by Lord Huan of Qi's righteous behavior, and thus many of them came to condole with the new Marquis of Wey. This happened in the twelfth month of winter of the eighteenth year of the reign of King Hui of Zhou.

The following year, the Honorable Hui declared his accession to the marquisate of Wey on New Year's Day: he became Lord Wen. He was reduced to an escort of just thirty chariots, and he had to live with ordinary people—a sad state of affairs for the ruler of a state. Lord Wen wore ordinary clothes with a simple cotton cap, eating only vegetarian food, rising early and going to bed late, doing his very best to comfort the refugees from Wey. Everyone praised his behavior. The Honorable Wukui now said goodbye and returned to the state of Qi, though he left behind him a force of three thousand armed men to guard Cao and prevent any attacks by the Di. When the Honorable Wukui arrived back in Qi, he had an audience with Lord Huan, at which he reported how simply the new Marquis of Wey was living. He also informed him of how Hong Yan had died. Lord Huan sighed and said, "How could such a terrible ruler find such a loyal subject? It is clear that this state is far from ready to be destroyed."

Guan Zhong came forward and said, "We now have all these refugees from Wey, so why not select a place to build a city for them to live in? That way, at one stroke we can guarantee their survival."

Lord Huan thought that a very good idea. He intended to call a meeting of the various lords, so that they could jointly undertake this task, but just at that moment a messenger suddenly arrived from the state of Xing to report an emergency there: "The Di army has attacked us again, and we cannot hold out much longer. Please rescue us!"

"Can we rescue Xing?" Lord Huan asked.

"The reason why the other lords are happy to serve us is because they know that Qi will save them when disaster strikes," Guan Zhong replied. "If we cannot save Wey and do not go to help Xing, you can forget about becoming hegemon!"

"If that is true, which of the two should I save first?" Lord Huan inquired.

"Once the state of Xing has been settled, you can find a new home for Wey, thus achieving something that will be praised for a hundred generations!" Guan Zhong said.

"You are right," Lord Huan exclaimed. He immediately sent a message to the states of Song, Lu, Cao, and Zhu, that they should all join with Qi to rescue Xing. All five armies were to assemble together at Niebei.

The armies of the two states of Song and Cao were the first to arrive. Guan Zhong explained his plan: "The Di are currently attacking across a wide area, and the state of Xing has so far been able to hold out against them. If we were to meet such a strong enemy head-on, it would surely be a lot of work; while if we go to the assistance of people who are so far holding their own, they will not appreciate our efforts. It would be better to wait until Xing can no longer resist the Di. Once they have collapsed and the Di have conquered Xing, they are sure to be exhausted. If we then expel the wretched Di and rescue Xing from disaster, we will get the maximum benefit from the minimum amount of effort."

Lord Huan thought his plan an excellent one, and he camped at Niebei under the pretext of waiting for the arrival of the armies from Lu and Zhu, while sending out spies to find out what was going on in Xing and among the Di.

A historian wrote a poem criticizing the fact that Guan Zhong did not go to the rescue of Xing and Wey earlier because it was part of his plan to establish Lord Huan's hegemony by fomenting problems that he could easily deal with. This poem reads:

> Saving people from disaster is the same as loosening the hangman's
> knot:
> If you are going to raise an army, then why should you delay?
> No hegemon ever matched up to a true king,
> They always looked to their own benefit, no matter what they said
> about justice.

The armies of the three states camped at Niebei for about two months. The Di army was attacking Xing day and night. The people of Xing were completely exhausted, so they broke through the encirclement and escaped. Spies reported back that the men and women of Xing were arriving in a great wave, and indeed a horde of refugees rushed to the Qi camp and begged for help. One man prostrated himself on the ground weeping: this was Shuyan, Marquis of Xing. Lord Huan lifted him to his feet and consoled him, saying, "I have come very late to assist you, and so it is my fault that things have reached this pass. However, I have been discussing with the Duke of Song and the Earl of Cao exactly how we will get rid of the Di."

He immediately ordered them all to strike camp and set off. The chief of the Di people, Souman, had now raped and pillaged to his heart's content, and so had no intention of fighting. When he heard that a great force was on its way, composed of the armies of three states, he simply set fire to the city and fled as fast as he could northwards. Thus, when these armies arrived on the scene, they saw the city reduced to a sheet of flame, while the Di people were already long gone. Lord Huan gave orders that the fires should be put out, and then he asked the Marquis of Xing, "Do you want to stay in the old city?"

Shuyan, Marquis of Xing, said, "More than half of my people have run away to live at Yiyi. I think it would be better if I moved there too, since that is what my people seem to want."

Lord Huan ordered that each of the three states would be responsible for one third of the construction of the city wall at Yiyi, so that the Marquis of Xing could make his home there. The construction of houses and official buildings, the establishment of a new shrine to the ancestors of the Xing ruling house, and the provision of cattle and horses, grain, silk, and so on were all the responsibility of the state of Qi. The city having been restocked, both ruler and people of Xing felt as if they had come home, and they praised the Marquis of Qi with thunderous acclaim.

When this had been done, the lords of Song and Cao wanted to say goodbye to Lord Huan and go home to their own states.

"The problem of Wey has not yet been settled," Lord Huan reminded them. "If we fortify this city for Xing and leave Wey unprotected, what will they think of us?"

The two lords said, "We await your commands."

Lord Huan gave orders for the army to move towards Wey, and each man carried a spade or a pick on his shoulder. Lord Wen of Wey came a long way to meet him, and when Lord Huan saw that he was dressed in ordinary clothes with a cloth hat, not even having changed into mourning clothes, he was silent in anguish for a long time. Then he said, "I have availed myself of the strength of some of the other lords and come here to build a capital for Your Lordship. Do you have any suggestions for a suitably auspicious location?"

"I have already performed a divination and discovered an auspicious site at Chuqiu," Lord Wen informed him. "However, it is not possible for a doomed state like my own to build a city there!"

"Leave it to me!" Lord Huan exclaimed. That very day he issued orders to the troops of the three states to go to Chuqiu and start work. Just as in the previous instance, they had brought the materials to build the city gates with them. They also reconstructed the court and the ancestral shrines of the ruling house, in the name of "restoring Wey."

Lord Wen of Wey deeply appreciated Qi's generosity in rebuilding his state, so he composed the song "Quince" in order to express his gratitude. This song runs:

You threw me a quince and I repaid you with a gem.
You threw me a peach and I repaid you with a precious agate.
You threw me a plum and I repaid you with a jewel.

At that time, people said that Lord Huan saved three doomed states. He established Lord Xi and thus saved Lu; he fortified the city of Yiyi to save Xing; and he fortified the city of Chuqiu in order to save Wey. It was thanks to these three signal successes that he became the first of the five hegemons.

Master Qianyuan wrote the following historical poem concerning these events:

After the Zhou dynasty moved to the east, all proper norms were
  smashed.
Lord Huan led the coalition to put a stop to Prince Tui's rebellion.
Now he saves three states otherwise doomed to destruction,
No wonder that he became the first of the five hegemons!

At this time Xiong Hui, King Cheng of Chu, had employed Grand
Vizier Ziwen with a view to putting the government of his kingdom in
good order, and once he had done so, the king was ambitious to con-
tend for hegemony in the region. When he heard that the Marquis of Qi
had ensured the preservation of Xing and Wey and people were singing
his praises even in Chu, King Cheng was very unhappy. He said to
Ziwen, "The Marquis of Qi has displayed his virtues and brought yet
more luster to his name, so people are giving their allegiance to him. I
live in obscurity east of the Han River and am neither virtuous enough
that people honor me nor powerful enough that they are frightened of
me. Right at the present time, it is clear that people care about Qi and
not at all about Chu. I find this deeply humiliating!"

"The Marquis of Qi has been working at his hegemony for almost
twenty years now," Ziwen reminded him. "Since he always has the fig
leaf of 'respecting the king,' the other lords are happy to obey him. You
are not yet in a position where you can openly oppose him. Zheng is
centrally located and at present acts as a barrier between us and the
Central States. If you wish to expand into that region, you will have to
capture Zheng."

"But whom should I employ for the job of attacking Zheng?" King
Cheng asked.

Grandee Dou Zhang announced that he would be willing to go. King
Cheng gave him an army of two hundred chariots and he set off at all
speed to Zheng.

· · ·

After Zheng had recovered from the near-disaster at the Chun Gate,
they spent day and night preparing for further attacks from Chu. When
they discovered that the kingdom of Chu had mobilized its army, the
Earl of Zheng was deeply alarmed, and so he sent Grandee Dan Bo to
take his army to defend the Chun Gate, while a messenger traveled by
night to report the emergency to Qi. The Marquis of Qi issued his
instructions that the lords should come for a meeting at Cheng, at which
they would plan the campaign to save Zheng. Dou Zhang was well
aware that Zheng had been making preparations for defense, and now

he also heard that Qi's army had come to the rescue, so he was afraid that the situation would not turn to his advantage and turned back at the border. King Cheng of Chu was absolutely furious, so he took off the sword hanging from his belt and bestowed it upon Dou Lian, with orders that he should cut off Dou Zhang's head in front of the entire army. Dou Lian was Dou Zhang's older brother, so when he arrived at the army camp he kept the king of Chu's orders a secret. He discussed the situation with Dou Zhang in private: "If you wish to escape punishment, you must immediately achieve some signal victory that allows you to atone for your past mistake!"

Dou Zhang knelt down and asked his brother what he should do.

"Zheng knows that you have withdrawn your army," Dou Lian explained, "so they will not be expecting you to come back any time soon. If you were to make a lightning attack on them, you would win a great victory!"

Dou Zhang divided his army into two groups, and he himself took personal command of the vanguard, while Dou Lian was responsible for the rearguard. He marched quietly over the border with Zheng, with the bells on his horses muffled and the drums silent. Purely by chance he ran into Dan Bo, who was reviewing the troops stationed at the border. Dan Bo realized that they were being invaded, but he had no idea which country was responsible. He mustered his troops as quickly as he could and then intercepted the attacking army, fighting a terrible battle. Things went much worse than he was expecting, because Dou Lian's rearguard arrived and came up behind the Zheng army, catching them in a pincer movement. Dan Bo could not withstand this assault; he was hurled to the ground by a single blow from Dou Zhang's iron baton and then taken prisoner. Dou Lian took advantage of his victory to put the enemy to the sword, and indeed more than half of the Zheng army died that day.

Dou Zhang put Dan Bo in a prison cart. After that, he wanted to head off at full speed for Zheng.

"We have achieved a great success in this surprise attack," Dou Lian reminded him. "However, if you want to escape the death penalty, are you going to put your trust in always being lucky?"

That very day they turned back, with the army singing songs of triumph. Dou Zhang went home and had an audience with King Cheng, at which he kowtowed and apologized for his crimes. He then presented his opinion: "The reason why we turned our army back was because we were trying to lure the enemy on and not because we were afraid of doing battle!"

"You have done well in capturing an enemy general, which outweighs your former offense," King Cheng said. "But given that Zheng had not yet submitted to our authority, why have you disbanded the army?"

"I was afraid that given the small size of our army, we could not be certain of victory," Dou Lian explained. "A defeat would cause them to despise our kingdom."

King Cheng was angry and said, "You are using the size of the army as an excuse, when in fact it is quite clear that you were too scared to do battle. I am now giving you another two hundred chariots. If you come back again without having taken the capital city of Zheng, I will refuse to see you."

"I hope that you will let my brother go with me," Dou Lian said. "Even if Zheng does not surrender, at the very least we will present the Earl of Zheng to you as a captive."

King Cheng liked the sound of this and agreed. He appointed Dou Lian as the commander-in-chief, with Dou Zhang as his deputy, and they reinvaded the state of Zheng in command of a force of four hundred chariots.

A historian wrote a poem about this:

Since the rulers of Chu had declared themselves kings, their power had
    grown.
He conquered many other states, but his ambitions were not satisfied.
What had Zheng done to deserve being attacked three times?
This problem could only be resolved by a hegemon-lord.

When the Earl of Zheng heard that Dan Bo had been taken prisoner, he yet again sent someone to Qi to ask for help. Guan Zhong came forward and said, "In the last couple of years Your Lordship has rescued Yan and saved Lu, fortified Xing, and given new land to Wey, and you have behaved with great generosity and virtue towards the people. You have also shown great righteousness in your dealings with the other lords. If you wish to make use of the armies of the Central States, now is the time. If Your Lordship wishes to rescue Zheng, you will have to attack Chu. If you want to attack Chu, you will have to assemble a coalition force with a large number of other lords."

"If I bring together a huge army taken from the other aristocrats, Chu is sure to make preparations," Lord Huan said. "How can I be sure that I will be victorious?"

"Cai has offended Your Lordship, and you have been wanting to punish them for a long time," Guan Zhong reminded him. "Chu and

Cai are neighbors, so you can advance all the way to Chu, proclaiming that you are on a campaign against Cai. This is what *The Art of War* calls 'appearing where you are not expected.'"

. . .

Some time prior to this, Lord Mu of Cai had married his younger sister to Lord Huan of Qi as his third wife. It happened one day that Lord Huan and Lady Ji of Cai were sailing around the lake on a small boat, amusing themselves by picking lotus flowers. Lady Ji of Cai splashed water on her husband for fun, and he ordered her to stop. Lady Ji knew that her husband was afraid of water, so she started to rock the boat, soaking His Lordship's clothes. He was absolutely furious and said, "I really cannot stay married to such a bitch." He ordered Shu Diao to escort Lady Ji of Cai back home.

Lord Mu of Cai then became angry in his turn: "To send a married woman back to her parents' home is the greatest possible insult and means that you must intend to break off all relations with us." He married his younger sister into the Chu royal family, and she became King Cheng of Chu's queen.

Lord Huan loathed the Marquis of Cai, thus what Guan Zhong said struck him deeply: "The two states of Jiang and Huang are not able to bear the violent assaults that they have suffered from Chu, so they have sent ambassadors with tribute to that kingdom. I would like to make a blood covenant with them, and on the day that I attack Chu, they can act as support from inside. What do you think of that?"

"Jiang and Huang are located far away from Qi and close to Chu," Guan Zhong said. "They have submitted to Chu's authority in order to survive. If they betray their treaties and follow us, Chu is sure to be furious with them and attack them. In that case, even if we want to help them, we are too far away. If we do not save them, we will betray the covenant that we have sworn. Besides which, you have already held a number of meetings for the lords of the states of the Zhou confederacy, which have been a great success. Why do you need to get help from these tiny little countries? It would be better to decline any offers of assistance from Jiang and Huang politely."

"To refuse their offer would be rude, given that they have come from so far away and admire me so much," Lord Huan said.

"In that case," Guan Zhong stated, "Your Lordship should inscribe my words on the wall. Then in the future you will not forget to go to the assistance of Jiang and Huang when they are in trouble."

Lord Huan made a blood covenant with the two rulers of Jiang and Huang, at which he secretly agreed with them on a date for an attack on the kingdom of Chu, in the first month of the following year.

"The state of Shu has assisted Chu's vicious attacks on us," the two lords said, "so people speak of them in one word: *Chu-Shu*. They must be punished too!"

"I would like to capture Shu first," Lord Huan announced. "That will clip Chu's wings."

He wrote a secret letter, which he sent to the Viscount of Xu. The state of Xu was located near to the state of Shu, but Lady Ying of Xu was Lord Huan of Qi's late second wife. Thanks to the alliance created by this marriage, Xu had become closely associated with the state of Qi, so Lord Huan was able to tell him all about his idea of an attack on Shu. Just as he had intended, the Viscount of Xu launched a surprise attack on the state of Shu, in which it fell. Lord Huan then ordered the viscount to garrison the capital city, with instructions to prepare to assist him in any emergency. The two rulers of Jiang and Huang stayed within their own borders waiting for the order to move.

Lord Xi of Lu then sent the Honorable You to Qi to apologize for his crimes and say: "Due to problems with the states of Zhu and Ju, I was not able to participate in your campaign to save Xing and Wey. Now I hear that you have made a blood covenant with Jiang and Huang, so I have sent this ambassador specially to express my good wishes. I am also happy to rush to the front, holding a whip in my hand, in your next military campaign."

Lord Huan was very pleased and secretly ordered him to participate in the attack on Chu.

. . .

At this time, the Chu army had already arrived back in the state of Zheng, and Lord Wen of Zheng wanted to ask them for a peace treaty, in the hope of preventing any further suffering among his people.

"You cannot do that. Qi has begun to mobilize its armies to attack Chu for our sake," Grandee Kong Shu told him. "They have behaved very well towards us, so it would be wrong of us to simply give up. We should sit behind our fortifications and wait." He sent yet another ambassador to Qi to report the emergency.

Lord Huan informed him of what he was planning to do and got him to spread the word that Qi would be coming to their assistance, in the hope of getting Chu to back off. When the appointed time came, various lords and ministers would lead a great army out of Hulao and set off in the direction of Shangcai, where they would join forces with Qi to attack Chu. The lords of Song, Lu, Chen, Wey, Cao, and Xu all agreed that they would mobilize their armies when the time came. They would proclaim that they were going on campaign against Cai, but the real objective of their attack was the kingdom of Chu.

The following year, which was the thirteenth year of the reign of King Hui of Zhou, on New Year's Day, after receiving the formal congratulations of his ministers at early morning court, Lord Huan of Qi discussed the campaign against Cai. He ordered that Guan Zhong should be the commander-in-chief and that he should lead Xi Peng, Bin Xuwu, Bao Shuya, the Honorable Kaifang of Wey, and Shu Diao out at the head of a force of three hundred chariots and ten thousand men. Afterwards, they would divide into their different units and proceed with the attack.

The Grand Astrologer reported: "The seventh is an auspicious day for the army to leave."

Shu Diao asked permission to take a small army out in advance of the main force to make incursions into Cai and raid their borders and then meet up with the armies of the other countries of the coalition. Lord Huan agreed to this. The people of Cai were relying entirely upon Chu, so they had made no preparations at all themselves. It was only when the Qi army actually arrived that they gathered a few soldiers and placed them on guard.

Shu Diao drew up his army in an impressive force at the foot of the city walls and shouted out his orders to attack the city, but when night fell, he withdrew. Lord Mu of Cai recognized Shu Diao, for in the past he had served Lady Ji of Cai in the Qi palace, and she had been very fond of him—when she was sent back home, he had escorted her. He was well aware that Shu Diao was a wicked and venal man. Therefore, in the middle of the night, he secretly sent someone with a cart full of gold and silk and begged him to take his army away. Shu Diao took the bribe and explained in great detail to Lord Mu how the Marquis of Qi had assembled a coalition force with seven other feudal lords and was intending to invade Cai and then attack Chu: "In the not-too-distant future, when the armies of all these states arrive, the walls of your capital will be trampled flat. You had better run away as soon as you can."

When the messenger reported this, the Marquis of Cai was deeply shocked. That very night he ordered the gates to the city to be opened to allow himself and his family to flee to Chu. His people were left leaderless, and resistance immediately crumbled as they began to run away. Shu Diao thought that he had done very well, and so he sent a message by carrier pigeon to the Marquis of Qi to announce that the city had fallen.

When the Marquis of Cai arrived in Chu, he had an audience with King Cheng and reported Shu Diao's words to him. When King Cheng had thoroughly understood Qi's plan, he gave orders for a muster of chariots and men to prepare for the defense of the capital, as well as ordering the recall of the Dou Zhang's forces in Zheng. A few days later the Marquis of Qi's army arrived at Shangcai. When Shu Diao had finished making his report, one after the other the lords of seven other states arrived, each in command of chariots and infantry that would assist in the coming battle. This was indeed a mighty army. These seven lords were Yushuo, Lord Huan of Song; Shen, Lord Xi of Lu; Wuqiu, Lord Xuan of Chen; Hui, Lord Wen of Wey; Jie, Lord Wen of Zheng; Ban, Lord Zhao of Cao; and Xinchen, Lord Mu of Xu. Together with the Master of Covenants, Xiaobai, Lord Huan of Qi, there were eight lords in attendance. Lord Mu of Xu was seriously ill, but nevertheless he had led his army to be the first to arrive in Cai. Lord Huan appreciated the efforts that he had made and insisted that he should be ranked above the Earl of Cao. That evening, Lord Mu of Xu passed away. The Marquis of Qi remained in Cai for five days in order to hold a funeral for him. He ordered that when the body was returned to Xu, they should inter him with the ceremonies due to a marquis.

. . .

The lords of the seven states advanced southwards until they arrived at the border with Chu. The only thing that they could see there was a man very formally dressed in an official robe and hat, who had stopped his chariot there and was standing by the side of the road. He bowed deeply and asked, "Are you the Marquis of Qi? I have a message for you; the kingdom of Chu sent me to watch out for you, and I have been waiting for a long time." This man was Qu Wan, a member of one of the Chu aristocratic houses and a grandee of that kingdom. He had been sent as an ambassador by the king of Chu to meet the Qi army.

Lord Huan was puzzled: "How did they learn of my army's arrival?"

"Someone must have leaked this information to them," Guan Zhong said. "If they have sent an ambassador here to meet us, they must have some sort of plan. Let me try and embarrass him into leaving, for that way we will not have to fight."

Guan Zhong got onto a chariot and drove it out from the ranks, whereupon he bowed respectfully to Qu Wan on his chariot.

Qu Wan began the discussion by saying, "When His Majesty heard that you were coming with your army to humiliate us, he ordered me to wait for you here. His Majesty commanded me to say, 'Qi and Chu are very different countries—Qi is located by the northern sea, while Chu is found close to the southern seas. They have never had any contact with each other. I do not understand why you have invaded my territory!' I now ask you for an explanation of your behavior!"

"In the past, King Cheng of Zhou enfeoffed our former ruler, the Great Lord, in Qi," Guan Zhong proclaimed, "and gave him the following mandate: 'Undertake to punish aristocrats of every degree and the chiefs of all the nine provinces in order to help and support the Zhou ruling house. Your lands stretch from the sea to the east to the Yellow River to the west and from Muling in the south to Wudi in the north. If anyone does not serve the king, do not forgive them!' Since the Zhou dynasty moved their capital to the east, the feudal lords have been increasingly lax in their observances of the rules. His Lordship has now accepted the position of Master of Covenants, with the intention of restoring the good government that prevailed under his ancestors. Chu is indeed located far to the south, but it is nevertheless your duty to provide tribute of sweet herbs, which is used in the royal sacrifices. Since you do not present this tribute, His Majesty, the Son of Heaven, has no means to strain the wine used in sacrifice. His Lordship would like to call you to account for this! In addition to that, King Zhao of Zhou never returned from his campaigns in the south, and that is also thanks to you! What do you have to say for yourselves?"

"The Zhou royal family have lost control of their kingdom, which is why people no longer present tribute to them," Qu Wan replied. "That is the way of the world. Why are you putting all the blame on us? Of course, His Majesty accepts that it is his responsibility that the sweet herbs have not been sent to the Zhou court. How would he presume not to give it, since you command him to do so? As for the fact that King Zhao of Zhou never returned home, that is the fault of the boat in which he was traveling. You will have to ask for information about that along the riverbank; it has nothing whatsoever to do with His Majesty! I now need to go back to report to my king."

When he had finished speaking, he turned his chariot around and withdrew.

Guan Zhong reported back to Lord Huan: "These Chu people are really tough—we cannot get out of this one by sophistry. We had better advance and try and put them under some pressure."

He gave orders that the eight armies should all advance until they reached Mount Xing, not far from the Han River. Then he commanded: "We will make camp here. Do not advance any further!"

"Since we have already gone this far, why not cross the Han River and do battle there?" the lords all inquired. "Why should we stay here?"

"Since Chu sent an ambassador to meet us, they must be prepared for our arrival," Guan Zhong explained. "Once our armies have joined battle, it will be impossible to draw back. If we make camp here now, we can keep an eye on what they are doing. Chu is afraid of the great force that we have assembled, and so they will send more ambassadors to us, and we can use this as an opportunity to make peace. We may have come here on campaign against Chu, but if we leave having made them peacefully submit to our authority, will that not be entirely acceptable?"

The lords did not really believe him, and the discussion broke down into an argument.

. . .

King Cheng of Chu had already appointed Ziwen as the commander-in-chief of his army, and he had mustered a very well-equipped and well-trained force that was camped south of the Han River. He was waiting for the lords to cross the river, and then he would attack. His spies reported: "The armies of the eight countries have made camp at Mount Xing."

Ziwen then came forward and said, "Guan Zhong excels at military strategy, and he will not advance unless he is certain of victory. If he has made the armies of the eight states halt and make camp, it means that he must have a plan. Let us send another ambassador to him, to inspect the strength of his forces and their morale. We can decide later whether to fight them or to make peace."

"Whom should we send?" King Cheng asked.

"Qu Wan has already met Guan Zhong once, so it would be appropriate for him to go again," Ziwen stated.

Qu Wan presented his opinion: "I have already accepted that we were wrong not to send the tribute of sweet herbs to the Zhou court. If Your Majesty wants to make peace with Qi, then I will do my very best to resolve all the disputes between our two countries. If, on the other hand, you are intending to go to war, then please send someone else."

"It is for you, my minister, to decide whether it is peace or war," King Cheng told him. "This is now beyond my control."

Qu Wan then went back to the Qi army.

Do you want to know what happened next to Qi and Chu? READ ON.

Chapter Twenty-four

*At the blood covenant at Shaoling, a Chu
grandee is treated with ritual propriety.*

*At the meeting at Kuiqiu, the Zhou king
is honored.*

When Qu Wan arrived back at the Qi army, he requested permission to have an audience with the Marquis of Qi face-to-face to discuss the situation.

"Since Chu has sent its ambassador back, it means that they must be hoping for a blood covenant," Guan Zhong explained. "Your Lordship should treat him with all due ritual propriety!"

When Qu Wan came into Lord Huan of Qi's presence, he bowed twice and Lord Huan responded politely, asking him why he had come.

"Your Lordship has come on campaign here because His Majesty did not present tribute to the Zhou court," Qu Wan said. "His Majesty has already accepted that he was at fault in this matter. If you would be prepared to withdraw your army by one day's march, my king will listen to your further commands."

"I am very pleased to know that you, sir, have assisted your ruler to restore the old norms," Lord Huan said. "I can now make my final report to the Son of Heaven."

Qu Wan thanked him and left. On his return, he reported this to the Chu king: "The Marquis of Qi has already promised to withdraw his army, and I have agreed that we will send tribute to the Zhou court. Please do not go back on your word, Your Majesty!"

A short time later, spies reported: "The armies of the eight states have struck camp." King Cheng sent them back again to investigate the situation, and they reported: "They have withdrawn thirty *li* and are now camped at Shaoling."

"If the Qi army has withdrawn, they must be terrified of me!" the king of Chu said. He was starting to regret having agreed to send tribute, but Ziwen said, "The lords of eight countries have just kept their word to one of your grandees. Your Majesty cannot possibly humiliate yourself by failing to keep your word to them!" The king of Chu fell silent. He ordered Qu Wan to take eight carts full of gold and silk to the armies of the eight states camped at Shaoling. In addition, he prepared one cartload of sweet herbs, which would be sent on in advance of the Qi army, to make it clear that they were resuming the practice of paying tribute to the Zhou king.

Lord Mu of Xu's body was sent home for burial. His son and heir presided over the funeral and then succeeded formally to the title, becoming Lord Xi. In recognition of Lord Huan's magnanimity, he sent Grandee Bai Tuo to Shaoling in command of the Xu army.

When Lord Huan heard that Qu Wan was coming back yet again, he instructed the other aristocrats: "Your chariots and men should be divided into seven divisions and stationed separately. The Qi army will camp at the southernmost position, so that if the Chu army attacks, we will take the brunt of it. You should wait until the drums of the Qi army sound and then strike your own. Make sure that your soldiers are fully armed and smartly turned out, so that we of the Central States present a most formidable appearance!"

When Qu Wan arrived, he had an audience with the Marquis of Qi and showed him the gifts intended for the armies of the Zhou confederacy. Lord Huan ordered that they be divided up and sent to each force. He also inspected the cartload of sweet herbs and commanded Qu Wan to take charge of it. He felt that he should be responsible for presenting it as tribute to the Zhou king.

"Since you are here, you should inspect the armies of the Central States!" Lord Huan said.

"I have lived my whole life in the deep south, so I have never been able to see the glory of the Central States," Qu Wan replied. "I would be delighted to inspect the troops!"

Lord Huan then climbed into an armored chariot with Qu Wan, so that they could review the troops of each of the states. Drawn up in formation, their ranks stretched for several dozen *li*. The Qi army sounded their drums, and then the drums in the other armies responded with an ear-splitting, thunderous noise. Lord Huan said happily to Qu

Wan, "Look at my forces. If I did battle with them, I would naturally be victorious! Anyone whom I attacked would simply have to surrender!"

"The reason why Your Lordship has become Master of Covenants over the feudal lords of the Zhou confederacy is because you have consistently proclaimed your loyalty to the king and acted with great magnanimity towards others," Qu Wan responded. "Given how correctly you have behaved towards the other lords, would they dare to turn against you? If you rely on brute force for your victories, even though Chu is a small and remote country, I would remind you that we have great mountains for our walls and the Han River itself forms our moat. Given the strength of our fortifications, even if you have an army of a million men, you will not necessarily be able to defeat us!"

Lord Huan looked somewhat ashamed of himself and said, "You really are a good man, sir! I would like to restore the old alliance between my state and yours. Do you think that would be possible?"

"You, my lord, have brought great blessings to other countries," Qu Wan replied. "Now if you wish for a blood covenant with us, how could His Majesty dare to refuse? Would it be acceptable if we decided on the terms now?"

"It would be fine by me," Lord Huan said.

That night Qu Wan stayed overnight in camp, and a banquet was held there in his honor. The following day, an altar was constructed at Shaoling. Then Lord Huan held the ear of the sacrificial ox in his role as the Master of Covenants, while Guan Zhong assisted him. Qu Wan represented the king of Chu on this occasion. The text of the covenant that they swore was as follows: "From now on, let us be allies from one generation to the next." Lord Huan was the first to smear his mouth with blood, and then the lords of the seven other states and Qu Wan followed him in order. When the ceremony was completed, Qu Wan bowed twice in thanks. Guan Zhong spoke privately to him, requesting that Dan Bo should be released back to Zheng. Qu Wan also apologized on behalf of the Marquis of Cai. Each side accepted the other's apologies. Afterwards, Guan Zhong gave the order to stand down the army.

On their way home, Bao Shuya asked Guan Zhong, "Chu has committed many crimes, of which usurping the title of king is the most serious, so why have you let them off with sending a cartload of sweet herbs? I really don't understand it."

"The rulers of Chu have now used the title of king for three generations," Guan Zhong replied. "I have been trying to get them to leave us alone—the same policy that I use with all other foreign peoples. If we upbraided them for changing their title, would they hang their heads and obey us? But if they didn't listen to us, the whole situation would end in armed conflict. Once you have gone to war, then one state would be invading the other, creating a disaster that would take many years to undo. I do not want to see the north and south embroiled in constant warfare! I was prepared to let them off with presenting one cartload of sweet herbs because it makes it easier for them to accept our instructions. We have gotten them to admit that they have behaved badly. That is quite enough to raise our reputation among the other feudal lords to the skies and to requite the mandate that His Majesty the king bestowed upon us. Surely this is better than becoming embroiled in endless conflict, is it not?"

Bao Shuya sighed deeply.

Master Hu Zeng wrote a poem about this:

> The king of Chu by the southern seas cared nothing for the Zhou
>   dynasty;
> Elder Zhong, on the other hand, was an excellent strategist.
> He made this treaty without resorting to force,
> Causing the Marquis of Qi to be praised by later ages.

A bearded old man wrote a poem criticizing the fact that the agreement brokered by Lord Huan of Qi and Guan Zhong did no damage at all to Chu, which meant that after the Qi army withdrew, Chu was free to invade the Central Plains, just as they had in the past. When that happened, Lord Huan of Qi and Guan Zhong did not raise an army to attack Chu. This poem reads:

> In your dealings with the south, you vacillated for several decades,
> Throwing your allies into complete confusion:
> Proclaiming that you will punish them while plotting to extend your
>   influence,
> Attempting to restore the good name besmirched by your brother.
> In the temple of King Zhao, his lonely soul suffers great pain;
> The states of Jiang and Huang represent a lasting reproach.
> What did this single blood covenant achieve?
> The Central States were still embroiled in bloody warfare.

When Grandee Yuan Taotu of Chen heard the order to stand down the army, he discussed this with Grandee Shen Hou of Zheng. He said, "If the route that this great army takes home runs through Chen and Zheng, we will have to give them food and clothing, which will cost more than we can possibly afford. It would be better if they went home along the coast, which would mean that Xu and Ju would have to provision them. That way our two countries will escape this imposition."

"You are absolutely right," Shen Hou said. "You should try and persuade them."

Yuan Taotu then spoke to Lord Huan. "Your Lordship has attacked the Rong to the north and Chu to the south, so if you were now to take your great coalition army and pacify the Yi peoples to the east, the lords there would be in awe of your military might. Would they dare not to pay court to you?"

"You are quite right," Lord Huan exclaimed.

A short time later, Grandee Shen Hou requested permission to have an audience with him. Lord Huan summoned him, and so Shen Hou came forward and said: "I have heard that one should not keep the army mobilized for too long, for fear of exhausting your people. Your soldiers have been serving you all spring and summer, in frost and hail and wind and rain, and the army is tired out. If you take them home through the states of Chen and Zheng, they will have to provision you and give your troops clothing and shoes, which is the least that they can do. If you were to try and go home by sea, the Yi peoples in the east might well decide to attack, in which case you would have to fight in most disadvantageous circumstances. Why should you do that? Yuan Taotu only cares about his own country, and that is why he suggested such a stupid plan. Your Lordship ought to consider the true state of affairs!"

"He almost managed to get me into real trouble!" Lord Huan said crossly. He gave orders to have Yuan Taotu arrested and ordered the Earl of Zheng to give the lands of Hulao to Shen Hou as a reward for his excellent advice. Grandee Shen Hou thus massively increased the size of his fief, which stretched the length of the country. The Earl of Zheng had to follow His Lordship's commands, but he was not at all happy about it. The Marquis of Chen sent an ambassador to give bribes to Qi and apologized again and again for his mistakes, so Lord Huan agreed to pardon Yuan Taotu. Each of the lords then returned to his own country. Lord Huan had been deeply impressed by all that Guan Zhong had done, so he took three hundred households away from the fief of the Bo family of grandees and presented them to him, to augment his holdings.

. . .

When the king of Chu heard that the allied army of the lords of the Central States had withdrawn, he did not want to give the tribute of herbs.

"You cannot betray your word to Qi," Qu Wan told him. "Chu has been the only state to break off diplomatic links with the Zhou king, and so far the only result has been to allow Qi to step into the breach and make themselves much more important than they were before. If we take advantage of this opportunity to open up our own lines of communication with Zhou, then we are on an equal footing with Qi."

"What is to be done about the fact that we are both kings?" the king of Chu inquired.

"Don't mention your title," Qu Wan said. "Just say that you are a foreigner living far away, and that will be fine."

The king of Chu followed his advice, invested Qu Wan as his ambassador, and gave him ten carts of sweet herbs, as well as gold and silk, to present as tribute to the Son of Heaven. King Hui of Zhou was thrilled by this development, and proclaimed: "Chu has refused to pay tribute to us for a long time. Now they are being so generous, it must be thanks to the beneficent influences of our former kings!"

He reported these events to the ancestral temples of Kings Wen and Wu, and afterwards gave a present of sacrificial meat to Chu. His Majesty said to Qu Wan, "Stay in the south and stop invading the Central States." Qu Wan bowed twice, kowtowed, and withdrew.

When Qu Wan left, Lord Huan of Qi sent Xi Peng to follow after him and report the submission of the kingdom of Chu to the Zhou court. King Hui treated Xi Peng with the utmost courtesy. But when he requested permission to be allowed to meet the crown prince, King Hui seemed unhappy about this. He ordered both Prince Dai and Crown Prince Zheng to appear. Xi Peng observed King Hui minutely, and he seemed confused and weak. When Xi Peng returned from his embassy to Zhou, he said to Lord Huan, "There is going to be a civil war in Zhou."

"Why?" Lord Huan asked.

"The Zhou king's oldest son is named Zheng, and he is the son of Her Late Majesty, Queen Jiang," Xi Peng explained. "Although he has already been formally appointed as crown prince and sent to live in the East Palace, ever since the death of Queen Jiang, one of His Majesty's secondary consorts, Lady Gui of Chen, has been much favored, and he has appointed her as his new queen. She has a son named Prince Dai, who is absolutely charming. The Zhou king loves the prince and calls him by the honorific title "Taishu"—that means that he must want to depose the crown prince and establish Prince Dai in his place. I noticed that His Majesty looked uncertain, which must be because he is worrying about this matter. I am afraid that we are going to repeat the history of King You and Bao Si. Your Lordship is the Master of Covenants; you must come up with some plan to prevent this!"

Afterwards, Lord Huan summoned Guan Zhong and discussed the situation with him. Guan Zhong said, "I have a plan to stabilize the situation in Zhou."

"What do you suggest?" Lord Huan asked.

"The position of the crown prince is threatened, and his faction has become isolated," Guan Zhong explained. "Your Lordship should now inform the Zhou king: 'The feudal lords would like to see the crown prince, so please send him to meet us!' Once the crown prince has been formally presented to us, it is clear that he will be the future king. Even if His Majesty wants to depose him, it will be very difficult to do so."

"Good!" Lord Huan exclaimed. He then sent a message to the other lords summoning them to a meeting at Shouzhi in the summer of the following year. He also sent Xi Peng back to the Zhou Royal Domain to say, "The aristocrats would like to meet the crown prince. This is an expression of their respect for the Zhou royal house."

King Hui of Zhou naturally did not want the crown prince to attend this meeting, but Qi was so strong and they had phrased their request in such a respectful way that it would be difficult to refuse. He simply had to agree. Xi Peng went back to Qi to report this.

. . .

The following year in the spring, Lord Huan sent Chen Jingzhong to go on ahead to Shouzhi and build a traveling palace at which the crown prince could stay. In the fifth month, the lords of the eight states of Qi, Song, Lu, Chen, Wey, Zheng, Xu, and Cao all arrived at Shouzhi. Crown Prince Zheng was also present, staying at his traveling palace. Lord Huan led the other lords in a delegation to decide the order of precedence. Prince Zheng refused time and again to take charge, and he insisted on using the rituals appropriate from a guest towards his host when he had an audience with Lord Huan.

"We all belong to minor houses," Lord Huan told him. "Having an audience with you, my prince, is the same as having an audience with the king. How could we dare not to kowtow to you?"

Prince Zheng refused to accept this honor, saying, "Please don't."

That night Crown Prince Zheng sent someone to summon Lord Huan to the traveling palace, whereupon he told him all about Prince Dai's plans to usurp his position.

"We will swear a blood covenant supporting your accession to the throne," Lord Huan assured him. "You have nothing to worry about."

Crown Prince Zheng was profoundly grateful and stayed happily at his traveling palace. The other lords did not dare to go home, so each had to stay in his own guesthouse; they took turns hosting banquets for one another and feasting each other's retinues. Crown Prince Zheng was afraid that he was putting them to a lot of trouble and expense, so he wanted to say goodbye and return home to the capital.

"The reason we are all willing to stay here with you is because we want His Majesty to realize that we support your position as the crown prince," Lord Huan said. "If we refuse to give up on you, that will prevent any conspiracy to depose you. We are now in the heat of summer, so you will have to wait until the cooling breezes of autumn for us to escort you back to the royal court."

A date was then selected for a covenant to be sworn, and it was decided that the eighth month would be auspicious.

When King Hui of Zhou realized that his son was not coming home any time soon, he understood that the Marquis of Qi intended to support his accession to the throne. He was very unhappy about this, and the queen and Prince Dai spent all day every day with him, making sure that he was fully aware of their opinions on the subject. The chancellor, Kong, Duke of Zhou, came to have an audience, and the king said to him: "The Marquis of Qi is said to have attacked Chu, but I do not believe it. Now Chu presents tribute to us, but it is much less than before. I am not sure that recent events prove that Chu is in any way inferior to Qi. Qi is now in cahoots with the other lords to keep Crown Prince Zheng abroad—what do they mean by this? Do I have any authority left at all? I would like you to send a secret message to the Earl of Zheng, asking him to seek an alliance with Chu. Tell him to work hard to support Zhou and not to let me down."

Chancellor Kong presented his opinion: "It is thanks to Qi's efforts that Chu now pays tribute to us at all. Why should Your Majesty abandon a long-standing alliance with your uncle, the Marquis of Qi, in favor of an agreement with a bunch of southern barbarians?"

"If the Earl of Zheng does not leave, the other lords will not abandon the field," King Hui said. "How else can we guarantee that Qi is not plotting something to our detriment? My mind is made up, say nothing more."

Chancellor Kong did not dare say another word.

King Hui sealed his letter with the royal seal and enclosed it in a box, which he handed to Chancellor Kong. Chancellor Kong had no idea of what the letter said, but he had to order someone to take it to the Earl of Zheng, traveling by the light of the stars. When the Earl of Zheng opened the letter and read it, this is what it said:

Prince Zheng has disobeyed my orders and set up his own faction at court. He is not suitable to be crown prince, and it is my intention to make Prince Dai my successor. If you, my uncle, would abandon your alliance with Qi and establish an accord with Chu, you can together support my younger son. In that case, I would be prepared to restore the offices at court formerly held by the earls of Zheng to you.

The Earl of Zheng said happily, "Our former rulers, Lord Wu and Lord Zhuang, both held hereditary positions as ministers at the royal court and were the acknowledged leaders of the aristocrats. Unfortunately, this situation was suddenly altered and we were relegated to the ranks of the minor states. Although Lord Li played a major role in restoring the king to power, he was not rewarded by being summoned to resume office. Now His Majesty gives this command to me, so in the not-too-distant future, I will be accepting the congratulations of all my ministers!"

Grandee Kong Shu remonstrated: "Qi sent its army into Chu on our behalf. It would be very ungrateful of you to betray Qi now and go to work for Chu. Besides which, it would only be right to support the crown prince. It is not a good idea for Your Lordship to be the only one to refuse to help him."

"Which is better, obeying a hegemon or obeying His Majesty?" the Earl of Zheng demanded. "Besides which, the king does not care for the crown prince, so why should I put myself out in his cause?"

"The kings of Zhou have always been the oldest son of the queen," Kong Shu said. "As Your Lordship well knows, King You loved Bofu; King Huan loved Prince Ke; and King Zhuang loved Prince Tui. However, if the people do not support the accession of a particular prince, any attempt to place him on the throne will simply end in disaster. It would be bad enough to see Your Lordship be the only one to refuse to support the accession of the crown prince, but please do not also follow in the footsteps of the five grandees who helped King You to depose his heir. You will regret it!"

"Who would dare to disobey an order from the Son of Heaven?" Grandee Shen Hou asked. "If you agree to a blood covenant with Qi, then you are offending against His Majesty's commands. If we leave, then the other lords are sure to wonder about the reason. If they are worried that something is going on, then they are sure to disperse without swearing a covenant. Besides which, just as the crown prince has supporters outside the Royal Domain, Prince Dai has his own faction at the royal court. If the two princes start fighting, it is not at all clear who will win. It would be better for us simply to go home and await further developments."

Lord Wen of Zheng followed Shen Hou's advice, and, making the excuse of an urgent matter that he needed to attend to at home, he left without saying goodbye to anyone. When Lord Huan of Qi heard that the Earl of Zheng had disappeared, he was absolutely furious and wanted to punish Zheng in the crown prince's name. However, Guan Zhong came forward and said, "The state of Zheng borders on the Zhou Royal Domain, so the king must have sent someone to do a deal with him. One person may have left, but that is no reason to disrupt our plans. The auspicious date for swearing the blood covenant is almost upon us—wait until that is over before you make any further plans."

"You are right," Lord Huan said. He immediately held a blood covenant on top of the old sacrificial platform at Shouzhi, together with the rulers of Song, Lu, Chen, Wey, Xu, and Cao. Crown Prince Zheng was present on this occasion, though he did not smear his mouth with blood. This made it clear that none of the lords would dare to oppose Prince Zheng's accession. The wording of the covenant said: "The participants in this covenant agree to join together to support the crown prince and bring peace to the royal house. May anyone who betrays this agreement be killed by the Bright Spirits!"

When it was over, Crown Prince Zheng went down the steps and bowed to them. He said gratefully, "Thanks to the beneficent influences of our former kings, you, my lords, have not forgotten your duties to the royal house, and you have become my friends. From the time of the founders of the dynasty, King Wen and King Wu, you have all done well in supporting us. I will never forget what you have done for me!"

The feudal lords all bowed and kowtowed. The following day, Crown Prince Zheng expressed his intention of going home, and the lords all sent chariots and infantry to guard him. Lord Huan of Qi and the Marquis of Wey personally escorted him out of the borders of the state of Wey. Crown Prince Zheng said goodbye to them with tears in his eyes.

A historian wrote a poem praising this:

His Majesty's partiality put the succession in danger;
The Earl of Zheng was happy to betray the cause of righteousness.
The covenant at Shouzhi confirmed the position of the crown prince,
The proper principles of good government thus escaped from harm.

When Lord Wen of Zheng heard that the lords had all sworn a blood covenant that meant that they could punish him for his disloyalty, he did not dare obey Chu's commands any more.

When King Cheng of Chu heard that Zheng had not attended the blood covenant at Shouzhi, he said happily, "Zheng is on my side!" He sent a messenger to Grandee Shen Hou, indicating his wish to restore his previous good relationship with Zheng. Grandee Shen Hou had at one time served in the Chu court and was an excellent orator. Although he was a greedy man, he was also very charming, and King Wen of Chu favored and trusted him greatly. When King Wen was on his deathbed, he was afraid that his successor would not be able to tolerate Shen Hou, so he gave him a white jade disc and told him to flee and seek asylum in a foreign country. Shen Hou then fled to Zheng and ended up working for Lord Li when he was in exile in Yue. Lord Li favored him and trusted him just as much as King Wen of Chu had, so when Lord Li was restored to power in Zheng, he became a grandee. Naturally, the ministers in Chu were all old friends and acquaintances of Shen Hou, and now that they wanted to open communications, they found that he was ready and waiting to persuade Zheng to abandon its alliance with Qi and throw its lot in with Chu.

Shen Hou spoke in private to the Earl of Zheng. "It is only Chu that can withstand the might of Qi. What can a royal mandate do to change that? If you do not handle this situation very carefully, you will find that you have made both Qi and Chu into your enemies. Zheng will then be truly doomed!"

Lord Wen of Zheng was completely misled by his words. He instructed Shen Hou to begin secret negotiations with Chu.

. . .

In the twenty-third year of the reign of King Hui of Zhou, Lord Huan of Qi led his allies among the feudal lords on campaign against Zheng, and they besieged the city of Xinmi. At that time Shen Hou was still in Chu, and he told King Cheng of Chu: "The reason that Zheng is prepared to give its allegiance to Your Majesty is because they are aware that Chu is the only country that can withstand the might of Qi. If Your Majesty does not rescue Zheng, I will have failed in my mission!"

The king of Chu accordingly discussed a plan of campaign with his ministers. Grand Vizier Ziwen stepped forward and said, "Lord Mu of Xu died in the campaign at Shaoling, which deeply upset Qi. If anything were to happen to Xu, Qi would do their very best to prevent it. Your Majesty would do well to send an army to Xu, for then the lords will be forced to go to their rescue, thereby relieving the siege of Zheng!"

The king of Chu followed this advice and personally commanded the attack on Xu, in which they laid siege to the capital city. When the lords heard that Xu had been surrounded, they abandoned Zheng to go to their rescue, and the Chu army then withdrew. Shen Hou went home to Zheng, thinking that it was entirely thanks to him that Zheng had survived. He was very pleased with himself and confidently expected to have his fief increased. The Earl of Zheng, on the other hand, felt that Shen Hou already had more land than was good for him, particularly after he had been rewarded with territory in Hulao. He was also not prepared to grant him a more senior title. Shen Hou could not refrain from complaining.

The following year in the spring, Lord Huan of Qi led his army back for a second assault on Zheng. Grandee Yuan Taotu of Chen had become an enemy of Shen Hou following his behavior after the attack on Chu. He now wrote a letter to Kong Shu:

The reason that Shen Hou wanted to make up to Qi was purely because he wanted to be rewarded with the lands of Hulao. Now he is trying to make up to Chu, causing the Earl of Zheng to renege on his promises and betray his alliances, which will only result in the outbreak of war, bringing disaster upon your country and your people. You must kill Shen Hou, for then the Qi army will go away without a fight.

Kong Shu showed this letter to Lord Wen of Zheng. In the past the Earl of Zheng had ignored Kong Shu's advice and thus run away without participating in the blood covenant, but since that time the Qi army had invaded twice, and he was feeling very ashamed of what he had done. He was perfectly happy to throw all the blame onto Shen Hou. He therefore summoned Shen Hou and upbraided him: "You said that only Chu would be able to withstand the might of the Qi army! Now they have invaded us time and again—where is the assistance from Chu?"

Shen Hou attempted to prevaricate, but the Earl of Zheng shouted to his guards to drag him out of the palace and behead him. He had his head placed in a box, which he gave to Kong Shu to present to the Qi army with these words: "I made the mistake of listening to Grandee Shen Hou's advice, and that is why I ended up betraying the alliance between our two countries. Now I have executed him and instructed my ministers to apologize to you on my behalf. I hope that you can forgive me!"

The Marquis of Qi was very aware of Kong Shu's brilliance, so he agreed to make peace with Zheng. He summoned all the aristocrats to a meeting at Ningmu. Lord Wen of Zheng was still thinking about the mandate that he had received from the king. In the end he did not dare to go to the meeting in person, but he sent his heir, the Honorable Hua, to participate in the meeting at Ningmu in his stead.

The Honorable Hua and his younger brother, the Honorable Zang, were both the sons of the Countess of Zheng. Her Ladyship was originally much favored by the earl, and so he appointed Hua as his scion. Later on, he married a further two junior wives, both of whom gave birth to sons. As a result, the countess gradually lost favor, and not long afterwards she became ill and died. A daughter of the Jí ruling house of the state of Nanyan had come to the Zheng palace as one of His Lordship's junior wives. Before she had been presented to him, she had a dream one night in which a very handsome man appeared, holding an orchid in one hand. He said to the girl, "My name is Bochou, and I am one of your ancestors. I now give this orchid to you as a sign that you will have a son and he will bring great fame to your state." Then he handed her the flower. When she woke up, the whole room was filled with a rich perfume, and when she told her dream, her servants all exclaimed: "You are sure to give birth to a son!" That day, Lord Wen of Zheng happened to catch sight of this girl as he entered the palace, and she pleased him. His entourage looked at each other and giggled. Lord Wen asked the reason for this, and when they explained, he was deeply interested in the dream and said, "What a wonderful omen! Let me make it come true!" He ordered that a bunch of flowers should be presented to her, and he said, "Let this be a sign of my affection for you." That night he summoned her to his bedchamber and got her pregnant, as a result of which she gave birth to a son named Lan, or "Orchid." As this young woman gradually advanced in His Lordship's favor, people called her Lady Jí of Yan.

Scion Hua saw how much his father loved her and was afraid that at some point in the future he himself would be demoted, so he went to Shu Zhan in secret to plot against his father's wife.

"It is Heaven's will if you succeed to His Lordship's title," Shu Zhan informed him. "All you have to do is carry out your filial duty." Afterwards, Scion Hua also went to talk to Shu Kong, who urged him to be filial too. Hua went home in a rage.

The Honorable Zang was a very strange character. At one point he collected some snipe feathers, which he wore in his hat. Shi Shu said, "Your clothing contravenes the rules of ritual propriety. I hope that you will not wear it again!" The Honorable Zang was annoyed by the blunt terms in which he had spoken and complained to his older brother about this. This is the reason why Scion Hua became alienated from the three grandees: Shu Zhang, Kong Shu, and Shi Shu.

When the Earl of Zheng sent Scion Hua to represent him at the meeting at Ningmu, Hua was afraid that the Marquis of Qi would be angry to see him rather than his father, so he did not want to go. Shu Zhan encouraged him to hurry up and set off. Scion Hua was very angry and tried to come up with some sort of plan to ensure his own safety. Thus, when he had an audience with Lord Huan of Qi, he asked permission to dismiss his entourage, saying, "The government of the state of Zheng is dominated by the three clans of Xie, Kong, and Ziren. When His Lordship ran away without making the blood covenant with you, this was in fact their idea. If you could kill these three senior ministers for me, I will guarantee that Zheng will serve Qi as a vassal state."

"Splendid," Lord Huan said.

He subsequently reported Scion Hua's plan to Guan Zhong. Guan Zhong kept saying, "No! No! The reason that the other lords obey you is because you always behave with ritual propriety and keep faith with them. For a son to disobey his father's orders is not ritually correct. To come to reaffirm a long-standing alliance and then use this opportunity to foment a rebellion backed by a foreign power is disloyal. Besides which, I have heard that the current representatives of these three clans are all wise ministers, and thus the people of Zheng call them the 'Three Good Men.' You are honored as the Master of Covenants because people trust you to do what is right. If you were to offend against the people's principles and act in a reckless and insensitive way, it would cause disaster. In my humble opinion, Scion Hua is the kind of schemer who will have to be gotten rid of. Your Lordship ought not to agree to anything that he wants to do."

"What you have told me touches on a great matter of state," Lord Huan told Scion Hua. "I will wait until I can talk to the Earl of Zheng in person and then make a decision."

Scion Hua turned bright red and the sweat poured down his back, but he had to say goodbye politely and go home to Zheng. Guan Zhong was disgusted by Scion Hua's wickedness, so he leaked the substance of his discussions with the Marquis of Qi to the Zheng ambassador and made sure that someone reported this back to the Earl of Zheng.

When Scion Hua reported back on his mission, he simply lied about it: "The Marquis of Qi was deeply angry that you did not go in person, so he is not willing to make peace with us. We had better try and reaffirm our alliance with Chu."

"You have betrayed our country, you bastard!" the Earl of Zheng shouted. "How dare you lie to me?" He ordered his servants to imprison Scion Hua in the Cold Palace. Scion Hua dug a hole in the wall and attempted to escape, for which the Earl of Zheng executed him, just as Guan Zhong had thought he would. The Honorable Zang fled to Song, but the Earl of Zheng sent someone to pursue him and killed him en route. The Earl of Zheng deeply appreciated the fact that Qi had spurned Scion Hua's plotting, and so he sent Kong Shu back to Qi to express his thanks and ask for a blood covenant.

Master Hu Zeng wrote a poem evaluating history, which reads:

The "Three Good Men" of Zheng were like the pillars of a hall:
If suddenly the pillars were to be removed, the hall would not remain
    standing.
Scion Hua disobeyed his father and plotted to seize sole control of the
    country;
After his death, all that remained was a reputation as an unfilial son.

This happened in the twenty-fourth year of the reign of King Hui of Zhou.

• • •

That winter, King Hui of Zhou became critically ill. Crown Prince Zheng was afraid that the queen would launch a coup, and so before this could happen he sent Prince Hu to report the problem to Qi. A short time later, King Hui died. Crown Prince Zheng discussed the matter with Kong, Duke of Zhou, and Liao, Duke of Shao, and they decided not to announce the demise of His Majesty, but to send someone secretly under cover of darkness to take a message to Prince Hu. Prince Hu discussed the situation with the Marquis of Qi, and he held a great meeting of many of the other lords at Tao, at which Lord Wen of Zheng came in person to take part in the concluding blood covenant. On this occasion eight feudal lords smeared their mouths with blood: the rulers of Qi, Song, Lu, Wey, Chen, Zheng, Cao, and Xu. Each of them then wrote an official document to state that he would send a senior grandee to Zhou. These grandees were Xi Peng from the state of Qi; Hua Xiulao from the state of Song; Noble Grandson Ao from the state of Lu; Ning Su from the state of Wei; Yuan Xuan from the state of Chen; Ziren Shi from the state of Zheng; the Honorable Wu from the state of Cao; and Bai Tuo from the state of Xu. The grandees of these eight states set off one after the other, forming a most magnificent spectacle. In the name of asking after the health of the king, they assembled outside the walls of the Zhou capital. Prince Hu hurried on ahead to report. Crown Prince Zheng then summoned Liao, Duke of Shao, to thank him for all his hard work, and they made the arrangements for the funeral of His Late Majesty. The various grandees all requested permission to be allowed to stay and have an audience with the new king. The dukes of Zhou and Shao assisted Crown Prince Zheng through the funerary ceremonies. The grandees then took advantage of the situation to announce that they had received orders from their respective rulers to condole with His Majesty and openly requested that Crown Prince Zheng should ascend the throne. His ministers offered their congratulations. He was thus crowned King Xiang. Although the queen dowager and Prince Dai were unhappy about this, they did not dare show any open signs of their displeasure. The following year was declared the first year of the reign of King Xiang of Zhou, and a notice to this effect was circulated to each state.

In the first year of the reign of King Xiang of Zhou, at the completion of the Spring Sacrifices, he ordered his prime minister, Kong, Duke of Zhou, to take the sacrificial meats and present them to Qi to thank them for their assistance. When Lord Huan of Qi heard this news, he assembled the feudal lords at Kuiqiu for a second time.

Lord Huan of Qi was on the road, and he happened to mention the situation in Zhou to Guan Zhong.

"The royal family has stopped maintaining proper distinctions between the children of the queen and the offspring of concubines, and this nearly ended in disaster," Guan Zhong told him. "Your Lordship has still not officially appointed an heir, and you should do so as soon as possible to avoid problems in the future."

"I have six sons, and they are all the children of concubines," Lord Huan mused. "The oldest is Wukui, the cleverest is Zhao. I have been married to the Senior Lady Ji of Wey for the longest, so by that measure I ought to appoint Wukui as my heir. Yi Ya and Shu Diao have spoken to me about this many times. However, I think Zhao is by far the best of my sons, and that is why I have not yet made any appointment. The decision is now in your hands, Elder Zhong!"

Guan Zhong knew well that Yi Ya and Shu Diao were corrupt and wicked men who had been bribed by the Senior Lady Ji of Wey, and he was afraid that if at some point in the future the Honorable Wukui did indeed become ruler, the government of the country would be ripped apart by factional fighting. The Honorable Zhao was the son of Lady Ji of Zheng, and now Zheng had been joined with Qi in a blood covenant, so in the future there should be peace between these two countries. Therefore, he replied: "If you wish your son to inherit the position of hegemon as well as the marquisate, you will have to appoint Zhao as your heir. You know how clever Zhao is, so you should establish him as scion."

"I am afraid that Wukui will cause trouble on the grounds that he is my oldest son," Lord Huan said. "What can I do about this?"

"It is all thanks to Your Lordship that the position of the Zhou king has been stabilized," Guan Zhong pointed out. "You have now called a great meeting to hold a blood covenant, so you should make use of this opportunity to select the very wisest of the feudal lords and entrust the Honorable Zhao to him. What disaster could threaten him then?" Lord Huan nodded his head.

When he arrived at Kuiqiu, the other feudal lords were all present already, including the prime minister, Kong, Duke of Zhou. Each was staying in his own guesthouse. At that time Yushuo, Lord Huan of Song, had recently died, and his scion, Cifu, had attempted to cede the title to the Honorable Muyi. The Honorable Muyi had refused to accept this, so Cifu had succeeded to the title as Lord Xiang of Song. Lord Xiang was most respectful of the commands of the Master of Covenants, so even though he was recently bereaved, he did not dare to refuse to attend and arrived at the meeting in the deepest black mourning clothes.

"The Duke of Song tried to cede the title to another man whom he believed to be more worthy," Guan Zhong remarked to Lord Huan, "so he must be a most noble character. He has come to attend this covenant in his black mourning clothes, so he clearly respects us a great deal. He is the right person to entrust with the job of supporting your heir."

Lord Huan followed his advice. He ordered Guan Zhong to summon Lord Xiang of Song to his guesthouse in secret, whereupon he informed him of the Marquis of Qi's intentions. Lord Xiang then went in person to have an audience with the Marquis of Qi. Lord Huan grabbed hold of his hand and entrusted the Honorable Zhao to his care, repeating his instructions over and over: "In the future, with your support, he will be able to preside over the state altars."

Lord Xiang was embarrassed and refused on the grounds that he could not possibly undertake so important a task. However, he fully appreciated the sincerity of the Marquis of Qi's wishes, and in his heart he agreed to accept this charge.

On the day of the meeting, everyone appeared in the most magnificent of robes and hats, the jade discs and pendants hanging by their sides chiming together tunefully. The aristocrats gave way to allow the representative of the Zhou king to be the first to ascend the platform—then the remainder followed in order of seniority. An empty place had been left there to represent the Son of Heaven, and the lords all faced north and kowtowed to it, just as they would at the royal court. Afterwards, they each took their own place. The prime minister, Kong, Duke of Zhou, lifted up the sacrificial meats and then took his place facing east, at which point he announced the new king's first commands: "The Son of Heaven has performed a sacrifice to the founders of the dynasty, Kings Wen and Wu, and now the sacrificial meats are presented to his uncle." The Marquis of Qi was about to go down from the platform to bow and accept this gift, but the Duke of Zhou stopped him, saying, "His Majesty further instructed me that, given that you are so advanced in years and have achieved so much in the service of the king, he gives you a dispensation. There is no need for you to go down and bow."

Lord Huan was about to agree to this, but Guan Zhong stepped forward from his place to one side and said, "Even if His Majesty is prepared to humble himself in this way, his subjects must still show their respect to him!"

"No royal prerogatives should ever be infringed," Lord Huan proclaimed. "I would never dare to forget my position as a royal subject, no matter what His Majesty may order." He quickly descended the stairs, bowed twice and kowtowed, and then climbed back up to receive the sacrificial meats. The other aristocrats were all deeply impressed by the reverence with which Qi performed these rituals.

Since the feudal lords had not yet dispersed, Lord Huan took this opportunity to announce a new blood covenant at which the "Five Prohibitions" of the Zhou dynasty would be sworn: "Do not block up a water source! Do not interfere in the sales of basic foodstuffs! Do not dispossess your oldest son! Do not appoint your concubine to be your wife! Do not allow women to interfere in the government!" The oath read: "Let those who swear this covenant with me abide by its wording." This was written down and the document placed on top of the sacrificial animal. Each of the participants then read it aloud, but they did not kill the beast or smear their lips with blood. The lords all obeyed his instructions to the letter.

A bearded old man wrote a poem that says:

Betrayal and suspicion were rampant in the Spring and Autumn period;
Pacifying Chu and respecting the royal house were simply slogans.
If it were not for Lord Huan of Qi's great victories,
Could anyone have forced the lords to keep their word?

When the ceremonies of the blood covenant had been completed, Lord Huan suddenly said, "I have heard that the first three dynasties in our history held the Feng and the Shan sacrifices. How were they performed? Would it be possible for you to explain them to me?"

"The ancients performed the Feng sacrifice on Mount Tai and the Shan sacrifice on Mount Liangfu," the Duke of Zhou said. "For the Feng sacrifice on Mount Tai, earth is piled up to make a platform, and then gold dust and jade batons are sacrificed to Heaven, to thank Heaven for all that Heaven has done for us. Heaven is high above us, so the place where the sacrifice is performed must be similarly elevated. For the Shan sacrifice on Mount Liangfu, the earth is swept and then the ritual is performed, to correspond to the position of Earth below our feet. The ground is covered with grass mats and rush trenchers form the sacrificial vessels, which are buried once the ceremonies are over in order to requite the blessings that we have received from Earth. The three dynasties arose because they received a mandate to rule and were protected by Heaven and Earth, so that is why we perform such rituals to requite them."

"The capital of the Xia dynasty was at the city of An; the capital of the Shang dynasty was at Bo; while the Zhou capital cities were at Feng and Hao," Lord Huan said thoughtfully. "Mount Tai and Mount Liangfu are both located far away from any of these cities, and yet they still performed the Feng and Shan sacrifices there. These two mountains are today located within the borders of my fief, and I have received great favor from the Zhou Son of Heaven, which would make it appropriate for me to perform these exceptional ceremonies. What do you think of my idea?"

The Duke of Zhou looked at Lord Huan's proud and arrogant bearing, and he replied, "If Your Lordship thinks that is the right thing to do, who would dare to disagree!"

"I will discuss this tomorrow with the other lords," Lord Huan said. The people present at this audience then all went their separate ways.

Prime Minister Kong, Duke of Zhou, then summoned Guan Zhong in secret and said, "It is not appropriate for a mere aristocrat to engage in the Feng and Shan sacrifices. Do you think that you can say anything to stop him, Elder Zhong?"

"His Lordship is a very competitive man, but he is susceptible to private advice if not to open remonstrance," Guan Zhong explained. "I will go and speak to him now!"

That very night he went into Lord Huan's presence and asked him: "Is it true that Your Lordship wishes to perform the Feng and the Shan sacrifices?"

"Why shouldn't it be true?" Lord Huan asked.

"Since high antiquity the Feng and Shan sacrifices have been performed by seventy-two individuals, from the sage-king Wuhuai down to King Cheng of the Zhou dynasty," Guan Zhong said. "These men all received the Mandate of Heaven and then held these sacrifices."

"I have attacked Chu to the south, my armies traveling as far as Shaoling," Lord Huan said crossly. "I have attacked the Mountain Rong to the north, extirpating Lingzhi and Guzhu; to the west, I have traveled as far as the deserts of Taihang—none of the other lords have done the like. I have led a coalition army on three occasions and held six great diplomatic meetings, so I have brought together the lords of the Central States nine times and united the world under my command. When the founders of the three dynasties received the Mandate of Heaven, did any of them do anything that can match my achievements? I would like to perform the Feng sacrifice at Mount Tai and the Shan sacrifice at Mount Liangfu to proclaim my successes to future generations. What is wrong with that?"

"In the past, those who received the Mandate of Heaven were first singled out by auspicious omens," Guan Zhong explained, "and only afterwards prepared the equipment that they would need to perform sacrifices like the Feng. That is why these ceremonies are so important and splendid. The auspicious grain that appeared at Haoshang, the auspicious rice growing at Beili: these are the right kind of good omens. When the couch grass growing between the Yangtze and the Huai Rivers is found to have a triple stem, then it is called Numinous Grass. It grows when the king has received the Mandate of Heaven and is used in the sacrificial vessels for the Shan sacrifice at Mount Liangfu. There are a total of fifteen different kinds of auspicious omens that can appear, such as the Bimu fish from the eastern sea and the Biyi bird from the western sea, which are then recorded in the history books to inspire future generations. There have been no recent reported sightings of phoenixes or kylins, but plenty of owls and other birds of ill omen. No auspicious grains have sprouted, but you can see weeds and brambles wherever you go. I am afraid that if you were to perform the Feng and Shan sacrifices under present circumstances, all the other aristocrats would simply laugh at you."

Lord Huan was silent. The following day he said nothing about the Feng and the Shan sacrifices.

When Lord Huan returned home, he announced that he had achieved an unparalleled success, so he rebuilt his palace on a much grander scale and made it even more beautiful. He now wore identical clothes and rode in the same kind of chariot as the Zhou king. The people of the capital became more and more critical of his unwarranted assumption of royal privileges. Guan Zhong then built a three-story tower within his own mansion, which was called the Three Allegiances Tower. The name referred to the allegiance that the people, the other aristocrats, and the barbarians had all shown to Lord Huan. He also built gatehouses at all the passes and added a platform in front of his ancestral shrine, where he could hold formal meetings with the ambassadors sent by the other lords.

Bao Shuya was worried about this and said, "Is it right that when His Lordship is greedy, you show yourself to be greedy too, and when His Lordship usurps royal privileges, you do so as well?"

"His Lordship has worked very hard and achieved great things, and now he wants to have a bit of fun," Guan Zhong pointed out. "If we were to tie him down too tightly with the prescriptions of what is and is not ritually correct, it would make him unhappy and dissatisfied. The reason why I am doing this is so that I will share in some of the criticism meted out to His Lordship."

Although Bao Shuya made agreeable noises, he thought that this was a mistake.

. . .

Let us now turn now to another part of the story. The prime minister, Kong, Duke of Zhou, said goodbye to the other participants of the meeting at Kuiqiu and went home. On the way, he happened to meet Lord Xian of Jin hurrying the other way. Kong said, "The meeting has already broken up."

Lord Xian stamped his foot and said angrily, "I live so far away that I never get to attend any of these grand events. It is really unreasonable."

"Don't be cross, my lord," Prime Minister Kong said. "Right now the Marquis of Qi believes himself to be the most important person in the world, and it has made him arrogant. But having waxed, the moon will wane; when water fills the basin, it will overflow. Qi's power is just about to be eclipsed—there is nothing to worry about in the fact that you did not attend this meeting."

Lord Xian then turned his chariot around and set off westwards, but he became sick on his journey, and when he arrived back in the state of Jin, he died. Jin then collapsed into civil war.

If you want to know how this civil war in Jin came about, READ ON.

Chapter Twenty-five

Clever Xun Xi destroys Guo after borrowing a road.

Poor Baili Xi is appointed prime minister after feeding his oxen.

Lord Xian of Jin had his mind poisoned by his wife, Lady Li Ji, and he was led astray by the advice given by his ministers, the "Two Wus," to the point where he became increasingly alienated from his heir and gave ever more of his love to his son, Xiqi. But Scion Shensheng was a thoughtful and obedient son, and he had on several occasions commanded the army in victorious campaigns, so there was nothing that anyone could do to get rid of him. Lady Li Ji summoned her lover, the actor Shi, and told him what she really felt about this situation: "I want to get rid of the scion and establish Xiqi in his place. Do you have any plan to accomplish this?"

"His Lordship's three sons are already far away at the borders, so how could they possibly cause trouble for Your Ladyship?" Shi asked.

"They are all young men at the height of their powers," Lady Li Ji pointed out. "They have experience in warfare and in government, and many friends at court. How could I dare to touch them?"

"If that is the case, then why not get rid of them one at a time?" Shi inquired.

"Which should I get rid of first?" Lady Li Ji asked.

"It has to be Shensheng," Shi told her. "He is a very kind and noble character. Since he is so noble, he will be ashamed to appear in the wrong, and given that he is so kind, he will not accept a situation where he causes someone else harm. Someone who is ashamed to appear in the wrong feels particularly humiliated when touched by scandal, while someone who cannot accept a situation where he harms someone else would rather suffer himself. Even though the scion has been sent away, His Lordship knows his son's character well, so if we were to slander him by claiming that he is plotting to rebel, we will never be believed. On the other hand, if Your Ladyship were to start crying in the middle of the night and then slander the scion while appearing to praise him, you would destroy his reputation in just a couple of sentences!"

According to plan, in the middle of the night Lady Li Ji did indeed start crying, and when Lord Xian asked her what was the matter, she refused to say anything. Lord Xian forced her to speak, but Lady Li Ji just said, "Even if I told you, you wouldn't believe me. The reason that I am crying is because I am afraid that I will soon cease to enjoy the pleasure of serving Your Lordship!"

"Why do you speak in such an inauspicious way?" Lord Xian asked.

Lady Li Ji wiped the tears from her eyes and said, "I have heard that Shensheng is a benevolent and kind man. Since he went to live in Quwo, he has been so very good to the people that they would happily die for him. He will certainly want to make use of that fact. Shensheng often says, 'Our lord has been bewitched by his concubine, and this is sure to cause trouble.' Everyone at court has heard him say so—you are the only one to be unaware of his opinion, my lord. I am afraid that in order to bring peace and stability to the country, he may well assassinate you. Why don't you kill me and apologize to Shensheng, thereby putting a stop to his conspiracy? You must not allow the people to suffer the turmoil of a civil war simply for my sake."

"If Shensheng is so kind to the people, why should he not be kind to his own father?" Lord Xian cried.

"That has been worrying me too," Lady Li Ji said. "But then I have heard people say that kindness among ordinary people is not at all the same as kindness among the nobility. An ordinary person would regard loving their family as kindness, but a ruler thinks of things that benefit the whole country. If you are thinking of benefiting the country, then how can you consider the demands of your own family?"

"He has always really valued his good reputation, so is he not afraid of destroying it?" Lord Xian demanded.

"In the past, King You did not kill Crown Prince Yiqiu but sent him to live in Shen," Lady Li Ji replied. "The Marquis of Shen then summoned the Dog Rong, and they killed King You at the foot of Mount Li, whereupon they installed Crown Prince Yiqiu as the new monarch, King Ping. He then became the founder of the Eastern Zhou dynasty.

Right up to the present day, King You's wicked reputation is known to everyone. Who criticizes King Ping?"

Lord Xian was horrified and got up, wrapping himself in his dressing gown. He said, "You are absolutely right! What should I do?"

"You had better declare that you have retired on the grounds of old age and let him take over the government of the country," Lady Li Ji told him. "That way he will have satisfied his ambitions to take control and may perhaps spare your life. Besides which, when Quwo and Yi were disunited in the past, was that not because of feuding among family members? It is only because Lord Wu cared nothing for his own family that the state of Jin was created. Shensheng is just as ambitious as he was. You ought to yield your position to him."

"No!" Lord Xian shouted. "The other lords admire me for my military might and the awe that I have inspired in them. If I now hand over the country in order to save my own life, where is my might? If I cannot even control my own son, where are my awe-inspiring qualities? If I have neither military might nor anything awe-inspiring about me, then I will be completely under the domination of others. That would be a fate worse than death! Do not worry; I have a plan to deal with this!"

"In recent years the Red Di people from the kingdom of Gaoluo have repeatedly invaded our country," Lady Li Ji said. "Why don't you appoint him as a general in command of the army to attack the Di and see if he really can manage his troops? If he is not successful, you can punish him for his failure. On the other hand, if he is successful, he will believe that he is a fine commander and take advantage of his victory to further his conspiracy. You can then execute him, knowing that the people will support your actions. By this plan you will be able to pacify the border regions with a victory over our enemies and find out whether the scion is a capable commander or not. Why do you not send him out on campaign?"

"Good idea," Lord Xian said. He gave orders that Shensheng should lead his army out of Quwo and attack Gaoluo.

The Junior Tutor to the Heir Apparent, Li Ke, was in court, and he remonstrated: "The scion is Your Lordship's deputy. If Your Lordship goes on a journey, it is the scion who should assume regency. It is also the scion's responsibility to oversee the palace meals provided in the morning and in the evening. You cannot send him out to deal with the Di, and you also cannot appoint him to command the army!"

"But Shensheng has already commanded the army on numerous occasions," Lord Xian pointed out.

"At that time he was commanding troops in support of Your Lordship," Li Ke said firmly. "It is not appropriate that he should be given an independent command."

Lord Xian turned his face up to the ceiling and sighed, saying: "I have nine sons, and I have not yet decided who will inherit my title. Do not say any more."

Li Ke withdrew silently and reported this conversation to Hu Tu, who said, "Scion Shensheng is in terrible danger!" He sent a letter to him, warning him not to do battle: "If you win this war, you will bring disaster down upon your own head. Go into exile!"

Scion Shensheng received this letter and said with a sigh, "My father entrusted me with command of the army not because he loves me, but because he is testing my loyalty to him. It would be a terrible crime if I were to disobey my father's orders. If I were to be lucky enough to die in battle, at least I would save my reputation."

He fought Gaoluo at Jisang and defeated them. Afterwards, Shensheng presented the booty from this campaign to Lord Xian.

"The scion is just as good a strategist as we suspected," Lady Li Ji said. "What are we going to do now?"

"He has not actually done anything wrong, so we will simply have to wait," Lord Xian told her.

Hu Tu was pretty sure that the state of Jin was heading towards a civil war, so he used the excuse of chronic ill health to stay at home.

. . .

The two states of Yu and Guo were neighbors, and their ruling houses were members of the same clan, making them very close allies. The lands of both these states abutted the territory of Jin. The Duke of Guo was named Chou. He was a very arrogant and bellicose man who repeatedly invaded the southern regions of Jin. The border officials reported the emergency, and Lord Xian was determined to attack them.

"Why don't you send Shensheng?" Lady Li Ji suggested. "He has an awe-inspiring reputation, and he is good at deploying his troops. He is certain to be victorious."

Lord Xian was quite sure that Lady Li Ji's advice was good, but he was afraid that after Shensheng had defeated Guo, his reputation would be even more well-established and he would be much harder to control. Lord Xian was vacillating, unable to make a decision, so he asked Grandee Xun Xi, "How should I attack Guo?"

"Yu and Guo are allies," Xun Xi replied. "If we attack Guo, Yu is sure to go to their assistance. On the other hand, if we were to attack Yu, Guo would certainly help them. I do not think we can be sure of victory if we have to fight on two fronts."

"In that case, I had better not attack Guo at all," Lord Xian said.

"I have heard that the Duke of Guo is a very debauched man," Xun Xi responded. "If Your Lordship were to collect some beautiful women, have them trained in music and dance, give them some nice clothes to wear, and present them to Guo with a humble request for a peace treaty, the Duke of Guo would be happy to accept. When he is busy enjoying himself with these women, he won't be paying any attention to the government of the country, and he is sure to react badly to any loyal remonstrance. If we then give generous bribes to the Dog Rong and encourage them to raid Guo, we can wait for an opportunity to destroy them."

Lord Xian took his advice and sent a group of women entertainers to Guo. The Duke of Guo wanted to take this gift, but Grandee Zhou Zhiqiao remonstrated: "This is the trap that Jin has set for Guo! Surely you are not going to swallow this bait, my lord?"

The Duke of Guo did not listen to him, but agreed to make peace with Jin. From this point onward he spent every day listening to music and every night in the arms of his new beauties, so he very rarely had any time to spare for government matters. Zhou Zhiqiao remonstrated again, and this time the Duke of Guo got angry and sent him to guard the pass at Xiayang. A short time later the Dog Rong, greedy for Jin's bribes, started raiding Guo's borders. When their forces arrived at the bend in the Wei River, they were defeated by the Guo army. The chief of the Dog Rong then raised a truly massive army. The Duke of Guo wanted to follow up on his previous victory, and so he led his own forces to prevent their advance, resulting in a prolonged stalemate at Sangtian.

Lord Xian again asked Xun Xi what to do: "The Rong and the state of Guo are now at a standstill, so can I attack Guo?"

"Yu and Guo are still allies," Xun Xi replied. "However, I have a plan that will allow you to attack Guo first and then to conquer Yu."

"What is your idea?" Lord Xian asked.

"Your Lordship should give massive bribes to Yu and get them to allow your army to go through their country to attack Guo."

"I have only just made peace with Guo, and I have no reason to attack them," Lord Xian pointed out. "Why would Yu believe me?"

"You should secretly order the people living in your northern territories to go and cause trouble in Guo," Xun Xi told him. "The border officials in Guo are sure to make a fuss. You will then have a reason to ask for the road from Yu."

Lord Xian followed his advice, and the border officials in Guo did indeed start complaining about the problems they were facing. Both sides started mobilizing their forces for an attack. The Duke of Guo was fully occupied dealing with the troubles caused by the Dog Rong, and he simply had no time to spare for this second problem.

"Now I have a very good reason to want to attack Guo!" Lord Xian said happily. "But I am not sure what sort of things I should offer to Yu as bribes."

"The Duke of Yu is greedy," Xun Xi replied, "but he will not agree to our demands for anything less than real treasures. There are two things that you must give him, but I am afraid that Your Lordship cannot bear to part with them."

"Please tell me what those two things are." Lord Xian said.

"Your two favorite possessions: your jade disc and your horses," Xun Xi replied. "Am I not correct in saying that Your Lordship owns a jade disc from Chuiji and a team of horses from Qu? You must use these two things to borrow a road from Yu. Yu will covet our jade and horses, and then they will fall into our trap!"

"They are my greatest treasures! How can I bear to give them to someone else?"

"I knew that you wouldn't agree to part with them," Xun Xi told His Lordship. "However, if we can borrow the road from Yu to attack Guo, then Yu will not go to their assistance and they will be destroyed. Once Guo is gone, Yu cannot survive independently—who will then own the jade and these horses? We are just temporarily sending the jade to another treasury and the horses to another stable."

"Yu has two particularly clever ministers, one named Gong Zhiqi and the other Baili Xi," Grandee Li Ke said. "If they work out what we are up to, I am afraid that they will find a way to prevent it. What do we do then?"

"The Duke of Yu is stupid and greedy," Xun Xi reminded him. "Even if they do remonstrate, he won't pay any attention!"

Lord Xian did indeed give his jade disc and his horses to Xun Xi and sent him to borrow a road from Yu.

. . .

Initially, when the Duke of Yu heard that Jin had come to borrow a road so that they could attack Guo, he was deeply angry. But when he saw the jade disc and the horses, he found his rage turning into delight. As he turned the jade over in his hands and gazed at the horses, he asked Xun Xi, "These are the greatest treasures of your country, and things of this quality are rarely seen in this world. Why are you giving them to me?"

"My lord is deeply aware of your grace's wisdom," Xun Xi flattered him, "and in awe of your grace's military might. He would not dare to keep these treasures for himself, but presents them to you in the hope that you will enjoy them."

"That may be so, but I am sure that you have some request to make of me!" the Duke of Yu said.

"Guo has repeatedly invaded and harassed us from the vantage point of their southern border," Xun Xi replied. "His Lordship, for the sake of the country, begged them for a peace treaty. Now, even though the ink on this treaty is not yet dry, they complain about the situation all the time. His Lordship is hoping to be allowed to take his army through your territory to punish them for this. If we are fortunate enough to defeat them, then the prisoners of war and booty will all be handed over to your grace. My lord hopes that he will then be allowed to swear a blood covenant with you, making us allies for many generations to come."

The Duke of Yu was very pleased, but Gong Zhiqi remonstrated with him: "You must not agree to this, my lord. There is a proverb: 'When the lips are gone, the teeth feel cold.' Jin has already annexed the territory of more than one state that was a member of the same clan. The only reason they have never dared to attack Yu and Guo is because you have been such staunch allies to each other. Once Guo is gone, disaster will quickly overtake us."

"The ruler of Jin has given me these treasures because he wants an alliance with us," the Duke of Yu said. "Why should I care about letting him borrow a road? Besides which, Jin is ten times stronger than Guo. I may lose Guo, but providing that I have this alliance with Jin, will everything not turn out for the best? Go away and stop interfering in my business."

Gong Zhiqi wanted to remonstrate again, but Baili Xi tugged at his sleeve to prevent him. Gong Zhiqi withdrew. Afterwards, he said to Baili Xi, "You could at least have put your oar in to help me, but instead you stopped me from speaking. Why is this?"

"I have heard that presenting good advice to a fool is like scattering pearls and jade across the highway," Baili Xi said. "The wicked King Jie killed Guan Longfeng and the evil King Zhou murdered Prince Bigan because they insisted on remonstrating with him. You were in danger there!"

"Yu is now doomed! Gong Zhiqi said. "Where shall we go now?"

"If you want to leave, you can," Baili Xi told him, "but you will have to go on your own, because taking me with you will simply compound your crime. I am going to stay here."

Gong Zhiqi then left with his whole family, telling no one where he was going.

Xun Xi returned and reported to the Marquis of Jin: "The Duke of Yu has taken our jade and horses and agreed to lend us the road."

Lord Xian wanted to command the attack on Guo in person, but Li Ke had an audience with him and remonstrated on this point: "Guo will be easily conquered now. There is no need to bother Your Lordship to go."

"What is your plan for the conquest of Guo?" Lord Xian inquired.

"The capital city of Guo is at Shangyang, and the route takes us through Xiayang," Li Ke informed him. "Once Xiayang has fallen, Guo cannot survive. Although I am lacking in any particular talent, I can certainly achieve this for you. If by some mischance I am not successful, I will accept any punishment that you choose to mete out."

Lord Xian appointed Li Ke as the commander-in-chief and Xun Xi to assist him, and they led an army of four hundred chariots to attack Guo. However, first they sent an ambassador to inform Yu of the date of their arrival.

"I feel ashamed that I have taken your treasures without doing anything in return," the Duke of Yu said. "I would therefore be happy to provide you with auxiliary troops."

"We would appreciate being given control of the pass at Xiayang much more than any auxiliary troops," Xun Xi told him.

"Xiayang is held by Guo," the Duke of Yu said. "How can I possibly give you control of that pass?"

"I have heard that the Duke of Guo is fighting a huge campaign against the Dog Rong at Sangtian and it is not at all clear who will emerge as the victor," Xun Xi said. "If your grace would announce that you are sending an army to assist them, but secretly allow our Jin soldiers to infiltrate, we can take the pass. I have one hundred armored chariots that you can use for this purpose."

The Duke of Yu agreed to his suggestion.

The general in charge of guarding the pass, Zhou Zhiqiao, did not imagine that there was anything wrong, so he opened the pass to allow the chariots in. There were Jin soldiers hidden in the chariots, and once they had all gone through the pass, they struck. By then, it was far too late to try and shut the gates. Li Ke threw his forces forward, advancing as quickly as he could. Zhou Zhiqiao knew that he had lost Xiayang, and he was afraid that the Duke of Guo would punish him for this, so he surrendered to Jin with all the troops under his command. Li Ke employed him to lead the way for their attack on Shangyang.

All this time, the Duke of Guo was at Sangtian. When he heard that the Jin army had broken through the pass, he immediately stood down his army. However, they were attacked on the retreat by the Dog Rong army and a terrible battle ensued, at which the Duke of Guo suffered a devastating defeat, escaping with only a couple of dozen chariots. He fled back to Shangyang to hide behind the great walls there, but he had no plan at all for how to deal with the crisis in which he found himself. When the Jin army arrived, they laid siege to the city. From the eighth month until the twelfth, Guo fought one losing battle after the other. Meanwhile the city starved, the officers and men were exhausted, and the people wept day and night.

Li Ke had a letter from Zhou Zhiqiao shot into the city, which encouraged the Duke of Guo to surrender.

"My ancestors were all loyal ministers to the Zhou king, and I will never surrender to a mere lord!" the Duke of Guo stated categorically. That night he had the gates to the city opened to allow him and his family to flee to the royal capital. Li Ke did not pursue them.

Finding themselves abandoned, the people of Shangyang were left with no choice but to welcome the Jin army into the city with bouquets of flowers and lit candles. Li Ke made arrangements to keep the populace pacified and prevent his soldiers from harming them in any way, and he ordered his troops to garrison the city. He had all the treasures in the storehouses of Guo loaded onto chariots and presented to the Duke of Yu, together with thirty female entertainers. The Duke of Yu was absolutely delighted with this gift. Li Ke also sent someone to report back to the Marquis of Jin, saying that he was ill and would be resting his army outside the city walls, and that once he had recovered they would set off again. The Duke of Yu sent him medicine and was constantly asking after his health. This went on for more than a month. Then suddenly spies reported: "The Marquis of Jin's army has arrived at the suburbs." The Duke of Yu asked why they had come, and the messenger said, "I am afraid that their attack on Guo has not gone very well, so His Lordship has come in person to take charge."

"I have been wanting to meet the Marquis of Jin face-to-face," the Duke of Yu said. "Now that he is here in person, it is like an answer to my prayers."

He rushed out to the suburbs to meet him with gifts of food. When the two lords met, they thanked each other profusely, which does not need to be described in any detail.

Lord Xian went hunting with the Duke of Yu at Mount Ji. The Duke of Yu wanted to show off to his guests from Jin, so he took all his soldiers and horses out of the city and held bets with the Marquis of Jin over the bag. That day in the middle of the afternoon, before the battue was over, suddenly someone reported: "Fire has broken out in the city."

"Someone must have set fire to their house," Lord Xian remarked. "I daresay they will put it out in no time at all." He suggested that they set up a second battue.

Grandee Baili Xi whispered in the duke's ear, "I am told that there has been some sort of uprising in the city—Your Lordship cannot stay here a moment longer!"

The Duke of Yu said goodbye to the Marquis of Jin and insisted on going home. As he made his way back to the city, he found refugees running towards him in panic, screaming, "The Jin army took advantage of your absence to make a surprise attack! They have captured the city!"

The Duke of Yu was furious and shouted, "Get our chariots back to the city as fast as you can!"

When they arrived at the foot of the city walls, they could see a single general standing at the gatehouse, leaning over the railing, his armor glinting in the sunshine, looking extremely serious. He shouted to the Duke of Yu: "First you gave us a road, and now you have given us your country. Many thanks for your generosity!"

In his rage, the Duke of Yu wanted to attack the gate. But then a sound like that of a watchman's rattle could be heard from the top of the city walls, and arrows fell like rain. The Duke of Yu ordered his chariots to retreat as quickly as possible and sent someone to round up the forces coming along behind him. A soldier reported: "The reason why the rest of the army has been delayed is because they have been under constant attack by the Jin army. Some people surrendered and some have been killed, and all your remaining chariots have been captured. The main force of the Jin army, under the command of the marquis, is just about to arrive!"

The Duke of Yu realized that it would now be impossible for him either to advance or to retreat. He just sighed and said, "I wish I had listened to Gong Zhiqi's remonstrance."

He turned his head towards Baili Xi, who was standing to one side, and asked, "Why didn't you say something to stop me?"

"You weren't prepared to listen to Gong Zhiqi, so why would you have listened to me?" Baili Xi pointed out. "The reason that I did not say anything then was to make sure that I would still be here with you today!"

As the Duke of Yu was caught in this dangerous situation, he noticed that a single chariot was speeding towards him. When he looked more closely, he realized that it was General Zhou Zhiqiao, who had surrendered from the state of Guo. The Duke of Yu looked terribly ashamed of himself.

"You made a dreadful mistake when you betrayed your alliance with Guo, and now you have lost everything," Zhou Zhiqiao told him. "If you are planning to seek sanctuary abroad, you had best make a deal with Jin. The Marquis of Jin is a very magnanimous and sensible man, who will certainly not hurt you. Since he feels sorry for you, he will treat you generously. Do not worry about that!"

The Duke of Yu did not know what to do for the best. Just at that moment, Lord Xian of Jin arrived in person and sent someone to ask the Duke of Yu if he would meet him face-to-face. The Duke of Yu had no choice but to go. Lord Xian laughed and said, "I am here to see that I get full value for my jade disc and my horses." He ordered that the Duke of Yu should be made to ride in a chariot behind his own and be taken to stay in the army camp. Baili Xi followed, as close as he could get. Some people criticized him for going, but he simply said: "I have been in His Lordship's employment for a long time, and I am doing this to requite his kindness to me."

Lord Xian entered the city and calmed the populace, while Xun Xi came forward with the jade disc in his left hand, leading the team of horses with his right hand.

"My plan worked," he said. "With your permission I will now return this jade to your treasury and these horses to your stables." Lord Xian was very pleased.

A bearded old man wrote a poem about this:

Although this jade disc and these horses were very valuable,
How can they be compared with a whole country?
It would not be right to praise Xun Xi for his clever ploy,
You should just laugh at the Duke of Yu for being so stupid!

Lord Xian returned home with the Duke of Yu as his prisoner, with the intention of executing him.

"The man is a moron," Xun Xi said. "What can he do to hurt you?" Afterwards, the Marquis of Jin treated him with all the ceremony due to a member of a ruling house living in exile, and gave him a different jade disc and another team of horses, saying, "I have not forgotten that you were so kind as to allow me to take my army through your territory."

When Zhou Zhiqiao arrived in Jin, he was appointed to the position of a grandee. He then recommended Baili Xi for office. Lord Xian also wanted to employ Baili Xi in his government, and sent Zhou Zhiqiao to communicate this to him.

"You will have to wait until the Duke of Yu is dead before I will take office with anyone else," Baili Xi said.

After Zhou Zhiqiao had taken his leave, Baili Xi sighed and said, "When a gentleman leaves his country, he does not live in an enemy state, let alone take office there! I will never take office in Jin!"

Zhou Zhiqiao heard what he said and thought him very short-sighted. He was extremely unhappy to have failed in his mission.

. . .

At this time Renhao, Lord Mu of Qin, had been ruling for six years, but he had not yet established a principal wife. He therefore sent one of his grandees, the Honorable Zhi, to request a marriage alliance with the state of Jin, asking for the hand in marriage of Lady Bo Ji, the oldest daughter of the Marquis of Jin. Lord Xian ordered Grand Astrologer Su to perform a milfoil divination about this, and he obtained the hexagram "The Marrying Maiden." The text said:

> The man cuts up his sheep, but there is no blood; the girl presents her basket, but there is no gift in it. The neighbor to the west reproaches us for not keeping our word, and there can be no amends.

Grand Astrologer Su made a play on these words, suggesting that since the state of Qin was located to the west and it said something about being reproached for not keeping one's word, it meant that this was not an auspicious omen. Besides which, the hexagram "The Marrying Maiden" is clearly an omen for the wedding. If you reverse the two trigrams "Fire" and "Thunder" that make up the hexagram "The Marrying Maiden," you get the hexagram "Polarizing." Both "Polarizing" and "Fire" are inauspicious. He suggested that His Lordship should not agree to this marriage.

Lord Xian then ordered the Grand Diviner Guo Yan to perform a divination using a turtle shell. Guo Yan inspected the cracks and pronounced it extremely auspicious. He proclaimed:

> The cypress and the pine are neighbors, and from one generation to the next they have treated each other as uncle and nephew. Three times they have settled our lord. This is auspicious for a wedding, but inauspicious for warfare.

The Grand Astrologer Su continued to stick stubbornly to the words of his divination.

"Last time, didn't you say 'You should pay attention to the turtle-shell divination and not to that obtained from milfoil'?" Lord Xian demanded. "If this turtle-shell divination is auspicious, why should I hesitate? I have heard that the ruling house of Qin has received a mandate from God on High, and so in the future this is sure to be a great country. I cannot refuse this marriage alliance!"

He agreed to send his daughter to Qin.

. . .

When the Honorable Zhi returned from his mission, he met someone on the road with a dark red face and a curly beard, who was ploughing the ground with a hoe held in each hand, biting more than a foot down into the earth. The Honorable Zhi asked him his name, and he replied, "I am Noble Grandson Qi, my style-name is Zisang, and I am a member of the ruling house of Jin."

"With your abilities, what are you doing wasting your time in the fields?" Zhi asked.

Noble Grandson Qi replied, "Nobody has ever recommended me for office."

"Would you be willing to come with me to Qin?" the Honorable Zhi asked.

"Knights die for the man who appreciates them," Noble Grandson Qi said. "If I could but get someone to recommend me, I would be happy to go anywhere."

They rode together in the same chariot to Qin, whereupon the Honorable Zhi spoke about him to Lord Mu, and he appointed him as a grandee. When Lord Mu heard that Jin had agreed to the marriage alliance, he sent the Honorable Zhi back to Jin with the wedding gifts, after which he was to escort Lady Bo Ji to her new home. The Marquis of Jin wanted one of his ministers to go with her.

Zhou Zhiqiao stepped forward and said, "Baili Xi has announced that he is not willing to take office in Jin. Since we don't know what exactly he is up to, it would be best if you sent him far away."

The Marquis of Jin included Baili Xi as one part of his daughter's dowry.

. . .

Baili Xi was originally a native of the state of Yu, and his style-name was Jingbo. When he first tried to find someone to give him an official post, he was already more than thirty years of age. He had married a wife from the Du family, and they had one son. Baili Xi was not at all wealthy and could find no one to give him a job, so he wanted to travel to seek better opportunities, but this would leave his wife and son without any support, which worried and upset him greatly.

"I have heard it said that men should be ambitious," his wife told him. "What on earth is a young and strong man like yourself doing, sitting and suffering at home with your family, when you could be out working? I can look after myself, don't worry about me!"

They only had one chicken left, but she killed it and cooked it for his farewell supper. There was no firewood in the kitchen, but she burned the plank they used to bar the door. She mashed up some yellowing pickles and steamed them to make a meal, and thus Baili Xi got to eat his fill. As they said goodbye, his wife held their son in her arms and grabbed hold of Baili Xi's sleeve. She then said with tears in her eyes, "Do not forget us when you are rich and noble!" Baili Xi then left.

He traveled first to Qi, where he tried to get a job with Lord Xiang, but found no one to recommend him. After a long time in terrible poverty, he was reduced to begging for food in the streets of Zhi. At that time, Baili Xi was already forty years of age. Among the inhabitants of Zhi there was a certain Jian Shu, who found his appearance remarkable and said, "You are no ordinary beggar!" He asked his name and made him stay for a meal. Over the food, they discussed contemporary issues. Baili Xi spoke extremely fluently, and the points that he made were apt and carefully considered.

Jian Shu sighed and said, "It must be fate that has reduced a man of your talents to such a situation!"

He decided that Baili Xi should stay in his house, and they became sworn brothers. Since Jian Shu was the older one by one year, Baili Xi addressed him as his elder. Jian Shu's family was not at all wealthy, so

Baili Xi went out to work as a herdsman for the village cattle in order that he should not be a burden on the household.

After the Honorable Wuzhi murdered Lord Xiang and established himself as the new ruler, he sent out placards summoning wise men into his service. Baili Xi naturally wanted to go, but Jian Shu said, "His Late Lordship has many other sons who are at present in exile, and Wuzhi has usurped the title in the teeth of their better claims. He will not be able to hold his position for long." As a result, Baili Xi didn't go.

Later on, he heard that Prince Tui of Zhou was very fond of oxen and that anyone employed to look after his cattle was generously rewarded, so he said goodbye to Jian Shu and traveled to Zhou.

"You must not entrust your future to anyone lightly," Jian Shu warned him. "If you take office with someone and then give up your job, you will be accused of disloyalty. On the other hand, if you suffer disaster with your lord you are simply stupid. Please be very careful! I will put my own affairs in order, and then I will go to Zhou to see you."

When Baili Xi arrived in Zhou, he had himself recommended to Prince Tui as being especially skilled at looking after cattle. Prince Tui was very pleased with him and wanted to appoint him as a household servant. Later on, Jian Shu arrived from Zhi, and he went with Baili Xi to have an audience with Prince Tui. As they left, he said to Baili Xi, "Prince Tui is a very ambitious man, but there is no way that he has the brains to carry out his plans. The people whom he employs are all flatterers and toadies who are going to cause a great deal of trouble. This regime will not last. You had better leave."

Baili Xi wanted to go back to Yu, having been separated from his wife for such a long time. Jian Shu suggested, "Gong Zhiqi, who is a minister in Yu, is an old friend of mine whom I haven't seen for ages. I would love to see him again. If you are going to go back to Yu, I will go with you." Accordingly, he accompanied Baili Xi back to the state of Yu. However, by that time Baili Xi's wife had become so poor that she was no longer able to support herself and had been forced to move elsewhere. No one had any idea where she had gone. Baili Xi was devastated.

When Jian Shu met Gong Zhiqi, he told him how clever Baili Xi was, and Gong Zhiqi then recommended him to the service of the Duke of Yu, who appointed him to the rank of a mid-level grandee.

"As far as I can see," Jian Shu remarked, "the Duke of Yu is a small-minded and arrogant man, so he will not make you a good master."

"I have been poor for a very long time," Baili Xi reminded him. "My situation can be compared to that of a fish that has found itself on dry land and which in a moment of desperation gets a ladleful of water poured over it!"

"If you take office in his government because you are forced to do so by poverty, it is very difficult for me to stop you," Jian Shu told him. "If in the future you want to find me, come to Minglu Village in Song. It is a very peaceful place, and it is there that I plan to go and live."

Jian Shu said goodbye and left, while Baili Xi stayed behind to work for the Duke of Yu. When the Duke of Yu lost his state, Baili Xi insisted on staying with him.

"I have already proved that I am stupid," he said, "so how can I add disloyalty to all my other mistakes?"

Afterwards when Lady Bo Ji married in Qin, Jin included Baili Xi on the list of her dowry. Baili Xi said to himself, "I could be helping this entire generation, but I have not been able to meet with an enlightened ruler who wishes me to help him achieve his ambitions. Now, in old age, I find myself part of the train of a new bride, just like a slave. What humiliation could be greater than this?" He decided to run away.

It was his initial intention to go to Song, but he found the roads leading there were blocked, so he went to Chu instead. He arrived at the city of Yuan, where he was discovered by some locals who had gone out hunting. They suspected that he was a spy of some sort, so they arrested him and tied him up.

"I come from the state of Yu," Baili Xi told them. "After my country was destroyed, I fled and have ended up here."

"What are you good at?" they asked.

"I know how to look after cattle."

They untied him and set him to taking care of their oxen, which grew fatter and sleeker every day. They were very pleased and reported his success to the king of Chu.

The king of Chu summoned Baili Xi and asked him, "Is there some sort of principle behind your success with these animals?"

"They need food when they are hungry, and you have to be careful not to exhaust them too much," Baili Xi replied. "You need to care about them—that is all."

"You are absolutely right," the king of Chu told him. "This applies not only to oxen, it should also work for horses." He sent him to work, raising horses by the Eastern Sea.

When Lord Mu of Qin saw that Baili Xi's name was listed among the people who would be accompanying Lady Bo Ji, but that he had not actually arrived, he was irritated.

"This man used to be a minister in the state of Yu, but now he seems to have run away," the Honorable Zhi explained.

Lord Mu asked Noble Grandson Qi about him: "You come from Jin, so you must know something about Baili Xi. What kind of person is he?"

"He is a very clever man," Noble Grandson Qi replied. "You can see how wise he is by the fact that he understood that the Duke of Yu would not listen to remonstrance, and so he did not bother; you can see how loyal he is by the fact that after the Duke of Yu went to live in Jin, he would not take office there. He is the kind of man who could bring good government to an entire age, but he has not yet met with the right opportunity!"

"How do I encourage Baili Xi to take office in my administration?" Lord Mu asked.

"I have heard that Baili Xi's wife and son are living in Chu, so he will certainly have gone there," Noble Grandson Qi said. "Why don't you send someone to Chu to find him?"

The messenger went to Chu and came back to report: "Baili Xi is currently living by the sea, herding horses for the king of Chu."

"If I send generous gifts, will Chu agree to let him come to me?" Lord Mu inquired.

"Baili Xi won't be able to come under those circumstances!" Noble Grandson Qi warned him.

"Why not?"

"The reason why the king of Chu employs Baili Xi to look after his horses is because he does not know how clever he is," Noble Grandson Qi explained. "If you go and ask for his services, offering them enormous bribes, they will realize that there is something special about him. If Chu knows that Baili Xi is a clever man, they will employ him themselves—why would they hand him over to us? Your Lordship should demand him back on the grounds that he is a runaway member of your bride's dowry. Just think about the way that Guan Yiwu was able to escape from Lu!"

"Good!" Lord Mu exclaimed. Then he sent an envoy to present five sheepskins to the king of Chu and say: "Baili Xi has run away from our country to seek sanctuary in yours. His Lordship would like to get him back to punish him as a warning to other people thinking about running away. Please take these five sheepskins as payment for your trouble."

The king of Chu did not want to do anything that might jeopardize the good relationship that he enjoyed with Qin, so he ordered people at the Eastern Sea to arrest Baili Xi and hand him over to Qin.

When Baili Xi was about to set off, the local people from around the Eastern Sea thought that he was going to be executed, so they clung to him, crying. Baili Xi laughed and said, "I have heard that the ruler of Qin has ambitions to become hegemon. Why should a man like that care about someone missing from his wife's train? If he has extracted me from Chu, it is because he is planning to give me a job in his administration. I am setting off on the road that leads to fame and fortune, so why should you cry?" He then got into the prison cart and departed.

When he arrived at the border with Qin, it transpired that Lord Mu had sent Noble Grandson Qi to go and meet him in the suburbs of the capital. First he had him released from the prison cart, and then he summoned him for an audience. His Lordship asked, "How old are you?"

"I am seventy years old," Baili Xi replied.

Lord Mu sighed and said, "It is such a shame that you are so old."

"If you want me to run after a flying bird or catch a wild animal with my bare hands, then I am indeed too old," Baili Xi told him. "On the other hand, if you want me to sit down and plan matters of state for you, then I am still quite young. Was not Lü Shang eighty years old and fishing beside the Wei River when King Wen of Zhou found him and took him home, appointing him to a senior ministerial position? Did he not in the end play a key part in establishing the Zhou dynasty? Have I not been lucky enough to meet you today, my lord, a whole decade earlier than Lü Shang?"

Lord Mu was impressed by his words. He sat up straight and asked him, "My lands are bordered by those of the Rong and Di nomadic peoples, and we do not participate in either the meetings or the blood covenants of the Central States. Please, can you instruct me in good government? If you can make us the equal of the other feudal lords, I will be extremely grateful!"

"Since you, my lord, do not care that I was once a prisoner of war captured from a lost state, or that I am in my declining years, and you are serious in asking me such a question, then I will do my very best for you," Baili Xi replied. "These lands are where the great kings Wen and Wu of the Zhou dynasty first came to power; the mountains here are shaped like hounds' teeth and lie across the land like an enormous snake—the Zhou dynasty was not able to keep them and abandoned them to Qin. In other words, Heaven has opened up the way for Qin. You live close to the Rong and Di peoples, and so your army is strong; you do not participate in meetings and covenants, and so your power has become concentrated. The territories of the Western Rong are several tens of times bigger than your state: bring this land under cultivation and you will have enough to eat; register their population and you will have an army. In that case there will be no one among the lords of the Central States who can rival you. If you behave with magnanimity and punish those who turn against you severely, you will be able to take complete possession of the Western regions. Having done this, you can strike awe into the Central States from your position safe amidst the mountains, waiting for the right moment to advance. Whether you show kindness to them or inspire awe through your military might will be entirely your choice. Then you will become hegemon."

Lord Mu now rose to his feet and said, "I am lucky to have you on my side, just as Qi is lucky to have Elder Zhong."

They spoke together for three days in a row and got along extremely well. Afterwards, Lord Mu appointed him to the position of a senior minister and employed him in the government of the state. From this point on the people of Qin called Baili Xi the "Five Sheepskins Grandee."

There is an alternative tradition that Lord Mu appointed Baili Xi to high office right when he was in the middle of a herd of oxen, or alternatively that Baili Xi was raising cattle in Chu and that Qin used five sheepskins to ransom him.

A bearded old man wrote a poem that reads:

It was amazing that Guan Zhong became prime minister straight from prison,
But his example was more or less repeated by Baili Xi.
From this point on Qin became a name to be reckoned with,
So you could say that he was worth every bit of his five sheepskins!

Baili Xi refused to take office as a senior minister and recommended someone else instead. If you do not know who it was that he suggested to take his place, READ ON.

Chapter Twenty-six

A song about a bar to the door allows Baili
Xi to recognize his wife.

After capturing the Treasure of Chen, Lord
Mu discovers the truth of his dream.

Lord Mu of Qin was deeply aware of Baili Xi's brilliance, and so he wanted to appoint him to a senior ministerial position. Baili Xi, however, refused, saying, "My own talents are less than a tenth of those of Jian Shu. If you wish your country to be well-governed, you should appoint him to a senior position and let me assist him."

"I know how talented you are," Lord Mu told him, "but I have never even heard about this Jian Shu."

"You are not the only one to be ignorant of Jian Shu's abilities, my lord," Baili Xi said. "Even the people of Qi and Song are not aware of how clever he is—in fact I am the only person who knows. I once traveled to Qi, because I wanted to have an audience with the Honorable Wuzhi. Jian Shu stopped me by saying, 'Do not do that.' I left Qi and thus escaped the disaster that subsequently engulfed the Honorable Wuzhi. Next I traveled to Zhou, because I wanted to meet Prince Tui, and yet again Jian Shu stopped me by saying, 'Do not do that.' I left Zhou and escaped involvement in Prince Tui's rebellion. After that I went home to Yu. I wanted to meet the Duke of Yu, and yet again he stopped me, saying, 'Do not.' At that time I was very poor, and I was desperate for a job bringing me some income, so I stayed and worked for His Grace, ending up as a prisoner of war held captive by Jin. If I had listened then to what he said, I would have avoided this disaster in which I almost got myself killed. This tells you that he is much cleverer than ordinary people. He is currently living as a recluse at Luming Village in the state of Song. You should make haste to summon him into your service."

Lord Mu ordered the Honorable Zhi to dress up as a merchant and take generous gifts to Song to recruit Jian Shu into his administration. In addition to that, Baili Xi wrote a letter explaining what had happened.

The Honorable Zhi packed his bag and headed for Luming Village, riding in an ox-drawn cart, with a second cart following on behind him. As he approached this place, he caught sight of a number of people ploughing the slopes, singing together. Their song ran as follows:

These mountains are high, but we do not have to climb them;
These roads are muddy, but we do not need to traverse them.
On this slope the waters are sweet and the soil is rich.
By our labor we raise the five grains,
Providing no disaster strikes, we will have enough to eat.
We enjoy our lives here, where no one cares if we are noble or base!

The Honorable Zhi heard this song while sitting in his chariot and thought it most unusual. He sighed and said to the driver, "There is an old saying that when a gentleman comes to live in a village, even the most vulgar customs are transformed. Now, as we approach Jian Shu's home, you can see that even the plough boys have a refined air to them, which makes me believe everything that has been said about this gentleman's qualities." He got down from the cart and asked the plough boys, "Where does Jian Shu live?"

"Why do you want to know?" they inquired.

"I have a letter from his old friend Baili Xi," the Honorable Zhi explained, "which he asked me to deliver."

The plough boys indicated the direction and said, "If you go right into the deepest part of the bamboo forest up ahead, you will find a stream on your left-hand side and rocks on your right, and in the middle there is a little thatched hut. That is where he lives."

The Honorable Zhi thanked them politely and got back on his cart. When he had advanced about half a *li*, he reached the place that they had described. As the Honorable Zhi looked around himself, he realized that the landscape was indeed exceptionally beautiful and refined.

The Recluse of Longxi wrote a poem about reclusion, which reads:

Living deep within the forest of emerald-green bamboos,
What more can you ask for in this life?
On every side white stones are piled up like clouds;

A pure stream trickles through this landscape.
You can entertain yourself watching the monkeys and gibbons,
And step through these glades with the innocent deer.
Although the world is filled with hurly-burley,
This reclusive gentleman is completely unconcerned.

The Honorable Zhi stopped his cart outside the thatched cottage and sent one of his servants to knock upon the gate. A small boy opened the gate and asked them, "Why have you come here?"

"I am here to see Master Jian," he explained.

"My master is not at home," the boy said.

"Where has he gone?"

"He has gone with two of the neighbors to see the spring at Shiliang, and he will be back in a short while," the boy announced.

The Honorable Zhi did not think it appropriate to go into the house in the master's absence, so he sat down on a rock to wait. The boy left the gate ajar and went back into the cottage. A short time later, he saw a tall and strong man with large eyes and thick bushy eyebrows approach along a path through the fields to the west, carrying two haunches of venison on his back. Zhi felt his appearance to be most remarkable, so he got up to meet him. The man put the two haunches down on the ground and returned the Honorable Zhi's salutation. Zhi then asked him his name, to which he answered, "My name is Jian Bing, and my style-name is Baiyi."

"Are you any relation to Jian Shu?" Zhi asked.

"He is my father," he replied.

The Honorable Zhi redoubled his respectful bows and said, "I am very pleased to meet you."

"What are you doing here, sir?" Jian Bing inquired.

"I have an old friend named Baili Xi," he replied, "who has just taken office in Qin. He asked me to take this letter to your father."

"Please come into the house," Jian Bing said. "My father will be home any minute now."

As he spoke, he pushed open the gate and allowed the Honorable Zhi to enter before him. Jian Bing then picked up the two haunches of venison and carried them into the cottage, where the boy took them off him. Jian Bing bowed repeatedly as he invited his guest to take the seat of honor. The Honorable Zhi started chatting with Jian Bing about farming and the cultivation of mulberries, then the conversation turned to military matters. Everything that Jian Bing said was clever and pertinent, and Zhi was amazed. He said to himself, "If the father is anything like as brilliant as the son, Baili Xi's recommendation is entirely deserved."

After tea had been served, Jian Bing sent the boy to stand by the gate and wait for his father. A short time later, the boy reported: "The master is back!"

Jian Shu came walking along with two of his neighbors. When he saw the two carts pulled up outside his door, he said in surprise: "Since when has our little village had any carts like that?" Jian Bing rushed out to explain what had happened. Jian Shu then came into the cottage with his neighbors, and, having introduced themselves, everyone sat down in their appropriate places.

"I gather from my son that you have a letter for me from Baili Xi," Jian Shu said. "Please could you give it to me?"

The Honorable Zhi handed over the letter. Jian Shu broke the seal and read it. It said:

I made the mistake of not listening to your advice and thus became caught up in the disaster that overtook Yu. Fortunately, the Lord of Qin is interested in recruiting good men, and he ransomed me from my fate of herding cattle and gave me a position in the Qin government. I know that I am not nearly as clever as you are, so I have recommended you for office here. The Lord of Qin is a man who believes in treating other people well, and to demonstrate this, he has sent Grandee the Honorable Zhi with gifts to welcome you into the fold. I hope that you will come out of your mountains and help me to achieve my ambitions. If you decide that you cannot bear to leave your forests, I will join you in Luming Village.

"How was Baili Xi able to make himself known to the Lord of Qin?" Jian Shu asked.

The Honorable Zhi explained how Baili Xi had been included in the dowry offered by the state of Jin, only to run away to Chu, and how the Lord of Qin had heard about how clever he was and used five sheepskins to ransom him. "My lord wanted to appoint him to a senior ministerial position, but Baili Xi said that he could not possibly take this job, given that you were so much more qualified, and he insisted that he would only take office once you have joined him in Qin. His Lordship armed me with a few trifling gifts to give you as a sign of his appreciation."

When he had finished speaking, the Honorable Zhi ordered his servants to bring in the gifts and his official credentials from the trunks in the carts, and they were all laid out in the cottage. The neighbors were both peasants who had spent their entire lives living in these mountains, and they had never seen such magnificent things. They stared at each other in amazement. Then they said to the Honorable Zhi, "We had no idea that a nobleman would be visiting! Please let us leave!"

"What do you mean?" Zhi said. "My lord is hoping that Master Jian will help him in the same way that the parched fields might long for the rain. I hope that you two will both join your voices with mine in encouraging him to take office in Qin, and I can assure you that your rewards in that case will far exceed what you see here!"

The two old men now spoke to Jian Shu: "Since Qin is so sincere in seeking out good men, you should not make this gentleman travel so far in vain."

"In the past, the Duke of Yu did not make use of Baili Xi's advice, and that is why he was defeated and his country destroyed," Jian Shu stated. "If the ruler of Qin is indeed sincere in his wish to employ good men in his government, Baili Xi is quite enough. I have long ago given up any idea of taking office and have no wish to go to Qin with you, so I hope you will take back all these gifts and make excuses to His Lordship on my behalf."

"If you do not go, Baili Xi will not stay with us!" the Honorable Zhi said.

Jian Shu muttered something, then he sighed and said, "No one ever realized what a talented man Baili Xi really is, which is why he has spent such a long time trying to find a job. Now, at long last, he has found an enlightened ruler to serve, and I suppose I must help him achieve his ambitions. Otherwise, the next thing I know Baili Xi will be pulling a plough here with me!"

The boy came in to announce: "The venison is cooked!"

Jian Shu took down some freshly brewed beer that he was keeping by his bedside and presented it to his guests. The Honorable Zhi took a seat on the west side, together with the two neighbors, and then host and guests toasted each other, eating and drinking their fill from earthenware bowls and using wooden chopsticks. They did not at all notice that it was getting late, and in the end Zhi stayed overnight in the cottage.

The following morning, the two neighbors held a party for them to see them off, and they all sat in the same positions that they had the night before. After some time, the Honorable Zhi began praising Jian Bing's intelligence and suggested that he should come with them to the state of Qin. Jian Shu agreed. He divided the presents offered by the Lord of Qin between the two neighbors and told them to look after his household: "I hope that we can be in touch soon after I leave." He instructed his family: "Make sure that you tend the fields carefully! Do not allow them to become overgrown with nettles and weeds!" His two neighbors said goodbye to him, wishing him good luck on his travels. Jian Shu got onto one of the carts, which was driven by his son, Jian Bing. The Honorable Zhi rode in the other cart, and they set off together.

They traveled along, and when they approached the outskirts of the Qin capital, the Honorable Zhi went on ahead to the palace, where he reported to Lord Mu of Qin what had happened: "Master Jian has already arrived at the Qin capital with his son, Jian Bing. Both of them are indeed remarkably talented men. I will go and bring them to you, and you can give them important jobs to do!"

Lord Mu was thrilled and ordered Baili Xi to go and welcome them. When Jian Shu arrived, Lord Mu went down the steps to greet him. Having arranged for him to be given a seat, he asked him, "Baili Xi has spoken to me many times of your brilliance. What can you teach me?"

"Qin is located far to the west with the Rong and the Di peoples for neighbors," Jian Shu said. "Your lands are located among mountains and your army is very strong. If you wish to advance, then you are in a very advantageous situation for battle; but if you have to retreat, you can easily defend yourself. The reason that you are not ranked among the most important feudal lords of the Zhou confederacy is simply because you have not yet displayed your magnanimity and military might. If others are not aware of your military might, why should they fear you? If they have not experienced your magnanimity, why should they be loyal to you? But if they neither fear you nor are loyal to you, how can you ever become hegemon?"

"Which is more important, military might or magnanimity?" Lord Mu asked.

"The two advance together," Jian Shu replied. "If you are magnanimous but lack military capabilities, your lands will be partitioned among other states. If you are militarily strong but behave brutally, your regime will collapse internally."

"If I wish to display my magnanimity and make my military strength known, how should I go about it?" Lord Mu inquired.

"Qin has been much affected by its contact with the Rong, and so your people know nothing about the rules of ritual propriety," Jian Shu said. "They do not understand their position in the world, nor do they distinguish between people of noble and humble birth. I will instruct them in these matters on Your Lordship's behalf, and then afterwards we can introduce them to punishments. Once they have been instructed, the people will know that they have to respect their rulers, but it is only once they have appreciated the kindness that you show to them that we can use punishments to make them fear you. That way you can make use of your people as you would your hands and feet. That is what Guan Zhong has taught and that is the reason why he is unequalled in the world!"

"If what you say is correct, then can I become hegemon?" Lord Mu asked.

"Not yet!" Jian Shu told him. "There are three prohibitions placed upon hegemons: they must not be greedy; they must not get angry; and they must not be in a hurry. If you are greedy, then you alienate people; if you get angry, then you cause resentment; while if you are in a hurry, you rush into things. If you have measured up the true value of things in your planning, what is the point of being greedy? If you understand your own position and that of other people, what is the point of getting angry with them? If you have weighed up what would be the right moment to act, why should you be in a hurry? If you can keep to these three prohibitions, then you are close to becoming a hegemon!"

"That sounds wonderful!" Lord Mu exclaimed. "Please, can you weigh up the current situation for me and tell me when would be the right moment to strike!"

"Qin has been established in the territory of the Western Rong, and this is a very auspicious region," Jian Shu said. "The Marquis of Qi is getting old, and his hegemony is in decline. If you were to bring good government to the people of Yong and Wei, my lord, then you can use that fact to extend your dominance over the Rong people, while punishing anyone who disobeys you. Once the Rong have submitted to your authority, you can wait for a suitable emergency to occur in the Central States, which will allow you to assume the mantle vacated by Qi and show the same magnanimity and justice to others. Then, even if you do not want to become hegemon, you will not be able to refuse this honor."

Lord Mu was very pleased and said, "I have found two men who can take charge of my people!"

He appointed Jian Shu to the position of Militia General of the Right, and Baili Xi became the Militia General of the Left. The two of them also held office as senior ministers, and indeed they were known as the "Two Prime Ministers." He also summoned Jian Bing and appointed him a grandee. From this time on, the "Two Prime Ministers" took control of the government and instructed the people in the laws of the land, promoting profitable ventures and removing evil influences. The state of Qin thus became well-governed.

A historian wrote a poem that says:

The Honorable Zhi recommended Baili Xi, and he recommended Jian
  Shu,
One after the other attracting each other to the Qin court.
If you are as good at recruiting brilliant men as Lord Mu of Qin,
You really don't need to ask for any further blessings!

Lord Mu knew that many of the kind of talented men that he needed were to be found in other countries, so he increased his efforts to seek them out. The Honorable Zhi recommended a man named Xiqi Shu from Qin for his abilities, and Lord Mu summoned him to court and gave him a job. Baili Xi had heard of the unusual talents of a man from Jin named Yao Yu, so he spoke privately to Noble Grandson Qi about him.

"Yao Yu never got anywhere when he was living in Jin," Qi explained, "so he has now taken office with the Western Rong."

Baili Xi was very upset by this news.

. . .

After her husband went traveling, Baili Xi's wife made her living by spinning and weaving, but then there was a famine and she could no longer carry on, so she was forced to take her son to look for food elsewhere. They kept on moving until they ended up in the state of Qin, where she made ends meet by taking in washing. Her son's name was Shi, and his style-name Mengming. He spent his time out hunting and getting into fights with the locals and never tried to get a proper job. When his mother tried to talk to him, he paid no attention to her. When Baili Xi became prime minister of Qin, she heard all about it and even once saw him from a distance riding on his chariot, but she did not dare to make herself known to him. His household was looking for a washerwoman and she took the job. She worked very hard and the other members of staff were very happy with her, but she never got to see Baili Xi. One day when he was sitting in the main hall, he wanted his musicians play for him in one of the side chambers.

"I know something about music and I would be happy to play," she told the other servants.

They took her to the side room, where she spoke to the other musicians. When they asked her what she could do, she said, "I can play the *qin* and sing." Accordingly, they gave her a *qin* to play. She performed a very elegant and melancholy piece, to which the other musicians all listened in silence, knowing that they could not match her skill. Afterwards, they wanted her to sing.

"Since I came here as a refugee, I have never sung once," she said. "Please tell His Lordship that I will only sing if he invites me up to the hall."

The musicians reported her words to Baili Xi, and he gave orders that she should come and take her place on the left side of the hall. She lowered her head and straightened out her sleeves, after which she began to sing:

Baili Xi, the Five Sheepskin Grandee!
I remember when we said goodbye:
I cooked our last chicken, cut up pickles, and burned the bar that closed our door.
Are you now so rich and noble that you have forgotten what I did for you?

Baili Xi, the Five Sheepskin Grandee!
You eat meat while your son starves,
You wear silk while your wife washes clothes.
Alas! Are you so rich and noble that you have forgotten what I did for you?

Baili Xi, the Five Sheepskin Grandee!
In the past, I cried when you left,
Today you sit keeping yourself away from me.
Alas! Are you so rich and noble that you have forgotten what I did for you?

When Baili Xi heard this song, he was amazed and summoned her to stand in front of him so that he might ask her about it. It was then that he discovered she really was his wife. The two of them hugged and were deeply moved by their reunion. After a long time, he asked, "Where is my son?"

"He is out hunting," she explained. Baili Xi ordered someone to go and find him. That very day, the three of them were reunited. When Lord Mu heard that Baili Xi's wife and son had been found, he gave him one thousand bushels of grain and a cartload of silk and gold. The following day, Baili Xi took his son to court to thank His Lordship for his kindness. Lord Mu appointed Baili Shi to the position of a grandee, and he was given command of the army together with Xiqi Shu and Jian

Bing. The trio was known as the "Three Commanders-in-Chiefs," and they were responsible for all military matters.

. . .

Wuli, the chief of the Jiang Rong, was a proud and arrogant man who repeatedly launched attacks or made incursions into Qin territory, and the Three Commanders-in-Chief joined forces to punish him. Wuli was defeated and fled to Jin, where he occupied the lands of Guazhou. At that time, the chief of the Western Rong was a man named Chiban. Seeing how powerful Qin was becoming, he sent one of his ministers named Yao Yu on a diplomatic mission there, to see exactly what kind of man Lord Mu was. The two of them were wandering through Lord Mu's hunting park together. Having climbed the Sanxiu Tower, he praised the beauty of the palace and its gardens.

"Did you make ghosts build this," Yao Yu asked, "or did you force people to construct it for you? If it was ghosts, you must have put the netherworld to a lot of trouble. If it was your people that built this, they must be exhausted."

Lord Mu was amazed by his comment and said, "You Rong and Yi barbarians have no rituals or music, nor indeed any proper regulations. How can you be well-governed?"

Yao Yu laughed and said, "The reason why the Central States are in such trouble is because they have rituals and music and proper regulations. The great sages created civilization and laws in order to tie down the ordinary people, which may be good government but only in a very petty sense. Later on when wickedness and licentiousness increased day by day, rulers used ritual and music to add prestige to themselves while taking advantage of people's fear of the laws of the land to cast all blame for any wrongdoing on their subordinates. People were angry about this, and that breeds rebellion. Among the Rong and the Yi peoples, things are not like that. The ruler treats his people with simple benevolence, while the people serve their ruler with loyalty and trust— ruler and people are as one. They have none of the appurtenances of power with which superiors can bully their inferiors, nor do they irritate each other in the name of civilization and law. Good governance that you cannot see is supreme good government."

Lord Mu fell silent. Then he withdrew to report this conversation to Baili Xi.

"He was always regarded as one of the most brilliant men in the state of Jin," Baili Xi remarked, "and I have often heard his name mentioned."

Lord Mu was very upset and said, "I have heard it said that if one of your neighbors has a sagacious minister, it is a worry for all enemy states. Yao Yu is brilliant and he holds high office with the Rong. What can we do to prevent disaster befalling us from that quarter?"

"The Court Historian Liao is very cunning," Baili Xi said. "He is the person you need to talk to about this."

Lord Mu immediately summoned the Court Historian Liao and told him what the problem was.

"The Rong chief lives in a poor and remote region, and he has never heard any music from the Central States," Liao said. "You could try sending him some women musicians, to distract him from his other ambitions. You should keep Yao Yu here on some pretext so that he overstays the time set for his mission. That way there will be problems for the government and it will generate mutual distrust between the chief and his minister. That way we should be able to gain not only the services of Yao Yu, but also the territory of the Rong!"

"That is brilliant!" Lord Mu exclaimed. Accordingly, he insisted that Yao Yu should sit with him on the same mat and eat from the same vessels, while Jian Shu, Baili Xi, Noble Grandson Qi, and so on took it in turns to ask him questions about the precise details of the terrain and the relative strengths and weaknesses of the Rong army. In the meantime, he recruited six exceptionally attractive women musicians, whom he dressed in the finest clothes and jewelry. He ordered the Court Historian Liao to present them to the chief of the Rong. The Rong chief, Chiban, was delighted and spent every day listening to music and every night having sex with his musicians, paying no attention at all to the government of the country. Yao Yu was made to stay in Qin for an entire year before anyone could be persuaded to allow him to go home.

The chief of the Rong was extremely displeased that he had come back so late, but there was no excuse Yao Yu could make: "I begged to be allowed to return all the time, but the Earl of Qin would not let me go."

The Rong chief suspected that he had been suborned by Qin, and the two of them became completely alienated. Yao Yu realized that the Rong chief was being corrupted by the women musicians and that he no longer paid any attention to matters of state, so he felt it his bitter duty to remonstrate with him. The Rong chief refused to allow him to speak. Lord Mu of Qin then sent someone to summon him into his service, and Yao Yu abandoned the Rong to give his allegiance to Qin. He was appointed to a ministerial position, working closely with Jian Shu and Baili Xi. Yao Yu presented a plan for attacking the Rong, and when the

Three Commanders-in-Chief arrived at the Rong borders, they found the information they had been given so precise it was as if they were traveling along a well-known road. The chief of the Rong, Chiban, was unable to make any effective resistance, and in the end he had to surrender to Qin.

Later on, someone wrote a poem that reads:

When the Duke of Yu ignored Baili Xi, he became a prisoner of war;
When the Rong chief lost Yao Yu, his country was destroyed.
If you are wondering about the difference that clever men can make to history,
Then please look at the examples of Qi and Qin.

Chiban, the chief of the Western Rong, was in fact the leader of all the Rong peoples and received their allegiance and labor. When they heard that Chiban had surrendered to Qin, they were very frightened for the future, and many of them in turn gave their lands to the state of Qin and accepted subordinate positions. Lord Mu held a great banquet for his ministers at which he issued rewards, and they all took it in turns to toast him. He was not aware of quite how drunk he was becoming; when he returned to the palace, he slipped into a coma, much to the alarm of the palace servants. When this was made known to others, the ministers all came to the palace gates to ask after his health. Scion Ying summoned the palace physician to check his pulse, which turned out to be completely normal, though his eyes remained tightly shut and he seemed to be capable of neither movement nor speech. The palace physician said, "This is most mysterious." He suggested summoning the Court Historian Liao to perform a beneficial sacrifice.

"He is suffering from catalepsy caused by an unusual dream," Liao said. "We will have to wait for him to come to of his own accord, for it is not possible to wake him. Sacrificing is also no use in these circumstances."

Scion Ying stayed by his father's bedside, never leaving to eat or sleep. On the fifth day, Lord Mu suddenly woke up with sweat pouring from his forehead. He kept saying, "How odd! How odd!"

Scion Ying knelt down and asked him, "Are you all right after sleeping for so long?"

"I have only been having a nap," Lord Mu said.

"You have been asleep for more than five days," the scion told him.

"Did you have any unusual dreams during that time?"

"How did you know?" Lord Mu asked in alarm.

"Court Historian Liao said that it would be so," Scion Ying said.

Lord Mu summoned Liao to his bedside and spoke as follows: "In my dream I saw a beautiful woman, dressed like the wife of a nobleman, with skin as white as snow. In her hands she was holding a tablet, and she said she had received a command from God on High to summon me. I went with her, and suddenly I found myself floating among endless billowing clouds, until I made my way to a great brilliantly painted palace with jade steps nine feet wide and hung with curtains made from ropes of pearls. The lady instructed me to make my bows at the foot of the steps and then, after a short time, one of the pearl curtains was pulled aside. Beyond it, I could see a great hall with pillars of pure gold, hung with silk brocade tapestries, all of the finest quality. There was a king present, dressed in an official robe and crown, sitting on his throne and leaning against a jade armrest. His entourage was lined up on either side of him, all most imposing and magnificent in appearance. The king gave his orders: 'Bestow gifts!' and then someone who looked like a eunuch presented me with an emerald goblet full of wine. It was incomparably delicious. The king gave his entourage a bamboo text, and I heard someone in the hall shout out my name and say, 'Listen to His Majesty's edict, for it is your job to bring peace to the state of Jin!' That announcement was made twice. The lady then instructed me to bow twice and led me out of the palace. I asked her name, and she replied: 'I am Lady Treasure, and I live on the western slopes of Mount Taibai in Your Lordship's own domains. Have you really never heard of me? My husband's name is Lord Leaf, and he lives at the city of Nanyang, coming to see me perhaps once every year or two. If you build a temple for me, I will make sure that you become hegemon and that your name is famous for the rest of time.' I then asked her, 'What is the problem in Jin that I am supposed to be putting a stop to?' Lady Treasure replied, 'That is one of the secrets of Heaven that I cannot divulge to you.' After that I heard a cock crowing with a sound as loud as a clap of thunder, and I woke up. I do not know whether this is an auspicious omen or not."

Court Historian Liao replied, "The Marquis of Jin is besotted with Lady Li Ji and has become estranged from his heir. Of course civil disturbances are to be expected there! Your Lordship has received a mandate from Heaven! This is the greatest good fortune!"

"Who is this Lady Treasure?" Lord Mu inquired.

"I have heard that in the time of our former ruler, Lord Wen, a man from Chencang was out hunting and captured a strange animal in shape not unlike a full bag and yellowish-white in color, with a short tail and many feet and a mouth like a beak. The man from Chencang intended to present it to Lord Wen, but then on the road he met two small children who clapped their hands and laughed, saying: 'You torment dead men, so what are you doing in the hands of a live one?' The man from Chencang asked what they were talking about, and the two children said: 'The name of this beast is Wei, and it usually lives underground, sucking the brains of dead men to obtain their essence, so that it may change its shape. You need to treat it very carefully!' The Wei then opened its beak and suddenly spoke in the words of men: 'These two children are called the Treasure of Chen. They are in fact the finest of pheasants, and a man who captures the boy will become king, while the man who captures the girl will become hegemon.' The man from Chencang then abandoned the Wei to run after the children, and they suddenly turned into pheasants and flew away. The man from Chencang reported this to our former lord, who ordered that it be recorded in a bamboo book and kept in the archives, which is where I read this story. Chencang is to the west of Mount Taibai, so if Your Lordship were to go hunting between these two mountains, you could make investigations on the spot. Then you will discover the truth of the matter!"

Lord Mu ordered that the records written on bamboo preserved by Lord Wen should be brought to him, so that he could have a look at them. Indeed, it was just as Court Historian Liao had said. He ordered that Liao should write a detailed account of his dream and that this too should be kept in the archives.

The following day Lord Mu held court, and his ministers all offered their congratulations. Lord Mu ordered that a chariot should be prepared, and he went out hunting at Mount Taibai. Wandering here and there, he eventually arrived at Mount Chencang. There the huntsmen spread their nets and caught a pheasant with particularly beautiful coloring, which a short time later metamorphosized into a stone bird without losing one jot of its color. The huntsmen presented this to Lord Mu. Court Historian Liao offered his congratulations: "This is Lady Treasure. 'The man who captures the girl will become hegemon'; is this not a portent? Your Lordship ought to build a shrine here at Chencang, in order to gain blessings from her."

Lord Mu was very pleased, and he ordered that the stone should be washed in orchid perfume, wrapped in a silk brocade cloth, and stored in a jade casket. He immediately ordered people to start cutting down trees to build a temple on the mountainside. He named this temple The

Shrine to Lady Treasure. He changed the name of Mount Chencang to Mount Baoji, or "Precious Pheasant," and commanded that sacrifices should be performed there every spring and autumn. At dawn on the day of these sacrifices you could hear the sound of pheasants throughout the mountain and for three *li* beyond. Every year or two you would also see a strange red light rising high into the sky there and hear a sound like thunder. This was said to indicate the arrival of Lord Leaf.

Lord Leaf was the spirit of the male pheasant who was said to live at Nanyang. More than four hundred years later, Emperor Guangwu of the Eastern Han dynasty was born at Nanyang. He raised an army to execute Wang Mang, restoring the dynasty and making himself the first emperor of the Eastern Han. This is the proof that the man who captures the male pheasant will become a True King.

If you want to know how Lord Mu of Qin put an end to the civil war in Jin, READ ON.

Chapter Twenty-seven

Lady Li Ji plots the murder of Shensheng.

*Lord Xian gives deathbed instructions
to Xun Xi.*

After Lord Xian of Jin conquered the two states of Yu and Guo, his ministers all congratulated him. Lady Li Ji was the only one left unhappy. She had originally wanted to see Scion Shensheng sent on the mission to attack Guo, but he had been replaced by Li Ke, who achieved an enormous success with very minimal effort. Right at that moment there was nothing that she could do about the situation. However, she discussed the matter with her lover, the actor Shi: "Li Ke is part of Shensheng's faction, and now he has achieved a great victory, making his position even more secure. I cannot possibly take him on. What should I do?"

"Xun Xi destroyed the two states of Yu and Guo using nothing more than a jade disc and a team of horses," Shi said. "He is far cleverer than Li Ke. His Lordship knows well that he was as important in achieving this victory as Li Ke himself. If we beg Xun Xi to act as tutor to the Honorable Xiqi and Zhuozi, we will be more than able to deal with Li Ke when the time comes."

Lady Li Ji requested permission for this from Lord Xian, and he appointed Xun Xi as Xiqi and Zhuozi's tutor. Then she spoke again to Shi: "Xun Xi has now joined our faction. However, as long as Li Ke is at court, he is sure to bring our plans to naught. Do you have some means to get rid of him? If Li Ke is removed, then we can deal with Shensheng."

"Li Ke may appear strong on the outside, but in fact he is a very hesitant man," the actor said. "If we can sway him by pointing out the advantages and the disadvantages of the situation, he will respond by refusing to take sides. Then we can make use of that fact. Li Ke enjoys a drink, so if Your Ladyship will arrange for a banquet of lamb and beef in his honor, I will get him drunk and test out his attitudes. If he falls for it, that is all to the good. If he does not fall for it, then I am just an actor who forgot my place and teased him a bit. He won't hold it against us."

"Good!" exclaimed Lady Li Ji. She prepared the banquet on behalf of the actor.

Shi had carefully prepared the words that he would use to invite Li Ke: "You, sir, have been rushing between Yu and Guo, so you must be absolutely exhausted. I would like to hold a party for you in the hope that you may enjoy at least a moment's leisure. What do you think?" Li Ke agreed.

The wine cups were set out at Li Ke's house, and he and his wife, Lady Meng, sat on the western side to show that they were the guests on this occasion. Shi bowed twice and handed him a beaker of wine, then stood respectfully to one side ready to top it up. They chatted and joked together very happily. When they had drunk so much that they became tipsy, Shi got up and started dancing. He said to Lady Meng, "If you would give me something to eat, I will sing a new song for you."

Lady Meng poured wine into a rhinoceros-horn goblet and handed it to Shi, after which she fed him a morsel of lamb. Then she asked, "What is the name of this new song?"

"It is called 'The Pleasures of Idleness,'" the actor replied. "If you would serve His Lordship according to these words, I can guarantee that you will remain rich and noble." He then cleared his throat and sang:

> The pleasures of idleness have palled on me;
> I cannot be as free as a bird.
> All the others have gone to the thickets,
> You alone have stayed by the single tree.
> Why are the thickets so dense and so lush?
> The tree invites the blows of the axe.
> When these blows start to bite,
> What can you do to change the fate of the tree?

When the song was over, Li Ke laughed and said, "What do you mean by the thicket? What do you mean by the single tree?"

"Well, you might compare it to a person whose mother was the principal wife of a lord who was originally destined to become the next ruler," Shi said. "In that case his roots would run deep, his branches would be closely packed, and a whole host of birds would come to roost there—you could then call that a thicket. But then if his mother died and people slandered him, disaster would threaten. In that case his roots would become shallow and his leaves drop, giving the birds nowhere to settle, just like the lone tree of my song." When he had finished speaking, he left.

Li Ke felt extremely uncomfortable and gave orders for the banquet to be cleared away. He got up and walked to his library, where he could be alone, pacing the room for a long time. That evening he did not eat dinner, but put out the lights and went to bed. He tossed and turned, unable to get to sleep. He thought to himself: "That actor, Shi, has been acclaimed both inside and outside the court, and he comes and goes from the palace without any restraint. There must be a reason why he sang that particular song today. He must have something to tell me. I will go tomorrow and pay a call on him."

It got later and later, and he was still on tenterhooks. He told his servants: "Go in secret to fetch Shi and bring him here. I want to talk to him."

Shi knew exactly what the problem was, so he quickly put on a hat and robe and went with the servants back to Li Ke's bedroom. Li Ke summoned Shi and told him to sit on the bed. With his arms wrapped around his knees, he asked him, "When you talked about the thicket and the lone tree, I have already worked it out—you meant the situation in Quwo, didn't you? You must know something . . . please tell me! Do not keep it a secret."

"I have wanted to tell you what I know for a long time," Shi replied, "but you are the tutor of the man at Quwo, so I did not dare to speak. I was afraid that you would punish me."

"If you tell me what is going on far enough in advance to allow me to make my plans and avoid getting caught up in a disaster, I will be deeply grateful," Li Ke told him. "Why should I punish you for that?"

Shi then leaned his head towards the pillow and said in a low tone: "His Lordship has already promised Her Ladyship to kill the scion and establish Xiqi in his place. Their plan is just about to come to fruition."

"Is it still possible to stop them?" Li Ke asked.

"Her Ladyship has His Lordship wrapped around her little finger," Shi replied. "You know that perfectly well. The two grandees, Liang Wu and Dongguan Wu, are much trusted by His Lordship—you know that too. Her Ladyship is in charge of the palace and the two grandees are in charge of the court. You might want to stop them, but how can you?"

"Even if it is His Lordship's wish," Li Ke exclaimed, "I cannot just stand by and watch the scion being murdered. On the other hand, I also cannot possibly support the scion in a fight with his father. If I just sit on the fence and do nothing, do you think I will be able to get through this crisis?"

"You will," Shi told him.

After the actor had left, Li Ke sat and waited until dawn, at which point he got out the bamboo strips that he had written all those years earlier. Counting up, he realized that it was now indeed ten years later. He sighed and said, "Divinations are really amazing things!" Then he walked around to the home of Grandee Pi Zhengfu and ordered his servants and attendants to leave them alone. He said, "Astrologer Su and Diviner Guo Yan's predictions have been entirely borne out!"

"What has happened?" Pi Zhengfu asked.

"Last night the actor Shi came to my house," Li Ke explained, "and told me, 'His Lordship is going to murder the scion and put Xiqi in his place.'"

"What did you say to that?" Pi Zhengfu inquired.

"I said that I am going to do nothing," Li Ke said.

"That is like noticing that a fire has broken out and deciding to fan the flames," Pi Zhengfu wailed. "This particular plot is aimed at you—you should have pretended to go along with it and found out what they are up to. You have been a mainstay of the scion's faction and crucial for him maintaining his position thus far. You could have taken advantage of this situation to change His Lordship's mind; who knows but it might have worked! Now that you have announced that you are going to do nothing, disaster will overtake the scion any moment now."

Li Ke stamped his foot and said, "What a shame! I should have come to discuss the matter with you much earlier." He said goodbye and got onto his chariot. Then he pretended to stumble and fall. For the next few days he did not go to court, claiming that he had injured his foot.

A historian wrote a poem that reads:

An actor danced in front of tables groaning with beef and lamb,
The scion was ruined by a single song.
Is it not laughable that such a senior minister had no idea what was
    going on,
And his neutrality led to the outbreak of war?

Shi reported back to Lady Li Ji, who was very pleased by these developments. That night she spoke to Lord Xian as follows: "The scion has been living for a long time in Quwo. Why don't you call him back to court? You can say that I would like to see him. If I show him some generosity, perhaps we can avoid all these constant conflicts. What do you think?" Lord Xian did exactly as she asked and summoned Shensheng back to court.

When Scion Shensheng received the summons, he set off at once and went first to have an audience with Lord Xian, bowing twice and asking after his health; then, when this ceremony had been completed, he went into the palace to see Lady Li Ji. She had prepared a banquet for him, and they spoke very happily together. The following day, Shensheng went back to the palace to thank her for the banquet, and Lady Li Ji again kept him for a meal.

That evening, Lady Li Ji went to Lord Xian in tears and said: "I wanted to establish good relations with the scion, so I asked you to summon him. I have treated him with all proper ceremony, and I really was not expecting him to behave so badly towards me."

"What has he done?" the horrified Lord Xian asked.

"I invited the scion to stay for lunch," Lady Li Ji sobbed. "He kept on drinking until he was half-drunk, and then he started teasing me, saying, 'When my grandfather got old, my mother, Lady Jiang, started an affair with my father. Now my father is getting old, so sooner or later you will be looking for someone new; who could be better than myself?' He then tried to grab hold of my hand, but I fought him off. If you don't believe me, then I will go for a walk with the scion in the park. You can watch from the tower, and you will see the truth of what I am saying with your own eyes."

"I will!" Lord Xian exclaimed.

The following day, Lady Li Ji summoned Scion Shensheng to walk with her in the park, for which she prepared by smearing a tiny bit of honey into her hair. Bees and butterflies clustered around her tresses.

"Do you mind trying to get rid of these insects for me?" Lady Li Ji said.

Shensheng, who was walking respectfully behind her, used his sleeve to flick them away. Lord Xian, who was watching from some distance away, thought he really was molesting her. He was furious and wanted to give immediate orders to have Shensheng arrested and executed. However, Lady Li Ji knelt on the ground before him and begged: "It was I who summoned him here, so if you kill him, it will all be my fault. No one other than yourself knows how he has behaved here in the palace. You will have to endure the situation a little longer."

Lord Xian ordered Shensheng to go back to Quwo, and he sent people to go there secretly to inquire if he had committed any crimes.

A couple of days later when Lord Xian had gone out hunting at Dihuan, Lady Li Ji came up with a new scheme with her lover. Afterwards, they sent someone to tell the scion: "His Lordship dreamed that your mother appeared to him and said, 'I am suffering starvation and have nothing to eat.' You must perform a sacrifice to her memory as soon as possible."

A separate shrine had been established at Quwo to the memory of Lady Jiang of Qi, so Shensheng held a sacrifice there for his mother and sent a messenger to take the sacrificial meats to Lord Xian. Lord Xian had not yet returned from his expedition, so the meats were kept in the palace. Six days later, Lord Xian came home.

Lady Li Ji had poisoned the sacrificial wine and meat, and she now presented them with the words: "I dreamed that Lady Jiang of Qi was suffering terrible torments from starvation. Since you had gone off hunting, I instructed the scion to perform a sacrifice for her. The sacrificial meats have now been sent here, and we have kept them for you."

Lord Xian picked up the beaker and was just about to taste the wine when Lady Li Ji sank to her knees and stopped him, saying: "This wine and meat have come from outside, so we have to test them."

"You are quite right!" exclaimed Lord Xian.

He poured the wine on the ground, and it bubbled and split. Then he had a dog brought in and gave it a lump of meat to eat. It died the moment it bit down. Lady Li Ji pretended to be unable to believe her eyes. She summoned a young eunuch and had him taste the wine and meat. The eunuch refused, but they forced him, and the moment he had swallowed them, blood poured from every orifice and he died. Lady Li Ji pretended to be horrified and ran around the hall, screaming: "Heavens! Heavens! Whatever happens, the scion will inherit everything sooner or later. His Lordship is old—surely he can wait a little longer! Why does he want to assassinate his own father?"

As she spoke, the tears streamed down her cheeks. Again, she fell to her knees in front of Lord Xian, and said in a voice choked with emotion: "The scion launched this conspiracy because he hates me. Let me take this meat and wine and die in your place, my lord. That way the scion will have achieved all that he wants!" She picked up the goblet as if she were really going to drink from it.

Lord Xian wrenched it from her grasp and dashed it to the ground, so overcome that he could not speak. Lady Li Ji collapsed in a tearful heap on the ground and said angrily, "How can the scion be so wicked? He is prepared to murder even his own father, so Heaven only knows what he will do to other people! Originally when you wanted to strip him of his titles, I was against it. Then when he assaulted me in the park and you wanted to kill him, I prevented it. Now he has almost murdered you! It is my fault that he got the opportunity!"

Lord Xian stammered out a few words as he lifted Lady Li Ji in his arms: "Get up! I will explain the situation to my ministers and then execute my wicked son."

He announced that court would be held immediately and summoned his grandees to discuss what had happened. Everyone came and filled the palace audience hall, with the exception of Hu Tu, who was living in reclusion, Li Ke, who was claiming that his foot had been injured, and Pi Zhengfu, who was off on some kind of mission.

Lord Xian informed his officials that Shensheng had made an attempt on his life. The ministers were well aware that Lord Xian had been plotting to strip his son of his title for ages, so they looked at each other but did not dare to argue.

Dongguan Wu stepped forward and said, "The scion has behaved very badly. I ask Your Lordship's permission to punish him."

Lord Xian immediately appointed Dongguan Wu as a general and ordered Liang Wu to assist him. They led a force of two hundred chariots to attack Quwo. He instructed them as follows: "The scion has had charge of the army on a number of occasions, and he is a brilliant strategist. You must be very careful!"

Although Hu Tu was living in reclusion, he sent people out to investigate what was going on at court. When he heard that the "Two Wus" were getting their chariots ready, he knew that they would be heading for Quwo. He ordered someone to go to report this to Scion Shensheng as quickly as possible. Shensheng discussed what to do with his Grand Tutor, Du Yuankuan.

"The sacrificial meats were kept in the palace for six days, so it is quite clear that the poison must have been introduced by someone in the palace," Du Yuankuan said. "You must appeal! Make sure that the ministers know the truth rather than sitting here waiting for them to come and kill you."

"If my father had to do without Lady Li Ji, he would not be happy," Shensheng said. "If I were to make an appeal and it were unsuccessful, this would simply compound my offense. But if my appeal were successful, my father would simply protect Lady Li Ji from all the consequences of her actions. I would not necessarily escape punishment, but I would certainly make my father deeply unhappy. The best thing that could happen now is for me to die!"

"You could go into exile abroad and wait to see how the situation develops," Du Yuankaun suggested. "Would that not be a good idea?"

"My father has sent these people to punish me without investigating whether I am innocent or not," Shensheng said sadly. "If I were to run away, I would take my reputation as an attempted parricide with me—people would treat me like a bird of ill omen! If I leave and succeed in convincing people that it is my father who is in the wrong, he will go down in history as a wicked ruler. To declare how badly my father has behaved would be to humiliate him in front of all the other lords. I am in an impossible situation whether I stay or go. If I expose what my father has done in order to absolve myself of the crimes of which I have been accused, then I am simply escaping punishment. I have heard it said that 'a benevolent man does not hate his ruler, a wise man does not place himself in impossible situations, and a brave man does not escape punishment.'"

In the end, he sent a letter back to Hu Tu, which said:

> I have committed a crime for which I will atone with my death. However, my father is old and Xiqi is still very young, and there are many dangers facing the country. I hope that you will do your best to guide the country through them. That way, even though I am dead, I will still be greatly helped by you.

When he had finished writing this letter, Shensheng turned towards the north and bowed twice, then he hanged himself. The day after his death, Dongguan Wu arrived with his army. When he discovered that Shensheng was dead, he arrested Du Yuankuan and put him in prison. Afterwards, he reported to Lord Xian: "The scion realized that having committed such a crime there was nowhere to go, so he killed himself."

Lord Xian ordered Du Yuankuan to testify as to the crimes that the scion had committed.

"He was innocent!" Du Yuankuan screamed. "The reason that I let myself be taken prisoner rather than committing suicide was so that I could prove that the scion was innocent! The sacrificial meats that he sent were kept for six days in the palace! Surely if they were poisoned, someone should have noticed something odd about them?"

Lady Li Ji, who was present but sitting behind a screen, shouted out: "Du Yuankuan led his student astray. Why don't you just kill him?"

Lord Xian ordered a guard to crush his skull with blows from a bronze hammer. The ministers all mourned him, but they did so in secret.

. . .

Liang Wu and Dongguan Wu now spoke to the actor, Shi: "The Honorable Chonger and Yiwu have always been on excellent terms with the scion. Now he is dead, but they are both still alive, which is very worrying." Shi mentioned this to Lady Li Ji and told her to slander the two young men.

That night, Lady Li Ji spoke to Lord Xian in tears. "I have been told that Chonger and Yiwu were both involved in Shensheng's conspiracy. They both blame me for Shensheng's death and are training their troops day and night so that they can make a surprise attack on Jin and kill me. They are hatching a treasonous conspiracy—you must investigate this, my lord!"

Lord Xian did not really believe this, but at early morning court the next day one of his ministers reported: "Your two sons came from Pu and Qu to pay court to you, but when they arrived at the gates, they heard what had happened to the scion and immediately turned their chariots around."

"If they left without a word to me, they must be part of this conspiracy," Lord Xian decided. He ordered the eunuch Bo Di to lead the army and go to Pu to arrest the Honorable Chonger. At the same time, Jia Hua would lead an army to Qu to arrest the Honorable Yiwu.

Hu Tu summoned his second son, Hu Yan, to his presence and said: "The Honorable Chonger has fused ribs and double pupils: such a remarkable appearance is a presage of his exceptional intelligence. In the future he is sure to achieve great things. Now that the scion is dead, the succession will proceed according to seniority. You should go at once to Pu and get him to flee into exile. You and your older brother, Hu Mao, must both assist him, for one day he will become the Marquis of Jin."

Hu Yan did as he had been ordered and headed for the city of Pu under cover of darkness to throw in his lot with the Honorable Chonger. Chonger was shocked by this latest development, and he discussed the prospect of exile with Hu Mao and Hu Yan. Just then Bo Di's forces arrived. The people of Pu wanted to shut the gates of the city and refuse to allow him in.

"We cannot disobey an order from His Lordship," the Honorable Chonger reminded them.

Bo Di forced his way into the city of Pu, where he surrounded Chonger's house. Chonger, Hu Mao, and Hu Yan rushed into the garden, pursued by Bo Di with a sword in his hand. Hu Mao and Hu Yan climbed over the wall first, pulling Chonger up after them. Bo Di grabbed hold of his sleeve, which the latter then hacked through with his sword. This was how the Honorable Chonger was able to escape unharmed. Bo Di took the sleeve back with him to report. These three men then escaped to the Di nomadic people.

The chief of the Di dreamed that a blue dragon coiled around the top of his city walls. When he heard that the Honorable Chonger of Jin had arrived, he was very happy to welcome him. A short time later a couple of small chariots arrived below the walls, one after another, and the occupants shouted out that they should open the gates as quickly as they could. The Honorable Chonger was worried that these were troops that had been sent after him, so he told the soldiers on top of the walls to shoot them dead.

One of the men at the foot of the walls shouted out: "We have not come to hurt you—we are knights of Jin who have come to serve you!"

Chonger climbed up to the top of the walls and looked out. He recognized the first of these men as Zhao Cui, styled Ziyu, the younger brother of the Grandee Zhao Wei, who was himself also a grandee of the state of Jin.

"I really was not expecting to see you here!" the Honorable Chonger said happily. He ordered them to open the gates and let them in: the famous knights Xu Chen, Wei Chou, Hu Shegu, Dian Jie, Jie Zitui, and Xian Zhen all entered. There were another couple of dozen men who had followed in their train helping them to get away, holding whips and carrying bags—this group included Hu Shu and others.

Chonger said in amazement, "His Lordship is waiting for you at court—what on earth are you doing here?"

Zhao Cui and his companions all said, "His Lordship has behaved appallingly, showing favor to that dreadful woman and murdering his scion, so the state of Jin is on the brink of a civil war. We all know you to be a good man, and that is why we have decided to follow you into exile."

The chief of the Di gave instructions to open the gates of the city. Once they entered, they had an audience with him.

"That you gentlemen have been noble enough to help me is something that I will never forget to the end of my days," the Honorable Chonger said with tears in his eyes.

Wei Chou came forward and presented his opinion: "You have been living in Pu for many years, and the people of that city would be happy to die for you. If you were to ask for assistance from the Di and they joined forces with the people of Pu, you could force your way into the capital. There are many people at court who are deeply unhappy with the way that things have gone, so you would certainly find support from some quarters there. You can get rid of that horrible woman who is poisoning His Lordship's mind, bringing peace to the country and security to our people. Would this not be better than spending the rest of your life wandering around as an exile?"

"You have a point in what you say," the Honorable Chonger said, "but I am concerned that this might be too great a shock for my father. I would not dare to behave in such a way."

Wei Chou was a brave man. Seeing that the Honorable Chonger was not prepared to follow his advice, he ground his teeth and stamped his foot, saying, "Lady Li Ji is not as fierce as a tiger or as poisonous as a snake, but if you are that frightened of her, when will you ever achieve anything?"

It was Hu Yan who explained the situation to Wei Chou: "He is not afraid of Lady Li Ji—he is worried about preserving his reputation."

Wei Chou was left with nothing to say.

In the past, someone wrote an "Old Poem" that praises the men who followed the Honorable Chonger into exile:

> This gentleman from the city of Pu was brought to disaster by slander;
> Carts and horses sped westwards, fleeing into exile as fast as they could.
> Who are these men with bags on their backs and swords by their sides?
> These heroes are all knights from Shanxi.
> The knights from Shanxi competed with each other to be part of his train,
> All men of exceptional appearance and remarkable talents.
> The civil officials were all of a caliber to fix the stars in their courses,
> The generals were such that they could ride the whirlwind.
> Lord Xian had never appreciated Zhao Chengzi,
> A man to bring you warmth on the coldest day.
> His Lordship had also never understood Sikong Ji,
> Who developed the "Six Secret Teachings" and "Three Stratagems."
> The two members of the Hu family were his blood relatives,
> Their strategies and plans brilliant beyond compare.
> The brave and martial Wei Chou was a tiger among men,
> Jia Tuo so strong that he thought nothing of lifting one thousand *jun*.
> Dian Jie was a proud and independent man,

While straightforward Xian Zhen could be trusted to speak out
  fearlessly.
As for Jie Zitui's honesty, who can compare?
The qualities of all these men stood the test of time.
They worked well together, finding themselves in harmony,
As they traveled together through the states of Qin, Qi, and Chu.
On the road, eating and sleeping, they were never apart,
They followed their master through the most trying of circumstances.
Since antiquity True Kings have always been supported by the gods,
And tigers and dragons have flocked to their standard.
If you plant a paulownia tree, the phoenixes will come,
So why should you worry about the idea of "thickets" and the "lone
  tree"?

From a very young age the Honorable Chonger had made the
acquaintance of many knights, whom he treated with the greatest respect.
From the age of seventeen onwards, he behaved towards Hu Yan as if he
were his own father, while treating Zhao Cui as his teacher and Hu
Shegu as his older brother. He had become friends with all the knights he
heard about, whether they were at court or not, so although he was now
forced into exile and found himself in a terribly difficult and dangerous
situation, a great many good men were prepared to follow him.

. . .

The Grandee Xi Rui and Lü Yisheng were good friends, while Guo She
was the Honorable Yiwu's maternal uncle. These three men traveled
independently to Qu to work for the Honorable Yiwu. When they had
an audience with him, they informed him that Jia Hua and his army
would arrive at any moment. The Honorable Yiwu then mobilized his
troops to defend the city walls. However, Jia Hua actually had no intention of arresting Yiwu, so when he ordered his forces to surround the
city, he did so in a deliberately inefficient manner, while at the same time
sending a secret message to Yiwu to say: "You must leave immediately.
Otherwise, when more troops arrive from Jin, you will not be able to
withstand their onslaught."

The Honorable Yiwu discussed the situation with Xi Rui: "Chonger
has gone to the Di. What do you think of the idea of me going to join
him?"

"His Lordship is trying to assert that the two of you have joined in
some kind of conspiracy against him, and that is why he is punishing
you," Xi Rui said. "Now, if you both end up in the same place, Lady Li
Ji is sure to have something to say about it, and the Jin army will attack

the Di. It would be better for you to go to Liang. Liang is located close to Qin, and Qin is a strong state and one that is allied to yours by marriage. When His Lordship dies, you can avail yourself of their support to accede to the title."

The Honorable Yiwu then fled to Liang.

Jia Hua claimed that he had gone in pursuit and simply failed to catch up with him. He reported back that the Honorable Yiwu had fled. Lord Xian was absolutely furious and said, "What is the point of having an army, if you can't even arrest my sons for me?" He shouted to his entourage to arrest Jia Hua and behead him.

Pi Zhengfu presented his opinion: "Your Lordship ordered that these two cities should be walled and allowed them to be garrisoned. That is not Jia Hua's fault."

Liang Wu also presented his opinion: "The Honorable Yiwu is not a particular source of concern. The Honorable Chonger, on the other hand, has a reputation as a brilliant man, and many knights have given their allegiance to him, to the point where Your Lordship's own court has become denuded. Besides which, the Di have been our enemies from one generation to the next, so if you do not attack them and kill the Honorable Chonger, there will be a disaster sooner or later."

Lord Xian pardoned Jia Hua and sent someone to summon Bo Di. When Bo Di heard of the punishment that had almost overtaken Jia Hua, he immediately asked permission to take the army to attack the Di, and Lord Xian agreed to this. When Bo Di's forces arrived at the Di capital, the Di chief had already stationed his army at Caisang, and they became locked in a standoff that lasted for more than two months.

At this point, Pi Zhengfu came forward and said, "Your Lordship has no reason to behave like this. Not only have you not announced what crimes your two sons are guilty of, but they have both already been forced into exile. If you now insist upon murdering them, what does this look like? You have not been able to defeat the Di, and all you have succeeded in doing is exhausting your own army. You have humiliated us before all the other aristocrats."

Lord Xian was gradually brought around to this new point of view. He summoned Bo Di and ordered him to bring the army home. However, Lord Xian still suspected that many members of the ruling house were secretly involved in either the Honorable Chonger or the Honorable Yiwu's faction, so in the future they would certainly not support Xiqi's accession. He therefore gave orders that all members of the ruling house were to be thrown out of the country; indeed, none of them dared to stay. After this, he felt able to appoint Xiqi as his heir, but apart from the "Two Wus" and Xun Xi, no one else accepted this appointment. There were many ministers who announced that their health was failing or resigned their posts on the grounds of old age. This all happened in the first year of the reign of King Xiang of Zhou, which was the twenty-sixth year of Lord Xian of Jin's rule.

That autumn in the ninth month, Lord Xian rushed to attend the meeting at Kuiqiu but still did not get there in time. On the way home, he became sick. When he arrived back at the capital, he went straight to the palace. Lady Li Ji sat by his feet and cried: "Your Lordship has alienated your sons and forced the rest of your family into exile in order to establish my son as your heir. If anything were to happen to you, I am just a weak woman and Xiqi is only little—supposing that your sons enlist support from foreign powers and try and come back? On whom can your son and I rely?"

"Do not worry!" Lord Xian told her. "Grand Tutor Xun Xi is a loyal minister and will never betray you. I will entrust little Xiqi to his care."

He summoned Xun Xi to his bedside and asked him: "I have heard it said that the most important qualities for a knight are loyalty and trust-worthiness. What do you understand by loyalty and trustworthiness?"

"Loyalty is serving your lord to the best of your ability," Xun Xi replied. "Trustworthiness lies in never breaking your word even if that means you die."

"It is my intention to entrust my son to your care," Lord Xian informed him. "Will you accept this charge?"

Xun Xi kowtowed and said, "I will do my very best."

A tear trickled from Lord Xian's eye, and Lady Li Ji's convulsive sobbing could be heard from the other side of the bed trappings. A few days later, Lord Xian died. Lady Li Ji hugged Xiqi and handed him over to Xun Xi—at that time he was only eleven years old. Xun Xi did exactly as His Late Lordship had requested and helped Xiqi to take charge of the funeral, at which all his officials lined up and wept bitterly. Lady Li Ji appointed Xun Xi to the position of a senior minister, while Liang Wu and Dongguan Wu became Marshals of the Left and Right and took their troops to patrol through the country to prevent any overt resist-ance, just as Lord Xian had instructed her to do on his deathbed. All matters of government, whether large or small, had to be referred to Xun Xi. The following year was the first year of the new lord's reign, and he informed the other lords of his accession.

How many days did Xiqi survive as ruler? READ ON.

Chapter Twenty-eight

Li Ke murders two infant rulers in succession.

Lord Mu pacifies a civil war in Jin for the first time.

When Xun Xi presided over the establishment of the Honorable Xiqi as the new Lord of Jin in front of his father's coffin, all the officials attended the funeral and wailed ceremonially. Hu Tu was the only one who refused to go, with the excuse that he was seriously ill.

Li Ke spoke privately with Pi Zhengfu: "Even though this child has now become the new lord, what will happen about his brothers in exile?"

"Xun Xi seems to be in complete control of the situation," Pi Zhengfu said, "so you had better go and find out what he intends to do." Accordingly, the two men got onto a chariot and went to Xun Xi's mansion together.

Xun Xi invited them in, and Li Ke made his representation to him: "His Lordship has just passed away, and the Honorable Chonger and Yiwu are both abroad. You are one of the most senior ministers in the country, so why did you not invite the oldest son to succeed to his father's position and establish the son of a base-born favorite instead? How will you persuade anyone to submit to his authority? They were prevented from expressing their opinions to His Late Lordship, but the faction behind his three older brothers hate Xiqi and his mother right down to the marrow of their bones. Now that Lord Xian is dead, they will be planning a rebellion. Xiqi's brothers will have the support of the state of Qin and the Di people, as well as that of the residents of the capital. What plans have you come up with to deal with this?"

"I have supported Xiqi purely because that was His Lordship's deathbed wish," Xun Xi explained, "so he has now become my ruler. I do not care about his exiled brothers! If there is anyone who does not agree with what I have done, they can kill me. In that way, at least, I will be able to requite our former lord's kindness to me."

"Dying is pointless," Pi Zhengfu retorted. "Do you really not have any better plan?"

"I have always repaid His Late Lordship with absolute loyalty," Xun Xi said proudly. "Even if dying is indeed completely pointless, at least I will have kept my word!"

The two men kept trying to persuade him, but Xun Xi's mind was made up. From start to finish, he just repeated the same thing, so in the end they just had to say goodbye and leave him.

Li Ke then said to Pi Zhengfu, "We have been good colleagues, but even though I have explained the delicacy of the situation so clearly, he simply will not listen. What should I do now?"

"He is working for Xiqi," Pi Zhengfu said, "and we are working for Chonger. Each of us is serving our own master. What is wrong with that?"

The two men made a secret agreement to send a trusted knight, dressed up as one of His Lordship's guards, to mix in with all the others. His mission was to stab Xiqi to death while he was attending to his father's coffin in his mourning hut. When the assassin struck, the actor Shi was by the young boy's side, and he drew his sword to defend him. Although he succeeded in slaying the assassin, both he and Xiqi were killed in this attack. In a moment, the whole party was in uproar. Xun Xi was some way away, wailing over the former lord's coffin. When he heard the news, he was deeply alarmed and immediately rushed over. He patted the boy's body and said sadly: "It was His Lordship's dying wish that I should support your accession, and I have been guilty of a terrible crime in not protecting you."

He attempted suicide by dashing his head against one of the pillars of the hut, but Lady Li Ji quickly ordered someone to prevent him. "His Lordship's body is lying in its coffin," she said. "Are you the only person who is not aware of that fact? Even if Xiqi is dead, the Honorable Zhuozi is still alive. You should support his accession."

Xun Xi ordered the execution of the couple of dozen men who had been guarding the party. That very same day he convened a meeting of all the officials, at which they discussed installing Zhuozi as the new ruler. At that time the Honorable Zhuozi was just nine years old. Li Ke and Pi Zhengfu pretended to know nothing at all about what was going on, and they did not attend this meeting.

Liang Wu said: "The death of this child was the result of Li Ke and Pi Zhengfu taking revenge for the death of the late scion. Now they have not come to this meeting, so the truth could not be clearer. I request your permission to take the army to punish them."

"Those two men are long-serving ministers of the state of Jin," Xun Xi reminded him, "and they are both well-connected and widely supported. Most of the seven senior grandees of our state are related to one or another of them. If you fail in your attempt to punish them, things will be made much worse. It would be better to ignore the whole situation, letting them imagine that they have gotten away with it, so that they proceed with their plan. Once the funeral is out of the way, we can formally establish a new ruler, and then with support from our allies we can get rid of their faction. Once that is done, we can deal with the pair of them."

As Liang Wu walked away, he said to Dongguan Wu, "Xun Xi is a very loyal minister, but he is not a good conspirator. He seems to want to let things drag on, but we cannot wait! Li Ke and Pi Zhengfu may be on the same side, but of the two of them Li Ke suffered the most with what happened to the scion, and so his hatred is correspondingly deep. If we get rid of Li Ke, Pi Zhengfu will not fight us."

"How do you plan to get rid of him?" Dongguan Wu inquired.

"The funeral cortege is now approaching the city," Liang Wu said, "so if you were to arrange an ambush by the East Gate, all we would need is one soldier to suddenly attack him once he has spotted him in the funerary procession."

"That's fine!" Dongguan Wu exclaimed. "I have a client named Tu'an Yi who can run at full speed while carrying a three thousand–*jun* weight. If I hold out the prospect of a title and money to spend, he will do this for us."

He summoned Tu'an Yi and explained what they had in mind.

Tu'an Yi had always been on good terms with Grandee Zhui Chuan, and so he secretly leaked the details of the plot to him. "Should I do this or not?" he asked.

"Everyone in the country was devastated by the terrible death of the innocent scion," Zhui Chuan reminded him, "and that was all the fault of Lady Li Ji. Now the two grandees, Li Ke and Pi Zhengfu, want to extirpate her faction at court and establish the Honorable Chonger as the new ruler, which is an entirely virtuous action. I will not let you help the wicked to punish the loyal by carrying out such a heinous crime. You cannot do something that will see you cursed by ten thousand generations, you cannot!"

"Ordinary people like me don't know anything about the bigger picture," Tu'an Yi said. "How would it be if I simply refused?"

"If you refuse," Zhui Chuan told him, "they will just find someone else. It will be better if you pretend to agree, and then, when the time comes, you turn your sword on them and help us to punish these wicked men. You will then have the honor of having supported the accession of the rightful heir. You will not only become noble and rich, but also be highly esteemed. Surely that is better than getting involved in such a wicked crime."

"You are absolutely right," Tu'an Yi said.

"Do you think you can carry this off?" Zhui Chuan asked.

"If you have any concerns about my loyalty," Tu'an Yi proclaimed, "let us swear a blood covenant!" He slaughtered a chicken and they smeared their mouths with blood.

When Tu'an Yi left, Zhui Chuan told Pi Zhengfu what had happened, and Zhengfu communicated this to Li Ke. They arranged that their own soldiers would be mobilized and primed to set out on the day of the funeral.

On the appointed day, Li Ke announced that he was too ill to attend the obsequies. Tu'an Yi then spoke to Dongguan Wu. "All the grandees with the exception of Li Ke will be attending the funeral. This means that Heaven must want him dead! Let me take three hundred soldiers to surround his mansion and kill him."

Dongguan Wu was very pleased. All that happened, however, was that Tu'an Yi pretended to surround Li Ke's house with the three hundred soldiers. Li Ke added verisimilitude to these events by sending a messenger to go to the tomb site and announce that he was under attack. Xun Xi was alarmed and asked what was going on, but Dongguan Wu simply said, "We heard rumors that Li Ke was planning to take advantage of the current situation to launch a coup, so we have sent one of our clients with a few troops to place him under temporary house arrest. If our efforts succeed, then you will get credit for putting down a rebellion. If they do not, you will not take any of the blame."

Xun Xi felt as if he had been stabbed to the heart. He carried out the remainder of the funerary rites in a daze. He sent the forces under the command of the "Two Wus" to help in the attack, while he himself assisted the Honorable Zhuozi to preside over his first court, in the hope that this would put the best possible gloss on the matter. Dong-guan Wu's troops were the first to arrive at the Eastern Market. Tu'an Yi came forward to meet him. With the excuse of needing to report on the progress of their plan, he came right up close, got Dongguan Wu into a headlock, and broke his neck. The army was thrown into complete chaos. Tu'an Yi then shouted: "The Honorable Chonger has already arrived at the foot of the city walls in command of an allied force of Qin and Di soldiers. Let us punish the corrupt and wicked people responsible for the terrible death of poor Shensheng and welcome Chonger as our new ruler. Anyone who supports this should come with me! Anyone against it can go home!"

When the army heard that Chonger had been proclaimed their new ruler, they all leaped up and were happy to obey his orders. When Liang Wu heard that Dongguan Wu had been murdered, he immediately rushed to court, for it was his intention to flee into exile with Xun Xi and the Honorable Zhuozi. However, Tu'an Yi came in hot pursuit. Li Ke, Pi Zhengfu, and Zhui Chuan all arrived at the same time, each in command of his own troops. Liang Wu realized that he would not be able to escape, so he drew his sword and tried to cut his own throat, but before he could kill himself, Tu'an Yi wrested the sword from his grasp and took him prisoner. Li Ke then raised his sabre and cut him in two pieces. Just at that moment Grandee Gong Hua, the general in command of the Army of the Left, arrived at the head of his own army to assist them. They cut their way through the palace gates together, with Li Ke leading the way, a drawn sword in his hand. The troops followed him, and the palace servants scattered in terror. Xun Xi remained calm, and he hugged Zhuozi to his chest with his left arm while holding his right arm so that his sleeve hid the boy's face. Zhuozi was whimpering with fear.

"What crime has this child committed?" Xun Xi demanded. "Kill me instead! I beg that you will leave His Late Lordship's son alive!"

"And where is Shensheng now?" Li Ke retorted. "Was he not also one of His Lordship's sons?" He turned his head to look at Tu'an Yi and said, "What are you waiting for?"

Tu'an Yi grabbed the boy from Xun Xi's grasp, threw him down upon the steps, and crushed him to death with a single stamp from his foot. Xun Xi was furious, and, wrenching his sword from its scabbard, he launched an attack on Li Ke. He too was beheaded by Tu'an Yi. They then cut their way through the palace, only to discover that Lady Li Ji had already fled to seek sanctuary with Lady Jia Jun. However, Her Ladyship shut the door on her and refused to help, so she went to the rear gardens, where she threw herself into the lake from the top of the bridge and drowned. Li Ke ordered that her body be exposed in the marketplace. Lady Li Ji's younger sister had never been favored, nor had she held any power at court, in spite of the fact that she had given birth to the Honorable Zhuozi. Her they did not kill, but she was imprisoned in one of the side rooms in the palace. They murdered every member of the "Two Wus" family and that of the actor, Shi.

A bearded old man wrote a poem bewailing what happened to Lady Li Ji:

> What was the point of murdering Shensheng,
> To allow a child to take over these lands?
> But both mother and child were killed in their turn,
> Just as described in the song "The Pleasures of Idleness."

There is another poem that bemoans the fact that Xun Xi upheld his lord's stupid commands and thus established two concubines' sons in power, to the detriment of his posthumous reputation. This poem runs:

> Surely it is not right to follow the stupid orders of a misguided ruler?
> And yet he stubbornly insisted on remaining loyal until death.
> What happened to the intelligence that planned the bribing of the Duke
>   of Yu?
> Thus a ruler and a minister ended up waiting to die together.

Li Ke summoned all the ministers to court to discuss the situation with them: "The two base-born children are now dead. Of all the sons of His Late Lordship, Chonger is the cleverest, and he is also the most senior. He should become our next ruler. All those grandees who agree with me should sign their names to this document."

"For this matter to be accomplished, we will need the help of Grandee Hu Tu," Pi Zhengfu reminded him.

Li Ke immediately sent someone with a chariot to fetch him. Hu Tu refused to go, saying, "My two sons followed the Honorable Chonger into exile. If I now play any role in bringing him back to the country, I will become an accessory after the fact in the assassinations of Xiqi and Zhuozi. I am an old man anyway. Chonger will only come back if mandated to do so by all the grandees of our country."

Li Ke seized the brush and was the first to sign his name to the document. He was followed by Pi Zhengfu, Gong Hua, Jia Hua, Zhui Chuan and more than thirty other grandees—in fact, not all of the junior people who wanted to sign were able to. They awarded Tu'an Yi the office of a senior knight and ordered him to take this official letter of appointment to the Di, and to escort the Honorable Chonger back to the country.

When Chonger noticed that Hu Tu had not signed, he became suspicious.

"They want to bring you back, so why don't you go?" Wei Chou demanded. "Do you want to stay in exile forever?"

"You don't understand," Chonger said. "There are many other potential heirs, not just me. Besides which, although the two boys have both been killed, their supporters are still out there. What is the point of going back if I am just going to be forced into exile again? If Heaven wishes to bless me, surely it will not leave me stateless?"

Hu Yan was worried that his reputation would be irreparably damaged if Chonger were seen to take advantage of his father's death to launch a coup, so he urged him not to go. The Honorable Chonger apologized to the envoy and said, "I fled into exile after offending against my father, so during his lifetime I was unable to perform the duties of a son, and after his death I have not been able to mourn him according to the proper rites. In the circumstances, surely it is not appropriate for me to take advantage of the chaos in Jin to take over the country. The grandees will have to establish one of His Lordship's other sons, because I do not want anything to do with this situation."

Tu'an Yi reported back with this message, and Li Ke wanted to send another envoy. However, Grandee Liang Yaomi now spoke up: "Any of His Lordship's sons will do as our next ruler, so how about Yiwu?"

"Yiwu is a greedy and unpleasant man," Li Ke said. "Since he is greedy, he is untrustworthy, while his unpleasant character means that people do not love him. Chonger is a much better choice."

"But he is cleverer than any of His Lordship's other sons, is he not?" Liang Yaomi said. The company all agreed, so Li Ke had no choice but to send Tu'an Yi to help Liang Yaomi bring the Honorable Yiwu home.

. . .

The Honorable Yiwu had been living in Liang, where the Earl of Liang had given him the hand of his daughter in marriage and she had given birth to a son named Yu. While Yiwu was staying with his in-laws, he was on watch day and night for developments in Jin, in case there was some kind of opportunity that would allow him to go home. When he heard that Lord Xian had died, he immediately ordered Lü Yisheng to attack the city of Qu and hold it for him. Xun Xi was so busy with other matters of state that he could not deal with this. Then he heard that

Xiqi and Zhuozi had both been murdered and that the grandees had sent someone to bring Chonger home. Lü Yisheng told the Honorable Yiwu about the document that they had prepared. Yiwu then discussed the situation with Guo She and Xi Rui, because he was planning to dispute the succession. Suddenly Liang Yaomi and his entourage turned up to welcome Yiwu back, so he slapped his hand against his forehead and said, "Heaven has snatched the country out of Chonger's grasp and given it to me!" He could not overcome his delight.

Xi Rui came forward and said, "Chonger has certainly not given up his claim to the title, so his refusal is highly suspicious. You must not trust him! The grandees are all still in power inside the state, and yet they are bringing you in from abroad to make you the ruler, so they will be expecting lavish rewards. The most important ministers in the government of the state of Jin are Li Ke and Pi Zhengfu. You will have to give them massive bribes or your position will be in great danger. 'When a man goes into the tiger's den, he had better be carrying a sharp spear,' so if you want to return to your country, my lord, you will have to have the assistance of a strong foreign power. Of the states bordering on Jin, Qin is by far the strongest. You should send an envoy to humbly beg for Qin for help in installing you in power. If Qin agrees, then you can go home."

Yiwu followed his advice and agreed to give Li Ke one million *mu* of land in Fenyang, while Pi Zhengfu would get seven hundred thousand *mu* in Fukui. This was all set out in writing, and then the document was sealed. He ordered Tu'an Yi to go back to Jin to report on the situation, while he kept Liang Yaomi behind, because he wanted him to take a letter to Qin to announce that the grandees of the state of Jin wanted him to become their new ruler.

Lord Mu of Qin spoke about this to Jian Shu: "I am the only person in the world who can bring an end to the civil war in Jin; that has been proclaimed by the dream given to me by God on High. I have heard that Chonger and Yiwu are both brilliant young men, so I should choose one to install in power. But which one is best?"

"Chonger is living with the Di, while Yiwu is in Liang," Jian Shu said. "These two places are both nearby, so Your Lordship could send someone to condole with them on the death of their father. That way you can learn something of their personalities."

"That would be good," Lord Mu agreed.

Thus it came about that he sent the Honorable Zhi to offer formal condolences first to Chonger and then to Yiwu. When the Honorable Zhi arrived among the Di people, he had an audience with the Honorable Chonger, at which he expressed his condolences as he had been instructed by the Lord of Qin. When the ceremony had been completed, Chonger withdrew and the Honorable Zhi then sent a message by the gatekeeper to say, "You should be thinking about how to take advantage of this situation to get back home. His Lordship would be happy to help you in return for a small douceur."

Chonger reported this to Zhao Cui, who said, "If your own people want you back, that is one thing. It is something quite different if you are installed by a foreign power."

Chonger went out and had audience with the ruler of Qin's envoy, at which he said, "His Lordship has been kind enough to send official condolences to me even though I am in exile, but he has humiliated me by his second message. Having been expelled from my country, I have no treasure to offer him—friendship is all that I have left. My father has only just died; under the circumstances, how can I be plotting a coup!"

He threw himself upon the ground and wept, kowtowed, and withdrew; from start to finish, he did not say a single word that could possibly be construed as indicating any selfish ambition. The Honorable Zhi realized that Chonger would not be playing along, and he was deeply impressed by his noble character, so he sighed and left.

Next he went to condole with Yiwu in Liang. When the ceremony was over, Yiwu said to the Honorable Zhi, "You, sir, received His Lordship's order to come and condole with me, so do you have any further instructions for me?"

The Honorable Zhi then tried the line about "taking advantage of this situation to get back home" on him, and Yiwu kowtowed and thanked him. Afterwards, he went in and reported this to Xi Rui, saying: "Qin has agreed to install me in power."

"What is Qin hoping to get out of it?" Xi Rui asked. "They are going to want something from us. You had better be prepared to bribe them with a large tranche of land."

"Won't giving them a large area of land harm Jin?" Yiwu inquired.

"Until such time as you have returned to your own country as ruler," Xi Rui explained, "you are just an ordinary subject of the Lord of Liang and you do not own so much as a foot of land in Jin! What is the problem with giving them something that actually belongs to someone else?"

Yiwu then had a second audience with the Honorable Zhi. Clasping hold of his hand, he said, "Li Ke and Pi Zhengfu have both promised to support my accession. I intend to reward both of them generously for this. If, thanks to His Lordship's support. I am able to take control of the state altars, I will give five cities beyond the Yellow River to him to add to his eastern border. I am happy to give the Lord of Qin all the former territory of Guo, as far south as Mount Hua and extending right up to the border at Xieliang, and yet this will only requite one tiny part of His Lordship's generosity to me." He took a document to this effect out of his sleeve with an appealing expression on his face.

The Honorable Zhi went through the motions of refusing, but Yiwu said, "I have here forty ingots of gold and six pairs of white jade pendants, which I would like to give to your entourage. I hope that you will speak well of me to His Lordship. Indeed, I will never forget your kindness to me."

The Honorable Zhi then accepted all his gifts.

A historian wrote a poem that reads:

The Honorable Chonger was virtuous and mourned the death of his
    father.
The Honorable Yiwu was greedy, and so he was thrilled by these events.
Simply by observing the way in which they received the condolences
    offered,
You can tell which of them would succeed and which would fail.

The Honorable Zhi returned with this document to show Lord Mu, and he described his audience with the two young men.

"Chonger is a much more noble character than Yiwu, so I will install him," Lord Mu announced.

"Is Your Lordship planning to install a new ruler in Jin because you feel sorry for this country?" the Honorable Zhi inquired. "Or is it because you want to make yourself famous?"

"Why should I care in the slightest what happens in Jin?" Lord Mu said in puzzlement. "I just want to make myself famous."

"If Your Lordship were feeling sorry for Jin," the Honorable Zhi explained, "you would want to select the best possible ruler to install in power. If your primary intention is to become famous, then you had better choose an ignoble character. In both instances you are putting a new ruler in place, but a brilliant man would outshine you, whereas a stupid person would always be in your debt. Which of the two is more beneficial for you?"

"You have really opened my eyes!" Lord Mu exclaimed. He then ordered Noble Grandson Qi to take a force of three hundred chariots out to install Yiwu in power.

. . .

Lord Mu of Qin's principal wife, Lady Mu Ji, was the younger sister of Scion Shensheng of Jin. From a very young age she had been brought up in the palace of Lord Xian's secondary wife, Lady Jia Jun, and she was a most noble and virtuous woman. When she heard that Noble Grandson Qi was going to install Yiwu in power in Jin, she wrote a letter for him that said:

> When you become the ruler of Jin, you must treat Lady Jia Jun well. Your brothers and uncles who have fled into exile to avoid the troubles in Jin are all innocent of any crime, so you should allow them all to come home. If in the future they achieve great things, this will only bring greater glory to you. Let them protect the borders of our state.

Yiwu was afraid of offending Lady Mu Ji, so he did exactly as she instructed him. At that time, Lord Huan of Qi heard that the state of Jin had descended into civil war, so he wanted to call the lords together for a meeting to plan their response. When he arrived at Gaoliang, he heard that the Qin army had already set out and that King Xiang of Zhou had also sent Prince Dang in command of an army that was heading for Jin. He sent Xi Peng to meet the Zhou and Qin armies, that they might install Yiwu in concert. Lü Yisheng also came out from the city of Qu to meet them. Afterwards, Lord Huan went home to Qi.

Li Ke and Pi Zhengfu asked permission from the senior minister Hu Tu to take charge of the ceremonies. They arranged that the officials would prepare the carriages to go to collect Yiwu at the border of Jin. Upon his entry into the capital city of Jiang, Yiwu was formally installed as Lord Hui of Jin, and this year was proclaimed the first year of his rule. The first year of Lord Hui of Jin's rule was also the second year of the reign of King Xiang of Zhou. The residents of the capital had long admired Chonger's noble character and were hoping that he would become their next ruler. Now Yiwu had replaced Chonger, and they were very disappointed.

When Lord Hui was established, he appointed his son Yu as the scion and made Hu Tu and Guo She senior grandees, and Lü Yisheng and Xi Rui as mid-level grandees, while Tu'an Yi became a junior grandee. The remaining ministers all kept their old offices. He sent Liang Yaomi to escort Prince Dang back to Zhou, and Han Jian to escort Xi Peng back to Qi, that they might each thank the ruler for his assistance in installing him in power. Only Noble Grandson Qi stayed in the state of Jin, because he insisted on being given the five cities west of the Yellow River. Lord Hui could not bear to lose them, so he summoned his officials for a meeting to discuss the situation.

At this meeting, Guo She stared meaningfully at Lü Yisheng. He then came forward and said: "The reason why Your Lordship wanted to bribe Qin was that you had not yet been able to return to your country, so the land that you offered them was actually not yours to give. Now you have been installed in power and the country is yours. If you don't give this land to Qin, what can they do about it?"

"Your Lordship has only just come to power," Li Ke reminded him, "so it would not be a good idea for you to betray the trust of a powerful neighboring state. You had better give them the land."

"Losing those five cities is like losing half the state of Jin," Xi Rui said. "Even though Qin is militarily very powerful, they certainly would not be able to wrest these lands from us by force. Besides which, His Late Lordship began his military campaigns from that territory—we cannot just abandon them!"

"Since you knew that those were His Late Lordship's heartlands, why on earth did you agree to hand them over?" Li Ke demanded. "Having agreed, will you not anger Qin greatly when you refuse to give them? Besides which, our former lord founded the country at Quwo, a very small parcel of land, but he then strengthened his government and was eventually able to conquer a number of other small states, thus becoming great. If Your Lordship will reform the government and maintain good relations with your neighbors, there is nothing to worry about in losing these five cities."

Xi Rui sighed and said, "Li Ke isn't speaking up on behalf of Qin, but because he wants his one million *mu* of land in Fenyang and is afraid that Your Lordship is not going to give them to him. He wants Qin to use as a precedent."

Pi Zhengfu elbowed Li Ke in the ribs, and he did not dare to say another word.

"If I don't hand over these cities then I betray my word," Lord Hui said, "but if I do hand them over then I am seriously weakening my position. How about I just give them one or two cities?"

"If you present them with one or two cities," Lü Yisheng said, "first of all you have not completely kept your word, and secondly it might well provoke open conflict with Qin. How about you try apologizing to them?"

Lord Hui ordered Lü Yisheng to write a letter apologizing to Qin. This letter said:

> Originally I promised to give five cities west of the Yellow River to Your Lordship. Now I have been so fortunate as to be able to return and take control of the state altars. Remembering your great kindness to me, I want

to fulfill my promise. However, my senior ministers all said, "Your lands are the territory of our former rulers. When you were in exile, how could you unilaterally agree to give them away to someone else?" I argued with them, but they did not accept my position. I hope that you will agree to a slight delay. I will never dare to forget your generosity to me.

"Who will go on my behalf to apologize to the state of Qin?" His Lordship asked. Pi Zhengfu was willing to go, and so Lord Hui agreed to this.

. . .

Originally when Lord Hui was trying to get back into the country, he agreed to give Pi Zhengfu seven hundred thousand *mu* of land in Fukui. However, since Lord Hui was not prepared to hand over the cities that he had promised Qin, is it likely that he was willing to give this amount of land to Li Ke and Pi Zhengfu? Even though Pi Zhengfu never said a word about it, he was very angry. He asked specially to be allowed to undertake this mission because he wanted to complain to Qin. Therefore, Pi Zhengfu followed Noble Grandson Qi back to the state of Qin, whereupon he had an audience with Lord Mu and presented the document with which he had been entrusted.

When Lord Mu had finished reading it, he was furious and said, "I knew that Yiwu would never make a good ruler. Now that bastard is trying to cheat me!" He wanted to execute Pi Zhengfu.

Noble Grandson Qi presented his opinion: "This is not Pi Zhengfu's fault. I hope that Your Lordship will forgive him."

Lord Mu was still angry, and demanded: "Who is encouraging Yiwu to go back on his word? I will rip him to pieces with my own bare hands!"

"Send your entourage away, my lord, for I have something to tell you," Pi Zhengfu said.

Lord Mu now began to calm down, and he ordered his servants to withdraw to the far side of the tapestry hangings. Afterwards, he waved Pi Zhengfu forward and asked him what was going on.

"All the grandees of Jin are deeply aware of Your Lordship's benevolence," Pi Zhengfu told him, "and would be happy to give you this territory, but Lü Yisheng and Xi Rui are preventing it. If Your Lordship were to send a diplomatic mission to Jin with generous gifts and then summoned the pair of them, making sure that no word of your actual intention leaked out, you could kill them when they arrive here. Your Lordship could then install Chonger in power, for Li Ke and I would throw Yiwu out of the country and act as your agents at court. We would then serve Your Lordship from one generation to the next. How would that be?"

"That is a wonderful plan!" Lord Mu exclaimed. "You have put my wishes into words!"

He sent Grandee Ling Zhi to follow Pi Zhengfu back to Jin with generous gifts, in the hope of luring Lü Yisheng and Xi Rui out of the country so that he could kill them.

Do you want to know what happened to Lü Yisheng and Xi Rui? READ ON.

Chapter Twenty-nine

Lord Hui of Jin executes all his government ministers.

Guan Yiwu discusses the prime ministership on his deathbed.

Li Ke's original idea was to make the Honorable Chonger the next ruler of Jin, but Chonger refused to come back, and Yiwu offered generous bribes in his efforts to return to the country, so he followed the wishes of the majority and set about seeing to his accession. Who would have guessed that once Yiwu was installed as Lord Hui, he would refuse to hand over any of the lands that he had promised, and would employ only his personal friends such as Guo She, Lü Yisheng, and Xi Rui in senior government positions, thereby alienating all the old officials who had served in the previous regime? Li Ke found himself in a situation that he simply could not accept. When he encouraged Lord Hui to give the land to Qin, this was clearly said with the good of the country at heart, but Xi Rui interpreted it as being said for his own selfish reasons. He was careful not to put his rage into words and tried to appear calm, but in actual fact he was furious. When he walked out of the palace gates, the mask slipped and he looked murderous. When Pi Zhengfu went on his mission to Qin, Xi Rui and his cronies were worried that he was involved in some kind of plot with Li Ke, so they secretly sent people to spy on him. Pi Zhengfu had anticipated the possibility that Xi Rui would send someone to check up on him, so he deliberately did not go to say goodbye to Li Ke. Li Ke sent someone to fetch Pi Zhengfu because he wanted to speak to him, but at that time he had already left the city. Li Ke chased after him but could not catch up with him.

Naturally, someone reported this news to Xi Rui. He had an audience with Lord Hui and presented his opinion: "Li Ke hates Your Lordship because you have taken away his power in the government and refused to give him the fields in Fenyang. Now when he heard that Pi Zhengfu had been sent on a diplomatic mission to Qin, he set off in hot pursuit, so he must be plotting something. I have always understood that Li Ke was a close friend of the Honorable Chonger and never intended to see Your Lordship succeed to the title. If he is indeed plotting a coup with Chonger, what are you going to do to stop him? You had better force him to commit suicide before he brings disaster down upon you."

"Li Ke put me in power," Lord Hui said. "What excuse can I now give for killing him?"

"Li Ke assassinated both Xiqi and Zhuozi," Xi Rui reminded him, "and he murdered Xun Xi: the man who received your father's dying commands. These are terrible crimes! You may be privately grateful for his assistance in ensuring your accession, but that should not prevent you from punishing him for his murders in the interests of justice. No enlightened ruler ever neglected the interests of justice in favor of some private gratitude. I request that you give me the order to punish him."

"Please do!" said Lord Hui.

Xi Rui went to Li Ke's house and told him: "The Marquis of Jin has commanded me to come and see you. The Marquis of Jin said: 'If it were not for you, I would never have succeeded to the title, and so I have always been cognizant of the enormous assistance that you have given me. However, you assassinated two lords and murdered one senior grandee, which really puts me in a very difficult position. I have now taken up the mandate of our former lords, so I cannot neglect the interests of justice because of my personal gratitude. Therefore, I wish you to commit suicide.'"

"If they had not died, would His Lordship be in power now?" Li Ke demanded. "Now you want me to take the blame, so how can I escape disaster? I accept my fate!"

Xi Rui attempted to force the issue. Li Ke drew his sword and paced around, shouting, "Heavens! I am innocent! Loyalty has now become a crime! If the dead do indeed have awareness, how can I face Xun Xi?" He then killed himself by cutting his throat.

Xi Rui went back and reported this to Lord Hui, who was very pleased.

A bearded old man wrote a poem that reads:

Given that working for the Honorable Yiwu got him killed,
Would it not have been better to die with Scion Shensheng?
He should have known that sitting on the fence would not work,
And made his reputation even worse than that of Xun Xi!

There were many ministers who were extremely unhappy that Lord Hui had killed Li Ke. Qi Ju, Gong Hua, Jia Hua, and Zhui Chuan all spoke openly about their resentment. Lord Hui decided that they would have to be executed, but Xi Rui reminded him: "Pi Zhengfu is still abroad. If you execute too many people, you will push him into open rebellion, which would be a bad idea. You will just have to put up with the situation."

"Lady Mu Ji asked me to look after Lady Jia Jun and to bring all my uncles and brothers back to the country," Lord Hui remarked. "Would that be a good idea?"

"Your uncles and brothers would like to contest your right to the title," Xi Rui warned him. "You cannot let them back into the country. On the other hand, looking after Lady Jia Jun would be a good way of requiting Lady Mu Ji's kindness."

After this conversation, Lord Hui went to the palace, where he had an audience with Lady Jia Jun. At this time, Lady Jia Jun was still very pretty, and Lord Hui suddenly found himself prey to overwhelming lust for her.

"Lady Mu Ji told me to enjoy myself with you," he told her, "so you cannot refuse!" He immediately took Lady Jia Jun in his arms, and the palace servants all left, giggling. Lady Jia Jun was terrified of Lord Hui, so she had no choice but to go along with what he wanted.

When he had finished, Lady Jia Jun said in floods of tears: "His Late Lordship's death left me a widow, and now I cannot even claim to be chaste. What happens to me is not important, but I beg that you will proclaim the late Scion Shensheng to have been innocent of all the charges against him. That way I can repay Lady Mu Ji's kindness to me and atone for my failure to preserve my chastity as a widow."

"The two brats have been killed," Lord Hui said, "so the former scion's innocence has already been proclaimed!"

"I have heard that the late scion is still buried in a shallow grave outside the New City at Quwo," Lady Jia Jun said. "Your Lordship should move his coffin to the cemetery of the Jin ruling house and give him a posthumous title, that his soul may rest in peace. That will also please the people of the capital!"

Lord Hui agreed to this. He ordered Xi Rui's cousin, Xi Qi, to go to Quwo and select a new burial site, and commanded the Grand Astrologer to select a suitable posthumous title. Given his filial piety and sense of duty, the title chosen was Gong, or "Respectful." His Lordship also ordered Hu Tu to go and perform a special sacrifice at Scion Shensheng's gravesite.

When Xi Qi arrived at Quwo, he prepared clothes for the body and a shroud, an inner and an outer coffin, as well as the full range of burial goods and wooden funerary statues. When he had Shensheng's body exhumed, he looked just as if he were alive, but the body stank unbearably. The gravediggers simply could not carry on working as they were overcome with nausea, their hands clamped over their noses.

Xi Qi burned some incense and bowed twice, saying, "In life you preserved your purity to the end, so how can you be impure in death? If death has caused you to become impure, that is not your fault. I hope that you will cease scaring the populace."

As he spoke, the foul smell abated and was transformed into a strange fragrance. Then the gravediggers redressed the body and placed it in its new coffin for reburial at Gaoyuan. The city of Quwo emptied as its people went to escort the cortege, and they were all in tears. On the third day of the funeral Hu Tu arrived, bringing all the paraphernalia for the sacrifice. As Lord Hui had commanded, he set up a spirit tablet, bowed deeply in mourning, and put in place a tombstone reading: "The grave of Scion Gong of Jin."

When the ceremony was over, it was Hu Tu's intention to return to the capital, but suddenly he saw row upon row of fluttering flags and line after line of soldiers massed around a group of chariots. Hu Tu had no idea who this could be, and he hurried to get out of the way. He noticed that a man with grizzled hair was riding in the second chariot, dressed in official robes and carrying a staff of office. The man got slowly down from the chariot and came over to where Hu Tu was standing, bowed, and said, "The scion would like to speak to you. Please come this way." Hu Tu scrutinized him and realized that this was the Grand Tutor, Du Yuankuan. In his amazement, he forgot that the man was already dead.

"Where is the scion?" he asked.

Du Yuankuan pointed to the huge carriage at the back and said, "That is the Scion's carriage."

Hu Tu then followed him over. He saw that Scion Shensheng was wearing an official hat and carried a sword by his side; he looked just as he did when he was alive. The scion ordered his driver to get down and help Hu Tu to climb into the carriage. Then he asked, "Do you still remember me?"

Hu Tu broke down in tears and replied, "Even passing strangers wept when they heard about how you died. What kind of monster would I be if I did not remember you?"

"God on High has appointed me to be the Master of Mount Qiao in recognition of my benevolence and filial piety," Shensheng said. "When Yiwu raped Lady Jia Jun, I became completely disgusted with him, and wanted to prevent him from reburying me. However, in the end I went ahead with it because that was what the people wanted. The ruler of Qin is a very brilliant man, so it is my intention to give the lands of Jin to him, provided that the people of Qin keep up sacrifices in my memory. What do you think of my idea?"

"Even though you hate the ruler of Jin," Hu Tu replied, "what crime have the people of Jin committed? What crimes have the former rulers of Jin committed? If you abandon your own family and entrust another clan with the duties of sacrificing to you, I am afraid that you will prove yourself unworthy of your reputation as a benevolent and filial man."

"What you say is absolutely correct," Shensheng answered. "However, I have already petitioned God on High to this effect. I am going to make a second petition now. If you will wait here seven days, there is a shaman who lives in the west part of the New City of Quwo that I will instruct to tell you the answer."

Du Yuankuan called out from below the carriage: "It is time for you to say goodbye!"

He helped Hu Tu to get down from the carriage, but all of a sudden he lost his footing and fell flat on the ground. In a flash, the carriages and horses disappeared and he found himself lying in the guesthouse at the New City of Quwo. He was very surprised and asked his entourage, "What am I doing here?"

"When you had finished the funeral sacrifice and the paper offerings had been burned," his servants explained, "all of a sudden you collapsed in your seat, and we could not wake you up no matter what we did. We lifted you up into a chariot and brought you here to rest. Luckily, you have now recovered."

Hu Tu realized that it had all been a dream. He thought the whole thing most peculiar, though he did not say a word about it to anyone.

However, he insisted on staying in the guesthouse on the grounds that he was not well enough to move.

On the afternoon of the seventh day, the gatekeeper reported: "A shaman has come from the city and is asking to see you."

Hu Tu ordered that the shaman be summoned, and told his servants to wait on the far side of the arras.

When the shaman entered, she announced: "I can communicate with ghosts and the spirits. The Master of Mount Qiao, who was in life Scion Shensheng of Jin, has requested me to give you the following message: 'I have made my second petition to God on High, who has agreed that he should suffer great humiliation and have his family line cut off as punishment for the crimes he has committed. No harm will come to Jin from this.'"

Hu Tu pretended that he did not understand what the shaman was talking about, and asked, "Who is it who is going to be punished?"

"The scion ordered me to take this message to you, but I do not know what it means," the shaman replied.

Hu Tu ordered his entourage to reward the shaman with gold and silk, and warned her not to say a word of this to anyone else. The shaman bowed in thanks and left.

Hu Tu then returned to the capital and went in secret to tell Pi Zhengfu's son, Pi Bao, what had happened. "His Lordship acts in such a wild and reckless manner that he will not last long," Pi Bao declared. "Will Chonger not then become our lord?"

Just as they were discussing this, the gatekeeper came to report: "Grandee Pi has returned from his mission to Qin, and he is currently having an audience with His Lordship at court." The two men then said goodbye and went home.

. . .

Pi Zhengfu returned to Jin at the end of his mission, accompanied by Grandee Ling Zhi of Qin and a number of chariots stuffed with gifts. When he got to the suburbs of the city of Jiang, he suddenly heard the news of Li Ke's execution. Pi Zhengfu became worried and decided that it would be best to go back to Qin and then consider what to do next. However, he was worried about his son, Bao, who was still living in the city of Jiang, and said: "If I leave, he will be in trouble." Given the dangers attendant on either option, he vacillated, uncertain of what to do for the best. By chance he bumped into Grandee Gong Hua out in the suburbs, and invited him to discuss the matter. Pi Zhengfu questioned him about what had happened to Li Ke. Gong Hua explained everything.

"Do you think I should go back to Jin or not?" Pi Zhengfu asked.

"Li Ke had many supporters, including me," Gong Hua replied, "and so far the only person who has been killed is Li Ke himself; the rest of us have not been affected at all. Besides, this is nothing to do with you—you had been sent on a mission to Qin at the time. If you are too frightened to go back to Jin, it will seem as though you are admitting that you are guilty of conspiracy."

Pi Zhengfu followed his advice and spurred on his chariot to take him into the city. He first made his report on his mission and then escorted Grandee Ling Zhi to court for an audience. He presented his credentials and the gifts. Lord Hui opened the letter, and this is what it said:

> The states of Jin and Qin are joined by a marriage alliance that makes us brothers-in-law, so it does not matter if the land belongs to one or the other. I quite understand that the grandees are loyal to their own state. It would not be appropriate for me to insist on obtaining this land if that will lead to a breach with your officials. However, I would like to discuss some long-standing boundary disputes with Grandee Lü Yisheng and Xi Rui in person. I hope that they will come as soon as possible so that this issue can be resolved.

At the end of the letter there was one final line: "I have returned the deeds of your lands to you." Lord Hui was a silly man, so when he saw how generous the gifts were and realized that Lord Mu had returned the deeds of his lands, he was absolutely delighted. He immediately agreed to send Lü Yisheng and Xi Rui to Qin.

Xi Rui spoke privately with Lü Yisheng: "This embassy from Qin is bad news for us. These generous presents and honeyed words are simply intended to lure us out of the country. If we go, then they will hold us hostage to force Lord Hui to hand over the lands."

"I agree that if Qin were simply trying to maintain good relations with Jin, they wouldn't go this far," Lü Yisheng said. "It must be that when Pi Zhengfu heard that Li Ke had been killed, he was afraid that he too would not escape, so he has come up with this plot with Qin. He must be hoping that Qin will kill us and then he can launch a coup."

"Pi Zhengfu and Li Ke were coconspirators," Xi Rui said. "Once Li Ke was executed, how could Pi Zhengfu not be scared? You are quite right. At least half the government belongs to their faction. If he is indeed plotting something, there will be other people involved. We had better get rid of the Qin ambassador and then investigate what is going on."

"Good!" Lü Yisheng said. He spoke to Lord Hui about sending Ling Zhi back to Qin as soon as possible.

"The state of Jin has still not been completely pacified," Lord Hui told him, "so you will have to wait a bit until my two ministers are free. I will send them to you at the first possible moment." After this, Ling Zhi had no choice but to go back to Qin.

Lü Yisheng and Xi Rui sent a trusted servant to keep watch on Pi Zhengfu's gate every night, to find out what he was up to. Pi Zhengfu thought that they had not noticed anything, so he secretly summoned Qi Ju, Gong Hua, Jia Hua, Zhui Chuan, and others to come to his house under cover of darkness and discuss their next move. They left in the early hours of the morning. The trusted servant reported exactly what he had seen.

"Well, it is easy to guess what they were up to!" Xi Rui exclaimed. "They must be plotting against us!" He discussed the situation with Lü Yisheng, and they sent someone to summon Tu'an Yi. When he arrived, Xi Rui said, "You are in real trouble. What are you going to do about it?"

Tu'an Yi was most alarmed and asked, "What trouble?"

"You helped Li Ke murder the child marquis," Xi Rui reminded him. "Li Ke has already been punished, and you are next on His Lordship's list. We felt that you had played a significant role in putting His Lordship in power, so we could not bear to see you killed—that is why we are telling you this."

"I am just an ordinary soldier," Tu'an Yi said with tears in his eyes. "I do what other people tell me to. I am not guilty of any crime! Save me!"

"His Lordship is so furious there is no doing anything with him," Xi Rui said. "There is only one way that you can escape punishment."

Tu'an Yi got down on his knees and asked what he should do. Xi Rui quickly helped him to his feet and then whispered in his ear: "Pi Zhengfu was involved in a conspiracy with Li Ke to put a new ruler in power. They were plotting a coup with the seven senior grandees of Jin that would get rid of His Lordship and install the Honorable Chonger instead. How about you go and see Pi Zhengfu and pretend that you are afraid of being executed, so that you can join in the conspiracy? If you can find out exactly what is going on and report it to the authorities, I will reward you with three hundred thousand fields in Fukui taken from the lands allocated to Pi Zhengfu. That way, not only will you not be punished, you will actually come out ahead!"

"You have saved my life," Tu'an Yi said happily. "I will do my very best, but I am not good at talking to people. What should I do?"

"I will tell you exactly what you have to say," Lü Yisheng said. He then composed a dialogue, which he got Tu'an Yi to memorize.

That evening, Tu'an Yi knocked on Pi Zhengfu's gate and said that he had a secret message to report. Pi Zhengfu refused to see him, on the grounds that he was drunk. Tu'an Yi stood in the middle of the gate and would not go away no matter how late it got, so in the end they let him in.

When Tu'an Yi saw Pi Zhengfu, he knelt down and screamed, "Save me!" Pi Zhengfu was most alarmed and asked what he was talking about.

"His Lordship wants to punish me because I helped Li Ke assassinate Zhuozi," Tu'an Yi sobbed. "What should I do?"

"Lü Yisheng and Xi Rui are in charge of the government now," Pi Zhengfu said. "Why don't you go and ask them for help?"

"This is all a plot on the part of Lü Yisheng and Xi Rui," Tu'an Yi told him. "I could kill them for it. What is the point of asking them for help?"

Pi Zhengfu didn't really believe him, so he asked, "What do you think you want to do?"

"The Honorable Chonger is a benevolent and filial man," Tu'an Yi replied, "and what is more, he has gained the trust of many knights. Everyone in the country would be happy to see him become our next ruler. In addition to that, Qin is angry because Yiwu has betrayed the agreement that he signed with them, so they would also be pleased to see Chonger take power. If you would write a letter, I will take it to Chonger under cover of darkness and get him to form an allied army with soldiers from Qin and the Di. Meanwhile, you can bring together the late scion's supporters and raise a rebellion in the capital. First you behead Lü Yisheng and Xi Rui, then you throw Yiwu out of the country and install Chonger. Would that not be wonderful?"

"Do you really think that you can carry this out?" Pi Zhengfu asked.

Tu'an Yi bit a hole in one finger so the blood spurted out, as he swore an oath: "If I betray you, may all my clan be executed in return!" After that, Pi Zhengfu trusted him. They agreed that the following night they would discuss the matter further. At the appointed time, Tu'an Yi returned to Pi Zhengfu's house. Qi Ju, Gong Hua, Jia Hua, and Zhui Chuan were already there, together with four men who had been part of the late Scion Shensheng's household: Shu Jian, Lei Hu, Te Gong, and

Shan Qi. With Pi Zhengfu and Tu'an Yi, there were ten men present in total. They swore an oath sealed in blood that they would unite to install the Honorable Chonger as their lord.

Later on, someone wrote a poem about this:

When Tu'an Yi came to beg for his life,
Who would have guessed it was part of Lü Yisheng and Xi Rui's plot?
A conspiracy requires conspirators;
One man's trick cost nine men's lives.

Pi Zhengfu hosted a banquet for them, and they all went home drunk. Tu'an Yi secretly reported back to Xi Rui, who said, "You have no concrete evidence yet for your assertions. You must make Pi Zhengfu put something in writing, for that would prove his guilt."

Tu'an Yi went back to Pi Zhengfu's house the following night and asked for a letter that he might take to Chonger. Pi Zhengfu had already written a letter and signed it—in fact, it bore the signatures and thumbprints of nine other men; the tenth was to be Tu'an Yi himself. Tu'an Yi asked for a brush that he might sign this letter too, and he sealed it with a thumbprint. Pi Zhengfu tied tape around the letter to seal it, then placed it in Tu'an Yi's hands and said, "Be very careful. Let no one know what you are up to."

Tu'an Yi received the letter as if it were a great treasure and went straight around to Xi Rui's house to give it to him. Xi Rui then hid Tu'an Yi in his house and, placing the letter securely in his sleeve, went with Lü Yisheng to see Guo She. They had already prepared exactly what they were going to say to him: "If you do not get rid of these people immediately, we will not be responsible for the consequences."

Guo She went that very night to the palace and had an audience with Lord Hui, at which he explained every detail of Pi Zhengfu's conspiracy. "Tomorrow morning at court you can punish him for his crime. This letter is all the evidence that you need."

The following morning, Lord Hui held court. Lü Yisheng and Xi Rui had already arranged for soldiers to lie in wait behind the tapestry hangings in the audience chamber. When the officials present had finished their ceremonial greetings, Lord Hui summoned Pi Zhengfu and said to him, "I know that you are plotting to force me into exile and install Chonger in my stead, and I am going to punish you for it."

Pi Zhengfu attempted to exculpate himself, but Xi Rui drew his sword and shouted: "You sent Tu'an Yi with a letter informing the Honorable Chonger of your plan, but His Lordship was in luck, and my people arrested him when he left the city. We found this letter when we searched him. It names ten coconspirators. Tu'an Yi has already confessed, so don't think that you can wriggle out of this one!"

Lord Hui threw the letter down on the table and Lü Yisheng picked it up, shouting out the names in the order in which they were signed, commanding the soldiers to arrest these men. As it happened, Gong Hua had requested the day off and thus was not present, but the other men were all arrested. These eight men looked at each other blankly, not knowing what to say, but aware that there was nowhere to hide.

"Take them out of the palace gates and behead them!" Lord Hui bellowed.

One of the men, Jia Hua, shouted: "His Late Lordship commanded me to attack the city of Qu, but nevertheless I let you escape. I am now asking that you repay this by not executing me!"

"In those days you were working for Lord Xian while secretly helping out His Lordship," Lü Yisheng said. "Now you are working for His Lordship while secretly helping the Honorable Chonger. The sooner we execute crawling worms like you the better!"

Jia Hua was left with nothing to say. The eight men were led out to be executed.

Gong Hua was at home when he heard that Pi Zhengfu's plot had been discovered and that he had been killed. He quickly said goodbye to the family ancestral shrine and set out with the intention of going to court to receive his punishment.

His younger brother, Gong Ci, said, "If you go, they will kill you. Why don't you run away?"

"It was I who encouraged Grandee Pi to go back home," Gong Hua told him. "It would not be gentlemanly of me to entrap someone and bring about his death, and then carry on living perfectly happily. It is not that I want to die, but I cannot bear the feeling of having betrayed Grandee Pi!"

He did not wait for them to come and arrest him but went straight to court and demanded that they kill him. Lord Hui ordered that he too should be beheaded.

When Pi Bao heard that his father had been executed, he fled for his life to Qin. Lord Hui wanted to kill all of Li Ke and Pi Zhengfu's relatives, but Xi Rui said, "It is an ancient principle that criminals should be punished but not their families. You have now executed these traitors, which is quite enough to strike fear into the hearts of the populace. Why kill any more people? Or are you planning to terrorize your subjects?"

Lord Hui accordingly pardoned the family members of each of these men and promoted Tu'an Yi to become a mid-level grandee, rewarding him with three hundred thousand fields in Fukui.

• • •

When Pi Bao arrived in Qin, he had an audience with Lord Mu, at which he threw himself down upon the ground and wept. Lord Mu asked him the reason for this behavior, and Pi Bao explained about his father's plot and the terrible fate that had overtaken him. Then he presented the following plan: "The Marquis of Jin has betrayed the generosity shown to him by Qin, and the nasty tricks that he has played while taking control of the country have terrorized his officials and alienated his people. If you were to go and attack him, his regime would simply collapse, and having removed him from power, you can do what you want with him."

Lord Mu asked his ministers for their opinion. Jian Shu replied, "To attack Jin on Pi Bao's word would be to assist a subject to assault his ruler, which is not a righteous thing to do."

"If the populace really does not support this regime, there will be a civil war in Jin sooner or later," Baili Xi reminded him. "Your Lordship should await further developments before making up your mind about what you want to do."

"I too am suspicious—can it really be true that he killed nine grandees in one morning?" Lord Mu asked incredulously. "Surely he would need the support of the people to do such a thing? Besides which, without support from inside Jin, will our attack be successful?"

Pi Bao remained in Qin, where he took office as a grandee. This happened in the second year of Lord Hui of Jin's rule, which was the third year of the reign of King Xiang of Zhou.

• • •

That same year, Prince Dai of Zhou bribed the Yi Rong and the Luo Rong peoples to attack the capital, to coordinate with the rebellion that he would start inside the city. The Rong people invaded and laid siege to the royal capital. Kong, Duke of Zhou, and Liao, Duke of Shao, did everything they could to hold the city, and so it was impossible for Prince Dai to communicate with the Rong armies. King Xiang sent ambassadors to report this emergency to the aristocrats. Lord Mu of Qin and Lord Hui of Jin were both hoping to cement good relations with the Zhou king, so they each led their armies to attack the Rong and save Zhou. When the Rong discovered that the armies of these lords had arrived, they set fire to the East Gate of the city and left.

When Lord Hui met Lord Mu, he looked very embarrassed. He had just received a secret missive from Lady Mu Ji in which she listed the offenses that he had committed, including raping Lady Jia Jun and refusing to allow his uncles and brothers back into the country. She concluded by telling him to mend his ways before he did irreparable damage to his hereditary alliances. Lord Hui was suspicious of what Qin was up to, so he stood down his army at the earliest possible moment. Pi Bao urged Lord Mu to attack the Jin army that very night.

"We have both come here to serve the king," Lord Mu told him. "Whatever private enmity there may be between us, this is not the moment to deal with it."

They then each returned to their own states.

. . .

At that time, Lord Huan of Qi had also sent Guan Zhong in command of an army to rescue Zhou. On hearing that the Rong invaders had already left, he sent someone to make a formal complaint to the Rong chief. The Rong chief was afraid of the might of the Qi forces, so he sent someone to apologize: "Would we Rong dare to invade the Zhou capital? We were invited by Prince Dai!"

Because of this, King Xiang forced Prince Dai into exile, and he fled to the state of Qi. The chief of the Rong also sent an ambassador to the Zhou capital to apologize for the trouble that they had caused and ask for a peace treaty, to which King Xiang agreed. King Xiang appreciated the major role that Guan Zhong had played in his accession, and now he had also helped him to make peace with the Rong, so he held a great banquet in his honor, at which he treated Guan Zhong with all the ceremonial due to a senior minister.

Guan Zhong refused to accept this: "The present heads of the two hereditary ministerial houses of Guo and Gao are both here. How can I possibly accept such an unwarranted honor?" He was resolute in his refusal, and in the end he would only accept the ceremonial due to a junior minister.

That winter Guan Zhong became seriously ill, and Lord Huan went in person to visit him. When he observed his emaciated appearance, he took hold of his hand and said, "You are obviously terribly ill. If you are so unfortunate as not to recover from this, to whom should I entrust the government of the country?"

By that time Ning Qi and Bin Xuwu had both died one after the other, so Guan Zhong sighed and said, "It is such a shame that Ning Qi is gone!"

"Surely there is someone other than Ning Qi whom I could employ." Lord Huan asked. "I was thinking about Bao Shuya. How would that be?"

"Bao Shuya is a gentleman," Guan Zhong agreed. "However, you cannot entrust the government of the country to him, because he is too sensitive to the flaws of other people's characters. To appreciate another person's good qualities is a wonderful thing, but if your disgust at their flaws is correspondingly deep, who will ever be good enough for you? If Bao Shuya sees someone make a single mistake, he never forgets it—that is a serious shortcoming."

"Then what about Xi Peng?" Lord Huan asked.

"He would be a good choice," Guan Zhong replied. "Xi Peng has never shown any sign of feeling himself humiliated by having to deal with his social inferiors, but he also never lets people forget that he is a member of the ruling house of Qi." After he said that, he sighed deeply. Then he continued: "Xi Peng and I have always worked together. Once I am gone, how can he survive on his own? I am afraid that you will not have Xi Peng with you for long, my lord."

"If that is the case, then how about Yi Ya?" Lord Huan asked.

"Even if Your Lordship had not mentioned him," Guan Zhong replied, "I would have something to say about him. You must keep your distance from Yi Ya, Shu Diao, and Kaifang."

"Yi Ya cooked his son for me to eat, which shows that he loves me more than he loves his own child. Why should I be suspicious of him?" Lord Huan asked.

"It is human nature to love your own children," Guan Zhong told him. "If he can bear to do this to his child, what will he not do to you?"

"Shu Diao castrated himself in order to serve me, which shows that he loves me more than he loves his own body. Why should I be suspicious of him?" Lord Huan asked.

"It is human nature to care about your own body," Guan Zhong replied. "If he can bear to do this to himself, what will he not do to you?"

"The Honorable Kaifang of Wey turned down the position of scion to a state of one thousand chariots in order to serve me," Lord Huan said, "because he regards this as a greater honor. When his parents died, he did not even go to attend the funeral, because he loves me more than he loves his own parents. Why should I be suspicious of him?"

"It is human nature to love your parents, and if he could bear to treat his own father and mother like this, what will he not do to you?" Guan Zhong said. "Besides which, most people would kill to become the ruler of a state of one thousand chariots. If he gave up this opportunity to serve you, it is because he wants much, much more. You must get rid of these people before they bring about a civil war."

"These three men have all served me for many years," Lord Huan said. "Why did you not say something earlier?"

"I did not say anything because I was trying to please Your Lordship," Guan Zhong replied. "You could compare these people to water and myself to the dam that holds them back and prevents them from flooding the place. If the dam is removed, there will be disaster. You must send them away."

Lord Huan withdrew in silence.

If you want to know what happened to Guan Zhong in the end, READ ON.

Chapter Thirty

Qin and Jin fight a great battle at Mount Longmen.

Lady Mu Ji climbs a tower to demand a general pardon.

When Guan Zhong became terminally ill, he instructed Lord Huan to keep Yi Ya, Shu Diao, and the Honorable Kaifang of Wey at a distance and to entrust all matters of state to Xi Peng. There was a member of his entourage who heard every word that had been said and reported this to Yi Ya, who then had a meeting with Bao Shuya at which he told him: "Elder Zhong became prime minister because you recommended him for office. Now he is ill, and His Lordship asked him who should take over. He said that you could not be trusted with matters of state and recommended Xi Peng instead. This is most unfair."

Bao Shuya laughed and said, "That is exactly why I recommended him. Zhong is loyal to the country and would not recommend his friends for selfish reasons. I have been employed as the minister of justice, with responsibility for removing incompetent and corrupt men from government—there is more than enough on my plate already. If I were to take over governing the country, would there be any place here for you?"

Yi Ya felt very humiliated and left.

The following day, Lord Huan went to see Guan Zhong again, but by that time he could no longer speak. Bao Shuya and Xi Peng were in floods of tears. That night, Guan Zhong died.

Lord Huan was moved to tears. "How sad it is about Elder Zhong!" he cried. "I feel as though one arm has been cut off!"

He ordered the senior minister, Gao Hu, to take charge of the funeral ceremony, at which he was buried with full honors. The lands that he had held during his lifetime were all transferred to his son, and the Guan family were made hereditary grandees.

Yi Ya said to Grandee Bo, "In the past His Lordship removed three hundred towns from your fief to give them to Guan Zhong as a reward for his efforts. Now Elder Zhong is dead. Why don't you speak to His Lordship and get these towns back? I will do my best to help you."

Weeping, Grandee Bo said, "I achieved no merit in the service of my country, and that is why I lost these towns. Even though Guan Zhong is dead, his enormous successes are still with us. How could I have the gall to ask His Lordship for the return of these lands?"

Yi Ya sighed and said, "Grandee Bo still obeys Guan Zhong even though he is dead. We really are being very petty."

Lord Huan of Qi remembered Guan Zhong's dying words and entrusted the government of the country to Xi Peng. However, just a couple of weeks later Xi Peng was struck down by a sudden illness and died.

"Was Elder Zhong some kind of sage?" Lord Huan inquired. "How did he know that Xi Peng would die so soon?"

He appointed Bao Shuya to take over Xi Peng's office, but Bao Shuya resolutely refused. "You are by far the most experienced minister in my administration," Lord Huan told him. "Who do you think would be better than yourself?"

"As Your Lordship is well aware," Bao Shuya replied, "my talents lie in appreciating the good qualities of others and punishing their crimes. If Your Lordship insists upon appointing me, you must get rid of Yi Ya, Shu Diao, and the Honorable Kaifang of Wey, for in no other circumstances will I accept this office."

"Elder Zhong also emphasized this point," Lord Huan said, "so of course I will agree to your request."

That very day he dismissed them, refusing to allow them to come to court and have an audience with him. Bao Shuya then accepted the post of prime minister. Just at that time, the Huai Yi people invaded the state of Qǐ and the inhabitants reported the emergency to Qi. Lord Huan of Qi joined forces with the lords of Song, Lu, Chen, Wey, Zheng, Xu, and Cao, and personally led the campaign to rescue the state of Qǐ, moving its capital to Yuanling. The lords still obeyed the orders that they received from Qi, because since Lord Huan had employed Bao Shuya, there was no change in the principles of government originally laid down by Guan Zhong.

. . .

Let us now turn to another part of the story. After Lord Hui took power in Jin, the millet and barley did not ripen properly in successive harvests, and so in the fifth year of his rule there was a terrible famine. The government storehouses and granaries were completely empty, and the people had nothing whatsoever to eat. Lord Hui wanted to beg for food from some of the other states. He remembered that while Qin was his nearest neighbor and the two countries were linked by a marriage alliance, the conflict between them since he had betrayed his treaty obligations had still not been resolved, and thus he was not in a position to request anything of them.

Xi Rui came forward and said, "It is not entirely correct to say that we have betrayed our treaty obligations to Qin, since we specifically informed them that payment would have to be delayed. If we beg them for grain and Qin refuses to give it, then Qin has let us down first and we would be justified in ignoring their demands."

"You are absolutely correct, sir," Lord Hui told him. Then he sent Grandee Qing Zheng to take a precious jade to Qin and ask for food aid.

Lord Mu summoned his ministers to discuss the situation: "Jin agreed to hand over five cities and has not done so. Now they have also come to beg for grain because they have been struck by a famine. Should I give them food aid or not?"

Jian Shu and Baili Xi both said, "All states are affected by natural disasters sooner or later. It would be immoral to refuse to help people who have been struck down by calamity. If you do this, you are sure to receive Heaven's blessings."

"But I have already done a great deal for Jin," Lord Mu reminded them.

"If your great generosity results in their feeling that they must repay you, will Qin suffer any loss?" Noble Grandson Qi asked. "And if it is not returned, the fault will be theirs. If the people of Jin come to loathe their own ruler, will they fight us? Your Lordship ought to give this grain."

Pi Bao remembered only too well the circumstances in which his father had died. He waved his arms and shouted, "The Marquis of Jin is a wicked man; that is why Heaven has sent down this disaster. If you take advantage of the famine to attack them, Jin will be destroyed. You should not miss this opportunity!"

"A benevolent man does not profit by taking advantage of others when they have gotten themselves into trouble," Yao Yu said, "and a wise man does not expect to achieve his aims by some unexpected stroke of good luck. You ought to give them the grain."

"The ruler of Jin has betrayed his treaty obligations to me," Lord Mu said, "but it is the people of Jin who are starving. I will not bring further disaster upon these wretched people just because I happen not to like their ruler."

He ordered that tens of thousands of bushels of grain should be transported along the Wei River, until they reached the conjunction with the Yellow River and the Fen River. From the Qin capital to the Jin capital, the boats advanced like a massive snake, so tightly packed that you could walk from one to the other, to save the famine-struck people of Jin. Everyone in Jin was overwhelmed with delight.

A historian wrote a poem praising Lord Mu's goodness:

> The wicked ruler of Jin was punished with a natural disaster,
> Yet wave after wave of relief traveled from Yong to Jiang.
> Who was the man who turned the other cheek?
> Lord Mu was indeed exceptionally virtuous!

In the winter of the following year, the state of Qin suffered a famine while Jin was enjoying the fruits of a bumper harvest. Lord Mu spoke to Jian Shu and Baili Xi: "Today I remember what you two said about a run of good years being sooner or later followed by bad. It is just as well that last year I gave the grain to Jin, for otherwise it would be difficult to ask them for food aid this year when we are suffering from famine."

"The Marquis of Jin is a greedy and untrustworthy man," Pi Bao reminded him. "Even if you beg him for food aid, he will not give it."

Lord Mu did not believe that such a thing was possible. He sent Ling Zhi to Jin with the gift of a precious jade to ask for aid. Lord Hui was just about to hand over the grain from west of the Yellow River in response to Qin's request, when Xi Rui came forward and said, "If you are going to give them this grain, my lord, are you also proposing to give them the cities?"

"I am just going to give them food," Lord Hui said. "Surely no one is expecting me to hand over the cities!"

"Why are you going to give them food aid, my lord?" Xi Rui asked.

"To repay them for their grain transport," Lord Hui said.

"If you think that Qin did well by you in sending you the grain transport," Xi Rui told him, "then they helped you even more when they put you in power in the first place all those years ago. If you ignore the really great help that you have received from them and repay the lesser assistance that they gave you subsequently, do you really think that will be acceptable?"

"Last year I received an order from Your Lordship to beg for grain from Qin," Grandee Qing Zheng said. "Lord Mu did not haggle in the slightest—he really is a most magnanimous man. If we now close our storehouses to them, Qin will be perfectly justified in hating us!"

"The reason that Qin gave us the grain was not to benefit us, but because they want those five cities," Lü Yisheng said. "If we don't give them the grain, Qin will hate us. If we give them the grain but don't give them the land, Qin will also hate us. If the result is the same either way, why should we give them anything at all?"

"To take advantage of the fact that someone else has suffered disaster is not benevolent," Qing Zheng said in horror. "To betray someone else's kindness is not just. If you are neither kind nor just, how can you expect to keep your state?"

"Qing Zheng is absolutely right," Han Jian said. "What would you have done, my lord, if Qin had refused to give us food aid last year?"

"Last year," Guo She told him, "Heaven betrayed us into Qin's hands by sending down a famine upon us. Qin not only failed to conquer us—they also gave us grain, which was really stupid of them. This year, Heaven has betrayed Qin into our hands by sending down a famine upon them. Why should we let slip this Heaven-sent opportunity? In my humble opinion, Your Lordship should meet with the Earl of Liang and take advantage of this situation to conquer Qin, dividing their lands between you. This would be by far the best plan."

Lord Hui agreed with Guo She's suggestion, and so he told Ling Zhi that he could not help them: "My country has been struck by famine for many years in succession, forcing many of my people to become refugees. This year the harvest was somewhat better, which has allowed some refugees to begin to move back to their old homes. However, we only have enough food for our own use; there is not sufficient to help anyone else."

"When you were suffering famine," Ling Zhi reminded him, "His Lordship remembered the marriage alliance that links your ruling house with ours; hence he did not refuse to open his storehouses just because you had not handed over the land. He simply said, 'I am sorry about the disaster that has overtaken you.' I really find it very difficult to have to report back that you are not going to repay the assistance that you received when you were in trouble."

Lü Yisheng and Xi Rui shouted, "You were involved in Pi Zhengfu's conspiracy and tried to tempt us with lavish bribes. Fortunately, your wicked plots were revealed and we did not fall into your trap. Now you are back again, trying to cheat us! Go back and tell your lord that if he wants any grain from Jin, he will have to deploy his army to get it!"

Ling Zhi had to swallow his anger and withdraw.

Qing Zheng left the court and said to Grand Astrologer Guo Yan, "The Marquis of Jin has behaved appallingly and angered his neighbor; disaster will soon overtake us!"

"This autumn," Guo Yan said, "Mount Shalu suffered a landslide and all the trees fell over. Mountains and rivers are the masters of the country. This may well be the first sign that the state of Jin is doomed!"

A historian wrote a poem criticizing Lord Hui of Jin:

Qin's boats brought relief to the poor and starving from far away,
But when they suffered famine, the result was not at all the same.
Since antiquity, there have been many men who have betrayed their
  benefactors,
But few have been as egregious as Lord Hui of Jin's treatment of Lord
  Mu of Qin.

Ling Zhi went back and reported this to the Lord of Qin, saying, "Jin is not only going to refuse to give us any food, they have also been in touch with the Earl of Liang with a view to raising an army for a joint attack on us."

Lord Mu was absolutely furious and said, "I had no idea that anyone could be so evil! I will destroy Liang first and then attack Jin."

"The Earl of Liang enjoys building things, and he governs a vast state," Baili Xi said. "He is endlessly working on fortresses and other lavish construction projects, but he does not have a sufficiently large population to bring these grandiose plans to fruition. His people hate him, so obviously he will not be able to provide military assistance to Jin. The ruler of Jin is a wicked man and his cronies, Lü Yisheng and Xi Rui, keep themselves in power by force. If they raise an army in Jiangzhou, that will ring alarm bells throughout the western regions. The Art of War says: 'Whoever attacks first will control the situation.' Your Lordship's wisdom is well-known; if you were to order your grandees to spread the word of how the Marquis of Jin has betrayed his treaty obligations, your victory is assured. With your reputation, taking over Liang will be as easy as shaking dry leaves off a tree."

Lord Mu thought that this was good advice. He mobilized his three armies and ordered Jian Shu and Yao Yu to stay behind and help Scion Ying look after matters in the capital. Mengming Shi led his troops out to patrol the borders to ensure that the Rong did not think of causing trouble. Lord Mu was in personal command of the Central Army together with Baili Xi, while Xiqi Shu and Baiyi Bing acted as their bodyguards. Noble Grandson Qi was in command of the Army of the Right, while the Honorable Zhi was in command of the Army of the Left. In total they had four hundred chariots in the field, all fully appointed. They proceeded to cut a swath through the state of Jin.

The emergency was reported to Lord Hui from Jin's western borders. Lord Hui asked his ministers, "Qin has raised an army and invaded our borders for no good reason. How do we stop them?"

Qing Zheng came forward and said, "The Qin army has come here to punish us because you have behaved so badly, my lord. Why do you say they are here for no reason? In my humble opinion, you should admit the error of your ways and ask for a peace treaty, giving them the five cities as a sign of your sincerity. That way we will not have to go to war."

Lord Hui was enraged by this. "I rule a state of one thousand chariots, and yet you are expecting me to give up my lands and beg for a peace treaty," he shrieked. "How do you expect me to rule the country in the future?" He then shouted out a command: "First behead Qing Zheng, and then send the army out to intercept the enemy!"

"If you behead the general before the army has even left their barracks, it will not be good for morale," Guo She told him. "It would be better to pardon him and let him go out on campaign, for then he may atone for his crimes by success in battle."

Lord Hui approved this suggestion. That day he held a great muster of horses and equipment, from which six hundred chariots were selected. He ordered Xi Buyang, Jiapu Tu, Qing Zheng, and Yi Xi to take command of the left and right wings of the army, while he himself and Guo She organized the Central Army. Tu'an Yi was placed in charge of the vanguard. When they left Jiangzhou, they advanced westward. The Marquis of Jin was riding a horse called Petite, which had come to him as a gift from the state of Zheng. This horse was particularly elegant, with a fine, glossy mane, and moved with a very stable gait. The Marquis of Jin was particularly fond of this horse.

Qing Zheng remonstrated with him: "In antiquity, whenever rulers went out on campaign, they rode horses born inside the borders of their own state. Such horses, having been born in the region, understand their masters, are familiar with their style of riding, and know the roads. That way, once battle was joined they would do what they were told and did not cause trouble. Today, you are on the eve of a great battle, my lord, and yet you are riding a foreign horse. I am afraid that this is a bad idea."

Lord Hui shouted at him: "This is the horse that I am used to riding. Stop making such a fuss!"

By this time the Qin army had already crossed the Yellow River and was proceeding eastwards. They fought three battles and were victorious each time. The generals who were responsible for defending this region had all fled. They kept on marching forward, and it was only when they arrived at Hanyuan that they made camp. When Lord Hui of Jin heard that they had already reached Hanyuan, he said with a furrowed brow, "Their invasion has already gone deep. What can I do about it?"

"It is your fault that they are here, so why are you asking me?" Qing Zheng sneered.

"If you are going to be rude, you can leave," Lord Hui told him.

The Jin army made camp ten *li* away from Hanyuan. They sent Han Jian out to find out how large the Qin army really was.

"Even though the Qin army is smaller than ours," Han Jian reported, "their morale is ten times better."

"Why?" asked Lord Hui.

"My lord, you originally fled to exile in Liang with Qin's help," Han Jian told him. "Later on, you succeeded to the title with Qin's assistance. Finally, you received famine relief from Qin. They have helped us three times, and yet we have done nothing in return. Their ruler and people are deeply angry, and that is why they have come to attack us. Their three armies all feel that we have betrayed them, and so their morale is very high. In fact, I should have said that their morale is more than ten times better than ours!"

"That is exactly what Qing Zheng said," Lord Hui replied crossly. "Now you are saying the same thing. However, I am determined to fight Qin even if it kills me." He ordered Han Jian to go to the Qin army with a message to provoke battle: "I have come here with a force of six hundred chariots, which ought to be enough to deal with Your Lordship. If you withdraw your army, I will let you leave unmolested. If, on the other hand, you do not leave, even if I wanted to avoid battle, I am not sure that I could restrain the knights in my three armies."

Lord Mu laughed and said, "The kid is pretty arrogant." Then he ordered Noble Grandson Qi to respond on his behalf: "You wanted a country and I gave it to you. You wanted grain, and I gave it to you. Now you want to fight, so who am I to say no?"

Han Jian withdrew and said, "Qin is in the right here. We did not know it, but we were marching to our deaths."

Lord Hui of Jin ordered Grand Astrologer Guo Yan to perform a divination about who should serve as his bodyguard. Every result was inauspicious, except when Qing Zheng was proposed.

"Qing Zheng is part of the pro-Qin faction," Lord Hui exclaimed. "How could I possibly give him this task?" He appointed Jiapu Tu to act as his bodyguard, with Xi Buyang to drive his chariot. They went to meet the Qin army at Hanyuan.

. . .

Baili Xi climbed up on the fortifications and surveyed the massed ranks of the Jin army. He said to Lord Mu, "The Marquis of Jin wants to kill us. It would be better if we did not do battle."

Lord Mu pointed up to the sky and said, "I have had enough of Jin kicking me around. If there is no such thing as justice, then I am doomed. But if Heaven has witnessed all that we have suffered, we are sure to win."

He drew up his army in battle formation at the foot of Mount Longmen. A short time later, the Jin army also went into formation. The two armies were in full battle array, and the generals each sounded the drums to advance their troops. The brave Tu'an Yi was the first to rush into the breach, holding an iron spear weighing over one hundred pounds in each hand, stabbing everyone in his way. The Qin army collapsed in the face of this onslaught. Then he ran into Baiyi Bing, and the two of them started fighting. After they had crossed swords about fifty times, their blood was up and both leapt down from their chariots, fighting hand to hand.

"Only one of us will leave here alive!" Tu'an Yi declared. "If anyone helps one of us, that person will stand revealed for the bastard he really is!"

"I will prove my heroism by taking you captive single-handedly," Baiyi Bing proclaimed. He shouted to his troops: "None of you are to come near me!"

The two of them then punched and kicked each other through the massed ranks of troops. Lord Hui of Jin noticed that Tu'an Yi was now completely surrounded by Qin soldiers, so he quickly instructed Han Jian and Liang Yaomi to attack on the left flank, while he and Jiapu Tu attacked the right flank, in cooperation with the Central Army. When Lord Mu saw that his army was caught up in the Jin army's pincer movement, he turned his troops in two different directions to meet the enemy.

Lord Hui's chariot happened to run close of that of Noble Grandson Qi. Lord Hui then ordered Jiapu Tu to get ready to fight. Noble Grandson Qi was a great warrior—how on earth could Jiapu Tu be expected to defeat him? Lord Hui instructed Xi Buyang: "Hold tight to the reins! I am going to help him!"

Noble Grandson Qi waved his spear and shouted, "Anyone who reckons they can fight is welcome to join in!" That shout was like a rumble of thunder splitting the heavens: Guo She was so frightened that he crouched at the bottom of his chariot, too scared to make a sound. Petite, hitched to the Marquis of Jin's chariot, had never been in battle before and was also terrified by the noise, so it paid no attention to the driver but started running wild, until it got itself stuck in a bog. Xi Buyang hit the horse as hard as he could with his whip, but Petite was not a strong horse and could not pull its hooves out of the mud. The situation was now critical, but just at that moment it happened that Qing Zheng's chariot drove across in front of them.

"Save me!" Lord Hui screamed.

"Where is Guo She?" Qing Zheng asked. "Why are you shouting at me?"

Lord Hui called out again: "Come and help me!"

"It was you who insisted on bringing Petite, my lord," Qing Zheng reminded him. "I am going to go and save people more worthy of the effort." He turned his chariot away to the left and raced off. Xi Buyang was hoping to find someone else to help, but just then they were encircled by the Qin troops, so he was not able to get away.

As Han Jian advanced his troops, he ran straight into Lord Mu of Qin's Central Army. He then fought with the Qin general Xiqi Shu. They crossed swords thirty times, but it was impossible to tell which of them would win. Yi Xi then arrived with his forces and the pair attacked in concert. Xiqi Shu was not able to withstand this onslaught and fell beneath his chariot on the point of Han Jian's spear.

"A defeated general is useless!" Liang Yaomi shouted. "We must join forces to capture the ruler of Qin alive!"

Han Jian paid no attention to Xiqi Shu, but set off with the Jin army in pursuit of the battle chariot that was carrying Lord Mu of Qin.

"What injustice!" Lord Mu said with a sigh. "How is it possible that I can today be taken prisoner by the Jin army?" Just as he was sighing a second time, he spied a group of warriors approaching from the west, consisting of about three hundred men.

"Do not hurt our benefactor!" they bellowed at the tops of their voices.

Lord Mu raised his head to look at them. What he saw was hundreds of men running like the wind, their hair wild and their torsos naked, with rush sandals on their feet. All of them were carrying enormous knives, and they had bows and arrows hanging from their waists. They seemed like the demon soldiers of the king of hell; and once they had arrived, they starting hacking their way through the Jin army. Han Jian and Liang Yaomi quickly turned to meet this new enemy. Then they saw another person arriving on a speeding chariot from the north: this was Qing Zheng.

"Stop fighting!" he screamed. "His Lordship is stuck in a bog at the foot of Mount Longmen and has been cornered there by the Qin troops! Go as quickly as you can to rescue him!"

Han Jian and the others had no more stomach for this fight, so they wrenched themselves out of the warriors' grasp and rushed to the foot of Mount Longmen to save the Marquis of Jin. They had no idea that Lord Hui of Jin had already been taken prisoner by Noble Grandson Qi, along with Jiapu Tu, Guo She, Xi Buyang, and the rest. Having been tied up, they were all marched into the main camp.

Han Jian stamped his foot and said, "If we had captured the Qin ruler, we could have done an exchange. Qing Zheng has really put us in a terrible position!"

"As long as our lord is here," Liang Yaomi declared, "we cannot leave!" He and Han Jian then put down their weapons and went to the Qin camp to surrender. They were imprisoned with Lord Hui.

The three hundred warriors had saved not only Lord Mu of Qin, but also Xiqi Shu. The Qin army took advantage of this success to make further attacks, under which the Jin forces crumbled. A mountainous pile of bodies lay at the foot of Mount Longmen; of the original force of six hundred chariots, only two to three hundred were able to escape. When Qing Zheng heard that the Lord of Jin had been captured alive, he secretly made his way out through the enemy lines. When he happened to come across Yi Xi, lying injured on the ground, he lifted him up into his chariot. The two of them then escaped back to the state of Jin.

A bearded old man wrote a poem commemorating the great battle of Hanyuan, which runs:

A pile of corpses lay below Mount Longmen,
Simply because a wicked ruler refused to repay his obligations.
Moral behavior determined victory and defeat on the field of battle,
From which it is clear that heavenly justice was upheld.

When Lord Mu of Qin returned to the main camp, he said to Baili Xi, "I did not listen to your advice and almost got myself into serious trouble with Jin."

Just then, the three hundred or so warriors came to kowtow in front of the camp.

"Who are you that you were willing to risk your lives for me?" Lord Mu asked them.

"Does Your Lordship not remember the loss of your blood-horses all those years ago?" the warriors replied. "We are the men who ate your horses."

It so happened that at one time Lord Mu had gone out hunting at Mount Liang, and overnight a couple of fine horses had gone missing. He sent an official out to look for them. Searching at the foot of Mount Qi, this man had discovered a group of more than three hundred natives eating horsemeat. The official did not dare to approach them but rushed back to report to Lord Mu: "If you send soldiers here immediately to arrest them, you will be able to capture all of them."

Lord Mu sighed and said, "My horses are already dead. If I punish them for this, then everyone will complain that I care more about animals than I do about people." Instead, he ordered that a couple of dozen jars of fine wine should be collected from the camp. He had a servant take them out to Mount Qi and give them to the natives with Lord Mu's compliments: "I have heard that it is bad for one's health to eat horsemeat without drinking wine. Therefore, I bestow this wine upon you."

The natives had kowtowed and thanked His Lordship for his kindness, and each drank his share of the wine. They all sighed and said, "His Lordship has not blamed us for stealing his horses, but worries about our health and makes sure we are given this fine wine. How can we ever repay His Lordship for his great kindness?"

So when they heard that Lord Mu had attacked Jin, more than three hundred of these men had rushed to Hanyuan to help in the fighting, risking their lives. When they saw that Lord Mu had been surrounded, they all fought like tigers to help him break free. This really is a case of:

If you sow pumpkins, you will reap pumpkins,
If you sow beans, you will reap beans.
If you do little, you will not be repaid much,
If you do much, you will be repaid a great deal.
And if you receive help from someone else and do nothing to repay them,
Are you any different from an animal?

Lord Mu looked up at the sky and sighed. "Even men from the wilds know that you should requite the benefits you have received from others," he said. "What kind of man is the Marquis of Jin?" Then he informed the assembled multitude: "Anyone who is willing to stay and serve me will receive titles and emoluments!"

The warriors answered as with one voice: "We are all men from the wilds, so although we are happy to repay Your Lordship for all that you have done for us, we do not want to serve you."

Lord Mu gave each of them a gift of gold and silk, but they refused to accept it and left. Lord Mu was very impressed.

Later on, someone wrote a poem about this:

Two armies met at Hanyuan, at the foot of the mountains;
The Jin soldiers surrounded Lord Mu, row upon row.
If in the past he had executed the men who stole his horses,
Would he today have escaped from this trap?

When Lord Mu counted up his generals, there was not a single one missing, with the exception of Baiyi Bing, who was nowhere to be seen. Lord Mu sent some officers out to search for him, and eventually they noticed a muffled sound coming from a cave. As they approached, they saw that Baiyi Bing and Tu'an Yi had rolled into the cave while locked in combat—although they were both exhausted, neither was prepared to let the other one go. The officers pulled the two men apart, lifted them onto waiting chariots, and drove them back to the main camp. When Lord Mu saw Baiyi Bing, he was already beyond speech. Someone had seen the pair of them fighting to the death and explained exactly what had happened. Lord Mu sighed and said, "Both of them were great knights!" Then he inquired of his entourage, "Does anyone know the name of this Jin general?"

The Honorable Zhi had been watching them from his chariot, so he now respectfully stated, "This man is Tu'an Yi. In the past, when you sent me to condole with the two sons of Lord Xian of Jin, the senior ministers ordered Tu'an Yi to meet me. I have had various dealings with him, so that is how I recognize him."

"Should we keep him and employ him in Qin?" Lord Mu asked.

"This man assassinated the Honorable Zhuozi and killed Li Ke," the Honorable Zhi reminded him. "In justice, you ought to execute him."

Lord Mu then gave orders that Tu'an Yi should be beheaded. His Lordship took off his brocade silk gown and draped it over Baiyi Bing's shoulders. He commanded Baili Xi to drive him back home to Qin in a covered carriage to get him medical attention. Baiyi Bing took some medicine, spat a couple of mouthfuls of blood, and was completely restored to health within six months. This all happened some time later.

. . .

Lord Mu of Qin had won a great victory, so he struck camp and sent someone to tell the Marquis of Jin, "You did not want to avoid me, and today I find myself unable to avoid you. I hope that you will come to my humble country and answer for your crimes!" Lord Hui hung his head in silence. Lord Mu ordered Noble Grandson Qi to lead a force of one hundred chariots to escort the imprisoned Marquis of Jin back to Qin. Guo She, Han Jian, Liang Yaomi, Jiapu Tu, Xi Buyang, Guo Yan, Xi Qi, and others all followed on behind, unprotected from the elements, their hair hanging down to cover their faces as if in a funeral procession.

Lord Mu sent someone to condole with the grandees of Jin and tell them: "Your ruler and ministers have informed me that if I would like to eat grain from Jin, I should bring my army in to collect it. I will be keeping your ruler as a hostage until such time as the grain from Jin is delivered—this is not excessive, surely? However, there are so many other suitable candidates that I am sure you can find someone better! There is no point in being too upset about the loss of this one!"

Han Jian and the others bowed twice, and then they kowtowed and said, "You seem to have forgiven not only His Lordship's stupidity but also the government that supported him: that is most kind! We swear by Heaven and Earth that we will obey your commands, and so we kowtow in acknowledgement of your generosity."

When the Qin forces arrived at the border of Yongzhou, Lord Mu summoned his ministers to discuss the situation with them: "I have received a mandate from God on High to bring peace to the state of Jin: that is why I installed the Honorable Yiwu in power. Now the Marquis of Jin has betrayed his treaty obligations and offended against God on High. I would like to use the Marquis of Jin in the suburban sacrifices to God on High, in order to thank Him for his blessings. Would that be a good idea?"

"That would be splendid, my lord," the Honorable Zhi declared.

Noble Grandson Qi came forward and said, "You cannot do that. Jin is a great state and we have taken their people prisoner, which is already quite enough to bring their vengeance down upon us. If you now kill their ruler, they will be even angrier. Jin has already suffered more at our hands than we have suffered at theirs."

"I was thinking that we should not just kill the Marquis of Jin but also replace him with the Honorable Chonger," said the Honorable Zhi. "That way we would get rid of an evil ruler and replace him with an excellent one. The people of Jin would soon realize the merit of our actions, so why would they be angry with us?"

"The Honorable Chonger is a most benevolent man," Noble Grandson Qi pointed out, "who is clearly very close to the rest of his family. Chonger was not willing to benefit personally from the circumstances surrounding his father's demise, so what makes you think that he would be happy to take advantage of his younger brother's death? If Chonger does not become the next Marquis of Jin, someone else will—why will that necessarily be any better than Yiwu? Even supposing he is willing to take power, he will want to punish Qin for our treatment of his younger brother. In that way, Your Lordship will destroy the last vestiges of the good relationship that you had with Yiwu and create a new enmity with Chonger. In my humble opinion, that would be a very bad idea."

"In that case, should I send the Marquis of Jin into exile?" Lord Mu asked. "Or imprison him? Or put him back in power? Which of the three would be best for us?"

"If you imprison him," Noble Grandson Qi replied, "then he is no different from any other ordinary criminal—there is no benefit to Qin from that! If you send him into exile, there will be endless conspiracies to put him back in power. You might as well restore him yourself."

"Does that not make this victory pointless?" Lord Mu asked.

"My idea is not that you should simply restore him to power," Noble Grandson Qi replied. "He will have to give us the five cities west of the Yellow River that he has promised us and send Scion Yu to live as a hostage in Qin before we can agree to a peace treaty. In that way, the Marquis of Jin will never dare to behave badly to us again. Not only that, when the marquis is dead and his son inherits, it will be we who ensure the succession of Scion Yu. That way, Jin will have to serve us for generations to come. What could be better than that?"

"Your plan will benefit us for decades in the future," Lord Mu told him. Accordingly, he arranged that Lord Hui should be sent to live in the traveling palace at Mount Lingtai, with a thousand men to guard him.

Once Lord Mu had made his arrangements for the Marquis of Jin, he wanted to set off home himself, but suddenly a whole host of palace eunuchs arrived, all dressed in mourning attire. Lord Mu believed that his wife must have died, and he was just about to ask them what had happened when the eunuchs, wailing, delivered this message from Lady Mu Ji: "Heaven has sent down disaster! The lords of Jin and Qin have abandoned the good relations between them and gone to war! It is a source of great shame to me that the ruler of Jin has been taken prisoner. If tomorrow morning the Marquis of Jin is dragged into the Qin capital in chains, then I will die that morning. If tomorrow evening the Marquis of Jin is dragged into the Qin capital in chains, then I will die that evening. I have sent these servants to meet Your Lordship's triumphant army. If you can pardon the Marquis of Jin, then you will also save my life. It is up to Your Lordship to make the decision."

Lord Mu was deeply alarmed and asked, "What is Her Ladyship doing in the palace?"

The eunuchs responded: "When Her Ladyship heard that the Marquis of Jin had been captured, she dressed the scion up in mourning clothes, and then the two of them walked out of the palace and climbed up to the top of the Chong Tower in the rear gardens. Her Ladyship is living in a little hut on top of the tower, and she has stacked dozens of bundles of firewood around its base. The people who are taking her food have to scramble up and down over these logs. She instructed us: 'I am waiting until the Marquis of Jin enters the city before I kill myself. I am planning to burn myself alive, to demonstrate my love for my brother.'"

Lord Mu sighed and said, "How lucky that Noble Grandson Qi urged me to spare the Marquis of Jin's life. Now I realize how close I came to losing my wife!" He ordered the eunuchs to take off their mourning clothes. They were to take the following message to Lady Mu Ji: "The Marquis of Jin will be on his way home any day now." Lady Mu Ji then went back to live in the palace.

The palace eunuchs knelt down before her and asked, "The Marquis of Jin is a greedy and unprincipled man who has not only betrayed his treaty obligations to His Lordship but also let you down in everything that you have asked him to do. It is his own fault that he was taken prisoner, so why were you so upset?"

"I have heard it said that benevolent people never forget their family members, no matter how angry they are," Lady Mu Ji replied. "Likewise, they never behave rudely, no matter how irritated they get. If the Marquis of Jin had gotten himself killed in Qin, it would have been at least in part my fault." All the servants were deeply struck by Her Ladyship's wisdom and generous spirit.

Was the Marquis of Jin able to return to his home? READ ON.